GRETTA CURRAN BROWNE was born and grew up in Dublin city. She left Dublin as a teenager and went to London to study drama. She started writing in January 1984 and had two articles and a short story published, which encouraged her to start writing her first novel, *Tread Softly on my Dreams*, in October 1984. It was re-issued by Wolfhound Press in 1998. She is married and has two children and does her writing at night when the world and her children are asleep.

Reviews of
Tread Softly on my Dreams

'Well and simply written, with feeling and humour, and the meticulous research illuminates the scene without ever intruding upon it.'
Sunday Telegraph

'I can honestly say it's one of the most enjoyable books that I've read for some time. I can't recommend [it] highly enough.'
Irish World

'A very fine achievement.'
Sunday Press

'An epic novel. Fast moving and as down to earth as a romanticised story can be, the novel is based on documented evidence. Gretta Curran Browne spent four years researching the novel ... her dedication has proved itself.'
IT Magazine

'A vivid and moving story. We will, no doubt, have more from this author.'
Irish Post

FIRE ON THE HILL

Gretta Curran Browne

Wolfhound Press

This edition 1998
Published by
WOLFHOUND PRESS Ltd
68 Mountjoy Square
Dublin 1
Tel: (353-1) 8740354
Fax: (353-1) 8720207

First published London, 1991

British Library cataloguing in Publication Data
A catalogue record for this book is available from the British
Library.

 Wolfhound Press receives financial assistance from The
Arts Council/ An Chomhairle Ealaíon, Dublin, Ireland.

ISBN 0 86327 676 8

10 9 8 7 6 5 4 3 2 1

Cover Design: Estresso, Dublin
Printed in Scotland by Caledonian Book Manufacturing

Dedicated with love to Paul, Ellena and Sean-Paul,
who, in winter and summer, were my cheerful
companions in all my wanderings amongst
the Wicklow hills.

ACKNOWLEDGEMENTS

I would like to thank my publisher, Mr Seamus Cashman, and all the talented staff at Wolfhound Press who, in every way, and in every department, have backed me whole-heartedly every step of the way.

To Sally Mimnagh, a lovely lady, who has continually given my work her tremendous support.

To Michael McLoughlin and all the journalists and booksellers, for the part each played in making my first Book Tour a wonderful event to remember, and helping me to realise a long-held dream.

For her personal assistance with documentation in Dublin Castle, I would like you thank with warmth and gratitude, Dr Philomena Connolly.

For providing me with copies of General Musters of 1811, 1814, and 1825; copies of entries in the *Index to Births, Deaths and Marriages — 1787-1905*; as well as various other relevant newspapers, I am deeply grateful to the Mitchell Library, Sydney.

For providing me with copies from microfilm of *Indictments, Information, and Depositions* of the Proceedings of the 1807 Trial in Sydney Criminal Court, I am deeply grateful to the Archives Authority of New South Wales.

For permission to publish an extract from 'The Three Flowers' by Norman G. Reddin, I am indebted to Walton's Music Gallery, Dublin.

For details of the 'Robin and Sea Whistle' incident on the Lugnaquilla Mountain, I acknowledge my debt to the account given by the grand-daughter of one of the persons involved, Mrs P. O'Toole, as told in *Béaloideas*, 1935 (National Library of Ireland).

Documents from the Irish State Paper Office, Dublin Castle, are reproduced herein by permission of the Director of the National Archives.

BOOK ONE

Part One

Let us go forth, we tellers of tales, and seize whatever prey the heart longs for, and have no fear. Everything exists, everything is true, and the earth is only a little dust under our feet.

W. B. Yeats, *The Celtic Twilight*

Chapter One

In autumn all things wither. In winter the earth sleeps as if dead. But in springtime life is renewed and young again.

So it is with the land, the eternal land that feeds mankind from generation to generation, shrugging off the dark shroud of winter's sleep to spring forth again with buds and shoots towards the fruitfulness of summer. Life, those who yearned hungrily for the abundance and continuance of life, knew it came only from the land, and the men who nurtured the land.

So it was with John Dwyer as he stood gazing over the fields of his farmland at Eadstown on the western side of the Glen of Imaal, a vast and lovely valley deep in the Wicklow hills.

He was a tall man, over six feet in height, strongly built, and still with traces of the handsomeness of his youth in his appearance. He turned as the figure of his twenty-four-year-old son stepped from the farmhouse into the yard, the eldest of his seven children, shrugging on his jacket and smiling.

' 'Tis going to be a good and warm spring, Daddy.'

John Dwyer smiled also. 'It is that, Michael. Where are you going?'

'To see Hugh Vesty.'

'Did you give him your promise? Will he be waiting for you?'

'I did, and he will.'

John Dwyer nodded resignedly. 'Then you must go. A promise is a promise, and not to be broken. But when,' he added, 'do you intend going up to Donard to see O'Casey the blacksmith for me?'

'Today,' Michael called back as he took the short cut across the fields in the direction of the high meadows. 'I intend to call on O'Casey today.'

'And suffer none of his nonsense. You will be firm with him now, won't you?'

'I will.'

'Do you promise?'

Michael's soft laughter came back to him. 'I do, Daddy, I surely do.'

John Dwyer was silent as he watched Michael walking away, a look of intense pride in his eyes. In Michael he saw all the wild energy of youth that he himself once had, and the son he once yearned to have.

His eyes followed his first and favourite son across the fields, a tall young man, with the lean strong body of a man who could reap an acre a day. The sun shone on his hair, not long and tied back as was the fashion in 1798, but cut in black curls which fell loosely around his neck.

Then his gaze moved from his son and rested on the distant cornfields, still young with springtime, and his eyes grew soft with pleasure.

Like all the other farmers of Wicklow, John Dwyer loved the land with a passion that never cools. A land that had belonged to their forefathers but was no longer theirs. Their inheritance stolen. Reduced from lords to land slaves rooting the earth for survival, their candlelit homes no more than a temporary sanctuary against the whim of a landlord who might one day decide to extend his gaming ground and turn them out, cast them into the depths of hell which was the lowlands and grass-barren streets of city beggars.

But when his mind is not idly pondering on ways to win back his inheritance, the Irish farmer thinks only of the land which he loves so deep in his soul he is not even conscious of it. He looks at it with the tender eyes of a lover while grumbling about its capriciousness. Damns it for a Judas for succumbing to the tyranny of winds or drought. Complains of too much rain, too much dry weather. Only in springtime, when the sowers bend under the morning sun does excitement glow on his face like an eager child's. And at summer's end, after threshing with the reapers in the mid-day heat and finally bringing in a good harvest, is his happiness as exalted and as satisfied as the young lover's after the glorious hard work of mating.

John Dwyer looked over his growing fields and smiled. The land was the source on which his life thrived; his wife and children the loves of his heart; his fields and animals were his friends – he wanted nothing more, satisfied with all that God had given him; a man content with his lot.

The air around him was soft and warm and as still as a young maiden asleep in the arms of her lover. A sudden memory from his youth made him lift his gaze again towards the high meadows, but his son was gone from sight.

It was late afternoon when Michael Dwyer arrived at the village of Donard on the north-west border of Imaal, in the company of his cousin Hugh Vesty Byrne; a tall, fair-haired young man of twenty-three, renowned for his ready smile.

When they reached the forge at the end of the square, Michael paused and gave a call into the dark interior.

The blacksmith stepped out, a squat, muscular man with a dome as bald as the crest of the moon. The rest of his head was clouded in a mat of brown hair turned grey for the most part. He was not much above five feet in height but he sported a huge moustache more suitable for a seven-footer. When he saw the two young men, he smiled nervously.

'Bless my soul!' he cried in a high pitch. 'If it isn't Michael Dwyer! God and Mary to you, avic. What brings you here?'

'It's about that suckling pig my father sold you at Christmas,' Michael said. 'Do you remember that?'

'What? When? At Christmas? That was a long time ago, wasn't it? In the winter, and now it's spring.'

'And now it's spring,' Michael agreed.

'So what could your father, in this lovely spring weather, have against me and the suckling pig he sold me at Christmas?'

'He thinks it's time you paid him for it.'

'The suckling pig? Did I not pay him for it?'

'You did not,' Michael said.

'Did I not? I thought I did. Ach, to be sure I must have!'

Michael glanced wearily at his cousin, then sternly at the blacksmith. 'Stop play-acting, Finbar.'

The blacksmith shifted nervously on his feet while he racked his brains for a reason or excuse. Michael Dwyer was a quiet boyo, but not one to mess with. Not that he was the troublesome type, far from it, but he could be as cold and as wild as the wind in winter at times.

'Well, avic?' Michael questioned. 'Now you are reminded that you did not pay for your Christmas feast, what do you say?'

In a sudden change of tone and mood, the blacksmith sighed tragically and laid his hand on Michael's arm, his face and voice depressed. 'Will you not come inside for a minute while I explain. Oh come in, Michael darling, come in and listen to me like a man, let you!'

7

Hugh Vesty Byrne smiled in amusement. Despite the dumpy blacksmith's muscular appearance, it was common knowledge that O'Casey had the liver of a chicken and the heart of a coward.

Inside the forge, O'Casey busied himself at the furnace with wooden cups and a jug of ale while he explained about his bad memory.

'Oh aye, 'tis a terrible affliction, sure enough. And what! – with business being so bad and the cat deciding to have her litter in the bellows! Lost me days of business, that did. Couldn't light the furnace.'

Michael stood gazing into the glow of the furnace while the blacksmith poured out the ale and his tales of woe and deprivation. Hugh Vesty, with his bent for teasing, urged him on, his face drooping in exaggerated sympathy.

'Poor man,' said Hugh Vesty sadly, 'you have your sorrows.'

'More sorrows than Job!' the blacksmith cried, then turned to Dwyer and prodded his chest. 'So now then, Michael darling, what would you say to a poor man whose finances have suffered so badly?'

Michael looked at the doleful face of the blacksmith, his eyes moving over the huge moustache that reminded him of the fleece of an old goat. 'I would say that you, unlike my father, have neither chick nor child waiting to be fed. So play the good neighbour and pay up like a decent fellow.'

'Now?'

'Yes, now.'

'Can I pay next month? Or maybe next week? I'll be in funds next month.'

'Now,' Michael repeated coldly.

The blacksmith wiped his hands on his apron, sighing loudly and unhappily as he dug into his pocket, withdrew his purse, and reluctantly paid up. 'My God,' he muttered tragically, 'but this is a hard life!'

'Oh aye, 'tis a life as hard as the Devil you have entirely,' said Hugh Vesty, patting the blacksmith's head and winking at his cousin.

Without waiting to drink the ale, Michael turned and moved through the dark forge out to the sunlight where he stopped and blinked at the sight of the dark girl walking towards him. She was accompanied by an older woman who was obviously her mother. Both dressed with taste and carried themselves with a gentle dignity.

Hugh Vesty also stood to stare at the girl, then his hands moved quickly to smooth down his tousled fair curls. O'Casey joined in the preening, wiping his hands across his apron as he pushed his way forward, then jutted out his chest like a rooster.

'Good day to you, Mrs Doyle,' he said in a fawning voice. 'And to you, too, Miss Doyle.'

Mrs Doyle paused to return the greeting graciously, but it was the girl who still claimed Michael's gaze. She was perhaps seventeen or eighteen, slim and tall, very appealing, very beautiful. She looked at him with dark eyes, soft, gentle, and warm, and for a moment there was a flickering return of interest, before she lowered her lashes and turned away.

Along with the others, Michael watched her walk on down the street, moving with an easy grace within a blue tailored habit, black hair hanging long and smooth to her waist.

The blacksmith's marble eyes danced with relish on the departing figure of the girl. 'Isn't she a darling!' he whispered, nudging Hugh Vesty. 'Don't you think so, avic, now you've seen her with your own two looking eyes?'

'Aye, but it was Michael here that she lowered the lashes to. You and me, old friend, never got a glance, good, bad, or indifferent.'

'What do I care for that?' said the blacksmith with a laugh. 'Sure wasn't she only playing coy to the hot passion in my eyes on her. And what's he beside me but an inexperienced long-legged colt next to a fine, mature champion.'

'Oh, no comparison,' Hugh Vesty agreed, then murmured under his breath, 'A thoroughbred next to a cart-horse.'

'Sure,' said the blacksmith in genuine conceit, 'I'm fifty-five years but I'm still in my beautiful prime.' He flicked his moustaches like an aristocrat. 'As fine and well bred as any man ever born in Imaal.'

'True for you, Finbar,' said Hugh Vesty, then spluttered out laughing.

'Hoigh!' the blacksmith cried furiously. 'I think 'tis me you're laughing at! How dare you laugh at an O'Casey!'

Michael was still watching the distant figure of the girl. The blacksmith prodded his chest. 'Make him stop laughing at me, avic.'

Michael glanced at O'Casey sideways. 'Doyle?' he said curiously. 'Is she the younger sister of John Doyle of Knockandarragh?'

9

'Aye, that's her, Mary Doyle. Just back from service in one of the big houses in Dublin. Her father sent her there in the hopes that some gentleman would snap her up and make him a rich man, but it seems young Mary never could settle for city life, spent all her time pining for the mountains.'

'Well, well,' Michael said with a smile. 'The last time I saw her she was a skinny little thing of about fifteen, gambolling over the hills like a wild young fawn.'

'Oh, she's changed, as you saw; lost all her frivolity.' The blacksmith nodded his head gravely. ' 'Tis lace-making and lavender baths and china on the table now. Doyle himself was here complaining just the other day, said Mary took a cloth and a jar of beeswax and polished him out of the house.'

'So what's wrong with cleanliness?' asked Hugh Vesty. 'You're a religious man. Isn't it as close as a skylark to Godliness?'

'Of course, 'tis the mother, Mrs Doyle, that's behind it,' the blacksmith went on. 'She has notions of grandeur, always has done. And now she's trying to make young Mary fit the same cut as herself. Did you see the way Madame was swishing along like one of the grand dames of Dublin? And Doyle himself nothing more than a penny-farthing farmer, for heaven's sake, only a mile away in the same Knockandarragh.'

'No need to be spiteful,' Michael told him quietly. 'John Doyle is a friend of mine. 'Tis offensive to hear to you speak of his mother that way.'

Startled, the blacksmith momentarily cowered under the rebuke, then laughed in a high quavering pitch.

'Ah don't be like that, avic. Sure I didn't mean no harm. No! Wasn't I only saying as how Mary has changed. And now that she's all grown up and has run away from service in Dublin, her father intends to recoup his losses by marrying her off. He has his own choice picked out for her. A well-to-do farmer, one with fat sows in his sty, good milk cows in his byre, and plenty of gold sovereigns in his box.'

'Poor girl,' said Hugh Vesty. 'Who is the farmer?'

'O'Riordan.'

'Poor girl,' said Hugh Vesty again.

'So you see,' the blacksmith prodded Michael in the chest, 'you'd be better to leave your mind off Mary Doyle. Her father is set on O'Riordan for her. Sure didn't I make a bid for her myself. Aye, I did! I may be older than O'Riordan but I'm bonnier looking and still in my prime.'

Again Michael glanced wearily at Hugh Vesty. 'Let's go,' he said. 'We've delayed with this beauty too long as it is.'

'All I'm saying, brothers,' continued the blacksmith, 'is that you have no chance there at all, neither of you. Not when her father turned even me down – and me an O'Casey!' His pitying expression confirmed his words; if an O'Casey was rejected, what chance had any other name?

'So why should we care?' said Hugh Vesty airily, moving to follow his cousin, who had turned away. 'We have our own little purties to court on the hills now spring is back.'

The blacksmith watched them as they strolled down the square, then move with ease up the steep hilly path directly opposite, the lines of their strong young bodies outlined in the red glow of the setting sun.

Who am I fooling? he said to himself. 'Tis they who are in their beautiful prime, not me. Devil roast them!

He turned and sulked back into the dark interior of the forge.

The following day Michael travelled from Eadstown to Knockgorrah, a journey of seven miles across country, ending with a wild and hilly path which struggled its way upwards around rocks and trees until it reached the remote and desolate area of the sheep hills, then spent itself at a low stone wall some yards from a small white thatched cottage surrounded by willow trees and wilderness.

At the door an old man stood waiting for his visitor with the eagerness of those who live alone. He was John Cullen, a mountain shepherd with woolly white hair that framed a face tanned by sun and wind. His pale blue eyes had a kind of virginal innocence in their expression, almost as if he had stepped from boyhood to maturity without experiencing the difficult years in between.

His waiting had the quiet stillness of a man who sits for hours on the deserted hills, hearing only an occasional bleating of sheep in the vast silence. But then, suddenly, he stood erect as his ears picked up the welcome sound of a human whistling on the path below.

Cullen stepped out and walked down to the low stone wall, his movements quick and vigorous. He put a hand to his brow and peered intently, then a delighted smile came on his face as his eyes took in the figure of a tall young man clad in buckskin knee-breeches and high mountain boots. Aye, it was Michael

11

for sure. No other lad had that walk of his – strong and lithe, like a mountain cat.

The old man smiled with relief, although he had never doubted that Michael would come. Being distantly related, he had known Michael Dwyer from the day of his birth and ever since. In days now gone the two had travelled together many times along the path of life, both sharing a deep love for the austere beauty and peaceful solitude of the wilderness, roving together over snow-covered hills in search of lost sheep, or sitting on the sunny banks of the Rivers Ow and Aughrim, watching in silent harmony as the salmon tried to elude the destiny of the nets.

They had been good friends, older man and boy, all through those years of bone-shivering winters and tranquil hot summers, but then childhood ended and the boy became a young man infatuated with the manly sports of his peers, displaying excellent skill with a pistol in the target contests, and a mastery over his competitors in the athletic exercises, especially in the hurling games which every man in Imaal turned out to watch.

Cullen absently scratched his chest as his eyes moved down the lush green slopes of the Glen of Imaal, twenty miles long, a green and lovely valley of silent lakes and dreaming meadows through which the River Slaney flows, rising on the Lugnaquilla Mountain then plunging in silver streams into deep mountain pools.

From a tree near the wall a bird sang in harmony with the whistling young man on the path below. Spring was in the air and everything stirred with the joy of warm fresh days and the promise of new life. And that life came from the land.

Cullen frowned as he turned his gaze back to the young man bending his steps towards him. Devil take the pistol shooting and the hurley games! he thought dismissively. What were they more than amusing diversions for Sundays and fair days. It was as a *farmer* that Michael was destined to survive. He was born for it. Had the God-given strength for it. A body only had to see him in the fields at harvest time, a scythe in his hand, muscles rippling through the skin on his back as he whirled the scythe in the air and swung it down to cut through the stalks with a speed and rhythm that was a joy to watch, the never-ending pivotal movements of his body and limbs swift yet calculated, the strike of the blade deadly accurate.

Closer now, Michael looked up at the old man, nodded and smiled.

Cullen suddenly turned and walked hurriedly back to the cottage, muttering to himself as if he had forgotten something important. Once inside he quickly made tea, an expensive drink he only made on special occasions, then placing the teapot on the fire-flag, he lifted the hot griddle breads from the gridiron over the fire, placed them on a chipped willow-pattern plate, and took his seat in the rocking-chair to the right of the inglenook, eagerly anticipating the pleasure of having a friend at his hearth. Life could be mortal lonesome for a solitary shepherd at times.

Michael sprang over the low stone wall, still whistling as he strolled towards the cottage. A milk-goat wandered out of the small adjacent barn and stared at him with soft yellow eyes, then twisted up her neck and offered her forehead. He obliged her with a gentle scratch.

When he entered the house, the old man smiled. 'I have the tea ready,' he said, 'and griddle bread as you like it.'

The interior of the two-roomed cottage was surprisingly clean and tidy for the habitat of a bachelor. In the long, low living-room the black oak dresser stood against the wall opposite the deep fireplace and a rectangular table stood between them. Against the far wall was a settle-bed on which the old man slept, although there was a four-poster in the bedroom which sported a cover of fine linen trimmed with Irish lace. But the heart and soul of the house was the turf fire which glowed warm and comforting in the hearth, above which hung a large faded picture of Christ carrying the lamb.

Within a minute Michael found a mug of tea and a piece of warm buttered griddle bread in his hands. Cullen watched him keenly as he tasted the tea and griddle bread, and when at last he swallowed and murmured his praise and appreciation, the old man sat nodding his head and smiling in satisfaction.

'You're late, but I knew you would come,' Cullen said happily, lifting the poker to stir the fire. 'You always do what you say you will do, come sun or snow, wind or rain.'

Michael was looking across to the far wall, at the settle-bed, neatly made up, but without its wooden day-time cover.

'Tell me something,' he said quietly.

The old man looked at him. 'Tell you what, treasure?'

'Why do you still sleep on that hard old settle-bed? Why deny yourself the pleasure of stretching out in the four-poster. 'Tis a sin to waste such comfort.'

13

Cullen shrugged. 'As well you know, Michael, the four-poster was my mother's bed, and I've never liked to use it.'

' 'Tis foolish of you all the same.'

The old man gazed into the fire with a reminiscent smile. 'I remember when she ordered that bed and made my father bring it on the cart from Dublin. It shamed the Da, God reward him, and amused the people greatly to see such a fine thing being carried up to this cottage. You see, the cart could not make it all the way up, so the Da and two neighbours had to carry it. Then, begor, we had to lift off the thatch to get it inside.'

Cullen smiled and took a long, reflective pull on his tea. 'But she loved the fine things, my mother. Aye, for sure. And I was her treasure.'

Michael looked thoughtfully at the old man, knew his loneliness. 'Are you ever sorry that you did not marry?' he asked.

Cullen glanced up, eyes clear and honest. 'There's not a sorrier man than me,' he said, 'from here to Glenmalure.'

Michael laughed. From here to Glenmalure was a distance of some nine miles over high and difficult mountains and not one human habitation on the whole route.

'Sweet-talking a woman is like most things in life,' Cullen said, 'there's a knack to it. I never had the knack. To me women always seemed troublesome creatures, noisy and confusing. Except my darling mother. Oh a mild creature *she* was. None kinder or more gentle in the whole of Imaal. And I'll ne'er forget the day she told me she was dying and me unable to stop her. Ach—' the old man shrugged, ' 'tis hard to be telling it! But if I could have found someone as gentle as her, maybe I would have tried harder to find the right words.'

Outside the sun was shining but inside the cottage was dim. Shafts of light sneaked through the two-foot square window and joined with the soft rays of the fire to cast a bronzed glow over the old man's face.

'I remember a time way back,' he continued, 'when I was about as young as yourself and a woman named Rosie Noonan set her hook at me. A big blowsy strap of a woman that talked so much I often thought the words would choke her. Oh, sorra the day she fixed her eye on me . . .'

Michael listened patiently as Cullen reminisced. He had heard it all many, many times before, but he smiled and widened his eyes in pretended surprise, giving an occasional murmur of disbelief or encouragement. He loved the old man.

14

At last Cullen paid tribute to his memories of Rosie Noonan, as he always did, with a shudder.

'So now then, treasure,' he said, reaching for his pipe, 'tell us what you've been up to these past two weeks. Are you still nudging and dallying with half the girls in Wicklow?'

Michael leaned back in the chair and placed a booted right ankle over his left knee, humour in his hazel eyes as he looked at the old man.

'Would you believe me,' he asked, 'if I told you I was not?'

Cullen considered, then chuckled. 'Not for a minute,' he said.

Chapter Two

Baltinglass Spring Fair was coming to a close. Throughout the day prices had been bartered for pigs and sheep and large sums paid for some of the finest horses ever seen in the three kingdoms.

Mary Doyle wandered over to where an old scribe sat on a wooden box busily writing the poems he still hoped to sell. He squinted badly, being blind in one eye, but his writing was neat and firm. He looked up at the dark-haired girl coming towards him, and smiled.

'Nearly done now, Mary,' he said. 'Only one more dip of the pen and I'll be finished.'

Mary sat on the edge of the box and peered over his shoulder, moving her lips slowly as she tried to read the words, a task she found very difficult, never having been to school, since it was considered that only males needed an education. Some fathers did employ a travelling hedgemaster to come into the house and teach their daughters in return for a few months' bed and board, but Mary's father had never believed in such nonsense.

'Can you read any better these days?' the scribe muttered as he wrote.

'A bit better,' Mary told him. 'When I was in Dublin I used to go see my aunt there, on my days off. She often made me try and read the newspapers to her.'

'Oh, she should never have made you do that!' The scribe looked outraged. 'Newspapers is full of lies and corruption not fit for a female!'

'I could only read a word here and there,' she assured him.

'Then shame on you, Mary Doyle! After all the Sunday afternoons I sacrificed trying to teach you. And it was not newspapers I wanted you to read, but the philosophers and poets – especially the poets.'

Mary sat silent, fearing he was about to launch into one of his lectures about the poets. The scribe turned his head to get a

16

better look at her, and met the worried gaze of her dark brown eyes.

'Are you still good at the sewing and lace-making?' he asked gently.

'Aye, I made a lace tablecloth in Dublin. My aunt sold it to one of the big houses in Stephen's Green for seven shillings and sixpence.'

When Mary gave him a bright, proud smile, the scribe thought her face one of the loveliest he had ever seen, a face so young and fresh it made him long for his own youth again, resent his advancing years now barren of all passion and pleasure. Only his memories and his poetry stopped him from becoming dry and withered like the rest of his age.

'Seven shillings and sixpence? God above, you don't need to read or write if your fingers can earn that kind of money.'

'Aye, and it's much easier than reading and writing,' Mary said, but the scribe was no longer listening; he was squinting at two of the gentry standing a few feet away, loudly discussing drenches, fetlocks and brood mares. The scribe hastily finished his poem, then bent down and scooped a spoonful of sand from a box and sprinkled it over the paper to dry the ink.

'Would you be interested in a fine piece of poetry, sir?' he shouted. ' 'Tis a good one! And only five dips of the pen did it,' he added proudly.

The two men moved on without favouring him a glance. The scribe shrugged, shook the sand from the paper, then looked again at the girl.

'Well, Mary,' he said, 'now all the selling is done, it's time for the singing and dancing. Will you be staying?'

'I suppose I must,' she said without enthusiasm, 'seeing as I have only just arrived. Will you be staying?'

The scribe nodded. 'I have more chance of selling a poem in the evening, when the lads are feeling romantic with the effects of the music and poteen and trying to win a girl.'

'I'd better find my mother and father,' Mary murmured, standing and drawing her shawl around her, then slipping a sixpenny piece into his hand, enough for three tots of whiskey. 'From the sale of my tablecloth,' she told him, smiling.

'Ah, Mary, no! Take it back. I'll sell a poem yet.'

The scribe watched her with his good eye as she strolled off, an unconscious swing to her hips and a lightness in her step.

17

'O Mary my lovely,' he muttered, ' 'tis yourself that's likely to drive the young bouchals to wild drinking tonight!'

The main camp fire had been set up on a hill just beyond the market square. Only the peasantry of Wicklow had remained to enjoy the final fun of the fair. Near this main fire the musicians played while young men and women danced, and some of the young men were the best dancers in Ireland. Large sheets of flat pine timber were placed on the ground so the steel-tipped toes of their hornpipe shoes could be heard clicking in time with the music. Many of the girls carried round wooden frames covered in goat hide which were normally used to carry meal to chickens, but now they held them over the fire to make the hide taut and used them as tambourines.

Around other small fires the older men were seated, smoking long-pipes and discussing the news of the day.

Trading finished, it was now time for the musicians and ballad singers to earn their money with the songs that were open to auction. A master of music was appointed to hold the hat while each man bid the choice of song that would please his partner. The man who bid the most placed his money in the hat and called the tune.

Mary found her parents sitting on wooden stools a little way from the main fire. Mrs Doyle inspected her daughter as she sat down: her red calico dress was still crisp and spotless, but she frowned disapprovingly at Mary's free-flowing hair.

'Why did you pull the pins out?' Mrs Doyle queried. 'You look like a gypsy with it hanging all around you like that.'

'Sure who's to see me?' Mary sighed, with exquisite indifference to half the young men on the hill gaping dreamily at her.

'Pat O'Riordan is to see you,' her father said testily. 'You look older with it pinned up, more responsible. Pat O'Riordan may—'

'Pat O'Riordan,' Mary said, 'couldn't tell the difference between a woman and a prize heifer.'

'And by the hokey, here's himself now!' William Doyle rose to his feet and thrust a hand towards the big red-faced man who approached their stools. 'Good evening to you, Pat! Wasn't Mary just talking about you?'

Pat O'Riordan flushed a deeper red as he looked at Mary.

His face shone as if it had been scrubbed mercilessly and his cravat appeared to be strangling him.

'Hello, Mary,' he said, sitting down beside her. 'Isn't it a grand fine night, praise be to God.'

'It would be hard to find fault with it, Pat,' her father answered when Mary said nothing, only nodded curtly.

Pat O'Riordan was forty years old with a thatch of fair hair, a red, thick neck and enormous hands. He accepted with thanks the wooden cup of whiskey that Mary's father had filled from a bottle at his feet, then talked for a time to Mr and Mrs Doyle about aspects of farming, but when William Doyle motioned his head silently and significantly in the direction of his daughter, Pat O'Riordan cleared his throat and said nervously,

'Well now, Mary, is it true what I'm told, that you're a fair hand at making the butter and the cheese?'

'No,' she answered, 'I'm useless at making the butter and the cheese.'

'Now that's not true, darling,' her father said quickly.

'Of course, it's a skill that's easily learned,' O'Riordan said. 'And how is your hand at milking the cows?'

Mary looked at him demurely. 'Bold things, they behave something terrible when I try it, Mr O'Riordan. And 'tis worse when I sing to them.'

O'Riordan frowned. 'Why is that? Most cows love a song. Makes the milk fall sweetly.'

'Aye, I know.' Mary seemed puzzled. 'But when I sing they get all excited and try to dance, swishing their tails and jumping and sending the bucket flying till ne'er a drop of milk can be got.'

'Oh, now,' O'Riordan said gravely, 'milking is a serious business and flighty songs don't help at all.' He puckered his mouth, then a hopeful expression came into his eyes. 'I have plenty of pigs. Do you by any chance get on with the pigs?'

'Oh, I do. I gave ours a wash down once.'

'Once!'

Mary nodded. 'Truly. On another occasion I took out their feed, but I didn't like that. The smell of the old potato skins made me feel quite sick.'

William Doyle almost convulsed at this blatant lying from his daughter. He said quickly, 'But isn't Mary a beautiful girl, Pat O'Riordan? Everyone hereabouts seems to think so. Some have even hinted they'd be prepared to hire a woman for the jobs if they could have a chance of Mary at their hearth.'

'Hire a woman!' O'Riordan erupted. 'God preserve us!'

Mary's mother was a good-natured, handsome woman, if a little vain and giddy. Her hair was arranged elaborately in the latest style, knotted at the nape with girlish curls wisping around her face.

'My Mary,' she said, 'has all the refinements of a lady, and you don't usually find a lady near a pigsty. Of course,' she patted her hair proudly, 'Mary used to be on the thin side, but I soon rounded her out grand by putting plenty of butter on her potatoes.'

'Plenty of butter on her potatoes!' O'Riordan choked. 'Oh, now,' he said, nervous again, 'I've never agreed with plenty of butter on the potatoes. It's a wasteful extravagance, surely?'

Mary caught sight of a group of young men approaching the fire: one was her brother. She raised her hand to wave. 'There's John,' she said, dropping her hand quickly as her eyes moved to the young man strolling at his side.

'And is it Michael Dwyer with him?' O'Riordan cried, eager to break up the conversation. The business of the match was not turning out as he had hoped. Beauty was a fine thing, but it could fly in a night. Strong arms and shoulders, good child-bearing hips, and a capacity for hard work were what a wise man looked for when dealing for a wife; and Mary Doyle was not up to that standard. Plenty of butter on the potatoes indeed! He'd not worked hard all these years to have a slip of a girl like Mary Doyle pauper him.

'Hello there, Michael,' O'Riordan called, as the five young men approached. 'Isn't it the grand fine night, glory to God?'

'It is,' Michael said, his eyes on Mary, 'a night for angels at your window.'

'But a drop of rain would come in handy now,' O'Riordan said, 'handy for the soil.'

'The devil with your soil,' said Mary's brother. 'Is it to dampen the fire and spoil the merrymaking you want?'

'And who are these boys with you, John?' Mrs Doyle asked her son, patting her hair again.

'Allow me,' John said with a brash air, and pointing to each man in turn, 'to introduce Michael Dwyer, Hugh Vesty Byrne, John Mernagh, and Martin Burke. All good and hearty friends of mine. And lads – my mother and sister Mary. You all know my father and Pat O'Riordan.'

Mrs Doyle smiled and nodded at each of the young men in turn, but Mary's dark gaze was fixed on Michael.

'Are you not joining the dancing?' he asked her in a low voice.

She stared back at him, lips half open to say she would love to join the dancing, but her father said, 'No, she's not – she's in the company of Mr O'Riordan.'

'Ah,' Michael said, then gave Mary a slight, rueful smile before turning away; her brother and his three companions following at his heels as he strolled back towards the camp fire and the merrymaking.

All over the slope of the hill, candles were being lit inside box lanterns as darkness fell. For almost half an hour Mary dismally watched the young people singing and dancing around the fire while her parents and Pat O'Riordan verbally battled in polite tones. She now desperately wanted to join the younger group, to join in and sing with them. Even the music seemed to have changed, no longer jigs and hornpipes, but vibrant, exiting music that made her edgy with restlessness.

'Did you hear that Michael Dwyer won a packet of money today?' O'Riordan said conversationally. 'At the target-shooting contest. Creighan, Coogan, and Case were the losers.'

'Creighan, Coogan, and Case,' repeated William Doyle with a frown. 'Aren't they militiamen? What was he doing sporting with militiamen?'

'Relieving them of every penny they had,' O'Riordan said. 'And most of it won from poor lads more used to handling a spade than a pistol. But sure, Michael's been shooting game over the mountains since he was ten years old, so they say.'

'How much did he win?' Doyle asked curiously.

'Enough to make the militiamen purple with fury.' O'Riordan suddenly chuckled. 'Cripes, but it was a pleasure to watch! They'd made a wooden life-sized replica of a man with a fat nose, eyes and mouth and even a beard drawn on. When Michael had won three rounds, Robin Case insisted they mark rings around every other hole in the wood, then drew a heart about the size of a kitten's head which was to be the hit. Creighan chipped an arm, Coogan missed altogether, but Case was bang on target, inside the heart. "Beat that," he said, so Michael did. He shot out the target's eye.'

'But if the heart was the hit,' Doyle said, 'then he lost.'

'That's what Case maintained, shouting and cursing like a

madman, so Michael let him have the purse; then suggested they stake everything they had won on the next round, just him and Case – for the other eye. All or nothing on one shot.'

O'Riordan held out his cup for another refill. 'Well, Robin Case accepted the challenge, placed his money on the ground, ordered Michael to do the same, then, after insisting on first shot, Case took careful aim with both hands and hit a shoulder. Cripes! Before Case could even utter a curse Michael had turned, swung up his arm and shot out the other eye without even waiting to aim, or so it seemed.'

'God!' cried Doyle, 'that's what you call a crack shot.'

'Aye, and a canny one too,' laughed O'Riordan, knocking back his whiskey and holding out his cup for yet another refill. 'Seconds later Michael had reloaded his pistol and pointed it straight at Case while he lifted up the money and backed away, a smile like a Kilkenny cat on his face.'

'Robin Case,' said Mrs Doyle thoughtfully. 'Isn't he a son of the Cork man?'

O'Riordan nodded. 'Aye, a son of the Cork man, but his mother is pure Wicklow.'

'Then Dwyer should have given half the money back,' snapped William Doyle, suddenly annoyed that O'Riordan was showing no further interest in Mary.

All Mary's interest was fixed on Michael Dwyer, who, unlike his friends, had not danced, although he was dressed for dancing. His buckskin boots had been replaced with shoes and brown wool stockings. He wore a cream shirt, brown whipcord knee-breeches and matching coat. He had his arm around the waist of a pretty girl with a mass of dark curls hanging over her shoulders who looked up at him adoringly. For a long time they had been talking and laughing together, but now they looked at each other solemnly, as if their topic of conversation had suddenly changed.

Mary sighed, feeling deeply depressed as she watched the girl's upturned face and wondered what she was saying so earnestly to Michael Dwyer.

'If you like her that much,' the girl was saying, 'why don't you just up and approach her and ask her to dance.'

Michael glanced sidelong at Mary, who sat with head bent as she fiddled with the fringe of her shawl.

'God help her,' the girl murmured, 'she looks fair miserable sitting there. And that red-necked bull of a man is paying no heed to her at all, just drinking her da's whiskey and spraying the fumes on the suffering mother. And sure, isn't he old enough to be her father?'

'I think I will,' Michael said slowly. 'I think I will ask her to dance, and bedamned to O'Riordan.'

The girl smiled as he walked purposefully towards the stools where the Doyles and Pat O'Riordan sat.

'Would you . . .' his voice scraped, 'would you care to join the dancing, Miss Doyle?'

Mary looked up, her expression bewildered as her eyes travelled past him to find the girl.

'No, she can't join the dancing,' William Doyle said impatiently. 'Haven't I said she's in the company of Mr O'Riordan.'

'Ach, take her to the dancing, Michael!' O'Riordan cried drunkenly. 'There's a good boyo!'

'God's curse on you, O'Riordan!' William Doyle shouted, almost as drunk. 'Is it only to drink my whiskey you want, while you send my girl off with another man?'

'Sure we've only done one bottle,' O'Riordan said. 'You've two more left, fair play to you.'

Mary had risen to her feet. She looked confused. 'What about that girl?' she said.

'Which girl?' Michael looked behind him to the crowd at the fire, then understood. 'Oh, you mean Anne Devlin? She's a first cousin. My mother's niece.'

'By God, O'Riordan!' bellowed Doyle. 'I'll curse you by sun and candlelight if you're playing games with me this night!'

'Playing games is it? All I'm asking, William Doyle, is for you to come and look at my lovely brown mare. She has haunches on her as sleek and lovely that would make a man shiver with pleasure.'

'Devil take your blasted mare! Her haunches are nothing as lovely and sleek as my Mary's. And as for my bottles – isn't it yourself that always comes empty-handed, I'm thinking!'

Mrs Doyle leaned forward on her stool. 'Take Mary to the dancing,' she said quietly to Michael. Then to Mary: 'I'm going to join the other matrons, dear. Your daddy and Mr O'Riordan will argue now until all the bottles are finished.' She patted her hair wearily. 'God's curse on the same drink, it has ruined many a good match. Although . . .' she lowered her voice to a whisper, 'despite what your daddy says, I do not consider Pat O'Riordan a good match for *my* girl.'

Mary smiled with relief, knowing that she now had an ally in the battle against the match with Mr O'Riordan.

Michael and Mary walked in a separate silence towards the camp fire. He caught her hand as they joined the weaving throng of dancers and Mary's cheeks flushed with pleasure as she was welcomed into the circle of young people. There was such happiness and gaiety in the air, light hearts and life pulsed all about her as they moved round the fire in dance after dance.

'Might you truly marry that miser?' Michael suddenly breathed as the music stopped.

'O'Riordan?' She made a face. 'No, never. Men like Pat O'Riordan don't marry women. They marry land or a dowry. Why do you ask?'

'Just wondering,' Michael said with the slightest of smiles.

They were silent for a moment, staring at one another, caught up in the heady potion of mutual attraction. 'What tune would you like?' he asked.

'Oh . . . something wild and gay.' She smiled. 'You choose.'

When she smiled, he noticed, her dark eyes narrowed at the corners in a very attractive way. 'Something wild and gay,' he repeated softly.

Suddenly he turned and called for a tune. Nobody bid against him, and he placed his money in the hat. When the fiddles and flutes struck up with a strong wild beat, Michael raised his hands over his head and began to clap them in time with the music, a challenge in the smile he levelled at Mary.

For a long moment she stood irresolute as Michael and the other young men began to stamp their feet like so many Cossack soldiers. Then the girls began to thump their tambourines, urging Mary on, and when Michael's cousin handed her a tambourine with an encouraging nod, a delicious madness swept over her and she stepped out to meet the challenge.

The circle of dancers fell back, yielding space and clapping hands as they watched the black-haired couple move around the circle of the fire's flames to the primitive beat of the music. They danced as if they had known each other all their lives or in another age. They danced like the gypsies, not even the wild Wicklow gypsies, but the ones who had come to Ireland from a place called Hungary in the quest for magic potions and good horses. And it was that night, the night of the Spring Fair in

1798, that many saw the wild recklessness that was in Michael Dwyer was also in Mary Doyle. Underneath those ladylike ways of hers, she was still a mountain girl.

Her shawl had fallen on to the grass and her firm breasts stood out under the tight red bodice, the mane of black hair swinging around her face as she danced, red skirt flying provocatively, matching in colour the huge vermilion flames of the fire as she whirled and twirled, revealing the frill of a white petticoat and fine bare legs stained bronze by the firelight.

Many of the old men almost swooned with pleasure, for she had the ankles of a thoroughbred dancing over the grass to the starting post, side-stepping and flinging up her slender neck and black glossy mane just like the black filly that won the ribbon at the Donard Races – when was it? Last spring, was it?

The matrons sat gaping as he put his arms around her and both leaned back from the waist, spinning faster and faster to the feverish excitement of the thumping tambourines. Then, with a high, strident, triumphant screech, the fiddles abruptly stopped – and Mary fell dizzily against Michael. He took the tambourine from her hand and laughed as he threw it high above their heads while the air thundered with whistling and hand-clapping applause.

The old scribe sat with a knowing smile on his face as he watched the pair of them, already wording a poem about the young bouchal and beauty who had danced so wildly. There was never a girl more ready for love than Mary Doyle, and any man who had watched her dance would see it.

O'Casey the blacksmith had watched her dance, and was so overheated he took a long gulp of his ale and wiped the sweat from his brow and huge moustaches.

' 'Tis not right for her to show her legs like that,' O'Casey barked at Mrs Doyle. 'If 'twere up to me, I'd bring the priest to her!'

Some of the matrons muttered in pious agreement, but most laughed, while Mrs Doyle ignored him. 'I was a fine dancer myself,' she told the other matrons, 'once upon a time.' She sighed sadly and patted her curls into place as she remembered her girlhood.

Maudlin with whiskey, William Doyle put his arm around Pat O'Riordan. 'Is she not beautiful?' he whimpered, tears rolling down his cheeks. 'My Mary.'

'You're beautiful,' Michael whispered into her hair, 'the

loveliest thing I ever saw.' His arms were around her waist, holding her close. The music was starting again, a buzz of conversation welled from the crowd as partners were chosen.

Mary was still breathless from the dancing and the excitement in her stomach caused by the closeness of his body which felt warm and strong and trembled with her own. She felt exhilarated, never in the wildest throes of her life had she ever felt this mad before, this reckless, this *wonderful*.

They were abruptly broken apart by two smiling girls who fell upon them. One was the cousin with black curls, Anne Devlin; the other was Michael's eighteen-year-old sister Cathy.

Ignoring Michael's protests they steered Mary over to the table laden with food and plied her with questions about herself. In the confusing excitement of the night, Mary exchanged laughter and information with the girls as she hungrily ate the food handed to her. She learned that Michael had three sisters and three brothers, and his father farmed a holding of fifty acres in Eadstown, in the west of Imaal.

Then the ballads started. Everyone began to move back around the fire. Some of the young men hovered around Mary, but Michael held out his hand to her, and when she grasped it, he held her hand fast, raising it slightly as he eyed the men, silently indicating his claim on her.

Songs of love and heartbreak were sung as the fire was fed and flared up again. Lips smiled and faces shone, shadowing when the flames lost their height. Then came the slow, melancholy songs that spoke of human bondage and lost freedom. Everyone joined in, swaying slowly to the music, their voices soft with an ancient sadness. And then the voices abruptly silenced – and only the lilting, painful music echoed over the dark hills as the strings of the fiddles whined and wailed and screamed under the moon and stars, trembling wildly with an old and bitter grief that made some of the old men around the smaller fires droop their heads and weep without tears, the music stirring their souls in the way that only music can.

Then the fiddles ebbed in their wailing and trembled into a fluttering whimper, and joined by the harmonising flutes, mellowed into a soothing melodic croon, lilting to almost a lullaby, and everyone breathed easy again.

The music changed, became young and lusty and joyful. The bódhran thumped, thumped, thumped, the mandolin twanged. The tune of the flute soared up and up and up like an albatross flying, *high* up in the sky. The tambourines clicked, clicked, clicked, and shoes were tapping, hands were clapping, skirts were swinging, eyes were smiling, lips were laughing . . .

And the old men muttered as they watched the young ones dancing merrily, all smoking their pipes and pretending to be glad that they were no longer a part of those heady days of youth that could never come to them again.

The main fire was fed once more, logs and dry branches that quickly flared into soaring red and gold flames. A young blind ballad singer, a pretty girl with an exquisite voice, smiled when the people called for her to sing. But as singing was the only way she had ever earned her supper, she waited until the pennies had stopped clinking into the hat before she strummed her mandolin, and the hill fell silent as her voice drifted sweetly on the air.

'There's an old, old serenade that only gypsies know,
    Calling through the forest glade from the long ago;
Once a roaming Romany sang that sweet song to me,
    Now my heart is sighing for his melody.'

The listening crowd round the fire swayed in happy unison as she sang, then all softly joined her in the chorus.

'Oh play to me, Gypsy, the moon's high above,
    Oh play me your serenade, the song that I love.
Oh sing to me, Gypsy, and when you are gone,
    Your song will be haunting me and lingering on.'

And all the time, as they stood hand in hand, Michael's fingers caressed and stroked Mary's fingers until she could feel herself flush with sensations she had never before experienced, could not define, bringing a quickening to her pulse and a heat to her blood. She resisted the urge to turn and look at his face, even though she knew that, like almost everyone else, he was staring into the fire.

'When I hear that serenade come stealing in my dreams,
I can see the forest glade beneath the bright moonbeams.'

Mary tried to concentrate on the words but all her senses

were focused on the warm hand holding hers, fingers tightly entwined and palm pressed to palm. Her whole body seemed to be on fire. Her head swam as the delicious music began to intoxicate her.

> 'Beside your caravan the camp fire is bright,
> So I'll be a vagabond just for tonight.'

He must have sensed more than heard her deep intake of breath. He turned his head and met her eyes. In the firelight they studied each other, saw what they wanted to see, spoke by silence.

Swiftly he stepped back and drew her outside the ring of the crowd into the darkness. They did not speak, but both trembled. He put his hands on her waist, then bent his head and his lips moved on hers, her head jolted back as if his kiss burnt her. Then that something which frightened her vanished with a snap, and arms, bodies, limbs, lips, joined in a frenzied pressure as they wrapped themselves into each other and kissed with a passion innocent of all shame.

And so lost were they in the exciting and unfamiliar world of each other, neither heard the warning sound of sudden silence from the music and singing until the circle of people broke asunder and the glow of the fire reached them.

And even then they continued cleaving together, until they heard a man's harsh, malicious laugh, and the dream was broken. Michael looked over her head and blinked, then in a flash he was alert and stared at the three uniformed militiamen standing a few yards away. He recognised them instantly as Creighan, Coogan and Case.

Robin Case stood with legs apart and fists on hips. A huge man, solid and powerfully built, with a certain fame for being a fire-eater.

'Romancing is it now, Dwyer?'

When Michael made no answer, Case gave a vicious little laugh. 'Such a shame to spoil your pitch, Dwyer, but we could not stop ourselves thinking about you, thinking that maybe it was a grand night to teach you a lesson, one you've obviously not yet learned – about staying in your shagging corn fields and not thinking you can ape your betters.'

Case gave another vicious laugh and looked at the shocked group around the fire. 'And what better place to teach you, we

28

said, than before all these people who think you're such a darling boy with a pistol in your hand.'

The people continued to stare at the three uniformed men. 'Anyone who interferes,' Case suddenly thundered, 'will be arrested and charged and without doubt transported or hanged!'

Mary was staring in white incredulity at the three militiamen. 'What is happening?' she whispered to Michael.

Michael kept his eyes on the yeomen as he moved her away from him. 'Go back to your mother, Mary. The entertainment these three heroes have in mind will not be fitting for a female.'

Mary moved away but hovered with the watching crowd.

'Only three against one?' Michael said wryly. 'You must be feeling mighty fearless tonight, Case.'

'Three against three more like!' Michael's cousin, Hugh Vesty Byrne, sprang from nowhere and locked his arm around Creighan's throat. A second later Martin Burke had captured Coogan in the same stranglehold.

Robin Case looked behind him at the two lads holding his yeomen. 'You're asking for trouble, Byrne!' he bawled.

'So are you, Case,' Hugh Vesty warned. 'Seek and you shall find.'

The yeoman hesitated. It was common knowledge that Hugh Vesty Byrne was the best wrestler in all Wicklow, and the most dangerous.

'We have no dispute with you boys,' Case said angrily. 'It's the sharpshooter here we want. But if that's the way you want to play it—' he turned back to Michael, 'I'll take him on my own.'

Mary stared at the huge man who was grinning at Michael with a cruel twist to his mouth.

'All right, Dwyer, let it be just you and me in it. A fight fair and square, man to man. Do you agree with that, Byrne?' he called over his shoulder to Hugh Vesty. 'A fight fair and square. And when I've finished with him, we walk away undisturbed by you and your friends, with no hard feelings.'

' 'Tis Michael you should be asking,' Hugh Vesty answered. 'It's him you want to murder.'

Case laughed, then spread his legs and bent them at the knees, his bulky shoulders hunched forward in the posture of attack, his hands beckoning to Michael.

'Come on, Dwyer, let's see how sharp you are without a gun

in your hand. Oh, come on, Michael *darling*. What's wrong with you, boy? Afraid?'

Michael's face had remained inscrutable, only his eyes betrayed the rage inside him. 'Man to man,' he said, carefully circling the ground with Case as he removed his coat and flung it aside. 'Fair and square.' He spread out his arms. 'No weapons.'

'No weapons,' Case said, his face full of contempt as he removed and threw down his pistol. 'I'll kill you with my bare hands.'

Martin Burke let out a laugh, for although Hugh Vesty was considered the best wrestler in all Wicklow, no one had yet equalled Michael Dwyer when it came to the foot and hip for a pitch-over.

Michael looked over at Martin and smiled almost lazily, then suddenly sprang at the yeoman and caught him off guard, gripping his shoulders and violently hipping him in an attempt to pitch him to the ground, but Case staggered backwards. Michael followed with a full drive to the stomach which doubled the yeoman on to his knees, groaning gutturally, head almost touching the ground.

'You came looking for trouble, and you got it,' Michael said. 'Now go home, Case.'

The man addressed made no reply, only slowly moved to his feet, half dazed.

Michael bent and picked up Case's pistol, turned to hand it over but Hugh Vesty's shout came a second too late. Michael's head jerked from the force of the yeoman's back-fist across his face, followed by a blast to the gut which sent him careening backwards.

'Kill him, Case! Kill the croppy upstart!' a yeoman shouted excitedly.

'Now that's not nice,' Hugh Vesty rebuked as he gave his captive a hard slap on the head.

Michael was on his feet, swaying slightly, but Case had fully recovered himself, crouching with arms half extended, moving forward like a loping gorilla. He lunged and caught Michael in a crushing bear hug, making him gasp as he stared into the yeoman's grinning face, aware that Case's iron grasp had sent many a man into a dead faint.

Wheezing painfully for breath, Michael moved his hands and arms inch by inch around the yeoman's waist until they were both in a crushing embrace, then with a surge of strength, he managed to lift Case until his heels left the earth.

'Now give him the foot and hip!' Hugh Vesty ordered, and Michael did.

Robin Case let out out a ferocious roar as he was pitched on to the ground. His eyes looked up at Michael as if insane. 'Bastard, bastard,' he grunted, moving on to his knees. In a second he had lunged at Michael's legs, clawing at his thighs and shirt and bringing him down in a brutal tackle before throwing his great weight full on top of him. And once he had him there, Case pushed down a hand and withdrew a pocket pistol. 'I'll finish you, you bastard!'

Michael stared at the small gun the yeoman clutched in one hand, thick stubby fingers moving for the hammer and trigger.

'You lying son of a loose mother!' Michael gritted, clawing and writhing with a superhuman effort to get a grip on the gun and his survival and finally wrenching it out of Case's hand.

'Bastard, bastard,' Case grunted, then swiftly jerked up his lower body and would have rammed a crushing knee into Michael's groin if Michael had not placed the muzzle of the gun against his shoulder and pulled the trigger.

A great gasp rose up from the crowd and for one long moment the yeoman stared down into the eyes of his adversary, eyes bulging like two blue moons, then the eyes drifted upwards and his body slumped down.

The two lay still for a moment, then Michael rolled Case off him and sprang to his feet, his breath coming in hard gasps. His shirt was ripped down the front, his naked chest stained with Case's blood.

'You croppy bastard!' Coogan shouted. 'You've taken his life!'

'He tried for mine,' Michael answered, throwing the gun down. 'But if it was to kill him I wanted, I would have aimed at his throat, not his shoulder.'

A woman rushed forward to examine Case. 'No, he's not dead,' she cried. 'Oh, thank God!' She peered closer. 'No . . . I don't think any of the vital parts are damaged. But he'll need a doctor to lift out the bullet.'

Two other women quickly joined her. One bent and ripped at her petticoat. 'Here,' she said, holding out a strip of cotton, 'use this to stop the bloodflow.'

'What are you doing?' Hugh Vesty demanded. 'Tending

and fussing him like that. He tried for Michael's murder!'

'That may be so,' a woman answered, 'but if he dies they'll have a sound reason to hang Michael, and the bla'guard is not worth swinging for.'

The women carefully removed Case's coat and dressed the wound, then Hugh Vesty ordered the other two militiamen to take him home.

Michael was standing with hands on waist and head down, drawing slow breaths into his lungs, but in the end he forced himself to look at Mary. Her face was stark white against her dark hair, eyes huge and black with shock. She was shaking like a person suffering from a bad chill.

He took a step towards her.

She took a step away from him.

'Mary . . .' There was a desperate appeal in Michael's voice, but she turned and ran. For a long moment he stared after her, then abruptly turned about and walked off in the opposite direction without a further glance at anyone.

He was halfway down the hill when his cousin Anne Devlin caught up and grabbed his arm. 'She's upset, Michael. She's not thinking straight.'

Michael looked at her. 'Did you see the way she looked at me, Anne? As if I was a . . . a brute of some sort.'

'It was the horror of it, Michael. She saw you near kill a man.'

'And what did she expect me to do? Lie there like a gentleman and politely let him murder me?' His mouth twisted. 'I was never that big a fool for a woman.'

His sister Cathy came running down to them, clutching his coat. 'Oh, Michael! Is your stomach hurt bad? Oh, Michael . . .' She reached out to touch the skin on his bruised ribs.

He brushed her hand aside and took the coat. 'Don't mention any of this to Mother or Daddy,' he warned her, then walked away.

'He's mortal upset about Mary Doyle,' said Anne Devlin as they stood and watched him go. 'He can't understand why she turned and ran from him.'

'And why should he understand?' Cathy snapped. 'We all saw the way of the two of them when the crowd parted. Would she have run to him and showered him with tears if he'd allowed his body to be smashed, I wonder?'

'The poor girl was shaking with shock,' Anne insisted.

'I could shake her some more for upsetting my brother only minutes after he'd near been killed by the same gun.'

Cathy clutched her skirts and marched furiously back up the hill. Anne Devlin followed her cousin at a slower pace, knowing only too well that the Dwyer family had a fierce feeling of love for each other.

Chapter Three

The morning was dull and grey after two days of rain. On the mountainside in Leoh, some miles away from John Cullen's cottage at Knockgorrah, Michael Dwyer stood with arms folded and listened patiently as the old man raged in fury at another shepherd.

'I can tell the cry of my own lambs,' Cullen stormed, 'and 'tis three of my lambs you have in that flock over there. I was slow in putting my mark on them.'

The other shepherd spat on the ground. 'All those sheep are mine!'

'Oh, you divil!' Cullen cried. 'You're new to these parts, and thinking I was alone with no kith or kin you thought you could do what you like to me. But let me tell ye—' Cullen squared his shoulders threateningly, 'any man who interferes with John Cullen or his sheep soon finds out he has Michael Dwyer to answer to!'

Michael pretended interest in a bird flying overhead as Cullen threatened away. Two other men had now arrived on the scene to listen to the quarrel.

'I have none of your blasted lambs!' insisted the shepherd.

'A good shepherd knows his own sheep like his own children.' Cullen turned to the two onlookers. 'Isn't that right, men?'

The two onlookers nodded solemnly.

'And the sheep know their own herd too. Those are three of my babies crying over there.'

'Bah to your talk,' snapped the shepherd. 'I've had enough of it!'

Cullen dropped his shoulders and turned to Michael. ' 'Tis no use, treasure, you'll have to sort him out for me.'

'And what are you going to do?' the shepherd snarled at Michael. 'Standing there like Solomon himself! Demand we cut the lambs down the middle and take three halves each?'

Michael shrugged. 'The solution is simple. Bring your flock over here and see if any of the lambs break loose and manage to get suck from Cullen's ewes. If you're any sort of a decent sheepman, you will know when a lamb is with its own dam.'

The shepherd eyed the two onlookers, unable to deny the challenge and maintain his honour. He nodded, then turned and marched towards his flock. Michael followed and helped to drive the sheep towards Cullen's small flock, stopping a few yards away.

Cullen let out a joyful laugh as three of the lambs broke from the flock and ran towards their dams. 'Look at them!' he cried, seconds later. 'Look at them nuzzling and sucking.'

Michael looked levelly at the shepherd. 'Those are not your lambs,' he said.

'Well damn my eyes, but I didn't steal them! They must have got mixed up with mine somehow on the hills.'

'A good shepherd knows his own sheep!' Cullen repeated sourly, then turned to Michael. 'Come along, my bouchal, let's you and me partake of some refreshment over by that rock. I'll leave Captain here to hold the flock.' He bent to the dog who cowered slightly. 'And do a better job this time!'

As they strolled away Cullen glanced venomously over his shoulder at the sheep-stealer.

'Did you get any honey?' Michael asked as they approached the rock.

Cullen nodded and opened his bag. 'Aye, I got a good supply from the bee-keeping woman only yesterday.'

Once Michael had eaten the oaten cake and honey which the old man gave him, he rose to leave. 'I have to get back. I have my own work to do now the rain has stopped. I told Daddy I would only be a few hours.'

'Will you come over tomorrow and walk the hills with me for an hour or so?' Cullen asked. 'Just to let that sheep-stealer know I have reinforcements at my beck and call. Some divils play sorely on a mortal if they think he's alone and defenceless. Oh, aye! But with you at my side, if he bothers me, I'll just spit at his feet and see what he does about *that*.'

Michael smiled. 'Not tomorrow,' he said. 'But I'll come for an hour or two the day after.'

The ground was damp and slippery from the rain. Mary walked slowly over the hills towards Dernamuck still full of confusion.

She had not seen Michael Dwyer since the night of the fair a week past, and since then there had been a kind of dull ache under her breast. She no longer knew how she felt about him. In a way she felt afraid of him. She still could not come to terms with the way he had deliberately fired the ball through the militiaman's shoulder.

Strands of hair blew around her face as she walked. She shook them back wearily. The morning was well on and still no sign of any sun to dry the land.

She sighed, her memories of that night a confused tangle of hot excitement and cold shock: music, wild dancing, warm lips kissing hers – then violence, terrible violence, and a gun being fired.

But worse, much worse than all the violence was the warning she had been given on returning home that night by her brother.

'Be careful in that quarter, Mary. When it comes to the men, Michael is a fine companion and a true friend, but 'tis common knowledge that he's nudging and dallying with perhaps half a dozen girls up and down Wicklow.'

Miserably she gazed around her, then gasped in shock – the subject of her thoughts was standing on the hill just above where she stood, leaning against an upstanding rock and contemplating her tranquilly.

She turned and blindly started to run, desperate to have no contact with him until she had sorted out her tangled feelings. Her shawl fell from her shoulders, she paused to pick it up, clutching a corner and letting it trail behind her as she ran on. Her feet slipped on the damp grass as she skidded, then stumbled and half rolled down the hill, letting out a sharp cry of pain as her face banged against the upjutting roots of a tree.

She lay with her face on the ground, not in the least surprised when his hands went to her shoulders and lifted her into a sitting position. All the time she had been running she had heard his footsteps closing in on her.

'Are you hurt?'

She shook her head. 'I'm not hurt. Go away.'

'You've grazed your face. It's bleeding a little.' He put his hand in his coat pocket, pulled out a white linen square and handed it to her.

She sat staring at the handkerchief, at the clean whiteness that told of a doting mother. Then the pain of her cheekbone broke the rigour of her posture. She pushed his hand and the handkerchief aside and moved on to her knees and stood up. 'I'm all right, I tell you. Just . . . go away!'

She bent and fumbled at the hem of her petticoat, her hands groping for the pocket which held her own handkerchief, and pressed it to her cheek.

He stood watching her silently for a moment, then told her, 'Robin Case, the yeoman, he's no longer in danger from his injury. His recovery is certain.'

She was looking at him now, hand to her cheek and head on one side. 'Have you ever killed anyone?' she whispered.

'Why should I ever kill anyone?' he asked, astonished. Then bending slightly towards her, 'What do you think I am anyway? Some brute that would kill without a thought?'

'You nearly killed that militiaman.'

'He nearly killed me.'

'But you had the gun! There was no need to fire it as you did.'

He looked at her as if thinking she was incredibly naïve. 'You saw the power of Case – a blow from that knee would have been worse than deadly. He'd have got the gun back in a second and would have killed me without a doubt. And being a militiaman, he'd not have been troubled with a trial for murder either.'

She stood silent, her brown eyes troubled.

'Ach, Mary,' he said tightly, 'stop looking at me like that! I would never hurt you, never offend you. You need never be afraid of me.'

'I'm not afraid of you,' she flashed angrily, 'I just . . . dislike you. You're violent and dangerous. Yes—' She suddenly knew what he was. 'That's what you are – dangerous!'

He rolled his eyes impatiently, but said nothing.

Her shoulders and arms were trembling. 'Oh, why don't you just go away!' she cried, the pain in her cheek beginning to throb.

'If that's what you want,' he said quietly.

'That's what I want.'

'Then I'll say goodbye.'

'Goodbye.'

'And I'll not be troubling you again.'

She watched him as he turned and left her, a wave of regret sweeping her at his final words; somehow she felt he was not the

37

type to make idle threats or false promises, and she wanted to rush after him and say she was sorry. But then, in contrast to her own remorse, she saw him walking quietly and easily down the hill, as if her rejection of him mattered hardly at all.

Michael crossed the meadows doing his best to shrug Mary Doyle from his mind, but in the depths of his hazel eyes confused emotions raged. Ach, why should he care? He would not spend his time apologising for what he was to anyone.

He began to run. He had his work to do at home and the day was half through. There'd be an evening in it now before he'd finish. He sprinted across the fields, slowing as he neared the farm and saw the family gathered in the yard. Instantly he knew something was wrong. Rebel had not lurched out to greet him, and that had never once happened in the five years since he had brought the dog to the farm as a pup. They all turned as he approached, their faces white with a kind of dread.

'Oh, Michael,' Cathy ran towards him. 'They did it just to spite you.'

He pushed past her and walked towards his dog. Rebel lay on his side panting hard, his big eyes staring up as if he had been hanging on to life for this last moment of seeing his beloved master. And now he saw him, he let out a piteous whimper.

Michael knelt and brushed a slow hand over Rebel's shuddering head, then over the black sleek body. He didn't need to ask who had done it. The militia had done it. They had cut off the dog's hind legs. His dog.

'Poor boy,' he whispered, 'poor boy, poor boy.'

The shivering dog looked up at him with moist eyes, threw back his snout and uttered a howl which tailed off into a series of shuddering whimpers. Then Rebel lay still.

The family stood in silence. Michael knelt staring at his dog with tears spilling down his face. Slowly he lifted Rebel into his arms then moved to his feet, turned and carried him over to a grass patch near the first field. John Dwyer motioned his children not to follow him, but twelve-year-old John-bawn grabbed a spade and followed his eldest brother like a young pup himself.

Michael set his dog down and took the spade from John-bawn. He drove it into the ground and sliced through the grass, lifting the squares and piling them neatly to one side, then shifted the earth until the hole was deep enough for a grave. He lifted Rebel and laid him gently down, then without any preamble moved back and began to spade the soil, finally placing the squares of grass back over the earth, pressing them down evenly with his boot. When he had finished he turned to see Cathy standing behind him.

'They pushed Mammy out of the kitchen,' she whispered, 'almost knocking her down. They took Daddy into the barn, four of them, to speak to him, they said. He looked quite shaken when he came out. He said they made threats, a great deal of threats, but he wouldn't disclose them to us.'

Michael moved his eyes from her angry face and looked over at his family. His mother, a tall and slender woman with cool hazel eyes and upswept fair hair that kept coming undone, stood hushing a sobbing young Etty, fifteen years old and almost as pretty as Cathy. His eldest sister Maíre stood beside them, her arm protectively around their mother. His two teen-age brothers stood whispering angrily together while his father walked across the yard towards him, then put a hand on his shoulder and spoke in the low calm voice that was usual for him.

'Come now, we have to talk, son. Just the two of us.'

They did not speak until they had reached the meadows overlooking the farmlands of Eadstown. They sat on a low stone wall and continued their silence for a time, listening to the cry of wild birds and distant bleating of sheep. A rabbit lolloped through the grass a few yards from their feet, paused to sit up and look round him, then dropped on all fours and sped out of sight.

Michael glanced sideways at the strong profile of his father. His lean tanned face showed lines which seemed to deepen with every season. He could still remember the days when his father's hair hung in long black curls down his back; a fine show of a man when he walked out of a Sunday in leather breeches and black wool stockings. Now the curls of his hair had lost their spring, were edged with grey, and the length was shorter, tied at the nape with a black ribbon.

'What were the threats?' Michael murmured.

'Oh, as you'd expect. Next time it will be you they punish, not the dog. First sight they get of you they will shoot you. And – well, no matter!'

'Did they hurt you at all?'

'Not much.'

Michael looked sharply at his father. 'What did they do?'

'No more than I could take.'

From his pocket his father withdrew a pipe already filled with tobacco, then a tinder-box. 'Don't forget, son,' he said, 'we are of the old race. The race that stood out in the war against Cromwell.' He puffed on the pipe and gazed at the hills. 'And aye, we are surely a tough race.'

It was something in his father's tone, something in the way his hand had trembled as he lit the pipe that made Michael sure there was something else. Something his father had not yet told him.

'What is it?' he asked.

'It's Dublin for you, Michael,' his father said, continuing to look at the hills. 'And from there, America. They'll not leave you alone now. The militia. They'll not rest until they have you.'

'America?'

'Where else? The French are friendly, but you can't speak the lingo. America is the country for young men.'

'No!' Michael rasped. 'No man – be he gentleman, Englishman, or Irish militiaman – will ever drive me from my homeland!'

'Better exiled than dead,' his father said quietly. 'Now listen. Michael, I have some money. It is yours. All of it. It will pay for a safe passage across the western ocean, and give you a start when you reach the land of the free.'

Michael could not believe what he was hearing. He stared as if mesmerised at his father, who kept his eyes fixed hard on the hills and spoke again in a low, choking whisper, as if the emigrant ship of his nightmares was already preparing to set sail.

'I'll think of you,' he said. 'And I'll weep for you.'

'No!' Michael jumped to his feet in rage. 'I'll never leave Wicklow!' he cried, smashing his fist into an open hand. 'Never, never, never!'

His father reached for him but he jerked away. 'Is that how the old race stood out against Cromwell, Daddy? By running? Well, not me! No, sir. Not me!'

'I'm thinking of you, Michael,' his father pleaded. 'God knows, it will half kill me not to have you here. But it is the way of things now. You have to go. Say you'll go,' he begged.

'No!' He swung away to run down the hill.

'Michael,' his father pleaded. 'Michael! Michael darling!'

Michael paused, then waited with thumbs in his belt until his father caught up and clutched his arm. 'Listen, son, I didn't tell you all the militia said. They said Dublin Castle has proclaimed martial law throughout the country. The notices will be up everywhere by tomorrow.'

'Martial law?'

Michael stared wide-eyed at his father, who nodded. 'You know as well as I do what that means, son. Under martial law the militia will be able to do whatever abomination they wish – and get away with it! They'll be given even greater powers, will rule Ireland more brutally and more powerfully than ever. And that's exactly what the politicians in Dublin want – to break us – body and spirit!'

Michael made no answer. He turned his head and let his gaze wander over the hills to his beloved mountains. He had been born, cradled, then grown from boy to man under the shade of these Wicklow Mountains: the Keadeens, Sugarloaf, Table Mountain, and his favourite of all – the Lugnaquilla, over three thousand feet, the second highest in Ireland. It was climbing those lofty childhood friends that had first developed the muscles in his limbs, given a sharpness to his vision as he sat on their crags and gazed into the far-off blue horizon or down to the green valleys.

All the hidden secrets of the wilderness were up there, secrets hidden to the stranger who could wander for days without ever seeing another soul, could die there and not be found for months. A savage, beautiful wilderness of dense pine forests and freshwater lakes, rare flowers and plantlife too beautiful to be suffocated in any gentleman's drawing-room. And most important of all – there were river streams to quench a man's thirst; deep mountain pools to keep him fresh and clean; wild game of every description to keep away hunger; wood in excess to burn and keep him warm; and sheltering caves as big and airy and bright inside as the Castle ballroom. And he knew every inch of those mountains. From the meadows at the base to the highest peak in the firmament.

'That's it then,' he said softly.

'You'll go?' his father said.

'To the mountains,' Michael said.

'What? *Live* up there?'

'Why not? They provide more hospitality than many a poor man's cottage.'

'Oh my!' said his father, a light of new hope in his eyes. 'Maybe you could live up there at that. Summer is on the horizon and the air up there will be sweet.' He looked at his son, then smiled like a boy. 'I was once a lad too, you know. I know what it's like to lie on the sweet heather and gaze at the stars. In fact, if your mother is to be believed, it was in a shady dell on Lugnaquilla that you were conceived.'

'Daddy!' Michael said in mock horror. 'Before or after you were married?'

John Dwyer laughed, the sudden relief of not losing his son to America as intoxicating as a bottle of poteen. 'After, boy, after the marriage. You can rely on that. Your mother was not one for a flighty tumble in the hay. She was always a good girl.'

For the life of him, Michael could not imagine his mother tumbling anywhere. Her emotions were always as cool and controlled as his own usually were; on the surface at least. He shrugged the thought aside as irreverent and grasped what his father was saying.

'A few good blankets, utensils for cooking, an extra set or two of clothes – you can always come home for clean clothes, at night, in darkness. But listen . . .' John Dwyer frowned, 'will you not be lonely? It can be very lonely up there at night if a body is alone.'

Michael smiled. 'I'll wager I'll not be alone for long. As soon as Hugh Vesty hears I've gone aloft, he'll be up there faster than a buck hare after a doe rabbit.'

'Aye, aye,' his father nodded a smile. 'You two are more like brothers than cousins, always have been. Still . . .' He heaved an anxious sigh. 'Let's go down and tell your mother now. She didn't know I was planning to send you to America, so she may not be too happy at you leaving home at all. And God, she can be as unpredictable as the weather at times!'

'Will you come back to see us now and again?' his mother said when they told her later that night, her face expressionless.

'Yes, once or twice a week, probably. At night. You can be assured that I will never endanger you.'

'Endanger me?' She tutted and put her hands back into the tub of soapy water. She was doing the weekly washing and wanted to get it wrung and hung on the lines over the fire now the family had gone to bed. 'You endangered me the day you were born,' she said, her back to him. 'All ten big pounds of you. Many thought I was for eternity, fetched the priest, and *he* was sure of it. Gave me the Last Rites.'

'I'll collect my things,' he said quietly.

'Aye, do that. And make sure to take a bar of carbolic soap. Mountains or no, I'll not have you going around looking like an unwashed beggar.'

When he re-entered the kitchen carrying his bag, she was still busy at the tub.

'Fare well,' he said softly.

'You too,' she replied, not turning round. 'Your daddy has your haversack. I've put some things in to keep you going. A pie, ham and cheese and such.'

'Thank you.'

'Well, off you go. It won't be an easy trek up the mountains in the dark.'

He turned and walked through the kitchen and parlour and opened the front door to the yard where his father stood waiting for him.

'Michael!'

'Aye.' He turned round.

Soapy hands were cupping his face, her lips touched his cheek. 'Your daddy and I will worry about you every livelong day,' she whispered.

'No need, Mammy,' he told her softly.

Oh, it was a long time since he had called her Mammy! Her arms went around him, clinging to him as tight as a drowning woman clinging to a log hurtling downstream. The Dwyers had a fierce feeling of love for each other, but Mrs Dwyer's love for her first-born was the fiercest of all, although she rarely displayed it.

'God go with you,' she whispered, then turned and left as abruptly as she had come, back to the tub, head bent low as she pummelled the same shirt she had been pummelling since the moment he told her he was leaving.

In the shadows of the yard his father stood holding the bridle of the horse Michael had asked him to get ready, his expression bewildered as he looked at the bottle-green riding cloak his son wore.

'Why do you need your horse?' he asked. 'I would've thought you'd make swifter progress up there on foot.'

'I'll send the horse back before dawn,' Michael told him.

'But before I go anywhere else, I'm going across Wicklow to Ballymanus. To see Garrett Byrne.'

'For what purpose?'

'You were the one who said it, Daddy – martial law has been proclaimed. And that will be the final act that leads to outright war in this country. And when the war starts, I'll be here to play my part.'

'War?' John Dwyer stared at him, aghast. 'War!' he repeated. 'And what's at Ballymanus?'

'The secret headquarters of the Wicklow Committee of United Irishmen. Garrett Byrne is their commander.'

Michael tied his bag to the horse, fixed his musket to one side of the saddle, long-barrelled gaming-rifle to the other, then checked the pistol in his belt.

John Dwyer couldn't think of a single thing to say. For hours he had relaxed in the knowledge that his son would be safe in the fastness of the mountains until matters cooled down – but now this! This was even worse than exile in America! Young men *died* in wars. Why, just the other day he'd sat in the tavern and listened to a wizened old Jock telling of the Forty-Five Scottish Rebellion, and the slaughter on Culloden Moor. Thousands of young Highlanders behind Bonnie Prince Charlie, thousands of fathers' sons, slaughtered by the army of the English Duke. Why should the Irish fare any better? And when – when did this mad notion to take up arms occur to his eldest and most beloved son?

It hit him like a bolt from the sky. 'This afternoon,' he cried. 'Up in the meadow when I told you of martial law and you said "That's it then". That's when you made this insane decision, wasn't it?'

'Yes.' Michael had swung into the saddle. He lifted the reins and looked down at his father.

'They've been asking me to join them for two years. I never committed myself, not completely. I never took the oath.'

'Oh, Michael . . . what chance have they? What chance have you? The Catholics have never won, never will. This is the Protestants' Promised Land and the Catholics' Egypt.'

'Nay, Daddy. The United Irishmen have as many Protestants in their ranks as Catholics. Their aim is one nation of United Irishmen of every religious persuasion. And the leaders – Lord Edward Fitzgerald, Tone, Thomas Emmet – all are wealthy Protestants who hate this filthy rotten system of inequality and separation.'

'God and Mary!' his father whispered. 'And 'tis these Protestant City boys who want you to be a private in their mock army?'

Michael leaned slightly in the saddle and patted his horse before replying. 'Not a private. A captain. Of the Wicklow Marksmen Division.' He chucked the reins and prodded the horse forward.

'Goodbye, Daddy.'

John Dwyer called out, raised a hand, ran after him, called out again, but only the thudding of hoofs answered him.

Part Two

'Twas hard the woeful words to frame
　To break the ties that bound us;
But harder still to bear the shame
　Of foreign chains around us.

And so I said, 'The mountain glen
　I'll seek at morning early,
And join the brave United Men'
　While soft winds shook the barley.

'The Wind That Shakes The Barley', Irish ballad of 1798

Chapter Four

In the Doyles' farmhouse on the hillside at Knockandarragh, Mary could not compose herself for sleep. She draped a shawl over her nightgown and sat by her open bedroom window staring at the mountains washed in green moonlight.

Night was truly one of Wicklow's beautiful moments, when the sun sets and the fields grow dark and candlelight shines from the small windows of whitewashed cabins dotted over the hills, the smoke from their chimneys sending the sweet musky smell of burning turf drifting across the sky like incense.

The bedroom door opened and her brother crept in. 'Mary, are you all right? Mammy is still fretting and frowning because you ate nothing at supper.'

When she made no answer he perched on the window ledge and gazed out at the night. At twenty-three, John Doyle was six years older than Mary, and still too shy to look a girl in the eyes.

'Tell me more about him,' she whispered.

John did not need to ask about who. Every day since the night of the fair, and despite his warning that she was not the only flower in Michael Dwyer's garden, Mary had persecuted him with questions about the man. A form of mania, his mother said it was, when he complained to her; a mania of confusion that attacks all young maidens in the first flush of romance. Some asked questions, some danced down lanes, and some came out in the reddest skin rash that disappeared as quick as their fancy.

John sighed, deciding to take his mother's advice and humour his sister until she grew tired of the subject.

'What more do you want to know?' he asked.

'Anything. Everything. You were at Mr Burr's school with him. Was he violent even then?'

John considered, then said quietly, 'Michael was never violent in any way. In truth, I rarely knew him to quarrel. During our time of going to school he was remarkably quiet, often serious and thoughtful, but he had a great turn for wit and humour and was a favourite with the lads. As I recall, he himself rarely provoked a combat, but he would never refuse a challenge or brook the slightest insult . . . A fellow did insult him once, a great brawny bully named Padraig Power, only a few weeks in the school, with a taste for fighting and strutting around boasting that he was the future heavy-weight boxing champion of Ireland.'

John smiled as he remembered. 'Hugh Vesty Byrne and some of the other boys had Power marked, noticed he picked only on the weak, and never started a fight unless he could see an easy finish. Then one day he saw Michael sitting under a tree with his nose stuck in a book and his knees under his chin. Michael would read anything in those days, books, road-signs, tombstones, anything that had a word written on it. So seeing him looking all quiet and bookish, Power goes up to him accompanied by a few henchboys and says:

' "Can you handle yourself, Dwyer? Are you any good at boxing?"

' "Buzz off," Michael told him, quiet-like. "Can't you see I'm reading?"

' "Reading! 'Tis only a coward that hides behind a book," Power laughs to his henchboys, then seeing a crowd of us had gathered to watch, he kicked the book out of Michael's hand. Troth, Dwyer was up on his feet in a flash. And I don't think the future boxing champion of Ireland knew what hit him, for Dwyer's fist that day was as fast as a whip. He knocked Power flat on his back with a full drive to the stomach that left him a corpse for almost half an hour. The master had a terrible job to revive him, but eventually did it with the third pail of water. Padraig Power got a terrible jeering afterwards, but fair play to him, he took it like a man and let the matter drop without further ugliness.'

John chuckled. 'Aye, those were the days, great days! Whenever a dispute arose after that, it was Michael they always chose as umpire, and deadly serious he would walk from one furious lad to the other, arranging the preliminaries and reminding them of the rules, then with a grin as wide as the Slaney he would raise his arm and give the order for the warriors to charge and may the best man win.'

'Was he any good at his lessons?' Mary asked.

'Hugh Vesty was the history expert,' John said with a smile.

'He could reel off names and dates and battles as if he'd been there. Troth, to listen to Hugh Vesty, you would think he'd sat in conference with Brian Boru himself! But Michael excelled in book-keeping and arithmetic and was a hero to all the dunces – seeing as he used to work most of their sums for them. The master never found out, and some of those dunces passed out of school with the highest marks in book-keeping and arithmetic. One eejit even went so far as to get a job in a small bank in Kildare. Lord knows how he fared when it came to doing his own counting.'

Mary's head was flopped on her knees in laughter. She raised her head to ask another question but John quickly pleaded fatigue, wished her goodnight and made a hasty retreat.

Mary remained sitting by her window as the moon began to sink, growing paler and paler until the fields lightened in the grey dawn and a familiar pattering sound was heard on the road beyond. Two sleepy drovers walked behind a herd of black and white cows, swinging their sticks and smoking pipes in the cool morning air. Minutes later a bent old woman came along the road wearing a black shawl that covered her head and trailed at her ankles; in her arms she carried a pink piglet. Another herd of black and white cattle followed her. It was market-day in Rathdrum, and the whole countryside was awake, ready to start the long walk across Wicklow to sell and buy. From downstairs in the yard she heard the sound of her father's voice as he selected the finest pigs and told the sows of his plans.

'A nice little jaunt in the cart now! A day out of the sty and into town. Won't that be a grand treat for them?'

The answering din of oinks and squeals was enough to wake her mother who popped her head inside the door.

'Ah, you're awake. Well don't just sit there. Get dressed and help me prepare breakfast. Your daddy has to be away to market and we both overslept.'

'What time is it?'

'Late. After five o'clock.'

Mary stayed in a kind of dream as she moved about the living-room setting plates and turning sizzling rashers in the pan on the gridiron over the fire. But when she stepped out to the yard to fill the kettle from the rain barrel, the cold light of morning dashed her eyes and sent waves of tiredness shivering through her.

She groaned; and wondered what madness had made her stay awake all night.

In the market at Rathdrum very little business was done, so preoccupied were the travellers who gathered in horrified groups before the government proclamations posted on every wall and door. By sunset, every person in Ireland had seen the notices proclaiming martial law.

Some 150 miles from Wicklow, inside his tent at the British military camp near Bantry Bay, General John Moore sat at his fold-table and sought to bring his private diary up to date.

He was thirty-seven years old, tall and fair-haired with blue, blue eyes, and even without the scarlet uniform one would have guessed he was a soldier from the way he held his body, erect from the hips, shoulders broad and level. His features, even when lined with tiredness, were eminently handsome.

He moved the candle on the fold-table nearer to the thick diary. He sighed. It was late and he was tired, but too unsettled to sleep. He blinked his eyelids and wondered why he had started the diary in the first place, in Gibraltar, in 1792. Maybe it was simply because a soldier never knew the day or hour when his name would be on the bullet, and he wanted to leave something behind. Or maybe it was just to have something to look back on in old age. He desperately hoped it would not be the last! Like all true soldiers, there was only one way he wanted to die – on the battlefield.

He turned the pages detailing his service in Gibraltar, Corsica, the West Indies. Now Ireland! He paused to read through some of the insertions he had made since his arrival in the country. It seemed such a long time ago, yet only a few months . . .

Dublin, December 1797 Upon Sir Ralph Abercromby being appointed Commander in Chief of the Army in Ireland, he requested that I be put on his staff, which was accordingly done.

On the 24th November we left London, arrived at Holyhead on the 28th, sailed and arrived in Dublin on 1st December after a most boisterous passage. An aide-de-camp from Lord Camden the Viceroy was waiting to receive Sir Ralph with the message that apartments were prepared for him at the Castle. Rooms were also, by Lord

Camden's order, offered to me, but I declined and came to this Dublin hotel where I thought I should be more my own master.

Camp at Cork, January 1798 Sir Ralph Abercromby invited me to dine during my stay in Dublin. He gave me different papers to read respecting the defence of the south against a French invasion. I left Dublin on the 6th instant and arrived here on the 8th. I heard from Sir Ralph of the very defective state in which he found the military preparation. No artillery were in a condition to move; even the guns attached to the regiments were unprovided with horses. No magazines were formed for the militia regiments, little or no order or discipline.

The army here has been considered little more than an instrument of corruption in the hands of the Viceroy and his Secretary. So much has this been the custom that even now, when the country is undoubtedly in a very alarming state, both from internal disaffection and fear of French invasion, it requires, I believe, all Sir Ralph's temper and moderation to carry on the necessary business. The mode which has been followed to quieten the disturbances in this country has been to proclaim the districts in which the people appeared to be most violent, and let loose the military who are encouraged in acts of great violence against all who are supposed to be disaffected. A complete line seems to be drawn between the upper and lower orders of the people.

Camp at Bantry, 16th February 1798 I accompanied Sir Ralph Abercromby to Bandon, where I took over command from General Coote. My command consists of three thousand men amongst which are twelve companies of light infantry of Militia.

When the Militia was first formed, had pains been taken to select proper officers and to introduce discipline they might by this time have been respectable troops; but, like everything else in this country, the giving of regiments was made an instrument of influence with the colonels, and they made their appointments to serve electioneering purposes. Every sort of abuse has been tolerated, and it is, I fear, too late to amend them. The

officers are in general profligate and idle, serving for
the money, and not from a sense of duty or military
distinction.

Bantry is beautiful!

Camp at Bandon Sir Ralph in his inspections of the
different military quarters observed the irregularities and
abuses which existed, particularly in the militia regiments. Sir Ralph reprobated the abuses which had been
practised and in strong terms forbade their continuance.
He ordered all generals to compel the officers under their
command to give the strictest attention to discipline,
good order, and conduct of their men, such as may
restore the high and distinguished reputation which the
British troops have been accustomed to in every part of
the world.

This order, addressed to the troops, gave offence. The
principal officers who had hitherto been used to compliments, could not bear the language of truth. But as the
above conduct has been used most violently and successfully in the north, the cry of the *gentry* throughout is that
nothing but strong measures will do; and upon every
murmur of the people they call upon the military and
urge them to every act of violence. Sir Ralph
Abercromby is determined this shall no longer be the
case.

Those who have the government of the country seem
to have no plan or system but that of terrifying the common people; they give us every power to act against them,
but the higher orders of the community are to be
indulged in every abuse.

Bandon An outcry has been raised against Sir Ralph for
his moderation. His recall has been talked of, and the
whole of his conduct arraigned. I wrote him a letter saying that should he be induced to resign, I intend not to
serve.

In his answer which I received yesterday, Sir Ralph
writes, 'They may force me to resign, but I shall not
lower myself by a compliance with their propositions.'
He then entreated me to make no hasty decisions with
respect to myself. Sir Ralph's conduct since his arrival in

Ireland has been exemplary, his motives honourable and upright. Should the Irish Government force him to resign, Ireland will repent it, but unfortunately when it will be too late.

Bandon The Commander in Chief of the Army has written to England asking to be recalled. I have written in the most pressing terms to Colonel Brownrigg asking to be withdrawn from Ireland. The measures likely to be adopted here will be the most odious, and whoever attempts to execute them with mercy and moderation risks giving displeasure and being ruined.

Sir Ralph begged I would be cautious. He would be sorry if anything we did should bear the appearance of party. He said, 'I shall be blamed for what I have done in this country, but I never felt more satisfied with myself or with my conscience. I meant to act well, and feeling this, the slander of the world does not affect me . . .'

'May I enter, General Moore?'

'Enter.'

General Moore looked up as the tent flap was lifted and his batman stepped inside holding a stone hot-jar in his hands; a young Irish recruit who took his new position as batman very, very seriously.

'Well?'

'Begging your pardon, General, but I thought you might like a hot-jar in your bed.'

General Moore inclined his head. 'I appreciate the sentiment, Prendergast, but I must decline. I detest hot-water jars.'

'Oh, indeed, sir. Why is that?'

'They go cold.'

'Oh they do, sir. *Indeed* they do. Perhaps – perhaps you would prefer a cup of hot chocolate instead?'

'No, thank you.'

'Or a large glass of whiskey maybe?'

'No, Prendergast.'

The young soldier shifted uneasily on his feet. 'Is it true, sir,' he asked gloomily, 'that General Abercromby has left Ireland?'

Moore turned his eyes down to his diary.

'Yes,' he said softly.

'And is it to Scotland he's gone, sir? He is a Scotsman, is he not?'

'Yes.'

'And is it General Lake that's now Commander in Chief?'

'Yes.'

An unhappy sigh wafted over to General Moore, who ran silent and deep for a long bitter moment. 'Poor creature I pity him,' General Lake had said of Sir Ralph's attempts to restore order and honour to the army in Ireland, 'he is quite in his dotage.'

Seeing the grim expression on his superior's face, the batman looked anxiously around the tent as if searching for something else to offer. His devotion to the young general went beyond all duty.

'Are you *sure* there is nothing I can get you, sir? Have you enough ink in your pot for your pen?'

With a hint of a smile, Moore looked at his batman. 'All I require, Prendergast,' he said tiredly, 'is for you to withdraw.'

The soldier clicked his heels. 'Then I'll wish you a good and peaceful night, sir.'

'Goodnight.'

When the flap had dropped, General Moore dipped his quill in the inkpot and wrote:

Bandon, 27th May 1798 I received orders in April to disarm the two Carberries which is all the country that lies from Crookham along the coast to Bandon. I expected that upon the appearance of the troops the people would have given in their arms but it had no effect.

My orders were to treat the people with as much harshness as possible, as far as words and manners went, and to supply ourselves with whatever provisions were necessary to enable us to live well. My wish was to excite terror, and by that means obtain our end speedily. I thought this better than to act more mildly, and be obliged to continue for any time the real oppression; and as I was present everywhere myself I had no doubt of being able to prevent any great abuses by the troops. The second day the people, after denying they had any arms, began to deliver them in. After four days we extracted sixty-five muskets. Major Nugent in Coharagh was obliged to burn some houses before he could get a single arm.

The terror was great. The moment a red coat appeared everybody fled. I was thus constantly employed for three weeks, during which I received 800 pikes and 3400 stand of arms, the latter very bad.

The higher class of people seemed all delighted with the operation except when it touched their own tenants, by whose ruin they saw they themselves must suffer, but they were pleased that the people were humbled. I found only two gentlemen who acted with liberality or manliness; the rest seemed in general to be actuated by the meanest motives. The common people have been so ill treated by them, and so often deceived, that neither attachment nor confidence any longer exists. The people have yielded in this instance to force, are now humbled, but irritated to a great degree, and unless the gentlemen change their conduct and manner towards them, or Government steps in with regulations for protection of the lower from the upper order, the pike and the gun will appear again very soon.

A few days later General Moore made another entry in his diary:

Bandon Disturbances have appeared in the north. These we hear are terminating favourably, but I now consider that a regular war in this country is certain.

Chapter Five

And so it started, only days later, the bloodiest civil war in Ireland's history, the rebellion of 1798.

The Doyles of Knockandarragh defiantly refused to leave their home as night after night the sky over the Glen of Imaal and the surrounding country was aglow with flames from cottages burned by the militia. So terrified were the peasantry of being burned in their beds, whole families vacated their homes at night to sleep in the fields.

Mary sat by the small table beneath the window. Her mother and father had gone to bed. The fire had been banked down for the night and the doors bolted. A rush candle stood in the centre of the table as she worked on a piece of lace under its glow. The clock on a shelf of the dresser ticked away, amplified by the growing silence of the night. Occasionally she heard the distant hungry cries of children and babies nestling with their mothers under the hedgerows.

Foolish, her daddy said it was, to spend so much time making pieces of lace instead of something more practical, but Mary loved lace. She loved all nice things. She loved neatness and order and peace and simplicity. She hated confusion and chaos. Outside was confusion and chaos, and it would get worse. Outside was a country at war, and how would it end?

She wondered about her brother John, who had not been seen for almost a week. Rumour said he was up in the mountains with Michael Dwyer. She quickly turned her attention back to the lace; the last person she wanted to think about was Michael Dwyer. He was a different sort of confusion.

A sudden furtive tapping on the window startled her. She sat very still for a moment, but when the tapping came again she laid down her crochet needle and lace and peered out through the window into the darkness.

'Mary, it's me – John.'

She sprang out of the chair and ran to the door, threw back the bolts.

'Oh John, we're near worried to death about you.'

He slipped inside and put a finger to his lips, motioned for her to keep quiet. 'I don't want the Ma and Da to know I'm back,' he whispered.

'Where have you been all this time?'

'I'm a private in the United Irish army, Mary. Sworn to fight for constitutional justice for the Irish people of every religious persuasion.'

He said it so solemnly she wanted to both smile and cry. 'Are you going back up the mountains?' she asked.

'No, but I need money badly. Can you lend me some? Some of the money you got for the lace tablecloth.'

'My lace money? Oh John, my lace money is all I have.' She looked at him closely. 'If you're not going back up the mountains, why do you need the money?'

'I'm going to Wexford.'

'Wexford?'

'Aye, the rich corn country. That's where all the real fighting is going on. The battles here at Newtonmountkennedy and Baltinglass were only skirmishes, with the militia turning tail as soon as they saw we were ready for them.' John made an agonised face. 'Could you get me some food, Mary? I'm famished. Anything will do.'

She bade him sit down at the long table, then set out a plate of thick bread and cheese and a tankard of ale.

'So?' Mary asked as her brother ravenously attacked the food. 'When and why did you decide to go to Wexford?'

'A number of us were up on Lugnaquilla last night,' he told her. 'At dawn Michael woke us and said we should be moving. He said it was the boys of Wexford who were the real soldiers. Did you hear about their brilliant success on Oulart Hill?'

'Aye.'

'And now we hear that large detachments of government troops are being sent down to Wexford.'

Mary stared at him, aghast. 'And Michael Dwyer wants you to go there?'

'Aye, he said a Wicklow contingent of the insurgent army was also marching south and we should start off at once to join them. But nobody responded to his call. Not even me. No one wanted to leave Wicklow.'

'Small blame to them,' Mary whispered. 'What did Michael say?'

'Nothing. Not a word. He just stepped out from where we had been lying, looked all around at the sky, then picked up his musket and without any more ado walked off alone in the direction of Wexford.'

'But Wexford is miles away! And how will he get there? From what we've heard every road in the lowlands is covered by troops on horse and foot.'

'We watched him in the same wonderment, and I tell you, Mary, I never in all my life saw such determination in a man. He took the path of the mountain range. Michael will get there, sure enough.'

'But he could be killed! And now you want to follow him?'

'Aye, I do! And I have four others waiting for me. Hugh Vesty Byrne, Martin Burke, John Mernagh, and Big Arthur Devlin. We all finally agreed that if Michael is prepared to join our Wexford brothers in the fight, we will too.' He pushed back his chair and stood up. 'I must go now.'

For a moment they stood silent, then put their arms around one another and embraced tightly.

'Mary . . . if anything happens to me, you'll look after mother, won't you? You know how silly she can be at times.'

'Happen to you . . . oh John!'

If thousands of government troops were being sent to Wexford, they would be armed with the best weapons and the largest cannons, and both knew that perhaps not one of the boys from Wicklow would come back.

'It's a noble thing to fight for the freedom of your people, Mary,' he whispered passionately, 'a magnificent and noble thing. For too long we have been stripped of all dignity, all rights, all power. If we shirk the fight now, we may live while our brothers in Wexford die, but it would be a long and miserable life to live with that knowledge – that we shirked the fight.'

'Is that what Michael Dwyer said?' she challenged fretfully.

John made no answer, just looked at her darkly. 'I hoped you would understand.'

Mary sighed and pulled away. In her view, patriotism and heroism were passions for young men and old soldiers, not women. 'I'll be back in a minute,' she said.

She entered her bedroom and walked over to a small lace-covered table on which stood a casket, a comb, brushes and a looking-glass. She raised the lid of the casket, lifted out a knotted lace handkerchief containing her treasured lace money. A flush of shame coloured John's face when she handed it to him.

'I don't want to take it,' he said, 'but 'tis a long way to Wexford and I'll need money to exchange for food.'

'Just come back safely, John. That's all I ask in return.'

Again they embraced tightly, and as John unbolted the door, Mary clutched his arm.

'All those nights up in the mountains,' she whispered, 'did . . . did Michael Dwyer ever speak of me to you? Ask you questions about me?'

Seeing the hopeful expression in her eyes, John wanted to lie, but answered truthfully.

'No, Mary, he never did.'

Michael travelled through deserted mountain country for an entire day, reaching Limerick Hill in the north of the county of Wexford by nightfall. He made his way to Mountpleasant which he knew to be the rallying point for the Wicklowmen marching south. There he joined General Garrett Byrne and the Wicklow Ballymanus Corps of almost two thousand men, all wearing a simple green cockade in their hats.

On being handed a green sash to denote his rank as a field officer, Michael decided to wear it around his waist. Then taking his place among the Musketry, he marched with the Wicklow men until they made contact with a division of the Wexford rebel force at Gorey Hill. He met many friends and acquaintances in that camp and spent an enjoyable night of hearty male camaraderie.

It was decided that drums would not be used to call the men to their divisions at daybreak, as the sound of drums might frighten the country people in the surrounding farms who had not as yet ever met a drill sergeant, and would be at a loss to know what the drumming meant.

At five o'clock the following morning, the standard bearers of each company readied their flags and, accompanied by a small guard, marched through the camp calling their men to arms.

'Men of the Leitrim Light Company to your colours immediately!'

'Men of the Ballymanus Corps to your colours!'

'Men of the North Wexford Monaseed Division to your colours!'

Michael's heart thumped with pride at the alert and eager way the men of each division jumped to the cry of their standard bearer. The order to march was given and every face smiled as the command was repeated from rank to rank throughout the columns. The combined Wicklow and Wexford forces were over ten thousand strong. Young men who had risen up from the deep sleep of slavery, prepared to meet their oppressors in a bloody red war.

It was ten miles north east to Arklow, where they found the royal line of the King's troops entrenched and barricaded, ready for battle. A number of the Wexford boys were cut down by fire from the English entrenchments as they attempted to cross a field and attack the fishery to the right, then a volley from the rebel artillery knocked out an English cannon.

General Needham was in command of the English regiments, but it was Captain Grogan of the Castletown Cavalry who attempted the first charge, discovering at the cost of his life that the rebels were formidable in open field battle. Charge after charge by the cavalry was defeated and dispersed by pikemen and musketry.

After four hours of desperate fighting, the rebels were the masters of the field; with the exception of the fishery occupied by Colonel Skerret and his fencibles, who kept themselves barricaded and under cover, giving no support to the rest of the English army overwhelmed by the rebels and now retreating under General Needham.

Triumphant cheers rose up as the redcoats hastily quit the town of Arklow.

Later that night, lying on the heather with their faces turned to the sky, General Garrett Byrne of the Ballymanus Corps and Captain Dwyer spoke scornfully of the caution of Colonel Skerret and his fencibles, who had barricaded themselves in the fishery, then waited till darkness before making their silent departure.

'Colonel Skerret will make a reputation for himself after today,' Garrett said wryly. 'Unlike General Needham, he can claim he stayed on the field to the very end.'

Michael gave a contemptuous smile and rolled on to his stomach. 'They might even make him a general,' he said.

Mary Doyle listened eagerly to every idle report, every piece of news that was brought back to Imaal by wounded men returning home from the south. The rebels had possession of the whole county of Wexford, as well as Carlow, Kilkenny, Kildare, and the Wicklow-Wexford boundary from Carnew to Shillelagh.

A copy of the proclamation issued by the rebel generals found its way to the people of Imaal.

> WE THE PEOPLE united for the purpose of procuring our just rights, are determined to protect the persons and properties of those of all religious persuasion who have not oppressed us, and are willing in both heart and hand to join our glorious cause. But let not our victories be tarnished by any wanton acts of cruelty, neither let a differing in religious sentiment cause a difference among THE PEOPLE – God save THE PEOPLE!

Mary joined the excited crowd outside the forge in Donard, asking questions with the others.

' 'Tis said the Gaels are fighting like the warriors of old!'

'Is the Green Flag truly flying on Tara?'

'Flying in an Irish wind.'

'Glory to God!'

Amongst the reports of the Wicklow and Wexford division, Mary could find out nothing about her brother John, but it seemed that Michael Dwyer took part in every battle fought, being highly remarked by the Wexford chiefs for his daring bravery, especially when it was reported he had advanced to within a few paces of the English cannon that covered the road in an attempt to dismantle it, and had almost succeeded before being engaged in a bayonet fight that erupted around him.

'Twisted and manoeuvred a desperate run,' O'Casey the blacksmith shouted proudly, 'a desperate run through the hails of grapeshot right up to the mouth of the cannon! A Wicklow boy, brothers! A lad from right here in Imaal!'

The crowd all talked at once, gesturing and babbling, caught up in the ecstasy of the miracle. The native boys of their land were beating the foreign overlords.

It was a brutal and bloody war with the death toll on both sides mounting daily. The city of Dublin remained quiet due to being under heavy military guard, soldiers to be seen on every street and corner, the guards doubled in and around the Castle. But all reports coming into the city claimed the rebels were fighting with military principles and proving the superior force. Then came the news that thrilled the people and terrified the masters in Dublin Castle – Wexford had fallen to the rebels. Wexford had been declared a republic.

Inside the state apartments of the Castle, the Viceroy Lord Camden endeavoured to control his mounting hysteria in the presence of General Lake and the Secretary of State, Lord Castlereagh, who was seated at a table beside the Chancellor, Lord Clare. Both men listened silently as the two men argued their case.

'The rebels could make a march on Dublin,' cried the Viceroy, 'and despite the imprisonment of their lawyer generals, there is a nest of United men within the city just waiting for you to move the troops out so they can rise. The organisation of this treason is universal. You must understand, General Lake, priority must be given to the protection of the capital.'

'The capital has been successfully disarmed,' insisted General Lake, his face showing signs of battle fatigue after his long argument with the Viceroy. 'Dublin has the largest garrison in the country, yet they are held here unused. It's madness, your Excellency, military madness.'

'How many more men have you sent south?'

'Two detachments under General Loftus and Colonel Walpole,' Lake answered. 'General Moore has been ordered to leave Cork which is relatively quiet, and march up to Waterford, then Wexford.'

'Good.'

'It is not *enough*, my lord!' Lake cried. 'We must move now! The situation in the areas surrounding Wexford is critical, and now Antrim and Down have risen. Before long the whole of Ulster, papists and presbyterians alike, will have joined this revolution. The latest report is that McCracken's rebel forces are only ten miles from Belfast!'

'General Nugent has command of the north,' returned the Viceroy stiffly. 'I have complete confidence in his ability to deal with the situation there.'

The two lords at the table exchanged glances. They now knew that Prime Minister Pitt was blaming the Castle's policy of hard rule for precipitating the rebellion, and the Viceroy in turn was blaming General Lake's earlier frenzy of brutal military excesses for sending thousands into the ranks of the United Irishmen.

General Lake was at the end of his patience. 'Your Excellency, the rebels are in control of Kildare, Wexford, Carlow and Kilkenny – they succeeded in taking New Ross and Tara – and lost them again simply through a lack of experienced officers. It is the success of their United confederates in the south which has encouraged the north to take up arms.'

The Viceroy's eyes ranged over the two men sitting at the table; his look begged for their assistance.

'I must confess,' said Castlereagh, 'we were not prepared for such a formidable effort on the part of the people. It would only need a landing of a small French force, with trained officers and good armoury, to give the rebel army the edge . . . and possible victory.'

The Chancellor agreed. 'Unless Mr Pitt pours more troops into the country soon, Ireland could be lost.'

Lord Camden drew in his breath. 'What about the capital?' he asked General Lake. 'There must be an adequate force to protect the city.'

'Your Excellency's safety will be our first consideration,' Lake replied.

The sarcasm was not lost on Lord Camden, but he affected to ignore it.

'Very well,' he said, 'you have my permission, General Lake, to move the troops south.'

The following morning, the packet boat brought heartening news from Prime Minister Pitt to the Viceroy of Ireland – ten thousand more troops were on their way.

The people of Wicklow now only spoke in hushed tones about any further reports of rebel victories, still excited, still exalted, but hushed – for the savage retaliation of the militia at home was reaching terrifying proportions. Most of the young men had gone to join the insurgents, so the militia confined their energy to flogging the older men, burning houses, and still driving the women and children to sleep in the fields.

As the various regiments marched through the towns and villages on their way south, the sheep and pigs on the farmlands were slaughtered to feed the soldiers. Cows and goats were commandeered to supply milk. The Irish militia corps ordered to join the royal lines compounded the devastation by setting fire to the corn and barley crops for no logical purpose other than amusement on their journey.

The Wicklow people wandered around their farms in horror and disbelief. All knew what the destruction of the crops and loss of the livestock would mean – poverty and famine.

Pat O'Riordan stumbled into the Doyles' kitchen like a man in a drunken frenzy, his normally red face as white as a laundered sheet.

'I'm ruined!' he cried. 'Paupered! They've taken everything! All my pigs! All my darling cows!' He put his hands to his head and clutched fiercely at his hair. 'My lovely brown mare! Ah! Ah! My lovely brown mare!'

'Take a hold on yourself now,' William Doyle commanded, placing his hands on O'Riordan's shoulders. ' 'Tis the same for us too. We've lost nearly everything.'

'You too? You too?' O'Riordan's face crumpled. 'Oh God help us, William. We're done for! They may as like have murdered us and be done with it.'

William Doyle's own despair and melancholy abated slightly at the arrival of his friend who had fared worse than himself.

'I have a drop in,' he said, taking a bottle from the dresser. 'We'll take comfort from it.'

'God bless you,' cried O'Riordan. 'Weren't you always the man to have the drop of comfort for a neighbour.' He sank down on the settle. 'And they wonder why we drink!'

Doyle filled the glasses.

'What was that noise?' O'Riordan demanded.

'What noise?'

'That grunt!' O'Riordan jumped to his feet. 'I definitely heard the grunt of a pig!' He charged out of the kitchen to the back yard where Mary was feeding three pigs.

'Pigs! You still have pigs?'

A lowing from the byre made the eyes pop out of his head. 'Cows! They left you with lovely cows too?'

'They left us with nothing,' Mary said. 'These are what we managed to hide in the house.'

'In the house? Even the cows?'

'Even two of cows,' Mary replied. 'They took the rest.'

William Doyle was sitting morosely drinking his whiskey when O'Riordan stumbled back inside. 'You cur!' he shouted furiously. 'You lied to me! You said you lost everything too!'

'Now, now, Pat, no need to get upset. It was my Mary that

saved us, God be thanked for her. Used her brain she did.'

'Mary? That slip of a girl!'

Doyle nodded his head, then explained how Mary had spied the soldiers advancing and seen them rounding up the livestock.

'So quick as a flash,' Doyle said, 'Mary whips in a few of the pigs and puts them in the bedrooms, then in she comes again, leading a cow, then another, right into this kitchen. Blood-an-ouns! I thought I was drunk when I seen Big Sheila and Rosie-Posie standing over there by the table, as calm as you like and swishing their tails.'

'Did the soldiers not enter the house?'

Doyle smiled. 'Now here comes the best part. Mary opens the door to them, her face all shiny and yella with chicken grease and mustard, and tells them they are welcome to enter in the King's name – but did the King know that this particular house was reeking with yella fever?'

Doyle threw back his head and laughed. 'Yella fever! They fled quicker than a buck hare after a doe rabbit.'

'Yella fever,' O'Riordan repeated, gaping around him stupidly. 'Who would have thought of it?'

'My Mary,' Doyle said proudly. 'God love her. A bit of brain can be better than a bulk of brawn sometimes.'

'You may say it,' O'Riordan replied, gulping his drink. 'You may say it again. And me thinking she was more decoration than use.' His chin slumped on to his chest. 'Oh God, what are we going to do, William?'

'God knows, but I don't.'

They began to drink heavily. It was no longer easy to imagine the Irish boys winning now, not with thousands of redcoats heading south. Trained soldiers against farmers! Cannon against pikes and muskets! Ach, sure maybe God was an Englishman after all? The plight of the Irish had gone on for so long, for so many centuries. Too long to be changed by one generation in one hot summer.

The drink had an opposite effect on each of the two men. Doyle became brighter, but O'Riordan's melancholy was as low as his brogues. He laid down his glass, placed his elbows on his knees, drew his palms down his cheeks and said in a tone of bitter sadness, 'We spend our days breaking our backs working the land, then they take three-quarters of all our earnings. And now that the livestock is gone, what will we sell to pay the rent?'

'You have money in your box still, haven't you?' Doyle queried.

'Not much,' O'Riordan confessed. 'What's left will only pay the September rent.'

Mary entered and ignored them, moving silently by the dresser as she poured a tumbler of milk to take up to her mother, who was recovering in bed from the fright of the military's visit.

Pat O'Riordan eyed her speculatively. Now he was dispossessed of his assets and had learned Mary possessed a brain, he began to notice other things about her. His eyes lingered on her bosom, the long line of her limbs, the voluptuous mouth red and ripe as a cherry. He was breathing heavily, like a tired dog.

'Have you finished lamenting, Daddy?' Mary said coldly. 'There's still work to be done.'

'Work!' Pat O'Riordan uttered the word with a mixture of ecstasy and frustration. 'She talks about work! And I saw her feed the pigs. I saw her with my own two looking eyes.'

When Mary had marched out of the kitchen, Doyle refilled the glasses, then looked bleakly at the empty bottle. 'I may not have lost everything,' he said, 'but I lost twelve good cows and the rest of my pigs. And the sheep on the hills will be gone for sure. The lad I employed as a herd after John left was no more than eleven or twelve. He'll have run for his life at the first sight of the soldiers.'

'God pity us,' O'Riordan murmured.

'Aye,' Doyle agreed. 'He should at least do that.'

The two men began to weep drunkenly, patting each other's arms and putting the sides of their heads together.

'You're a mighty friend for a man to have, William Doyle,' said O'Riordan tearfully. 'A mighty friend.'

'You too, Pat,' sniffed Doyle, wiping a hand across his eyes. 'You'd be one of the best if it were not for your unnatural meanness.'

'And to prove how sincere I am in my sentiments,' O'Riordan said, 'I've decided to wed your Mary after all. She has fine qualities I never noticed before – and have you still the fine dowry you put by for her?'

Doyle turned his head and stared at him. 'Wed my Mary?'

'At the altar!' O'Riordan spat on his palm, then offered it to Doyle, 'Let's spit and shake on it this minute.'

'I'll spit in your eye!' Doyle shouted, jumping furiously to his feet. 'What? A beggar like you with neither pig nor cow in your yard asking to wed my girl! I'll see you to hell first!'

O'Riordan stared at him, dumbfounded and half-sobered with shock. 'But . . . but William, you've been after me to marry her for months!'

'That was when you were a man of substance, but now you've nothing! And a man who has nothing to offer is entitled to nothing in return.' Doyle was beside himself at the audacity of it. 'I'd give anything to a poor neighbour in need – but not my daughter! Go on, get away with ye before I take my pike to you!'

O'Riordan rose unsteadily to his feet. At the door he turned and stared at Doyle, anger flushing his big face.

'And to think I nearly brought a bottle of my finest whiskey to this,' he blurted. 'They never found my whiskey – oh no! I've six bottles under my bed. But God done it that I didn't bring a bottle to this house this day. Sure He knew it would be a holy waste!' And he stumbled out.

Doyle made to lunge after him but was checked by Mary's hand on his arm. He turned and stared at her. 'Did you hear what he said to me, Mary? Did you hear?'

Mary nodded. 'And to think I nearly brought a bottle of my finest whiskey to this! But God done it . . .' She choked with laughter.

'Ah, stop cackling like a hen, darling,' Doyle said, sinking heavily down on the settle. ' 'Tis a sad day when a man discovers a friend could be so meanspirited.'

'But look at this way, Daddy. Aren't you glad now that I have always resisted your attempts to make that miser your son-in-law?'

Doyle lifted his empty glass and stared at it gloomily. 'Well, I tell you, Mary, if the devastation of this war keeps on, with people losing crops and livestock and livelihoods, I may end up having to marry you off to a comfortable Protestant.'

'You'll marry me off to no one,' Mary snapped.

'I may be forced to, darling. Your mother and I have always said it would be a man of substance that got you.' He threw back his head and drained his glass. 'A man of substance now. I'll settle for no less.'

Chapter Six

Camp at Cork All our forces are now to be turned against Wicklow and Wexford. I received an order to march to Cork. I arrived here same day with the Light Battalion and two six-pounders. The rebels are in considerable force in the county of Wexford. It is said that in the different actions they have faced danger with uncommon bravery. We have hitherto certainly acted in too small detachments, which is certainly playing the enemy's game, who must wish to have time to form their troops.

Camp at Fermoy I received orders to move forward to Clonmel, from thence to Waterford. Our troops, mostly militia, are extremely undisciplined. My whole time is taken up instructing them in their duties, and inciting the officers to exertion. The march from Cork was quite disgraceful. Tomorrow we proceed to Waterford, thence Wexford.

Camp near Wexford The country through which we passed was rich and beautiful, though perfectly deserted. The soldiers, contrary to all orders, quitted their divisions and set fire to many houses. It was shocking to see such a fine cultivated country deserted of its inhabitants and in flames. I have succeeded in preventing this from happening since, and our last marches have been conducted with regularity. General Johnstone has sent word that I shall be immediately joined by the Queens and the 24th, which have landed from England.

At break of day, in the British military camp near Wexford, the reveille broke the slumbers of over a thousand soldiers. General John Moore, who had slept fully clothed and booted, sprang up from his bed which was simply a blanket spread over a truss of straw.

Without waiting for breakfast, he rode out to examine the picquets and patrols on duty during the night, and was pleased to see that his orders had been obeyed and no spirits had been consumed. He then did a tour of the cooking-sites to ensure the soldiers were adequately provided for.

After his own brief breakfast, he collected his officers for a campaign conference, then ordered Lieutenant-Colonel Wilkinson to patrol towards Tinterns and Clonmines to reconnoitre the surrounding countryside, and to make contact with the English troops he expected.

Wilkinson's patrol returned two hours later. 'The place seems totally deserted, General, apart from one straggling party of rebels who looked half-dead from fatigue.'

'Did you engage them?'

'We had no choice but to engage them. The fools began firing. We killed all of them.'

'Any sign of our troops?'

'Not a glimpse, sir.'

'How long can I wait?' Moore said impatiently. 'My orders are to join up with them and proceed to Taghmon, seven miles nearer Wexford.'

'The men will appreciate the rest while we wait, sir,' Wilkinson said.

General Moore frowned. 'We can rest when the rebellion is over, Wilkinson, not before.'

By 3 p.m. the sun was blistering, there was no sign of the expected troops, and the men were getting edgy. General Moore paced thoughtfully back and forth outside his tent, while his batman paced silently back and forth behind him.

'This dust and heat is intolerable, General,' Prendergast finally ventured. 'Indeed it is! I declare to God I have never known an Irish summer like it.'

General Moore turned and looked at him absently, then made his decision.

'Strike camp!' he commanded.

'I can wait no longer,' he informed his officers. 'My orders are for me to be at Taghmon this day. I have no wish to disappoint any plan by failure on my part. We have a thousand men, sufficient to hold our ground against the rebels if we meet any.'

'Yes, General.'

They had not marched above a mile when they spied a detachment of rebels, a force as large as their own. General Moore immediately ordered the Yagers to advance and skirmish, while he commanded the Light Infantry militia.

'Roll forward the guns!' he ordered.

'Roll them where, exactly, General Moore?'

Moore stared in astonishment at the militia officer. 'To the most commanding sitation, of course! The crossroads!'

The rebels made their charge and it seemed like a great cloud of dust was sweeping towards them.

'Advance!' General Moore shouted, then gaped in disbelief as the Light Infantry militia made no move.

'Advance, damn you!' he roared.

Still they hesitated, clutching their weapons nervously.

'We have no experience of open field battle,' an officer of the militia told him. 'We are unaccustomed to fire.'

'So now you can get accustomed to it!' Moore shouted, swinging down from his horse. 'Any soldier who does not follow me,' he warned, 'will face a white-feather court martial if he survives!'

He placed himself at their head and led the charge himself, running like a sprinter and jumping over a ditch with his horse galloping beside him; and every man of the Infantry, animated not only by his threat but by his spirit, followed at a run.

The battle erupted and went on for most of the afternoon. From his position at the front, Moore managed to hold the rebels at bay, but the fire to his left was getting hotter by the hour. Messages for reinforcements kept coming.

Bending low, he ran over to his brigade-major.

'Go and find out the true state of the left, Anderson. If it's as bad as they say, let me know immediately. I don't wish to leave the front. I am sure the rebels are just waiting for a favourable moment to fall on me.'

Anderson set off, and returned at the double. 'It's absolutely vital that you go to the left at once, sir. The entire area is in confusion and disarray. The fire of the rebels is well supported.'

'I thought they had few guns?' Moore snapped.

'I'd say one firearm to every twenty pikes,' Anderson replied. 'But some of their gunsmen are the best sharpshooters I've ever encountered. Most have been shooting game since their infancy, I'm told.'

'And we're to be the game now,' Moore said wryly, then ordered Anderson to stay and keep control of the front. Seconds later he had mounted his charger and galloped to the woods near Foulkesmill, on the left, where he met the rest of the Light Infantry militia and some dragoons, all in retreat, with the rebels following close, and firing.

General Moore came at them at speed, and pulled up sharp, commanding them to halt. Thrown on its haunches, the horse dashed the dust up with its forefeet and for a moment every soldier halted, their attention on the rider, his blue eyes piercing as he looked beyond them at the enemy's advancing ranks.

'If you cannot defend yourselves against Irish farmers,' General Moore shouted angrily, 'how will you defend yourselves against French soldiers if they land?'

Every soldier stared at him, transfixed. The splendid figure of the British commander astride his horse, his scarlet coat covered in dust, his furious blue eyes refusing to consider defeat, somehow struck up a faster beat in their British hearts.

'Jump out of the road and make a front each side of it,' Moore commanded the infantry. Then to the dragoons, 'Turn and prepare to advance!'

When they did, he placed himself at the head of the dragoons, withdrew his sword and held it high, put his horse into a trot, which set the tempo for the mounts of the cavalry lined up behind him; then when he was ready to make the push, he gave a mighty '*Huzza!*' and led the charge.

The tide immediately turned. They drove the rebels back, and back, and back. Several times a number tried to make a stand, but failed.

By nightfall, General John Moore had gained the battle and the ground, and the rebels had retreated with the dust.

On the grassy bank where his friend and brigade-major sat, General Moore sank down in exhaustion. 'How many men did we lose, Anderson?'

'Not half as many as the rebels.'

'Did any surrender?'

'A few. We gave them quarter.'

Moore lay back on the grass and put his hands behind his head. 'Allow them rations and rest,' he said, 'but inform them that, as our prisoners, they will have to march with us until we can conveniently hand them over to the authorities. At dawn we march to Taghmon – a day late.'

'We shouldn't be here at all,' Anderson said grimly. 'What glory is there in defeating an army of farmers and peasants? Do you credit, that at the end of the contest some of the rebels were attempting to fight us with only sticks in their hands – against muskets and sabres!'

'A pity the militia have none of their courage,' Moore said, closing his eyes. 'I tell you, Anderson, it was the combined brutality of the government and militia that started this war, and now they look to us to finish it for them.'

'General Moore?' a voice said. 'I have the pot boiling – would you like a cup of hot chocolate now?'

Moore opened his tired eyes and looked into those of his young batman who was bending over him anxiously.

'Or a drop of mountain dew perhaps – poteen! I have a bottle of it in my bag, sir, and a kick of ten mules in every sip! Indeed and indeed it has.'

Moore looked sideways at Anderson who was grinning, then both officers burst out laughing.

'Damn the hot chocolate, Prendergast,' said General Moore. 'Bring over the ten mules!'

Meanwhile, General Lake had blitzed his way down to Enniscorthy in County Wexford. Before leaving Dublin he had made it clear to his officers that he was not interested in the business of taking prisoners. Village by village, town by town, the rebels were fought back towards their compatriots in Wexford. Each village the army marched through was left behind in flames. Mercy was out of the question.

The insurgent army was rapidly diminishing. Great numbers of peasants who had joined the rebels fled back to their homes, their courage swallowed up in terror once they heard of the British reinforcements – and worse – a troopboat of Hessians had arrived. His Germanic Majesty, George the Third, had been sent German mercenaries by his relative the King of Prussia to help him defeat the Irish.

On reaching Enniscorthy, General Lake waited for reinforcements before making his attack. All around Vinegar Hill a depleted force of twenty thousand rebels was encamped; some quite old, many only children carrying sticks, waiting to take on the royal forces.

Down below, General Lake was growing impatient. General Moore and two English regiments had not arrived. He decided not to wait for them. He raised his sword, a bugle sounded, and the battle began.

All day the guns thundered around Vinegar Hill. The rebels stood back to back, desperately fighting government troops on three sides. The British regulars were amazed as rebels made charge after charge down to the very mouth of the cannons. But courage was no match for armoury, and as the day wore on the piles of dead rebels numbered thousands. Many of the old men and young boys, in accordance with the code of war, put their hats on their pikes and sticks and walked down the hill in surrender. General Lake sat astride his horse and watched them, then raised his sword – and swiftly turned it down.

The cannons exploded.

The battered remnant of the United army knew they were beaten. They were covered on all sides but the west, and to the west they made their escape, still firing.

Wounded rebels made their way through woodland and forests to the shelter of the Wicklow Mountains. Mary Doyle raced over the hills to the O'Briens' house. She found young David O'Brien sitting by the hearth surrounded by neighbours, a rough bandage on his arm, a pained expression on his face as he answered their questions about the massacre on Vinegar Hill.

'Oh man!' said O'Brien. 'There were so many dead bodies, so many!'

'My brother John?' Mary asked, pushing her way through, 'Do you know what happened to him?'

O'Brien turned to her. For a moment he did not answer her, for it seemed an eternity since he had seen a girl so breathtakingly fresh and comely as Mary Doyle. Her lovely brown eyes were searching his, her lips trembling.

'No, Mary,' he said softly. 'I can't recall seeing John after we arrived at Vinegar Hill.'

'Was he not among those who got away?'

'I don't know. Even before the chiefs gave the word to retreat we knew we were done. Then it was every man for himself.'

'And Michael Dwyer from Imaal here?' asked a man. 'Is he dead or alive or what, do you know?'

'Michael Dwyer? The last glimpse I had of the Captain was on Vinegar Hill. He was fending off a redcoat's sabre with a fierce swing of his musket.' O'Brien swallowed and looked into the fire. 'I doubt if he's alive now to tell the tale.'

People began to name their sons. O'Brien confessed to those he knew to have died, if not on Vinegar Hill, in the battles preceding it. A loud keening and wailing rose up inside the house.

'What about the wounded?' a woman cried hysterically. 'Our sons could be among the wounded taken to the hospital houses.'

'There was only one hospital house,' O'Brien said. 'General Lake ordered it burned to the ground with all inside. He was not disposed to taking prisoners. Any wounded left on the field were put to death where they lay.'

He put his face in his hands and began to weep. 'All those dead . . . so many, so many . . .'

Mary walked slowly out of the room, out of the house. Evening was falling and the last trills of the song thrushes echoed over the blue hills.

When she entered the house at Knockandarragh her parents stood erect, their faces white with dread, their hands unconsciously reaching out to each other.

'John?' Her mother finally whispered.

'He couldn't say. He saw him at Vinegar Hill . . . but not after that.'

Her parents clung to each other and sobbed.

Mary moved as if in a dream and somehow found her bedroom. At the window she stared at the mountains like a person blind, yet it was not only her brother she saw before her eyes, but a tall young man with black hair fending off a redcoat's sabre with a fierce swing of his musket.

The blue of the mountains had turned deeper, intensely mauve. Tears formed in her eyes, for never had the mountains looked so beautiful, or so melancholy.

The evening star was burning in the sky; and darkness was falling over the Glen of Imaal.

Chapter Seven

He had swung his musket in the same way he had swung his scythe in the cornfields, swish, swish, swish, the aim of the swing deadly accurate, and they had fallen back like sheaves.

He was lying on the heather of a hill near Carnew, awake, staring up at the sky of fading stars.

'*We surrender! We surrender!*' The voices still rang in his ears, young boys with hats aloft marching down the hill in surrender. General Lake astride his horse watching them, the hypnotic continuous roll of the English drum. Lake's sword held to shoulder, sword raised, sword swiftly brought down to point at the ground. Cannons exploding. Shouts, screams, blood, limbs flying, flesh burning. Death. Thousands of deaths. Honourable surrender, dishonourable slaughter.

A bird chirped in the branches above his head, then chirped again. Soon the air rang with a multitude of birdsong. In the distance a number of cockerels were crowing competitively. The sun could just be seen above the mountain tops and already the air was warm. The insurgent camp contained over two thousand men of the surviving body of four thousand which had separated into two divisions at Enniscorthy.

Since the defeat at Vinegar Hill, wounded rebels had taken off in small groups for their homes, but the division Michael was with had been involved in a number of battles as they pushed their way towards the safety of the Wicklow Mountains – marching and countermarching, heading first along the coast roads to Wicklow, then doubling back inland towards Wexford – all to confuse the enemy.

The men were roused from their slumber and soon the entire camp was on its feet. All were greatly fatigued from the long march which was made worse by the unusually hot weather and lack of food. Most of the stored crops in the farms they had passed had been burned by the soldiery, and the new crop was far from ripe.

77

A rough roll-call of the men disclosed that at least a hundred more had deserted in the night, back to their homes and families; no longer believing this small army of insurgents could hold out until French reinforcements arrived. But the French had given the United Irish Executive in Dublin a promise of assistance, and the leaders urged the men to give no surrender until all hope of a French landing proved false.

The rebels marched on through forest and woodlands, spending the night on Kilcomney Hill, and were again woken by the wild laughter and singing of the birds. Stiffly, the men roused themselves to their feet and prepared for another day of marching.

Scouts were sent to reconnoitre the surrounding land. They returned with word that the King's troops were advancing from several directions to surround and attack the camp. The morning was misty, making it difficult to distinguish the number and strength of the royal lines. To stand and fight would be extreme madness. There was nothing to do but make one desperate effort to cut their way through the pass at Scollagh Gap.

'If our advance guard of sharpshooters and pikemen can beat off the cavalry coming through,' Michael said to the leaders, 'then the rearguard can hold back the others until we are all clear.'

'There's too many females in this camp,' one said. 'It's going to be hard enough bringing our wounded through as well as these women.'

Michael's eyes ranged over the number of females that had joined the rebel camp: wives and sisters who had left burned-out homes and had nowhere else to go.

'Look on the bright side,' he said cheerfully. 'At least we won't have to cook our own food when we manage to get some.'

The order was given to march. At Scollagh Gap the enemy's cavalry came charging through the pass shouting ferociously, but were swiftly driven back by the counterattack of rebel sharpshooters, who kept up a brisk fire from their positions behind the rocks, until the retreat through Scollagh Gap was completed.

They continued to push on towards the Wicklow Mountains. The long journey was constantly interrupted by skirmishes with the cavalry when sharpshooters would jump behind a hedge or tree and fire volley after volley until the cavalry retreated. Nowhere else in the world were the British cavalry placed at such a disadvantage as in Ireland, due to the smallness of the fields and the high hedges surrounding on every part.

At White Heaps, on the southern slope of Croghan mountain, the men cheered when they saw the other division of the United army advancing towards them from the direction of the gold mines, led by the Wexford commanders, Fitzgerald and Perry. Michael was particularly delighted to meet up again with Garrett Byrne and the survivors of the Ballymanus Corps. And much to everyone's relief, this division brought with them sacks of flour.

A camp was set up, fires were lighted, and the women set to the task of making griddle cakes and slim bread. The wounded were brought to the centre of the camp to be tended by a young Protestant from Monaseed who insisted he had studied surgery. He used a goose-quill for a probe and swore the application of whiskey would emit all germs from any wound immediately.

Michael was sitting amongst a group of his most constant and trusted companions – Hugh Vesty Bryne, Martin Burke, John Mernagh, Sam McAllister, and John Doyle of Knockandarragh. All joked feebly about the hunger in their stomachs.

'Our rebellion is two years too late,' Hugh Vesty said, staring in the direction of the gold mines where a deserted military camp still stood. 'If we had gold now, even those farmers who are against us would sell us food. Begor, with pure gold in our hands I think we could even buy ammunition from the redcoats.'

The men all gazed in the direction of the mines. In 1796 a large gold nugget had been found near the slopes of Croghan Valley which led to a minor goldrush yielding over three thousand ounces of gold.

'Of course,' sniffed Martin Burke, 'we all know where that gold went – to the bloody Castle.'

'And according to old man Cullen,' said Hugh Vesty, 'the leprechauns have been on the warpath ever since. How can they leave their little crocks of gold for those they favour when their underground mines have been plundered?'

John Doyle was far more interested in a small group of females sitting around one of the fires. 'Do you see that little heroine in the blue dress,' he said, 'she would surely make us some more bread if we asked her.' He nudged Michael. 'She was giving you plenty of the come-hither earlier, Captain. Ask her to make us some more bread, will you?'

'Ask her yourself,' Michael replied, sitting erect as Garrett Byrne walked towards them, carefully holding a tankard in his hands.

'A nice tankard of mulled ale for you, Captain Dwyer,' said Garrett with a smile.

'And what about us, General Byrne?' demanded Hugh Vesty. 'Is there no nice tankard of mulled ale for us? We're of the Ballymanus Corps too.'

Garrett Byrne shook his head. 'Sorry, lads, but there's only enough for the captain.'

'That's favouritism!' Hugh Vesty cried. 'Favouritism out and out.'

'It's consideration,' Garrett said. 'Because while you boys are sleeping tonight, Michael will be standing with the others on outpost duty.'

'Outpost duty!' Michael almost spilled his ale. 'Ah, have a heart, Garrett,' he pleaded. 'If I do picquet tonight I'm liable to fall asleep standing up.'

The lads looked greatly amused. 'Orders is orders, Captain,' said Hugh Vesty. 'So drink down your nice tankard of mulled ale and take up position at the outpost like a good soldier boy.'

John Mernagh yawned extravagantly. 'While we stretch our weary limbs and—' yawn '—have a nice—' yawn '—sleep.'

Michael drank down his ale, lifted his musket and sprang to his feet, then looked Garrett Byrne coldly in the eye. 'If it's not a court martial offence to ask,' he said, 'what made you pick me?'

Garrett Byrne shrugged, then smiled. 'Favouritism,' he said.

As they were now approaching his own part of the country, General Garrett Byrne of the Ballymanus Corps was given supreme command by the Wexford chiefs. He decided to march towards Aughrim, and all accepted his decision.

It was twelve days since the battle of Vinegar Hill, twelve days of marching and countermarching in the fierce heat on little food, ending with nights sleeping on the hard ground; exhausted limbs revived only by occasional swims in the glistening rivers and aquamarine lakes. Since the retreat from Enniscorthy they had marched and countermarched more than a hundred miles which was made harder by the hunger and privation they had suffered in the preceding month.

At the place where the Rivers Ow and Derry meet to form

the Aughrim River, is Aughrim itself, situated at the junction of several mountain valleys; a beautiful place, not far from the Vale of Avoca.

But when the insurgents entered the neighbourhood of Aughrim, they stood in shock and horror at the number of dead bodies lying over the fields and highroad. Women lay with their stomachs ripped open, babies and children beside them. It was clear they had been dead for some days.

It was too much to take. The slaughter at Vinegar Hill had been something else, men who had taken up arms against the Crown and lost. But these were nearly all women and children, a few old men – savagely murdered.

They were all poor, shabbily dressed and no shoes. Strangely, from their postures, it appeared as if only the children had fought against death. Many of the women and old men had their hands outstretched in pathetic and hopeless supplication for mercy.

In their physical and mental exhaustion it was simply too much for the men to take. They couldn't talk. They couldn't cry. Most fell over the ditches and were violently sick.

Michael stared down at the bodies of two young girls no more than fourteen or fifteen years, sisters probably; both had the same freckled skin and beechnut-coloured hair. They had their arms around each other in a last act of protection and comfort as the bayonets drove into them.

He couldn't even be sick. The sorrow went too deep. They were so young, so very young. Like all the other men, his tears would come later, and they would never forget. The death fields of Aughrim would live with them for ever. That's how it was in this land of long memories, amongst a people who knew that the war of Cromwell had never finished – a war to wipe out an entire race of people, the native people of Ireland.

A small boy was found hiding in a barn, so terrified it took a great deal of patience and soothing before he could speak, and when he did, he told them that the people had been murdered two days previously by the Rathdrum Militia.

A general cry of vengeance rose up amongst the men, who demanded an immediate march to Rathdrum, but the chiefs managed to calm them, suggesting the Rathdrum Militia might be better served later if they first made an attack on the barracks at Hacketstown where much-needed powder and ball cartridge could be had.

This objective agreed upon, it was decided that a simultaneous attack would be made on Hacketstown from three sides. Captain Dwyer was chosen to lead one section of the attack and given independent command. Michael accepted the decision and drew off with a contingent of men to spend the night in preparation two miles east of Kiltegan while the main body lay at Ballymanus.

During the night, Michael's seventeen-year-old brother James made a visit to the camp. He brought with him ten sheep which were killed and roasted and divided amongst the tired and hungry insurgents. The succulent cooked meat soon made men of them again.

James responded to Michael's earnest inquiries about the safety of the family by saying all were well except their father, who had had an accident with the scythe in the fields and had now almost lost the use of his arm.

'And mother and the girls?' Michael asked. 'Are you sure they are well and safe?'

'Aye, but we all go about our business armed to the teeth. Even Etty is quite handy with a pistol now.'

Michael bit his lip. 'Is Daddy hurt bad?'

'He's all right. He has the six of us to help him with the work. He worries bad about you, though.'

Michael escorted James back down the hill, away from the view of the men, and there the two brothers hesitated for a moment, then threw off their male embarrassment and embraced tightly. James was almost in tears.

'You can never come home again, Michael. They know you were at Wexford and are watching the farm, I'm sure of it. Case and his friends have pledged their oath to your murder.'

Michael acknowledged the inevitability of the threat with a careless twist of his mouth. 'Don't worry, avic. They will not find it so easy to kill me as their confederates killed those defenceless women and children at Aughrim.'

Then he stood to attention, a grim smile on his face. 'I must say farewell now. I have a battle to command in a few hours.'

'God grant you life and victory so,' James whispered, 'for the truth is, Michael, our safety lies with your safety. They know if they violate the girls while you and the cousins are alive, they will be made to pay for it.'

'Violate . . . ?' Michael stared at him. '*Rape?* Don't say the evils of Wexford are happening in Imaal.'

'Every evil dreamed by the devil is happening in Imaal,'

James blurted. 'At first it was just house burning, their favourite sport; then floggings and half-hangings. Many of the Highland regiments do their best to keep things under control, but since the Hessians arrived the women are no longer safe in house or field. And now some of the redcoats are indulging lustily in the sport too.'

Even in the moonlight, James could see his brother's face had turned white. Michael rubbed a hand angrily across his eyes. 'We *have* to get that ammunition tomorrow,' he whispered, then turned on his heel and marched away.

'Now remember,' he said in final orders to his men, 'in any situation, the first blow well struck is often half the battle.'

When dawn broke, Michael moved his men to Kilmecart Hill, half a mile north of Hacketstown with the Dereen River flowing in between. Sharpshooters were placed in the front, pikemen at the rear. Through his spy-glass he could see numbers of the Ballymanus Corps moving in quietly from the east, with the Wexford colours advancing from the south-east. He kept his eyes on the Ballymanus division as his ears waited for the signal to strike.

When the signal of musket shots was heard, Michael led his men forward with a run, fording the shallow river and over the bank to see a line of troops drawn across an open field in readiness.

'To your knees!' Michael commanded. 'Slap at them!'

The line of marksmen all fell to one knee and fired at once. An instant gap was seen in the royal lines.

'Down every man!' Michael shouted.

The entire body fell to the ground as an answering volley whistled over their heads with no hits.

'Forward!'

Mary's head ached almost as much as her legs and shoulders as she walked across the wide yard to the barn and slowly climbed the ladder to lie on the hay in the loft. She moved on her knees and peered through a small opening in the side of the barn; from this height she had a good view of the surrounding land. There was a house on fire in the distance, choking up its last black clouds in the afternoon sunlight. Burning buildings were now a common sight. She lay back on the hay and closed her eyes, relishing the peaceful stillness of the empty barn.

Her mother and father had been nigh on useless for three days, ever since the battle at Hacketstown, convinced that John must surely be dead. Large and small parties of exhausted rebels had passed through Imaal on their way to the fastness of the mountains in Glenmalure, stopping only briefly to drink the water and eat the bread which they greatly appreciated. But none could repay the Doyles with any heartening news of John since they had last seen him at Hacketstown.

The battle at Hacketstown had lasted for ten hours, they said, ten long hours of the most daring bravery but, as always, courage was no match against artillery. All had agreed they would stand strong and not entertain defeat until the last of their ammunition was fired. And although the rebels had succeeded in taking the town, it had proved impossible to dislodge the main garrison. Frontal attacks on the barracks had resulted in heavy rebel casualties.

Generals Byrne and Fitzgerald, and Captain Dwyer had commanded, and never did three men strive harder to obtain a victory, but the most reckless and bold attempt, they said, was made by the intrepid Captain Dwyer and two Wexford brothers named Laphen, who planted ladders against the barracks and had scaled them almost to the top when they were repulsed, the ladders thrown back with the men ascending them, forcing them to leap to the ground and return fire lying on their backs.

The following day the people groaned to hear the opinion of the military commander at Hacketstown, stated in the press, that had the rebels persisted for a further half-hour, the garrison would have been forced to surrender.

But with no more ammunition, the rebels had withdrawn, bringing their wounded and some of the dead with them. Many more dead were left behind which the military piled into over thirty farm carts and buried the bodies in a large sandpit at the top of Church Hill.

Was John Doyle in that pit? His parents were sure he was, otherwise why had he not been amongst the returning groups? All the chores had been left for Mary to do while her parents sat and gloomed, see-sawing from weeping despair to chattering hope, then back to weeping despair. For three days Mary had risen at four, cooked and cleaned and carried turf buckets, lit fires, milked cows, fed the pigs and hens, churned butter, almost everything short of spooning the food into her stricken parents' mouths. Then falling into bed only to lie awake through the night wondering about her brother.

There was death in the air. The land stank of it. Stumbling across dead bodies in a field or outside a cottage was now almost as commonplace as smoke-blackened houses. According to the reports, the long-dreamed-of war for liberation had resulted in approximately thirty thousand rebel dead, and three thousand women and children murdered.

Mary stretched her tired limbs and closed her eyes. 'I mustn't think about it,' she told herself quickly. 'If I think about it any more I'll go mad.'

She drew a deep breath and allowed her fatigue to take its due of her.

She awoke some hours later and, for a moment, could not remember where she was. The rafters above her head told her she was in the barn. She sat up and glanced through the opening in the wall, saw that the sun had disappeared behind the mountain peaks.

Moving hastily on to her knees, she crawled over to the ladder and began to descend. The sound of footsteps made her pause three steps from the bottom and turn her face to the open door, swallowing her breath at the sight of the smiling face. Her heart lurched as he murmured a caressing word she did not understand.

'*Liebling.*'

She climbed down the remaining steps, taking a pace backwards as a second Hessian entered the barn. She stood speechless with terror at the expressions on their faces. They were grinning and moving towards her, talking in amused asides to each other in their foreign tongue. Through the corner of her eye she spied the pitchfork standing against the wall. Instinctively her hand reached out and grabbed it. She held it in front of her, grasped tightly in both hands and slightly raised.

The Hessians eyed the pitchfork warily. The younger one made a vague, ineffectual gesture towards her. She raised the fork higher, trembling, every inch of her.

The muttered asides struck up again. The younger one wiped a hand against his breeches and swallowed noisily as his eyes roved over the provocative lines of her body. But it was the second Hessian who moved to grab the pitchfork from her. She swiftly thrust the fork hard into his chest, making him shriek and jump back.

Mary stared at the blood appearing on the Hessian's blue tunic, momentarily shocked at her own violence. The younger soldier saw his chance and sprang, grabbing the pitchfork out of her hands, then threw it aside and roughly pressed her down on to the straw. When he straddled her she struggled wildly, tried to cry out but found it hard to breathe; his mouth was devouring hers like a savage. She fought him frantically, hitting his shoulders and face as his hands palped her body and plucked at her skirts.

Twisting her mouth free she screamed hysterically, knowing she could not stop him, he was too strong, too brutal with lust. He tugged impatiently at the side buttons on his breeches, pausing to give her a stinging back-hand across the face and kick her knee aside.

Mary's mind seemed to slip into a red darkness as terror over-whelmed her. It was the most jaw-clamping terror she had ever known, to be thrown down as if she was nothing more than a piece of flesh, with no human feelings inside that flesh – as if she were not a young virgin girl at all, but some animal that must be slapped and kicked into doing the master's bidding. She made one final effort to fight back as the Hessian plucked and pulled at her clothes, then suddenly he stopped – stopped panting, stopped moving, stopped breathing altogether. He made one last guttural sound in his throat, then his body slumped over hers, his face falling into her neck.

She drew in a mouthful of air, opened her eyes. For a moment she stared uncomprehending, then a quivering cry of relief escaped her as her vision focused on the tall young man with black hair bending over the Hessian.

Michael Dwyer withdrew his knife from the Hessian's back, then threw it down on the straw. He put his hands under the dead man's armpits and slowly lifted him off Mary, giving her time to shove down her disarrayed clothes and quickly pull herself to a kneeling position before the Hessian was thrown face down on to the straw beside her.

Trembling violently, she stared at Michael Dwyer. He ignored her and lifted his knife, coldly cleaning the blade on the Hessian's coat. Her glance now took in five other men standing behind Michael Dwyer, and to the side of them, her brother, standing over the other Hessian, also dead.

John came and squatted beside her. 'Are you all right, Mary? Did he . . . ?'

'No, I'm . . .' The relief of being rescued in time and the

sight of John alive was all too much for her to handle with dignity. She put her arms around her brother and began to bawl like a baby, burying her head into his shoulder.

'Don't be crying now,' John pleaded. 'You know I hate it when you cry like a childybawn. And the violators have been justly dealt with.'

Hugh Vesty Byrne gave a small derisive laugh. 'And no doubt the King of Prussia will be told they died nobly in action.'

John pulled Mary to her feet. 'We haven't been into the house yet. Are the Ma and Da all right?'

Mary nodded, wiped a palm over her wet face. 'They'll be so glad to see you, John,' she whispered. 'For the past month they feared you were dead, and for the last three days were sure of it.'

'We should bury these two now,' Michael said, 'in case any more Hessians are in the area.' He turned to John, not wishing to experience yet another family reunion after the emotional scenes in his own house and Hugh Vesty's. 'Give us the spades,' he said, 'and we'll do the job while you go see your people.'

Mary began to thank the rebels for her rescue but Michael was already dragging the body of one of the Hessians towards the door of the barn. He seemed tense and edgy, ordering Hugh Vesty to take up outpost duty near the field wall.

The hysterical scene inside the Doyles' house was deafening when the prodigal son entered. Mary immediately set to the task of peeling a large pot of potatoes and turnips as her parents sobbed and hugged her brother. When they had calmed a little, she listened as they plied John with questions. She had warned him to say nothing about the Hessians.

'Where have you been atall, John agra? Were you at the business at Hacketstown?'

'I was.'

'So why the delay? The other rebels passed through here two days ago.'

'We had to see to the wounded and bury those that later died. And the other boys wanted to look in on their families and get a change of clothes.'

'Is that right?' William Doyle looked annoyed. 'So being a good friend and a bad son, you left your own family till last.'

'Ach no, Da! But now I'm home I'll be staying. Those boys will be on their keeping in the mountains for God knows how long. I just wanted to share with them a bit longer.'

Mary hung the cauldron of vegetables on one of two cranes above the fire, next to a pot which contained a large joint of boiling bacon. 'And how is it,' she asked, 'that you can now stay at home and they cannot?'

'Their names and faces are known,' John replied, 'but I'm just one of the thousands. Like you said, not even rebels could tell you any news of me. If the military call I will just do the old Irish bit and act like a simpleton. I'll say I wandered up to Meath after a girl I was smitten with, but her father showed me the heel of his boot.'

'Woe betide any man who would do that to my son!' William Doyle shouted furiously.

'God save all here,' said Big Art Devlin walking into the kitchen, followed by John Mernagh, Martin Burke, Michael Dwyer, and a golden-haired young man wearing a green cravat who bowed to Mrs Doyle and said in an Ulster accent, 'Thank you kindly for the hospitality of your board and hearth, ma'am.'

Mrs Doyle stretched her arms to welcome them with a wide, dramatic gesture. 'Well now, you poor boys! Sit down and rest yourself after your terrible war.'

She smiled at each man in turn, then looked lovingly at her son. 'I was wondering if maybe we could all say a decade of the rosary together before supper, in thanksgiving to Our Lord and his Blessed Mother for sparing all your lives.'

The young Ulsterman threw an embarrassed glance at Michael Dwyer.

'My friend here, Sam McAllister, is not familiar with the rosary,' Michael said. 'He is a Protestant, and a deserter from the Antrim Militia stationed at Arklow.'

'The militia?' Mrs Doyle gaped at Sam McAllister. 'We knew that some of the militia did desert,' she said, 'but why? What was your purpose when you enjoyed such a privileged position?'

'The intelligentsia in Dublin have a name for it,' McAllister replied. 'Conscientious objector – to injustice and tyranny.'

'Then you shall always have a welcome in our home, Mr McAllister,' said William Doyle solemnly. 'And is it Michael Dwyer standing there with you? And Burke and Mernagh too. Welcome, boys, but tell me, whatever happened to Hugh Vesty Byrne? A laugh and a half he was at times. Dead is he?'

'Hugh is doing sentry duty outside,' Michael told him.

'Would you save him some food please, Mrs Doyle?'

'Certainly I will.' Mrs Doyle lifted her apron and dabbed at her eyes. 'All I know at this moment is that you brought my son home safely when thousands of other boys died. And I would not dream of embarrassing Mr McAllister by forcing him to join in the practices of our religious faith. We will eat immediately.'

Mary placed two loaves of white-brown bread on the long table with a dish of golden butter, followed by the meal. In the centre of the table she set a bowl of hot salty bacon water in which they could dip the potatoes.

'We have no salt,' she said apologetically. 'It's become like gold dust since the rebellion began. The soldiers have taken it all from the storehouses.'

Michael was looking round at the long, low parlour/kitchen which was spotless and shining. The black oak dresser gleamed with the beeswax polishing his mother swore by, providing a mirrored background to the patterned plates and cups on the shelves. Beneath the front window was a small table containing a piece of half-finished lace. In the corner stood the usual spinning-wheel, also polished to a satin finish.

'Can the lads rest up here through the night?' John Doyle asked his father. 'They'll be leaving before dawn.'

'Sure they can,' Doyle cried. 'Won't it be a grand excuse to have a drink and a bit of sing-song later – as a sort of celebration for the return of my hero son from the wars. Youse won't find me meanspirited – not like some I could mention!'

During the meal the men talked of the rebellion. 'A main contribution to our failure,' Michael said quietly, 'was that our military strategy was so poor. No reserves were held back to take over from exhausted men. When one of the enemy's soldiers fell, another stepped into his place. But whenever any of our men fell, it simply diminished our numbers.'

Throughout the conversation Michael's eyes avoided Mary, but her eyes rarely left his face. He looked thinner than when she had last seen him, and the skin of his face and arms was no longer lightly tanned, but burned a dark bronze. She sat silent, obliquely watching him, feeling happy and miserable at the same time.

William Doyle's humour was mighty now that his son was back. When supper was over he brought out a bottle of whiskey, then started to sing, waving his hands and swaying from side to side, encouraging the others until they joined in; all except Michael, who leaned back in his chair and watched Mary as she stooped before the fire and lifted the boiling kettle off the crane.

There was a weariness about her, in every movement she made. Gone was the well-cut young lady he had first seen in Donard, and the exciting girl of the fair. Her black hair was tied back simply with a blue ribbon, and her face, he noticed, was very pale. A trace of a sad smile played about his lips. She was still the loveliest thing he ever saw.

She laid the kettle down on the fireflag, straightening slowly as if her back ached, then suddenly she was looking at him. He saw a colour like bright roses come into her cheeks as her dark eyes stared directly into his. He was surprised by the altered look on her face, wondering why she was staring at him in such a strange way, wondering if she still felt disdain for him . . . even now. And not realising he was looking at a girl suffering from the most intense of all passions – first love, he managed to gaze back at her, neutrally.

She moved over to the table to stand beside him.

'I want to talk to you,' she whispered.

'Go ahead,' he said casually.

Her bosom heaved in an impatient sigh.

'Not here.'

'Listen to this!' shouted William Doyle from the other end of the table. 'This was always a good one!' then began to sing in a loud rumbling voice a romantic song Mary knew well. Michael's eyes were turned to her father, who grinned like a mule and spread his arms as he directed a verse first to his wife, then his daughter.

Unbeguiled, Mary turned away.

Darkness was falling. She lit the candles then sat down by the small table at the window and lifted her lace, untouched by the jolly atmosphere in the room. Even Mrs Doyle looked tipsy on her one glass of whiskey, smiling and humming along with her husband. When the song ended to hand-clapping applause, Doyle laughed and embraced his wife, who chuckled and ordered him to behave.

'My William,' she announced smugly, patting her curls into place, 'was always a romantic young fella.'

Every male stared at the big heap of a man sitting at the top of the table, knocking back his whiskey and smacking his lips with relish.

Michael rose to his feet. 'I'd better go and relieve Hugh Vesty,' he said.

Mary watched him stride out of the room, feeling only miserable now. She set aside her lace and moved listlessly to the hearth.

Hugh Vesty's smile was as wide as his face when he entered, and after quickly devouring the food Mary placed before him, thanked her heartily and sat back to enjoy his whiskey.

William Doyle was on his feet, gripping Sam McAllister's shoulders. 'Will I show you how wrestling is really done?' he said. 'Don't mind all that nonsense about Hugh Vesty Byrne being the best wrestler in Wicklow. Now watch carefully, Hugh Vesty, and maybe you'll pick up a good tip or two and all.'

Hugh Vesty threw back his head and laughed; and Mary slipped quietly out of the room.

Michael was not at the field wall as she had expected. She peered around the fields, then in the moonlight she saw him standing by a tree. He was leaning motionless on his musket, head bowed and eyes fixed on the ground.

The night was very still and warm with only a slight breeze moving softly through the long ferns and yellow gorse on the hills, the yellow gorse that bloomed all year round. For a change, she observed, there was no fire from a burning house lighting the sky. She climbed over the low wall and approached him slowly and nervously.

He lifted his head and they stood looking at each other, enclosed in the silence of the hills. Her mouth moved slightly, but no sound came through the congestion of words in her throat. He went on looking at her, calmly waiting for her to say whatever was on her mind.

Unexpectedly, her eyes filled up with tears, lost in the wordless spell of confusion that Michael Dwyer always managed to cast over her.

'Oh, Michael,' she cried at last, her voice husky, 'I was not wrong when I said you were dangerous. Today you proved it, when you killed that man.'

'That was no man,' he said coldly. 'All violators are less than animals. If I hadn't killed him, your brother or one of the others would.'

She made no reply, just drew a long slow breath.

'What did you want me to do, eh?' He looked at her contemptuously as he asked the question. 'Discuss the matter politely with him? Not a chance! On our way back from Hacketstown we learned of four other girls who had been raped. One was beaten up so badly she will never see again.'

'Oh!' Mary put her hands to her face. 'Hessians?' she whispered.

'Hessians, militia, redcoats, what matter? Underneath the cloth they were swine.'

'Oh, Michael,' she cried. 'Michael, Michael . . .' then she sagged and moved close to him, turning her face into his shoulder and weeping. Still keeping a hand on the musket he moved the other round her waist and held her, bringing his face down against her hair. And they stood that way for a long time, until her weeping ceased and she became tranquil.

'Where will you go from here?' she eventually whispered.

'Glenmalure.'

She gave a little sigh and bowed her head, her heart full of desperation and pain, her mind blank of all but the certainty that tomorrow he would be gone again, to Glenmalure, miles and miles away, with no sure prospect of running into him again for maybe months, maybe never.

'Tell me,' he whispered, 'what was it you wanted to say to me?'

She lifted her head and gazed at him with lips parted, eyes as wide and thoughtful as when she gazed on the mountains. Then without warning she slid her arms around his neck and kissed him on the mouth. And with that kiss said everything she had wanted to say. And it was at that moment they heard a ferocious roar from the direction of the house.

'Curse you, Hugh Vesty, you took me off guard! Come back, ye devil, you've broken my hip!'

Hilarious laughter. The bang of a door. Silence. Then a long low whistling call from the yard.

'That's Hugh Vesty,' Michael whispered, laying the musket aside and putting both hands on her waist. 'Ignore him and he'll have the decency to go away.'

They stood facing one another, their bodies touching. He dipped his head and gently put his lips to her mouth, as gentle as the touch of a butterfly, too gentle for Mary, who moved her hands over his shoulders with greedy fingers. It was an invitation, and he took it; wrapping his arms around her and kissing her in the sensual way she wanted him to, the way he had kissed her at the fair.

It was Mary who at last, trying to draw breath, pulled her face away, but still clung tight and let him trace a line of kisses down her cheek and neck.

'Will I see you again?' she whispered urgently.

'Oh yes.'

'When?'

'I don't know.' He moved his mouth softly over her hair. 'We'll be on our keeping in the mountains of Glenmalure until the French arrive.' He could feel the warm softness of her breasts pressing through his shirt and closed his eyes. 'But I'll send word to you.'

'When?'

'I can't say exactly when. A week; maybe less.' He drew in his breath. 'Mary . . . I can feel your heart thumping.'

'Yours too,' she breathed, not moving an inch, 'beating like a drum.'

'You're shameless,' he whispered, 'throwing yourself at a poor country boy this way.'

She drew back her head. 'Are you complaining?'

'Not a bit.'

'Did you think of me at all?'

'When?'

'All the time you were in Wexford.'

'Oh surely,' he said with a smile.

She was not so sure; her happiness ebbed.

Both turned their heads when Hugh Vesty's whistling call came again.

'Is he still there?' Michael exclaimed. 'I declare to God that man has no decency whatever.'

'I should go,' she said, suddenly unnerved and moving out of his embrace. 'My daddy may also come out. Will you get in touch with me soon?'

'Yes.'

'Truly?' she said earnestly.

'On my soul.'

She looked at him a bit doubtfully, suddenly remembering her brother's warning that he had romanced other girls, then walked away without appearing to give them a second thought. Then she also remembered something about females that the young Ulsterman named Sam McAllister had said during supper.

'The camp in Glenmalure,' she said to Michael, 'will there be females there as well as men?'

'Yes,' he answered honestly. 'Many have been with us since Wexford.'

'Camp followers?'

'Some.'

'Oh!' It was more a gasp than a word. She stood for a moment looking vacantly about her, her fingers twisting together. Then abruptly she turned to go.

She was only a few yards gone when Michael caught her arm, his tone puzzled. 'Mary, what is wrong with you?'

'Maybe I've changed my mind about seeing you,' she retorted. 'Maybe I don't want to be just another low and brazen camp follower.'

He smiled. 'Oh sweet girl, you could never be that.'

Like a mesmerised young fawn she stared at him, seeing only the amused smile of his mouth and the tanned skin of his throat and the black hair curling loosely round his neck; and her jealous heart ached.

He touched her face with his fingertips. 'You are always ready to believe the worst of me, aren't you?'

The enraged, hurting look melted from her eyes and she almost smiled. She was ready to believe *anything* of him – anything at all. He was the most unpredictable of men, quite unlike any other person she had known. He had whupped a yeoman and killed a Hessian in two of their four meetings, yet there was none of the fierce sniffing and sneering of many of the toughies she had seen prowling around Imaal. He was as cool as a river, his face as unrevealing of his thoughts as a secret wishing-well.

His eyes were fixed on her face, measuring her, and to her sudden delight she saw something more in his eyes than mild curiosity – she saw a shadow of anxiety. In that moment all her doubts were resolved. He not only wanted to see her again, but was *anxious* that he should.

Impulsively, her hands went around his waist. 'Love me or leave me,' she said in a whisper, 'but whatever you do, do it true. Don't play around with me. Don't make a fool of me.'

'Don't be silly, Mary,' he said softly. 'Of course I won't.'

'Truly, Michael?'

'Truly. And why should I? A lucky man like me. You're the loveliest thing in all Wicklow.' A sudden smile broke on his face. 'And I know just the place where we can meet.' He told her about Cullen's cottage at Knockgorragh. 'It's as isolated and untroubled as Heaven. Only the shepherds and the sheep

know those hills. 'Tis a fair walk, but it's safe from the soldiery.'
He smiled again. 'And you'll love the old man.'

'I love you,' she whispered.

For a fleeting second the shadow of anxiety was back in his eyes, but then she thought she must have imagined it, for he took her face in his hands and kissed her gently. 'I did,' he whispered, 'think of you in Wexford. And many a day and night before Wexford.'

She smiled happily.

'But you must go now,' he said, frowning over her head into the darkness. 'I'm supposed to be on outpost duty, and Hugh Vesty is sitting on the wall watching us like a blasted ghost!'

She turned with a jump as if really expecting to see a ghost; and Hugh Vesty began to whistle like a nightingale.

A last brief kiss, then she clutched her skirts and ran back towards the house, almost colliding with Hugh, who had risen from the wall and now came towards her.

'Everything all right?' he asked casually.

When she made no reply and ran on, Hugh shrugged and sauntered up to Michael. 'A lovely warm night, wouldn't you say, Captain?'

'It is,' Michael replied, 'a night for angels at your window.'

'If you happen to have a window,' Hugh Vesty drawled. 'And I don't. But I have been watching you, Captain, and while I was so doing, I began to wonder what little game you were playing.'

Michael could not help smiling at his cousin. They were the very best of friends and there had always been a good-humoured rivalry between them.

'And the only thing I could conclude,' Hugh continued, 'is that what happened in the barn today – you springing on that Hessian before anyone could bat an eyelid – was a case of protecting the sweet fruit until the time was ripe to pluck it yourself.'

Michael narrowed his eyes. 'Oh, mind your tone and tongue, Hugh,' he warned coolly, then bent and picked up his musket, his eyes slowly scanning the land, ears straining against the light breeze. Satisfied, he leaned against the tree and looked at his cousin.

'A fine sentry you've been,' Hugh said in disgust. 'Musket thrown to the wind while everyone in there is depending on you for their safety.'

Michael was unmoved. 'Were you worried, Hugh? Even for a minute?'

'For a minute I was,' Hugh said, 'and even longer. That's why I stayed outside.'

'And what brought you out in the first place?'

'Well, being the true and loyal cousin that I am, I came out to share this with you.' Hugh withdrew a pipe from his pocket and a tinder-box. 'Never dreaming, mind, that I would find you dallying with the daughter of the house.'

'Where did you get the tobacco?' Michael asked. 'I thought you had none.'

'I didn't. I got this from Doyle's pipe.'

Michael stared at him. 'You mean, after the man shared his home, table, and bottle with you – you whipped the tobacco out of his pipe!'

'Ach, sure what's the harm? He wasn't using it at the time. And 'tis only a venial sin, not a mortal one.'

'So what happens when he goes to smoke his pipe and finds the bowl empty?'

'No problem. I filled his bowl with turf dust from the turf bucket. With the whiskey that's in him he'll not notice the difference.'

Hugh fingered the tobacco in the pipe-bowl and leaned against the tree beside Michael. After a silence he said thoughtfully, 'That Mary Doyle is not a bad looking girsha, but you know, when all is reckoned up, she couldn't hold a candle to my Dymphna.'

Michael gave an audible snigger. His rivalry with his cousin often led to Hugh telling the biggest lies imaginable. 'Is this the buxom strap who chased you over the hills then vowed to wait and wed you?'

'And that's not all she's going to do either,' Hugh said smugly. 'She's going to bring me wealth. She'll be coming with a large dowry.'

'If she's that exquisite, why is her father prepared to pay handsomely the man who takes her?'

'A dowry, in case you still don't know, cousin,' Hugh said patiently, 'is a tradition between gentlemen. A contribution to a man for providing a home and board for another man's daughter. A tradition, of course, between those that have it to give.'

'All the same,' Michael said, 'her name would worry me ragged.'

'Why so?'

Michael fixed his eyes earnestly on his cousin and said in a low tone, 'She was named after Saint Dymphna, wasn't she?'

'Aye, I suppose so.'

'And do you know who Saint Dymphna is, Hugh?'

'No.'

'She's the patron saint of lunatics.'

'Eh?'

Michael narrowed his eyes. 'Makes you wonder about that fine dowry, doesn't it now?'

'Lunatics?' Hugh smiled uncertainly. 'You're lying!'

'God's truth. Go in and ask Mrs Doyle, off guard, who or what is Saint Dymphna the heavenly patron of.'

'Devil swallow you, Dwyer, I'll do it just to spite you!' Hugh turned and fled across the grass still clutching the pipe, a fearful frown on his face.

The men and Mrs Doyle were sitting around the hearth when Hugh Vesty marched in. Mary had retired to her room.

'Here's the culprit!' cried William Doyle. 'I wouldn't be surprised if you've crippled me for life,' he complained, 'throwing me over like that!'

'Mrs Doyle,' Hugh Vesty cried, 'would you know who Saint Dymphna is?'

'Saint Dymphna?' Mrs Doyle puckered her brow. 'Faith, but I've not heard of her, dear. 'Tis only Our Blessed Lady that I ask to pray for me.'

William Doyle stopped rubbing his thigh and looked up with a grimace of pain. 'I know who she is. My mother was very attached to Saint Dymphna.'

'Who is she the heavenly patron of?' Hugh demanded.

'Those poor unfortunate creatures that go dancing off in the dark of night thinking they're moon faeries – lunatics.'

'You cur!' Hugh cried. 'I should have broken your blasted neck!' He wheeled and stormed out, but by the time he reached Michael leaning on his musket and shaking with silent laughter, Hugh had composed himself.

'Well aren't you the jealous varmint, Dwyer,' he said airily. 'It has always annoyed you that I'm the better wrestler, so now you're trying to prove you have the better woman because she is named after the Queen of Heaven while mine is named after a saint who favours lunatics.'

Michael burst out laughing.

'Arrah, be easy will you.'

'Oh come on, Hugh, light your pipe. I feel in humour for a smoke.'

'Then go and whip some tobacco from your darling Mary's daddy. Why should I share my venial sin with you when 'tis me will have to answer for it?'

'Let's not fall out, Hugh,' Michael said. 'I didn't mean to upset you.'

Hugh Vesty looked at him suspiciously, then lit the pipe. 'Ach,' he said with a sudden forgiving shrug, 'you can't help your jealousy, I suppose. Here, you can have the first few pulls.'

Michael grinned and took the pipe. 'That's the spirit, Hugh. No sense in letting any lunatics come between blood cousins.' He laughed, and quickly drew on the pipe, then almost choked.

'This is not tobacco. It's blasted turf dust!'

'What?' Hugh Vesty grabbed the pipe and drew on it, then exhaled with an exclamation of indignation. 'You're right – *turf*!' Hugh's disgusted eyes glared towards the house. 'Oh, the cheat! No wonder that old bag of bluff sat singing his head off while I swapped his turf for more turf. Devil take him, if he can afford whiskey he can surely afford a screw of tobacco.'

'Maybe he just smokes the turf when he's out of tobacco,' Michael suggested. 'Same as you do.'

'Ach, no matter,' Hugh said nonchalantly. 'I'll have plenty of tobacco when my Dymphna brings me her dowry. But I don't think you'll be so fortunate, Michael, not if you intend to wed Mary Doyle. I doubt if that turf-smoking father of hers will be giving away any fine dowries.'

'Dowries be damned, Hugh,' Michael said seriously. 'I've no intention of marrying anyone.'

Chapter Eight

The valley of Glenmalure is three miles long and a mile wide, with the River Avonbeg flowing through it. A picturesque place bounded by high mountains of which some stand perpendicular and others almost hang right over the valley, making many a stranger fear he might be crushed if any of the enormous masses of rock were to be dislodged.

The rebel camp in Glenmalure now included thirty deserters from the Antrim Militia as well as deserters from thirteen other regiments. Sam McAllister, the young Antrim man with the green cravat, was drilling some of the men, severe in his reprimands of those who were slow in reloading their weapons. Michael and Hugh Vesty stood by a tree a few yards away, watching them.

'You were talking mighty mild about the Highlanders last night,' Hugh murmured, continuing to watch McAllister. 'Some of the boys are getting worried, fear that you're weakening.'

'Then let them go their own road,' Michael answered. 'Take my word, Hugh, the most decent soldiers in this country today are the Highland regiments. They carry out their business as humanely as they can, consistent with their duty. You never hear of the Highlanders murdering their prisoners, or burning and looting, or violating the women.'

Hugh sniffed. 'Aye, I suppose you're right. Sure 'tis only fifty-odd years since their own rebellion. Most of their grandfathers were probably out fighting at Culloden behind Charles the bonny Prince.'

Two more deserters from the Antrim Militia were led into the camp, rushing up to Sam McAllister and speaking urgently to him. Michael and Hugh Vesty exchanged frowns, then McAllister came over to Michael.

'The troops are mustering at Blessington,' he said, 'in readiness to attack us at first light tomorrow.'

'I just *knew* this would happen!' Michael cried. 'But would anyone listen to me?'

A week previously, Garrett Byrne of Ballymanus had left the glen with a large contingent of men in order to march to the counties of Louth and Kildare. Commanders Perry and Fitzgerald had returned with another division to Wexford where mass hangings were being carried out by the military under the command of General Lake.

Michael could not understand what had motivated the leaders to leave the stronghold of the Wicklow Mountains, where neither artillery nor cavalry could be brought to bear against them – to march out into open country such as Louth and Kildare where the enemy's cavalry would have every possible advantage.

'If our forces remained here,' Michael had said, 'we could muster to maybe six thousand strong and be ready to move as a reckonable army when the French arrive.'

But only his own division, and a Wexford captain named Miles Byrne supported his argument. To the rest of the men, the undaunted bravery of these Irish commanders simply served to make them even more beloved, and hundreds volunteered to go with them.

Now the rebel camp at Glenmalure was to be attacked.

With a thoughtful frown, Michael swept his eyes over the land around him. During the glacial period two mountains had been formed at each side of the Glenmalure valley; the Lugnaquilla to the west, and Mullacor to the east . . . and the Lugnaquilla stood between Glenmalure and Imaal – a retreat, if necessary.

He strode over to where some of the Wexford group were sitting and spoke to the eighteen-year-old captain in command of that division. Despite his youth, Miles Byrne was considered such a crack soldier he had been ranked up to captain before he had even reached Vinegar Hill.

'The troops are amustering in Blessington,' Michael told him. 'We have to prepare.'

Miles Byrne moved to his feet and glanced towards a camp fire to his right. 'We had better inform the general then,' he said in a wry tone.

Before they had left the camp, Garrett Byrne and the Wexford chiefs had appointed Michael as a sort of Governor of Glenmalure, entrusting the sick and wounded to his care, but the self-appointed leader of the rebel camp was a man named

Joseph Holt; a Protestant who had fought many a good battle since the start of the rebellion, although he had not been part of the force on Vinegar Hill. Joseph Holt was forty-two years old, heavily built with a beard growing under his chin. He had a large following and insisted his men called him 'General'.

Michael did not like Holt. He considered him a braggart and could not dispel his mistrust of the man once he had learned that Holt's wife was a relative of George Manning of Ballyteigue, a shooting-and-burning yeoman.

Joseph Holt was holding court around a fire when Michael and Miles Byrne approached him. He rose to his feet and greeted the two captains warily.

Holt did not like Dwyer either: especially when he caught the amused look on his face when the men saluted their general; or the lithe, easy way Dwyer had of walking – like a cat. Joseph Holt hated cats. You never knew when they were going to make a spring.

Michael informed Holt about the warning of an attack. 'Our position here is strong,' he said, 'but they know that well and will be ready to act in proportion. I would advise that we go out and meet them and cut them off.'

Holt considered. 'Meet them where?'

'Knockalt. If we split into two divisions, you could head for Imaal, thereby having the Lugnaquilla behind you for retreat if their numbers are too great. If not, give them a firm front while I catch them at the rear.'

Holt agreed to the plan and discussed the arrangements. At the conclusion he looked speculatively at Michael for a moment, then said brightly, 'I think you should be promoted in rank, Captain Dwyer, to lieutenant-colonel.'

Michael gave a slow, sardonic smile. 'My rank of captain was conferred on me by General Garrett Byrne of the Ballymanus Corps of the United Irish army. In committee, approved and voted by delegates. I have no time for courtesy titles, . . . General.'

'The men gave me my rank,' Holt snapped. 'I earned it.'

'Then lead your men,' Michael said, 'to Knockalt at dawn, and give the enemy a good day of it, like a good general.'

The animosity between the two men was plain for everyone to see. Holt narrowed his eyes as Michael strode away; then, conscious of his men watching him, Holt laughed, 'Isn't he the cock of the walk now?'

When none of the men ventured to mock Dwyer with him, Holt shrugged. 'Well, my boys,' he said cheerfully, 'we will just have to separate the captains from the generals tomorrow – on the battlefield.'

Later that night, when darkness fell, Michael and twenty of his men left the camp, then split up and went through the surrounding neighbourhoods. Many of the rebels were scattered throughout the houses for the purpose of taking a few nights' rest and meals with their families. All were warned that troops were ready to move in and they should return to the camp immediately.

As dawn was breaking, Joseph Holt and three hundred men moved across the head of Glenmalure to the Three Lakes and down the Glenreemore Brook to Knockalt in the King's River valley. There Holt placed his men behind the banks and waited; watching the troops advancing through his spy-glass.

When the King's troops had reached the banks of the river, the marksmen of the Leitrim light company rose and gave them a volley. Holt loudly ordered the pikemen to charge en masse across the river where the battle became sword to sword and pike to bayonet.

Holt had decided to handle the King's troops on his own before Dwyer arrived, but now he realised it could not be done and was getting anxious. Men were dying around him and things were getting sticky.

'Where the blazes is Dwyer?' he shouted. 'He's well late and he knowing we are depending on him.'

Michael was late due to a skirmish with a band of militia on the way, but an exultant bellow rose up from the rebels when he and his sharpshooters appeared on the hills to the rear of the troops and sent down a volley.

Many of the Rathdrum Militia who accompanied the English army in this expedition became terrified when they saw Dwyer, knowing well they would be the first to be picked off. Confusion and cowardly disorder prevailed in their ranks as they wheeled and attempted to flee back to Rathdrum, forcing the English trumpeter to sound the retreat, which brought another cheer from the rebels.

'Keep slapping at them!' Michael commanded, determined to get as many of the Rathdrum Militia as he could in retribution for the slaughter at Aughrim, then gave hot pursuit for a distance of two or three miles to those militiamen who broke ranks and ran like rabbits over the hills.

*   *   *

'Pick up all weapons,' Michael ordered his men as they returned to Knockalt. 'Every gun, cartridge box and sword to be collected from the fallen to rebuild our supplies.'

As they approached the banks Sam McAllister came up to him. 'It's Hugh Vesty. He's been hit.'

The bullet was embedded in the thigh and Hugh Vesty had lost a lot of blood. Hugh tried to grin as Michael examined him, but tears of pain brimmed his eyes.

'You'll be all right, Hugh,' Michael told him. 'I'll take care of you.'

When they had carried Hugh across the river and a mile beyond to a small field, they laid him down under cover of a high hedge. It was decided the rest of the men should return to Glenmalure after Holt, but Michael and six others elected to stay with Hugh Vesty who was in deep pain and losing too much blood for such a difficult and arduous journey across the mountains.

Michael and Sam McAllister ran to a house half a mile away. A man was in the front yard feeding some hens, pausing to stand and stare as the two rebels approached. Michael threw a secret sign. For a moment the man hesitated, then threw an answering sign, showing he was a United man.

'I'm Michael Dwyer.'

The man's face lost its wariness. He smiled. 'Aye, I was thinking you might be him. You fit the height and description.'

'Spirits?' Michael said urgently. 'Any kind, whiskey, poteen, anything. But quickly, man. We need it bad.'

The man frowned. 'I've mountain dew. A quart jug, almost full.'

'That'll be fine. Quickly.'

The man entered the house and emerged a minute later followed by his wife. Silently he handed the jug over and Michael thanked him. As he ran off the man shook his head in utter disappointment.

'Sorra the day,' he said to his wife, 'but isn't it true that all heroes have feet of clay. I'd always heard that Dwyer was a very sober lad, but you saw it with your own eyes, Judy. Shaking and begging for any kind of spirits.' He shook his head again. 'Wait till I tell the men.'

'We have poteen,' Michael said when he returned to the hedge. 'Rip the leg of his breeches open.'

Hugh Vesty let out a groan as the material was pulled away

103

from the torn flesh. Michael held the jug to Hugh's mouth. 'Drink as much as you can to numb the pain,' he said, 'while we operate.'

'Operate!' Hugh almost choked on the poteen. 'Who's going to operate? I see no doctor!'

'We've no time for doctors, Hugh. We'll have to do it ourselves.' Michael withdrew a knife sheathed inside the top of his boot. 'Of course, we could leave you here to bleed to death, or for gangrene to set in, if you prefer.'

'Your bedside manner is not the best I've encountered,' Hugh complained, then gulped at the poteen frantically for almost five minutes. When he gave the nod, four men held him down while Michael poured the spirit over the blade of the knife.

Hugh emitted an agonised grinding sound through clenched teeth as Michael carefully probed away the breech-cloth inside the wound, then he fell silent.

'He's gone unconscious,' said Sam McAllister. 'His fingernails dug into my palms so hard he's drawn blood.'

'It's better that he's fainted and can feel nothing,' Michael said, then slowly and carefully extracted the bullet.

The wound was dabbed with poteen, then a strip from Hugh's shirt was torn and also soaked in the spirit before being wrapped tightly around the thigh. Michael gazed down in concern at his cousin's face which was very white against the sandy curls loosely framing it.

'Don't die on me, Hugh,' he said in a whisper. 'Don't die, avic.'

Martin Burke flopped down on the grass and said sadly: 'No man would ever dare to insult the poor, the stranger, or the feeble, in the presence of Hugh Vesty Byrne. Generous to the extreme, true to his word, and faithful to his friends. That's Hugh Vesty.'

'Will you shut up!' Michael snapped.

Martin Burke stared at him, taken aback. 'What's wrong with you, Michael? I was only saying—'

'I know you were, Martin, but you were saying it like an obituary!' He looked down at the white face of his cousin. 'And I'll not let Hugh Vesty die. I'll cut my veins and give him my own blood if I have to.'

They waited until dusk before carrying Hugh back to the camp where he was put in the nursing care of a pretty girl named Sarah.

The following night, an expedition was decided to bring salt and provisions back to the camp. General Holt was to have command, and Captain Dwyer to stay with his men and defend the camp.

A number of the Wicklow and Wexford boys were muttering amongst themselves. They had received word that Holt's wife was in Pierce Harney's house at the head of the glen and were convinced she was in the process of making terms with the enemy in Rathdrum on behalf of her husband.

' 'Tis because some of her relatives are militia that nobody trusts her,' the Wicklow men insisted. 'Holt might lead us into some ambush and get rewarded by the enemy with a pardon.'

Michael listened to all this with great attention, then, with the Wexford boys, resolved on a plan to test the general.

The leaders had obtained horses and, at dusk, two hundred men were mustered for the expedition. Two captains, Miles Byrne and James Doyle of Ballynecor rode beside Holt.

'Where do you intend to march?' they asked the general.

'To the Seven Churches.'

The two captains exchanged glances. Whatever location Holt had decided upon, they had resolved not to go there. They objected strongly, insisting that neighbourhood was far too poor, and full of militia.

Holt looked over the men, perceiving that the majority were made up of Wexford lads. He shrugged. 'Where then?'

'As far as Greenan Bridge,' suggested Miles Byrne, 'and from there we'll turn into the richer country parts which have not suffered badly from the war, and may still have salt and provisions to spare.'

Many hours later, when the men straggled back to the camp, some wounded, Miles Byrne reported the night's proceedings to Michael.

'It was pitch dark,' Miles said, 'and myself and James Doyle were riding each side of Holt, listening to him telling us his plans, all the great things we should do that night before returning to the camp. He wanted to burn every isolated house where the enemy could take up position, especially those with slated roofs. We disagreed, insisting it was bad policy to destroy any habitation whoever the owner, but scarcely had we got the words out when we spied flashes of light like so many stars from the pans of the enemy's firelocks, within range of us, and instantly the whizzing of balls over the heads of our ranks. We soon discovered the discharge came from the English army which had marched to Rathdrum to reconnoitre our position and had reached the Bridge of Greenan. On hearing the noise of our column advancing, it had halted in silence and waited our approach.'

'What was Holt's reaction?' Michael asked.

Miles Byrne smiled. 'I shall never forget Holt's presence of mind and exertion on this occasion. He cried out with the voice of a stentor, ordering our men to march en masse across the bridge, giving orders to the gunsmen at the same time. The Rathdrum Militia who were with the English army deserted them again, and we on our side had the greatest trouble to rally our ranks and stop them from disbanding. Some feared they had got into an ambush because a pistol shot was heard at the rear of our men. But finally, after a hard burst of fighting, we got into the marshy fields on the left side of the bridge, although, in the darkness, we did not realise the enemy was already retreating.'

'How many injured?'

'Only those you see. It was the clopping of our horses which saved us from the first dangerous volley the army sent out. In the darkness they thought we were all mounted and took too high an aim.'

Michael blew a silent whistle. 'It's very fortunate for Joseph Holt that he had not chosen the route,' he said.

'Aye. In view of what happened, he'd have been accused of bringing us into an ambush and would be court-martialled by now. Instead, he has all the praise for getting us safely out of it.'

Holt's loud laughter rang over the camp and Michael put his head into his hands. 'Oh heaven help us,' he groaned. 'His bragging will know no bounds now. Sleep is out of the question.'

Miles Byrne grinned. 'All credit, though. He served us true and well.'

'Yes,' Michael allowed, 'but some men are just unbearable in victory.'

Five days later, Joseph Holt and a large contingent of his men set off on an expedition to Meath, where strong fighting was going on between factions of the United Irish and His Majesty's armies.

Once again, the sick and wounded in the Glenmalure camp were entrusted to Captain Dwyer's special care, along with defence of the camp, which he carried out vigorously; for every time the military attempted to reconnoitre the land near the entrance to the glen, Dwyer was sure to be on their flank, or in position before daylight, awaiting their arrival.

The men at Glenmalure then received word that Holt's force in Meath had been cut to pieces and scattered. The general himself had received a bullet wound and was last seen lying face down on the battlefield.

But the news that brought tears to every man's eyes was that the United divisions at Louth, Kildare and Wexford had been dispersed and totally defeated. Garrett Byrne of Ballymanus had been forced into hiding. Commanders Perry and Fitzgerald had been hanged.

The entire camp was devastated. Michael removed himself to a lonely part of the mountain and sat there throughout the night in the company of Sam McAllister. Occasionally the two men talked, but mostly sat in silence. Despite the difference in their religions, Michael and McAllister had a true friendship which did not have to be borne out with conversation.

In the days that followed, wounded men who had been with the Irish commanders made their way back to the camp at Glenmalure, hungry, wounded, and exhausted. Michael convinced them they could rest and sleep at ease. He would ensure the pass to the glen was well guarded and defended.

Then, to his astonishment, Michael saw the stocky figure of Joseph Holt. He was climbing the steep rise to the camp in the company of a handsome young woman wearing a green riding-habit who, Michael later learned, was a gentleman's daughter whom Holt had met on the mountains during his lone flight from Meath back to Glenmalure.

Michael greeted Holt with genuine delight. 'We thought you were killed.'

'Kill Holt?' The general looked disgusted at the very idea.

The girl giggled.

Michael peered at Holt's head wound. 'How bad is it?'

'Not bad at all. Just a graze.'

'But you were seen face down on the battlefield.'

'Aye, and so the enemy ran right past me.'

'Clever fellow.'

'Without a doubt.'

Again the girl giggled.

For a moment Michael met her brazen eyes, then looked at Holt. 'Who's your friend?'

Holt put an arm around the girl's waist. 'My new aide-de-camp!'

Michael stood to stare after them while the general and the laughing girl were welcomed joyfully into the circle of Holt's remaining men.

Sam McAllister came up to Michael and also stared.

'Who is that?'

'The generalissimo. Returned from the dead.'

'I can see that. But who's the doxie with him?'

'Our latest recruit.'

'A handsome heroine.'

'Aye.' Michael glanced at McAllister and smiled. 'And just wait till you hear her giggle.'

'Nice?'

'Very fetching. If you happen to be a rooster listening for a hen.'

It was early morning and the night mists had not yet risen. Michael and a small party of his men were crossing the mountains and scouting the land, unable to see for a distance of more than a few yards but hoping to shoot some game for breakfast. They could hear nothing but the dawn chorus of the birds and the echoing sound of river water falling into the glen.

Moving quietly through the mist, they suddenly came within a few feet of two officers and two privates from the 100th Foot Regiment of Highlanders.

The Highlanders clutched their muskets and stood their ground. They too had been out shooting game without success and had unconsciously wandered much farther than they should have done, across a strange heath well beyond their lines.

For a long moment the two sides silently contemplated each other, the soldiers visibly astonished by the peaceful attitude of the armed rebels who outnumbered them three to one.

Michael leaned on his musket and addressed one of the officers.

'You have been out sporting?'

'Yes.'

'You were foolish to have strayed so far from your camp.'

'We are off duty.'

'Off duty?'

'Yes.'

Michael shrugged. 'Then I'm sorry for our accidental meeting. You have nothing to fear from us. You are at your liberty to carry on – but in the direction of your camp.'

The soldiers hesitated, looked confused, wondering if they were to be the game in some kind of chase.

Sam McAllister and James Doyle of Ballynecor urged them to go. 'We will not harm you,' McAllister said, 'but you are very unwise to sport so far from your quarters.'

The two officers and two privates looked greatly embarrassed, but politely acknowledged their obligations and moved off, continually looking over their shoulders at the rebels, who were strolling away in the opposite direction. There had been no taunting, no insulting language, and no act of violence whatever.

The rebels had a sound reason for acting as they did. The Marquis of Huntly commanded the 100th Regiment of Foot. He had always shown a kind disposition to the common people and reacted sternly against their oppressors.

The sun was up and the mountains shimmering when they returned to the camp carrying three rabbits. As they approached Holt's section, who were having a breakfast of stir-about, the general himself was being attended by the gentleman's daughter, her green riding-habit now with military epaulettes sewn on the shoulders. It had been given out by Holt that she was a determined rebel, although no one had yet discovered the heroine's name.

One of Holt's officers responded to Sam McAllister's query with the information that she should be referred to simply as 'the general's lady'.

'The general's what?' Michael said, one eyebrow moving upwards.

'The general's lady,' the girl repeated, seeming highly gratified at hearing her distinctive title.

Michael's eyes moved insolently over the girl's green habit and fixed on her military epaulettes. 'I hope you don't expect us to salute her,' he said to Holt.

'Pay no heed to him,' Holt told the girl as Michael and his party moved off. 'Hasn't he always had a dry and sarcastic tongue on him.'

'Has the captain got a woman himself?' she asked curiously.

'Not that I know of,' Holt replied, catching her hand. 'He's too busy chasing redcoats and rabbits.'

'He's jealous so,' the girl decided, then giggled hysterically as Holt pulled her down on to his lap.

It was amazing how quickly Hugh Vesty Byrne returned to health and humour. And according to Hugh Vesty (who would not say how he knew) 1798 was turning out to be the most glorious summer of the entire eighteenth century – weatherwise.

Michael wandered across the camp to an overhanging tree where the pretty Sarah was sitting by Hugh Vesty's bed of ferns.

'How goes the leg, Hugh?'

'Grand, avic. I'll be scaling the heights in no time.' Hugh smiled. 'But my ministering angel here is worried about the sun getting in my eyes. Will you yank that branch down a bit more, Captain, and hold it for a while.'

'Devil I will,' Michael replied. 'I'm off for a swim. I'll see you this evening.'

'This evening? Why so long?' Hugh Vesty frowned. 'Oh, I know where you're going! 'Tis mighty risks you're taking. And man, you're tired! You've been on sentry duty for the past three nights.'

'I'll drop down somewhere on the hills,' Michael told him. 'Ten minutes of sleep and I'll be as right as rain in a drought.'

Hugh Vesty did not doubt it. Many times during the rebellion he had seen Michael completely exhausted and near sinking under his fatigue, but after a short sleep of less than an hour he would arise as fresh as ever and ready to take on an army.

'And they call us the dirty Irish,' Hugh said to Sarah as Michael strolled off for his daily swim, 'the Anglo gentry in their mansions. They look at our animals and our small cottages and our children dancing barefoot in the mud and rain and they sniff in disdain. But it is they who are not clean, for they rarely wash below their necks or beyond their silk-ruffled wrists. Powders and perfumes are their fountains. You never see a gentleman stripping off in naked glory and diving into a cold mountain lake or a warm river for a swim. Leastaways, I never have.'

'Nor I,' Sarah murmured.

Her cheeks were blushing hotly, but Hugh's eyes had closed, his fair head back against the bole of the tree as his mind launched back into the yesteryear, to the tales and traditions of his Celtic forebears.

'In the long-ago,' he told her, 'in the days when Ireland was a land of scribes and poets, the Celts considered water to be as essential as life-blood. For as the body cannot survive without blood, neither can it survive without water. The land too shrivels up and dies without water. And so water became a holy thing, a blessing from the sky which gave it. And every Celt, knave or king, ritually bathed his body every day whether sun shone or snow fell . . . But then the invaders came, and when they saw our young men and maidens swimming innocently naked in the lakes, they called us dirty savages.'

Sarah found everything Hugh Vesty said enthralling. 'How do you know all this?' she breathed.

'From the scholastic scribes and poetic shanachies,' he answered. 'Like many another, I spent my young years seeking them out. The master of our wretched little barn-school had only enough time to teach us the beginning and end of an historical tale, so to learn what happened in the middle, a body must go to the people who know it, and keep it alive from generation to generation, like the turf fire in the hearth that is never allowed to die.'

Sarah was gazing at him with eyes as soft as lamps, wondering if there was any way she could get him to see her as a maiden and not a comrade. It suddenly occurred to her that maybe the shanachies or those with the secret knowledge might have the cure to stir his fancy.

' 'Tis said the shanachies know all about the powers of herbs and charms,' Sarah said softly. 'Is that true?'

'Herbs definitely, charms perhaps, but why waste a shanachie's time with such things?' He opened his eyes and looked curiously at her. 'Would you not prefer to ask about the youth of our culture and flame of our history?'

Sarah bowed her head, knowing it was useless to explain to Hugh Vesty that not everyone had his love for the history. He would never believe it; and not only that, he would think it a shame and a scandal and insist it betrayed a lack of patriotism.

So she changed the subject and asked him a question about something she had often wondered.

'Is there a girl in it? In the times Michael goes off alone for hours?'

'Aye, there's a girl in it, sweet enough,' Hugh murmured. 'A neat-looking wench and himself is a bit cracked about her. But I tell you, Sarah . . .' he lifted her hand and smiled roguishly, 'she couldn't hold a candle to you.'

*   *   *

111

The back wall of John Cullen's cottage at Knockgorragh snuggled right into the mountainface, but a winding narrow path at the side led down to the Lech River, a branch of the Slaney banked and hidden by huge ancient whitethorns.

Mary moved out of their shade and strolled across to a patch of long ferns and lay down, closing her eyes and letting the heat of the sun play on her face. She had found this secret and enchanting place two weeks back when, too impatient to wait for Michael in the house, she had wandered down here. They had met five times since his return from Wexford; twice in the house above, three times down here. And down here they were free of all eyes, all ears; just the two of them, alone with the wonders of nature.

Nothing moved, not a breath of wind. The wild flowers in full scent and full bloom stood in perfect silence; only the sounds of the wilderness disturbed the stillness of the day. Bees droned through the flowers, birds chirped and laughed, insects clicked and rasped, while the music of the river water bubbled softly, softly, down to the Slaney.

The heat turned sweltering. Her hair clung damply to her neck, her blouse stuck to her skin. She raised her head and squinted her eyes. The mountain peaks looked red in the fierce rays of the sun. She pondered on moving back to the shade of the whitethorns but, languid with heat, was too tired to move.

She lay back and closed her eyes, patiently waiting, listening to an amorous wood pigeon coo a silly saucy note to his mate. She sighed and lifted the damp masses of her black hair away from her neck and let her arms rest above her head as her mind drifted off on a haze of dreamy thoughts about the rebel captain. She was crazy about him, spent all her days and nights dreaming wild dreams about him. He filled not only her heart but her whole sky from one end of Imaal to the other. No other person existed for her under the sun.

A family of bluetits in a branch near by had been watching her curiously. She had been still for so long, one ventured down to hop on her head, flying away in fright when she moved slightly.

But still, she thought with a frown, even after the last five meetings, she still felt unsure of him, despite the fact that he travelled from Glenmalure to Cullen's house in Imaal to see her, a distance of eight or nine miles over difficult and deserted mountains. A long way to travel for the honey and griddle-bread the old man always gave him on his arrival. A long way for only one short hour with a sweetheart.

Bracken crunched behind her. She tensed behind her closed eyelids, felt the increasing rhythm of her heartbeat pounding away as the footsteps drew nearer. Nobody could come down here without passing John Cullen, and the old man was sitting guard outside the house above.

For a moment there was silence, then the tall ferns rustled around her, and even when the sun was blocked out and the shadow fell over her face, she kept her eyes closed. She knew he was standing at her feet, looking down at her. She waited for him to speak, but instead she heard him move and felt him stretch the length of his body beside hers on the ground, felt his cool breath on her cheek.

Her eyes fluttered open. He was propped on his elbow, smiling into her face, the sun shining behind the dark curls of his hair like an amber halo.

'Don't speak,' he whispered.

She was quite silent. Her eyes held that ecstatic tender look that women often wear when they contemplate something or someone they love. He lifted a thick handful of her hair and let it fall slowly from his hand to float around her.

'You're lovely,' he whispered in a tone of fascination, 'the loveliest thing I ever saw.'

For answer she moved her arms around him, seeking the lips she had kissed to bruising in her dreams, her love burning as hot as the sun. When his mouth took hers it was gentle at first, then male and hungry; and she forgot everything, all capacity for thought swamped by the intensity of her feelings as she responded.

Somewhere on the hills sheep bleated, one after the other. Up above Cullen's goat also bleated, as if calling something, but she heard only the laboured sound of her breathing as he moved to his feet and walked away from her, over to the whitethorns and shady bank of the river.

Staring after him, she sat up and buttoned her blouse, her hands shaking, her whole being overwhelmed with guilt and misery. In all their other meetings when they had kissed and embraced she had sensibly and practically called a halt before the danger point was reached, but today . . . today she had felt hot and young and irresponsible and allowed him to do things

113

she had never allowed before, things that had made them both tremble with emotion until they were kissing as if they would eat each other alive.

But when he moved to bring about what they both wanted, the sin of it had suddenly chilled her and brought her back to her senses with a rush of fear. Panting with panic she had pushed him away, pleaded with him. And he had sat back on his heels, trembling, every inch of him; looking down at her through his lashes in frustrated anger.

Then he had left her.

She got hurriedly to her feet and almost ran towards the river. He was crouched at the bank's edge, splashing his face with the cooling water. He gave her a brief glance, then turned his gaze back to the water.

'I'm sorry,' she said in a tight aching voice, 'truly sorry. I should never have provoked you with my shameless behaviour. But it would be wrong, a sin, a mortal sin, and although I know it was all my fault—'

'Mary,' he said in a flash of weariness, 'don't start a long Act of Contrition about it, please.'

She stared at him, and only then noticed how tired he looked. As the silence grew she could sense him retreating from her, second by second, and panic churned through her.

'I love you, Michael, I truly do,' she whispered.

She awaited some response.

There was none.

'Do you love me?'

Again there was no response, for Michael's eyes were fixed hard on a silver shape lodged halfway under a river stone only two feet from where he was crouched. Slowly he dropped his hand into the river and let it rest there for a moment, until his hand was as cold as the water.

Then smoothly and silently, like a knife sliding through butter, his hand moved slowly under the babbling water until it reached the belly of the fish, his face tight with concentration as he gently lapped a finger again and again along the cold belly, as if it were part of the lapping water itself, fooling and soothing the trout into sleepiness, then as the fish slid dreamily over his palm – he clutched hard, and flicked him out.

He held up the twisting fish, moved to his feet and turned to her with a smile. 'Just what Hugh Vesty needs to put the oil back in his limbs – a nice sizzling trout for his supper.'

'Why can't he catch one himself then?' she said in sullen resentment of Hugh Vesty and the fish that had interrupted his reply to her question.

'Oh, Hugh is not up to much these days,' he answered quietly. 'Too stiff to tickle a trout anyway.'

He drew the knife from inside the top of his boot and turned his back to her while he put the fish out of its misery.

She leaned against a tree and watched in silence while he wrapped the trout in a number of large dock leaves, then crouched to wash his knife then his hands in the babbling river water.

'Do you love me?' she repeated, her voice low and troubled.

He turned to look at her.

'Say it, Michael,' she pleaded. 'Say if you love me.'

'I love the ground you walk on,' he said.

A smile hovered uncertainly on her lips. 'That could be taken two ways,' she said. 'The ground I walk on is Wicklow.'

'And I cross its treacherous mountains twice a week just to see you,' he reminded her, and the old teasing raillery was back in his voice as he rose and moved towards her. 'And the pity is, you don't even appreciate it. All I get from you at the end of my travels is a ravishing that even a saint could not resist, then you push me away, to console myself with the tickling of a trout—'

'Say it, damn you, say it!' Her hands had closed into fists, reaching up to pummel him. He grinned as he caught them, drew them down to her sides.

'I'm wild about you, Mary, too wild, that's the problem.'

She knew what he meant. It was her problem too.

'We could get married,' she suggested in a whisper.

'Married?' He stared at her. 'I can't get married, darling.'

The amusement in his voice upset her. 'Why not? Other rebels do! Have done since coming back from Wexford.'

'Good luck to them so.'

He let go her hands, moved back a pace, turning his head to watch the skimming water for a thoughtful moment before turning back and meeting her eyes very seriously, then very seriously he spelt out his situation to her.

'I'm on my keeping in the mountains, Mary. Surrounded by the enemy. I live on my wits and my will to win, but I never know the day or the hour when I will catch a bullet or a bayonet, and lose. There's an army of men up there in Glenmalure, men

115

who have lost everything by joining us, and many are under my command. I have responsibilities and obligations enough without the added responsibility of marriage.'

'So where does that leave us?' she asked.

His eyes closed, he sighed. 'I haven't a notion at this point.'

She gazed at him with her dark smoky eyes, loving him so much she felt lightheaded and sick, empty-bellied from being unable to eat. The sickness of first love, her mother called it. First love going nowhere.

'I must go now,' he told her, then bent to pick up the carefully wrapped trout and stuffed it into his jacket pocket. 'Will you wait here for me?'

She waited while he ran over to where they had lain to pick up his musket, the musket she had not even noticed he'd been carrying. She stared at the gun as he walked back to her. It told her more about their chances together than words ever could. Always his musket by his side, or a pistol in his belt. He couldn't take a swim in the river without being armed to the teeth. And having her as a wife would not be his heart's desire after all, but an added obligation and responsibility. Well, now she knew.

He slipped an arm around her shoulders as they walked back in silence. She glanced up at him briefly but, as always, except in their tender moments, the thoughts of his mind were not reflected in his face. She wished she knew whether he truly loved her or not.

Her coolness continued. It kept them separate from each other, even when his arm went tightly round her waist as they climbed up the steep, narrow rise to the side of the house. She abruptly broke loose and walked swiftly round to the front where old man Cullen sat on his stool. Deliberately she knelt down on the grass beside him.

It was then Michael truly felt her withdrawal from him. He always kissed her goodbye, but she knew he could never bring himself to kiss her in front of the old man.

'Married!' Michael almost laughed at the word as he made his way back to camp – except it wasn't funny.

A rough track wound up the mountain for a quarter of a mile then dipped deeply where a stream fell into a deep, azure pool. He occasionally had to put his hand on the ground behind him as he descended past clumps of yellow gorse and granite boulders, all the time wondering how long he could cope with that beautiful body of hers. She was beginning to play havoc with him, pushing him to the limit of physical endurance, then sulking like a child.

Her sulking. Cheek!

Chapter Nine

General the Marquis Lord Cornwallis stood rigidly on deck and studied the view as the ship approached Dublin's north wall. Gulls screeched menacingly overhead. His eyes moved quickly from right to left inspecting the shoulders of his scarlet tunic. He knew from experience that the gulls were indiscriminate with no regard whatsoever for rank.

Already the noise of the city rushed out to greet him: the clatter of horses and the grinding of wheels. The voices on the quayside became clearer; the brogue more distinct.

Cornwallis sighed. He had agreed to come to this wretched country as reluctantly as he had gone to fight the colonials in America, but Mr Pitt wanted order restored to Ireland, and Cornwallis intended to see that he got it.

At last the ropes were dropped and the gangplank raised. Lord Cornwallis squared his shoulders and prepared to meet his welcoming committee.

It seemed as if the entire city had turned out to catch a glimpse of the great general. The word had spread quickly. With service in America and India behind him, Cornwallis had been sent by Prime Minister Pitt to sort out Ireland.

The crowd watched in silence, all attention concentrated on the grey-haired man; large and sixtyish and looking every bit the general. In profile his face was fleshy, his nose long, the cool gaze steady. It was only when he moved that the authority of the man weakened a little; his erect posture was marred by a slight limp.

The state apartments of Dublin Castle were refreshingly cool. Lord Cornwallis sipped his soup and obliquely studied his dining partners. It was indeed a lunch for the lords! Camden, Castlereagh and Clare.

The three men gave him a full report on the state of the country and, as he listened, Lord Cornwallis carefully weighed up each man. The Viceroy, he decided, was too weak to govern; allowing himself to be ruled by a set of violent and hot-headed men. The Chancellor's naked bigotry was offensive, gloating about the flogging of Catholic priests. And then there was the Secretary of State, Lord Castlereagh, the most powerful and talented politician of the three.

'As for my friend Lord Castlereagh,' Cornwallis later wrote to London, 'he is so cold that nothing can warm him.'

Lord Cornwallis conversed amiably, but as soon as lunch was over he rose and removed a letter from inside his tunic which he handed to Lord Camden.

'I have been instructed by the Prime Minister to give this personally to the Viceroy.' He bowed. 'Good day, gentlemen.'

Lords Clare and Castlereagh stood watching as Lord Camden read the letter, his face turning pale as he digested the contents.

'Well?' said Castlereagh.

Camden slowly refolded the letter. 'It appears we must part company, gentlemen,' he said quietly. 'I have been relieved of my post as Viceroy of Ireland. Lord Cornwallis is assuming civil and military control of the country.'

The morning mist on the mountains was so thick it was impossible to see beyond the ridges. Every man in the Glenmalure camp was tense and edgy as they prepared to move out. Intelligence had been communicated to Michael the previous evening that they were to be surrounded in every direction by Highlanders, Hessians, and all the troops England had at her command.

Michael had discussed the situation with the other leaders: Joseph Holt, Miles Byrne, and Captain Corrigan of the King's County who commanded the deserters from that regiment.

They agreed they would have to abandon their stronghold in Glenmalure and move on. It was imperative to avoid any further engagement with the enemy and risk depleting their forces before the French arrived.

'Our only hope is to fight our way over to Imaal and the Lugnaquilla,' Michael said. 'We can hold out there as well as here.'

Corrigan agreed. 'The mountains there are the highest in the county and nearly uninhabited, without roads or any means of approach by horses. Even their infantry would find it hard.'

Michael smiled grimly. 'And it takes good lungs to breathe

119

the pure air up the 'Quilla, and sound limbs to climb it.'

The word was given throughout the camp. Wounded men, scarcely able to walk, came and asked what they were to do. None but the most vigorous of men would be able to undergo the fatigue of crossing the mountains.

'We cannot carry our sick and wounded,' Michael told them. 'If we try, we will all be doomed. All we can do is endeavour to get you away before the troops arrive.'

A small army of the strongest men had worked until after midnight, helping the wounded down the hills to places of shelter and refuge in the neighbouring villages. A number of the deserters, fearful of their fate if captured, decided to escape also.

Hugh Vesty walked with a limp but he refused to leave Michael; and the pretty Sarah refused to leave Hugh.

The heroine in the green habit had disappeared. Two nights previously Mrs Holt had made an unexpected visit to the camp to see her husband; and minutes later, much to the amusement of Michael and his men, 'the general's lady' was seen arunning in her epaulettes, then seen no more.

The men had spent the rest of the night under arms and on the alert, and now they began to form into line to start their journey. Joseph Holt was no longer in supreme command. They all looked to Captain Dwyer and his men to lead and guide them, being natives of these mountains and glens, but Michael was nowhere to be seen.

He was some way down the hillside at one of the outposts, in the company of the Wexford captain, Miles Byrne. Both were talking patiently to a distressed woman who had arrived from Wexford with her three small children.

'You know me, Captain Byrne,' she wailed. 'You know me to be from your own district of Monaseed.'

'Aye, Mrs Mulloy, but what can I possibly do for you?'

'Give me protection! I have nowhere else to go. My husband was killed at Vinegar Hill and everything I have in the world has been burned and destroyed, except my children. I was told you had a command in these mountains and that's why I came.'

'We're moving out,' Michael said. 'It would be impossible to take yourself and those three little ones over the terrains.'

The woman began to sob. 'But what shall we do? We haven't eaten for days!' When the children saw their mother crying they began to wail too. Michael and Miles Byrne exchanged despairing glances. They were duty-bound to help the wife of a man who had died on Vinegar Hill.

'Go to the house of my family,' Michael said, 'at the farmlands at Eadstown. Anyone will tell you where it is. Tell my mother and father that my dog is buried in the grass patch near the first field and that I buried him there myself. Tell them to give you and the children food and shelter.'

'Then you must return to Wexford,' advised Miles Byrne. 'If you go to the house of my cousin Pat Bruslawn, his wife will give you refuge until matters can be sorted out. Do you know where they abide?'

The woman nodded, wiped a hand across her wet face. 'Aye, I do. May God bless ye. And you, too, Captain Dwyer. You are not even from Wexford.'

'The whole of Leinster is indebted to Wexford,' Michael said. 'But you must go quickly. This camp is no longer safe. Look down there!'

The mists were clearing and now the enemy could be seen in great force moving along the pathways of the mountains.

The woman became terrified and gathered the children to her, ushering them away from the outpost. Miles Byrne rushed after her and caught her arm. He withdrew the sword he had won in battle and handed it to her. Her eyes widened as she stared at the mother-of-pearl handle.

'For Mulloy,' he said. 'Sell it and use the money for his children.'

Highlanders were approaching from the direction of the Seven Churches, whilst the English forces from Rathdrum approached from the mouth of the valley. The rebels moved quickly as they followed Michael across the Fraughan Rock glen and the mountains leading to Imaal. For almost two hours the soldiers pursued them doggedly, but on reaching the Lugnaquilla and getting some distance up the mountain, the rebels turned and halted, some forming into lines of battle while sharpshooters took up positions behind rocks.

Down below the British commander called a halt, aware the rebels now possessed the advantage.

Michael stepped forward a few paces and sent down a slow and audacious salute to him, his smile wide.

General John Moore looked up at the figure of the rebel and heaved a sigh. 'He's right,' he said to his officers. 'No point in going on. From their elevated position they could pick us off with their gaming-rifles as easily as they do the geese on the lakes.'

A triumphant cheer rose up from the rebels as the troops began the retreat down the mountains. Many rushed forward to slap Michael on the back but he ignored them, urging all to resume the march. Sam McAllister kept pace beside him as he led the climb upwards, both occasionally looking over their shoulders to ensure the troops were not following.

Suddenly Michael and McAllister looked at each other, and grinned; then Michael struck up a jaunty song, a song which echoed and was repeated by the column of relieved men.

> 'Up the rocky mountain,
> And down the rushy glen.
> We'll keep them in commotion
> Until the French come in.'

As soon as the word spread that the United camp had moved from Glenmalure to Imaal, twenty sheep, three sacks of potatoes, and a barrel of ale were sent up. The men who brought them fell exhausted on to the heather, laughing loudly. One was John Doyle of Knockandarragh. He left the following morning at dawn, bearing on his person a written message for Mary which, on his arrival home, he insisted she could read nowhere else but in the privacy of the loft in the barn.

'Damn Dwyer,' John said sullenly, sitting down on a pile of hay. 'Sometimes he can take his high spirits and pranks too far.'

Mary fell back on the hay in laughter when John turned and lifted his shirt so she could read the message written on the skin of his back.

'One of the men had quill and ink,' John grumbled, 'but no writing paper. Well can you read it? If you can't there is nothing I can do to help you. He deliberately put it on my back so I couldn't see it. Said it was personal and private.'

Mary slowly moved her finger under the words, mouthing them silently as she tried to read the simple message. In a short time she had the gist of it.

> If I could
> marry anyone
> Mary Doyle

'Have you done?' John demanded. 'If so, you can help me to wash it off.' He groaned miserably. 'Ink is desperate hard to get off the skin, even with pig soap. I'll have a rash for days probably.'

Mary's face beamed as her finger moved slowly and she read the message again.

They had spent two nights on the Lugnaquilla. Michael awoke to the sound of Hugh Vesty's voice loud with indignation.

'Oh, the devil! Oh what a sneaky varmint that man is! He must have done it in the dark of the night!'

Michael moved to his feet and joined his cousin, who was standing peering through his spy-glass across towards the valley's entrance into Imaal.

'What is it?' Michael asked.

'Take a look.' Hugh Vesty handed him the spy-glass. 'He must have taken the route around the lowlands so nobody would know what he was up to.'

Through the glass Michael saw the white military tents and flags of the 100th and 60th Regiments, known to be commanded by General John Moore.

Michael lowered the glass. 'No wonder that man is a general,' he said slowly. 'He knows his business.'

Hugh Vesty whipped the glass out of his hand. 'When you've finished praising the redcoat perhaps you'll tell us what we can do? He's set up camp at the head of the glen! He's got us trapped! The rest of the soldiery are probably camped at Glenmalure. We can't move outside Imaal.'

Michael pondered the situation. ' 'Tis hard for the Wexford and Meath men,' he said finally, 'but me – I'm happy to stay in Imaal just as long as General Moore wants. I live here.'

'Oh, very droll,' Hugh snapped, following him over to the camp fire where kettles hung from a tripod. 'Be serious, Michael, what are we going to do?'

'Sit it out, and repulse any attack. That's all we can do. General Moore will shift soon enough.'

Hugh Vesty looked at him curiously. 'Oh aye? And who's going to make him do that?'

'The French,' Michael said.

'The blasted French are taking their blasted time,' Hugh said. 'Every week we hear that Tone is on the seas with a French army.' He sat staring at the steam rising from the spout of a hissing kettle. 'Do you honestly think the French will ever come?'

Michael shrugged. 'Hope is green.'

Darkness had fallen. In a small forest clearing on the hill overlooking the mouth of the glen, Sam McAllister lay on his stomach in the shadows staring down at the little fires of the English military camp. Michael came running through the bracken and fell down beside McAllister, spy-glass in hand.

'Well?' McAllister asked.

'Two six-pounders for sure, and a howitzer. Two battalions of the Hundredth and Sixtieth Regiments. I'd say the whole make about fifteen hundred firelocks.' Michael put the glass to his eye, biting his lip as he peered at the camp.

'General Moore is a decent man,' McAllister said suddenly. 'I wish it was not him we were up against.'

Michael lowered the glass. 'You know him?

'I've met him. We were one of twelve companies of light infantry militia stationed down in Bandon when he came to take over command from General Coote. The men of the regular army were quite impressed with him, not so some of the militia companies.'

A dog howled in the distance. Michael turned his eyes back to the military tents. It would be interesting to find out as much as possible about the personality of the British commander. 'Tell me about him,' he whispered.

'Oh, he's tough but fair-minded. And a true soldier, I'll give him that.' McAllister rested his chin on his folded arms. 'There was some trouble down at Bandon, before the insurrection ignited into full flame. Rumours were spreading wild that the French had been sighted off the coast and the whole camp was on the alert. Usually the commanding officers do little but shout orders, not so General Moore. He mounted his charger and rode miles down the coast road, examining every bay, wood, road, and path, and comparing them to his maps. Then he appointed the spot where every company should form in case the alarm was raised by night or day. And until these arrangements were completed he neither rested nor dined, then was always up before the reveille to see that his orders had been obeyed and the camp in order. And throughout those nights of alarm his batman was hardly troubled – he slept fully clothed and ready, pulling off his boots only.'

'So why, if he is so admirable,' Michael murmured, continuing to look at the military tents, 'did you desert him?'

'It was no Army commander I deserted,' replied McAllister defensively. 'It was the militia – the poxy *militia*!'

Michael reached out and put a calming hand on McAllister's golden head. 'Easy, man, easy. Just tell me what you know about the British general, and the militia be damned.'

McAllister was silent for some moments, then said quietly: 'Well, I have to tell you this about the militia, but it's all credit to General Moore. A company of the Westmeath militia were also stationed at Bandon, and someone in that company sent an anonymous letter to General Moore complaining of injustice from their officers, saying they had held back money due to them. Moore responded by ordering all militia regiments to parade next morning, and told us when we had complaints, we should not make them in anonymous letters, a conduct unbecoming to soldiers, but should make them in a decent and manly manner.

'He then pitched upon two men from each company to go with him to his tent and explain their grievances, and ordered the captains to attend with their account books. It turned out that it was not the captains of the Westmeath who had held back the money, but the colonel, Lord Westmeath. And despite his lordly status, General Moore sent his findings to the colonel, and requested him to pay up.'

Michael looked surprised. 'Then why did some of the militia regiments dislike him? If he went to all that trouble on their behalf?'

'Because he committed the most grievous of all sins,' McAllister said, 'in Ireland anyway. He spoke out about religion.'

'Ah.' Michael sighed.

'General Moore had heard about a certain secret meeting which had taken place the night before, then gave a speech to all troops the following morning. He said that if such meetings were intended to form a union to defend their country, they were unnecessary, as they as soldiers were already sworn to do it. But if it was to create a distinction and separation from the Catholics, it was wicked; and for a man to boast of his religion was ridiculous. A man was a Protestant or a Catholic, he said, because his parents were before him, and his religion was determined for him before he had any choice in the matter, therefore he could claim no merit whatsoever in the distinction.'

'True for him,' Michael whispered.

' "Any man," General Moore said, "may fairly pride himself on being just and honest, but not on the colour of his religion." If they followed the doctrines of one or the other they would be good and upright.'

'Is he a Protestant himself,' Michael asked, 'like you?'

'Not like me,' McAllister said indignantly. 'I'm a Presbyterian.'

Michael sighed. 'Oh, what does it matter, Sam? Protestant, Presbyterian, Episcopalian or Catholic. Why should it matter what a man believes in his soul?'

'It matters in the militia,' McAllister said grimly. 'Any man who applies to join is asked his religion even before his name.'

Down below, on the far side of the military camp, General John Moore was strolling along a leafy lane in the company of Lord Huntly. A small patrol of the 100th Regiment ambled behind as bodyguards.

'Your opinion of Cornwallis?' Lord Huntly asked.

'He is as upright and worthy as Sir Ralph Abercromby,' Moore answered, 'with a solid belief in discipline and fair play. I like him well.'

Music drifted over the air, the music of fiddles. They turned a bend in the road and came across a cluster of white cabins, their windows and doorways bright with light. A number of old men sat smoking long-pipes outside a cabin that looked and smelled suspiciously like a shebeen. The men looked round, saw the uniforms, muttered nervously amongst themselves, then a voice cried in relief.

'Sure 'tis the Marquis of Huntly himself. A long life to ye, me lord! And what brings ye away from yer camp and down here all the way?'

'Now see here,' Lord Huntly said warningly, 'you haven't got anything you shouldn't have in there, I hope. There's a strange whiff in the air.'

A young woman came out of the shebeen holding a basket of purple heather. She gazed at the two officers without any sign of intimidation or malice, then smiled at the scarlet-coated officer.

'Come now, General,' she said in a voice like a song, 'and

buy the heather from me. It will bring you luck and fortune.'

General Moore looked at her, saw she was quite pretty. 'Not,' she added, 'that a fine, good-looking handsome man like yourself would need much luck now; not with the maidens, anyhow.'

The British commander smiled, took the sprig of heather she held out to him, then shoved his hand in his pocket and withdrew a full crown.

The girl stared at the crown, then remembered her manners. 'Oh, may the saints smile down on ye!' she sang, dipping a curtsy.

Lord Huntly chuckled as they walked on. 'Vanity, vanity, all is vanity,' he said. 'And how fragile is a man's vanity against the charm of Irish flattery. But, you know, in their own strange way I often suspect they mean it. In your case, General, she most certainly *did* mean it.'

'I suspect her real interest was drawing our attention away from the illegal shebeen,' General Moore said wryly, the sprig of very expensive heather twisting in his fingers. 'You like these Irish, I'm told.'

'I admit, I am rather fond of the beggars,' Huntly replied. 'When they're not being hostile and trying to boot the Crown out of Ireland, that is.' He smiled. 'But have you noticed how good-looking these mountain people are, what? These are the real Irish, the ones who have been here since the pagan days. A passionate, hot-headed people, certainly, but left to themselves they love nothing more than their land and their saints and their music and singing.'

When General Moore made no reply, Lord Huntly furrowed his forehead. 'On the other hand, they can be damned confusing too. It's impossible to get a straight answer from one of them, and if they ever heard of the word compromise, they never bothered to learn what it means. But can they bargain! No one in the world can do it better.' He chuckled. 'Ever see an Irishman attempting to buy a bull on market day, what?'

General Moore confessed he had never had the experience.

'Well, I'll tell you. An Irishman will get up before first light and travel for miles to buy a bull he has heard some other farmer is selling at such and such a fair. When he gets there, he ambles casually up to the farmer and starts a conversation about everything except the bull. The weather, the crops, the high taxes and tithes. You name it, they'll talk about it, but not the bull. Finally, when a good rapport has been established, the man will suddenly stare at the bull as if only just noticing it. "And who the blazes brought that old thing to market," he will say in utter contempt. "Surely the fool doesn't expect to get any sort of a price for it!" '

General Moore smiled and looked up at the pagan hills, lapsing into his own thoughts as Lord Huntly continued the tale.

Eventually, the marquis sighed, then pitched his brows in a sudden frown. 'But see here, General, you slipped up back there. One has to be constantly on one's guard with these people, especially the women. Ah, yes, the women.' Lord Huntly cleared his throat emphatically.

General Moore's eyes had never left the undulating outline of the hills. He was so silent that Huntly suddenly wondered if he was letting him ramble on merely out of politeness. It disgruntled him, for he liked the general enormously. A nice man and a great soldier, by God!

He hummed a cough. 'What are you thinking?' he questioned softly.

'That these Irish are not the simple people you portray. Don't forget that it was in these Wicklow hills that Elizabeth's army suffered a damnable routing. And if those fellows up there mean to carry on a brigand war in the style of their ancestors, then we may find the air a bit hot.'

The marquis rubbed his nose irritably. 'Of course, you are right,' he said. 'But see here, General, this is seventeen ninety-eight. They haven't a cat in hell's chance of beating us now. Good Lord, we wiped them off the map in Wexford—' He stopped suddenly, noticing the strange way Moore was looking at him.

'Do you ever think about Culloden?' Moore whispered.

Huntly froze and paled, 'No, sir, never!' he snapped rudely. 'Never, never, never . . .' There was a silence, then Huntly cried, 'Christ! What's the ruddy point in men like us thinking about Culloden?'

'But sometimes I do,' General Moore murmured. 'Sometimes I think that Charles Edward must, in his later life, have wished that he had died on Culloden Moor, died the death of a soldier fighting for his country.'

'They were a credit to Scotland, those highlanders of forty-five,' Huntly said. 'They charged bravely and without hesitation towards Cumberland's forces, but what chance had they against grapeshot and cannon balls! And Cumberland, the bastard, ordered no quarter. At the end of the slaughter the highlanders lay dead on the field in piles three and four deep. All for Scotland and Bonnie Prince Charlie. All for nothing.'

The patrol of Highlanders ambling behind heard every word their commander had said. For all his British bluster, he was as Scottish as Edinburgh, and they knew from his voice that he was getting upset.

'Blast these Irish,' Huntly said, shifting the subject angrily. 'Why can't they just be decent and toe the ruddy line? Damn me if they aren't the most belligerent race I've ever come across, fighting and shouting about their bullshit republic like that dirty little bastard Napoleon—'

'Napoleon?' General Moore seemed to come awake at the name. 'It would suit me far better to be out fighting Napoleon than these Irish. What honour is there in defeating the defeated? But trained French soldiers . . .' He smiled at Lord Huntly. 'Now that is more my field of play.'

Chapter Ten

The insurgents had been camped on Lugnaquilla a week when the proclamation of the new Viceroy, Lord Cornwallis, appeared in the press offering 'protection' to all those who surrendered their arms and returned to their allegiance. Any man who came forward and signed a document attesting his loyalty would receive a 'Certificate of Protection' and be allowed to return to his home and industry unmolested and without threat of charges.

Within days Michael saw the numbers in his army dwindle from over two thousand to nine hundred. Miserably he watched the men depart the camp but made no attempt to persuade them to stay. Who could blame them? Even if the French were to land tomorrow, they would already be too late. A rebellion of almost thirty thousand dead too late.

He peered though his spy-glass in the direction of General Moore's camp. 'You clever varmint,' he muttered bitterly. 'You and Cornwallis with you. More than one way to skin a cat, eh General?'

General John Moore was much too far away to hear him; he was at Dublin Castle, giving his report to the Viceroy.

The usual pomp and grandeur of former administrations was noticeably missing at the Castle. Like all his staff, Lord Cornwallis dressed in regimentals and boots. He received General Moore warmly, and the two sat down for almost an hour discussing the state of the country and the army.

'I directed Colonel Campbell with the first flank battalion to encamp at Seven Churches,' Moore informed Cornwallis. 'Colonel Stewart with the Eighty-ninth to Glenmalure, and part of the Toreby to Hacketstown. The Hundredth and Sixtieth are with me at the Glen of Imaal. I'm not without hopes that by holding out pardon to those in arms and treating kindly the inhabitants, I shall be able to get them to deliver up their arms and return to their work. The good conduct of the Highland regiments to the people, and the affable manner of Lord Huntly, has done much to reconcile them. When we arrived many of the houses were deserted, but in a short time we had the pleasure to see them inhabitated again.'

'And the rebels in the mountains?' queried Cornwallis.

'About a thousand have already surrendered their arms and received Protection Certificates, and more are coming in daily. I'm convinced the country could return to tranquillity if the gentlemen of the estates would treat the people with justice, and the militia regiments could just behave themselves with tolerable decency.'

'Behave themselves?'

Moore nodded wearily. 'I am constantly obliged to reprove their violence which seems to prompt them at every instant to gratify their revenge upon the inhabitants.'

'Soldiers?' Cornwallis cried in astonishment. 'Soldiers of victory seeking revenge!'

'The militia may wear the uniform,' General Moore said contemptuously, 'but I doubt if it will ever be possible to make real soldiers of them. In my opinion, it was their harshness and ill-treatment that drove the farmers and peasants to revolt. Yet they seem to have learned nothing by the lesson and are as ready as ever to recommence their former ways.'

Lord Cornwallis listened carefully to the man sitting opposite him. He had known many fine officers in his time, but, by far, General John Moore was one of the finest. Everything about him was real, solid, and unbending, and no other commander was more popular with his officers.

'The insurgents still holding out in Wicklow,' Cornwallis said, 'their numbers are still large enough to make trouble. Is it difficult to get at them?'

'Very difficult. Our best plan is to continue our invitation for them to surrender.'

'If they have not done so already, why should they later?'

'If the Protections won't do it, the elements will. The summer will soon be gone and it can get very cold up in the mountains at night. And now they believe the French misled their Dublin Executive with false promises of assistance.'

Lord Cornwallis nodded. 'Very well. Induce them to surrender and I will deal with the behaviour of the militia. Now, General Moore . . .' Cornwallis rose to his feet, 'I would be most obliged if you would consent to dine with me.'

General Moore inclined his head. 'I should be delighted.'

'Simple army fare,' Cornwallis warned. 'No lordly banquet. Fat men make slow soldiers.'

At the door Cornwallis turned and levelled a grin at General Moore. 'But I am told that there is a very good burgundy in the Castle cellars. We'll give it a sniff and try it out, shall we?'

General Moore smiled. 'If you insist, my lord.'

Later that night Lord Cornwallis wrote to London on the subject of the outstanding insurgents in the Wicklow Mountains:

> General John Moore and Lord Huntly with the 100th and 60th Regiments can be depended upon to try either to subdue or invite them to surrender, for the shocking barbarity of some of our national troops is more likely to provoke a rebellion than to suppress it.

Michael stood surrounded by his men and curiously watched the young man who climbed up the ravine towards them. He had been one of the first to surrender and they wondered at his return. He approached Michael diffidently, and handed him a letter.

'It's straight up, Captain. No tricks.'

Michael kept his eyes on the messenger as he ripped open the seal, his face stony. The messenger lowered his eyes and Michael did likewise, to read the contents of the letter:

> I have this day surrendered myself to General John Moore, who has engaged to obtain my pardon, and permission to quit Ireland and go reside in a foreign country. It is at the General's request I now write; he promises to obtain the same terms for you or any of the other chiefs who will avail themselves of this opportunity.
>
> > Yours
> > Garrett Byrne.

Michael looked up slowly. 'Did the man who gave you this letter give it to you in the presence of General Moore?' he asked.

'He did.'

'Was he a prisoner?'

'He was.'

'Was it Garrett Byrne of Ballymanus?'

'Yes.'

Michael swung away. The men formed a circle around him, waiting for his decision. When he turned back to the messenger he was trembling with rage.

'You can tell General Moore that the Protections he is using to lure men back to the allegiance of the Crown are turning out to be their death warrant! Only this afternoon, George Fenton made Andrew Doran *eat* his Certificate of Protection before he shot him! That's what the militia think of General Moore and his Protections. Moore and Cornwallis with him!'

The messenger stared at Michael, then around at the men. ''Tis true,' said a man, 'I saw it all from behind a tree. I was on my way to surrender.'

'You can't blame General Moore for that!' the messenger cried. 'He's a decent and fair and honest man. A man of honour!'

'Then go back,' Michael said, 'and tell Garrett Byrne that I wish him well, and truly hope his faith in the fair general is not unfounded.'

William Doyle could not believe it when he looked up from bellowing the fire to see Pat O'Riordan standing in the doorway with a bottle in his hand.

'Is it Armageddon then?' Doyle asked sarcastically.

O'Riordan gave a sheepish smile. 'No, William, it's me, Pat.'

'Aye, I can see that. And a bottle in your hand! I can only think it must be the world's end and you want help in drinking your precious whiskey before the divil can get a taste.'

'Still feeling sour are you?' O'Riordan moved closer. 'I came to tell you my good news, and let you share in my celebrating.'

'What good news?'

O'Riordan sat down on the settle with a gloomy face, his shoulders hunched. ''Tis not the same, William, without company. The drink goes sour on the tongue when it's not mulled with friendly company.'

'What good news?' Doyle demanded.

O'Riordan looked up at him, his red face pathetic. 'The return of my fortune.'

'By the hokey . . .'

'By Lord Cornwallis. He's promised to compensate every farmer for stock taken by the soldiers. On condition that he proves he has never taken up arms or sworn the oath of the United Irishmen.'

'Oh, the darling man!'

O'Riordan nodded, still dazed by it all. 'I didn't believe it when I was told. So I went up there meself, to Dublin, bold as brass. I had to wait five days but then he saw me in person, Lord Cornwallis.'

'You're lying!'

'I'm not,' said O'Riordan. 'And he did now. A minute only I was granted, after five days of waiting, but a whole minute it was. I showed him the bill, the cost of my lost stock and my lovely brown mare. One hundred and five pounds, four shillings, and eight pence. All the money that me and my father ever managed to save.'

'What did he say?' Doyle was on the edge of himself. 'Lord Cornwallis?'

'He kept the bill and bade me return the next day. So I did. Return the next day. His secretary, a young man in scarlet regimentals, said His Excellency was otherwise engaged, then he handed me a banker's draft for one hundred and five pounds, four shillings, and eight pence.'

'Oh, the darling, *darling* man!' Doyle was rubbing his hands. 'Will he do the same for me?'

The tears were rolling down O'Riordan's face. 'He returned my fortune. Lord Cornwallis. He did now. May God forever bless him. I'm a man of substance again.'

'I'll get the glasses!' Doyle shouted hysterically. 'Oh Pat! I can't tell you how I've missed you. The drink has been souring in me too with my misery.'

He sat down on the settle next to O'Riordan and by the time the bottle was near finished, the two men had an arm around each other, swaying sideways as they drank toast after toast to Lord Cornwallis.

'May God strike me dead if he's not the best Englishman ever born!' Doyle cried. 'Him that's going to compensate me.'

O'Riordan slapped his knee. 'And the darling General Moore.'

'And what's so darling about General Moore?' Doyle crooned.

'He sent his soldiers to take all my eggs and milk for his camp – and they paid me, paid me fairly.'

'Oh, may the saints shower a thousand blessings down on him!' Doyle cried. 'Does he want any bacon, do you know?'

'He wants Michael Dwyer.' O'Riordan sipped his drink.

134

'The soldiers told me. They said he wants the rebel captain to surrender, but he won't.'

'Won't surrender to the darling General Moore?' Doyle was frowning at the cheek of it.

'Do you know how it is, Pat,' he said informatively. ''Tis men the likes of Michael Dwyer that got us into this war in the first place. Him and those rebel lawyers up in Dublin – planning rebellions for us land slaves to fight! What do poor Irishmen want with Yankee and Frenchy politics? Answer me that. Bloody rebels!' Doyle shouted furiously. 'What have the United Irishmen ever done for us?'

'Michael Dwyer stopped the militia brutalising me once,' O'Riordan said. 'Him and his friends stopped them.'

Doyle's mounting fury against the rebels abated slightly at this, but it returned to its height when O'Riordan said, 'But he didn't save my stock. Or return my fortune.'

'Bad cess to him!' Doyle shouted. 'He never done nothing for me neither, only led my son to the brink of death in Wexford.'

'And brought him back again!' Mary stood in the doorway, her face white with anger. 'And saved me from the Hessians while you sat moping in here, no use to anyone. May God forgive you, Daddy, but you're a shameful turncoat.'

'Now, now, Mary,' O'Riordan said. 'We were only saying—'

'Aye, saying that Michael saved your hide but not your stock! How could he save your stock and he in Wexford? Tell me that, you great big heap of an ungrateful bull! And why should he do anything for the likes of you anyhow?'

'Mary, oh now, Mary, my pulse.' Doyle was flabbergasted at his daughter's rage. He staggered to his feet. 'Don't take on like that. Now Mary, come you back here!'

'What did she mean about Hessians?' O'Riordan asked when Doyle flopped back down on the settle.

'I haven't a notion. I saw no Hessians. Only the ones that were stationed beyond Donard.' He lifted the bottle and poured the remainder into the two glasses. 'Ach, pay no heed, Pat. She's not herself these days. Goes around in a dream like a simpleton.'

'Did you see the way her eyes flashed at me?' O'Riordan said. 'As black as the night.'

Doyle caught the expression on O'Riordan's face and sat erect, his brain working furiously. 'True enough,' he said, 'I did, for sure.' He pursed his lips for a moment, then moved them in the direction of O'Riordan's ear. 'Listen now,' he whispered. 'Listen while I tell you, Pat.'

'Tell me what?' O'Riordan whispered back.

'That's the way it is with women.'

'What is?'

'Their eyes flash that way . . . when they're taken with a man.'

O'Riordan stared at Doyle. 'Do you think she is, William? Taken with me?'

Doyle nodded. 'I'm sure of it. Did you hear the passionate way she shouted at you? I've never heard Mary that passionate afore. 'Tis only you could have inspired it.'

O'Riordan chuckled, delighted, rubbing his big hands around the glass. 'And wait till she hears I have my fortune back.'

'She'll be mad about you!' Doyle insisted. 'But of course . . .' he squared his shoulders and lifted his chin, 'that's all by the way if I'm not satisfied with her choice. 'Tis the father that makes the match.'

A silence rested over the room, then O'Riordan voiced a sudden idea. 'Will you come over to my place, William,' he said fawningly, 'and I'll open another while we talk some more. Sure isn't shame on me for bringing only one bottle to the house of she who looks like a queen, can dance like a gypsy, and work like a slave.'

'It'll be no land slave that gets her!' Doyle shouted. 'It'll be a man of substance.'

'And isn't that what I am again?' O'Riordan cried. 'I've forty rented acres, and now I have my fortune back I can rebuild my stocks. And even with the three-quarters of the profits I have to give the landlord, plenty of hard work will see me managing again.'

Doyle narrowed his eyes cunningly. 'I'm satisfied,' he said, 'for the most part. But you're right, Pat,' he looked at his empty glass, 'we should go over to your place and talk in more detail, I'm thinking.'

William Putnam McCabe, an elegantly dressed man, was escorted across the camp to Michael by two sentries.

'You should surrender,' McCabe said without preamble. 'It is useless to hold out any longer.'

136

'You've got a nerve, McCabe,' Michael said in a low voice. 'It was you and your Dublin friends that first came to us and talked about rebellion. Well we drilled and we trained and we fought your rebellion! Now you come and tell us to go down on our knees to the British general. It is his camp you've just come from, isn't it?'

McCabe nodded. 'All I can say is that I was sincere before the rebellion, and I'm sincere now. We have to adjust our views according to events.'

'Adjust our views?' Michael gave a contemptuous smile. 'I know others like you. Men who have one creed in the morning and another by nightfall. What were you offered?'

'My liberty, in another country.'

'Oh! The goddess Liberty again! That's what *you* and your friends offered us once upon a time, when you talked of rebellion – Ireland's liberty! Are the illustrious Executive Committee in Dublin of the same mind as you?'

'I've had no communication with the Executive. I doubt if they will ever change their views, not the likes of Emmet and Russell. They're fanatical idealists bent on a democracy we will never win.'

'Shove your talk of idealism. Shove your view that we will never win! And I tell you bluntly, McCabe – if I were Thomas Emmet or Tom Russell, I wouldn't trust the likes of you farther than I could spit!'

McCabe almost recoiled from the impact of Michael's contempt. He was spared from making a defence by the appearance of Hugh Vesty.

'The men are murmuring,' Hugh said. 'They want you to go to the camp and see General Moore.'

'For what purpose?' Michael snapped.

'They believe the general will ensure their Protection Certificates are honoured. They are tired and hungry and want to go home, if they can do so safely.'

'Then let them go and view the terms of the Protection Certificates themselves.'

'Sure you know most of them couldn't read the certificate even if you put spectacles on them,' Hugh said.

'You're a chief,' McCabe said to Dwyer. 'It's your duty to go down and parley their terms.'

Michael turned and faced the men. 'Is that what you want?' he demanded. 'After all this time we've held out – even in the face of defeat? For me to go with hat in hand to the British camp?'

The men stood in silence, the majority hanging down their heads.

'Sure, Captain,' a voice reasoned, 'you rarely wear your hat anyway.'

'A vote by a show of hands of those who want to parley for surrender.'

Michael looked over the raised hands, then turned angrily to McCabe and nodded. 'So be it.'

'When shall I tell General Moore that you'll be coming?'

'Tell General Moore that he will see me when he sees me. You have run your errand, the men have made the decision, but I will choose the time.'

He chose the following evening. Hugh Vesty, Martin Burke, John Mernagh, and Big Arthur Devlin went with him. Sam McAllister also wanted to go but Michael refused.

'No, Sam. Rebels is one thing, deserters another. Better wait and see what transpires.'

The men were mustering around him, loudly volunteering their opinions on what he should say to the British general.

'If we do not return,' Michael shouted, 'you will know we have been deceived, and that General John Moore is as rotten and as treacherous as Castlereagh!'

When they entered the English camp, escorted by a flank of soldiers, only Michael was allowed to enter the general's tent; the others were ordered to wait outside.

The Marquis of Huntly and two officers of the 100th Gordon Highlanders were also in the tent with General Moore, who stood behind a fold-table. He looked at the rebel captain without smugness or rancour, although a little surprised.

Based on the militia's description of him, 'A despicable Irish savage, devoid of all humanity and manners,' General Moore had expected a wild-looking fellow from the hills, uncombed, unwashed, face grim under a weather-beaten hat that he would only remove when finally requested to.

But the dark-haired young man who stood calmly before him appeared to have nothing of the peasants' boorishness about him. He was clearly acquainted with water, stood like an officer, and neither wore nor carried a hat. He looked around the tent, his eyes taking in each man in turn, his expression as cool and disdainful as some lord who has discovered a camp of trespassers on his land.

'I have been expecting you,' General Moore said, his voice smooth and very British. 'I'm glad you decided not to wait any longer.' He separated a paper from the pile on the table, then cast the rebel a polite look of inquiry. 'You have come to take out a Protection Certificate I hope?'

'The men wish to know and consider the terms.' Michael met his eyes look for look. 'That's all I came for.'

'Come, come, Dwyer!' Lord Huntly said. 'Surrender and save us all a lot of trouble. Take out a Protection and return home to your farming.'

'Protections, my lord, do not seem to be as useful as they were intended to be.'

Lord Huntly frowned darkly. 'You are, of course, referring to Fenton, who made that unfortunate fellow eat his Protection then shot him. Fenton has disappeared, but we intend to catch the beggar and bring him to justice.'

Michael looked unconvinced.

General Moore pushed a certificate across the table. 'Those are the terms,' he said. 'They are quite fair.' Michael lifted the certificate and read it.

THIS IS TO CERTIFY that the Bearer hereof has surrendered himself, confessed to his being engaged in the Rebellion and has given up all his arms; has taken the Oath of Allegiance to His Majesty, His Heirs and Successors, and has abjured all former Oaths contrary thereto, and has bound himself to behave for the future as a peaceable and loyal Subject; in consequence whereof this Certificate is given to the said . . . in order that his person and his property may not in any way be molested.

Signed by General . . . dated . . . 1798 and this Certificate to be in full force so long as the said . . . continues to demean himself as a peaceable and loyal Subject.

Michael looked up.

'Well?' General Moore asked. 'Will you sign it?'

'No, sir. I could not agree to all the conditions.'

'Such as?'

'The Oath of Allegiance to the King of England.'

'George the Third is also King of Ireland,' Lord Huntly reminded him.

'Then he treats his subjects badly and unfairly,' Michael said. 'The Catholics are seven-eighths of the population, yet only Protestants are allowed the rank of citizens.'

'Mr Pitt hopes to bring about the emancipation of your people,' General Moore said. 'As does Lord Cornwallis.'

'I doubt if even Billy Pitt and Lord Cornwallis could win against the Ascendancy in this land,' Michael answered, 'supported as they are by the government and militia. And that apart, from what we hear, old German George can't even hear the word Catholics without foaming at the mouth and ranging into another bout of insanity.' He gave a crack of a smile. 'Emancipation inagh. I'll believe that the day I'm allowed to keep more than one quarter of the profits I earn on my crops, and Lord Wicklow is allowed to sell me the farm my family has lived on for centuries – before Wicklow had any English lord on it!'

'That's for the politicians to decide,' Moore said, 'not soldiers. Our job at present is to oversee a return to normality. Order must be restored to this country at all costs.'

'That's a matter of opinion, General. If it is the old order you wish to restore, then you missed the point of this rebellion, and a lot of young men died for nothing.'

'My orders are to bring you back to your allegiance,' Moore said steadily. 'I would prefer to do it by fair means, if I can.'

'Why fair?' Michael asked. 'Foul means have worked very successfully so far.'

They stood, the two of them, their eyes locked and neither flinching: a perfect portrait of the long battle between the two countries. The dark Irish rebel who refused to knuckle under, and the scarlet-coated general representing the power of Britain in all her regimental glory.

'We cannot just leave you to your own devices,' the general said. 'Surely you can see that.'

'Why not just leave us altogether?' Michael answered in a low voice. 'And while you're at it, take Cromwell's militia with you.'

'We are being very fair with you insurgents,' the general said.

'Your army killed almost thirty thousand of us,' Michael reminded him.

'We had no choice. You took up arms against the Crown and war is war. We will do it again, if you force us.'

'Well I've no doubt you'll try,' Michael replied. 'Oh sure, maybe we were not ready, and maybe we did not have what it takes, this time. But when we did decide to make a thrust, we gave you a good crack of it. And, no doubt, will again.'

Moore's face was stony. 'Why do you persist in this lunacy? We outnumber and outgun you and always will. You are like lemmings rushing towards a whirlpool of your own destruction.'

Michael closed his eyes and clenched his teeth for a moment. 'When will you people ever learn that the British coat is not the only style,' he rasped. 'And no matter how far your armies march, no matter how hard you try, you will never make the British coat fit every back!'

Lord Huntly was so astounded he broke into a smile. 'Knock me down if it isn't often the case,' he said to the two Highlanders. 'Speak to an Irish farm boy and he invariably responds like a damned orator!'

It was one of Huntly's usual back-handed compliments, but Michael's eyes blazed wild with anger.

'Don't you patronise me, you bloody hypocrite! The whole damned lot of you! Marching through the world waving your civilised British Constitution in the face of every nation on earth – yet to us all you fling are the Penal Laws! And when we refuse to kneel down and grovel under those stinking laws, you come marching in with your drum-rolling red armies to whup us into line like those black slaves in America; the slaves you British keep fretting about and yelling about setting free—' he leaned across the table, his face closer to General Moore, 'while you blow our brains out, then bang on to ensure all our noses are returned nicely to the mud. For that's all we are to you – ignorant land slaves on King George's Irish farm.'

General Moore had never flinched in the face of the enemy and he did not now. He stood as calm and unbending as a granite statue, seeing only a young man smouldering from years of humiliation.

'We've seen the pictures you English draw of us in your newspapers,' Michael rasped, 'looking like a load of brain-battered apes that make all London laugh. Uncivilised savages unfit to govern ourselves. You *hypocrites*! You know full well we were a land of poets and scholars when London was just a dung-heap for wild mules.'

'You ruddy fool!' Lord Huntly's cheeks were crimson with rage. 'You are venting your spleen on the wrong British general! Speak to him again in that manner and, by Christ, I'll have you taken out and flogged!'

'Aye, do that,' Michael cried. 'Let's make it clear who still flays the whip in Ireland. And when you've finished, why not string me up on your British flag pole for all to see – why not string us all up! Give the militia another celebration to jump along banging their victory drums.'

'Now see here, Dwyer,' Huntly cried, 'you are pushing your ruddy luck too—'

'Enough!' General Moore commanded in a voice that jolted the tent to utter silence. He stared at the rebel captain in a way that had wilted many a soldier, but Michael had never learned how.

'I was under the impression that you came here to discuss the future of your men and the Protection Certificates,' Moore said quietly, 'not for a battle of insults. If that is what you came for, then I certainly hope you didn't expect me to engage in the name-calling contest, did you?'

The sheer dignity and calmness of the man amidst the rage in the tent was as mind-stopping as a cold January swim.

Michael found himself staring at the general as he sat down in his chair, stretched his legs, folded his arms, then looked up at him questioningly.

'The Protections. Do you mind very much if we now talk about them?'

'Well . . .' Michael almost smiled, 'I have a notion we will whether I mind or not,' he answered.

'If you lay down your arms against all further acts of rebellion,' Moore said slowly and emphatically, 'and take out the Protections, you can return safely to your homes and families. Surely you would prefer that to living up in the wilderness?'

'Of course I would.'

'Then take out a Protection.'

'If I don't?'

'If you don't, then I am forced to let you go; and hope you will quickly come to your senses. I'll not break my word by taking you prisoner and thereby risk losing the trust of the rest of the inhabitants. As I have said, order must be restored here at all costs.'

'Of all the luck.' Michael gave a crack of a smile. 'Your reputation is a true one after all, General.'

142

'And what about your reputation?' Moore asked. 'It is said you have committed many violent deeds.'

'Perhaps I have,' Michael said coldly, 'but it was the more violent deeds of others that sired them.'

General Moore frowned, unfolded his arms and sat up. 'We are well aware of matters under the former administration, and what is going on even now in the militia. But under Lord Cornwallis things will change.'

'Will they?' Michael doubted it. 'When Sir Ralph Abercromby was commander in chief of the army and made a public denouncement of the conduct of the troops, they forced him to resign. The Viceroy Camden called him a Scotch beast.'

Lord Huntly and the two Highlander officers frowned fiercely in unison.

'Lord Cornwallis is in command now,' Moore said. 'And, believe me, the unpardonable acts of the militia against the inhabitants will not be tolerated any longer. Not if Cornwallis has anything to do with it. Not if I have anything to do with it.'

Michael was staring into the blue eyes of the general, knowing he meant it. He may hate the uniform, but damnit, he could not help liking the man. But then . . . there was one thing which would instantly kill that liking and forever seal his hatred of the man and uniform both.

'May I ask you a personal question, General Moore?'

'You may ask, but whether it will be answered depends on its pertinence.'

'Were you with General Lake at the battle of Vinegar Hill at Enniscorthy on the twenty-first of June?'

General Moore thought about it, knew why the question was asked, and decided to answer it truthfully.

'On the twenty-first of June, my regiments were resting on the Taghmon, after scoring a triumphant victory over a division of your United confederates at Foulkesmill the day before.'

'You were not in the battle at all?' Michael questioned.

General Moore frowned, and stared off into space. When he had reached the camp at Taghmon, orders were waiting for him. Taghmon was a central situation and his was to be a moving corps. He had not ridden into Wexford itself until 2nd July, and then only to dine with General Hunter, who was endeavouring to pacify and conciliate the minds of the people, while other generals were sending out detachments to burn and destroy. The following morning he had ridden over to Enniscorthy to see the position that had been held by the rebels.

Wexford was out of sight the finest country he had seen in Ireland. Well cultivated and enclosed in woods; both farmers' and peasants' houses good and neat. It was strange that a part which showed so much industry should have been the most disturbed, and he was filled with melancholy to discover the houses deserted, the fields deserted, not a man, woman, or child in sight. Like Wicklow, it was situated on the Slaney, the countryside quite beautiful. And Vinegar Hill stank with thousands of dead bodies in unburied heaps.

'No, I was not at the battle of Vinegar Hill,' he said.

A small breath escaped Michael. He lowered his eyes and stared at the Certificate of Protection.

'It is in your interest to put the past behind you now,' General Moore told him firmly and quietly. 'You are not to seek revenge for any wrongs done to your women, but induce the people to give information, and the persons accused shall be proceeded against according to martial law. The rebellion is over. Face it. And remember, it is not your duty to seek redress against the militia.'

Michael had retreated into a silence, his fingers moving absently against the corners of the certificate. General Moore knew he was getting close, had reached some part of the Irishman, his defences had subdued, lost their edge, but there was a bitter darkness still there . . . still there.

He pressed the truth home.

'Our army is well armed and can be backed with massive reinforcements of men, ammunition, and artillery. All you truly have left is zeal and ardour, and although they might win you a battle here and there, they will never win you a war, much less a country. Be wise, assemble your priorities and your men, surrender your arms, and go home.'

'Come now, General, it's not that simple.'

'Why not?'

'You are forgetting about the fanatical hatred of the militia.' Michael lifted his head a bit sadly. 'I have as much chance of standing in the golden corn again and smiling on the land as a goat has of getting into heaven.'

'Whatever did you do to rise them to such a fury?' Lord Huntly asked curiously. 'Apart from the rebellion?'

Michael gave a slight smile. 'Well, I was beginning to get tired of watching them flashing their spurs like fighting game-cocks, strutting around and flapping their feathers like lords of the roost. So one day when they crowed, I answered the call, with a pistol. A short flash of spurs, and the game was mine. But don't you know, there is one thing the militia cannot live with, and that is one of us being cock of the walk. Even if our moment of glory is in our own barnyard.'

Lord Huntly pitched his brows. 'Can't you people ever answer a question straight and simple? Good Lord, I ask about the militia and get told about ruddy roosters!'

General Moore and the two Highlanders were smiling but the marquis had utterly missed the point. 'Now see here, Dwyer, that's the trouble with you Irish. You lack the order of the British mind and are too apt to go off into imagery and fantasies.'

'Sure we do, my lord, but don't be too hard on us. We are only descendants of simple poets and scribes, not solid Roman soldiers.'

'Quite,' Huntly muttered with a frown. 'The bastards never did come over here, did they.'

Michael lifted the certificate then looked at General Moore. 'Do these terms apply to everyone . . . even deserters?'

'The terms apply only to civilians. Deserters of the King's uniform will face a court martial.'

Michael thought of his comrade Sam McAllister. 'And death?'

'That is the usual punishment for deserters.'

'And what is the punishment for the likes of George Fenton who commit murder, and those other soldiers who murder and rape?'

'Soldiers who desert, soldiers who disgrace the army by the murder or rape of civilians, will be dealt with by the army, and only the army.'

Michael stared at him sombrely for a long moment, then nodded. 'Do I have your permission to leave, General?'

'Yes.'

As Michael lifted the flap, General Moore called him back. 'I shall expect to hear from you and your men soon,' he said, eyebrow raised.

The day following Michael's visit to the British military camp, a proclamation was posted in all towns and villages of the county of Wicklow.

> Whereas I have received information that George Fenton of Captain Hume's troop of Militia did inhumanly murder, without provocation, Andrew Doran of the Glen of Imaal, who had received Protection from the Government. I do therefore, being specially authorised thereto, promise a reward of 100 guineas to any person who shall apprehend the said George Fenton and deliver him up to His Majesty's officers in this County in order that he may be brought to immediate and condign punishment.
> Given under my hand at camp in Glen of Imaal.

GENERAL JOHN MOORE

Chapter Eleven

Three days later the camp on Lugnaquilla was reduced to two hundred men, a further eight hundred having surrendered themselves to General Moore and receiving a Protection Certificate.

Michael moved alone across the fields, along the sheltering path of the high hedgerows. He walked easily, disturbing the crickets with his feet until he came to the isolated dwelling of a widow and her daughter.

The widow was sitting at her door, knitting. She spied him as he bent to run past her wall. 'Will you stop your cod-acting, Michael,' she called, 'and come in for a while?'

He straightened and gave an impatient shrug. 'I can't,' he said. 'I'm on an urgent mission.'

'Is there a woman in it?'

'Aye.'

'Ach, if she likes ye enough she'll wait. Come on in and have some refreshment, just for a few minutes. 'Tis mortal lonely for company a body gets up here.'

Michael hesitated. He wanted to refuse, but when it was desperately needed the widow had given food and shelter to himself and his comrades. Hospitality could not be repaid with unfriendliness. And besides, he had eaten little in the last twenty-four hours and was feeling hungry.

'Have you honey?' he asked.

'I have. And griddle cakes to go with it.'

'Then I'll come in for a few minutes.'

'God bless ye.'

She bade him sit to the left of the inglenook, chattering incessantly while she prepared his light repast, plying him with questions and supplying the answers herself before he had a chance to open his mouth.

'You don't need company,' he told her. 'You could have an argument with yourself all the livelong day and still curse the winner.'

She laughed and handed him the food and drink. 'Now tell me, avic? Is it still up on the 'Quilla ye are? Of course ye are. 'Twill be very hard for ye when the weather turns, but then ye know that. Have ye blankets? Did yer mother give ye some? Ah, God bless her, and pity her too for having such a cross to bear – her man now with a useless arm. But when all's said—'

'Where's Rosie?' Michael interrupted.

'Lying on her bed asleep. She says she's sick. Sometimes I think she puts it on.' The widow looked at the bedroom door and screwed up her eyes. 'Always on her bed these days is Rosie. No company for her mammy at all.'

She looked back at Michael with a sad smile. 'She was asking about ye last week, she was now. I had to try and explain—'

'*Whisht!*' Michael held up his hand to quieten her, his face tight with concentration as he listened to the silence outside the open cottage door. The widow listened too, then opined: 'The birdsong is lovely at this time of year. Oh! The serenades I've heard while sitting at the door—'

Michael sprang to his feet and fled out of the house.

'What?' The widow rushed after him out to the yard which was silent and vacant, then she put her hands to her face and shrieked in terror. A band of militia were approaching the wall, led by George Fenton.

She ran back into the house. A few seconds later Fenton burst in and challenged her. 'Dwyer was here, wasn't he?'

'Was he, yer honour? Who?'

'We scouted him from the meadows below. Black hair and strolling like a lord. It had to be Dwyer.'

'I don't know who he was, yer honour. Just a man. A stranger. He came by and asked for food and I couldn't in all decency turn him away. But then he just ups and flies out of the house like an arrow. Who was he, yer honour? Michael Dwyer ye say? Oh, Lord protect us – they say he's a wild character.'

'You noisy fool!' Fenton snapped. 'Keep your red rag still or I'll silence it for ever!'

The woman fell into a pose of humble submission, promising to do as she was bid. The widow's daughter was dragged off her bed and thrust into the living-room with an order to stand beside her mother. Rosie did so obediently, then watched the soldiers with puzzled interest as they searched the house.

They searched and searched, bayoneted beds and laundry piles. Box drawers were ripped out, dressers torn apart, and such destruction done that the widow's red rag was prompted to fly again.

'How could a man six feet high get into a box drawer?' she queried, then followed Fenton and his men outside, while the hens screamed and flapped and ran for cover into the house.

The farmyard was searched, bayoneted, trampled, ricks and haystacks charged, carts overturned, until Fenton became incensed. 'He must be here somewhere. If he had run up the bare hill we would have spied him.'

'Perhaps the faeries are in it?' the widow wondered aloud. 'I've heard tell of whole armies of them lifting up a man they have charmed and flying away with him over the clouds and into the Land of Faery. Didn't it happen to Oisin, son of Finn the Fianna Chief? Up Oisin went, over the rainbow and into the Land of—'

'Dwyer is here all right,' said a yeoman with a smile. 'Look over there.' He had perceived movements in a small haystack in the field adjoining the holding. Fenton instantly ordered his men to advance and fire a volley into the stack.

When the acrid smell and smoke of the gunpowder cleared, blood could be clearly seen splattered over the hay. 'We've got him! We've got Dwyer!' Fenton cried, clawing at the hay in a frenzy, only to stare in utter dismay at his victims – a beautiful pointer who had chosen the sanctuary of the stack to have her litter of pups.

'Bessie! Ye've killed our Bessie!' the woman wailed. 'The best and only friend my Rosie has. *Ceád mile* curses on ye!'

'Where is he?' Fenton demanded savagely. 'Where is Michael Dwyer?'

'I don't know Michael Dwyer,' the woman insisted. 'Not if he was to stand before me now would I know him from Adam.'

'He must have escaped,' said a yeoman wearily. 'He knows every dip and fox hole in these mountains. We're just wasting our time here and the woman doesn't even know him.'

'Mi – Mi – Mi – chael' said the widow's daughter, coming out of the house. 'Rosie love Mi – Mi – Mi – chael.'

Fenton turned and stared at the girl who was about sixteen years old with a rosy face and hair the colour of the haystack.

'Do you know Michael Dwyer, girl?'

Rosie nodded her head.

'Michael Dwyer?' Fenton repeated.

Rosie nodded again.

'Do you know where he is?'

Rosie nodded and smiled.

She turned and ran into the house. Fenton made to follow her but she emerged within seconds clutching a doll made of straw with two long plaits very similar to her own. 'Mi – Mi – Michael done for Rosie.' She held up the doll with a proud, innocent smile.

The widow gaped in horror at the straw doll which Michael Dwyer had plaited and looped one night for Rosie as the girl sat at his feet and she herself had whiled the time chatting to his comrades. She turned her eyes back to Fenton, and knew the game was up.

'You're a harbourer,' Fenton said. 'You know the penalties for harbouring rebels.'

'No!' the widow screamed, backing away. 'I'm not a harbourer. He's been to the English camp. General Moore has given him a Protection. Everyone down below says he did.'

The name of General Moore seemed to freeze Fenton. 'General John Moore is a disgrace to his uniform!' Fenton gritted. 'We all know about him and Michael Dwyer. Three times that croppy has been to the British camp, three times when English and Highland soldiers talked to him as if he were as good as themselves, three times—'

'I heard it was only two times,' the woman argued instinctively. 'Some say it was only once. And others say 'tis you that General Moore—'

A back-hand across the face abruptly silenced the woman. 'Even if you're not a harbourer,' Fenton shouted, 'you're clearly a sympathiser. And by rights, under martial law, I should burn and destroy this house and mete out justice to you and that simpleton.' He looked contemptuously at Rosie, who was staring over at the bloodstained haystack with perplexed eyes.

'But I won't,' Fenton went on. 'I shall be merciful, and allow you to convey a message to Dwyer and his friends.'

'I don't know where he is,' the woman wailed. 'I'm only a poor widow and if you burn my abode—'

'You can get word to him. Your sort always can. And when you do, tell him that neither General Moore nor a Certificate of Protection will save him. Every militiaman from Rathdrum to Baltinglass has pledged to see him dead.'

'B – b – bessie?' murmured Rosie, wandering across the yard towards the haystack.

The widow stood with her apron clutched over her mouth as she watched Fenton and his men march away. She moved as if in a dream, slowly following them, standing to hide behind the bough of an elder tree until the fields and trees way below had swallowed them up and they were lost from sight.

She turned back and sauntered across to the yard in a puzzled daze. There she stood peering around her for some minutes, then exclaimed loudly: 'Where are you, Michael darling? Come out, agra! Wherever in the world you have hid yourself for one wonderful man, come out, my pulse! The blackguards have gone. I saw them off with my own two looking eyes.'

Next to the sty containing a sow and four piglets was a small wooden shed-sty containing a huge boar with a fearsome appearance and yellow tusks. He was ten years old and the full of the sty. He now crashed through the wooden half-door and bolted past the woman. Michael followed on all fours, his knife in his hand. He rose to his feet and gave the woman a sheepish grin.

'God forgive me,' he said, 'but I've given that poor fellow a terrible time.'

'Holy Mother! You mean ye were in with the boar? Under their noses?'

Michael twitched his own nose into a disdainful sniff, then explained how he had run straight for the boar's sty, knowing he was armed with only one pistol against many, and the odds were certainly against him. He had squeezed behind the huge boar, knife in hand, marking the daylight at the half-door of the sty and prodding the pig with his knife every instant a militia-man attempted to peer inside, making the boar rear ferociously, then clinging for dear life to prevent the pig from bolting and revealing all.

'Blood-an-ouns! But you must have the strength of an ox!'

'Sure he's all flab,' Michael told her.

'Ah, the poor old boy. I hope ye didn't hurt him too bad with your knife. But isn't he the darling for saving yer life?'

'And I'm indebted to you too,' Michael said.

'Did ye hear it all? Everything they said? Sure you must have done if you were in with the boar.' She gabbled on in her nervous way, questioning and answering herself, and Michael wandered over to where Rosie was standing by the haystack, sobbing quietly over the dead pointer and her pups. He put his arm around her shoulder.

'Look at that!' he whispered suddenly, pointing to a small rabbit standing on its hind legs and peering at something in the far hedge.

Rosie turned a tear-stained face and stared at the rabbit, then smiled as the rabbit dropped on all fours and wiped a tiny paw over its whiskers. She called out to the rabbit, who threw her a glance, then shot across the field in a blur of grey fur.

'Chase him, Rosie,' Michael urged. 'Go on! Anyone can catch a rabbit if they run fast enough.'

Rosie heard the challenge in his voice and hurtled off with her skirts clutched up to her knees. By the time she returned some time later, panting and gasping and shaking her head, Michael and the widow had buried the pointer and her pups and the haystack stood as before, if not as full, bearing no outward sign that could jog Rosie's memory.

'Ye'll get me another dog?' the widow whispered. 'As soon as ye can.'

Michael nodded. 'I will. You can rely on it.'

'Any breed. A mongrel will do. Just so long as it's kind and playful and will love her. The pointer was my man's dog. Used to take it with him when he went out shooting rabbits and grouse.'

'Do you see the way that boar is looking at me?' Michael said suddenly. They were standing by the door of the shed-sty and the boar was back in residence, his face surly. 'A dirty look if ever I saw one,' Michael said. '*He* knows who his friends are – and I'm not one of them.'

The woman laughed. 'His poor rump is very sore after your knife. Now tell me, are you still going to see the woman?'

'Aye, my mother.' Michael sniffed again. 'And she's very particular about cleanliness. I'll need a swim, then a fresh set of clothes.' He made a scowling face at the surly pig. 'I may be indebted to you, avic, but I don't have to smell like you.'

The boar reared up his snout in a ferocious grunt, then suddenly moved on to his feet.

'Oh God above!' Michael turned and fled from the yard, making a lightning spring over the wall as the boar bolted after him. He did not even pause to wave the widow farewell as he ran over to the cover of the hedgerows and made for the home he had not seen for many a long day.

nother six miles, through trees and sheltered fields,

Michael made his way towards the farmlands at Eadstown, until the aromatic smell of burning turf in the air told him he was almost home. At the top of a bracken-covered hillside he paused and looked down at the grey-slated roof of the farmhouse huddled in the centre of the ripening fields, smoke drifting out of its chimney. It seemed content in its place, like a grey old huddled man enjoying a tranquil smoke in the afternoon sun.

And as he stood there, looking down at his home, there was a sadness and regret in him for what might have been. To work in the field, and live off the yield, he would have been content with that, if he had been allowed to do so in peace. Now it was too late.

He looked up and listened as a thrush trilled a lusty call to her mate. Smiling, he put his fingers to his lips and whistled an answer, seductive and melodious; smiling when the mate went swooping past in furious search of his rival.

Suddenly a corncrake rasped in the wheat, and he moved on, down to the home fields and the bohereen which led to the yard of the house. His eyes had carefully scanned the land as he walked, but no danger lurked from the red militia.

Beyond on the high meadow, about half a mile or so away, he could see the dark figure of his father outlined against the sky. James and Peter hovered each side of him, gaming guns in their hands, while Etty danced beside them like an excited faery in May time.

What were they doing? He narrowed his eyes and focused hard. His father was agitated, he could see, raising his good arm and pointing his hand as if ordering Etty back to the house. Her head shook, shook again, then she flopped down and sat as still as a statue.

He was at the barn now, moving with a quiet and easy step, when the door of the house opened and a woman stepped out, a dark-haired woman of about forty years, and the biggest woman he had ever seen – knocking on six feet two and stronger than an ox: Midge Mahoney!

He side-stepped into the barn like a man in a fright, his back pressed flat against the door. He would rather face the militia than Midge Mahoney! A terrible woman! And mad about men – especially young men. And fierce in her anger if she was thwarted. 'Troth, she only had to give a man a belt of her boozalem and he'd be knocked out for sure.

'Midge!' cried a voice. 'Midge, wait!'

It was his sister Cathy's voice, breathless and excited. 'Myself and Maíre have something to ask you, Midge . . . about the knowledge.'

'You may throw out any notion of hearing any of that, Cathy Dwyer!'

'Oh, Midge, please. We're mortal desperate!'

'Desperate is it? Oh well then, that is something for me to ponder on, but I'm in a frenzy of a hurry.'

After a silence, Midge cried, 'Ach, let it never be said that Midge Mahoney turned her back on any of her poor female sisters in need. What is it, acquanies? Romance?'

'Romance,' Maíre gushed in confirmation.

'Can ye cross my palm? The knowledge flows more freely if the palm of the teller is crossed . . . in accordance with the tradition.'

'We can,' Cathy said. 'We've been saving from the egg money. A threepenny piece each. Will that do it?'

'Begor, but it will!' Midge laughed, a great bark of a laugh like a man. 'But hush now, and mind, let ye not tell your saintly mammy that you came to me for the knowledge. Show me the money . . . Well – what are you waiting for? Cross my palm with it.'

He heard Midge fire a walloping spit at the money and only had time to step back into the dark corner of the barn before her great shadow loomed like a gigantic bird of ill-omen across the floor.

'We'll talk here quickly,' Midge said in hushed tones, 'for as I said, I'm in a frenzy of a hurry.'

He knew the talk would be female and personal and in all decency and honour he should reveal himself; but Midge Mahoney was a law unto herself, and a nightmare he had fled from ever since the day he had passed her house and she had got him into the bedroom on the pretence of lighting the fire for her, and there she had grabbed him in a clinch that had nearly broken his ribs and all his bones in the struggle to escape. And her poor little husband working only a field away, too timid and terrified of her to object when she made lusty eyes at other men . . . A terrible woman.

And there she stood, like a great dark vulture, her lank hair scraped into a knot at the back of her head, while his sisters flapped around her in readiness for the parley.

Maíre spoke first, her voice hesitant. 'I've no young man in sight, as yet, Midge. But I want to know the knowledge before he looms – to save time, so to speak.'

'And ye, Cathy? Have ye a lad, or only a dream of one, like yer sister?'

'I have a lad,' Cathy said, 'although he's not mine yet, that's why I want the knowledge. 'Tis John O'Neill, a friend of my brother Michael. He's nineteen, but 'tis only since he came back from Wexford that I've noticed him. Overnight he seems to have greatly changed, from a boy to a man.'

' 'Tis war,' Midge said. 'War turns many a boy into a man. And many a man into a grave. But those that come back are hardened men. Wild men! And there's nothing wrong in a man being wild, for wildness is of the land and the mountains and the winds that drive the great ships across the seas. You may throw your pretty poets in the river, give me a wild man that's powerful and passionate and as strong as the storm—'

'Do you have the knowledge?' Cathy interrupted impatiently. 'To stir John O'Neill's fancy? For he's not once looked my way since returning home armed with General Moore's Protection Certificate.'

'And ye so purty! What's wrong wid him? Is he a man at all? They say many a corpse has walked back from a war.' A note of warning crept into Midge's tone. 'Are ye positive that you want him now? For the cure to his coolness is powerful. Begor and it is. As powerful as it is simple.'

'Oh, I'm positive,' Cathy said. 'He only has to look at me to bring a sweat to my brow and a trembling to my knees.'

'Then 'tis you that needs a cure,' Midge said dryly, 'and 'tis only himself can give you that. But here is the knowledge – all you need is a little bit of the musk.'

By bending his head just a fraction, he could see the great figure of Midge Mahoney in the doorway, standing with arms folded under her ton of a bosom while she regarded his two mesmerised sisters with a look that said it was surely that simple.

'Mimulus?' he heard Cathy say in astonishment.

'Mimulus,' Midge repeated. 'Or as them with the knowledge call it – *grah na mamalog* – the love flower. So go ye up to the high meadows and find some. Then boil the petals into a thin brew. And whether you invite him to sit at your table, or chance to pass him in the fields holding a friendly snack of soda bread in your basket, let you put a few drops of the brew in the making of the food. And if you do that, he'll end up eating you instead of the food – he'll be that in love with you.'

Cathy gasped. 'That powerful is it?'

'Sure it is,' Midge insisted. 'And let ye also put a few drops of the musk on yer body too, for it'll drive him wild!'

'Are you sure?' Cathy sounded uncertain. 'He's very shy is Johnnie O'Neill. As shy as can be, with the maidens anyway.'

'Oh they're the worst!' Midge warned. 'Shy as a violet when courting, blushing like a rose when kissing, shaking like a nervous young colt at the altar, but once in the marriage bed – stallions!'

'Oh, Gawney!' Maíre cried in terror.

After a moment Cathy found her voice, furious and shocked. 'You're disgusting, Midge Mahoney! How dare you speak about my Johnnie in that vile low fashion! He's holy and chaste and would never act – oh, you're disgusting!'

But Midge simply blasted a laugh that shook the barn and every bulging proportion of her massive body. 'Aye, but not as daft as those holy people who will tell you that Adam never rode Eve and that Cain and Abel came from the seeds of an apple!'

'Oh, Mrs Mahoney!' Maíre was almost in tears of mortification. 'If Mammy heard you talking like that she'd flay you with an ash branch and us as well for listening.'

'I knows what I know, and I've told youse what I know. All youse should know for sixpence anyway. And I know the cure for your dry skin, Maíre, the herbs and flower oil that will cure it. Shall I tell ye? Seeing as ye have no shy violet to romance yet.'

Maíre was tempted, the silence betrayed it. Cathy too.

'Will it cure blemishes?' Cathy asked.

'Even boils!'

Michael leaned back into the shadows and rolled his eyes with impatience. The talk was getting ridiculous now, roots of daisies and buds of the primrose boiled up and mixed into an ointment with butter. He wished Midge would hurry up and shove off. For a woman in a frenzy of a hurry she was amazing in her idleness.

When the knowledge advised that lips painted in the juice of a raspberry could look very red and tasty to a man – drive him wild – he was tempted to reveal himself and make a run for it, past the vulture, and was only checked from doing so by the horror and shame that Cathy and Maíre would feel if they knew he had heard the all of it.

'So go ye up to the meadows and find the love flower, Cathy acquanie, and with a few drops outside you, and inside him, ye'll find romance and passion undreamed of!'

When they at last moved off he slid in relief round the door of the barn, then out of the yard and scanned the land. His father, the boys, and Etty were still up on yonder meadow. Cathy and Maíre were now heading in that direction, falling against each other with giggles as they ran; while Midge Mahoney stalked up the bohereen singing at the top of her corncrake voice.

'Ate a bit of bread, ate a bit of bacon,
For 'tis love went in the making . . .'

And so, when he slipped noiselessly inside the open door of the kitchen, Michael found his mother alone, bending slightly over the table, sleeves rolled up, baking bread. He stood with his shoulder against the wall, silently watching her. Down came another strand of the upswept hair that always managed to come undone no matter how tight the knot. In the track of sunlight from the window it looked very fair, fairer than he remembered. And her face, her once lovely face with the lines of age edged around her eyes and mouth, looked flushed and tired.

She would have been up and working, he knew, since dawn; and there was in her every movement a resigned weariness that seems to come to women after years of childrearing and caring and housework. She would have gone through the day bustling about the house, giving orders to his brothers and sisters, fussing over his father, cooking and washing, cleaning and polishing, churning and spinning, sewing and knitting; never pausing in her work while she spoke. And that's how it was for her, every day of her life, a mother of seven, and wife of one.

In her hand she held a heap of soda, an abstracted frown on her face as she lifted a thumb to crush it in her palm, but then a tremor came to the corner of her mouth and she whispered through trembling lips: 'He's not mine . . . No, he's not mine.'

He stared at her in silent puzzlement, and it was then a chicken strayed into the kitchen and pecked at his boot, and she looked up, and the heap of soda slipped unnoticed through her fingers.

For an instant the sunlight seemed to have leapt into her eyes, cool hazel eyes of brown-tinted green, the colour of the woodlands, the colour of his own; but then an expression settled on her carefully arranged face that betrayed nothing more than slight surprise.

157

'Is it you, Michael?' she said, her voice a soft vapour.

'Aye, Mammy.'

'So why were you standing there as silent as a ghost? For a moment I thought you were one.'

'I was looking at you, at your hair. In the beam of light it looks the colour of ripe wheat.'

'On with you,' she said with a dismissive smile. 'You're talking like a mother's son. Come closer, boy, and you'll see I'm almost as grey as a badger.'

'You look tired,' he told her, moving towards the clean hearth and bright fire, a simmering cauldron of stew on the crane. 'Will you not sit down for a while?'

'No, I'm grand, pet. You sit down and I'll get you something to eat. You're losing flesh, son, and you must be tired yourself after all those mountain miles you've crossed.'

It had always been useless to argue with her. And so he sighed and sat down on the settle, then bent to stroke gently the head of a big black buck cat which sat in the centre of the hearth, his paws drawn under him, staring into the fire.

'A king of a cat, you are, avic,' he said in admiration, but the cat simply slanted him a superior glance before returning his gaze to the depths of the fire.

'Oh, Michael! You have the smell of the sow on you!' his mother cried in disappointment, for she came of a breed of women who took pride in how clean her menfolk and children were turned out; and until this one ever married and the responsibility passed on to another, his appearance would still be a mark of credit or shame against her.

' 'Twas on the journey over here,' he said, 'and I falling in with an old boar who was not in the least appreciative of my company.'

But she was not amused or interested in the whys or wherefores, her mind already grappling with the linen and breeches she must dig out from the linen-box to give him.

'Into the bedroom and strip off,' she ordered, 'and I'll fling some things into you in a minute.' Then busily and efficiently she moved through the house; and when he emerged from the bedroom and came back into the kitchen some minutes later, she threw him a look of satisfaction before bending over the crane and ladling him a plate of her stew. As he sat down and ate the food his eyes moved around the comfort of the kitchen that he had not missed until now.

'Did you have any trouble coming over,' she asked, sitting down on the settle and lifting her knitting.

'What sort of trouble?'

'The usual sort. Militia trouble. Did you spy any of them?'

'No,' he lied with convincing innocence. 'Not hilt nor hide of one of them. Have you had any trouble here?'

'Just searches. Regular searches of the holding. Two or three times a week. And no knocking on the door, of course. Just the usual kicking-in that will one day take the door off its hinges.'

His eyes grew dark, but he made no comment, just laid down his knife and fork on the plate and moved over to sit beside her on the settle. 'What's Daddy doing up on the high meadow?' he asked curiously.

'After a fox. A daredevil of a one that keeps attacking the hens at night. Five he's killed now, and two chickens. Your daddy will not be down until he catches him. Jamie and Peter have the guns, for he could not do it himself and he with only one good arm.'

She laid her knitting on her lap and stretched her legs with a sigh, unwittingly kicking the black cat that sprang to his feet with a hiss and a snarl and stared malevolently at her, his tail high.

'There's evil in that cat of yours,' she said irritably. 'Look at his eyes now. He thinks he owns the place.'

'He's a king of his kind and he knows it,' Michael whispered, bending forward to stare into the feline eyes, a slow hissing sound coming through his teeth which matched the sound of the cat, who arched his back at the challenge.

When the cat suddenly sprang with a snarl, his mother let out a cry of fright, but she saw her son smiling with delight as he caught the animal in a tight grip and held him struggling to his chest, whispering, whispering, words of praise and admiration, until the cat went still and Michael slowly set him back down on his rightful place in the centre of the hearth with a gentle stroking motion.

'You should never try to humiliate a cat,' he told her. 'If you master a dog, he will look up to you. But if you try and master a cat, he will look down on you. They are a proud animal, and must be allowed to keep their self-respect.'

'Is that right?' she responded sardonically. 'Then the old Irish proverb is true so – nature breaks through the eyes of a cat. And that one's nature is too conceited. Did you hear how he purred when you told him how great he was.'

'Well, let's be truthful, since the day that buck came here, there's not been even a shadow of a rat sighted, has there?'

'Not one,' she agreed.

'Then give him the credit and respect he deserves.'

His mother looked into his smiling face, but she did not smile back, just heaved a sigh, then, like the cat, turned to stare in sombre contemplation of the farthest region of the fire's red depths; while Michael sat in contemplation of her.

She was strong, his mother, a strong-spirited woman, and occasionally very cold. She was one of three sisters who had married three Wicklow farmers, John Dwyer, Brian Devlin, and Sylvester Byrne. Oh yes, at times she could be chillingly cold. She could silence her brood with just a look, sternly upbraiding them for their faults, and giving little lectures that always had an underlying moral to them. She despised the vice of vanity, and on the surface repressed any pride she had in her children, or even her husband, whom they all knew she adored.

'What did you mean,' he said softly, 'when you said to the soda in your hand . . . he's not mine. Who isn't yours?'

She didn't answer, only continued staring into the fire with a bead of sweat beginning to glisten along her upper lip, her chest beginning to heave in a quick-breathing motion as if her breath was choking her.

'Mammy?'

Finally the breath escaped through her lips and she looked at him, her expression intensely weary, and something more, something which made him reach out and cover her hand with his own and clutch it tightly. 'Tell me? What did you mean – he's not mine?'

So she told him of her personal nightmare and agony. 'Every time the word comes of another lad killed, I scramble over the fields and walls, praying and praying to Our Father in Heaven, and when at last they tell me the name of the dead son, so far I have always been able to say, no, he's not mine. Thank God, *he's not mine!*'

'Oh, Mammy,' he said helplessly.

But she threw off his hand and stood up before the fire, a dangerous shaking in her shoulders as she rested her hand and brow on the mantel. 'But then I ask myself, after I have prayed all the livelong day and most of the night for your safety, why should He, who did not spare His own beloved son, spare mine!'

He didn't move, didn't speak, and when she turned to look at him, the anguish and tears and overflowing love on her ravaged face sent him into a stupor of pain that held him stunned, but when she sagged and shrivelled he jumped up and caught her inside his arms, murmuring assurances to her as she wept in a way he had never dreamed she could weep, for he had never once known her to shed a tear.

'I'll not die for my country,' he told her. 'No funeral drum will beat slowly over my young grave. No fife will blow a melancholy anthem over my dead flesh. I intend to *live* for my country, so help me God I do. And that will be my supreme revenge on our enemies. Every last man jack of them.'

'It's all right, Michael.' She could feel the rage building in his body. 'I believe you,' she said, wanting desperately to believe him. And then, her emotion exhausted, she gently pushed him away, sinking down on the settle and wiping the tears from her eyes with a trembling hand, pretending it was all nothing more than the tiredness and blabberings of a foolish old woman.

Still struggling with his feelings, he slumped down beside her, not in the least surprised when the buck cat, who had been disturbed once again, sprang on to his lap and rubbed against him with a comforting meow. He bent his head low and stroked the animal, who curled into the warmth of his stomach with a rumble of purring, then narrowed his feline eyes in hostility at the woman.

"Tis older I'm getting for sure,' she said softly. 'Older every day.'

'Myself also,' he answered.

She looked at him with a shadow of a smile, then looked away. He too looked away, for the rare display of their emotions had left them suddenly shy with one another.

'Give him a stroke to show him how fine you think he is,' he urged her, his eyes on the cat.

'I'll not indulge his vanity,' she retorted with a sniff. "Tis a whack of a broom on his haughty head he'll get one of these days.'

She lifted the knitting that had fallen to the floor and sought to change the subject. 'I hear there's a special girl in your life these days.'

'No guessing who told you that. Hugh Vesty's mother?'

'Aye, in sisterly talk. Only natural when speaking about one son and the other.'

'Hugh Vesty has too slack a mouth when it comes to my business.'

'The daughter of Doyle of Knockandarragh,' she went on. 'I don't know the family at all, but I'm told she is admired by many for her beauty.'

When he made no answer, seemingly more interested in the cat, she continued, 'I'm told many men have asked for her hand in marriage, but her daddy, a possessive man, has driven them all away.'

'Lord Huntly has sent a message requesting to see me,' he said quietly. 'At the British camp. As soon as possible.'

She laid down the knitting and stared at him. 'Can you trust him?'

'Aye, he's not a bad old plume. He insists on giving all the lads that surrender a loaf of bread to carry them home over the mountains, then warns them he'll hang them if he ever sees them again.'

'They say General Moore is a decent man.'

'Aye, I suppose he might be. I just wish he was Irish and on our side of the battle line. But he is proud of his scarlet uniform and seeks only honour and victory for the British army to which he is sworn. To that end, he tries to be fair and just, but he's mad bent against the militia and some of the redcoats for disgracing the same uniform with their rapes and murders.'

'I wonder why Lord Huntly wants to see you,' his mother whispered in a nervous tone.

And suddenly he wanted to know too – but not enough to miss seeing his father. Without a thought he threw down the drowsing cat, who complained furiously, then strolled out of the house in languorous disgust.

'You say that Daddy'll not be down until he catches the fox?'

'Nay, he can't afford to keep losing the fowl at the rate the fox is killing them.'

'Would it not be wiser to lie in wait for it, at night-time?'

'He's tried that, but the cunning devil never showed, not until the morning when your daddy had stepped inside for a bite of breakfast, then within minutes we heard the screaming of the hens. He'll not be down until he catches it, no matter how long it takes. He's gone stupid with fury.'

'Then I'd better see if I can give him a hand,' Michael said with a grin, checking his pistol. 'Although when I get up there I'll take a gaming-rifle off one of the boys. Did you know the

162

long-barrelled gaming-rifle gives a clear four hundred yards further distance than a musket.' He nodded at her. 'Aye! I tested mine just the other day.'

A dour quietness fell over her as she looked into his enthusiasm. Then the challenge of the fox spurred him to the door.

'Goodbye, son,' she said quietly.

He turned and looked at her. 'Next time you hear of a kill, don't run over the fields to find out, for it won't be me. Just stay in your place and say a prayer for the dead.'

And with that he was gone, and she wearily wondered at the rash confidence of young men who ran headstrong into battle screaming victory, and still yelled victory, even as the sabres cut them down.

Cathy and Maíre were the first to return, faces flushed and smiling as they whispered together. Then Etty, who complained furiously about Michael chasing her halfway back to the house with a threat of a ducking in the river if she returned. 'And me over fifteen!' she declared indignantly. 'And as good with a pistol as any man.'

Then James and Peter who looked gloomy and said the fox had gone to earth well and truly.

Then the youngest, twelve-year-old John-bawn, who sidled in covered in grass and burrs and carrying a dangerous-looking catapult, finally confessing that he too had been stalking the fox, on the other side of the woods, unbeknownst to his father.

James expressed his high opinion of such an action by complimenting John-bawn with a hard whack on the head, and confiscating the catapult. 'You stupid fool! We could have shot you by mistake.'

'Although . . .' Peter said to his mother, 'Michael did say he reckoned the lair would be in the woods, and went sniffing in that direction when we left.' He gave a sudden affectionate laugh. 'With poor Daddy creeping after him like an excited old hound.'

'Your daddy is not that old,' his mother reproved demurely, a hand moving to tidy her hair as she spoke of her husband.

Supper was served and eaten and the dishes cleared away, the tension thickening as the hours rolled by and darkness fell. Throughout, one or other of the boys kept watch by the open door, peering towards the meadows which led to the woods. A full green moon had swung up and settled just above the bare black hill of the high meadow.

By half-past ten the girls had gone to bed and only the boys and their mother remained in the kitchen. She sat by the fire, the buck cat once more in his place at the centre of the hearth stretched in sleep. A number of times she glanced up at the clock, the sound of its ticking deafening her in the tense silence.

At a quarter to eleven, she murmured to the boys that they should go to bed, but none of them moved or answered, not even John-bawn, who lay sprawled on the straw mat by the open door, sniffing the air and peering into the darkness like a young dog, while his brothers stood in stony silence and continued to stare as if mesmerised at the great orb of moon just above the bare black hill.

Shortly after eleven the shot rang out. Just one shot. And not from as far away as the woods, but the high meadow. No one made a sound, just stared round at each other in an interplay of eyes that showed their disbelief. But they had seen it! With their own eyes, James and Peter and John-bawn had *seen* the kill as it happened.

'God save us!' their mother cried.

John-bawn sprang to his heels and ran like a river, with James and Peter hurtling after him.

Ten, maybe fifteen minutes later, they returned, laughing and whooping at the top of their voices as they came through the yard. She moved round the fire and busied herself at the cauldron, ladling a plate of stew in readiness for her husband, who had not eaten since dawn.

When she glanced over her shoulder he was standing in the door frame, an exultant smile on his face as he held up the dog fox.

'That son of mine is a bloody hero!' he cried. 'I was almost giving up and suddenly he spies the varmint, then tracks him like lightning, right down here to the homing fields, leaving me floundering up in the woods. But he doesn't even try to pick him off in the fields – too dark for a certain hit, he reckoned. So what does he do then, that son of mine?'

'Tell me,' she said with a touch of a smile.

'He employed a military tactic! "When the conditions are against you," says he, "then endeavour to draw or drive the enemy on to a more favourable field of battle." So he lets the varmint know he's tracking, and heads him off in a chase back up to his lair in the woods, knowing the devil would have to make a run for it across the bare black hill of the high meadow, and then he got him – in that fleeting instant when he was outlined as clear as a fox running across the moon – bang!'

The noise of the boys was deafening, all three talking at once as they examined the chicken killer.

'I hope you don't intend to bring that dead thing in here,' she said. 'And where is the hero now? Gone to the British camp?'

'The British camp?' Her husband frowned at her in puzzlement. 'He said nothing to me about the British camp. Last I seen of him, he was making for a moonlight swim in the river.'

It was almost two in the morning when Michael reached John Cullen's cottage at Knockgorrah and tapped out a rhythm on the window, pursing his lips and giving the hoot of an owl.

A screwed-up face appeared at the glass. 'Who is there?' Cullen called. 'Who's at the window?'

'The angels,' Michael murmured.

'Is Michael the Archangel in it?' Cullen asked, always enjoying these little games of verbal intrigue and capable of prolonging them endlessly.

' 'Twill be Gabriel blowing his horn if you don't open your door, old man,' Michael said impatiently.

'I'll be with you in a shout! Just let me put my topclothes on.'

A minute later Michael heard the chains rattling and the bar being lowered. Cullen opened the door and stood to peer round his shoulder but Michael pushed him inside with a reproving tone.

'I'm hardly likely to come acalling with the yeos close behind, especially after what happened to me today.'

'Will I light a candle?'

'Nay, the heart is still in the turf.' Michael moved over and kicked at the huge smouldering turf-brick, bringing it to a blaze while Cullen chained and barred the door.

'Where are you from?' Cullen asked as he poured out two cups of whiskey.

'The British camp. I went there after seeing the family.'

'Did you take out a Protection? The whole glen is wondering if you did.'

'No, I never did. Even Lord Huntly now advises me that it would be unsafe for me to live at home. He says the militia are incensed against me and will shoot me on sight, no matter what.' Michael smiled wryly. 'As if I didn't know that.'

'What else did they say? Was General Moore there?'

'Aye. They asked me to persuade Holt and his men to surrender, and if I were to join the British army, they would endeavour to get me into a foreign regiment.'

Cullen let out a nervous laugh. 'That would be a turnabout, wouldn't it? You in a scarlet uniform.'

'The cavalry,' Michael said thoughtfully. 'I have a fancy for the cavalry. Charging along on a strong-muscled horse and shouting a mighty huzza! as I give the natives the run. Yes, that would suit me grand.'

He leaned back in the rocking-chair and stretched his legs as he considered. 'India probably. They would probably choose India, being as far away as it is from Ireland. No bigoted yeomen in India, you know. Only dusky wenches who kneel at a man's feet in total obedience.' He sighed gustily. 'Who could refuse it? Good horses, assured victories, and dusky wenches . . .'

'God and Mary!' Cullen gulped at his whiskey. 'Is this what it's all led to? You running cat-tail after General Moore in the hope of riding good horses and dirty wenches? Shame on you, Michael of my own Imaal. The county of Wicklow has spawned a turncoat.'

'But listen, John, don't be hasty in condemning me till I tell you this.' Michael leaned towards Cullen with deep seriousness. 'General Moore has agreed that you can come with me. As my manservant. To carry my sword and such. 'Tis unheard of for a man wearing the royal colours to move around India without his servant at his heels.' He sniffed blithely. 'And you know exactly how I like my whiskey. No water.'

'You gout!' Cullen screamed. 'You blister on a pig's arse!'

'I know an old boar who'd agree with you there!' Michael threw back his head and laughed, but Cullen was so upset he jumped up and made to run into the bedroom, tripped in the darkness and fell on his hands and knees.

'Sure I'm only jesting,' Michael said, lifting him to his feet.

'And you think it's funny?' Cullen cried. 'Upsetting me like that and making me fall over?'

'I won't do it again,' Michael said in a humble tone. 'I'd be too frightened of that wild temper of yours.'

'Stop your grinning!' Cullen shouted. 'You're a desperate lad altogether, jesting like that. You don't give a thraneen for the feelings of others; troth, you don't.' He sat down again and lifted his cup. 'Did they really suggest that you join the army?'

'Aye, they did.'

Cullen moved his head from side to side. 'For a while there I thought you were serious about turning your coat in India.'

They sat for a while in silence, then Cullen asked. 'Are you going to see Holt? Where is he?'

'Somewhere in Glendalough. Shortly after we reached Lugnaquilla he drew off with some of the men and formed his own camp on the other side, then moved off altogether.'

'Why was that?'

Michael shrugged. 'Holt is a general. He didn't want to share command with any of the United captains. He went in search of another roost.'

'Will you do as they asked, persuade him to surrender?'

'Indeed I won't.' Michael began to scratch his chest uncomfortably. 'What Holt does is his business, not mine.'

'What ails you?' Cullen demanded. 'Scratching like that?'

'The lucra dhu,' Michael said. 'I had a swim tonight and while I was getting dressed one of them came on me.'

'By the hokey – did it go near your throat?'

'No, I sent it running. But I can still feel its touch on me.' Lucra dhus were small black-bellied green lizards of four inches long occasionally found in the rushes near water. Michael shivered at the memory. 'Can I go to bed?' he asked.

'Rub some salt on your chest first,' Cullen advised. 'To take the evil influence of the lucra dhu away.'

Michael was almost as superstitious as Cullen and did as he was bid. Salt was powerful at warding off evil. A flick of it over your left shoulder every day kept bad luck away. Even the Protestant clergy who went to a house to exorcise evil spirits brought their little bit of salt along.

'Isn't that why the militia took most of it out the storehouses,' Cullen said, wrapping up his bag of salt again, 'to make sure we would lose our rebellion!'

In the bedroom, Cullen lit a rush candle and placed it on the floor before the fireplace. He knelt down, and with surprising strength, pushed back a large slab of stone. 'Take the candle,' he said. 'I've put a fresh mat of straw on the floor and two good heavy blankets for under and over.'

Michael nodded and lifted the candle, then stooped down and walked through the fireplace and along a narrow passage into a small cavern inside the mountain which had its own natural airlets.

When he was through, Cullen shifted the stone slab back into place, then returned to the living-room, chuckling to himself as he lay back down in the settle-bed.

'Galloping horses, servants, and dirty wenches! Troth, but he's a card and no mistake.'

General John Moore could no longer fight it. He knew he was ill and allowed his batman to help him on to his bed.

' 'Tis the weakening fever you have, General,' his young attendant cried anxiously. 'And sure I know what done it. The exertion and fatigue and lack of sleep you suffered in Wexford in the fierce heat, then being caught in that downpour the morning you rode out to check the camp. It's the weakening fever, true enough. Indeed it is! No mortal could push himself as you did and remain strong.' He poured a large glass of whiskey. 'Here, General, drink this down and it will help you to sleep.'

But General Moore was already asleep, despite the tremors of his body and the perspiration streaming down his face.

Prendergast tucked the rug around him, then pushed back the fair hair and placed a palm on his superior's brow.

'God,' he whispered, 'he's boiling like a kettle!' Then ran out into the night in search of Lord Huntly and a doctor.

The illness confined General Moore to his tent for five days, after which time a coach and four was sent to him by Lord Cornwallis, ordering him to return to Dublin where he could be attended by the Viceroy's personal physician, and where he could avail himself of a week's comfortable respite from duty at the Viceregal Lodge in Phoenix Park.

General Moore prepared to write a letter of refusal. He had fought off the fever and felt able to cope again, if still a little weak and shaky in the legs. There was nothing he would like more than a few days of luxurious living in Dublin – to sleep in a decent bed in a comfortable room – instead of on a straw truss in a cheerless military tent. But it would be wrong to take advantage of his friendship with Cornwallis and leave his post, albeit in the care of the very able Lord Huntly.

He was halfway through the letter of gracious refusal, when his friend and brigade-major entered the tent.

'Are you going to Dublin?' Anderson asked.

'No.'

'Pity.'

Anderson held up a letter which had also arrived with the coach and four. He looked sadly at General Moore. 'It's good-bye then, my friend. The powers that be think I deserve a change. I am being posted home, to Bristol.'

General Moore didn't know whether to laugh or cry; to congratulate or complain. They had fought many campaigns together, all over the world. Now he was to be left in the terrible confusion that was Ireland, without his most loyal and steadfast friend, Anderson. However, both men knew that orders were not to be argued with, but obeyed.

'I shall miss you, need I say.'

'Perhaps we will join up together again soon,' Anderson said. 'The business in Ireland is more or less finished.'

'When do you leave?'

'Today. I am instructed to journey in the coach with you to Dublin. Collect my papers from General Cornwallis, then, after four days' leave in the fair city, take the packet boat to Holyhead on the seventeenth.'

'Four days leave – in Dublin?'

'Not that I know anyone there at all,' Anderson said dismally. 'I could go to the theatre, perhaps. Maybe even catch the eye of an actress or two. They say the Dublin doxies dislike the scarlet uniform so much they can't wait to tear it off the man wearing it.'

He smiled weakly, but General Moore was gazing at the unfinished letter. Suddenly he rose to his feet, dizzy for a second or two, then lifted the flap and beckoned to his batman, who was busy polishing his saddle. 'A word with you, young fellow.'

Prendergast came at the double. 'Yes, General.'

'How do I look, Prendergast?'

'Shall I bring you a mirror, sir?'

'Just tell me, Prendergast, how do I look?'

'Oh, fine and splendid, sir! As grand and well again as ever. Indeed and indeed you do!'

'Is that the truth?'

'The truth? Why no, General. If it is the truth you want, then you look as weak and pale as a man just had the fever.'

'Then pack my bag, boy. Lord Cornwallis insists on my having a week's leave in Dublin. Major Anderson and myself will be leaving in the coach within the hour.'

He turned back into the tent and smiled at Anderson. 'They'd never tear the uniform off a general, would they?'

'Maybe not. But I have heard of one or two gallant generals who very kindly spared them the exertion.'

Anderson grinned.

Chapter Twelve

It happened over a period of five days. Five days when former insurgents who had been given Protection Certificates by General Moore were dragged out of their homes, brought to the militia barracks in their districts, given a five-minute drumtrial, then executed. The militia and yeomanry forces blitzed through Wicklow on a burning campaign that left the inhabitants reeling.

Knots of young men clambered up the ravines like scurrying ants and flocked into the camp of Lugnaquilla, scarcely able to talk from the fatigue of their frantic climb.

'Captain! Captain!' A man ran across the camp to Michael. ' 'Tis young Kavanagh! They've hanged him at Baltinglass and have his head stuck on a spike outside the barracks as a warning and example.'

'Thomas Kavanagh?'

'Aye. Him and two others. Three of them at once – hanged and spiked! 'Tis a shocking sight.'

Michael stared at the man in horrified shock. Thomas Kavanagh was one of the finest young men he had ever known. Like himself, Kavanagh had fought in the rebellion not for any great revolutionary ideal, but simply to win the basic rights due to all men, whatever their nationality and creed. He had longed to return home to be with his young bride, and for that reason he had surrendered and vowed to live in obedience, in exchange for a Protection Certificate. Now he was dead.

The newcomers to the camp had formed a ring around him; and all seemed to be shouting at him at once.

'We trusted them and their Protection Certificates and look what we got for our trust!'

'There's murder and rape going on down there, Captain. Worse than ever before. Any woman found wearing a green skirt or dress is having it ripped off her back on the road. Men are being flogged and half-hanged.'

'General Moore may do and say what he likes, but the militia and yeomanry forces are cursing him to Hades with all the venom of savage devils!'

'They despise him for putting the reward out on Fenton. They're calling him a traitor!'

'And they say Huntly is the biggest gobshite to come out of Scotland since Abercromby!'

It went on until Hugh Vesty, Martin Burke, and John Mernagh broke through the group and ordered them to silence. 'Let there be no more screaming like banshees,' Hugh Vesty ordered.

'Easy for you to talk, Hugh Vesty,' a voice said. 'You haven't seen what we've seen. And why won't the captain give us a word of opinion?'

Hugh Vesty picked out the lad who had spoken and pointed a finger at him sternly. 'None of your impertinence, O'Mara.'

'You'll let me speak, brother,' a gruff, rumbling voice from the back of the group said. Immediately the refugees broke asunder to let the man through. 'You'll let me speak, brother, for, comical as it may appear, I have been chosen to speak on behalf of the people.'

'Ah, Kenny!' Hugh Vesty cried in embarrassment. 'It's damn low for anyone to send you climbing all the way up here.'

'I offered and I was chosen,' Tom Kenny said with dignity. He was a man of twenty-eight and his appearance somewhat grotesque, yet only a few months ago he had been a handsome fellow – until the militia got him.

Kenny had never been a rebel, but shortly before the rebellion the militia had charged a friend of Kenny's with being a United Irishman and, after burning down his house, went in pursuit of the rebel, who had fled to a cave near Kenny's house with his pregnant wife. Their daughter Peggy was born prematurely that night but survived, and it had become known as 'Peggy's Cave' ever since. A few days after Peggy's birth, Kenny was on his way to the cave with food for the fugitives when the militia suddenly appeared on the road. Some cows were grazing near by and all Kenny could do was pretend to be in the act of milking them – a thing he had neither clue nor practice at, for milking was women's work. The militia jeered him heartily, then strung him up on a nearby tree. He had hung there for hours until he was discovered and cut down. He had survived, but was left with a damaged voice-box and a severely crooked neck he could not straighten.

'Speak on, brother,' Hugh Vesty said gently.

'It's little enough I have to say,' Kenny rumbled, 'and it's to the captain I'll say it, and it's this. There is no longer any law in Wicklow but militia law. And we are not prepared to take any more of that. No matter what Cornwallis says, no matter what the British general says, we know our only hope of real protection in the face of murder, rape, and torture, is from the boys on the mountains. You Wicklow boys went to Vinegar Hill and fought for Ireland. Now we ask you to fight for the people of Wicklow. We have lost faith, lost confidence in all but you. We consider you to be our sole defenders, and now we look to you for help.'

Everyone looked at the captain, who stood with arms folded, calm and motionless. Kenny's words appeared to have induced no emotion in him at all.

'Well, brother?' Kenny moved forward and looked up into Michael's face from his twisted angle. 'Are you going to stand by while your people suffer, while three of your comrades are mutilated in Baltinglass?'

Michael turned away and walked slowly over to a crag from which he could look out far across Wicklow. In the direction of Rathdrum, cottages were burning at irregular intervals for as far as the eye could see. How easy it was to fire a peasant's home, crowned as it was by golden thatch. His eyes misted as his gaze flickered on the red beacons of flame lashing their straggly tongues up to the blue sky.

Then his eyes cleared and he turned and walked back to the men who had returned to the camp for protection and sanctuary. 'When you surrendered,' he said quietly, 'it was not to a militia tyrant, but to an honourable man – General John Moore. You gave him your signature and swore the Oath of Allegiance before him. 'Tis on your own heads if you break it.'

The militia were in Donard, ten of them, lounging outside the tavern, laughing as they held their tankards and watched the screaming blacksmith down on his knees in the centre of the little square, being prepared for the boiling pitchcap.

'You should do his whiskers first,' laughed one. 'Scald them off first will you, George, and give us a peep at the man hiding underneath.'

'Holy Mother save me!' Finbar O'Casey screamed, eyes shut tight. 'O God protect me! Our Father who art in—'

'How goes the pitching, boys?' a voice drawled.

The grip on the blacksmith's collar loosened and he opened his eyes to see the solitary figure of Michael Dwyer at the end of the small square, leaning against the wall of the corner house. He was wearing his bottle-green riding cloak with black-edged shoulder cape, his black slouch hat set at a jaunty angle as he observed the blacksmith's plight with an unconcerned eye.

Every soldier jerked alert, hand on musket straps, but the solitary figure seemed content just to lounge and watch, as cool as the breeze that blew the steam from the boiling bucket of pitch in his direction.

'Michael!' the blacksmith screamed hysterically, his face suffused with blood, eyes bulging. 'They're going to pitch me!'

Michael looked at him, unmoved. 'You should keep better company, Finbar,' he warned. 'When it comes to violence, these boys are the masters.' He slanted a smile at the militia. 'Is that not right, avics?'

'Are you alone, Dwyer?' shouted the militia captain.

Michael shrugged. 'I'm as you see me.'

'Then step forward, Dwyer, and produce your Protection.'

'My Protection?'

'Do you have one?'

'Aye, I do,' Michael said. 'And here it is, avic.' From the folds of his cloak he snapped up a musket and fired.

The blacksmith was flung on his face. The saliva dribbled like a stream from his mouth as he clutched his hands over his head and lay in a quivering lump while more men ran into the square and chaos erupted around him: gunfire, cross-fire, shouts; then more running feet, running away.

Not daring to raise his head, the blacksmith opened his eyes and scanned the ground around him: three men lay dead, all militia. He snapped his eyes shut when a red uniform fell down on the ground before him.

'Don't kill me! I took no part. Only drinking.'

'Why did you have to spike them? Kavanagh and the two others! Was it not enough to hang them. *You savages!*'

'That wasn't us! That was Baltinglass! It's only the ones at Baltinglass.'

The blacksmith peeped open an eye, quivering as he watched Michael Dwyer down on one knee, a hand clutched to the militiaman's throat.

'Only Baltinglass my eye! Cottages are burning from Rathdrum to Aughavannagh. Men with Protections are being shot from Roundwood to Coolamaddra – and Donard was about to have a pitchcapping. And you lot are supposed to be the upright lords of the law!'

'Let me go! Please! I took no part.'

'I'll let you go all right, but only so you can tell Fenton, Case, and every other yeo and militiaman that I got their message. And you can oblige me by taking one back.'

'I'll take it. Let go my neck. The message, I'll take it. What is it?'

'Those three lying over there are for the three on spikes in Baltinglass. And from now on, it will be one apiece for every man after that. Same goes for the burned houses. The war's back on and your lot fired it. In Wicklow anyhow.'

'I'll tell them, I'll tell them!'

'And you'll tell them something else, bucko. Any yeoman or militiaman that hurts my family in any way, or attempts to arrest my daddy on some buckshee charge, will have to keep looking over their shoulders from that moment on, because I'll be coming for them – and as sure as the dawn I'll get them! And you tell them so, straight and true. Now on your feet!'

When the feet of the militiaman had sent up the dust, the blacksmith still did not stir. Not even when Michael gave him the toe of his own boot and told him to rise.

'Is it asleep you are?'

' 'Tis dead I am,' the blacksmith whined. 'Brutally murdered.'

'By the hokey,' Michael said in amazement, 'I never saw a dead man shiver like that.'

'I'm murdered, I tell ye,' the blacksmith wailed. 'I'll never be able to stir again. The shock my heart got was too much. Just leave me here to expire in peace.' He stretched out his arms and lay flat. 'Go tell the people, Michael. Tell them how I was brutally treated at the hands of the red overlords. Tell them how I was left on the threshold of eternity.'

'If you insist, but they're all in hiding at the minute by the looks of things.'

' 'Twas the militia made them run, but they'll be out soon enough. Go call them, Michael. Tell them how dead and dying I am.'

Michael strode over to the tavern where the keeper, his hands still shaking with fright, was handing out tankards of ale to Hugh Vesty and the others.

'Poor old Finbar!' the keeper said, looking over at the black-smith. 'He was the first one to run and the first one they caught. But he'll have to get up from there. He's blocking the square entirely.'

'He is,' agreed Hugh Vesty. 'There's not much of him in height, but widthways you could cross the Slaney on him.'

Michael conversed in low tones with the men, then walked back to the prostrate blacksmith and contemplated him calmly.

'Are you dead yet?' he asked.

'As good as dead, avic,' the blacksmith whispered.

Michael sighed wearily. 'Troth, even the actor-boys on the Dublin stage don't take this long to die. Is it a medal or a ballad you're after or what?'

'I'm murdered, avic,' the blacksmith whispered hoarsely. 'Murdered in my prime. Murdered, murdered, murdered . . .'

His eyes slowly closed, his mouth fell slack, the rise and fall of his breathing stilled.

Michael looked at him silently for a long moment, then called over to the tavern. 'Hugh, Sam, Miles, find some spades as quick as you can, while I lift this poor old hero into the fields.'

Up shot the blacksmith's head. 'What are you going to do?'

'Bury you,' Michael told him gently. 'Isn't it murdered you are? And what else can we do with a dead man but bury him.'

'Devil roast you, Dwyer!' The blacksmith scrambled to his feet. 'Is that any way to talk to a man who's suffered as I have! A poor martyr near pitchcapped and dead!'

'Well damn my eyes,' Michael drawled. 'Is it Lazarus or the blacksmith himself?'

' 'Tis the mortal hard man ye are, Michael Dwyer, mortal hard.'

'Hard times make hard men,' Michael informed him.

'My God,' the blacksmith whined, 'but this is a hard life!' He stared at the still steaming bucket of pitch and began to shiver again. 'Oh, thank God you came when you did, Michael. 'Tis my life you saved, quick enough.'

'Pity I did,' Michael answered. 'If you'd been dead I could have just taken your horse in payment for burying you. Now I will have to plead for the loan of it.'

'My horse? What do you want to do with my horse?'

'Ride it, you fool.'

The blacksmith looked down again at the bucket of steaming

pitch. Tears suddenly moistened his marble eyes and ran down his face. He felt overcome by a genuine and terrible pity, not only for himself but for all people who suffered and lived in fear.

Slowly he lifted his eyes from the bucket of pitch and looked at Michael in the way he would to a woman with whom he had suddenly fallen in love.

'You can take the horse and keep it as your own, Michael. You may have shown me no pity but you saved my life, and I'll not forget that in a hurry. Now tell me, is it to war you're going?'

'No,' Michael replied. 'Rathdrum.'

Inside Dublin Castle, General John Moore faced Lord Cornwallis with his typical outer calmness, but his eyes were livid.

'According to my officers, the militia ran riot. In the past week, throughout the county of Wicklow men have been taken to trial on the flimsiest evidence and executed in the most barbarous manner. Hundreds have been clamped in gaol, and others have been forced to quit their homes again and take to the mountains. It is proving simply impossible for His Majesty's officers to check the violence and atrocity of the militia who are still shooting men after seeing their Protections.'

The Viceroy drummed his fingers irritably on the desk. 'Such a cursed country this is,' he said, 'but I believe the word of your officers. I have a report here from John Blanchford, son-in-law to the statesman Henry Grattan.' Cornwallis put on his spectacles and lifted the letter.

'He says he rode out from where he was stationed towards the village of Roundwood, and saw in all directions the houses of the peasantry burning. Not a human being was to be seen for a circuit of eight miles. He found some farmers shot and asked the yeomen present why they had been killed. They could give no reason, other than that they had set their houses on fire and shot them as they ran away.'

General Moore sighed in a kind of fury.

'Blanchford,' Lord Cornwallis continued, 'also says he drew the attention of his superior officers to instances of rape and murder in the militia corps, but was told that "it would be dangerous to punish the militia".'

The Viceroy threw down the letter, his lips back on his teeth.

'But as long as I hold military and civil control of this bogland – every officer, every private, every yeoman, every member of the militia, and every civilian, will answer to me.'

He looked steadily at General Moore. 'You had better return to Wicklow at once.'

An order was issued immediately by the Viceroy, preventing any court martial carrying out sentence until the evidence had been reviewed by himself or a general. The country magistrates and the militia were incensed.

Lord Cornwallis granted an audience to a yeomanry officer named Murray from Rathdrum whose fury was naked.

'Five days ago, your Excellency, they came to within one mile of Rathdrum and burned a number of yeomen's houses betwixt there and the mountains – commanded by one Michael Dwyer. The poor yeomen were ordered outside at gunpoint and made to stand and watch their homes going up in flames. And now to add insult to injury, some of the general officers have actually refused to assist us with troops to prevent these reprisals.'

'I have the report of those officers,' Lord Cornwallis said coldly. 'They insist that such outrages are caused by the continual burning of peasant houses by the militia and country gentlemen of rank.'

'The peasants must be kept in their place, your Excellency.'

'And where do you consider their place should be, if they are continually burned out of their homes? In the fields? Or is the truth that you wish to drive them even beyond the fields, possibly off the earth altogether?'

'They are little more than savages, your Excellency, with their pagan customs and idolatry of the soil. I've seen grown men kissing the earth and crying like babies after a good harvest. They are not civilised! They must be kept in their place! General Lake, at least, agrees with us there.'

Lord Cornwallis turned puce, his eyes glittered. '*I* am now commander in chief of the army in Ireland,' he stormed. 'Not General Lake!'

The yeoman looked startled, but stood his ground. 'What is to be done about Michael Dwyer?' he asked.

'Michael Dwyer?'

'Yes, Michael Dwyer – one of General Moore's pets. And if I may be allowed to say so, your Excellency, it is General

Moore, along with some more of our generals, who are contributing to the ruin of this once happy country.'

'No, sir!' Cornwallis exploded. 'You may *not* be allowed to say so!'

Michael was sitting on a lonely part of the Lugnaquilla, away from the rest of the men, idly smoking a long-pipe and watching a falcon gliding easily as it marked its prey down below. Michael narrowed his eyes as he waited for the handsome-winged bird to swoop and make his attack, wondering if it were a fieldmouse, a bird, or a small rabbit he was marking.

His concentration was broken by a young man named Michael Kearns, who came over to him in great haste, clutching a paper. 'They're everywhere, Captain. By all accounts, in every town and village. I found this one stuck on a hedge below on my return from Aughavannagh.'

Michael's face was expressionless as he read the latest government proclamation which was brief and to the point:

MICHAEL DWYER, a Captain of the outstanding Rebels still in Arms in the Mountains of Wicklow. About twenty-five years and five feet eleven inches high, square shoulders, broad-breasted, rather long-legged, black hair, black eyes. Born in Imaal. Five Hundred guineas for taking him.

'Must have have been the militia who described you so thoroughly,' Kearns said. 'Anywise, only a militiaman would say your eyes were black.'

Michael's long-pipe had gone out. He took out his flint and steel, and when the pipe was relit he resumed his observation of the falcon. It was now hanging motionless and, although Michael knew the bird could stay suspended like that for a long time, he felt positive it was getting ready to make a thrust.

Kearns stood gaping at him. He had been to Vinegar Hill and back with Michael Dwyer, and his courage and superb coolness in the face of danger were amazing. But this was different, this was not a fight of army against army, this was the government and its army against one man. And now that there was a rich reward to be had as well as rabid revenge, the militia would not rest until they got him.

Seeing Dwyer still engrossed in his study of the falcon,

Kearns moved away to take the news to the rest of the men.

'Is it true?' Hugh Vesty shouted, rushing towards Michael. '*Five hundred guineas!* Man, every bounty hunter in Leinster will be after you at that price.'

'Well damn you to hell!' Michael cried angrily. 'Look at him go! And I missed the swoop with you warbling like that.'

Incredulous, Hugh Vesty stared down at him. 'If you could just look at yourself, man, sitting there watching birds and calmly smoking. Don't you know what this means, Michael? It means that you are now a government certified outlaw!'

'What law?'

'Five hundred guineas! God, but you'll be famous.' Hugh sat down beside him. 'Where's the proclamation? The only other I ever saw like that was the one for Lord Edward Fitzgerald. Give us a look at it. Don't be shy now. Let me see.'

'I can't,' Michael murmured. 'I lit my pipe with it.'

The following day Michael was on the point of dropping down from the steep curved path that led to John Cullen's cottage when he saw her. She was some little way from the side of the house, not the side that led down to the Lech River, but the side that sat betwixt the shade of Lugnaquilla and Table Mountain. She was gathering fraughans, a small black fruit which grew in elevated places, and dropping them into a basket.

He caught his breath, then stepped back swiftly under cover of a huge whitethorn bush and crouched down, moving on to his stomach and sliding under the bush, folding his arms under his face as he watched her.

There was a pensiveness about her as she picked the fruit. Now and then her long black hair fell over her face and she shook it back with a swing of her head, pausing to gaze searchingly in the direction of Lugnaquilla. Just the sight of her made him feel weak. He had never had a feeling for any girl like he had for her. He watched her with a sense of wonder, the wonder of her gentle dark beauty which always made him catch his breath on seeing her again, and the wonder why she had still come, despite the proclamation.

Time drifted by: the line of fruit in the basket was getting higher. She knelt back and gazed long at the high mountain ridges above him, then her shoulders slumped and she bowed her head, staring at the ground near her knees. She stayed that way for a long time, then suddenly she hunched her body forward, clutching her hands round her waist, shoulders shaking; and he knew she was crying. He closed his eyes, drawing on all his will-power and cold discipline to stop himself from going down to her.

Old man Cullen came out of the barn at the side of house and walked up to her, stooping to catch her elbow and urge her to her feet. She had her back to the ridge as they stood talking together, Cullen was rubbing his chin and shaking his head in puzzlement. Then she moved and he knew she was leaving to go back to Knockandarragh.

He watched her sadly, as Cullen did, slowly walking towards the low stone wall. There she turned and looked back, a breeze blowing in her hair as she raised her hand in farewell to the old man. Michael tried to quell the flood of emotion that was rising in him. He should never have come. *She* should never have come. He had been convinced she wouldn't, and only came to prove it to himself. But there she had been – young and tense and as lovely as a new flower – waiting for a lover who did not have the heart to face her.

When she was out of sight, he slid sideways and pushed himself to his feet, dropping down from the ridge on to the path and startling the old man whose head jutted round as he approached.

'Ah, musha, she's gone,' Cullen said. 'You've just missed her.'

Michael nodded.

'She waited nigh on three hours. Just like the last time.'

'It was impossible to come the last time.'

'She was crying.'

'Aye, I know.'

Cullen turned his body fully towards him, his blue eyes moving up to the ridge above the path, finally pausing on the whitethorn bush. He drew in his breath and looked coldly at Michael as realisation dawned.

'How long were you up there?'

'I don't rightly know. A long time. Since the first few layers of fraughan.' They both glanced down at the basket of black fruit almost full. After all that hard work occupying herself, she had left it behind.

'Well,' Cullen said, 'I may never have learned the knack of sweet-talking a woman, but, by God! I never learned how to be cruel to them either.'

He turned and walked vigorously towards the house. At the door he swung round and shouted, 'You don't give a thraneen for anyone's feelings, do you! Why did you do it? Stay up there all that time and not come down to her?'

Michael could not believe it. Cullen was seriously taking another person's side against him. Never had he done that. Not since as far back into childhood as he could remember.

Cullen walked back to him. 'Eh? Tell me why? A true and gentle girl like that being treated like a doxie!'

Michael stared at him, saying nothing, but the muscles of his face and throat were all in motion. And suddenly Cullen knew.

'Ah, treasure,' he whispered, 'curse me for a fool. Come inside, let you.'

Once inside the cottage, the old man poured two cups of whiskey in the same way a woman would pour the tea; as a booster. He took his seat to the right of the inglenook and sighed heavily.

'Aye, you're right, for sure,' he murmured. 'Mary is not the type for nudging and dallying, she's for marrying.' He leaned towards Michael. 'But would it not have been better to come down and tell her.'

'Five hundred guineas should tell her better,' Michael said quietly.

'It won't tell her that you love her, love her enough to lie staring at her for hours.'

'Ach!' Michael shrugged his embarrassment. 'It will tell her that I'm not going anywhere near a priest or a marriage bed.'

'It was not right to hurt her like that,' said the old man sternly. 'And you've hurt yourself just as bad. I can see it. You know the girl loves you true.'

'But where's the future in it?' Michael said. 'I've nothing to offer her. No home where I can live safely, no security of any kind – nothing but a pile of hills and mountains. And five hundred guineas says I won't have them for long.'

'Perhaps, perhaps.' Cullen took a long reflective pull on his drink, his eyes shrewd. 'But what do *you* say, Michael of my own Imaal?'

Michael turned his head and looked at him, a slow smile breaking quietly over his face. 'I say they'll never catch me in twenty years.'

His words were put to the test less than an hour later, as he made his way back to camp along the hills near the Black Banks leading to the Lugnaquilla. About to turn off round a high rock, he saw a large party of militia heading towards him and only had time to step back behind the rock and press himself into the cleft, pistol in hand, while the soldiers passed by within four yards of him.

Face turned sideways, he watched the marching column continue on in the direction of Stranahely, then tucked the pistol back in his belt and strolled away in the opposite direction.

Chapter Thirteen

When he first heard the news, Michael Dwyer smiled. A distant smile that had little trace of humour. In truth he found it hard to believe, even if men *were* riding as fast as the wind from the province of Connaught carrying the same news to an astonished Dublin.

A week previously, on 22nd August, the French had landed in the west. Three frigates. A small force. Only one thousand men, but all trained soldiers of the French republic – the Great Nation, as they called it. A second expedition was following from Brest, commanded by Theobald Wolfe Tone, the founder of the United Irishmen, who had gone to France in the hope of persuading Napoleon to send help to Ireland. But only General Humbert had arrived so far, and the Green Flag was flying in Killala.

'Too late,' Michael said to his comrades. 'The French have come three months and a red bloody rebellion too late.'

But every person in Wicklow was on the alert. Even as they worked in the fields in preparation for the harvest, they thought and spoke of nothing else save what was happening up in Mayo.

The first news they heard was that the French had been successful at Ballina, where the militia were routed speedily. On marching into the town General Humbert was appalled to find the dead body of a young peasant lad strung up on the door of his house.

'Who did this?' the Frenchman asked.

'The militia did it,' answered voices in the crowd that had come to gape in awe at the French soldiers. 'The militia did it before ye came.'

Humbert stood before the corpse for some minutes, then stepped forward and kissed the dead youth's face. 'See, people of Irlande,' he said, turning, 'see how we honour your dead.'

Humbert marched his army, which had now been joined by

every Irish farm boy in Mayo, on to Castlebar, the county town of Mayo; where General Lake and a force of his men were waiting for them. Cannons were in position, musketeers ready, and all watched the road from Ballina. But General Humbert was too experienced a soldier for that. He made his approach to Castlebar by way of the mountains to employ the element of surprise.

As soon as the French troops appeared over the ridges the cannons fired wildly. The French and Irish made their charge down from two sides, then along the sheltering ditches and charged the enemy guns at bayonet point.

The people of Castlebar, watching from their windows, stared in stunned amazement as the redcoats turned and ran, leaving their cannons, muskets, and reputations behind them. So complete was their panic at their first close sight of French soldiers, that they fled down the narrow streets of the town and out to the country with the French and Irish racing after them. Even General Lake was forced to leave his bags behind and take to his heels. Within days a song commemorating the most disgraceful defeat in British military history was penned entitled 'The Races of Castlebar'.

'And who won the Races of Castlebar?' rebels in Wicklow would shout.

'General Lake!' came the laughing reply. 'He did sixty-three miles in seven hours! Now there's a two-legged racing champion that would put many a four-legged thoroughbred to shame.'

Michael peered through his spy-glass. The military tents of the 100th and 60th regiments had gone. Camp abandoned. General John Moore had left Imaal.

Lord Cornwallis had also left Dublin Castle, for the midlands, taking General Moore with him – the big guns were rolling out to meet the Frenchman and stop him reaching the capital province of Leinster. Every garrison had been stripped to the bare essentials, leaving only a thousand infantry in Dublin. Law and order would be maintained by the shooting-and-burning militia corps, some thirty to forty thousand strong.

Inwardly and outwardly Cornwallis fumed at Lake's defeat at Castlebar. All reports blamed the Longford and Kilkenny militia regiments, who, under a very trifling fire, had given way and fled – then the rest had followed their example. The flight of the British army was total and disgraceful, and all their cannons and ammunition had fallen into the hands of the enemy.

When his carriage reached Athlone, Lord Cornwallis received a report that the French had advanced to Hollymount, and had again beaten General Lake.

He hobbled into General Moore's tent, a cloth shoe on his bandaged foot which was swollen with gout, making it impossible for him to ride a horse efficiently.

General John Moore stood tall and strong, his blue eyes intense with the anticipation of battle. French soldiers! They would not make him run!

'I want you to be my advance guard,' Cornwallis told him. 'And you will report only to me.'

Moore smiled. 'Yes, my lord.'

'It would appear that the Frenchman is aiming for the Shannon,' Cornwallis murmured thoughtfully, 'then through the midland counties, then on to his main target – Dublin.'

'If he makes it to the capital,' Moore said, 'Ireland is lost.'

'But the impudent bastard won't make it to Dublin, will he, Moore?'

'No, my lord.'

'And we shall give those interfering Froggies a ruddy good drubbing to remember, eh Moore?'

Again General Moore smiled. 'Yes, my lord.'

'Splendid!' Cornwallis cried, his humour brightening. 'I'm glad to see I have at least one good commander I can rely on.'

As always when a battle was imminent, General Moore slept that night fully clothed and ready, pulling off his boots only. At dawn the following morning he mounted his charger in preparation for the march.

Behind him he had the first and second flank battalions of the 100th Regiment, flank companies of the Warwick and Bucks, the Roxburgh Fencibles, and a detachment of the Hompesch. The 2nd and 29th Regiments were following from Wexford.

General Moore sat astride his charger with his right hand held high, then looking over his scarlet shoulder at the men, gave a grim smile as the drums rolled and brought his arm forward to signal the martial march of the Advance Corps.

French soldiers! They would not make him run!

*　　*　　*

When it came to military strategy, Lord Cornwallis was as good a tactician as Humbert. He ordered General Lake's army, and Major Crauford's cavalry, to head north on the coast roads, then double back inland to catch the Frenchman at the rear. Which they swiftly did. And now Lake and Crauford were as close as a donkey's tail to the Frenchman and his army, and Cornwallis's army was advancing towards him. Just outside Granard, at a place called Ballinamuck, General Humbert found his road blocked, front and back.

It truly had been a glorious Irish summer – weatherwise. A golden summer producing one of the richest harvests of the century. And even now the September night was sweetly warm, the dark sky smothered with a myriad of silver stars that sparkled like diamonds.

Michael and Hugh Vesty had walked some long miles from their camp, pacing grimly over the silent hills and fields towards a small unlicensed shebeen in the remote area of Manger where they were greeted with surprise by some of the young men of the neighbourhood. Delighted at this visit from the most famous glensman in Wicklow, they competed for Michael's attention and endeavoured to drown him in mountain dew.

Inebriety had never been a weakness of either cousin, but tonight they didn't give a tinker's curse about anything. Grimly they drank glass after glass and said little as the locals gabbled; listened dourly as some relapsed into melancholy song; and sighed with relief when most had left for their beds.

Only two or three remained, seating themselves around the habitual fire and murmuring quietly amongst themselves as they threw covert glances at the two cousins. Ach, sure who could blame them looking so stretched? Defeat was a bitter taste to swallow.

The door flew open; two Highlanders marched into the shebeen.

Sudden fear and consternation showed on every man's face except the two rebels, who calmly eyed the soldiers. Their pistols lay under their hands on the table, loaded and cocked.

The locals sat in petrified silence, waiting for Dwyer to flick up his gun, but instead he simply smiled and said: 'What took you so long, avics?'

One of the Highlanders looked dourly at the keeper of the shebeen. 'Two more glasses and a bottle,' he said.

'Who's paying?' the keeper queried.

'I am,' Michael said.

'Then no charge.'

The keeper and the men around the fire watched in astonishment as the four men moved to a small table at the far end of the room, sat down and began conversing in low tones.

'Who did it?' Michael asked.

'Who d'ya think? General Lake.'

'It was definitely Lake himself who did the dirty work at Ballinamuck?'

'And Crauford. Lake can't take all the credit. Crauford's blade was dripping as freely as a hoore's favours.'

Michael's face was dark as he listened to the two Highlanders relate the final defeat of the French and Irish at a place in the midlands called Ballinamuck. A short burst of hard fighting for the reputation of the Great Nation of France had sufficed before Humbert placed his hat on his sword in surrender.

'And what about the Irish boys?' Michael said. 'They surrendered too, did they not?'

'They surrendered.'

'But unlike the French, they were all killed?'

'Most o' them. Poor stupid buggers. Cut down like pigs in a slaughter house. A filthy business.'

'Cut down like pigs in a slaughter house,' Michael said in a bitter tone, 'the brave lads from the West who wouldn't believe there had been a rebellion down in Leinster.'

'They fought gallantly.'

'Before or after they surrendered?'

'Before, o' course.'

'If they surrendered,' Hugh Vesty cried, 'why were they killed? The French surrendered but they weren't put to the sword! From what we hear they're being treated like lords in a Dublin hotel while they wait to be shipped back to France.'

The two Highlanders exchanged glances.

'The Irish were rebels in arms,' one said quietly. 'Not soldiers protected by the code of war. They were separated from the French prisoners. A great huddled mass staring in disbelief as the shouting cavalry charged towards them with sabres drawn.'

Michael could see it all, just as it had happened at Vinegar Hill. General Lake astride his horse, watching the spalpeens walk down in surrender, the hypnotic continuous roll of the

English drum. Lake's sword held to shoulder, sword raised, sword swiftly brought down to point at the ground. Shouts, screams, blood, death. Honourable surrender, dishonourable slaughter – his fist smashed down on the table. '*Bastard!*'

One of the Highlanders refilled his glass. 'Have a drink, laddie. Only thing to do about it now.'

'Were you part of it?' Michael asked. 'The slaughter of the Irish at Ballinamuck – your regiment?'

'Aye, against the French, swift enough, but what happened after – most of us ended up puking.'

'And Cornwallis?'

'No there. Moved off to Lord Longford's place at Castlepollard.'

'And General Moore?' Michael whispered. 'Did his regiment sharpen their swords on any prisoners?'

'Nae. Not Moore's style that. He was with Cornwallis over in Castlepollard. General Lake was commander in the field.'

'Where's General Moore now?'

'In Westmeath. Stationed there in case of further trouble.'

'What about the others? The prisoners who were not killed? You said most of them, not all of them.'

'Och! There was only a few left. Leaders. United Irishmen. They were sent to Dublin for trial. Some were sent back west to the Irish militia in Mayo. Others were just made to draw straws.'

'Straws?'

'Those who drew the short straws were hanged there and then.'

'Jesus!'

'That's it, man. No more. It's over. And we're off duty.'

Hugh Vesty called for another bottle.

'Who's paying?' asked the keeper.

'I am,' said one of the Highlanders. 'Only fitting to end our time here with a farewell stupor of Irish mountain dew.'

Michael raised a brow. 'You're leaving Ireland?'

'You're welcome to it. Scotland will seem like faeryland in comparison.'

'When do you go?'

'Tomorrow. Not soon enough. Just our regiment.'

The other Highlander smiled. 'Och! I canna wait!'

Michael lifted the bottle of poteen. 'You said it rightly at the beginning, avic – let's get totally and gloriously screwed!'

And they did. All four of them. The keeper stood with quizzical expression as he watched the two rebels and two Highlanders; opposing warriors, drinking like bosom chums. All sick to the teeth and seeking release in the careless pleasure of getting stupefied. But poteen was like white fire. It could make a man do anything, send him into a trance for days even. The Irish boys could take it, maybe; but could the Jocks?

The keeper folded his arms and watched.

Time moved on, conversation amiable. One of the Jocks started to grin and speak slyly, followed by an obscene roar of laughter from the other three. Ballinamuck was dead. They were conversing about more pleasant things.

It was after three in the morning when they finally raised their hands to the keeper in farewell. He was amazed they could still stand, let alone speak clearly. And blood and turkeys – the Jocks were holding their own as if they'd been weaned on the stuff!

At the door one of the Highlanders turned and stared at Dwyer, then with a swaying motion clutched his shoulders with both hands, whether in friendship or simply to support himself the keeper couldn't be sure.

'Here in Wicklow, Michael, and off duty, many a Hielander will turn a blind eye to ye. They don't like bein' back-up boys to the militia, and many like ye well, think you're a cunning bastard and a crack soldier.'

Michael drooled a grin and kissed him drunkenly on the cheek. The Highlander laughed and drunkenly kissed him back, then both doubled up with laughter.

'But I warn ye, Dwyer!' the Highlander levelled a thump at Michael's shoulder. 'On duty, with their regiments, the honourable regiments of the mighty Hielanders, they'll take you if they find you, and kill you if they have to.'

'More power to them,' Michael said carelessly. 'On duty and with my regiment, I'll kill them too if I have to.'

'Your regiment? Och, ye bluidy madman! The rebellion's finished.'

'For you, maybe. But here in Ireland's green valleys the song of resistance will still be sung. And let me tell you something – do you know why the Anglo gentry like to see you Highlanders come marching in here – do you know what they say about you Jocks? Shall I tell you? Because on my oath there's not a servant lad or kitchenmaid that's not heard them say it.'

190

The keeper stood sharply erect. The mood was grimming.

'Oh hold yer whisht there, laddie! We know right well what they say. They say we're the best bluidy soldiers in this shagging bogland of yours!'

'Aye, the best men for the job, that's what they say. Only they express it this way: It takes a Celtic savage to kill a Celtic savage – so bring in the Jocks!'

The silence was dark. The Highlander moved his lips to snarl an answer, then clammed them shut as the significance of the words sunk in.

'And you did them proud, didn't you? At Ballinamuck you did the job just how they like it – slaughter!'

'That were no' us! The slaughter! That were Lake and his boys!'

'Michael—!' Hugh Vesty had stood dumbstruck, but he came out of his shock and swiftly intervened.

'What the blazes are you playing at, Michael? If you felt like that why did you come here tonight? These boys have helped us in the past. Are taking a risk at this very minute by drinking with us – and you with five hundred guineas sitting on your black stupid head!'

Hugh looked at the grim faces of the two Highlanders and held up his palms. 'He doesn't mean it, lads. Not personally. Believe me. But deprived of Lake's neck to break, he's punching it out on you.'

The keeper narrowed his eyes nervously. The Highlander who had fallen foul of Dwyer's wrath sucked in a breath, and for a moment it looked as if he might unloose a few punches into Dwyer's gut, but instead he reeled over to the keeper.

'A drink?' he shouted. 'And none of your mountain dew either. Scotch!'

'Scotch?'

'Scotch, ye bastard! Scotch! The good stuff, ye bastard! Scotch from Scotland, ye bastard! Are ye bluidy deaf?'

In less then a minute the keeper was dusting down the only bottle of Scotch he possessed. Two quick slugs later and the Highlander swung round and shouted furiously: 'Well, ye bastards! Am I to drink alone?'

One by one the three men joined him and the relieved keeper set up more glasses which the Highlander slopped to the brims.

'I'm sorry,' Michael said, 'I shouldn't have gone for you like that, Neil . . . I'm sorry.'

191

Neil knew the apology had not come easy.

'Och, yer a bastard, Dwyer. Yer a papist pig and a soddin' rebel and a sarcastic bugger all rolled into one. Christ only knows why I like ye!'

'Because we're alike,' Michael supposed. 'You and me. Both lads from the glens.'

'Have another drink, ye bastard.'

Two more shots of the good stuff, and Hugh Vesty and the other Highlander were in earnest conversation about Scottish history while Michael and Neil slumped shoulder to shoulder on the edge of a table.

'My heart may belong to Scotland,' Neil said, 'but my body, mind, and soul belongs to the regiment. And ye know, Dwyer, that if I came face to face with ye on the battlefield, I'd not hesitate to ram a sword through yer belly or blow yer brains out.'

'Aye, it would be one or the other of us,' Michael agreed. 'Good thing you're going home tomorrow.'

'Aye, I forgot about that!' Neil brightened. 'Hame to Scotland! Let's celebrate – one last shot for the long road hame to Scotland!'

The Scotch was long gone. The dregs of a bottle of Irish was now drained in what the tavern keeper counted as the seventh last shot for the road. The one called Neil was stocious, slumped against Dwyer with a vacant grin on his face while Dwyer quietly sang him a lullaby.

> 'We'll sing a song, a soldier's song,
>   That will help us march to freedom.
> We'll fly our flag, our rebel flag.
>   That will—'

'Hold yer gab right there, laddie!' Neil cried indignantly. 'I'll no' listen to nae jaunty little song of insurrection! If ye want to sing, Dwyer, sing me a Scottish song!'

'I only know rebel songs,' Michael told him. 'Or love songs.'

'I want a Scottish song,' Neil cried. 'A Scottish love song.'

'Then go your own road, avic. Back to bonny Scotland. Because I'm looking for sleep now. But listen, if you ever come back to Ireland—'

'Christ, but I'll ne'er come back to this abattoir!'

'Nor I,' said Hugh Vesty's companion. 'I'd desert first!'

'Ah, don't be like that,' Hugh Vesty said cajolingly to him, then draping an arm around his shoulder, struck up a song which brought a yelp of delight from Neil.

'Oh there was a handsome Highland lad . . .'

The other three instantly fell in with a hand-clapping beat and Hugh grinned and started again.

> 'Oh there was a handsome Highland lad,
> Of the name of Bold Rabby Muldoon
> Came to Ireland with his regiment
> And lost his heart to a girl in Macroom
> A beautiful blue-eyed Irish lass
> She slayed him with her charms.
> And alone with her in the bending grass
> He lustily surrendered to her arms
> Saying what a . . .

. . . *'Fine girl you are!'* They all chorused.

The keeper stood at the door of the shebeen and took a last look at them, the Highlanders staggering in one direction, the rebels in the other.

'Stocious,' he muttered, 'the bloody four of them. Stocious!' He smiled as he turned indoors. It had been an interesting night though. And they had paid him for every drop. Fair play to them.

The night air and the poteen worked together like a boxer's south-cut to the jaw. The two rebels began to waver in their stride, eyes moving upwards and seeing stars, thousands of them.

'Isn't it the grand fine night,' Hugh Vesty said. 'All those stars.'

'It is,' Michael said. 'A night for angels on your pillow.'

'Angels on your pillow?' Hugh Vesty frowned. 'Who let them in? They've always been at your window before.'

'A figure of sp – speech,' Michael said.

'A figure and a face of an angel,' Hugh murmured, 'that's what my Sarah has. And grand it would be to have her on my pillow tonight.'

Michael smiled sidelong at him. 'What happened to the divine Dymphna and her rich dowry?'

'Devil take her rich dowry. 'Tis my poor Sarah I'll have, or nobody at all.'

They did not speak again as they walked in the lightening dawn, both becoming increasingly fogged with the effect of their potations. Hugh Vesty put a hand to the sandy curls drooping over his forehead.

'Listen, Captain,' he whispered, 'if 'tis all right with you, I think . . . I think I'll just drop under this cosy hedge and indulge myself in a short repose.'

Michael gave no answer and continued on alone, his eyes half closed, the effects of the poteen becoming more over-powering with every step. At Coolamaddra he wandered up to the house of a man named Brian Reilly; a United man who had two daughters. And one of them – the sexy one – was already feeding the hens in the front yard.

She was very pretty with rosy cheeks and chestnut hair which fell around her shoulders. She stared at him with sur-prised blue eyes as he slumped into a sitting position on the wall and stretched his legs.

'Why, Michael,' she said softly, 'what notion brings you here? Wandering alone as if every militiaman was at sea and not out searching for you.'

'Hospitality for a hunted man,' he said quietly. 'That's all I ask.'

She swayed up to him. 'What kind of hospitality, pray?'

He gave her a roguish smile. 'Safe harbour to drop my anchor and lie in port awhile.'

'Oh, the poetry!' she purred. 'Stop or you'll make me faint.'

' 'Tis me who's about to faint.'

'Oh, aren't you the cool one,' she accused with a frown. 'Turning up here after months without a glimpse of you.' She sat down on his knee and draped her arms around his shoul-ders. 'It's been a long while since I last saw you, sweetheart.'

'Where's your father?' he whispered.

'You haven't been dallying with some other maid, have you?'

'Where's your father?' he whispered again.

'Still abed.' A saucy smile came on her face. 'Why do you want to know?'

'I need his shelter, and some sleep.'

She giggled and poked him in the ribs. 'Stop acting like a tired old fogey and tell me all your newses. It's been a long time since I've seen you, darling. Where have you been?'

'I've no humour for talking,' he whispered. 'I think . . . I think I may be drunk. At the minute my mind is a fog of confusion.'

She laughed. 'Did you have that much? What was it, whiskey or mountain dew? Wait, let me guess.' She bent her lips to his.

They heard a man groan as they kissed. Brian Reilly stepped out to the yard, yawning and rubbing his eyes. The girl jumped away.

' 'Tis Michael Dwyer, Da,' she said quickly. 'He needs somewhere to sleep.'

'Come in then,' Brian Reilly called. 'What ails you, Michael, sitting there for all to see.'

Michael moved to rise, then sat down again and inhaled the air deeply into his lungs, his hands clutching the wall.

'He's a bity shaky in the legs, Da,' the girl said. 'Dewed as a bog.'

At Brian Reilly's boom of laughter, Michael winced painfully and put a hand to his head. He mumbled apologies as the older man came to assist him indoors. Reilly's elder daughter was kneeling at the hearth, pouring bubbling water into a teapot.

'Will you have some breakfast, Michael?' Reilly asked.

'Nay, just a bed, thanks.'

'Over here then.' Reilly led him into a room off the kitchen which contained two single beds.

'My daughters' beds. You have my permission to use either of them.'

Michael slanted a grin at Reilly. 'Decent man. I'll remember you said that.'

Reilly boomed another laugh and punched him in the arm as the girls tittered like birds. 'Ho, you rascal, I'll be changing my mind if you're not careful.'

But the punch had sent Michael slumping face down on to the nearest bed where he fell into an immediate deep sleep.

Reilly was up in the hills with his sheep, and the two girls sitting spinning in the kitchen when tramping footsteps were heard outside. The youngest girl rose and moved over to look through the window.

'Highlanders!' she whispered. 'A whole regiment of them. Two are coming up here!' The eldest girl sprang to her feet and poked her head inside the bedroom where Michael lay with his face pillowed on his arms in sleep. She hastened back to the spinning-wheel and hissed at the younger girl.

'Sit down and act natural.'

The Highlanders walked in without knocking. They eyed the two girls at their spinning, then glanced around the kitchen. One of them turned right and opened the door to Reilly's bedroom, leaving it open as he entered and began to search inside. The other walked over to the room where Michael lay. He had his hand on the knob when the younger girl jumped to her feet and checked him.

'Why soldier! Surely you don't intend to enter a female's beddaroom improperly dressed now?'

The Highlander, a handsome fair-haired young fellow, looked at her quizzically. 'How d'ya mean? Imprawperly draised?'

She leaned her back against the spinning-wheel, letting him see her figure to advantage as she smiled at him prettily.

'You've no breeches on.'

The Highlander glanced down at his kilt.

'And 'tis only a vagabone or a married man that enters a lady's beddaroom without his breeches on,' she told him in a voice as sweet as a lullaby.

The soldier eyed her speculatively, a hint of a smile on his lips.

'But now, if you were to exchange your kilt for the knee-breeches I'm sure I wouldn't mind marrying you myself,' she crooned. 'And even in breeches, couldn't you still show off those fine strong legs of yours?'

This brought the Highlander over to the spinning-wheel. 'And what's your name, bonny lass?'

'And here's another fine bouchal!' the older girl cried as the second Highlander stepped into the room. 'God, but the saints must be smiling down on this humble abode in Coolamaddra today!'

The Highlanders grinned and began to join in the badinage, their minds totally diverted from the object of their search as the girls flirted with them outrageously. It went on until the older girl moved to the open front door and drew their attention to a party of soldiers moving off in a hollow below the house.

'Lads, agrah,' she said, 'would that be your regiment moving away now?'

The two Highlanders moved to the door, then bade a hasty farewell. 'We'll be back,' they called cheerfully.

'Make sure you do!' the elder girl shouted, tossing her dark-red hair. She stood smiling as they hurried away, then turned back into the kitchen, face beaming. 'Oh, God!' she gasped, 'but wasn't that dark-haired one a beautiful specimen entirely.'

Her younger sister walked into their bedroom, peered through the open window at the back. 'Michael's gone,' she said when her sister entered.

'He was here when I looked in last. Only about ten minutes ago. Fast asleep and out to the world.'

'Well he's gone now.' The younger girl sulked. 'He's probably at the Little Slaney already, if the eye could just see him.'

Michael was almost at the Little Slaney River. For half a mile he had run like the wind along the hedges of the fields from Coolamaddra. He jumped over the stepping-stones of the shallow river, then raced on towards Camara. When he finally climbed the steep ravine and reached the camp on Lugnaquilla, the men sent up a wild cheer.

'We thought the militia had you,' Sam McAllister said in relief, but Hugh Vesty Byrne was livid.

'You deserting hound! You left me lying under a hedge while you sallied off somewhere. Where were you?'

Michael fell down on the heather. 'Sleeping,' he said.

'Under a hedge?'

'Nay, in a damsel's bedroom, on a soft bed.'

'Whose bed?' Hugh demanded with a frown. 'Whose soft bed were you in?'

Michael stretched his body and put his hands behind his head. 'The bed of one of Reilly's daughters. And let me tell you, Hugh . . .' he rolled his eyes, 'it was nothing short of bliss!'

'Oh, you lecherous varmint!' Hugh cried furiously. 'And there was me, cold and damp under a hedge and awakened by an ugly bullock snorting and sniffing and making me shift in a hurry.'

'But, Hugh, 'tis the charmed life I have,' Michael explained serenely. 'Seeing as I'm favoured by them that's in it.'

'Them that's in it? You mean . . . the lepos?'

The men were all laughing now. It was always amusing when the two cousins started riling each other.

'The leprechauns,' Michael confirmed. 'You see, it all started on the day they captured me near the Faery Rath when I was a wee childybawn—'

'Oh, someone shut him up!' Hugh wailed. ' 'Tis enough I've suffered with a fierce head from mountain dew and a sniffing bullock and a long run before climbing this monster. 'Tis not you and a damsel's soft bed I want to hear about, you deserting cur!'

Michael laughed. 'Ah, don't be like that, Hugh of the Clan of Feagh McHugh O'Byrne. Is it my fault if I descend from the great Sept of Duibhers – the finest warriors in Ireland whose sons became High Kings of Leinster. Ah yes, very fond of the Duibhers are them that's in it. And let's face it, avic, the lepos know their business – there is no comparison between a damsel's bed and a sniffing bullock.'

The raillery went on for some time, but later that night, around the fire in one of the mountain caves, Hugh Vesty insisted on apprising the men of the truth of the matter.

'Although the Duibhers date back to the highest and oldest lineage,' Hugh said, 'there is little record of them doing anything more than hunting, warring, and romping after women over the green meadow plains. One prince of Ossory was even known to have sired twenty sons, not to mention how many daughters!'

'Fair play to him,' said a voice. 'Was that before Patrick came and said only one woman from now on?'

'It was,' Hugh confirmed. 'Before Saint Patrick brought us Christianity.'

'Bad luck he ever found us then,' a voice said gloomily.

'But forgetting the Duibhers,' Hugh continued, 'the Clan of Feagh McHugh O'Byrne is remembered with great pride by all Leinster. Because it was the O'Byrnes who carried on mountain warfare and refused to submit to English rule. And it was during the reign of Elizabeth that the Gaelic lord Feagh McHugh O'Byrne won a crushing victory over the English at Glenmalure.'

Hugh raised his chin. 'And not only am I a Byrne on my father's side. My mother's maiden name was also Byrne.'

'Then so was Michael's,' said Sam McAllister. 'Your mother and his are sisters. So he can claim to be a descendant of the mighty O'Byrne clan of Wicklow too.'

'Maybe so.' Hugh sniffed. 'But in truth he's a Duibher out and out. Anyway, 'tis not the Duibhers but the Clan of the Gaelic lord Feagh McHugh O'Byrne that Ireland remembers with affection, especially since the incident which happened on Christmas Eve in the year of fifteen ninety-one.'

'Fifteen ninety-one?' Michael said, knowing the story well. 'Imagine that now. Only a mere two centuries ago. 'Twill be modern tales he'll be telling us soon.'

Undeterred, Hugh went on. 'It happened at the Glenreemore Brook in the King's River valley. The night was cold and bright with snow and the wind had teeth in it. And it was two of my own ancestors that found two small boys in the snow who, they later discovered, had escaped from imprisonment in Dublin Castle. One boy had frozen to death – he was Arthur, son of Shane O'Neill the Lion of Ulster, and him they buried there and then.

'The other boy was badly frost-bitten but still alive, just. And him they carried back to the Fananierin of Feagh McHugh O'Byrne in Glenmalure, where they nursed and fed him, and even trained him how to hunt before a party took him home to his own people in the north. And that boy later became one of Ireland's great heroes – Red Hugh O'Donnell of Donegal.'

'Red Hugh!' Many of the men looked at their own Hugh with frank admiration. Red Hugh O'Donnell of Donegal was a chivalrous tale all of its own, and the tale was told, and discussed into the night along with other tales of the shanachies.

Michael stared into the flames of the fire and drifted. Not back to the yesteryear, but to a farmhouse on the hillside at Knockandarragh where the girl of his dreams lay, fast asleep by now. He had not seen her for almost a month, and he had no intention of ever seeing her again. But at times he craved her. Only to see her, talk to her, nothing more. More would mean decisions and the breaking down of his defences.

There was no room for emotional attachments in his life, no place for love if you were a rebel on the run ... But still, whatever he did, wherever he went, he could not stop himself remembering her: her soft voice, soft body, soft brown eyes, the shy way she smiled; and the conflicting surge of happiness and fear he always felt whenever she had said she loved him. Foolish girl! Love was for ladies and gentlemen, not land slaves.

He blinked his eyes. Hugh Vesty's voice came back to him, still holding court as he laboured the merits of one Irish hero against the other. Foolish man! Ireland was coast to coast with heroes. Thirty thousand dead heroes in one year alone. And the few thousand at Ballinamuck – must never forget the brave boys from the West who had marched with the French and died at Ballinamuck.

He studied the fire, remembering how easily the blushing colour came to her cheeks. But she had looked very pale that day she had turned at the wall and waved farewell to Cullen.

Someone threw a log on the fire, flames flared around it as a warm blast of emotion coursed through him. Never had he loved a girl before, but he loved her, wished he didn't. Pointless. Nudging and dallying, not marrying. Mountain warfare and marriage never did mix well. And now with a price on his head, he had no choice but to stay out, in the fight, under arms. More logs were thrown on the fire. The flames were smothered.

Miles Byrne, the young Wexford captain, came up to Michael the next day and quietly informed him that he was leaving. 'There's no reason for me to stay in Wicklow now,' Miles said. 'The winds no longer blow fair from France.'

Michael was sorry to lose Miles Byrne and it showed on his face. 'Will you go back to Wexford?'

Miles nodded. 'Aye, just to see my family, but if I stay there the yeos will bury me. Even Mulloy's wife knew I had a command in the rebel army. My half-brother Edward has a business in Dublin. I'll go to him and lie low for a time.'

'What kind of business?'

'Timber. But I've often done the books for him. He'll employ me as a book-keeper without hesitation.'

Michael considered him thoughtfully. 'Is that what you want to do?' he asked curiously. 'Book-keeping?'

'Given the choice, I'd be nothing other than a soldier, but the United Irishmen are finished, for the present anyhow, and I'll never wear scarlet.'

'You could always wear French blue,' Michael suggested.

'Nay. Better to lose myself in the crowded streets of Dublin for a while. You could do that too, Michael, same as me.'

Both men smiled. Miles knew it was a ridiculous suggestion. Nothing could ever persuade Dwyer to leave the mountains of his own Wicklow. Only a war for liberation had done it before. Nothing less would do it again.

The two captains looked at each other, wanted to show a gesture of affection and brotherhood, but merely shook hands briefly.

When darkness fell, Miles Byrne moved off over the mountain in the direction of Wexford.

Michael ran after him.

'Miles.'

'Aye.'

'Good luck, avic.'

Miles Byrne smiled.

'You too, Michael. Good luck.'

Chapter Fourteen

'That's the way of it, Michael. They've been drinking and talking about it for many weeks, but now that Da has drunk O'Riordan dry, they've sealed the match. The wedding is to happen in three weeks' time – one week before All-Hallows' Eve.'

Michael reeled around a tree and held the bole, stunned as he stared at John Doyle. 'O'Riordan and Mary?' he whispered. 'My Mary!'

'*Your* Mary! She's hardly that. Twice she went to Cullen's house by arrangement but you never showed, and never a message from you since. She says you just cut her adrift without a word of explanation or farewell.'

Michael stood silent and defenceless against the truth of it.

'Anyway . . . she says she is truly over you now. Never wants to lay eyes on you again.'

'So why have you come here?' Michael asked.

John hesitated for a second, then shrugged. 'Just to let you know the score. I didn't want you calling me to account afterwards for not telling you. After all, 'tis you that's been courting her, not O'Riordan.'

'Has Mary agreed to the match?'

'Nay! She has no say in it anyhow. She plans to run away to Dublin. She says she'll have no problem getting employed as a maid there.'

Michael looked towards the group of his men a few yards off, some sitting around playing cards, others standing with eyes sharpened on outpost duty.

'What do you expect me to do about it?' he said in a flash of frustration. 'You can see our position. We have to keep on the move because now all of us have a price on our heads. Fifty guineas for each of the others and five hundred for me. So it will be me that the militia will want to bolster their purses with.'

John suddenly realised how foolish he had been to come

here. How naïve Mary had been to imagine there was hope of anything more than a romantic interlude with Michael Dwyer. He was the famous Insurgent Captain of the Wicklow Mountains, an outlaw, and every bounty hunter in Leinster was after him.

'Aye, I understand,' John said.

Michael met his eyes, saw in them the same dark brown of Mary's eyes.

'Do you?'

'Yes, I do!' John said strongly.

'Then explain it your sister, John. Explain why men like me can take no chances or make no choices – not since the first day we decided to fight back. We can never have normal lives again.'

After a silence, John agreed. 'Better to let Mary head off for Dublin. In time she'll no doubt meet a nice young butler or pantry boy and settle down to domestic peace.'

'Best all round.' Michael's voice was bleak. 'I couldn't live in a city, though. All that stench and noise. They say you never hear a bird sing in the city.'

'That's exactly what Mary says; you never hear a bird sing in the city.'

'How is she?'

John looked at him. 'Straight on?'

'Straight on,' Michael said. 'How is she?'

'White with unhappiness, hardly ever speaks, locked away in her own silent bewilderment. She's heartsick in love with you, Michael, despite what she says. I've heard her crying many a night.'

Michael spent the next minute suspended between self-loathing and misery, withdrawing into his own private world of remembering; wished he had not been so cruel that day of the fraughans, watched her crying and made no move – wished he had gone down and kissed her face dry. Too late now.

'She just can't understand why you did it,' John said emotionally, 'cut her adrift without a word of farewell. But I gave her fair warning, as long back as the spring I warned her not to dally with . . .' John's voice tailed off as he realised what he had said, embarrassment red on his face. 'Is there anything . . . anything you want me to tell her?'

Michael stuffed his hands in his pockets and looked around him. 'Just tell her how it is,' he said quietly.

John shrugged. 'Very well, I'll tell her.'

Without another word, he moved off, pausing briefly to talk to the men at the outposts before making the descent. He was almost at the back wall of the house at Knockandarragh when Michael caught up with him. John jerked around with a fright, then relaxed into a relieved smile.

'I'll tell her myself,' Michael said.

The autumn evening had a chill in the air. A hush lay over Imaal and not a whisper of wind rippled the grass. It was two weeks before All-Hallows' Eve.

Michael sat astride his horse, reins held loosely as his gaze distanced on the brow of a hill. The rebels' horses were stabled in various places throughout Imaal, but the complement of twelve men who waited with him had collected their mounts and now sat silently, also watching the hill. Under his cloak, Michael wore the brown whipcord suit he had worn the night of the Spring Fair at Baltinglass, having collected it earlier in the day from his tearful mother, who insisted he also wear the fine leather gaiters she had purchased for him.

A dog barked in the distance, as did the hound parading up and down the farmyard behind the mounted men and their captain, who also held the reins of a riderless bay.

A murmur of relief rose up from the men when the dog bounded over the swell of the hill keeping pace beside John Doyle's horse as he galloped down to them, with Mary sitting pillion behind him.

When John drew rein, Michael swung down and helped Mary to dismount, then lifted her on to the empty saddle of the waiting bay before remounting his own horse. Not a word had passed between them, but now he met her eyes.

She smiled shyly, looking beautiful in her blue fitted habit and loosely draped blue cloak. Her black hair was no longer straight and smooth, but cascading over her shoulders in shining ebony ringlets.

He smiled back, and chucked the bridle to her.

Hugh Vesty reared his horse and led the dash towards the ruins at Castleruddery where, on the banks of Green's River, stood the isolated little house of the parish priest of Imaal.

Father Richard Murphy was an old and wise man who bore the marks of many beatings on his body. His black cassock was old and darned in places, but immaculately clean; he wore it as proudly as a king robed in velvet and ermine. He sat in his chair and considered the young couple, then looked at John Doyle and the four groomsmen, Hugh Vesty Byrne, Sam McAllister, John Mernagh, and Martin Burke.

'Why do you need four groomsmen?' he asked Michael.

Michael smiled. 'To stop a dispute. And the more the merrier, Father.'

The priest turned his attention to Mary. She stood with her hands pressed in the form of a church steeple against her lips, her eyes fixed nervously on the floor.

'Where is the bride's father?' the priest asked. 'It is unusual for a brother to give a girl away when her father is alive and hearty.'

'You know my circumstances,' Michael said. 'It is not a normal wedding, and we cannot delay here long.'

'Oh, now I understand!' said the priest, nodding his head. 'The bride's parents know nothing about this intended marriage.' He sat back in his chair. 'It seems to me, that what we have here, is a case of abduction.'

'Abduction my eye!' Hugh Vesty cried, then demurred, 'Not at all, Father. Mary is willing and able.'

'Oh but she is not able, Hugh Vesty,' the priest corrected. 'She is not twenty-one years old. Are you, Mary?'

Mary shook her head. 'Eighteen,' she whispered.

'So she must have her father's consent. You must understand, boys, I am not a rebel like ye. I have a duty to all my flock. I don't want William Doyle breathing down on me and accusing me of aiding and abetting in the abduction of his beloved daughter.'

A long time passed as John Doyle and the four groomsmen endeavoured to persuade the stubborn priest. Tears of desperation crept down Mary's face. Michael took her hand and held it fast as they listened in silence to the argument. The men outside became restless and occasionally poked their heads inside the parlour to inquire as to the delay.

Of a sudden Michael let go Mary's hand and pushed his way through the pleading men. John Doyle was almost on his knees in supplication to the priest. 'Father, a word in private?' Michael said. 'In the scullery.'

The priest looked up at Michael's face, saw the anger there, and grudgingly consented.

In the scullery, Michael stood with his back to the door. 'I do not wish to be disrespectful, Father, not to a priest, but when my emissary came to you last night, you agreed to perform the marriage.'

'Ah yes, Michael, but since then I've had time to consider. Doyle, you know . . . a good and devout man.'

'Ah.' Michael sighed in understanding. 'And I'm not.'

'You're a dead man, Michael. And sorry I am to say it, for I baptised you. But it is only a matter of time before the militia get you.' The priest looked at him sadly. 'Now listen to me, it wouldn't be fair to Mary. She would be left on her own. And a widow is not so much sought after as a maiden. But now, do you honestly expect her to live with you in the mountains? Come to your senses, man. Send her home.'

'Mary has left home, Father, for the sole purpose of marrying me, and I have no intention of sending her back again. We came to you in faith, but whether you perform the marriage or not, Mary and I are going to share the bed of honour tonight, and if that's a sin, then on your head be it.'

The priest glared at him in astonishment. 'Do you mean to stand there, cool as you like, and dare to tell me that even without the wedding – you intend to sin with her!'

'A sin or a sacrament – it's your decision. We came to be married.'

The priest was astounded. He fumed, admonished, lectured, then seeing the unmoved expression on Michael's face, wearily agreed.

'Oh, very well,' he said with a sigh. 'I'm sure you intend to carry out your threat to take her to your mountain hideout, and God alone will consider it my duty to see she goes there a matron and not a maiden.'

Michael smiled.

'There's just one other thing, Father. It seems Mary is very partial to hymns. I promised her that you would sing a hymn at the wedding.'

'A hymn? Now you want me to sing a hymn?' The priest flopped his arms and looked around for a place to sit down, but there was none. 'Lord preserve us from such audacity!' he cried.

'You are well known for your beautiful voice,' Michael told him. 'You sang at her First Communion and she has never forgotten it.' He reached out and lifted the priest's hand in his own, gently pressing a gold sovereign into the palm. 'A hymn, Father, please. My wedding gift to Mary.'

The priest looked into his eyes, then sighed. 'Which hymn does she want?'

'The hymn of the mountain people,' Michael answered.

'I'll weep tears over this one day,' the priest decided. 'I know it. And warn your men not to mention a word of the hymn to William Doyle. Performing the marriage of his runaway daughter is one thing. Singing at it is another thing entirely.'

The four groomsmen and John Doyle all solemnly bowed their heads and joined in the prayers as the couple kneeled on the parlour mat under a picture of Christ the King.

Michael took Mary's hand and, prompted by the priest, pledged his vows to her in a quiet but sure voice.

'I, Michael, take thee, Mary, to my wedded wife, to have and to hold from this day forward, for better or worse, for richer or poorer, in sickness and in health, forsaking all others, till death us do part.'

When Mary had made her pledge in the same quiet but sure voice, Hugh Vesty dropped the gold ring which had belonged to Michael's grandmother, apologised profusely in hushed tones, then exhaled with relief when it was finally slipped on Mary's third finger.

The priest concluded the ceremony, then holding his hand over the couple, raised his voice in a sudden thundering which left even the men outside in no doubt as to the authority under which he had solemnised the union.

'*In nomine Patris, et Filii, et Spiritus Sancti!*'

'In the name of the Father, and the Son, and the Holy Spirit,' Sam McAllister murmured in English.

'Amen.'

For a moment there was a holy silence, then Michael raised his eyebrows at the priest by way of reminder. Father Richard nodded, cleared his throat, then sang in the deep beautiful voice that Mary had always loved, the hymn of the mountain people: the twenty-third psalm.

> 'The Lord is my Shepherd, I shall not want;
>   In green meadow pastures he lets me lie.
> Beside the still waters he leadeth me;
>   And there he revives my soul . . .'

Mary knew there could be no big barn dance where the entire district gathered and both sets of parents and aunts and uncles, cousins, and friends joined in the wedding festivity until the small hours. But she didn't mind. She had all she wanted. She had Michael.

She emerged through the door of the priest's house with a radiant smile on her face. The men outside smiled too as they looked at her. Most of them had their own girls, considered them pretty or even beautiful, but all agreed there was something especially stunning about the captain's Mary.

The sky was dark when they rode back to the farmyard and dismounted. The wife and daughters of the farmer were waiting and almost smothered Mary in tearful embraces and kisses, wishing them both well and not to spoil their wedding night by worrying about the militia – not at all!

The farmer, a towering hulk of a man, known to the rebels as Midget, stood with arms folded and spoke solemnly to Michael. 'The word is out,' he said. 'And the word conveyed to me to pass on to you is this: if you stay out, Michael, and keep up your fight against the militia, you and your men will be supplied with everything you need by the people of Wicklow. You will have your rations supplied as regularly as the soldiers in the barracks. And as to your lovely wife,' Midget added, 'every hearth will glow with a welcome for her if ever she needs one.'

Michael glanced at Mary who was still surrounded by the chatter of the females. He had explained the situation clearly to her a week ago, the night he had followed John down to Knockandarragh and she had come out to him, looked at him with her soft dark eyes, and in that second he had known the game was up – defences smashed by a sudden sweeping smile, all his cold discipline dissolved by warm trembling lips pressing against his own. Surrender to arms, battle over. Slayed by a beautiful girl. Poor Rabby Muldoon – you and me together, avic.

He could not stay in any one place for long, he had explained to her. They would be unable to live together on a regular basis. If they established a home, the yeos would watch it, and watch her, night and day. He would continue to live with his men, and she would have to lodge with his family and friends. It would be a grim life, being wife to one of the 'Rebels still in Arms in the Mountains of Wicklow' – as Cornwallis's latest proclamation called them.

She had taken no time over her decision. Just smiled. She would still take the rebel in arms in the mountains of Wicklow.

Michael nodded to the farmer. 'Thanks, Midget.'

'You're welcome, avic.'

They made the rest of the journey on foot, leaving Midget and his sons to see to the stabling of the horses throughout Imaal. At spaced intervals on the hillside leading up to the wilderness of Knockgorragh, men broke away in pairs and took up outpost duty. Only six of them continued on with the wedded pair to join in the celebration supper that Michael's mother had sent over to John Cullen's house. Hugh Vesty's sweetheart, Sarah, had laid it all out, and now bustled round the room, joking gaily as she took command of the proceedings and heaped slices of roasted beef on to plates.

'And according to Michael's mammy,' Sarah announced, 'that fruit cake is just stocious with brandy.'

'What about the other men?' Cullen asked. 'Have they wet their lips on a drink yet?'

'They had their shindig with the captain last night,' Martin Burke told him. 'While *we* did outpost duty.'

Michael and Mary barely spoke to each other throughout the supper, and as the night wore on and the liquor flowed and Hugh and Sarah danced to the music of Cullen's fiddle, they held hands under the table and joked and laughed with the others, hiding their burning impatience to be alone. Only once, as their fingers twined tightly, did their eyes meet and the look exchanged between them made the wait seem endless.

By two o'clock in the morning, John Doyle had escorted Sarah through the darkness to her home, and only Hugh Vesty and Sam McAllister remained at the cottage door. Mernagh, Burke, and Big Arthur Devlin had moved out to sleep in the small barn beside the house.

'Youse'll be warm enough out there,' Cullen assured Hugh Vesty as he prepared to chain the door. 'Indeed you will! Sure wasn't it on a bed of straw that St Joseph and Our Blessed Lady slept at Bethlehem.'

'And where is it yourself is sleeping?' Hugh murmured.

'Where?' Cullen gathered his white bushy eyebrows together. 'Where I always sleep. In my settle-bed.'

Hugh looked over Cullen's shoulder into the room. Michael was standing with his hand on the hearth-breast and his foot on the fender, gazing into the flames of the fire. Mary stood beside him, tensely blushing like a bride on her wedding night. Michael turned his head and threw an uncomfortable look at Hugh Vesty.

Hugh Vesty smiled. 'I'll say goodnight, Captain,' he called cheerfully. 'And while I'm at it – I'll take this little virgin with me.'

Cullen made the most violent struggle as Hugh Vesty and Sam McAllister seized him and carried him bodily to the barn. 'Sure what ails you,' Hugh Vesty cried. 'Don't you want to be a man amongst men?'

'Let me go, you gouts!' Cullen screamed. 'Let me go!'

They let him go on to a pile of straw just inside the doorless barn. Cullen scrambled to his feet and made to run past them. 'I'll not be turned out of my own abode!' he cried indignantly.

They caught him and propelled him back down. ' 'Tis for your own good,' Hugh Vesty declared. 'That little house is not a fitting place this night for a saint like you.'

'And didn't you say Michael could have your house for his wedding and honeymoon?' McAllister said.

'Aye, but I didn't expect to be turned out myself,' Cullen cried. 'Blood and turkeys, there's gratitude for you. And himself never lifted a hand to stop youse!'

Hugh and Sam roared with laughter at the old man's indignation. 'Are you stupid, man?' John Mernagh murmured. 'Now the captain's wed her, he's going to bed her.'

'I know that, you great tumour on a bullock's nose! Didn't I tell him Mary could have the four-poster – my mother's bed – and let me tell ye, there's not many I would let sleep in *that*!'

'You stay here with us,' Hugh said cajolingly, sitting down and putting an arm around Cullen. 'Have a drink and tell us about Rosie Noonan. The one who caught you up on Table Mountain and nearly made a man of you.'

' 'Tis not right to make fun of him, Hugh,' said Big Arthur Devlin. 'Here, old man, have a drop of comfort.'

Cullen ignored the bottle and made a great show of shivering. 'I'm cold,' he grumbled. 'I can only sleep on my own mattress.'

'Ach, stretch out your limbs and think of poor St Joseph in his barn at Bethlehem,' said Hugh Vesty. 'He didn't whinge like you. A better man and a better saint entirely.'

This rebuke fixed Cullen. 'Twas nothing less than a sin to complain about sleeping in a barn when the Holy Family had been thankful for the same. He grabbed the bottle from Art Devlin and gulped long. 'You're desperate lads,' he moaned. 'You don't give a thraneen for the feelings of others. Like himself in there in my house. He's as bad if not worse.'

'Ah, don't be codding,' Burke said. 'Everyone knows you love Michael like a darling son.'

'Not everyone!' Cullen cried. 'The militia think I hate him like the devil. Ever since that great display me and himself put up that day of the Spring Fair. Oho! Will anyone ever forget *that*!'

'The time you threatened to shoot the cur if you ever saw him again?'

'And the blow I gave him! Troth, the yeos were delighted when I swung my stick and hit him a larrup on the head. I nearly gave the game away by rushing to see if I'd hurt him bad, then remembered in the nick of time and warned him he'd get more of the same if he ever came near *me* again.'

Sam McAllister had heard of the incident. 'The militia reckon you'd sell Dwyer for a drink if you were given the chance.'

'Aye, and I might an' all! After tonight. Getting his boys to turf me out of my own abode.' He took another swig of the bottle and wiped his mouth. 'All the same, though,' he said suddenly, 'but isn't she a lovely gentle girl, that Mary Doyle.'

'Mary Dwyer she is now,' Hugh whispered in his ear, 'but never you mind about her. Tell us about Rosie Noonan?'

'Rosie Noonan?' Cullen shuddered and took another drink. 'By the holy nation – an odd body *she* was; structured like a haystack about to collapse. It was on account of her I swore off women. That day on Table Mountain, she put her great paws on me and I've been a different man ever since.' He pursed up his mouth and looked solemn as he remembered. 'Of course, it was the fine new breeches I wore that done it.'

The men had stretched and began to slumber, but Hugh Vesty was agog. 'The fine new breeches?'

'Aye, and she near pulling them off me. "No!" says I, " 'tis nothing I'll have to do with you or the likes of you, Rosie Noonan." But sure, with the heat and the fright and the botheration that was on me, I hardly knew what I was doing and, my shame, I slapped her.'

'Oh you tyrant!' Hugh gasped.

'Aye, 'tis bad when a man strikes a woman.' Cullen lay back next to Hugh Vesty and stared upwards. 'But then, she was no gentle woman – she could drain a tankard of ale quicker than any man I know. And that day on Table Mountain, she stood over me like the Whore of Babylon, looking down and taking tatters off my good name and that of my mother and father and using language that would make a soldier blush.'

'You poor man,' Hugh said. 'You did right to belt her.'

'Oh, mortal cheeky she was! "Helup owa that, me young hero," she shouted. "What's the matter wid ye? Sure wasn't I told it was the breeches made the man and I only wanted to see what kind of man those fine new breeches had made of ye!" '

Cullen flushed at the memory. 'Oh, sorra the day she fixed her eye on me. I spent years running from her. She gave up in the end, saying as how I wasn't worth the salt in her sweat.'

'You had a lucky escape, I'm thinking.'

'Don't I know it! Troth, I'd rather be hung! But what she did on Table Mountain was nothing to what she did up on the Lugnaquilla.'

'What was that?'

'I'll not tell you.' Cullen closed his eyes and shook his head positively. 'Michael is the only one who knows what she done up on the 'Quilla. And if you don't know, then it shows he kept his word to me. Not another mortal would I tell, not if it was my last breath.' He twisted on to his side and put his hand under his cheek. 'Goodnight to you now, avic.'

'And to you, old man,' Hugh said in disappointment, then turned on to his stomach and folded his arms under his face.

A mellow green moon had risen over the mountains of Imaal. A sleepy silence hung over the barn. In the darkness and the stillness, from the cottage a few feet away, a young girl's distant cries of love floated out to the night.

Cullen sat bolt upright. 'Bejabers, what's he doing at all? Upsetting a gentle girl like that?'

Hugh yanked him back down. 'Sure he's only being nice to her.'

Cullen's white brows were bunched over his darting eyes as his ears strained to the heightening cries of the girl, and never having experienced the ecstasy of loving for the first time, he did not grasp that she was innocent in her passion to all the living world outside.

'He's hurting her – the gout!'

'Indeed he's not,' Hugh snapped. 'She's on a moontrip by the sounds of it.' He whispered reprovingly, 'And shameful it is that you should be listening, old man. Michael would not expect such a sacrilege from a saint like you.'

In the darkness Cullen blushed to the roots of his white hair. He made a timorous sign of the cross over himself, then muttered in a bewildered voice, 'I meant no harm, God knows, but it sounded as if he was upsetting her. And I wasn't listening in that way; troth, I wasn't.' He turned and peered at Hugh Vesty. 'You won't say anything to him, avic, will you now?'

'No, old man, I won't say a word.' Hugh grinned slyly. 'Not if you tell me what Rosie Noonan did – up on the 'Quilla.'

Cullen considered, then sighed deeply. He sat up and reached for the bottle and took a long gulp. 'Troth, but it's hard to be telling it, and the sin that was in it – God will punish her!'

Cullen took another gulp at the bottle and wiped his mouth. 'Howsomever, it happened this-a-way . . .'

Throughout the telling, Cullen occasionally cocked a curious eye at Hugh Vesty's face, and satisfied with the gaping shock he saw there, nodded his head solemnly and continued.

Half an hour later, Hugh Vesty whispered a very sympathetic goodnight to the grave-faced old man, then rolled on to his stomach and positioned himself for sleep. He lay still for some minutes, then his body began to shake uncontrollably with silent laughter.

Chapter Fifteen

The honeymoon at Cullen's house lasted only one night. Michael's first care in the weeks that followed was always to lodge Mary in a safe house with one of the farming families, where she would remain in concealment until he came to move her on.

'If they once find out who you are, and where you are,' he told her, 'they will set you in order to catch me.'

Mary made no protest, no complaint, seemingly satisfied with her nomadic life just as long as she saw her husband frequently. Her only anxiety was for his safety. At times she kept the entire family who harboured her awake through the night while she paced up and down worrying about his safety.

'They'll never catch him,' the family assured her wearily, finally persuading her to sleep, and liking her all the more for her devotion.

Michael and nine others rode early over the land of Colvinstown on the southern slope of Kilranelagh Hill. Leading the party was a young man named Adam Magee who generally took on the task of cooking for the men; he was a cheerful youth, and a great favourite of them all.

Magee rolled off joke after joke and kept them all laughing as his feet dangled from the stirrups and a number of small tin vessels jangled from a string around his neck.

'Now my thirsty comrades,' Magee called, as he drew rein. 'It is here, at this magic crystal well, to which the faeries once rode upon a blast of wind, that I shall administer to your refreshment.'

The blarney rolled off Magee's tongue as he imperiously drew up the bucket from the well, dipped a tin vessel inside, and was about to hand it to one of his comrades when the warning was given.

'Mounted troops!' someone shouted.

Michael turned and saw a troop of the Humewood Horse, followed by a party of infantry and cavalry coming over the hill. 'Back on your horse, Magee!' he commanded.

Adam Magee mounted with a running jump and the rebels rode up to the hills of Kilranelagh and Keadeen at a gallop. At the Rath of Crossoona they dismounted and turned their horses loose, slapping them up the mountains, and taking cover themselves in the ditches of the Rath, giving the troops a burst of well-aimed fire which halted their advance.

As the cross-fire went on, Michael could see they were being encircled: the horsemen held the highway, infantry flanked the hills on either side. Ten against a hundred – bad odds. They had no choice but to retreat, down the sloping ground to the east, firing and reloading as they went amidst volley after volley from the pursuing troops.

Adam Magee stumbled, fell to the ground with the string of tin drinking vessels around his neck. Within seconds a group of yeomen converged upon him and emptied their firelocks into his body.

Michael and Andrew Thomas, who were pace for pace, turned together and stared at the blood-spattered body of young Magee.

'Slap at them!' Michael roared, standing at full height and firing and reloading with such amazing speed and taking a man down with each blast that the knot of yeos ran for cover.

Michael took advantage of their hesitation to turn and run towards the ditch where his men were keeping up a brisk fire. As they climbed over the hedge, the cavalry charged down to them, giving them no time to spare. Michael and Andrew Thomas sat astride the hedge and with the others kept up such galling fire that the cavalry drew back.

The rebels resumed their retreat, running and firing all the way to the bog's rushy boundary where they took up posts behind turf clamps, but their ammunition was almost exhausted and their fire slackened. Now they saw the enemy commencing an entry upon the bog at differing points.

'It's useless to remain here,' Andrew Thomas said. 'No ammo, no defence. And they've got us cut off on two sides.'

It was hopeless and the men knew it. The small band had held the greater number off miraculously, but, without ammunition, the contest was over.

Michael looked around him, thinking furiously. Behind

them was the ridge between Keadeen and Carrig Mountain, but if they made a move upwards they would be picked off handsomely. The wind blew coldly at his back and he shivered slightly. And then it came back to him, the words of poor young Magee: ' . . . *and the faeries came upon a blast of wind.*'

Michael smiled as another old Irish saying came into his mind: '*May the wind be always at your back.*' And the wind was at his back now! His eyes quickly scanned the land around him: next to the turf clamps was a line of hayricks in a field leading to a farmhouse.

'When I give the command,' he rasped over to Andrew Thomas, 'put everything in your guns and keep firing until you've nothing left. But keep me covered. Repeat the command.'

The command was repeated with a bewildered frown from man to man.

'What are you going to do, Captain?'

'Get us out of this,' Michael said. 'The wind is with us – blowing in the face of the enemy.'

Andrew Thomas looked dubious, but made no protest.

'Fire!' Michael shouted, and when his men obliged, he bent down and made a weaving run towards the farmhouse where the peasant family were huddled in the kitchen, the farmer holding a fowling-rifle in the posture of defence. When he saw who had entered his home, he lowered the gun.

'A torch?' Michael said urgently. 'As quick as you can.'

The farmer sprang to the hearth and lifted a clump of tightly plaited straw and put it to the flames. 'Here you are,' he said, handing over the burning torch.

'I'll have to fire the ricks,' Michael told him.

'Do whatever you like,' the farmer retorted, 'but don't let them get you, avic! 'Twould be criminal after the show you boys have put up out there.'

'Now listen carefully,' Michael said. 'Empty your rain-barrels around the area surrounding the house and soak it well. I'll start as far back as I possibly can from the field.'

When all the rain-barrels had been turned over, he ran back along the line, firing the hayricks and turf clamps and brush-wood as he went.

'And there they blow!' he cried, as the wind caught the flames and within minutes the entire bog was ablaze, keeping back the troops and sending up a dense blanket of smoke, under cover of which Michael and his men retreated up to the ridge between Keadeen and Carrig Mountain. On the ridge they were clear of the smoke, but much too far away for a hit. Some of the rebels waved the soldiers an audacious farewell.

Two cavalry officers sat on their horses staring up at the retreating rebels. 'Damn my eyes,' one said, 'but that Dwyer is everything they said he was!'

'A cunning and arrogant bastard,' a yeoman shouted furiously, 'who should be hung, drawn, quartered, and fed piecemeal to the dogs!'

The two cavalry officers looked at the puce-faced man, then at each other. 'Well, in my view,' said one, 'he is worth a wager on his capture. Five guineas says he will not be taken this side of Christmas.'

The other cavalry officer accepted the challenge. 'You're on,' he said. 'Five guineas says he will.'

In one of the lonely fastnesses deep in the mountains, Michael approached the small farmhouse of an old couple who lived alone. It was the time of the false dawn, that eerie time before the real dawn, and a number of his men were camped a few hills away.

He rapped out a rhythm on the door, whistled like a lark, and waited for the chains to be unlocked. The old farmer opened the door and smiled at him, then beckoned him inside where his white-haired old wife was moving about in her settle-bed in the corner.

'Mary's asleep,' the farmer whispered. 'Will you have some oaten cakes and buttermilk with us first and a bit of a chat.' He turned to his wife and said commandingly, 'Stir yourself, woman!'

'Aye, I'm coming along,' she said in a sing-song voice. 'What's the newses, Michael agrah?'

Michael shook his head and put a finger to his lips, then moved towards the small room off the kitchen. It was dark inside, the slatted wooden shutter over the small window being closed. He moved quietly to the bed and bent over her sleeping form, unable to see her for the profusion of black hair spread over her face and shoulders – all the signs of a restless night. Pausing to inspect his musket, he laid it on the floor beside the bed, then quietly undressed.

Mary felt the bed sag and the body stretching against her

217

own. She opened her eyes, seeing only darkness until the hair was brushed back from her face and warm lips touched her. 'Michael!' she breathed.

'Don't speak,' he whispered with a smile, loosening the draw-string of her nightgown. 'We'll talk later.'

In the living-room the old couple looked at each other gloomily, knowing he would not come back out again to brighten their dawn with a chat and a gossip about whatever was happening outside their own little wilderness. They enjoyed the rebel's company more than the girl's, for there was something about the girl that disturbed their normally placid emotions.

'Never mind,' the old man said a gentle low voice. 'Reckon we'll catch him for the newses on his way out, eh?' His tone had softened now that he was alone again with his wife, for he loved her dearly, and only spoke commandingly to her in the presence of other men.

A meek and gentle couple, they ate their breakfast in silence, until the old man lifted his head and looked towards the bedroom door, then looked away and stared into his memories, still able to remember the pure joy of young love when satisfied in the ecstasy of mating.

'Do you remember when we first wed,' he whispered thoughtfully, 'a half a century it must be now, and your father said that when we went to our bed at night, the old bed with the creaky springs, we often sounded as if we had a party of leprechauns making fun between the sheets with us.'

'Musha, it must be that long ago,' his wife responded thoughtfully. 'I was seventeen then, and now I'm sixty-eight. Or is it seventy-eight?'

' 'Tis sixty-nine you are,' her husband said gently. 'I should know, because I was eighteen then, and now I'm seventy.'

'Musha, but you have a wonderful memory, Paudeen. Mine is no longer reliable, and it keeps playing tricks on me . . .' She looked at him sadly. 'As well you know.'

'Some things are best forgotten and left buried under the years,' he said sadly.

'But I remember when we were wed,' she said brightly. 'You had a head of brown curls on you that many a girl would envy.' Then the sad look returned to her faded eyes. 'Now you're an unholy sight with that wiry white hair.'

' 'Tis the same colour as yours,' he said, looking at the white hair coiled into a knot on top of her head.

'Oh no,' she insisted, 'mine is a pure white and very soft, yours is a greyish white and wiry.'

And so their conversation continued in its usual trivial themes, until the birds began to hail the rise of the sun, and the old couple struggled to their feet and moved outdoors towards the daily round of work their little holding demanded. By noon both were giddy and tired but, reluctant to disturb the young sleeping newlyweds, the woman quietly wrapped a lump of cheese and a loaf of soda bread in a piece of muslin, while the old man crept about collecting his rod and his string and his treasured box of worms, then both set off at a turtle's pace towards the small lake three hills yonder, in the hope of catching a few nice fish for their supper.

Shortly after noon Michael awoke. Thin strips of light filtered into the room through the slats of the window shutter. He lowered his eyes and gazed drowsily at the girl who was his wife. She had her back to him, her voluptuousness hidden from him. He slowly printed his fingertips down her slender back and over her hip. She turned to him, her eyes fluttering open with a smile.

'Look what you done to me,' he whispered in pretended hurt, pointing his shoulder towards her and showing where her fingers had dug into his skin.

Two crimson flames of embarrassment flared in her cheeks and she croaked a sound of denial, sliding under the sheet to hide her face and her shame.

'So well you should feel guilty,' he teased. 'I swear you're more dangerous than the militia.'

'The militia?' The sheet came down, her eyes wide and anxious. 'Have you seen any of them lately?'

'Not hilt nor hide of one of them for weeks,' he lied.

'Truly?'

'Truly,' he lied.

'Have you come to take me somewhere else?' she asked.

'Do you want to go somewhere else?' He looked at her curiously. 'You've only been here four days.'

'I know, and the old couple have been very kind to me, but . . .'

'But what?'

She bit her lip and hesitated, unwilling to complain after she had vowed to accept *any* situation forced on her if they married.

'Mary, answer me.'

'I feel so lonely here,' she blurted. 'Can't you take me to a family where there are daughters? Someone young to talk to? The old couple only talk about the yesteryear, and when I talk to them in the long evenings the woman gets confused and thinks I'm her dead daughter.'

Michael listened to her quietly, his eyes never leaving hers. 'Mary, I'm sorry,' he whispered. 'It was the desolation of this place that made me choose it, the safety of the wilderness . . .'

'I could go to Cullen's,' she suggested. 'I like him greatly. He treats me like a daughter too, but his mind never wanders. He always knows who I am.'

'Cullen's place is the ultimate sanctuary,' he told her. 'But we can't go there too often.'

His head dropped back on the pillow as he thought about it. She twisted close to him and watched him staring into space. 'I'll move you out of here tonight,' he said suddenly. 'To a family with three lovely daughters, chirping and chattering non-stop, plenty of good food, and the house shining with beeswax polish.'

She stiffened against him, drew back her head. 'Three lovely daughters? Do you know them well?'

'Intimately,' he confessed.

Her face was stony.

'My sisters,' he said.

'Your family?' Her smile was like sunshine.

'Your family too,' he reminded her. 'My daddy and brothers will take care of you. And my mother—'

'Let's pick some flowers for her!' she cried impulsively. 'For your mother. A whole basketful to put on her table.'

'Mary, it's early November—'

But she was sitting up, reaching over to the chair where her clothes were neatly folded. 'Marigolds bloom nearly all the year round,' she said. 'The wind only has to blow at the seeds of the dead ones or the faeries drop a few, and more grow. Nice golden marigolds. Come on, we'll find and pick them together.'

He wanted to laugh. A rebel roaming in the wilderness picking flowers! But she was smiling at him, her brown eyes wide with pleading.

A strong dose of poteen can make a man do anything. Love is even more powerful. He helped her to find and pick the marigolds. They found some growing in patches here and there, and when she decided she had enough to fill a bowl, he took her hand and led her back to the house through a small wood where he lingered to hold her and kiss her goodbye.

'I love you, Mary.'

She smiled. She knew now that he did, although he rarely said it.

'You're my most cherished possession,' he whispered. 'The only precious thing I have.'

Mary weighed the words against the man. 'What's wrong, Michael?'

He looked at her a little awkwardly. 'About going to my mother's . . . I may not be able to visit you there. It's too dangerous.'

'Oh . . . ! Not at all?'

'Once in a while, maybe.'

They began to walk on. 'How long will I have to stay there?' she asked.

'A month or so. Too long and suspicion will be aroused.'

'You will come, though. To see me. Soon?'

'As soon as I can, but, Mary . . .' they had reached the yard outside the house and his self-consciousness was beginning to colour his cheeks. 'When I do come . . . we won't be able to make love.'

She stared at him, equally embarrassed. 'Why not?'

'In my mother's house? With my younger brothers and sisters in the next rooms . . .' He tried to smile.

'But, Michael, we're married!'

'That's beside the point,' he told her. 'And anyway,' he added softly, 'I don't want my family to know how I feel about you.'

She bowed her head to hide an irritable frown. Only an Irish mountain boy would shy away from letting the world know he loved his wife.

'I'll stay here,' she said quickly, 'with the old couple. I don't want to go to your family if it means we'll have to hide our feelings for each other. And worse, rarely see each other. I'll be fine here, truly I will.'

'No,' he said firmly. 'You'll be happier at Eadstown. Look there!' He pointed to where some marigolds were growing thinly at the edge of the field.

'I'm only happy when I'm with you, Michael,' she said shakily, but he had moved away towards the flowers.

*   *   *

Michael Kearns and Farrell Reily were standing by some pine trees on the opposite slope watching him at the edge of the field. Both young men were devoted to Dwyer, and had come to escort him back to the camp.

'Who would have thought it?' Kearns muttered. 'A hard man like the captain turning so soft. Man! It makes me want to cry.'

'If she can get him to pick flowers, she can get him to do anything.'

'She got him to marry her.'

'And what a stupid thing that was! A rebel with a price on his head and men under his command in a day and night fight against the militia, taking on the care of a wife.'

'And doesn't he take good care of her too? Checking on her almost every day and staying with her for hours longer than the agreed time.'

'Aye, and she may look like a gentle madonna, but underneath she's a wild creature. Did you hear about the way she danced with him at the Spring Fair? Like a gypsy. The blacksmith from Donard said he had to jump in a barrel of rainwater afterwards.'

'She'll make the captain bite the dust one of these days,' Kearns decided. 'You mark my words. He's so charmed with her, he'll end up taking too many risks and find his neck in a halter.'

Reily agreed. 'And 'twill be that lovely heroine that sets him.'

Michael Kearns looked at Reily, frowned, then narrowed his eyes angrily as he watched the captain running towards them.

'Not while I'm around she won't,' Kearns said grimly.

Mary was welcomed warmly into the Dwyer family. The girls took to her immediately, especially Cathy, who reckoned that any girl who chose to live on the run through love of her big brother must be genuine after all.

Michael's father had completely lost the use of his arm now, it hung limply down his side, but he still managed to do his work without complaint, and bore himself with a dignity that Mary admired.

Mrs Dwyer liked her new daughter-in-law's neat and tidy ways, although she thought her beauty a little indecent. Very kindly, she persuaded Mary to wear her long hair coiled up at the neck and to always keep her bodice covered with a shawl, even in the house.

'Pay no attention,' Cathy whispered with an amused grin, but Mary did as she was told. She desperately wanted Michael's mother to like her.

Their first disagreement came a week later when Mary learned that Michael was camped in a house near Donoughmore, only five miles away, and she prepared to go and see him.

'You're acting very unwisely,' Mrs Dwyer said sternly. 'And it is as dangerous for you as it is for my son.'

Mary could not be dissuaded, convinced the dangers were nothing like as real as everyone made out.

'Michael says he rarely sees a redcoat,' she insisted. 'Last we spoke he hadn't seen hilt nor hide of one of them in weeks.'

When she had gone, Mrs Dwyer looked at her husband, then at her sons and daughters. 'Someone will have to have a word with Michael,' she said coldly. 'Sparing her from worrying is one thing, but making a fool of her, and allowing her to put himself in danger is something else entirely.'

She pulled her shawl around her in an angry motion. 'And when her ladyship returns, I'll set her to rights, quick enough.'

But when Mary returned some hours later, breathless and beaming, Mrs Dwyer could not bring herself to utter even one word of rectitude.

'Did you see him?' Cathy asked.

'Aye, just for a few minutes. The look-out men were a bit strange in their manner, but Hugh Vesty saw me and brought me in.'

Cathy looked astonished. 'You did that trek and stayed just a few minutes!'

Mary nodded, smiling. 'That's all I wanted. Just to see him for a few minutes.'

Again Michael's mother exchanged a significant look with the members of her family. 'Come along, Mary,' she said kindly, 'and help me peel the potatoes.'

Later, when Mary and Etty were in bed, Mrs Dwyer kept her eyes on her knitting as the rest of the family questioned her in hushed tones as to what she had said to Michael's wife about her recklessness.

'I said nothing,' Mrs Dwyer replied without pausing in her knitting. 'Your daddy and I decided it was up to Michael to tell her. And anyway, she was so pleased with herself I didn't have the heart to correct her.' She paused and looked towards the fire. 'And another reason I did not correct her,' she said softly, 'is that I remembered – and let none of ye forget – that Mary ran away from home to that marriage. Away from a comfortable home and a mother she must be sorely missing, to be cast amongst strangers from one end of Imaal to the other. And not a word of regret or complaint as I've heard.'

She turned her head and looked coolly at each of her family. 'So if you think I'm going to upset her, in any way, while she is here in Michael's home, you've got another think coming.'

'Oh, Mammy,' Cathy grinned, 'Michael knew what he was doing when he brought Mary to you.'

The following morning, Michael's father was working in the yard outside the house when he spied a soldier running across the fields. He stood erect as he watched him, his eyes peeled to every movement of the soldier, who frequently looked back over his shoulder as if being pursued. When he drew near, John Dwyer saw that he was a private of the Clare militia which was stationed at Baltinglass.

By the time the soldier reached him, breathless and terrified, the rest of the family had come into the yard.

'I have deserted from those bloody fellows,' the soldier gasped. 'I am now determined to fight for my country against them. If you will have the goodness to tell me where your son the captain is I will go straight to him.'

John Dwyer looked steadily at the terrified man, then said quietly, 'Perhaps it would be better for you to go back to your regiment.'

'But I have just told you – I have deserted!'

'That is your affair,' said John Dwyer.

'Please – just send me to your son! I have nowhere else to go. He has deserters from other regiments with him. He is the only man we can trust once we desert those murderers.'

The entire family stood in silence. None would dare speak unless bid to by their father. 'As to my son that you allude to,' John Dwyer said, 'I know nothing about him.'

The soldier looked greatly distressed. 'Well then, can you direct me to some person who will put me on the right way?'

'I have told you, I know nothing of my son or anyone else who might know his whereabouts.'

The soldier accepted defeat, looked over his shoulder

again, then bid them a hasty farewell and ran off.

'What was it, darling?' Mrs Dwyer asked her husband.

John Dwyer shrugged. 'I may have only one arm, but I have two good eyes. That fellow did not start looking over his shoulder until he saw that I was observing him.'

Mrs Dwyer turned to Mary. 'Do you see how it is now, Mary? The militia will get up to any trick to entrap Michael. Even soldiers masquerading as deserters.'

'Are you sure he was false?' Mary asked her father-in-law.

'No,' he replied. 'I am not entirely sure. But when it comes to Michael's safety, Mary, we take no chances.'

Mary coloured under the veiled rebuke, but in the fierce obsession of her love, she was still determined to seek out Michael whenever she could discover where he was camped.

The soldier ran along the road, slowing his steps when a youth came walking towards him carrying a little basket which contained small wares he sold to gain a livelihood.

'Do you know where the captain is?' the soldier asked. 'I have deserted the militia and wish to join him.'

The youth was a little simple, but he acted even more simple now and stammered, 'What captain would that be, sor?'

'Captain Dwyer of course! I'd serve with none other. Where is he camped?'

'Well, sor,' the youth replied, pointing, 'some say he is beyont thataway, but others say he is ahint thisaway.'

'Look now,' the soldier cried, 'I will buy all your basket if you take me to him. I'm desperate, man! His father would not believe me, but the regiment will kill me if I go back now.'

'Buy all my basket?' the youth gasped. 'Everything? Even the sewing threads?'

'Everything.'

The youth hesitated, bit his lip, screwed up his face. Opened his mouth to speak, then closed it again.

'Is it frightened you are?' asked the soldier. When the youth nodded, he persisted, 'Would you prefer to wait until darkness before you take me to him?'

The youth nodded again.

The soldier dropped his shoulders in relief. 'All right. Now if you meet me here, at this very place, as soon as dusk has fallen, I will buy all your basket and Captain Dwyer will be very pleased with you.'

The youth smiled, gave his promise to return at dusk, with his basket, and take the deserter to the famous Insurgent Captain of the Wicklow Mountains.

'Michael Dwyer is like a warrior prince to us, sor,' the youth said proudly. 'A prince now. Same as a king's son.'

'Dusk, and no later,' the soldier said, smiling.

When dusk came down, the private from the Clare militia was punctual to his appointment, accompanied by five others who were eager to go with him to Dwyer's camp. They waited all through the night until dawn, then set out to find the youth. Always walking the roads with his basket, he was easy to trace. An old woman told them where he lived.

'And he sallied off before you could give him the money for the boot-brushes and combs, sir? Tunder-an-poteen, but isn't he the stupid boy altogether? Putting ye to all this trouble to keep your honour by him.' She clucked her tongue in annoyance. 'And his poor mammy desperate for a penny or two.'

The youth's name was Doyle. He lived at Ballyhubbock, one mile distant from the Dwyers' farm at Eadstown. Through a break in the trees they saw the ramshackle cottage, made of mud and limestone and covered in a yellowing whitewash. The private from the Clare militia knocked once, twice, then impatiently, a third time.

The door opened a crack, a woman's face peeped out. She peered at the militiaman, her eyes narrowing into slits as she looked beyond him to the five uniformed figures standing a few feet away.

'I paid me rent,' she said in an urgent whisper, 'two months late I admit, but I paid it only last week to Mr Shaughnessy, who collects for Lord Wicklow, every penny of it, and not a farthing short!'

The militiaman smiled at the woman and his voice was kindly. 'Your rent is not my concern.' Then he explained the object of his visit.

Her mouth dropped into a gape. 'Never waited for the money?' she cried.

'No, just wandered off.'

She shook her head and her voice returned to a whisper: 'He was like as not dreaming, making up silly songs in his head. He's always making up songs in his head and singing to the fields. But—' her head jutted out a belligerent few inches – 'he's a lovely boy, my boy!' she said defensively. 'A good-natured boy, my boy. And very good to his mammy.'

'I'd like to speak with your boy,' he said. 'Just a few words.'

'He's asleep,' she whispered. 'Just give me the money – he always does.'

'Could you wake him and send him out . . . I need to speak with him . . . on a personal matter . . . in private.'

The woman paused, munched her lips thoughtfully for a moment, then nodded. 'I'll send him out. You can give him the money while you talk.'

A minute later the youth stumbled out, bleary-eyed, wearing only his winter small clothes: flannel knee-drawers and vest.

'You broke your promise,' the private said.

'I know, sor, but then I got to thinking about it, sor, and it worried me that Captain Dwyer might not like it – me taking ye to where he is. He can be a hard martyr with people who cross him.' The youth rubbed his eyes.

The militia private turned away, nodded at his companions.

The youth peered curiously at the five men who instantly raised and pulled back the flints of their muskets, a second later the crash of gunfire blew the youth's flesh to pieces, actually splattering it against the white walls of the cottage.

The plot to entrap Michael Dwyer had failed, and, two days later, the militia officially commented on the incident: 'The youth was an unfortunate victim of the militia's diligence in attempting to catch the most desperate rebel in the county of Wicklow. A rebel whose violence against decent and law-abiding citizens would not be tolerated!'

Captain Corrigan, a deserter from the King's County Militia who commanded a small camp of deserters from that regiment, came to see Michael and showed him a letter.

'It was brought to me today,' Corrigan said. 'I can only think it must have been written by one of the servants of Lord Powerscourt.'

Michael read the letter:

Captain Corragen, I take this opertunity to let you know that Mrs Holt has been in Pours Court this week past and has General Holt's *Pardon* from Lord Pours Court without dowt, and if you and Captain Dwyer does not

mind her and him you are all Lost. Sir you may Depend
on this as the most sertan truth.

Michael looked up. 'It could be just vindictiveness. Joseph
Holt has many personal enemies.'

'Explain about Holt,' Corrigan demanded.

Michael explained that Joseph Holt was a smallholding
farmer who, in the years previous to the rebellion, had occasionally worked as a bounty hunter, bringing in robbers,
although Holt insisted he did it for the common good, and
never took the rewards. The first the rebels knew of Holt was
when he came to them claiming that a neighbour, a Protestant
squireen, had burned his house to the ground because he suspected Holt of being a United Irishman, which he was not.
Then Holt, in his vengeance, took the United oath. He showed
brilliant military strategy, led many a good campaign against
the enemy, and was soon elected General by his men.

'His wife, on the other hand,' Michael added, 'is one Hester
Long, and related to George Manning of Ballyteigue – a yeoman who set fire to my uncle's house knowing that he was alone
and unconscious in his fever bed. Now George Manning is of
the same type of man as Hunter Gowan, the biggest croppy
hater in Wexford. My friend, Miles Byrne, could tell you all
about Hunter Gowan and his thirteen daughters who are such
gentle creatures they actually tittered and grinned while they
prepared the croppies' heads for the boiling pitchcap.'

'But Holt fought for the rebels,' Corrigan said in puzzlement.

'Aye, but he had nowhere else to go. It was join the rebel
camp or lie in the ditches with his family. All credit to the man
for the smart fight he put up for the United Confederates. But
I've heard that wife of his talking about my lads, telling Holt
they were nothing more than Papist ruffians – despite the fact,
and she knows it, that a third of them are Protestants.'

Michael looked coolly at Corrigan. 'And you know what
they say – tell a bird by its song, tell a woman by her language.
And to me, that kind of talk stinks of hidden bigotry.'

Captain Corrigan looked again at the letter. 'And she's been
to see Lord Powerscourt. I think we had better pay a visit to
General Holt. Where is he?'

'Well, like myself, he moves around a lot. But my spies tell
me that, at the moment, he is camped in Glenmalure.'

* * *

Now the weather was turning cold, Holt had set up his own personal headquarters in Pierce Harney's house at the head of Glenmalure. When Michael and his men approached, they could hear loud shouting coming from within the house. Groups of men were arguing fiercely in the yard outside.

'Good security they have here,' Michael remarked to Hugh Vesty. 'Not one sentry on outpost duty.'

On entering the house they found it packed with men. Mrs Holt was standing in the corner, sobbing. Her husband was on his knees in the centre of the room, about to be shot.

'Shoot the traitor!' John Harmon shouted, but Pierce Harney put his hand up for silence when he saw Dwyer and his men, accompanied by Captain Corrigan.

'He's a traitor, Captain Dwyer!' Harmon shouted. 'And it's all down to his wife here!'

Amidst the babble of voices, it was then stated that a number of men had Holt under suspicion for some time, especially when his wife began to visit the camp and whisper to him. And upon her arrival that afternoon, they had searched her coat and found a letter inside, arranging the terms of his surrender to the enemy.

'While his men are holding out, sleeping in the cold and damp, the general is making terms for his own pardon, and that means one thing – disclosures of names. *Informing!*'

Michael asked Holt if the charges were true. Holt seemed confused, whether it was from terror of the men clamouring around him, or lack of a suitable reply, it was hard to tell.

'We should never deceive each other,' Michael said. 'We are all public property to each; every act goes towards strengthening or destroying the whole of us. In our fight of resistance, we suffer danger, hunger, the hazard of the elements, but we never suffer a man who trades in his own comrades.'

'It was me!' Mrs Holt cried. 'It was me who went to the wife of Captain La Touche and asked her to approach Lord Powerscourt about a pardon.'

'And bring in a bounty of names in exchange!' Harmon cried. 'Details of our hideouts. Everything.'

'No! No!'

The men were bursting to a fury, but Hugh Vesty Byrne was greatly indignant with them.

'You can't just shoot a man like that! Are we as bad as the militia? That can shoot a man without trial or investigation? A pack of murdering hounds around a lone fox? If you kill Holt now, without benefit of a fair and just investigation, you are contravening the honourable oath of the United Irishmen! And furthermore . . .'

Michael turned up his eyes and sighed. Hugh Vesty – descendant of Feagh McHugh O'Byrne – could be powerful when he wanted to be.

'. . . can a man be blamed,' Hugh asked, 'if it his *wife* who endeavours to obtain his pardon? And is that pardon conditional upon circumstances that would endanger any other person? Have any of you bothered to find out?'

The men looked confused. Finally John Harmon looked at Michael. 'We trust you, Captain Dwyer. What do you say?'

Michael looked long at Joseph Holt – the poor rooster had turned into a quivering chicken.

'Let the general go,' he said tonelessly. 'Any man who harms him will be brought to immediate court martial.'

Within seconds Hugh Vesty and all of Michael's men had their firearms cocked and pointing. Holt's men were instantly subdued. The majority were pikemen, not the sharpshooting gunsmen of Dwyer's division.

'Not only has Holt fought in our front lines,' Michael said, 'and risked his life bravely in leading our men safely in and out of battle . . . he is also a Protestant. And if you harm him, what will the world say of us? They will say that we are a savage set and too besotted with bigotry to let a Protestant live, although he was fighting for us.'

'His religion has nothing to do with it!' Harmon insisted.

'Nevertheless,' Michael answered, 'that is what people will say.'

Holt's men were greatly pacified. It was true, Holt had led them and fought like a lion in his day; they had even made him their general. Many hung their heads, while others moved to assist Holt to his feet.

Joseph Holt stood before Michael, shorter and looking up at him, drawing great gasping breaths. He both feared and hated Dwyer, and now Dwyer had held the balance of his life in his hands, and had given it back to him, he despised him even more.

Michael saw the hate and was indifferent to it. 'You are a Protestant,' he said quietly to Holt, 'and that alone has saved you.'

The rest of the men began to rally around Holt, offering him their apologies. Michael turned abruptly and walked out of the room.

Pierce Harney and John Harmon came after him, insisting he stay and have a drink. Hugh Vesty suggested they sit on the wall and have a smoke while they were at it. Captain Corrigan and the others agreed. They needed something to take the bad taste away after what had just happened, and before they returned to their own camps.

Later, as they sat on the wall finishing their smokes, they could hear the thundering voice of Holt admonishing his men severely.

'I did not expect that I should ever witness anything like this event,' Holt roared. 'I was elected your chief because you thought me best calculated to serve you. I have not disappointed your expectations. I have brought you through many difficulties, always safely, often with victory.'

'True enough, General Holt!'

'My fidelity, I thought above suspicion, but I have been treated like a traitor and degraded to the situation of begging for my life, had I condescended to do so. But I would *not*, no I would *not* beg for my life at your hands. My life was not worth saving if I was to be degraded.'

'What a load of bullshit,' Corrigan murmured.

'I have, therefore,' Holt cried, 'decided to resign the command of men who know not how to value an honest leader. I am ready to become a private, and now you have nothing to do but to choose another chief. I hope you will find a man so honest as myself, and one more able and willing to serve you.'

The men inside the house and in the yard began to murmur amongst themselves. Some accusing others of starting it all. And poor Mrs Holt could not be blamed for her devotion to her husband.

'A cheer for General Holt!' a voice cried. 'We will have no other general. He shall be our chief! And let any man show his face who will insult him!'

'He's a traitor!' Harmon shouted. 'The letter on his wife proves it.'

The disagreement went on and on, and Michael and his men listened, slightly amused, and greatly disgusted. Holt's voice became muffled. Michael called out to John Harmon who was standing at the open door. 'What is he saying about General Moore?'

Harmon sniffed. 'Saying how he turned down General Moore's humane proposition, and now it is too late. All because he was *burthened* with the care of others.'

'No, I could not,' Holt thundered, 'continue to be the leader of such a band of . . . ruffians . . . that cannot restrain their outrage and cruelty. I could never be sure of my own safety. You have broken out in *mutiny* and even threatened the life of your commander!'

'The mutiny on the *Bounty* must have sounded something like this,' Sam McAllister reflected. 'I'll wager Captain Bligh sounded just like Holt does now . . . poor Fletcher Christian.'

The men cajoled Holt, assured and reassured him, convincing him of their sorrow and renewed loyalty to him.

' 'Tis disgraceful how you have acted towards our commander!' a voice shouted. 'If it were not for the arrival of Captain Dwyer, the general would now be on a fast trip to eternity. Shame on you, making General Holt suffer like that – and he already with a tormenting bowel complaint!'

'Oh you were right about the bullshit,' Hugh Vesty said to Corrigan.

The men in the yard all turned their heads curiously as Dwyer and his men sent up a roar of laughter.

In that same month of November 1798, General Joseph Holt of the United Irish army, surrendered to Lord Powerscourt.

Michael decided to move Mary from Eadstown in case another raid was made on his family home. In the darkness of the night, he escorted her to the house of a family in Imaal who had no daughters, but four young sons, who fell over themselves in the rush to make her feel at home.

In the tower in Dublin Castle, Joseph Holt was visited by Lord Cornwallis, Lord Rossmore, Lord Monck, and other officials. The Castle publicly announced that Holt had made 'interesting disclosures'. He revealed the identities of twenty-six rebels from the County of Wicklow still at liberty.

Nevertheless, Lord Cornwallis did not pardon Joseph Holt, had never agreed to pardon him, but neither did he send him for trial. In return for his honourable surrender and the disclosure of names, Holt was informed that he was to be transported to Botany Bay in the antipodes, as a free settler.

Michael and his men waited, but it was speedily learned that of the names Joseph Holt had sworn against, Michael Dwyer's name was not one of them, nor any of the men associated with him.

In his camp at Athlone, General John Moore received a summons to attend at haste upon Lord Cornwallis at the Viceregal Lodge in Phoenix Park.

Upon his arrival in Dublin, Moore was apprehensive. Although Lord Cornwallis had always treated him with the utmost kindness and distinction, he had written a letter applying to Cornwallis for leave to return to England. Ireland was still plagued with rumours of another insurrection but, without further help from France, another rising was unlikely. And at present Napoleon was too busy squaring up to Nelson in Egypt. And Nelson was giving him a beauty of a drubbing.

Just the thought of it made Moore sigh with impatience. He was convinced there would be no further action in Ireland, and considered it nothing more than a loss of time to stay here, when there was service abroad more active.

Lord Cornwallis was in his office.

Even here at the Lodge, Moore observed, Cornwallis lived without pomp and ceremony, but in the simple manner of an army general surrounded by aides-de-camp. Cornwallis breakfasted at nine, and immediately after retired to his office and his papers with his military secretary Colonel Littlehales, and his private secretary, Captain Taylor. One hour later various officers, military and civic, were shown into him in succession.

General Moore did not have to wait. Littlehales immediately brought him in, then vacated the room in which Lord Cornwallis sat behind a desk, a letter in his hand, his face grim. He motioned his head towards a side table on which stood a tray of china and a teapot.

'Tea?' Cornwallis offered, without looking up. 'It has just been made and is therefore fresh.'

'No, thank you, my lord,' General Moore replied in a pensive tone.

'You have already partaken refreshment before coming here?'

'No, my lord. I was told to make haste.' Moore attributed Cornwallis's churlish tone to the letter he was holding, and his heart sank. 'I heard about the atrocity in Wicklow,' he said quickly. 'The youth shot to pieces by militia. It brought back to mind another and equally sickening incident which happened in the Glen of Imaal shortly after the Leinster rebellion.'

Cornwallis looked up, his eyes as cold as pebbles in a pool.

'A servant boy named Malone,' continued General Moore. 'A primitive young boy and very innocent in his manner. He presented himself to me and requested to surrender and receive a Protection Certificate, although it was penny plain he had never been on a battlefield in his life.'

Moore smiled sadly. 'I asked him a few droll questions about the action he had seen, and my officers and I had a little amusement with him when he began strutting up and down the tent and telling us what a great and fearless rebel he had been. But in the end we gave him his Protection Certificate. No doubt his purpose was simply to show it to other servant boys. We also sent him away with ten shillings, which we had decided amongst ourselves was worthy of the entertainment we had received.

'Less than half an hour later two of my soldiers brought him back with his Protection Certificate rammed into his mouth and a bullet in his head. The ten shillings, of course, was gone.'

Cornwallis was staring. 'Did you find out who did it?'

'My soldiers saw it. A party of militia who happened on the boy near the camp and also decided to have some entertainment with him, but of a brutal kind; making him go through the rebel pike drill, before they suddenly shot him, then ran away after taking the money.'

Cornwallis was turning a dangerous shade of purple. 'Did you find those men and bring them to justice, sir?'

'I certainly did. That is why I am not the militia's most favourite general officer.'

'Indeed you are not.' Cornwallis spoke absently, then, fearing his words might be misconstrued, he went on, 'London believes we no longer need so many troops here in Ireland, and that some should be withdrawn.'

General Moore opened his mouth to agree politely with London, but Cornwallis continued, 'The truth is, we need even more troops here than we have at present, and not to control the natives, but the militia and many of the Anglo-Irish country gentlemen of rank who believe it is more enjoyable to end the hunting season with a rebel's severed hand to stir the festive bowl of punch instead of the customary fox's tail.'

General Moore's face turned a sickly shade of pale.

Cornwallis sighed. 'Indeed, sickening is too weak a term for it.'

'I sometimes think, my lord, that if I were an Irishman, I should be a rebel.'

Cornwallis was not amused by or sympathetic to the thought. He ignored the remark, returning to British military affairs. 'But then, General Moore, our troops are greatly needed in the war against France.' He sighed irritably. 'Such a pity the scheme of giving Protections failed so badly here. If it had succeeded, there would not be so many rebels in the Wicklow mountains still refusing to surrender.'

'I feel myself that the Protection scheme might have met with success,' Moore ventured, 'if the maintaining of it had been left in the hands of the Highland regiments and not the militia. The Highlanders commit no atrocities and are respected, and often liked, by the people.'

'The Hundredth Gordon Highlanders, as you know, has now been renamed the Ninety-second.'

'Whatever their name, they are an excellent regiment,' Moore said.

'They will be leaving us shortly,' Cornwallis said. 'Which is a pity. As you say, an excellent regiment.'

Which brought the commander in chief back to the letter in his hand. 'This letter,' he said, 'has upset me greatly.'

General Moore glanced to the letter which he assumed was his own letter requesting leave to return to England, when Cornwallis explained.

'This letter is from London, requesting a recall of some of my troops, and also yourself, General Moore. It seems His Majesty's ministers feel that you are needed in the great contest against France. You are being given a command to proceed to Europe on a secret expedition.'

Moore was so astonished he could not answer at first, then managed to croak, 'A secret expedition?'

'Well, it is, of course, secret as far as the world is concerned. But I shall save you weeks of suspense by telling you that your destination is the Helder, under the command of Sir Ralph Abercromby. The Marquis of Huntly and his Ninety-second

Regiment of Foot will be one of the many regiments that go with you.'

The utter delight on Moore's face stirred Cornwallis to a begrudging smile. 'You will naturally have a few weeks' leave in England before you sail, and whilst you are there, I may add, you have been invited to dine with Prime Minister Pitt at Walmer Castle.'

General Moore knew he was smiling like a Cheshire cat at the thought of going where the action was. Then he observed the look on the commander-in-chief's face, and said very honestly:

'My lord, if there was a chance of further employment here in Ireland, there is no other man under whom I would sooner serve.'

'Most kind, most kind,' Cornwallis muttered, then smiled warmly at the person he considered not only to be a splendid man, but a truly great soldier.

'I do understand how you feel, Moore. You are a soldier, and have no wish to be a policeman. The apprehensions for Ireland seem to be over. And so Europe beckons. But firstly, you are to give up the command of your garrison to Brigadier-General Scott, and supreme command of your district to Brigadier-General Meyrick, who is on his way down from Galway. You will leave Ireland on the eighteenth.'

'Yes, my lord.'

When General Moore had left and Captain Taylor had entered, Lord Cornwallis hunched his shoulders under his epaulettes and gave his secretary a doleful look. 'A letter, Taylor, to Pitt's Secretary for War.'

When Captain Taylor was ready to write the letter to Henry Dundas, Lord Cornwallis said sourly: 'Tell him he can have whatever ruddy troops he wants – and General Moore – who is a greater loss to me than all the ruddy troops put together!'

Captain Taylor murmured a 'Yes, my lord,' then wrote:

I am sure you know me too well to suspect that any selfish consideration could weigh a moment with me against the general interests of my country. You may have all the troops you ask, and General Moore, who is a greater loss to me than the troops. But he will be of infinite service to . . .

Just outside the town of Baltinglass, in a gloomy tavern which also served as a general store, a number of the militia were

236

drinking heavily. The tavern keeper was tense and irritable, waiting for them all to clear off and go home to their beds. With head bowed but eyes darting furtively around the room, the keeper paced silently back and forth behind the small wooden counter. Every so often his eyes shot to the door as if dreading another customer.

Finally there were just two of the militia left, sitting by a barrel near the fireplace. The keeper watched them carefully, at least, one of them in particular, his eyes cold.

He turned his head sharply as an English soldier in scarlet regimentals quietly entered the dim room and moved to the wooden counter, his back to the two men at the fireplace. The keeper gritted his teeth as the soldier arrogantly clicked his fingers at him. 'Whiskey.'

For a moment the keeper peered at him, then nodded subserviently. His eyes darted to the fireplace as he placed a glass on the counter, lifted a bottle and poured.

'Have you anything under that counter?' the soldier inquired softly.

'I do,' the keeper answered just as softly.

The soldier gave a slight smile.

'But 'tis not mountain dew,' the keeper said, eyeing the two men at the fireplace. 'I serve only tax-paid legal whiskey in here.'

The soldier lifted his glass, dismissing the keeper from further conversation by fixing his eyes downwards on the counter as he sipped slowly.

One of the militia by the fire turned his head and stared resentfully at the straight scarlet back of the young English soldier.

'Bloody English regulars,' he murmured. 'Think they're a cut above the rest of us.' He lifted his glass and said loudly and belligerently, 'Here's to the militia and yeos, may they never fall! And be damned to General Moore and Lord Cornwall!'

His mouth stayed opened as he looked at his friend and laughed soundlessly, delighted with himself. 'There now,' he said, 'poetry!'

The soldier by the counter made no response, just kept his back to the fireplace.

'Poetry! And the savages think they're the only ones who have the poetry.' The militiaman turned to the keeper. 'What's that saying you peasants have about poetry?'

'As long as poetry is our heritage, and Ireland is our native land.'

'Ahahaha! Ahahaha!' The soldier at the fireplace thought it hilarious, while his friend kept drinking as if half-asleep.

The keeper continued in a dignified voice: 'It was Finn who said it, I think. He was of course referring to the red deer. Saying as how they should never be killed – not as long as poetry is our heritage and Ireland our native land.'

'Piss to you and poetry and your red shagging deer!' the militia-man sneered.

'Now, now, private,' the keeper said sternly. 'No need to be abusive.'

'Private me arse! "Lance-corporal" if you don't mind.'

The keeper met the eyes of the English soldier by the counter. 'Fancy that now?' he said. 'A private in the Clare militia stationed at Baltinglass promoted to lance-corporal!' The keeper jutted his chin towards the soldier by the fire. 'And was it your bravery that got you promoted? But sure now, it must have been.'

'Ahahaha! Ahahaha!' The lance-corporal was beginning to think that everything the keeper said was hilarious, but his companion staggered to his feet.

'I'm away to my bed,' he mumbled, giving his shoulders two or three shrugs, then walked slowly to the door as if there was an invisible line marked on the floor which he must keep to at all costs.

The lance-corporal watched him. 'Ahahaha! Upon my soul, there goes a man who can't take his drink!' He looked slyly at the English soldier's scarlet back. 'He must have more English blood in him than his mother told him about. Ahahahaha!'

The keeper moved to put the whiskey bottle away, but the English soldier held his glass over the counter. 'While you have the hammer in your hand,' he said softly, 'put another nail in that.'

The keeper smiled secretly as he poured the liquid into the glass. The militiaman by the fire had not heard the request. He was staring into the fire, his mouth open as if he was about to let out another laugh.

There was silence for a few moments, then the lance-corporal turned round to speak again to the keeper – but he had vanished into the shadows. On top of the counter behind which he had stood sat a small basket of wares.

The tavern was empty save for the English soldier, who had

removed his hat, and now stood facing the former private of the Clare militia.

'I'm told that you were looking to find me, avic.'

The former private of the Clare militia stared at him: about twenty-five years, about five feet eleven inches high, square shoulders, broad-breasted, rather long-legged, black hair, black eyes, born in Imaal . . . He made a choking sound as he realised that the five hundred guineas he had dreamed of was standing before him, dressed in scarlet regimentals. He stared wildly as the basket was carried towards him and dropped on the barrel.

'You offered to buy the whole of this basket. Even went to the boy's house to make payment for it. But you didn't pay, did you, avic?'

The soldier's eyes darted to where his brace of pistols were lying on the barrel, the basket covered them, held down by the rebel's hand.

He swallowed noisily, remembering all the rumours he had heard about Dwyer: about his ability to disguise himself so completely that he had often walked through the streets of Baltinglass and Rathdrum without anyone recognising him. Others said he could alter his appearance entirely by simply changing his facial expression and walk. And now it looked as if he must have friends amongst the English as well as the Jocks.

'What are you going to do?' he croaked, seeing Dwyer had made no move to withdraw his own pistol.

'I'm going to be fair, give you an even chance. Man to man. No weapons.'

'Fair! You call this fair? I've had a skinful of drink and you haven't!'

'It's fairer than you deserve,' Michael said contemptuously. 'There were six of you against one lad who was defenceless and unarmed when you murdered him.'

'No! No! Now listen, Dwyer, it didn't happen the way you were told. It was the others – bastards every one of them. They did the business before I could stop them. That's the truth, believe me, that's the truth.'

'The truth is that the boy died because of you, and because of me. And now it is time for you and me to settle the score.'

'Settle the score? In what way?'

Michael looked at him coldly. 'If you beat me, you can shoot me. Blow my flesh against the walls even.'

The militiaman rose to his feet, wiping his mouth with his hand as he backed away. 'And if you beat me . . . ?'

'Oh, I will beat you,' Michael quietly assured him, then viciously kicked the stool out of his path. 'I'm going to beat the life out of you.'

Chapter Sixteen

It was Christmas Eve. Michael had arranged to meet Mary at John Cullen's house at Knockgorragh. It was the only place they felt safe to be alone without a bodyguard, not only because of the desolation of the location and the cavernous passage from the bedroom, but a host of other places outside the house where a man could conceal himself without easy detection.

Cullen was delighted. Having the two of them spend Christmas with him would make it like a family. He ventured up to the bee-keeping woman and renewed his supplies of honey, then called over to Eadstown and was fed heartily by Michael's mother.

On returning home, Cullen put the half of suckling pig she had given to him on the spit to roast, then set off to see the man who 'stilled the mountain dew'. He returned some hours later, gloriously drunk, clutching two bottles of the illegal poteen.

When Mary arrived it was dark. She found the door wide open and Cullen sprawled on the floor unconscious, his arms outstretched. Thinking he was dead her stomach leapt with fright, but slowly steadied when the old man let out a blissful snort. It took two cups of black tea before he could open his eyes and think clearly. 'Oh bad cess to that stillman!' he cried. 'He'll put me in an early grave yet.'

'Why did you drink so much?' Mary demanded sternly.

'I only intended to taste it, treasure,' Cullen explained. 'You see, Mary, 'tis unwise to buy any of the stillman's poteen without tasting his new brew and reflecting on its quality and texture. Some of it can be very good, but others only quite good. Oh, my poor head!'

She poured him another cup of tea. Michael came in a few minutes later carrying a number of dead partridge which he and the lads had shot that morning. 'Covey after covey of them were flying above us on the wind,' he told them with a smile, 'and we having had no breakfast and carrying guns in our hands. 'Twas like a godsend. We were on them in seconds, bringing them down like manna from heaven.'

'Good lad!' Cullen cried. 'And your mother's sent you over a big fruit cake and half a suckling pig. We'll have a grand time.'

Michael looked at Mary. 'Aye, we'll have a grand time,' he said.

She wanted to reach out and touch him, put her arms around his waist, but knowing his dislike of physical displays of affection in front of others, she held tightly to herself and only smiled at him. She had seen him a number of times since leaving the old couple's house in November, but only for a few minutes, and always with some of his men or some of the harbouring family close by. Tonight would be their first time alone since the day of the marigolds.

'Light the Christmas candle, Mary, and put it in the window,' Cullen said. 'And, Michael, you go and light the fire in the bedroom. I meant to do it myself earlier, but sure I can't mind everything. Then you can rebuild the fire in here while Mary makes the supper.'

Michael stared at him. 'Is it Lord of the Manor you are or what?'

'No, treasure, just overhung a bit.' Cullen sighed. 'But I'm bearing it well. Ah, there now, isn't that nice?'

Mary had lit the Christmas candle which was three candles melted together at the base and held in a single holder. Michael watched her as she put it on the small shelf of the window, his gaze moving down the shining curtain of black hair that reached her waist.

'That'll show them,' Cullen said, a catch in his voice, 'poor Saint Joseph and our Blessed Lady. If they had come to Wicklow instead of going to Bethlehem, not a door would have been closed to them and the Holy Child.'

Mary kept her back to Michael, but in the reflection of the dark window their eyes met. They stared at each other, saw what they wanted to see, spoke by silence, their gaze held in the reflection of the candleglow.

Cullen broke the moment by again telling Michael to light the bedroom fire. Michael turned abruptly and did as he was bid.

When he came out of the bedroom she was spreading a cloth on the table, bending far over so her hips under the blue dress seemed to swell over the edge. He stood quite still in the doorway, watching her slender fingers slide over the cloth as she smoothed away the folds. She straightened and turned to the dresser, lifting down plates. His eyes lingered on the thrust of her breasts against the tight blue bodice. He remembered the days he used to look at her clothed body and wonder, but now that he knew made just looking at her exciting.

He moved into the room and busied himself washing his own hands in the ewer in the corner, took the bowl outside, emptied it and refilled it from the rain-barrel.

'We'll have some of the roasted pork tonight,' Cullen said. 'And the partridge done in the herbs when we get back tomorrow.'

Throughout the preparation of supper, whenever Cullen's attention was distracted, Michael would touch her in passing, her arm or her shoulder, and her cheeks would flush as they looked at each other in silence; he saw that the accumulated longing of weeks was burning in her too, and she was eager for his love.

Cullen was talking to him, his cloudy eyes on the spitted pork sizzling above the fire in the wide hearth, gesticulating with his pipe as he talked.

'The wind and rain was in her eyes, she told me, and her poor mule was facing it glumly. But she lashed the beast on, for being a mountain woman it was against her principle to turn back. On they went in the fleecing wind and rain, herself and her mule, and a strong mule he is too. Troth, he needs to be, for the bee-keeping woman has a very loving heart when it comes to her food . . .'

Michael pretended to listen, but scarcely heard the words as he stood looking into the fire, his mind lost in thoughts of her naked body locked in his embrace. He turned his head and saw she was no longer in the room.

Cullen was speaking to him again, and again he pretended to listen, but the old man's voice sounded afar off, the words vague and meaningless, as he stood looking into the fire as if in a dream, thinking of all the nights in the past weeks he had lain amongst his comrades thinking of her, remembering the warm lavender fragrance of her body lying within his arms, longing for their next reunion and the exquisite joy he always found between the warm young thighs of his sweet Mary, his beautiful wife.

Cullen's voice droned on. He made no answer, for the old

man required no answers, his story directed at the meat sizzling on the spit, the pipe emphasising in the same direction. He turned his head again, his eyes resting on the bedroom door.

Firelight was the only light in the bedroom, flickering and mingling with shadows on the bed and walls. She was turning back the bedclothes when he came up behind her and closed his arms about her waist. She uttered a little gasp of fright and turned her head to look at him, unable to turn her body in the tightness of his embrace.

'I was letting the heat of the fire at the sheets,' she whispered. 'They get cold and damp when a bed lies unused.'

Then she felt his lips on the side of her neck. She leaned her head back against him and closed her eyes, her lips parted, her body trembling. His lips moved down her neck, sipping at her skin as his hands moved up from her waist to her breasts, caressing them sensuously until her nipples felt as hard as raspberry buds in spring.

'This pork is going to be mostly crackling if it's not tended soon,' Cullen called.

Her eyes opened, and the whole room seemed to pause with her in the silence.

'And the potatoes, Mary,' Cullen said as she rushed into the room and over to the cooking pot, 'shouldn't be left to go too soft.'

'They're fine,' she said shakily, 'fine, fine . . .'

When supper was finally served, Cullen continued the endless tale he had left off earlier.

'So, herself and her mule were still plodding it over the hills when who did she meet but Tattam the tinker, and being mountain people, neither could pass the other without civil conversation. Troth, both found it hard to pass each other at all, seeing as the same stormy wind that was pushing him forward was also shoving her back. Howsomever, this way and that way, they got talking, and it was then that she learned about Green the cooper . . .'

The two lovers at the table were not listening as they looked silently at each other. Between his eyes and hers there was only one thought, only one vision. She smiled secretly at him, the light from the candle on the table framing her face in a soft suffused glow, and the sheer beauty of her face inflamed him. He reached out and stroked her cheek with his finger, while Cullen closed his eyes and shook his head in disgust at the behaviour of Green the cooper.

Supper over, Cullen moved to the fire and lifted the poker. 'We'll say the nightly blessing now,' he said, 'then you can check that the bolts and chains on the door are locked tight, Michael.'

Then the old man raked the turf fire, and said the prayer that was a nightly occurrence in most mountain cottages.

> 'I save the seed of the fire tonight,
> And so may Christ save me.
> Let nine of the mightiest angels
> Round the throne of the Trinity,
> Protect this house and its people
> Till the dawn of the day shall be.'

Cullen smiled, sighed, laid down the poker and moved over to lie on his settle-bed for a few minutes, complaining of the weight of the poteen on his bones. 'Ach, Christmas is a grand time,' he said happily, stretching on to his back. 'Sure even the militia take a holiday from murdering at Christmas. Peace and goodwill to all men, if only for a day.'

Michael crossed to the door and secured the bar and chains while Mary cleared the table, then he placed more turf-bricks on the fire before sitting down in the rocking-chair to the left of the inglenook.

'Everywhere you go, everyone you meet,' Cullen yawned, ''tis happy Christmas here, and happy Christmas there. Ah, don't be talking . . .'tis the best time of the year. Isn't that true, Michael darling?'

''Tis true enough,' Michael answered softly, his eyes watching the old man carefully, noting the drooping eyelids, the slackening mouth.

On the crane above the fire the kettle was boiling. Holding a cloth Mary bent and fussed with it and laid it on the fire-flag. Michael slowly rocked as he sat watching her, unable to take his eyes off the girl who had enraptured him, captured him, and now belonged to him.

He glanced again at Cullen, and abruptly stopped rocking. 'He's asleep,' he whispered. 'Out to the world.'

As if to confirm this, Cullen began to snore serenely.

Mary looked over her shoulder at the old man, then, turning back, tilted her face to Michael. As they studied each other the fire crackled loudly, the kettle's wet base spat and hissed on the fire-flag.

He held out his hand to her.

She rose, allowing him to draw her between his knees, then, bringing both his arms around her waist, he made her his prisoner. She held his face in her hands and they dwelt in each other's eyes, their bodies trembling.

'Oh, Michael,' she whispered, her voice a shiver. 'I thought today would never come.'

'Myself too,' he whispered.

He pulled her down to his lap and for the first time they kissed in the presence of the old man, and with such hunger and need, she was half undressed when he swung her up and carried her into the bedroom.

Outside the hills were draped in silence, no bird or creature moved in the black cold, only the silver mould of moon travelled on its endless nocturnal course.

Inside the bedroom they lay in blissful drowsiness, united in the exhaustion of their passion, but it didn't take them long to come back to individual consciousness. They had no wish to sleep, for time was scarce, time was everything, and they could not be sure if or when they would enjoy such happiness again.

In soft murmurs they exchanged news. Mary could not understand his laughter when she told him that John O'Neill had proposed marriage to his sister Cathy, and both sets of parents had agreed to the match. Then he informed her that Hugh Vesty was truly in love with Sarah now, pined for her poetically. And by the looks of things, Sarah felt the same way about Hugh. No – marriage was out of the question. Although her family were behind the rebels, they would surely outlaw her for marrying one.

A fleeting shadow of sadness crossed Mary's face. Michael saw it and closed his eyes for a moment, his question barely audible. She shook her head positively. She had no regrets.

The room began to cool, the cold air making her shiver and move further under the bedclothes. She put her hands against his chest and curled into him for warmth. He drew away teasingly, grinning, refusing to be treated as a bed-warmer, then slipped out of bed, tugged on his breeches and moved over to build up the fire. She slid up the pillow and watched him dreamily as he crouched before the hearth. He put his hand into one of the two fuel buckets at the side and fed straw and sticks into the red embers, then turf-bricks. The straw and sticks ignited, flickering golden light over his face and black hair as he coaxed the fire until the room was warm again.

He noticed her watching him and smiled at her happily as he moved into the living-room, and felt the chill. He did the same to the fire there, preparing it slightly differently so it would smoulder and not flame, ready to be brought to life with a few blasts of the bellows in the morning.

She murmured out to him. He caught her words. She was hungry. He bent over the old man, who was still on top of the settle-bed, sleeping the slumber of the righteous, his arms clasped around his body, hugging out the cold.

He lifted the old man's rug-cloak off the hook in the corner and spread it over him, then moved to the dresser and cut a large slice of the fruit cake and put it on a plate. His eyes fell on the two bottles of poteen and he deliberated silently, then he smiled and lifted a bottle. Sure wasn't it Christmas.

She was singing quietly to herself when he returned and handed her the plate, then he sat down on her side of the bed and unplugged the bottle of poteen, but he did not drink it, just stared at the bottle's rim as he examined the strange sensation bubbling in his chest. It flashed on his mind that it was simple happiness, which surprised him, for he was usually happy enough in his own way, but not like this . . .

The fire in the hearth was blazing fiercely, its light flickering on the bed, the sweet musky smell of the turf permeating the room. He had never liked this room, an unlived-in, unslept-in room, empty and cold. Even on his wedding night it had not touched him enough to notice it, blinded as he had been by the lovely candlelit face and body of the virgin young girl in the bed. But now he was noticing it, and saw it as warm and enchanting.

Something is happening to me, he decided, something dangerous. I'm losing my grip. He knew many thought him hard, and naturally so, for he lived hard. And now here he was, inwardly bubbling like a female with a happiness that had somehow transmuted a shabby little room in an old thatched cottage into a tiny corner of paradise.

He looked down at the bottle in his hand, and smiled at the nonsense of his thoughts. And he hadn't had even a drop!

She was munching the last mouthful of cake and looking at him. 'Why are you smiling at that bottle?' she asked.

He turned his head and looked at her, the blanket held tight to her body under her armpits, always shy with him except in passion. 'You wouldn't believe me if I told you,' he said.

'Oh, I think I would, Michael.' Her head moved knowingly up and down. 'And did you notice the curtains I made for our little haven?'

'Curtains?' He turned and stared at the small recessed window, at the two delicate lace curtains, then back at her. 'There's never been curtains on that window since Cullen's mother died,' he told her. 'What did he say when he saw them?'

'He hasn't seen them yet. I hung them while he was sobering up. But I'm sure he understands that I need something to do in the long evenings while you're gallivanting up the mountains. And I have no windows of my own to make them for. Do you think he will mind?'

'Not a bit. He'll be delighted. Although they may remind him of his mother, and he may start to cry, but don't take it personal.'

She made a face after her first taste of poteen, giggled after the fourth and fifth taste, then when she had stopped counting, convulsed with shocked laughter when he broke his oath to Cullen and told her what Rosie Noonan had done up on the Lugnaquilla. Finally, a crimson flush came to her cheeks and her dark eyes rolled with the burn of the white fire in her stomach.

He looked at her speculatively, wondering if he should have allowed her the poteen after all. 'Are you all right, darling?'

She looked into his eyes, and gave him the wanton smile of a temptress.

It was not long after dawn when Cullen awakened them, rapping on the bedroom door and shouting, 'Are youse getting up or what?'

Exhausted, they stirred and opened their eyes, the sobering dawn informing them they had fallen asleep and the night was gone. Murmuring, they nuzzled into the warmth of each other and went back to sleep.

Later, Cullen rapped louder. 'Come along now. Only heathens stay abed on Christmas morning.'

Mary made an effort to rouse herself. 'Sometimes I wish I was a heathen,' she moaned tiredly.

'God forgive you,' Michael whispered. 'Saying a thing like that on the birthday of Jesus.'

'I have the breakfast ready,' Cullen called, 'and the fire blazing. We have to get a move on if we're going up to Dublin.'

The air was cold and sharp and the land desolate of all people as they made their way on foot across the mountain paths to Donard. Mary and Cullen held back while Michael descended the rest of the hill alone, pulling his black slouch hat down over his brow as he cut sideways across the hill until he had a good view of the little square below.

The network of conspiracy, and the support for Michael Dwyer was so strong in Wicklow, that already the people had certain signals and passwords to welcome or warn him.

If he had sent word and was expected in the neighbourhood of a harbourer's house, and it was safe to approach, a small fire of withered bracken or heather was lit in the yard or on the hillside near the house. Another signal of safety was for a woman to stand at the door combing her hair.

Outside the forge, O'Casey the blacksmith sat huddled over a small fire of bracken, meticulously combing his magnificent moustaches, finishing each side with a great sweeping flourish.

Michael grinned, and ran back to the other two. 'I declare to God but that Finbar surely missed his calling,' he told them. 'He would make a great actor on the Dublin stage.'

The blacksmith yawned tiredly as he led out a horse and attached it to a canvas-covered two-wheeled cart known as a jingle, but then his eyes lit up like stars as Michael entered the square, after scouting the road, and walked back towards Cullen and Mary, who stood waiting for their transport.

O'Casey was now Dwyer's greatest admirer. He spoke about him continually, doted on every good word others said about him, and flew into a frenzy of threats if anyone did less than praise him to the skies.

When Cullen climbed into the cart, sitting on a pile of straw behind the bench, settling back under the canvas and lighting his pipe, O'Casey did not appear to see him. Nor did he notice Mary as she climbed up to the bench. But when Michael's turn came, the most agile of the three, O'Casey sprang to assist him aboard by offering his hand and shoulder and even his head as a mounting-stool.

Michael pretended not to hear or see him crouched there like a humble serf. He swung up to the bench and lifted the reins, then, after pulling up the collar of his greatcoat and lowering the hat on his brow, he chucked the reins and nodded a grin at the blacksmith. 'Happy Christmas, avic.'

'And to ye! A happy Christmas now – and a safe one.'

'Why do we have to go into Dublin?' Mary asked as the jingle rolled smoothly along the road towards Blessington.

'Because it is too dangerous to go anywhere in Wicklow – Christmas Day or not,' Michael replied. 'Dublin is full of Wexford boys who fled there after the rebellion, but they have to remain concealed on Sundays, for that is the day the yeos search for them. And you know the saying – needs must when the devil drives.'

'Still, won't it be grand,' Cullen said, 'spending a day in the big city.'

They approached Dublin through Brittas, Rathfarnham, and Harold's Cross, and a more innocent sight could not be seen than the young married couple driving along with a white-haired old man sitting behind them, happily smoking his long-pipe.

They came to a halt in the yard of Edward Kennedy of New Row, a half-brother of Miles Byrne, the Wexford captain who had left Michael in the autumn. The lad who unstrapped and stabled the horse informed them that Miles had gone on earlier.

'Miles will get a surprise when he sees us,' Michael said to Mary as they walked through an area of Dublin known as the Liberties. Cullen walked briskly beside them as they headed down to the quays of the River Liffey and stopped outside a tavern named Adam and Eve's.

Mary pulled hesitantly on Michael's hand as he led her inside the smoky tavern where a number of men sat around barrels in conversation. Cullen urged her on towards the door at the back of the room. Behind the door was a small passage which led to another door, guarded by two armed men who ushered them into a large room full with people.

When Mary saw the Christmas candle and the crib, a relieved smile spread over her face and she quickly pulled the hood of her cloak over her head.

'Just in time,' Cullen whispered, himself and Michael removing their hats as a young French priest, standing by the makeshift altar, held up his hand, and spoke in Latin:

'In nomine Patris, et Filii, et Spiritus Sancti.'

Since the brutalities of the Penal days only sixteen years

before, when Catholics could be put to death for practising their religion, places such as this abounded in Ireland. The tavern was merely a front for the small chapel behind it. Even now the practice of the faith was still frowned upon, and could be dangerous in many of the rural areas where the priests lived under a constant threat of floggings and possible death.

Much to Mary's sadness there were no hymns, no singing at all, just the soft accented voice of the priest.

'*Dominus vobiscum* – the Lord be with you.'

'*Et cum spiritu tuo,*' the people answered. 'And with you.'

'*Sursum corda!*' The priest smiled. 'Lift up your hearts.'

As the Mass progressed and the bread was broken and shared, Mary began to feel faint through lack of sleep, began to dream, to pray fervently. Dimly she could hear the sound of the people saying the Pater Noster and the Credo as she whispered silently and feverishly.

'Please don't let him be done to death. Let us both live to see our old age in peace, and let us live to see our children's children.'

When the Mass had ended, Miles Byrne was delighted and surprised to see them, and even more surprised to learn that Michael had married. He smiled nicely at Mary and shook all hands warmly, but would brook no refusal when he insisted they all return to his stepbrother's house for Christmas dinner.

As they made their way through the tavern, Cullen caught the arm of another man. 'Bejabers! will you look who it is? Ha'penny Hallet himself!'

The two men fell on each other, laughing loudly as they slapped each other on the back.

'This is the scoundrel,' Cullen informed Mary, 'who once lived in Wicklow and kept me up throughout a long night in a card game for a magnificent pair of brogues, which in the heel of the hunt I won, but sure when I got them home I found they were three sizes too big for me.'

''Tis not my fault if you didn't take the time to try them on,' Ha'penny shouted.

'No matter,' Cullen laughed. 'I sold them for three chickens.'

'But lookit here, Johnny, we have another game going this evening. Out in Rathfarnham. Will you come to it?'

The old man looked pleadingly at Michael, who responded with a shrug.

'Aye, I will!' Cullen cried excitedly. 'What's the game?'

'Twenty-five.'

'What's the opening stake?' Michael asked curiously.

'What the opening stake always is at Ha'penny's card games,' Cullen retorted. 'A ha'penny!'

The welcome that Michael and Mary and Cullen received at the home of Miles Byrne's stepbrother was warm and generous. Edward Kennedy's house was snug and comfortable with a drawing-room-type parlour on the first floor. As soon as dinner was over, Cullen begged a thousand pardons and gave a hundred 'God bless ye's', as he prepared to take himself off to his rendezvous with Ha'penny Hallet.

As Rathfarnham was on the route home, Michael told Cullen he would collect him later. 'But you must be ready to leave as soon I call for you,' he warned. 'And no begging for just one more game or I'll leave you there.'

'Don't worry, treasure,' Cullen called back excitedly, 'I'll be on my mark with my pockets loaded by the time you come for me.'

Miles Byrne was chuckling. ''Tis comical the way he speaks to you, Michael, calling you endearing names as if you were just a wean.'

''Tis the old way,' Michael said. 'And 'tis not for me to try and teach an old dog new tricks.'

Everyone smiled in agreement, then toasted Cullen's success at the game.

Around the fire in the large parlour which seemed to have piles of old books in every corner, the whiskey and sherry flowed freely and the talk naturally centred on the rebellion in Wexford and the galling defeat of the United Irishmen. Still, it was Christmas Day and the topic moved on humorously, the laughter coming easily.

'By the way,' Miles Byrne said, 'is it true what I hear that some of your boys have left and joined the English army?'

'Aye, about twenty, using false names. Stationed somewhere in the south of England.'

'I'm surprised.'

Michael shrugged. 'Those who wanted to leave us had no homes to go to,' he said, 'burned out by the militia. And some men are not cut out for the hazards of the mountains. Man, it can be grim up there in winter, believe me. I've seen some of my strongest lads near crying with the cold of their hands.'

'Why do you do it?' Edward Kennedy queried. 'Why do you stay out?'

Michael ran deep and silent for a long moment as he studied the fire, then said quietly, 'My main reason, I suppose, is to avoid the assassination I would surely suffer if I ever decided to return to live at home.'

'But if you surrendered . . .'

'Nay, I'd rather go down fighting than finish up my days in the rat-infested hold of a prison ship.'

Only Edward Kennedy saw Mary's face drain of all colour as she stared at Michael.

'Talking about ships,' Kennedy said, in an attempt to change the subject, 'I've just obtained a copy of a booklet written by Edward Christian. Did you ever hear about the mutiny on the *Bounty*?'

Michael confirmed he had. 'But only that Fletcher Christian took over the ship and sailed away. I never found out the whys or wherefores.'

'It was a great scandal,' Kennedy said. ' 'Tis a wonder Captain Bligh is still in the Navy.' He adjusted his spectacles and peered at Michael. 'Would you like me to tell you the whys and wherefores of the story? I've read everything ever been printed on the matter.'

Miles Byrne flashed Michael a look, urging him to *please* say yes.

'Aye, that might be interesting,' Michael said earnestly. ' 'Tis not a lot I know about ships and foreign climes. And Christmas afternoon around a warm fireside is very fitting for a story or two.'

Edward Kennedy's chest swelled a little, his cheeks flushed with anticipated pleasure. He possessed that ancient, almost wild craving for freedom at the heart of every Irishman, but clamped as he was here in the noisy streets of Dublin, working to secure a livelihood, he vented that passion by reading avidly of the great explorers like Christopher Columbus and James Cook. Although, every Irishman knew that St Brendan landed in Newfoundland only fifteen hundred miles from Galway Bay, and then America, before Columbus ever did.

He moved over to a cluttered bookcase saying somewhat proudly as he lifted out a number of books. 'I have here three volumes on Captain Cook's voyages to the South Seas. William

Bligh was with Cook on one of those expeditions, you know. And in Cook's opinion, Bligh was one of the best nautical navigators he had ever come across.'

Mary glanced at Michael in blank bewilderment.

'And did you know,' said Kennedy, 'that when Columbus landed at America in 1492 on the flagship *Santa Maria*, he had on board an Irish wolfhound, and a young man named William of Galway.'

'What was an Irishman doing on a Spanish ship?' Michael asked.

'Ah well,' Kennedy smiled, 'wasn't there a great smuggling racket going on between Ireland and Spain at that time. Brandy and wines in return for wool and Irish marble. It's probable that William of Galway ended up in a Spanish gaol and was then released to the Italian, Columbus, as one of his sailors.'

Mary was getting very confused by it all. 'And was this man Bligh on the ship too?' she asked. 'The ship of this Columbus man?'

The three men looked at her strangely, then Michael smiled and reached out to lift her hand, held it fast as she blushed hotly, knowing she had said something ignorant and stupid.

Edward Kennedy also flushed as he looked at Mary's crimson face, thinking how lovely she was. 'Forgive me,' he mumbled, 'but sure it's my fault for rambling on the billow of thought. Shall I tell you the story of the *Bounty* now, for it is a great story, although, as yet, it has no ending.'

Mary nodded, too ashamed to meet his eyes, knowing that, despite her nice dress and cloak, Mr Kennedy and Miles Byrne had seen her for the ignorant mountain girl that she was.

'It happened only nine years ago,' Kennedy said, 'and the *Bounty* was destined for a place called Otahiti in search of a breadfruit that Cook had previously discovered there . . .'

Mary stared into the fire and drifted away over the oceans as she listened to the tale of twenty-four-year old Fletcher Christian, and Captain Bligh only ten years older.

She listened engrossed as the story went on until the point where Fletcher Christian staged what Edward Kennedy described as the most famous mutiny in naval history, and returned in the *Bounty* to the beautiful coral-ringed island of Otahiti and the dusky native girl whom Christian had fallen in love with, named Isabella.

'It's a terrible crime, mutiny,' said Kennedy. 'And Christian must have known that he could never return to England from that day on. He came from a very high-ranking English family, you know. A close friend of the Wordsworths, they do say.'

Mary came back to her surroundings and blinked at him. 'What happened to them after that? Fletcher Christian and Isabella?'

'It would be grand to know,' Kennedy answered wistfully. 'The last sight of them was had by the islanders of Otahiti, when the *Bounty* sailed away again, apparently in search of some deserted island where Christian intended to start a new English settlement. Ships have been on the look-out for years, but neither the *Bounty* nor Christian have ever been seen since.'

'And Captain Bligh?' Michael asked.

'Bligh returned and reported all to the Admiralty and the King. He was hailed as a hero, and acclaimed by the Admiralty, and for a time he received great affection and public sympathy for being the victim of so desperate a mutiny. But then, in the heel of the reel, people began to wonder why so many young officers from high-ranking English families had mutinied with Christian. And now that Edward Christian has published a pamphlet publicly accusing Bligh of persecuting his brother to a point beyond human endurance . . . well, 'tis still a subject for talk everywhere.'

Mary was sorry when the time came to leave; the talk in Wicklow rarely ranged beyond Wicklow. She silently accepted the Christmas present of second-hand storybooks that Edward Kennedy gave to her, too shy to tell him that she would be unable to read a word of them.

'And I have a present for you, Captain Dwyer,' Kennedy said, taking a small paper parcel out of a drawer.

Michael looked greatly embarrassed as Kennedy pushed the parcel into his hand. 'What is it?'

'Open it and see.'

Michael slowly opened the paper and stared down at the strangest-looking whistle he had ever seen.

'It's a sea-whistle,' Kennedy said, face beaming, 'given to me by the captain of a ship that trades between here and America.'

'I couldn't take it from you,' Michael said, pushing the whistle back into Kennedy's hand. 'It wouldn't be right.'

But again Miles Byrne flashed Michael a look, and Kennedy insisted. 'It is of little practical use to me, here in the crowded streets of Dublin, but it may help you sometime in the mountains.'

Michael didn't know what to say, so he said nothing, just nodded and accepted the gift. 'But I warn you,' Kennedy said urgently, 'do not blow it inside a dwelling, for its sound is meant to carry across the waves to other ships.'

A slow smile began to move over Michael's face. 'I think I have a notion why you are giving this to me.'

Kennedy smiled. 'You were a comrade in arms of my young half-brother here, fought back to back with him on Vinegar Hill. He speaks of you often with great respect. My home is always open to you, especially if you ever need a place to hide.'

'Thank you,' Michael said, 'I will remember that, but I hope it will never be necessary.'

In the yard Miles grasped Michael's hand. 'It's been a real pleasure seeing you again, avic. And your lovely wife. May God keep up your luck.'

Michael smiled. 'Aye, yours too, Miles.'

As the horse and cart rolled through the dark streets, Mary linked Michael's arm and whispered dreamily, ' 'Twould be nice, wouldn't it? Finding some beautiful island to live on, like Otahiti.'

'We live on a beautiful island,' he told her, 'the Emerald Isle.'

' 'Tis no peaceful paradise,' she sulked.

Michael smiled sidelong at her. 'Oh, I don't know. It has its moments.'

When the jingle pulled up outside the large barn near a lonely house in Rathfarnham, the excited noise coming from inside was like that of a haggard full of crows. Michael jumped down and murmured to a man standing by the door.

Cullen finally came out wearing the expression of a child dragged out of a sweet shop. 'I'm on a winner's run!' he cried petulantly.

'Then run back and we will carry on alone,' Michael said. ' 'Tis not that long a walk from here to Imaal. You'll do it by tomorrow night.'

Cullen considered, then shuffled up to the small carriage and climbed up Michael's side of the cart on to the straw behind the seat. 'Did you have a nice day, treasure?' he whispered to Mary.

'Oh, it was grand! Mr Kennedy reads books something

fiercely and buys piles of them second-hand. Some of them are full of wonderful stories and he gave us a few as a present. He was telling us all about what happened to a man called Fletcher Christian on a ship called—'

'Huh! that's nothing to what happened to me! Look at the fine waistcoat I won! What do you think of it now?' Cullen proudly pulled back the lapels of his coat.

'It's too dark to see, man,' Michael said, chucking the reins. 'Did you win any money?'

'Aye, two shillings, but this waistcoat was the prize of the night. Our entrance fee paid Ha'penny for it. I had my heart set on the waister as soon as I saw it, but then so did another fellow. In the heel of the hunt there was just him and me in it – but 'twas me that had the cards. Oho!'

'Was he annoyed? Ha'penny Hallet?'

'Oh no, 'twasn't Ha'penny. 'Twas a man named Michael Lennard and sure he took it in good sport, fair play to him. A servant to the Emmets he is. Have you heard of them and their darling son now in Kilmainham Gaol for being a leader of the United men?'

Michael glanced at Mary and turned up his eyes. 'Everyone's heard of Thomas Emmet,' he said.

Cullen withdrew his long-pipe and tinder-box and began to smoke. 'But 'tis the youngest son that Michael Lennard has the great grah for, Robert Emmet. Mortal fond of him Lennard is. But d'you see, young Emmet is on the run now, away in France. It seems that some stag informer gave Emmet's name to the Castle as being one of the Executive Council of United Irishmen.'

'And isn't it the long tongues that both you and that Lennard have,' Michael said sternly, 'discussing secret information like that.'

'No one heard us. Just him and me talking quietly over a drink after the waistcoat game.'

'Mary has just heard you now,' Michael snapped.

'Sure Mary wouldn't say nothing. Would you, treasure?'

Mary was asleep. The long enjoyable day full of good food and sherry and stories of faraway islands, preceded by a sleepless night, had all taken their due of her.

Michael pulled her into him and cushioned her head on his shoulder. He drove the jingle with one hand around her and the other holding the reins.

257

All around the night was silent. All nature asleep. Only the rhythmic clopping of the horse disturbed the peace of Christmas night. The only lights were the stars in the clear sky and the lanthorn that hung on the front of the cart.

They had passed through Blessington, and were on the road to Donard. Michael's hand absently moved up and down Mary's arm, wondering if he should chance another night at Cullen's. No – with the fire lit and blazing, he would be unable to use the cavern in an emergency. She lay against him all soft and warm and he sighed regretfully.

Although, he thought tiredly, not even Mary could keep him awake tonight.

'There's another card game coming up,' Cullen murmured. 'In Tallaght. I promised Ha'penny I would go up for it and stay over.'

Michael half-turned his head to look at the old man. 'When is it?' he asked. 'The game?'

'Cock-step-along.'

'Twelfth Day?'

'Aye.'

'Oh, man,' Michael said, hiding a smile, 'you can't go.'

'Can't go? Why not?'

'Well, Mary and I were only saying on the road from Dublin to Rathfarnham, that we would come and stay with you again on Twelfth Night. I even said I would try and catch a pheasant for our dinner.'

Cullen sucked on his pipe for a time, then said in an uncertain tone, 'I told Ha'penny I would be there and he's put my name down; and the number of entrance payments decides the main prize ... howsomever, if you want me to spend Cock-step-along with you two, then I will.'

'Ah no,' Michael responded quickly. 'On second thoughts, you go and enjoy yourself. Mary and I will manage on our own.' He grinned at the road ahead. 'It won't be the same without you, of course, but 'tis not often you get invited to a big card game.'

'You may say it!' Cullen answered. 'And 'tis not often I can take the time to go up there either. I'll have to use that lad again as a herd.'

'How long will you be away?'

'Just a day and a night.'

Michael smiled up at the stars. ' 'Tis long enough.'

The scene in the Doyles' kitchen at Knockandarragh was far from peaceful. William Doyle had drunk himself into a rage and now sprang to his feet, his eyes wild as he glared at his son.

'Bring him to me!' he shouted. 'Bring him to me and I'll smather him to pulp. Go on! Bring Dwyer to me so's I can kill him stone dead.'

'William dear,' Mrs Doyle cried, 'no good will come of all this shouting.' She put her apron to her eyes. 'And you've been shouting for months.'

'Two months and ten days!' Doyle informed her. 'That's how long it is since that son of yours took her away to wed that rebel who has neither land nor lamb to call his own.'

'Oh, he has now, William,' Pat O'Riordan corrected. 'His father's farm is rightly his now. And under normal circumstances, him being the eldest son, the lease would have been signed over to Michael as soon as he took a wife.'

'Took a wife? Took a wife! He took my daughter without a by-your-leave to me! That's what Dwyer did!'

'Oh that's what he did,' O'Riordan confirmed. 'And he did me out of a wife that cost me nearly twenty bottles of whiskey in the parleying.'

'Ah, Pat!' the wind seeped out of Doyle's sails as he slumped down next to his friend. 'Ah, Pat, you know I would have had it otherwise. As God is my witness, there's no other man on this earth I would want for a son-in-law.'

'Quare oul son-in-law,' John Doyle muttered. 'He's nearly as old as yourself.'

'Don't antagonise him, dear,' Mrs Doyle pleaded to her son.

'And you were in on the conflab too, woman!' Doyle thrust a finger at his wife. 'You knew all about her meetings with him up the mountains. Getting up to God only knows what in the long grass.'

'Shame on you!' Mrs Doyle cried. 'Mary is a good girl.'

'She's no good girl now, is she? Married to that rebel. She knows the score now! And the unholy flames to that priest who said the prayers over them! May he take a drink of holy water and choke on it.'

'God forgive you!' O'Riordan cried in sudden panic. 'Talking about a saintly priest like that! I'll not stay in this house another minute if that's how you're going to talk.'

Doyle's head sunk into his neck. He knew he had gone too far but he was quivering with hysteria. 'I didn't mean it,' he wailed. 'I didn't mean it.'

'God knows you didn't,' O'Riordan soothed. 'Wasn't it the sorrow and torment in you talking, and not wickedness. God is very understanding.'

After a long silence Doyle turned and stared at O'Riordan. 'Wait now, Pat,' he whispered. 'Wait'll I tell you.'

'Carry on,' O'Riordan whispered.

'It was on the eve of the sixteenth of October, two months and ten days ago, that my Mary snuk out of this house with that boyo there, and secretly married Michael Dwyer. I say secret, mind, but it seems that everyone in Imaal knew about it, except meself and the militia.'

'And me,' O'Riordan put in quickly, having listened to the story endless times and resentful of the way he was always excluded from the betrayal.

'Devil take you!' Doyle cried. 'Meself and you then. And since that day she has not come near her daddy or mammy.'

'You told me to tell her that you would thrash her alive if you ever saw her again,' his son cried.

'And of course, William,' O'Riordan added, 'she could not come back near this house for a month after the wedding anyhow. 'Tis the tradition. A bride must not see her parents until a month after the wedding.'

'A month? 'Tis two months and ten days, you cur!' Doyle cried. 'And don't be talking! Is this not Christmas Day?'

O'Riordan nodded. 'It is of course. Although it's almost gone now.'

'And even on Christmas Day she doesn't come near her daddy or mammy. The brat! The ungrateful shameless brat who is now somewhere up those mountains with Michael Dwyer and not giving a tinker's fiddle for the two people who sired, birthed, and reared her! The jezebel! Oh 'tis true when they say women are responsible for all the sin in the world.'

' 'Tis in their nature,' O'Riordan said gloomily. 'Look back to Eve and what she did to Adam. Only for that hungry hussy and we would all be having a great time in the Garden of Eden now.'

'If you keep on like this in front of Mother, I'll smash you!' John Doyle shouted at his father.

'Ah don't be talking,' Doyle blurted. 'Wasn't it your mother who lured me all those years ago? Cooing and blushing and

260

opening her eyes wide to me over the sides of bacon in me cart.'

'I'm going to bed,' Mrs Doyle said, patting her hair. 'And to show you how sinful I can be, William Doyle, you can sleep in Mary's bed in future.'

'Ah now, darling, don't be like that, my pulse!' Doyle jumped up and tried to embrace her. 'Isn't it just upset I am, Anne my lovely. Mortal upset at the way that daughter of yours has treated me.'

'She was in love with Michael,' Mrs Doyle said, 'and could not stomach the sight of O'Riordan – saving your presence, Pat – and near sick to dying she was at the thought of marrying anyone but Michael Dwyer.'

'Michael Dwyer?' The name was like a match to a fuse in Doyle's brain. 'My Mary was a modest saintly girl until that villain made her show her legs at the dancing. He's the devil himself! A lovely virgin girl until that devil put his eye on her. Ask any militiaman and they'll confirm it. The devil himself! And I'll wager that neither of them made an appearance at any Mass today. No doubt he persuaded her against it, saying it was too risky or some other excuse. Sure he'd likely frazzle up if a drop of holy water fell on him.'

John Doyle made to lunge at his father but his mother clung to him. 'No, John, for my sake, please. Hold your temper.'

' 'Tis the militia that are the devils,' John shouted. 'But what do you care about that? All you and O'Riordan care about is your stock and your money and your stinking drink.'

'And my darling daughter,' Doyle shouted. 'I cared about her but I lost her to the devil.'

'I lost her too,' O'Riordan butted in. 'And it cost me twenty bottles of whiskey in the parleying. All for a girl I didn't even get a sniff of, let alone a kiss or a day's work from.'

It was too all too much for William Doyle, this constant reminder of how he had not come up with his part of the bargain in the end. And it wasn't even his fault! The unfairness of it drove him wild. He put his hands to the lapels of his coat and pulled them back, jutting out his chest as if baring his heart to the bullets.

'Bring him to me!' he cried. 'I don't care what they say about him being a hard martyr and leaving that militiaman almost dead in the tavern at Baltinglass. I'll fix him! I'll boot him to hell and back and then I'll run my pike through him!'

As if to prove his point he ran out of the house and returned a minute later clutching a pike.

'Oh Mother of God!' O'Riordan exclaimed. 'He's lost his sensibles.'

'Bring him to me!' Doyle barked at his son. 'And I'll show your darling captain whether I can present arms as good as any man.'

'For the love of God,' Mrs Doyle sobbed. 'Isn't this a shameful way to be carrying on Christmas night.'

'And I'll tell you what else I'm going to do,' Doyle cried. 'I'm going to find out where Dwyer is, then I'm going to collect myself five hundred guineas on him!' He turned to O'Riordan. 'The devil take you and your hundred whatever pounds it was! I've got me a son-in-law that's worth five hundred guineas and no mistake!'

The silence was sudden. All stared at him in shocked disbelief.

It was finally O'Riordan who broke the stone-like appearance of the people in the room. 'You would do that, William?' he said gravely. 'Turn informer? A Judas to one of your own people?'

'To your own daughter's husband,' Mrs Doyle whined, 'knowing you would leave her a widow in her youth.'

'A stag,' said John Doyle, 'to your own son-in-law. You called him that yourself.'

'He's no in-law of mine or anyone else's!' Doyle cried. 'He's a bloody outlaw! Isn't there a proclamation to prove it?'

'Well if you won't accept him as your son under the law,' O'Riordan said quietly, 'you can't deny that he's your son under God. They were joined together in the holy sacrament of marriage by the priest. And what God has joined together, let no man put asunder.'

Doyle looked at O'Riordan as if he had just had a revelation. 'What God has joined together,' he mumbled, wonder in his eyes. 'Then, by God, 'tis true . . . he is my son—' he dropped the pike as if it burned his hands.

A few seconds later he was sitting on the settle next to O'Riordan. 'My heart is broken,' he said in a voice hoarse with tears. 'Not to have known or seen my girl married. Not even to have had the honour of handing her over. And truth to tell, I'd nothing personal against himself. How could I blame him for being a rebel and my own son a hero of the Wexford rebellion!'

He put his head into hands. 'But not to have come and seen me on Christmas Day. She must know I meant none of my threats against her. Sorra the day when I'd strike my own flesh.'

'Did you mean it?' O'Riordan whispered. 'About the five hundred guineas?'

'What?' Doyle's head snapped up. 'Sell my own son-in-law? 'Tis you should be sold as a fool! 'Twas all only words, Pat, wooorrrrrds! Stupid meaningless words that slip out when the brain's not minding the mouth and the tongue goes rambling off on its own. 'Tis not wooorrrrrds I want – 'tis my daughter! I want to see her again and know that she's all right and still loves me.'

Mrs Doyle joined in her husband's weeping for she too missed Mary terribly. But staring at them both, John suddenly felt great pity for his father. He was like a crying lonely child whose little pet has been stolen by a bullyboy.

'If I'd only been told about her and himself I would have agreed to the match,' Doyle said. 'I would! And so would Pat. Wouldn't you, Pat?'

O'Riordan nodded. 'For Michael Dwyer I would. Begor, but I would not dare to disagree.'

Doyle stared at the floor for a long moment, then turned to O'Riordan. 'Wait now, Pat,' he whispered. 'Wait'll I tell you.'

'Go ahead,' O'Riordan whispered.

'He's a hard martyr – the same Michael Dwyer.'

O'Riordan nodded. 'But never hard on the weak. Not as I've heard.'

'And a good fighter.'

'Knows how to handle himself, sweet enough. That night in the spring when George Fenton and his militia boys came to my place for a bit of blood and bruising, Dwyer and his pals arrived on the scene from nowhere and gave them what they came for.'

'A tough Christian!' Doyle declared.

'He saved my hide that night,' O'Riordan said. 'Cripes! Fenton had a fierce grip of me by the hair and my legs were trembling under me when Dwyer sprang on him from no-place like a cat. And, begor, the spurs were on the other heel *that* night! Three times Dwyer put Fenton down, then helped him to his feet for the fourth which sent Fenton tumbling into the pigsty for a long snooze. Hugh Vesty made short work of the others. Him and Mernagh and Burke along with him.'

'A great bunch of lads!' Doyle exclaimed. 'May they live long.'

'Long and strong,' O'Riordan said, 'for they'll not tolerate bullies handling them that can't handle themselves – especially Dwyer. Underneath that granite way of his, when it comes to his own people of Wicklow, he has the heart of corn.'

'My son-in-law!' Doyle shouted proudly.

'And married to my own betrothed,' O'Riordan cried. 'Which, when you think about it, William, makes us sort of related, doesn't it?'

William Doyle sighed. 'Father of the bride and fiancé of the bride and neither of us invited to the wedding! 'Tis sorely we've both been treated, Pat; musha it is. But sure, all we can do is take it like martyrs!' He slapped his hands on his knees and called for a ballad. In a trice both men were singing and putting the sides of their heads together.

Mrs Doyle and John exchanged glances. 'I think we should go to our beds, dear,' she whispered wearily. 'For I have a feeling this is going to be the longest Christmas night your daddy ever rued.'

The two men on the settle paid no attention as Mrs Doyle and John left the room. 'At least we still have each other,' O'Riordan said when the song ended. 'A woman is one thing, but a man's drinking partner is more reliable in the long run.'

'Shall we open another bottle, Pat?'

'Aye, William. And shall we share a twist of tobacco as well?'

'If you have some. I'm all out of it and smoking the turf. You see, Pat, it was Mary who always gave me the tobacco at Christmas. I was sure she would come along with some today.'

'The turf will be grand,' O'Riordan said, withdrawing his pipe.

The walk across the mountain paths from the forge at Donard was long and cold. Cullen led the way, holding the lanthorn of which three sides of the glass were covered so as not to be spotted from the land below. Michael and Mary followed closely behind.

Once inside the cottage, Michael quickly brought the banked-down fires in both rooms to a blaze while Cullen tended the goat who was waiting by the barn door and crying piteously to be milked.

'God forgive me for forgetting you,' Cullen muttered. 'If 'twere not for the other two, I'd bring you in and give you a heat by the fire.'

Cullen's dog lumbered out from the back of the barn and began to whine. 'Come on you, inside,' Cullen pleaded. 'They'll not object to you. Come on now, there's a good boy.'

When he entered the cottage Mary had heated a small pot of milk and was pouring it into three cups.

'Will you look at that now,' Cullen cried, pointing at the dog. 'It must be cold for him to come inside. Ne'er a bit of company is he for me, but a great dog with the sheep.'

Michael sliced a large chunk of the cold roasted pork and bent to feed it to the dog, whom he was sure was a bit touched in the head, for unlike other dogs, he could not bear to be indoors. The barn was the nearest he ever came to being enclosed by walls. ' 'Tis a sheep in dog's clothing, you are, avic,' he whispered, 'not a dog like other dogs.'

'We never had the partridge,' Cullen said, spicing his own and Michael's milk with a warming dash of whiskey. 'Mary and I will have to eat one tomorrow. You take the rest back to the lads, Michael. I put them in the cold salt water so they'll still be fresh.'

'I'll make a partridge pie for us,' Mary told the old man. 'Or would you rather it in the herbs?'

'Either way suits me, treasure. Get yourself to bed now.'

Mary nodded tiredly. 'Goodnight,' she said.

'And to you,' Cullen yawned. 'God bless you now and sleep well.'

After Cullen had stoked the fire and said the nightly prayer, Michael sat talking quietly while the old man undressed down to his flannel undergarments and climbed into the settle-bed.

'If I don't show tonight the lads will get worried,' Michael said.

'Same as you would about them. Will you take the lanthorn?'

'Aye, but sure I'd know my way up the mountains if I was blind.'

Cullen chuckled. 'Myself also.'

When Michael entered the bedroom no candles were burning. Mary had undressed by the light of the fire. He sat on the edge of the bed and whispered to her.

'Stay here with the old man and have a good rest. I'll come back in two or three nights and move you on. And listen . . .' he smiled, 'Cullen is going up to Tallaght on Cock-step-along. Staying overnight. We'll have this place to ourselves.'

The dog in the living-room began to whine loudly. Cullen

called to Michael to let him out. 'He only came in for a bit of food. He'll not stand for a locked door.'

Mary listened as Michael let the dog out then chained the door again. When he came back into the bedroom he said with a bemused smile, 'That dog is definitely a bit mental, you know.'

She didn't smile back, just frowned at him darkly. 'Are you really going up the mountains tonight?'

'I must go, Mary. Hugh Vesty and the others will be watching for me.'

'Don't go,' she pleaded in a whisper. 'Stay here with me.'

'I hate to leave you, darling, but we agreed to be disciplined about things.'

She sat up in her nightgown and put her arms round his shoulders. 'Just to sleep,' she coaxed softly. 'I'll keep you warm.'

'Oh, Mary . . .' Just the thought of the cold trek up the cold mountains made him hesitate. 'No. I can't,' he said emphatically, and she knew he meant it. 'I can't.'

She felt the touch of his lips as he kissed her farewell, and she avidly responded to his kiss, lifting his hand from her waist and guiding it over the warm softness of her breast, using every weapon to battle down his resistance.

'Will you stay?' she whispered a few minutes later.

'No,' he said, stripping off his coat.

And later, as he lay asleep in her arms, her black hair tumbling over his shoulders, she smiled smugly. There were some battles the captain could never win of late – and she was becoming ruthless in her tactics. She put her face against his head and closed her eyes as she softly sang a love song in her native tongue.

> *'Siúl, Siúl, Siúl a rún,*
> *Siúl go sochair agus siúl go ciúin . . . '*

Chapter Seventeen

Now Christmas was over, determined efforts were being made to capture Michael Dwyer. If the desperado could just be caught, the soldiery were convinced the other rebels would be as easy to round up as a herd of sheep.

In a small cave on the eastern slopes of Lugnaquilla, Michael lay asleep. On either side of him lay Hugh Vesty and Sam McAllister. They were as comfortable as birds in a nest, lying on a bed of clean straw and good bedclothes that had been brought up to the cave by a neighbouring farmer named O'Toole.

O'Toole's young son was also in the cave, shuffling around the fire as he prepared to make his captain's breakfast. Only the four were inside this comfy cavern; the rest billeted in houses throughout Imaal and other caves on other mountains. By and by the light of a winter sun broke through the bush of heather which concealed the entrance.

Michael awoke to the sound of the clattering kettle and stirred, looking over his shoulder at young O'Toole. 'All right, avic?'

'Aye, Captain, but stay where you are. 'Tis a lovely speckled trout I'll be grilling for you now, a lovely speckled trout. The fire is spitting nicely, but stay where you are till I'm done.'

Michael smiled at the young recruit, at his utter seriousness. Some served with a sword in their hands, others with a speckled trout.

'You're a good lad, avic.'

'So my father says,' O'Toole answered with a smile.

The voices awakened Hugh Vesty and Sam McAllister, who began to mumble and stir. They slid up the blanket that covered two sacks of chopped-up hay which served as their pillows. Hugh Vesty fired a delighted smile at the four trout O'Toole was preparing to spit.

'When did you tickle those?' he asked. 'You must have been up and out early.'

'Dark and early,' O'Toole answered. 'But stay where's youse are till I have them done. Easier for me to work around an empty fire.'

Hugh Vesty grinned. 'You're a good lad, avic.'

'So the captain says. So the captain says.'

The three men stayed where they were, talking and laughing together, as happy as the day is long. Michael fingered the green cravat around Sam McAllister's neck. 'Do you never take this thing off?' he asked curiously. 'Troth, I've seen you stripped for a swim wearing nothing but that green cravat.'

'And that's why it always looks so clean,' McAllister replied.

'And that's why the men have nicknamed you "the man in the green cravat",' Hugh Vesty said. 'Isn't that right, Captain?' But Michael's attention was concentrated on a robin that had flown in and was busy jumping around the quilt over them. He held out his palm to her, but she bustled and hopped and flew out again.

'Did you see that now?' Michael murmured. ' 'Tis unusual to see a robin so high up in the mountains.'

On that she flew in again. Hugh Vesty grabbed at her, and then McAllister, but she would have no play or petting, just hopped and bustled over the quilt. Again Michael held out his palm to her, but she rustled her feathers and set herself fiercely at him as if she was preparing to attack him.

'Oh, she's turned wicked looking,' Hugh Vesty declared. 'Wicked!'

She had, Michael could see. 'There's something in this,' he said slowly. 'Something has sent her flying up here, flying in here, for cover.'

Young O'Toole sprang to his feet and ran to the cave's entrance. He manoeuvred his head outside the hiding heather.

'Captain!' he cried, pulling back. 'The southern end of the hillside is red with soldiers!'

The three men jumped to their feet, dragged on their belts and boots and reached for their guns.

'What will we do – stay in or go out?' Sam McAllister asked. 'If we stay in and stay silent, they probably won't find us.'

'But they might,' Hugh Vesty cried, 'and if they do, we've had it.' He clutched Michael's arm. 'Let's make a fight and then a run for it through the brushwood.'

'Wait till I see how the land lies,' Michael answered.

'Let's fight and run!' Hugh Vesty pleaded. 'I've got me a

woman that's crazy in love with me, and heart-scalded she'll be if I don't show up at our rendezvous tomorrow night!'

'Stay where you are and stay silent,' Michael commanded, then dropped to his knees and crept out of the cave where he fell on to his stomach and weaved his way over to a boulder where, by moving his head slightly, he could see down the rushy slope.

For a moment he saw nothing, then he spied a flash of sunlight in one spot, then again in another, and another, near a clump of pine trees down the slope. Winter sunlight flashing on naked steel. Bayonets!

Within seconds he picked out the dashes of red dappled amidst the tall bronze ferns, and began to count. One . . . two . . . three . . . four . . . five . . .

Young O'Toole weaved over to him behind the boulder. 'Are we killed, Captain?' he whispered.

'Are we hell.' Michael shook his head irritably, and resumed the count again from one to five, then continued, 'Six . . . seven . . . eight . . . eight.' He blinked his eyes, then looked wryly at O'Toole.

'My, but you do exaggerate, boy,' he said in a dry whisper. 'The hillside is red with soldiers indeed. There's only eight of them! And they're not even real soldiers, just yeos.'

'But, Captain,' O'Toole gulped. 'That's two apiece. And the yeos are viciously vicious!'

'Aye, vicious cowards,' Michael said, then his hand gripped O'Toole's jaw tightly and his eyes warned him to stay easy and silent.

O'Toole's wide eyes never left his captain's grim face as he watched him marking the position of the yeos, waiting for them to come within gunshot range, O'Toole supposed.

The silence that settled on the slope was nerve-wracking, and despite the winter sunlight, the air was as heavy as before a storm. When O'Toole next looked down the slope his eyes saw what Michael was seeing; his mouth dropped into a gape – the yeos were only thirty yards or so away, crouched red figures stalking upwards like determined predators in search of elusive prey. A tawny hare made a rapid dash for cover and O'Toole gulped his breath nervously.

'Captain, they're almost on us!' he breathed, but Michael only nodded and slowly pulled at the drawstring of a leather pouch attached to the belt round his waist, his eyes never straying from the oncoming yeos.

O'Toole stared at the object in his captain's hand, then made a hasty sign of the cross over himself. 'God and Mary,' he whispered, 'but your brain has gone daft, Captain. I'll not stay here to watch you killed before I'm killed myself.'

As he moved to make a run for it, the tumultuous roar of an army of screaming men rose into the air and echoed and echoed in a roar that seemed to shake every ledge of the mountains.

The yeomen turned and fled wildly down the mountainside without firing a shot or looking back, spurred on by the terror of being surrounded by Dwyer's rebel army who had obviously been spread out for miles and waiting to ambush.

But when they eventually stopped running and looked back, the land was desolate, the air silent again. It was only then that Coogan's wits cleared enough to realise there was not a man in view. He stared at each petrified yeoman in turn, then put a hand on Creighan's shoulder and gripped it.

'The place is deserted,' he whispered. 'No army of men could roar like that and stay in hiding.'

Creighan agreed. 'A roar like that would spur any man's legs into battle, even if his heart and head wanted to stay put.'

'But I heard them,' Coogan said in a cowed voice. 'I heard them with my own two hearing ears. Did you hear them too, men? That roaring ghostly army?'

They all confirmed they had, why else had they run? One laughed a bit shakily. 'Ghostly army? Are you suggesting it was ghosts that fleed us?'

'It could well have been,' Coogan said slowly, his eyes darting around him nervously. 'They say these mountains are haunted with the dead spirits of their slayed ancestors; especially this mountain, the Lugnaquilla. Ghosts that rise up and scream vengeance whenever the spirit moves them. 'Tis even said they can scream a charge at a man until they send him over a ledge to his death.'

'Nonsense!' a yeoman said contemptuously. 'Dwyer and his friends hide up these mountains without a care in the world. And 'tis common knowledge the savages are more frightened of ghosts than humans.'

'But 'tis also common knowledge that Dwyer is in with them,' Coogan cried with a superstitious shudder. 'A woman once confided to me that she had it on the soundest authority that Dwyer had sold himself to them – lock, stock, gun-barrel and soul! And that's the reason he has always lived such a charmed life and can hit the eye of a target without even aiming his gun.'

'Them? Them? Who's them he's supposed to have sold himself to? Surely you don't mean the little people the stupid peasants are always wittering about?'

But Coogan did, for he had grown up in Ireland amongst Irish peasants and servants, as had his mother and father and grandfather and all his ancestors before him, since the days of Cromwell.

'The lepos!' he said emphatically, calling to mind everything he had heard in his time from chattering cooks and kitchen-maids. ''Tis said they know all the hidden secrets of the world, but they give nothing for nothing, not even their protection. 'Tis said they can raise the spirits of the dead with just a whiff of wind. But they're mischievous and cunning sprites, descending as they do from a queen that was a degenerate faery. Kicked out of the Land of Faery she was—'

'Will you hold your soft tongue, man!' a yeoman snapped irritably. 'We came to find Dwyer and find him we will. But first, this is what we'll do. Down below, in that old shack in the hollow, lives an old crone who keeps a bloodhound for company. We'll get it and bring it back to this here slope of the Lugnaquilla, and if it's ghosts or mortals that's lurking up there, the bloodhound will soon sniff them out.'

'Smart thinking!' Creighan exclaimed, then looked at Coogan as if he suddenly found him a great let-down of a friend. 'Ghosts indeed!'

Fifteen minutes later they arrived back at the southern end of the slope, the bloodhound tugging at his leash in an attempt to chase a rabbit that blurred past him.

'Come on, you cur!' his handler snapped. ' 'Tis better game than a rabbit we're after.'

Up above, Michael and O'Toole were still watching them, joined now by Hugh Vesty and McAllister, who crouched behind clumps of brushwood with guns primed. Once again O'Toole gulped in his throat to see the captain so unperturbed about the danger sneaking towards them.

Michael was calmly marking the advance of the yeos, an amused smile on his face. Five minutes later he broke his tranquil contemplation of the enemy and put the sea-whistle to his lips.

Again the tumultuous roar of an army of screaming men rose

271

into the air and echoed and echoed in a roar that seemed to shake every ledge of the mountains – and the bloodhound was the first to turn and run. His companions had no problem in deciding between bravery and retreat and overtook him in the flight back down the slope.

Michael fell back against the boulder, shaking with laughter, but O'Toole's teeth were still chattering from the blast of noise that sounded like a great reserve of men screaming a war cry. 'Blood and thunder, Captain!' he whispered. 'They must have heard that all the way to Wexford.'

Hugh Vesty came on the scene amazed. 'I wouldn't have believed it without seeing it! They ran as if a pack of mad ghosts were after them!'

'And I doubt if their breeches are still white,' McAllister opined. 'What say you, Captain?'

But Michael just laughed and laughed until the tears came to his eyes.

It was some minutes later when they moved back inside the cavern and O'Toole busily resumed his task of preparing breakfast.

'They'll not come near this part of the 'Quilla again,' Michael said, lifting a small bowl of water on to a flat stone ledge and lighting a candle. 'They'll spread the word that it's haunted by mad ghosts or wild lepos.'

'I've never come across a whistle like this,' Hugh Vesty said as he inspected the object that was three times the size of an ordinary whistle. 'What kind of a whistle is it?'

'A sea-whistle.'

'And where did it come from?'

'Where else but from a seaman. Come and hold this candle for me.'

Hugh was still staring at the whistle as he moved to hold the candle above the bowl of water, while Michael pulled his knife-razor from his belt and flicked it open.

A vain race, these mountain people, it was common practice for all young men and maids, no matter how poor, to carry a comb on their person, but unlike the females, few of the men carried mirrors. And when the morning was grey or cloudy and a sunlight reflection in a river or stream was not possible, a candle held over a bowl of water served as well as any mirror.

'So it's a sea-whistle from a seaman,' Hugh said. 'But where did you get it?'

'It originally came from the captain of a ship that sails the western ocean between here and America,' Michael said, bending over the bowl and rubbing soap on his face. 'But it was given to me by a well-wisher on Christmas Day.'

'Did you know the sound it would make?'

'I tried it out myself last week, the day after Christmas, while travelling through a desolate part of the mountains on my way to see the family at Eadstown.' He skimmed the razor down the side of his face. 'I nearly died myself with the fright it gave me.'

While Sam McAllister also inspected the whistle, resisting the urge to give it another blast, Hugh Vesty suddenly remembered his sweetheart Sarah, and what he wanted to ask Michael about her. But Michael was smiling at his reflection in the bowl of water, and began to sing quietly to himself as he shaved his face.

> 'Up the rocky mountain,
>   And down the rushy glen,
> I sent the yeos arunning
>   With the help of ghostly men.'

He looked up, first at Hugh Vesty, then at Sam McAllister, then once again he laughed until tears came to his eyes.

The Christmas candle which burned brightly in the window of the small old house near the bank of Green's River could be seen for some long minutes before Michael reached it. There was a clear moon in a clear sky which lighted his steps as he moved along the edge of the dark water.

Inside the house Father Richard Murphy shuffled from the scullery back into the parlour, bent almost double from an attack of stiffening rheumatism in his bones, not to mention the odd twinges of pain he still occasionally felt from his old flogging wounds.

He sat down and huddled over the fire. He was getting old, old and weary, and God would excuse him for the two bottles of claret that were keeping him company this Christmas. He had bought the claret with the money he had received for singing a hymn at a wedding. And no doubt it would not be long drunk before he sang at the same young man's funeral. Without even realising it, he quietly sang the first few words.

'*Requiem aeternam dona eis.*'

He sat back in his chair and lifted the glass of claret from the side table, resting his head against the wing as he stared into the fire.

'May you live long, Michael,' he whispered, raising his glass. 'May God spare you in mercy and forgiveness.'

The rich taste of the claret recalled memories of his days as a young student priest in the seminary in France. In those days it was a crime of death to give a Catholic an education, or even to help in sending him abroad to receive one. The Irish were an ignorant race, and had to be clearly seen as an ignorant race. How else could England justify her invasion and oppression of a country that had once been the brightest light of learning in the Western world, had sent her scholars, philosophers, writers and poets to enrich and enlighten a Europe struggling in the Dark Ages?

Another sip of the claret and he was back in France, back in the seminary where his education had led him. His father had said the Irish people's fascination with their religion was like Eve's fascination with the forbidden fruit. Once denied, always yearned. But it was not true, not for him. His fascination, his *love* for his religion came from the word of the written Gospels, and through reading them, he had come to a love of God that defied description, defied floggings, had even once defied expression in words, until that day in the French seminary chapel, when he had been chosen to sing the Corpus Christi.

He could see it still, the dark chapel with the candles burning brightly, the incense burning on the air. And the hush that fell when he had stepped up to the altar, hands raised high as his love for his God had poured out through his singing voice, the voice that had reduced every priest in the chapel that day to tears.

Through the candlelit window of the house, Michael stood looking in at the old priest who sat staring into the fire, a far-away look in his eyes. He was not as old as he looked, he had simply grown old before his time, old and grey. But then he had been flogged many times in his life, and many times he had defied his persecutors by singing at the top of his voice while the tongs of the cat had ripped into his flesh.

The man in the chair closed his eyes, and Michael was jerked out of his contemplation, fearing the priest was falling asleep. But, suddenly, he heard him begin to sing a hymn in the strong voice of a young man, a voice so beautiful it made Michael catch his breath, for he had never heard Father Richard sing in such an emotional way. And he recognised the hymn. It was the Corpus Christi.

> *'Lauda Sion, Salvatorem,*
> *Lauda ducem et pastorem*
> *In hymnis et canticis . . .'*

Michael stood with his back to the wall and gazed up at the dark sky as the hymn went on verse after verse. Somehow he felt it would be a sacrilege to interrupt before the end. So he waited and listened, and in the imagery of his Celtic mind he imagined it was just how a male angel might sound, a strong male angel singing at the throne of Heaven.

The priest had stopped singing a full five minutes when Michael quietly slipped into the house. The old priest stirred himself and looked up, bemused at the sight of the young man who entered the room.

'Musha, Michael, are you still alive?'

'I am, Father. Are you?'

The priest smiled. 'Well sometimes I do wonder.'

'I would have knocked,' Michael said, 'but I thought I would spare you the journey to the door.'

'That was kind of you. There is some good left in you so.' The priest motioned to the opposite chair. 'Sit down and keep me company a while. It has been a lonely Christmas for me. Once the Mass was ended, everyone went to the jollity of their homes. But the priest, the priest lives alone.'

'And so it was you who chose it that way, Father.'

'So it was. And I have no regrets, my son. No regrets.' The priest motioned to the claret. 'Would you like a glass?'

'No, Father, it would be too foreign a drink for a country boy like myself.'

'I have no spirits.'

'I have no wish for drink. I am travelling abroad alone and must keep my wits about me.'

'Did you go to Mass on Christmas morning?'

'Aye, in Dublin, in one of the secret penal chapels.'

'Ah, that is cheering to hear. There is some good left in you so.'

Twice he had said that now. Michael looked at him curiously. 'Do you truly think I am that bad, Father?'

'You have killed men, Michael. You have committed the ultimate sin.'

'And the redcoat? The soldier in his uniform? Does he not commit the ultimate sin when he kills, time and time and time again?'

The priest sighed. 'You are getting angry, Michael. And I have no heart for anger this night. For this night, after many years, I have again sung the Corpus Christi.'

'Aye,' Michael murmured, 'so you have.'

'But as your pastor, I will answer your question. The soldier in his uniform believes he is serving his king. So let his king stand before the throne of Heaven and answer for the thousands, maybe even millions, of deaths that have been committed in his miserable mortal name. But you, Michael, you will have no King George the First, Second, or Third standing beside you on Judgement Day to explain why you did it. You will stand alone. And only you will be able to answer as to why you committed the ultimate sin and broke the Fifth Commandment of God as given to Moses.'

'You have me judged to hellfire already, Father.'

The priest was silent for some minutes, his hand clasped over his black cassock, his eyes thoughtful. 'But then, Michael,' he continued more gently, 'perhaps when God looks down on what is happening in Ireland, has been happening in Ireland for so long, the injustice, the rapes, the torture and the murder, he may understand that only a saint or a Christ could turn the other cheek.'

'You turned the other cheek,' Michael reminded him. 'When they whipped the skin off your back, you took it with a song.'

'Not a song – a hymn!' The priest lifted his glass. 'And I was not saint enough to turn the other cheek. No, not me! I was as defiant as the Jews who sang the Psalms of David while being whipped by Pharoah's soldiers. And every word I sang thudded into my persecutors like the plunge of a musket-ball, until they were screaming with rage and ready to kill me stone dead. And they would have done, but for an act of providence which brought Lord Huntly riding through that part of the woods and calling a halt with the most obscene string of curses I had never before heard, not even from a drunken Irishman, let alone a Scottish marquis.'

Michael smiled. 'Aye, Huntly is not a bad sort.'

The priest sighed. 'A good man and a fair one. A credit to Scotland.'

'But you are lucky to have such a weapon as your hymn-singing,' Michael said. 'If I sang it would only amuse them. They would know they had whipped me senseless.'

'But you will never allow them that pleasure, will you, Michael?'

'No, Father.'

Michael lifted the poker and stirred the fire. For a while the bright flames seemed to hold his interest.

'How is Mary?' the priest asked. 'Is she well?'

'She's beautiful, Father.'

'Ah, you are in love with her, I can see.'

Michael smiled. 'She is my wife.'

'The two don't always go hand in hand.'

'No, not when others bargain the match.'

'Is she reconciled with Doyle yet?'

'No, she believes it is a choice between him or me. She has chosen me.'

'And that is how God has commanded it. That a man will leave his father and mother and cling to his wife, and a woman will leave her father and mother and cling to her husband, and the two will become one flesh.'

'So you told us, Father, during our wedding ceremony. You never let up from being the priest, do you?'

'No, Michael. I have sacrificed everything others consider important to be a priest. And that is what I am. That is all I am.'

'Do you forgive me, Father, for forcing you to marry us?'

'I forgive you, Michael. I forgive you every wrong you have ever done. But others may not be so forgiving. That is what you should worry about.'

'Then I confess, Father, that it doesn't worry me in the slightest, not a bit. Mary wanted me and I wanted her. We had no other choice. Like you, we have no regrets.'

'Ah, so you think I speak only of Mary. But, no matter! I am glad to see that she has brought you happiness of a kind, warmed some of the cold anger out of you.'

While the priest sipped his wine Michael looked into the dying fire and pondered on the happiness of a kind that Mary had brought him. Happiness he had not thought possible.

'And did you manage to spend Christmas Day with her?' the

priest asked. 'Your first Christmas as man and wife should have been spent together. Were you able?'

'We were able,' Michael answered, continuing to look into the fire. Two nights and a day they had spent together. And on both nights, from starry sky to grey dawn she had enslaved him, wrapping the warmth of her love around him even as she wrapped the warmth of her body around him. He closed his eyes at the ecstatic memory of it – then flashed them open as he remembered where he was – in the house of a priest!

'Shall I feed the fire for you?' he said quickly, moving out of the chair and down to the turf bucket.

The priest sat with his fingers knitted together beneath his chin, his eyes shrewd. He had a notion of the memories that had catapulted his young visitor on to the floor with a flush on his cheeks. But why should he feel ashamed? Had he not just told him that the word of God was that the two should become as one flesh?

He recalled the solitary features of his own life. He had never known the love or affection of a woman, and he had never missed or yearned it; for he had a greater love to fire his soul. He had vowed never to give a singular love to one person, but a collective love to his whole flock.

He wanted to lie back once more and close his eyes, dwell in the glow of the glorious dream he often had of late, a glorious dream of joyful people singing triumphant hymns as they marched in glory to the mountain top; marching in joy towards their Redeemer – His arms outstretched and His whole body surrounded in golden light as He welcomed them to the true and only liberation that awaited all of mankind.

He breathed deeply. His bones ached. Such were the dreams of an old Irish priest with the scars of eighteen whipping sessions on his back. Once again a tune came into his head and he began to hum.

'Do you know it in English?' Michael murmured.

The priest kept his eyes closed. 'Know what, my son?'

'The hymn you are humming – the Corpus Christi.'

When the priest gave no answer and lapsed into a silence, Michael moved back to his seat and assumed he only knew the hymn in Latin. He sat looking at the prematurely aged old man in the opposite chair, and again wondered if he was going to sleep.

The fire he had nurtured came to a blaze and its light caught the lines on the priest's face, tight with concentration. Michael turned his eyes to the flames of the fire, wondering if the priest was maybe praying.

> 'Sing forth, O Sion, sweetly sing
>   The praises of thy Shepherd-King,
> In hymns and canticles divine;
>   Dare all thou canst, thou hast no song
> Worthy his praises to prolong.'

Oh, it was beautiful! The voice so pure, so softly melodic, so filled with a quiet love and pain. Michael leaned back and shut his eyes as verse after verse of the Corpus Christi was sung in English. And when it came to the last verse, he could not be sure if it was the beauty of the voice or the words themselves that had brought the lump to his throat.

> 'Come then, good Shepherd, bread divine
>   Still show to us thy mercy sign;
> Oh, feed us still, keep us thine;
>   So we may see thy glories shine
> In the fields of immortality . . .'

They sat in silence staring into the deep fire, then spoke a few more words before the priest did fall into a sleep. Michael searched around for a covering for him, found his cloak in the bedroom and draped it over him.

He was halfway out of the door when he remembered why he had come in the first place. Hugh Vesty had sent him. Hugh Vesty and a few others were waiting on the hills yonder. Hugh Vesty had begged him to use all his powers of persuasion on the stubborn priest, just as he had done on the night of 16th October, behind the scullery door.

And he had not managed to say one word to the priest about Hugh Vesty.

Hugh Vesty would kill him!

He eventually found paper and a quill in a writing-box, and wrote a letter of appeal to the priest, explaining the reason for his visit.

In the rural areas of Ireland, the twelfth day of Christmas was commonly known as 'Cock-step-along' because from then on the daylight was said to lengthen each day by the length of the cock's step.

Despite the cold, Mary stood waiting at the open door of Cullen's cottage. The old man had left that morning for his card game in Tallaght. Every so often she went back inside and tended the fire, her expression satisfied as she looked around the room which was warm and cosy and shining with beeswax polish.

'Twould be so grand to have a home of our own, she thought wistfully, as she returned to the door. A home for just the two of them, day in and day out.

She was sighing with impatience, about to turn indoors again, when she saw him – dropping down from the ridge on to the steep path; a gaming-gun in one hand and a pheasant in the other. And then she was running towards him, covering his face with her lips and talking and laughing at the same time.

Inside the cottage he pressed her away from him. 'I have something to tell you,' he said with a smile. 'Hugh Vesty and Sarah were married last night. At Green's River.'

Mary clapped her hands with delight, then her face straightened. 'What about her family?'

'Well, of course, they knew nothing about the elopement beforehand. But when they found out, they rushed over to Green's River and arrived before the wedding took place. Naturally the priest refused to marry them if the parents objected. Hugh and Sarah were almost in tears. But to everyone's surprise her parents did not object. On the contrary, her father spent ten long minutes telling everyone that Hugh Vesty Byrne was the greatest wrestler in all Wicklow – and not only that – he had fought with great valour on Vinegar Hill – had survived the battles of Ballyellis and Hacketstown after that – not to mention his fine humour and good looks. It was only the priest who shut him up in the end, with a thunderous *In nomine Patris*, and the wedding began.'

'Will she be living on the run with him? Or in harbourers' houses?'

'Neither. Her parents said she can remain at home living with them until the future sorts something out.'

'Oh, won't that be grand for them,' she said moodily, her eyes downcast as he slipped off his coat and hung it on the hook in the corner.

'Were you his groomsman?' she asked.

'Naturally.'

'Did he have any others?'

'No, just myself. Although a number of the other lads were there.'

'Was there a celebration?'

'Aye, with the family; but McAllister and myself were on outpost duty most of the night.'

She raised her black eyebrows at him. 'Then you must be very tired so?'

He smiled an intimate smile and pulled her inside his arms. 'Not a bit.'

Chapter Eighteen

He arranged to stay with her twice in the week after that, in the homes of various harbourers, but the visits were not a complete success, not like Christmas and Twelfth Day.

The change in Mary, it seemed, happened overnight. She became tense and fractious, suddenly tired of being moved from pillar to post. She wanted her own home, she said, day in and day out. Insisted it *was* possible – in America.

He tried to reason with her. Pointed out that it took money to get to America, and any money he had was tied up in his father's farm. Besides, he could not look to his own safety and ditch his men up in the mountains, men who had been with him since the rebellion, and had stuck by him, day in and day out.

She accused him of caring more for his men than he did for her. She accused him of not seeing her enough, of not allowing her more than five minutes in his company when she sought him out.

'And it is dangerous for you to seek me out!' he told her. 'If you were to lead the militia to me, other men besides myself could get killed. You *knew* this was how it would be, Mary. You knew!'

'I didn't know!' she screamed. 'I didn't know a whole week might go by without seeing you.'

'I come only when I feel it is safe to do so,' he told her wearily. 'I am more concerned about your safety than I am about my own. Do you know what they might do to the wife of a rebel leader?'

Over the following few weeks her behaviour became even more baffling to him, constantly sending messages to his camp asking that he come to her at once, then speaking to him hardly at all when he arrived, as if her mind was constantly focused on some faraway dream. He endeavoured to humble himself to her every wish, but she became silent and remote and unattainable, even in bed, where she continually offered the pain in her head as an excuse, and fell asleep within minutes of her head touching the pillow, leaving him staring at the ceiling in utter bewilderment, unable to understand the sudden whirlwind of her moods. The idyllic, almost unreal magic of Christmas was gone. The honeymoon seemed to be over. For Mary anyhow.

The entrance leading through to the cave on the north side of the Keadeen Mountains was covered by a huge bush of heath which was changed as soon as it withered. Inside the cave, the walls had been lined with moss to keep out the damp and cold. The men's equipment stood along the walls in military order, and mattresses of ferns lined the floor. A warm fire burned in the centre. This was only one of a number of caves which Michael and his men had fitted out as hideouts. There were others on Luggelaw, Knockamunnion, Leitrim, Oakwood, not to count those on Table Mountain and Lugnaquilla.

Some way down the hillside, Michael Kearns and Farrell Reily were once again on outpost duty, passing the time discussing incidents of the Wexford rebellion.

'You weren't at the battle of Ballyellis, were you?' Kearns asked with a curious expression, knowing well that Farrell Reily had not joined the action until afterwards.

'No, but you've told me plenty enough about the great day you had,' Reily retorted pettishly.

'But did I ever tell you about a lad named Harry Neil?'

'Harry Neil? No then, but he must be the only man at Ballyellis that you have not told me about,' Farrell Reily said, reluctantly smiling, for himself and Michael Kearns were often put on outpost duty together, and Kearns was a great companion when it came to the talking.

'Harry Neil was a great lad with horses, but useless at fighting,' Kearns said. 'And it was while the battle was raging on the field at Ballyellis that Harry sees a trumpet on the ground, and sees also the horses of the enemy prancing wildly. So Harry whips up the trumpet and blew the blast that orders the cavalry to fall in, and several of the poor horses attempted to fall into line amidst the chaos of the battleground. Then Harry blows for them to fall out and sets them prancing wildly again. And so it went on, with the horses dancing in and out, in and out.' Kearns smiled at Reily, 'He had a great sense of humour did Harry Neil. And although you could say that he was more a spectator than a fighter at Ballyellis, he did more for us with his trumpet-blowing than others did with their swords.'

Farrell Reily was grinning. 'What happened to him?'

'Killed, I think,' Kearns answered a bit sadly. 'I never saw him again after the battle anyhow. Some say that he . . . well, damn my eyes, but look who's coming!'

Kearns was looking grimly at the girl in the dark blue cloak weaving her way towards them.

'She just won't stop until she sees him, will she?' Farrell Reily said quietly. 'Not only does she send for him every few days, she's beginning to follow him everywhere. She'll make him bite the dust quicker than any militiaman.'

'Not while I'm around,' Kearns said. 'Myself and the captain have been through too much together. I'll not let her put a halter round his neck.'

Mary came up to them, pink-cheeked and breathless, a smile on her face.

'What do you want?' Farrell Reily snapped.

'To . . . see Michael,' she stammered, her smile disappearing at his tone.

'I'll go and get him. You wait here.'

When Reily had gone, she twisted her fingers together and looked vacantly around her, shocked at their open hostility. Kearns leaned on his musket and ignored her. He had always found her very sexually attractive and for this he unconsciously blamed her, but not as much as he consciously disliked her for endangering the captain.

'You are acting very stupidly,' Kearns said quietly, 'always seeking him out like this. Don't you realise that it will not be long before the spy and the informer begin to follow you, hoping your movements will lead them to the captain?'

'I . . . I just wanted to see him for a few minutes.'

'All the lads are annoyed about you. 'Tis our lives you are putting in danger as well.'

'But I can see him if I want . . . I am his wife.'

'So what! We all have our wives and girlfriends too, but they know their place. Sensible women who wouldn't *dream* of putting any of us in danger. Why don't you take a leaf out of Sarah's book? She doesn't follow Hugh Vesty around. *She* cares too much about him to put her own selfish whims before his safety.'

Mary stared whitely at him, tears moistening her eyes. She rapidly blinked them back when she saw Michael and Farrell Reily coming down to her.

Kearns and Farrell Reily watched as Michael escorted her back down a short distance and stopped by a tree, his head lowered as he listened to her silently.

'Looks like she's telling him what I said to her,' Kearns muttered.

'What did you say to her?'

Kearns repeated the conversation. 'Then she looks at me with tears in her eyes, and I was sorry I had spoke then. But someone had to tell her sometime.'

'You did right,' Reily said. 'And look – he's smiling at her. She mustn't have told him.'

They watched as the captain and his wife stood quietly talking. 'Have you noticed how he never kisses her?' Farrell Reily said. 'Not even a peck on the cheek.'

Kearns nodded. The captain had flirted openly and outrageously with other girls in the past, but he never displayed any emotion towards his wife in front of the men.

Farrell Reily sighed. 'It's rude to keep staring at them. Tell me some more about Wexford?'

Kearns shrugged. 'I've said enough about the rebellion for one day. Why don't you tell me something, just for a change.'

Farrell Reily leaned on his musket. 'Do you ever miss being a carpenter?'

'I wasn't a trained carpenter. I was an apprentice carpenter to a master craftsman.'

'But do you ever miss it? The old whittling and sawing?'

'Aye, I do too. I wouldn't mind turning this here pine tree into a nice table. Did I ever tell you about the beautiful chair I made for my mother from black bog-oak? Oh, it was lovely, high-backed Jacobean style with roses carved on the head-rest. And inside one rose I even carved her initials. She started crying when she seen it. Then the militia came in one night on one of their routine inspections and smashed it to pieces. It was me who was crying then, and I didn't stop crying for at least a day. Then last spring, just before the rebellion, on the day of my twenty-first birthday, I started another chair, but God knows when I'll ever get the opportunity to finish . . . oh would you look – the captain's kissing her!'

Farrell Reily gaped. 'Well, by God, he is, and a beauty of a kiss it is too . . .'

Kearns looked at Reily and shook his head sadly. 'He's done

for. The noose is ready. And she'll lead him to it like a dog on a leash.'

'Divil a clip,' Reily cried, 'not even Hugh Vesty throws decency to the wind and kisses his wife in front of us in that way – and you know what an amorous buck *he* is!'

'The captain is a frightened man if you ask me,' Kearns said. 'That's the way a man kisses a woman when she's threatened to leave him. I bet that's what she's done, threatened to leave him if he doesn't do whatever she wants.'

'She's going.'

Michael came strolling back towards them, his manner calm and relaxed, turning his head and pausing as Rory Derneen came running up the hill after him. The two fell in step together, the captain smiling at whatever Derneen was breathlessly telling him. And although he would never admit it to Farrell Reily, Kearns experienced a great wave of relief.

Ten seconds later he was pitched flat on his back from the foot and hip Michael gave him as he passed.

Up in the cave, Hugh Vesty was sitting around the fire, laughing with John Mernagh, Martin Burke, and Sam McAllister.

'It was a terrible thing you lads did at my wedding,' Hugh said. 'And nothing will convince me that Dwyer was not behind it.'

Mernagh grinned. 'Wasn't he standing innocently on outpost duty minding his own business?'

'Ach! don't give me that. He was in high spirits right enough.'

On the night of a marriage, it was custom for the lads and girls to whistle and sing outside the bedroom of the wedded couple until drinks were handed out to them. If the couple were too lazy to comply with the custom, then . . .

'He blocked up the chimney and smoked us out!' Hugh Vesty cried. 'We never did that to him on his wedding night, did we now?'

But Hugh could not help laughing at it, now that a space of time had rekindled his humour, and Sarah had thought it hilarious. 'Even if she was tipsy,' Hugh muttered.

Rory Derneen came running into the cave.

'Hugh Vesty, I think there's trouble abrewing. The captain has just given the most violent pitch-over to Michael Kearns, nearly broke his back!'

Hugh sprang to his feet. 'For what reason?'

'Kearns spoke rudely to the captain's wife and it's caused

286

himself some annoyance. He's called Kearns to account.'

When Hugh Vesty and the others reached the outpost, Kearns was still down on one knee with Reily bending over him. Michael was nowhere to be seen.

'What's going on?' Hugh Vesty demanded.

Farrell Reily answered. ' 'Tis the captain's wife who is the cause of all the trouble, but he can't see no fault in her. Always following him whenever she can find him out.'

'If she were *my* wife,' Kearns shouted, almost in tears, 'I would make her stay away! There's no need of informers awhile she keeps coming after him.'

'Then act like a man and voice your grievances directly to him,' Sam McAllister said. 'Not to his wife. And 'tis lucky you are that you got off with just a pitch-over.'

'Kearns is right,' Hugh Vesty said quietly to McAllister. 'The men are very displeased and even his family are unhappy at the reckless way Mary is carrying on. It can't be allowed to continue.'

'Then tell him so,' McAllister said.

Hugh Vesty gaped at McAllister. 'I'm not going to tell him! If you feel he should be told, you tell him.'

After a pause, McAllister turned to Farrell Reily. 'Where's the captain now?'

'Went wandering off up yonder.'

Sam McAllister finally found Michael on a lonely part of the mountain, leaning against a tree. McAllister approached him quietly, and Michael made no move to look in his direction. The light of day was withdrawing into the shadows and the air seemed silent and melancholy.

'Kearns is almost crying,' McAllister said, 'and not from the hurt of the pitch-over.'

'He only got what he earned,' Michael answered, looking straight ahead.

'Maybe so. And yes, I agree, he was wrong to take it upon himself to speak to Mary. But you know, Michael, of all the lads in the camp, Kearns is the one who would risk his life for you. His action was deplorable, but his intentions were well meant.'

When Michael made no answer, McAllister drew in his breath to broach the subject. 'Michael, I understand how you feel about Mary, but she is behaving—'

'Sam,' Michael turned to look at him, 'one thing I'll not do is discuss my wife with you or any other man in this camp.'

'Fair enough. But what about the men? Many are feeling nervous—'

'Then let them go their own damn road!' Michael snapped. 'No one is forcing them to stay.'

'It would be a shame if you and Kearns fell out. You two have been friends a long time.'

'Friends do not take it upon themselves to correct a man's wife. God, when I think of the audacity of him, not to mention his bad manners, I could strangle him! It was only *my* feeling of friendship for him that stopped me.'

In the lull that followed, McAllister heard footsteps behind them, but once again Michael did not trouble himself to turn around. Kearns looked abashed.

'I'd like to speak with the captain,' he said in a subdued voice to McAllister.

A trace of a smile came on McAllister's face. 'Go ahead.'

'If it's all the same with you, Sam, I'd as lief speak with him alone.'

McAllister nodded, and moved off.

Down below the men waited.

'Kearns is too hot-headed,' John Mernagh said.

Martin Burke agreed.

But nevertheless, most of the men in the camp liked young Kearns, and were greatly relieved when they saw him and the captain strolling back together, with Kearns smiling broadly as he chattered on in his usual way.

Hugh Vesty and McAllister smiled at each other, and the men returned to whatever they had been doing before the incident had occurred. Tranquillity had returned to the camp, and all were comrades in arms again.

Two nights later, murmurs of discontent again rumbled amongst the men when a lad from Ballinacrow came to the camp and told Michael that his wife wanted to see him urgently.

Michael left immediately. When he had not returned by midnight, Kearns was livid.

'She's done it again! She doesn't give a damn if he gets captured and killed just as long as he keeps dancing to her tune!'

'Enough of that,' Hugh Vesty snapped, but he too was angry

288

at his cousin's imprudence. Michael was blind to Mary's fool-
ishness and that was dangerous. The men depended on his
leadership, and already a number were suffering badly from
living out in the cold and damp; coughs and colds, and now two
had signs of pneumonia.

'She knew what he was when she married him,' Mernagh
said quietly. 'And his first duty is to the men who have stuck
with him through everything.'

'They've only been married a few months,' Hugh muttered
in excuse.

'And lookit the day Kearns's own girlfriend came afollowing
him – he chided her and sent her away. He expects the same if
not better from the captain.'

Michael Kearns had moved to the far end of the cave and was
talking to some of his friends. 'The captain needs to be given
practical proof of the danger his wife's visits and summonses
could cause,' he said.

'How do you mean?'

Kearns winked. 'Keep Hugh Vesty and the others talking,
and I'll tell you all about it tomorrow.'

The men looked hesitant.

'Don't worry,' Kearns urged. 'The captain will be shaking
my hand and thanking me afterwards.'

'If you think you can outsmart him, then you're a fool,
Kearns.'

But Kearns was not to be reasoned with. He had formed his
plan and now slipped out of the cave and began to run quickly
in the direction of Ballinacrow, where the captain's wife was
being harboured. In his mind he worked out the text of a long
sermon he would give to the captain afterwards.

Mary was staying in the house of a man named Brien. Two of
his sons were doing sentry duty outside. Kearns threw a secret
United sign as he approached, and the sons relaxed. He fell into
conversation with one and said he had an urgent message for
the captain.

'Is the family asleep?' Kearns whispered.

'They're all long asleep by now. Shall I go in and get
Dwyer?'

'No, no!' Kearns rasped, holding up his hand. 'I'll just nip in
and whisper the message to him. Won't be a minute.'

Kearns moved slowly and silently through the living-room
where Mr Brien lay snoring in the settle-bed in the corner.

When Kearns crept into the dark bedroom off the kitchen, he sucked in a nervous breath and closed the door silently.

His eyes quickly adjusted and he could see the two figures in the bed, lit by the brilliance of the moon beaming through the window. He could tell by their breathing and postures that both were asleep; the captain on the nearside, lying on his front.

Creeping swiftly to the bed, Kearns thrust a hand around Michael's neck and cried in the voice of a yeoman, 'I have you at last, Dwyer! And long have I been searching for you!'

His arm was seized in a fierce grip and a second later the muzzle of a pistol pressed into Kearns's throat.

'Ca-ca-captain! 'Tis me – Kearns!'

When Michael perceived whom he had, he complimented Kearns with a hearty curse, then after a moment's silence he whispered: 'It is well I did not shoot you, you fool.'

Kearns tried to nod his head in agreement but the gun was still pressed into his neck, his arm still locked in the iron grip.

Michael slowly drew away the pistol, slipped it back under his pillow, then looked at Kearns without any sign of emotion. 'What was your purpose in coming here?'

'I was trying out an experiment, Captain.' Kearns's voice was bleak. 'And 'twas nearly a sad experiment, for me.'

'You have acted very inconsiderately,' Michael said coldly, 'but I tell you one last time, Kearns . . . if you ever interfere between myself and my wife again, or enter a bedchamber where my wife is sleeping, you will regret it sorely.'

'After that,' Kearns said later, 'I did not ask to make my experiment the text for the wise sermon I intended to preach to him.'

Mary lay absolutely still, her eyes wide and terrified. When Kearns had closed the door ever so softly behind him, Michael turned his head and looked at her. His heart sank. He could see another tantrum was brewing.

He tried to appease her, but she pushed him away, just as she had done earlier. She turned her back to him and began to weep.

'Don't turn away from me again,' he whispered. 'If you would just tell me what's wrong with you.'

'I don't know,' she cried. 'All I know is that I'm tired and miserable. And your men get abusive whenever I try to see you for a few minutes.'

'You could be followed. That's what worries them. And, Mary, they are right.'

She spun around to face him. 'You take their side against me? Your precious friends against me? No wonder you don't want to try and get away to America.'

'Oh, don't start that again.'

After a long silence, he said steadily, 'Just tell me what you want from me, Mary. And not America, for I'll not leave Wicklow, even for you.'

'I want to go back home.'

He stared at her coldly. 'Back to your father?'

'No, to my Mammy. I need to see Mammy. I need a woman to talk to.'

'You have Mrs Brien to talk to.'

' 'Tis not the same as talking to Mammy. I can't talk intimately to strangers.'

'Strangers? Everyone has treated you with all the kindness of a daughter. You said so yourself.'

'I know. But it's not the same as talking to my own people. I want to go back home.'

'Then you shall go back home.'

'Truly?'

'Truly,' he whispered tiredly.

He took her in his arms and rubbed his face gently against hers until she had stopped weeping. His lips sought and moved on hers and for a moment she responded, then again pushed him away.

'What's the matter with you, Mary? At Cullen's on Twelfth Day everything was wonderful with us, wonderful . . . but for weeks now you've not let me touch you.'

A maelstrom of emotions chased across Mary's face, but her eyes evaded his. 'I'm just tired, Michael, bone tired. And my head is aching near to bursting.'

He lay back, supine and silent; and realised his own head was throbbing with the problem that Mary had become.

There were no words spoken the following morning as they made their way along an isolated route to Knockandarragh. It had rained in the night and a dismal dreariness covered the land. He walked silently beside her, only taking her hand whenever they had a difficult climb or descent. Mary glanced at him nervously, wondering what he was thinking.

The back of the house came into view. He stopped by a tree.

'There you go,' he said, motioning with his head to the house. 'Your own home again.'

'Will you come in with me?' she asked tentatively.

He shook his head. 'If I am with you, your father will stand against you. But if you go in alone, you will just be his darling Mary back from her escapade.' He looked at her steadily. 'Do you have any wish to see me again?' he asked.

At first she thought he was being sarcastic, but looking into his face she realised he was being very serious. 'I'd like to see you this evening,' she said quickly. 'Meet me at Cullen's, just after dusk, about four o'clock. I'll feel better this evening, Michael, surely I will. And we'll have a long talk, and I'll tell you all what happens inside.' She cleaved to him for a moment, before turning away.

He watched her walk down to the low stone wall and climb over it. A sudden roar crashed through the air as Doyle himself came out of the barn. For a moment he and Mary stood staring at each other, then she was in his arms and Doyle was crying loudly, 'Oh, my darling, my darling, my darling!'

Mrs Doyle came out in her nightgown. All three seemed to be wrapped into each other, laughing and hugging and crying. Their emotion was so shameless, so enveloping, so complete, neither of the parents seemed to look or question where the husband was. And Mary did not look back as they scooped her into the house.

He stood alone by the tree for some time, then turned away, and carefully keeping under cover as much as possible, he made his way towards his own family at Eadstown.

'But why would she just turn cold on you?' Cullen said in bewilderment. 'Answer me that?'

It was almost midnight, and Mary had not arrived at John Cullen's house. Michael silently studied the fire.

' 'Tis some mistake,' Cullen said. 'That father of hers probably tied her up and locked her in the bedroom.'

'No,' Michael answered. 'She can twist him around her little finger as easily as she did me. The novelty of marriage just wore off for her, and that's the truth of it. She got tired of being moved from pillar to post, tired of me and the life that goes with me.'

'She knew that's how it would be,' Cullen said. 'She knew it would not be easy.'

'She didn't know anything beyond her own romantic notions. But I knew how it would be. I should never have married her.'

Cullen was wringing his hands together fretfully. 'And all this trouble with the men. Something will have to be sorted out.'

'Something has been sorted out.' Michael stood up and lifted his coat from the hook and withdrew a purse of money from the pocket.

'I went to Eadstown today. This is my share of what's left of the year's money. Will you take it to her tomorrow? And tell her that my share of the farm's profits will be paid to her every quarter-day.'

Cullen stared at the purse with mouth open. Michael threw it on the table and shrugged on his coat. 'What are you doing?' Cullen cried. 'Where are you going?'

'Back to my men. Where I should have been these hours past.'

'What about Mary?'

'What about Mary?' Michael pulled up the collar of his coat. 'She's gone back home to her daddy and mammy that she should never have left in the first place.'

Cullen sprang to the door and tried to bar his way. 'What are you saying, Michael? You're confusing me something desperate.'

Michael practically lifted him out of the way. 'I'm saying it's over! The marriage is over! The love part anyhow. She's made that clear enough.'

'No, treasure, no! 'Tis just teething troubles. All married couples get out of twist now and again. Wait now, wait, when will you be coming back to see me?'

'Not for a while, old man. You can leave any message for me at Eadstown.' Michael opened the door and bent his head against the blast of cold February air and disappeared into the night.

'For better or worse!' Cullen shouted. 'You both made the vow!' but only an owl answered him, and it wasn't even a man imitating an owl either.

As if in a daze Cullen moved back indoors, wringing his hands and looking around the room where they had had such a grand time at Christmas. Michael's visits were like sunshine to him, sunshine in a dreary life. And even better when Mary came too. Now what had happened?

Cullen was so upset he took down the whiskey, drinking and muttering to himself. 'Who would have thought it? A sweet and gentle girl like Mary acting the tyrant.'

*   *   *

When Mary arrived at the isolated house in Knockgorrah the next morning, just after daylight, holding her side and breathless from her hurried journey, Cullen refused to look at her.

'Is Michael still asleep?' she asked, heading for the bedroom door.

'He's not here,' Cullen muttered dourly.

'Do you know where he's camped today?'

'He didn't mention it.'

Mary's fingers began to twist together as Cullen put on his greatcoat and prepared to leave. 'What's wrong with you?' she whispered.

'What's wrong? You ask me what's wrong after the way you've been carrying on!' He spun around to face her. 'You've upset Michael something sorely these past weeks. I should have stayed here on Cock-step-along and not lost my money and lovely waistcoat up in Tallaght. But lookit here, Mary, 'tis a bad thing when a woman tries to come between a man and his friends.'

'I never did—'

'Women don't understand the love there is between comrades. Aye, love! When men have fought together, seen their friends killed, come through dangerous times together, saved each other's lives – a kinship develops that is strong and binding. They begin to love each other like brothers. Not out of the same hatch maybe, but all in the same boat. Brothers in peril.'

Mary tried to speak but Cullen went on: 'Going on about wanting your own home and he not knowing if each day will be his last. And asking Michael to leave Imaal! Michael is as much a part of these Wicklow Mountains as the Lugnaquilla itself. 'Twould kill him to leave, and you know it!'

'I know, it was foolish. I was just dreaming because—'

'Dreaming? Is that what you were doing last night? He waited from four of the clock until after midnight but you never came. When he walked out that door he had tears in his eyes. And *that* is a rare sight. I'm very annoyed with you, girl!'

'I couldn't come,' Mary managed. 'I got sick just as I was leaving and Mammy made me go to bed and forced me to stay there until she sent for the doctoring woman. And by the time she had finished I was too weak and it was too dark and too late to come . . . and I couldn't send a message because my brother John didn't come home until the small hours.'

294

Mary's legs began to tremble. She reached for the table, sitting down heavily. Cullen narrowed his eyes sharply as he looked at her. All the colour had drained from her face leaving her skin a startling white. Her eyes were wide and looked black as black against the paleness of her skin.

'What ails you?' Cullen said in sudden concern. 'Are you still feeling sickly?'

'I'm going to have a baby.'

Cullen stared at her. 'A baby? Oh, wait now. A baby? Does . . . does himself know?'

Mary put her palms to her cheeks and shook her head. 'I thought I might be, in January, and I kept going to the camp to tell him, and I kept sending for him to tell him, but somehow I never did. I kept thinking that it would be stupid to worry him until I was sure. My body has acted strangely before.'

Cullen hadn't a clue what she was talking about. 'Are you sure now?'

'Aye. Mammy examined me and she was sure. And then when the doctoring woman came she said I was pregnant by three months. Since early November.'

She stood and began to pace up and down, talking frantically to herself as if Cullen wasn't there.

'I could have talked to the women at the houses, but I didn't feel I knew them well enough. And I wanted to find out from Mammy if it was dangerous to let him love me if I was pregnant, that's why I wouldn't . . .'

She turned desperately to Cullen. 'Oh, why did he get upset last night? Why did he not realise something must have happened? Why did he not trust me?' Her voice spiralled hysterically on each question.

'I don't know what to say to you,' Cullen mumbled, unable to handle the situation. 'I knew it was all some big mistake but he thought the worst. Especially after the confusing way you've been behaving and misbehaving. He left that purse of money for you, and said his share of the farm's profits will be paid to you each quarter-day.'

Mary stared in puzzlement at the purse of money still lying on the table, her black brows downwards. 'What are you talking about? Money every quarter-day?'

Cullen was all of a fluster. His hands moved over his face and then clasped together. 'It's how he thinks you've gone home to your mammy and daddy for good and final. He thinks the marriage is over, the love part anyhow. Oh, Mary, could you not have just been simple and told him what you suspected, instead of all this complication?'

The cry that Mary gave was half a wail, half a scream; a savage cry of disbelief. She made to run out the door but Cullen caught her, his arms surprisingly strong. She struggled fiercely with him, screaming hysterically.

'Stop it, Mary,' Cullen begged. 'No use upsetting yourself more by running wild. You'll not find him if he doesn't want to be found.'

'I have to find him,' she wailed, 'to tell him how wrong he is, tell him that I'm carrying his child. I was going to explain it all last night, as soon as I was sure.'

'I'll try to find him,' Cullen assured her. 'I'll try to find him for you. Sit down and rest awhile, treasure. Sit down, sit down . . .'

Mary let herself be led to the chair by the hearth, her crying loud and unchecked. When she quietened the old man said, 'I'll be off now. You'll just sit quiet while I'm gone, won't you?'

She nodded and wiped her face with her palm. 'You'll bring him back here with you? Promise you will? Promise?'

The old man nodded and gave his promise, not at all sure if he could keep it.

The camp on the Keadeens was deserted. A fresh bush of heath placed over the small entrance, instructions given to a trusted partisan family to renew the bush whenever necessary. One of the secrets of the rebels' survival was their policy of keeping constantly on the move. And early that morning Michael and his men had moved to the camp on Knockamunnion, just below Table Mountain, while old man Cullen was miles away, plodding up the Lugnaquilla.

Chapter Nineteen

The snow had started to fall as the men reached the camp on Knockamunnion, and three days later, on the morning of 14th February 1799, it was still falling.

Inside the cave where a fire burned warmly, Michael was sitting alone on his bed of ferns away from the other men, reading a book by the light of a candle when Michael Kearns came and sat beside him.

'I've decided to quit,' Kearns said. 'I can't stay out in arms any more.'

Michael lifted his eyes from the book. 'You know our principle. Never to give obstruction to any person who wishes to leave us.'

'My mind's made up,' Kearns said in a distressed tone. 'I've decided to try and escape the severity of the laws of this land. I'll go to Dublin first, then, hopefully, America.'

'If that's what you want.'

'There can be no realisation of our former hopes of liberty,' Kearns blurted. 'The beggarly French invasion failed, and no hope of another. Only death awaits us here.'

'I shall be sorry to lose you,' Michael said quietly. 'You were a fine comrade.' He smiled slightly. 'And a good friend.'

Kearns looked even more distressed. 'Here,' he said, 'take my musket and a few rounds of ammunition. It is all I have to give, but I want you to have them.'

'You will need them yourself, to see you to safety.'

'I want you to have them!' Kearns insisted. 'I shall be fine. Not even the militia will be out in this weather.'

Michael took the gun and rose to his feet. Kearns gave him the ammunition, then turned abruptly and moved back to the main group, shaking their hands in farewell. They had all known about Kearns's decision to leave some minutes before he had approached the captain, and despite his occasional hot-headedness, all were very sad to see him go.

As Kearns reached the entrance, he turned and looked back at the captain, and saw him with his coat on, collar turned up, and pulling his black slouch hat lower over his eyes. 'I'll come part of the way with you,' Michael told him.

Kearns stared at him in surprise, then nodded a smile.

They moved in silence down the mountains, discovering the snow to be even deeper than they had thought. They more or less slid down the rest of the way, but on the more level land the going was slow and laborious.

'Are you sure you want to carry on?' Michael asked.

'Yes,' Kearns said.

'Then you have only one way of getting there before spring-time.' Michael climbed up on to the wide top of a low hedge and began to do a wobbling walk as if he were on a tightrope. Kearns let out a laugh and jumped up behind him.

''Tis better if you run,' Michael called. 'Gives the feet less time to sink into the hedge.' The two of them clowned like children as they proceeded, but they made fast progress running along the snow-matted top of the hedges instead of plodding through the deep snow below.

After four miles, Michael turned to leave his comrade to travel on alone. Kearns had decided he would stop for a few hours at the house of a man named Brady in Ballinacorbeg whose son had been out with them until a few days ago. Sadly, Kearns held out his hand in final farewell.

Michael clasped it. 'Good luck, avic.'

'You too, Captain. And thanks, thanks for always being beside me or in front of me on the battlefield, and thanks for coming so far with me now.'

'You're welcome,' Michael said lightly, and made a scrambled jump up on the hedge. Kearns stood and watched him go, a tall black-coated figure against the white snow. Michael paused and looked back, waved, and started to wobble exaggeratedly as if he were overbalancing.

Kearns laughed and waved, then shoved his hands into his pockets and hunched his shoulders as he watched the captain until he was out of sight.

On the morning after Michael Kearns's departure, there was another heavy fall of snow. The men had sat around the fire discussing the situation. It was madness to continue living out in the freezing weather, and the two young lads showing signs of pneumonia should be taken home, whatever the risk. It was finally agreed that all but the leaders should go down to the houses until the bad weather had passed. Hugh Vesty and Martin Burke headed the group that was gathered to take one of the sick lads home, Michael and Sam McAllister prepared a blanket stretcher for the other.

'When we get our boy home,' Hugh Vesty said to Michael, 'I intend to seek out a few days in the warm company of my wife.'

Michael made no comment or reference to his own wife, simply carried on with the task of knotting the four corners of the blanket which lay underneath his sick comrade, to the blanket covering him. This done, the four corners were lifted by four men, and all prepared for the journey through the snow.

'Every man for himself and God for us all,' Michael told the men as they parted, then the two parties set off in opposite directions.

By that afternoon, the sick boy had been delivered safely into the care of his family, and Michael and his eleven comrades were climbing up the steep hills towards Derrynamuck, all drenched with snow. They made fun of it, making an improvised hurling ball with a lump of rock-hard snow and tossing it to each other with the butt of their muskets, until it disintegrated. Michael then proceeded to rub a handful of snow into the face of Thomas Clerk, a deserter from the 9th Dragoons who had the nickname, 'the Little Dragoon'. Another rebel, known as 'Hughie the Brander', came to the Little Dragoon's assistance, then Sam McAllister joined in until all the men were rolling in the snow and laughing like lunatics.

'Oh, look there!' Michael said, suddenly seriously. 'I reckon that's a sheep.'

Under a great swell of snow, a small hole had appeared with whispers of smoke flittering through it. Instantly they knew it to be an airhole kept open by the hot breath of an animal. They dug at the hard snow with the butts of their muskets, then clawed the snow back with their hands until they had the shoulders of the helpless ewe out of the hole. The ewe began to cry loudly. Michael gentled her until eventually she was completely free, and he led over to the shelter of a mearing dyke.

Up above, three houses nestled on the hillside. The first was a farmhouse owned by a family named Hoxey. Michael was well known to these residents who had supported him faithfully in the past. Patrick Hoxey immediately welcomed some of the men to take shelter in his house, but as he had a travelling tailor and his apprentice staying, there was room for only two.

Further up the hillside was the larger house of the Toole family: six more were readily given shelter there, and up a long winding path near the top was the small two-roomed cottage of Miley Connell and his wife and two children.

The front door of the Connells' cottage opened into a small porch which had two doors at either side of the main one. The door to the left led into a square low kitchen, while the door to the right led into a bedroom.

Michael, Sam McAllister, John Savage, and Patrick Costello were ushered inside. 'We'll squeeze you in somehow,' Connell declared cheerfully, while his wife made them strip off their wet coats and partake of bowls of hot mutton stew.

Later, Patrick Hoxey and the tailor staying with him, a man named Lawler, made the journey from the bottom house up to the top house and asked Michael if a picquet was needed for the night. If so, they would do it, and be glad of the chance.

Michael stood at the door and looked over the white land. From the Connells' house, situated as it was behind the bend of the winding path leading up the hill, the Tooles' and Hoxeys' houses were hidden from his view; as was the road leading up here to Derrynamuck.

'I wouldn't have thought any sane person would be out tonight,' he said, 'even the soldiery. But the Tooles' house is best situated for a defence. If there is any danger, give the alarm to the men in that house first.'

The tailor was barely able to conceal his delight at becoming one of 'Dwyer's men'. And being a travelling man, he would now be able to inform the families he stayed with that he was not *just* a tailor! He pushed his spectacles further up his nose. After tonight, he would be able to say that he had seen active service in the army of resistance!

Travelling tailors were a common thing amongst the country people. The tailor was paid so much for a coat or a suit along with his bed and board. Usually the whole family was fitted out so he could be in residence for as long as three or four weeks. He would be less likely to be hurried on if he had an interesting tale to contribute to the evening conversations while he did his hand-stitching. But a tailor who had risked life and limb with Michael Dwyer! – Lawler's chest swelled at the thought of it.

Lawler the tailor now presented Michael with a solemn countenance and a slow salute of his hand. 'You can rest aisy and rely on us, Cap'n Dwyer,' he said gravely.

When he held the salute, Michael stared at him quizzically for a moment, then jerked to attention and returned the salute. Lawler's face beamed as he turned and marched away, arms swinging like a soldier.

Later, when the woman and children of the top house had gone to bed, Michael and his three comrades played a few hands of fifteen and twenty-five with Miley Connell, who eventually threw down his losing cards in despair and brought out two comfortable old ticks from the bedroom.

'It'll have to be two apiece on each of these,' Connell said, 'but there's plenty of room.'

Michael and McAllister looked around the small room which was not big enough to swing a cat o' nine tails, but they made no complaints, just grinned at Connell. 'Aye, there's plenty of room.'

Miley Connell nodded. 'I'll bring the blankets now.'

They pushed the furniture against the walls and spread the straw mattresses on the floor in the centre of the room. After bidding Connell goodnight, Costello and Savage climbed sleepily under their blanket, while Michael and McAllister remained sitting by the fire, each with a warming tot of whiskey in his hand.

Sam began to talk about his life in Ulster while Michael listened with silent attention, occasionally lifting the poker to stab the heart of the fire and stir the flames. He questioned Sam curiously about the Antrim glens.

McAllister smiled. 'You boys think Wicklow is the last place God made, but let me tell you, there are parts of Antrim that would take your breath away; the lush glens, the mountains and the beautiful sea coves . . .'

When McAllister eventually finished eulogising about Antrim, Michael said softly: 'We'll go there, Sam, in the summertime, when the air and sea are warm. Just you and me travelling together, to your own lovely Antrim.'

McAllister held up his glass and smiled. 'I'll drink to that,' he said.

Patrick Hoxey and Lawler the tailor were doing outpost duty down by Hoxey's barn and near freezing to death. The novelty of being a rebel was beginning to wear off Lawler.

'God sakes,' he said through chattering teeth, 'could we not keep an eye out from the bedroom window?'

Patrick Hoxey's lips were too numb to answer. His eyes moved up the hillside. The candles has long been extinguished in the Tooles' house, but the top house was around the bend and hidden from view.

''Tis w-w-warm inside,' Lawler the tailor said, 'and we c-c-could have a drop of the parliamentarian while we keep w-w-watch.'

Hoxey's lips still refused to move, so he nodded instead. Some minutes later the two men were propped by the bedroom window, feeling the warmth seeping through them and the life coming back as they sipped the whiskey.

'God sakes,' Lawler tutted, filling his glass again, 'not even the divil would venture out on a night like this. Never mind the redcoats.'

'That's not the point of the argument,' Patrick Hoxey returned. 'We have to be on our guard just in case.'

Lawler shifted his position and the cat sprang from the floor on to the bed. For a moment Lawler stared at it, then said suddenly,

'Cats is queer animals. Did you know that you should never ask a cat a question?'

Hoxey looked at him curiously. 'Why is that?'

'A widow woman I made a cloak for was telling me. If you ask a cat a question, and 'tis a female cat, and she answers you back, 'tis fourteen years' bad luck you'll have brought on yourself.'

Hoxey creased his brow, then said: 'Did the widow woman have a few straws short in her hayloft, I wonder?'

'Oh, I did wonder the same thing,' Lawler said quickly, then jutted his head towards the ceiling and tutted, 'God sakes!'

In the Glen of Imaal and the surrounding areas there were a number of families called Lynch who were constant, true, and reliable friends of Michael Dwyer. But one man – Patrick

Lynch – hated Dwyer beyond measure. Some years previously there had been an eviction, the poor family turned on to the hills because the rent could not be paid, and the rule among the people was that no man would take up residence on a holding where an eviction of children had taken place. This rule caused great trouble to the agents of the English landlords, for if the holding was not worked, the mountain would take back its own and the furze and bracken would soon swamp the land.

Patrick Lynch had immediately taken up residence after the eviction, and had suffered the whistles of derision whenever Dwyer and his friends passed him. No other inhabitant of Imaal could condescend to speak to the traitor who had walked over an evicted mother's threshold.

Lynch had brooded and smouldered, but now he saw his chance to get even. He had seen Dwyer and his men clowning in the snow earlier that evening. For hours he had shivered as he watched two of the three houses on the hill at Derrynamuck, waiting for the candles to be extinguished, and thereby comfirming the band of rebels were set for the night.

Not daring to be seen anywhere near a yeoman or a barracks, Lynch took his information to Reverend Edward Blake of Humewood, who immediately ordered his carriage and travelled with all possible speed to the headquarters of the Glengarry Fencibles at Hacketstown.

Roderick McDonald, a colonel in the Glengarry (1st British Highland) Regiment, and Captain Hugh Beaton, listened silently as the minister gave them the information.

'There have been complaints, you know,' Reverend Blake said, 'about your lax attitude to these barbarians who terrify innocent God-fearing people. The loyal people of Wicklow expect you to do your duty – your duty to your King and to the honour of the regiment that you are so proud of – the regiment of His Majesty's First British Highlanders!'

In less time than it takes to brush a sporran, a company of one hundred infantry of the Glengarry Fencibles was preparing to set out for Derrynamuck, under the command of Colonel Roderick McDonald and Captain Hugh Beaton.

The Highlanders suffered painfully on their march to Derrynamuck. Some were nearly crying with the cold and the severe night air which cut sharp in their chests when they breathed. But the Green Tiger of Imaal had to be captured and brought in – the honour of the regiment was at stake.

They were covered in snow and in foul humour when they quietly and carefully approached the area. Although still night, visibility was clear due to the whiteness of the land.

The two picquets sitting on outpost duty in the bedroom, Hoxey and Lawler, had by now fallen asleep and the Highlanders were presented with no obstruction as they silently surrounded the three houses.

'Thirty to each house,' Colonel McDonald commanded in a whisper.

Inside Hoxey's house, James Byrne, the nineteen-year-old apprentice to the travelling tailor found himself sleeping between Ned Lennon and the Little Dragoon. The arrival of the rebels had been a great diversion from cutting and stitching, especially when Mr Lawler abandoned the scissors for a musket and marched off to do 'active service in defence of our boys still fighting the enemy'.

At first young Byrne had been disappointed that the captain himself had not elected to stay in Hoxey's house, but the two rebels who had remained had been as good as a holiday, telling him tales and singing him songs and exchanging verbal volleys amongst themselves until Byrne was sure his sides were going to split open from the laughing. Musha, 'twould be mortal dreary having only Hoxey and Mr Lawler for company when they had gone.

What had awakened Byrne he could not say afterwards, but he now opened his eyes and blinked as the colourful figure of a Highlander glided past the window.

'Lads!' he whispered loudly, reaching to shake them, 'I think I saw a kiltie gliding past the window there.'

Ned Lennon and the Little Dragoon stirred each side of him, assured him he was dreaming, then Lennon made a bleary-eyed query, 'Was he blowing his pipes by any chance?'

'No, he just sort of . . . glided past . . . silently.'

'Oh, well then, 'tis the ghost of Lugduff you saw. He has a habit of gliding, snow or not.'

A second later all three saw another Highlander move past the window and the two rebels were out of the bed reaching for their guns. The Little Dragoon scrambled on his hands and knees across the floor then stood with his back flat against the wall as he looked sideways through the window. His eyes opened wide before he turned them back into the room and whispered,

'We're surrounded by a large force of Highlanders.'

A knock was heard at the door, then the firm voice of Captain Beaton, demanding their surrender. This was followed by the crying of children and the sudden wail of a terrified woman from one of the bedrooms.

'If you do not surrender,' Captain Beaton warned, 'I will be forced to burn the house over you, and the suffering of the women and the children will be on your heads.'

Lennon now looked at the Little Dragoon and said in a resigned tone, 'It can't be helped now, but it looks like we have lost. No point in making the family suffer for our bad luck.'

They agreed to surrender. Lennon shouted through the door to Captain Beaton. 'What do you want us to do?'

'Open the door just a few inches and hand out your arms one by one, with the butt end foremost.'

Captain Beaton himself cautiously received each weapon as it was handed out. When he was convinced the house was disarmed, he pushed open the door and ordered his soldiers to tie up the three men in the room, which they did, using hay ropes and a tie used for tying a cow up to her fodder.

When Hoxey and Lawler were marched into the room, the travelling tailor protested indignantly at the 'trussing up' of his apprentice.

'A boy training under my own master craftsmanship, destined to be one of the finest handstitchers in the County Wicklow; and definitely not a rebel.' He nodded his head at the ceiling and tutted in disgust, 'God sakes!'

Captain Beaton questioned young Byrne and asked to see his tailor's kit. Bryne motioned with his head towards the dresser where his sewing-kit lay. Captain Beaton inspected the kit, but decided that the apprentice's hands would remain tied. He had, after all, been found in the house of a harbourer.

They were all ordered to stand outside where Captain Beaton warned, 'Any kind of signal to your comrades in the houses above and you will be instantly shot.'

Another Highland officer was carrying out the same performance at Toole's house where the six men inside were having a council as to whether they should give resistance. John Ashe and Walt McDonnel insisted they should fight it out.

'The captain will give no surrender,' Ashe said. 'You can be sure of that.'

At that moment, the female section of the Toole family begged the men in one heartrending plea to give themselves up.

'Every man of your party is a prisoner along with your captain,' said the Highland officer. 'You may as well come out peacefully.'

'You have our captain?' Ashe cried incredulously.

'Yes.'

'Well let him come and speak to us,' Ashe shouted. 'And if he commands us to do so, then we will surrender.'

'No,' said the Highland officer. 'He has already been marched off.'

The men hesitated, shocked.

'Ah, God,' said Walt McDonnel, 'the captain taken! 'Tis a day for the devil.'

'If we surrender,' Ashe shouted out to the officer, 'do we have your word that the property will not be destroyed and no harm done against the family?'

'You have my word.'

They all agreed to surrender, all except Hughie the Brander.

'We're coming out,' Ashe shouted.

'First hand out your weapons, through the window, the butt foremost.'

When this had been done, the door was opened and the five rebels were bound tightly.

'Now,' said the officer, smiling, 'we will go and get your captain.'

All the occupants of the Connell house further up on the hill were sleeping soundly, oblivious of the cordon around the house which was now strengthened by the detachments who came up from the other two houses.

Colonel Roderick McDonald commanded this operation personally. There was no way Dwyer could escape, but he was taking no chances with the rebel's reputation for evasion of capture.

When the knock came on the door, Michael sprang to his feet at the same moment as Sam McAllister. Through the window, both saw the line of soldiers.

'Are you in there, Dwyer?' McDonald called.

'You know that I am,' Michael replied matter-of-factly, tugging on his breeches over his small-clothes.

'The house is surrounded. All your men are prisoners. I call on you to surrender.'

Michael and McAllister had reached for their guns, standing with their backs flat against the wall either side of the window.

''Tis the Glangarry's,' Michael whispered.

'Will you surrender peacefully, Dwyer?'

The voice of another Highlander rose up. 'We mean business, Dwyer! We do!'

Michael looked at McAllister. 'Now there's a friendly laddie trying to warn us of the facts of the matter. The Highlanders are here to do the business, to the death if necessary.'

'Hold your tongue, Corporal!' McDonald shouted furiously.

Michael turned his eyes again to the window. Some twenty feet away from the property ran a low stone wall. Behind it a line of kneeling Highlanders had their muskets trained on the house, the colours of their uniforms and large plumes in their hats standing out against the white hills behind them.

The terrified family now came rushing in to the rebels, the woman and children screaming and Miley Connell pleading with Michael to surrender.

Michael turned and rammed the butt of his musket through the window, breaking the glass. Colonel McDonald loudly commanded his men to keep clear of the two windows and the door.

'Who's the commanding officer?' Michael shouted.

'Colonel McDonald.'

'Then listen to me, McDonald. I occupied this house by force and without the consent of the family. Will you allow them to pass through the cordon unharmed?'

'Will you surrender peacefully?'

'Will you let the family pass out safely?' Michael returned.

'Very well.'

John Savage and Patrick Costello stood rooted to the spot. 'Do we surrender, Captain?'

'Every man must make his own choice,' Michael said. 'Those who wish to surrender, pass out now with the Connells.'

While Savage and Costello deliberated, Michael shouted through the window, 'The family is coming out!'

Sam McAllister held the door ajar while the family squeezed through and scurried up to and past the cordon behind the wall.

'Captain, what do we do now?' Costello cried. 'The entire male population of the Glengarry glens must be out there.'

'Our surrendering now won't save us,' Michael said realistically. 'It will be a bullet or a halter if we do. One way or the other, death has come to us. Let us meet it like men.'

'Very well, very well,' said McAllister. 'I am ready.'

'Myself also,' said John Savage.

'Well, Dwyer? That's the family,' McDonald shouted. 'How many men are there?'

'To my reckoning,' Michael answered, 'there's a hundred without and only four within.'

'Then I call on you to surrender in the name of the King. I am not prepared to waste time on a night like this. What do you intend to do?'

'Fight until I die,' Michael answered, raising his gun. 'And here's at you, avic.'

The sound of gunfire from the top house raised a loud cheer from the rebel prisoners standing outside the two houses down the hill. Despite shouts from the Highlanders, some of the Toole family ran up the hill to see what was happening.

The battle went on and on, and Colonel McDonald warned his men to stay clear of the range of the door and windows. They now took the additional precaution of entrenching themselves behind a cowhouse, half left from the house, and from this outhouse they managed to pour in a stream of bullets through the window, killing John Savage.

Michael and McAllister gave an answering burst and a number of Highlanders were injured. The rebels' volleys were so fast and furious that Colonel McDonald smiled at his men.

'Their own fire will do them in the end,' he said. 'The house is low, and they will eventually set it on fire with their continual discharge.'

As time went on, the long and hard resistance being put up by three or four men, and from a house so ill-suited for defence, finally made Colonel McDonald lose his temper.

'Set fire to the roof-thatch at the four corners,' he commanded.

Inside the house the situation was getting desperate. The men were aware the house was on fire, although it blazed slowly on account of the snow and wetness of the thatch. The room began to fill up with smoke until it was hard to breathe. Two tubs of butter on the table began to melt and run into oil over the floor. Portions of burning thatch began to fall in on them, making it impossible to reload their weapons with any degree of safety.

Pat Costello suddenly lost possession of himself. He found a spade and began digging up the floor in an attempt to make a tunnel. Michael was crouched beneath the window. 'Stop that, Costello. You're only digging your way to hell.'

A second later, a succession of bullets through the window sent Costello reeling against the back wall, then slumping down in a bloodied heap.

Michael and McAllister stared at their two dead comrades. ''Tis just you and me in it now, Captain,' Sam whispered.

'Och! you bluidy fool, Dwyer!' Colonel McDonald shouted impatiently. 'Why don't you just surrender?'

'And have the yeos use me for target practice in the centre of Rathdrum or Baltinglass?' Michael shouted. ''Tis you who's the fool McDonald, if you think I'd give them such an ecstasy.'

A clamp of turf near the hearth caught fire and blazed towards the flames above. The smoke inside the house became dense, making the two rebels cough fitfully. They were fast approaching the highest point of human endurance, but they had resolved to give no surrender with life, and were now resigning themselves to perishing in the flames.

'We haven't a chance,' gasped McAllister. 'We can't even reload our pieces without setting ourselves on fire.'

'Never say die, avic,' Michael whispered, 'not unless it is the last breath in your lungs.' He dragged the table across the floor and crawled under it, protected from the falling pieces of burning thatch as he recharged his musket. McAllister choked a laugh and also crawled under the table, reloading his gun as Michael sprang to the window and gave a burst of fire.

And so they continued, reloading under the table and firing from the window until a bullet found McAllister and smashed through his arm, sending his musket flying into the air and landing on the fire with a bang. He reeled back with a cry of pain and seemed stunned at the amount of blood gushing from his arm on to the floor.

Michael crawled across the floor and reached for him, barely able to see his comrade in the smoke. 'Ah, Sam, Sam . . . where did they get you?'

'In the arm. The blood is running like a stream. And my gun is gone.'

'But mine is still hot and angry,' Michael rasped, moving to reload his gun, then back to the window; back and forth, until McDonald shouted.

'Only one gun answering fire! Only one man left alive in there!'

As Michael moved to make another spring at the window, McAllister reached out with one hand and pulled him back down to the floor where he was half lying. 'Listen, Michael . . . I want you to do something for me.'

'Anything, avic, anything.'

'Try and escape.'

'Escape? Are you crazy, man? There's no escape from this.'

A volley of bullets crashed through the window over their heads.

The numbness was disappearing from McAllister's shattered arm and the pain began ripping through him. 'Listen,' he said, 'I know the way of the Highlanders. I was stationed alongside some of them before I deserted. I know the way they think.'

'Aye, so do I,' Michael answered. 'The honour of the regiment comes first.'

'They'll not give the militia the pleasure of hanging you,' McAllister said. 'Not when it is them who have pulled off the coup of catching you. But they'll not let you live either. They found you here and they'll finish you here. As soon as you walk out that door, they'll give you everything they have.'

They both ducked as another volley ripped through the walls.

'You'll not outfight this one,' McAllister rasped. 'Your ammunition is almost gone and they have plenty. They'll get you with a bullet in the end. And what about Mary? How do you think she will feel when she hears you died from a musket-ball inside a burning cottage.'

'Oh, Mary will feel fine,' Michael answered bitterly. 'She'll be free to marry again. A nice steady man who'll provide her with a nice steady home day in and day out. Her fling with a rebel was short and sweet. Now she wants what her father always wanted for her – a steady man of substance.'

'Then do it for me,' McAllister said. 'Try and escape with your life for me. A moment ago you said you would do anything for me. So here's what I want you to do . . .' McAllister gasped for breath. 'Load your gun and give it to me. I will open

310

the door while you get on your hands and knees. As soon as I open the door the Higlanders will think it is you and every one of them will discharge their muskets – especially if I go out firing. It will take them thirty to forty seconds to reload. You make the spring and try to escape while they are doing so.'

Michael shook his head positively. 'No, Sam, I love you from the heart, you know that, but I'll lose or save my own life. And I'll not save mine by sacrificing yours.'

'I'm done for anyway,' McAllister rasped. 'I'll not fight my way out of this with a smashed arm. I'm finished, but you could still have a chance.'

'No,' Michael said again. 'No, no, no!'

A clump of burning thatch fell down a few inches from McAllister, who sprang to life and shuffled across the floor. At the door he pulled himself to his feet. 'Give me the gun,' he said.

Michael weaved across the floor and stood irresolute before him. Shouts could be heard outside and a volley of bullets blasted through the wall only inches away.

'He must be hit or suffocated,' McDonald shouted. 'He's stopped answering fire.'

'Die if you must, Michael,' whispered McAllister, 'but live if you can. Don't let me walk out of there for nothing.'

Michael's eyes were fastened on McAllister's green cravat. It was certainly the end for one or both of them. Briefly the two men embraced each other, then McAllister clapped Michael on the back with his good hand. 'Don't let me down now,' he said. 'Give me the gun.'

Michael handed over the loaded firearm, and as McAllister reached to open the door, he looked at Michael and smiled. 'Now let me see how fast a spring you can make.'

A billow of smoke belched from the cottage as McAllister stepped out firing one shot. The soldiers did as he had anticipated, and let him have the full pelt of their ammunition. He staggered and twisted like a man doing a dance under the hail of bullets which riddled his body. For one terrible moment, Michael stared at him, but as soon as the firing stopped he made the spring.

A cry of surprise rose up as a rebel was detected running through the smoke down the passage at the side of the house which led to the fields.

'Black hair and taller than the others – Bluidy hellfire! – it's *Dwyer*!'

Michael's progress was halted by a ladder in his path, resting across the two walls of the passage. As he bent to throw it aside, a volley from the detachment on the high ground behind the house whistled over his head, completely cutting away the thatch from the corner of the barn.

He ran like a deer across the field. A powerful Highlander threw down his gun and set after him, and got so near in the chase that twice Michael felt his hand on his shoulder. The two of them paced it out, stride for stride, gasping breath for breath, one behind the other – and the determined Highlander was oblivious of the furious shouts of McDonald and Beaton, who found they could not fire a volley without bringing their own man down.

When the Highlander's hand touched his shoulder for the third time, Michael stepped sideways and gave him the trip, sending the soldier stumbling on to his hands with a cry as his ankle twisted under him. A few moments later Michael himself slipped on a patch of ice and went down as a hail of bullets whistled through the air above him.

He jumped up and turned sharp right, plunging down the sloping snow and springing into the fields beyond until he reached the Slaney, one of the deepest parts of the river. He plunged into the swelled icy waters and swam across, and disappeared into the bushes on the opposite bank.

The pursuing Highlanders took one look at the freezing water and the chase was abandoned. When they returned with the news to McDonald, who was now outside the Tooles' house, the colonel roared furiously,

'So he got away after all? Well damn my soul if he isn't the *luckiest* and the *pluckiest* rebel I ever encountered!'

The rebel prisoners sent up a delighted cheer, for which they were rewarded with violent blows on the head with musket butts. The three families were rounded up and ordered to march with the prisoners, but not before the men were questioned.

'Six rebels, you say?' McDonald said to Toole.

'Aye, your honour. Six rebels.'

'So why were only five taken out of the house?' McDonald asked the Highland officer.

'Ah, sure maybe it was only five, your honour,' Toole put in quickly. 'I've never been much good at the sums.'

'Search the house!'

They found Hughie the Brander hiding up the chimney. He

was quickly tied and, on reaching Hoxey's house, ordered to stand in line behind the tailor and his apprentice.

'Now then,' McDonald said, 'which of you harbourers or rebels will offer to lead us by the most convenient and least hazardous route to Baltinglass Gaol?'

'I'm not a harbourer or a rebel,' said the tailor's apprentice, 'but I am from Baltinglass.'

McDonald studied young Byrne. 'Do you know the shortest and easiest route?'

'Aye.'

'Good laddie.' McDonald smiled. 'And I promise you the munificent reward of blowing your brains out if you lead us one step wrong.'

'God sakes!' the tailor tutted, and was rewarded with a hard whack on the head from McDonald.

Michael was in a pitiable condition. In the freezing temperatures he was dressed only in whip-cord knee-breeches and the flannel waistcoat of his small-clothes, drenched from head to foot after his swim in the freezing Slaney.

He made for Seskin, just outside Camara, where a relative of his father lived, also called Dwyer. When he reached the house, Mrs Thaddeus Dwyer let out a startled cry to her husband.

'Thaddeus! 'Tis Michael. Come quickly!'

Thaddeus Dwyer came out of the bedroom and stared at Michael, at his naked chest and arms under the wet waistcoat, then down at the lacerated bare feet which were bleeding profusely. 'My God, what's happened to you, Michael?'

Michael was trembling violently. 'McAllister,' he croaked, 'he took the bullets to save me. My comrade, Sam McAllister . . . he did a shot-jig at the door so I could escape.'

Mrs Dwyer fired a command at her husband. 'Thaddeus, bring him over to the fire, while I heat up some scalteen for him.'

'Scalteen?' Michael croaked, as Thaddeus threw a blanket around him.

'Aye,' she answered. 'Scalteen would make a corpse warm.'

A detachment of the 89th Regiment, stationed at Davidstown, had seen Dwyer in the distance running across the snow towards the house of his relative. As Mrs Dwyer turned around to lift a vessel to put the milk in, through the window she saw the soldiers rapidly approaching and gave a shout of warning.

Michael was out of the house in an instant, and the chase was on again. It could only have been his years climbing the mountains and his youthful love of any kind of athletics that gave him the edge over the soldiers, despite his lacerated feet. He ran like the wind, in and out through the trees heading north-east to Stranahely, up to Cavanagh's Gap, and on and on and on towards the remotest part of the mountains.

A number of volleys had been fired at him, and now the redcoats gave up the pursuit when they saw traces of blood in the snow. 'He's been hit,' they said. 'And anyway,' they added, 'no man could survive up there in these temperatures, without hat or shoes and dressed only in knee-breeches and waistcoat.'

The following day the word was given out all over Wicklow by the ecstatic militia: Michael Dwyer, the Wicklow desperado, had been served justice by officers of His Britannic Majesty, and leaving a trail of blood behind him, and in the fashion of the mountain animal that he was, had disappeared into the mountains so he could crawl into a cave to die.

The travelling tailor and his apprentice were allowed to return home, as were the women and children. Hoxey, Toole and Connell were flung in the gaolhouse. The eight rebels taken at Derrynamuck were court-martialled.

Colonel McDonald informed the court that he had commanded a company of the Glengarry Fencibles on the morning of the 16th instant to Derrynamuck. Of the twelve rebels in the three houses, eight surrendered with arms and ammunition, and all acknowledged they belonged to 'Captain Dwyer's company'. Three others were shot, and Dwyer himself escaped.

Thomas Clerk was identified as a deserter from the 9th Dragoons by officers of that regiment. Derby Dunn and Walter McDonnel were identified as deserters from the Antrim militia stationed in Arklow.

Sam McAllister could not be identified, as a deserter or otherwise, for so lacerated were his features after receiving over fifty bullet wounds, he had been buried on the hillside of Derrynamuck.

The prisoners were each called upon separately to give their defence. All answered they had nothing to say.

The three deserters were sentenced to be shot by soldiers from their own regiments; the rest to be hanged, except Hughie the Brander, who saved his life by agreeing to turn informer against another rebel awaiting trial.

Details of the court martial were sent to Lord Cornwallis, who confirmed the sentences, and the seven men were executed.

Chapter Twenty

Like a demented creature blinded by a single purpose, Mary moved as fast as she could across the snow-covered mountains, searching, searching, searching. Her hair and cloak and the hem of her dress were soaked but she seemed unaware, oblivious, blinking away the snow as she clawed at the drifts under rocks to see if they led into a natural cavern where he might be hiding. He was *not* dead. She was liable to fly at anyone who even hinted that her Michael might be dead.

Her father plodded and stumbled behind her, knowing it was useless to try and stop her, but endeavouring to stay close in case she came to grief herself. Finally she halted, staring wildly around her in desperation.

William Doyle pleaded with her. 'The sky's turning dark. Will you not come home now, Mary?'

'No! No! No!' she screamed. 'I'll not go home until I find him!'

After a further hour, her father pleaded again in a whimper, his face blue with cold. ' 'Tis no use, Mary. Any longer and we too might perish.'

She made no answer, only tossed her head from side to side, but the path she took now led to John Cullen's house at Knockgorragh.

The old man greeted them with many nods of the head, his white hair unkempt and on end, his eyes puffy and red-rimmed. He poured three tots of whiskey as Mary and her father divested themselves of their outer clothes, and shivered and steamed before the heat of the fire.

'The boys have been out for two nights and three days,' Cullen said, his voice a croak. 'Ever since they heard what happened. Hugh Vesty, John Mernagh, Andrew Thomas, and Martin Burke. They came to me twice then went back out again. They'll not stop searching until they find him, and 'twill be here they will come if they do. Dear God . . . but Hugh Vesty is like a madman.'

Mary sat silent, her eyes wide as she studied the fire and listened to Cullen and her father, who seemed to take great comfort from each other.

'And what did ye think of the brave McAllister?' Doyle said. ' 'Twas one of the Toole family who met and told me about it. Saw it all. Said the snow was red for yards with his blood. Said the poor lad was twisting and jumping for ages before he fell.'

'Kept on his feet as long as he could so that Michael could get away,' Cullen said, nodding his head up and down. 'Kept their attention distracted, do you see?'

'Aye. The whole glen is talking about him; the man with the green cravat. Antrim he came from. A Protestant.'

Doyle suddenly shook himself like a dog. 'Bring over the bottle there like a good man. 'Tis near dead I am myself after traipsing the hills since dawn.'

'Ah don't be talking!' Cullen cried, moving towards the bottle. 'The love between comrades is a fine thing. And didn't McAllister prove his love for Michael – may he be in heaven this minute.'

'Who?' Mary demanded shortly, 'May who be in heaven?'

'Sam McAllister.' Cullen looked at her contritely. 'I wasn't referring to Michael, treasure.'

Doyle helped himself to more of the whiskey. 'I don't suppose anyone thought to wake him? McAllister?'

'Sure he has no family from what I'm told. Only a widowed mother up in Antrim – God help and console her – and two of the boys have set out to give her the terrible news.'

Doyle heaved a sigh. 'They laugh at us and our wakes, the English. Laugh at how the women pray and the men drink and sing. But sure any mortal would need a drop of comfort at the loss of a loved one.' He took a drink. 'And what could be better than a prayer for the departed and a song to cheer those left behind? Answer me that.'

'You have the right of it,' Cullen agreed. 'A prayer for the one gone to a new life, and a drink and a song to cheer those left behind in this valley of tears. Aye, aye, the brave and darling Sam McAllister. The whole of Wicklow is praying for him. And 'tis Wicklow that will never forget what he did for a Wicklow boy at Derrynamuck.' Cullen nodded his head. 'You mark my words.'

Mary wandered into the cold bedroom and lit the fire; in no way as good or efficient as Michael used to light it. She remained kneeling before it for a long time, listening to the non-stop murmur of the two men in the living-room. Suddenly she hunched her body forward, clutching her hands round her waist, shoulders shaking as she cried her heart out.

It was long after dark when the cottage door crashed open and the boys carried Michael inside. 'A mattress!' Hugh Vesty shouted. 'Bring a mattress over to the fire. Quickly!'

Cullen jumped up and almost fell in his haste as he ran into the bedroom and pulled a straw tick from under the four-poster. Mary followed him out as he dragged it across the floor to the hearth.

White-faced and rigid, she stared as they gently laid Michael down on the mattress, dressed in Hugh's topcoat.

'Is he . . . is he . . . ?'

'Unconscious,' Hugh Vesty answered, 'but not dead.'

'Where did you find him?'

'On Lugnaquilla. Making his way here by the looks of it. A snowdrift had almost covered an old ewe who was sitting over him, breathing her hot breath on to him. Only for that he might truly be dead now instead of almost dead.'

'No wonder Jesus loved sheep,' Cullen croaked. 'Tender creatures.'

'Will he make it?' Mary whispered nervously.

'Only time will tell,' said Mernagh. 'God knows how he's survived as he has.'

Mary knelt down and put her hand to Michael's cold cheek. 'Oh, Michael, Michael . . .' Her whole being cried as she bent over him, covering his head with the long curtain of her hair as she rubbed at his cold face. 'Michael, my Michael, I couldn't live with the thought of not seeing you again. I know I couldn't go on without you . . .'

For a moment the men looked uncomfortable, then Hugh Vesty said gently, 'He needs warmth, Mary. Let the heat of the fire at him.'

'Aye, darling,' her father said, lifting her away. 'Stand back and leave this to your daddy. 'Tis the start of the pneumonia he will have if not the end from it. Put water on to boil and hand me that bottle of whiskey.'

Everyone watched in silent amazement as William Doyle removed his jacket, then rolled up his sleeves before lifting one of Michael's arms as he proceeded to take off Hugh's coat and the flannel waistcoat. When he had finished, Doyle poured some of the whiskey into his hands and began to massage it into Michael's chest, moving his palms in slow circular movements.

' 'Tis heat, heat, heat, he needs to bring the life back into his blood. And there's heat in more things than a fire.'

The men sprang to life and reached for the bottle. Hugh Vesty worked on an arm while Mernagh and Burke massaged the whiskey into Michael's legs. Andrew Thomas ran outside and filled a cauldron with water from the rain-barrel and hung it over the fire before kneeling to blast the turf with the bellows until the flames licked the base of the cauldron and the kettle.

'Oh, his poor feet,' Mary wailed, 'they're cut to bits.'

'Aye,' said Hugh Vesty, 'that was the blood the redcoats saw, the blood running from his feet. Divil the day one of them would ever be lucky enough to catch him with a bullet.'

When Mary had tended and dressed Michael's feet in cotton strips from a sheet, she knelt behind him and massaged his shoulders, her head reeling from the smell of the spirit. When the water boiled she cut the rest of the sheet into pieces and dipped them into the cauldron, placing the hot clothes over Michael's body until the sweat glistened on her own face. The room was steamy from the hot water Cullen kept going. Condensation ran down the walls and dripped everywhere.

'If this doesn't bring him round, nothing will,' said William Doyle, pouring whiskey on to a spoon and pressing it to Michael's mouth, pushing the blue lips open and slowly feeding the spirit into him until he saw a twitching of the face muscles and Michael gave a slight cough.

Everyone looked at each other and smiled with relief. 'Where there's life there's hope,' Cullen croaked, tears streaming down his face. 'Come on now, treasure, wake up, wake up!'

When Michael slowly opened his eyes he looked strangely at the face bending close to his.

'You're all right, son,' William Doyle said softly. 'We thought you were a goner, but you're back with us now. Praise be to God.'

Michael tried to move and gasped, his face contorting in agony from the pain of his warming muscles. When he returned to consciousness again, he was in the bedroom, the fire blazing, and Mary's dark eyes looking anxiously into his. A ghost of a smile came to his lips as he drifted back to sleep.

For three days he hovered between life and death, shivering

violently and rambling in delirium as the fever of pneumonia raged to its peak. At times he murmured piteously to Sam McAllister, at others tenderly to Mary, then piteously to McAllister again.

Throughout those three days and nights Mary sat holding his hand, wiping his sweating face, kissing his lips, refusing to move or sleep herself although she was clearly on the verge of total collapse.

The other men had stayed at Cullen's house and watched her, full of admiration for the determined girl, and quietly threatening to throttle anyone who criticised her again. Her pale, anxious face looked hollow-eyed and exhausted, but now as she felt his cool brow, she knew the worst was over.

She smiled a tired smile as she looked up at the men.

'He's going to be fine,' she whispered smugly, 'fine and well again. They'll not beat my man. He was not born to be beaten. He's a survivor, a winner, out and out.'

The men grinned and agreed with her; but better to let everyone keep thinking he was dead, they decided, especially the soldiers. It was the best protection he could have until he was fit again.

'What say you, Mary?' asked Hugh Vesty.

Mary made no answer. Her head was slumped on Michael's chest in exhausted sleep.

Hugh Vesty and the others left Cullen's house that same night. As the days passed Michael's strength returned slowly. He insisted on leaving the bed. He wore calf-skin moccasins on his bandaged feet as he hobbled out to the kitchen to sit by the fire with Cullen.

Michael's sadness over McAllister was still with him, and Mary understood that, that and his silences; but she could not understand his distant attitude towards her. He treated her with a reserved politeness; rarely smiled, and spoke to her only when he had to, or when she spoke to him first.

At night she lay awake, listening to his breathing as he slept, wondering why he had never kissed her since his recovery, never even tried to embrace her. He was a strange and confusing man, a law unto himself, not one to be taken for granted. She lay twisting the gold band he had placed on her finger. Unending love? That's what it was *supposed* to signify, the endless circle.

By the end of a cold but polite fortnight, her heart was near bursting with the pain and confusion of it all.

Sometimes she would watch him as he sat and stared into the fire or read one of the books Mr Kennedy had given to them, and it would take all her self-control to stop the tears running down her cheeks. Derrynamuck had changed him, changed everything. He no longer loved her. She was sure of it.

She was standing by the table, her face flushed with steam and the sleeves of her dress rolled up as she pummelled a tub of washing, when she became aware of his eyes on her. She met his gaze and smiled nervously.

'I can't give you what you want, Mary,' he said softly. 'A hearth and home and wedded life day in and day out like other people. I told you so in the beginning.'

'You're all I want, Michael,' she answered, her fingers twisting around the suds in the water. 'Even if it has to be only now and again.'

He returned to staring at the fire. After a long silence he murmured, 'I'll have to go back out one day. I won't be able to stay here for ever.'

'No . . . I suppose not.'

She lowered her head and pummelled the washing furiously. She had agreed to take him on any terms as long as he married her. And he had, and it had been wonderful, wonderful, until she had spoiled it by looking for more, more than was in his power to give. It was only when she thought she had lost him after Derrynamuck that she knew she could stand anything, cope with anything, as long as he was there, as long as she could see him every now and again – her Michael, alive and well – whether he loved her or not.

The nightmare of those three days after Derrynamuck came back to her. She paused in her washing activity and looked up to reassure herself that he really was there, and he was, looking at her thoughtfully.

Across the room their eyes held, and for a moment she felt they were one again. Her sudden smile was like bright sunshine in the dimness of the cottage, slowly fading when he turned away and lifted the turf bucket, then rose and limped out of the room without a word.

A few mornings later, after Cullen had gone to see to his sheep, Michael came in from outside with his arms full of chopped wood and stacked the logs on the hearth to dry. His eyes strayed to the bedroom door, surprised that she had still not risen.

He sat down and dropped his head into his hands, wondering why she stayed when he treated her so coldly. Why had she come back to him at all? Simple wifely duty, he supposed.

He wished she would go back home. It was taking all his discipline to keep his distance from her, stop himself from reaching for her in the night, but he had fallen into her feminine trap once before, allowed her to dominate him, to bend his will to hers until he was ready to promise her almost anything. He had even considered America – that night – lying beside McAllister he had been ready to consider America if it would bring her back to him. But not now. The die was truly cast now. He would never give up or give in now.

He shook his head to clear it. His mind was all jumbled up with dead men, and one dead young man who wore a green cravat; all jumbled up with a woman who filled him with bleak despair and aching love. But Derrynamuck could happen again, and again, and one day it might be a dead man they brought back to her. Better to loosen the strings now, ease away gently. Better for her in the long run, or the short run, whichever it was to be.

He took his hands from his face and frowned as he looked again towards the bedroom door. It was unlike her to stay abed this late.

When he entered the room she was lying with her eyes wide open, staring at the wall.

'Mary?'

She made no response and he moved closer, sitting down gently on her side of the bed.

'Are you not getting up today?'

'No.'

'Oh.' He too looked at the wall, then back at her. 'Why not?'

'I'm too tired,' she said miserably.

'Perhaps you should go back home,' he suggested quietly.

'Do you want me to go?'

He drew a shaky breath. 'Well . . . it might be better for you. You don't have to keep slaving after us here. Cullen and I will manage fine and—'

'All right, I'll go,' she whispered, moving to the other side of the bed and pushing back the covers.

He remained sitting with his back to her while she struggled out of her nightgown and into her clothes, then gathered up the combs and few belongings she always kept at Cullen's. She lifted her cloak from the hook on the bedroom door. He heard her footsteps . . . and the sound of the outer door slamming behind her.

He lifted his head and looked sadly around the room which still held traces of her; a small bowl of dried heather on the window ledge, and the little white lace curtains each side. Even the turf and wood buckets on the hearth were placed neatly side by side, handles forward, in the tidy way she liked them.

He had moved into the living-room, was standing by the fire, his hand on the hearthbreast and staring into the flames when she walked back into the cottage some time later. He turned to look at her.

'Mary,' he said in surprise. 'I thought you'd be almost at Knockandarragh by now.'

She hit him with her fist as hard as she could. 'You *bolgach*!' she cried.

'Mary!' he gasped in shock.

'How dare you dismiss me like some doxie you've grown tired of!' She flung herself at him in frustration and rage, almost knocking him off his feet as she aimed blows at his face and chest with her fists. He endeavoured to restrain and calm her until she savagely bit his hand.

'Oh, you bitch!'

'A bitch is a dog,' she flashed, 'a decent dog, but you ye pup you're nothing!'

Suddenly he smiled at her, his old smile, and all the anger seemed to seep out of her. She started to cry. He caught her to him and wrapped his arms around her shoulders as she babbled accusations at him. He admitted he had been cruel to her, had coldly ignored her, but he had done it for her sake not his.

She struggled to hit him again but he held her in a tight grip, one hand around her waist and the other in her hair as he rocked her against him, listening silently as the hiccupping tirade of accusations continued.

No, he finally confessed, he didn't know how he could have done it, been so unkind and deliberately hurt her, but he was confused, all jumbled up inside since Derrynamuck, since *before* Derrynamuck.

Now she was silent, her head back, staring at him in understanding, then she muttered on a cracked note, 'Oh,

323

Michael, Michael, do you still love me? I must know.'

'I thought I did,' he whispered, 'before Derrynamuck ... but I didn't realise just how much I do until I heard that door slam behind you.'

'Say it, Michael. Say it.'

'I do,' he whispered, trembling, hardly able to speak. 'I love you, Mary. I've never stopped loving you. But ... I'm still a rebel, a man on the run, and I can't give you the steady life you want.'

'You may keep your steady life,' she whispered. 'Poor compensation that would be, without you. I'll sleep in the ditches, Michael, I'll sleep in caves, I don't care what hardship awaits, as long as I have you.'

'I would never let you sleep in ditches and caves,' he said gently.

'I know that,' she confessed. 'But I thought I would say it anyway.'

He gave a little sigh. 'Then I'm glad your heroism goes no further than your tongue. For I have enough martyrs to haunt my dreams. I couldn't bear another one lying in my bed.'

'You've been thinking a lot about death these past two weeks,' she said.

'Not death itself, but dead men.'

She clasped her hands behind his neck and whispered, 'Then hold me tighter and think only about life, Michael. Because I'm going to have a baby, our baby.'

He stared at her stunned.

'You're not pleased?' her voice broke.

He pressed her back a little from him, his gaze moved over her. 'But you don't look ... not the slightest.' He stared at her again. 'How long have you known?'

She quickly explained why she had wanted to go back home to see her mammy, her fear of making love in case it was dangerous, the unconscious nesting instinct that had made her yearn for her own hearth, the sickness that had prevented her from meeting him at Cullen's, the hurried journey the following morning and ...

Michael spun into the rocking-chair and sat with head bowed while looking at his joined hands.

'I know I should have told you before,' she said, 'but I thought I would wait until you were well again ... and then I wasn't at all sure if you still wanted me, let alone me and a baby.'

He looked up slowly, his face ashen. 'Oh, Mary, I feel so ashamed, so ashamed of what I've thought about you, how coldly I've treated you. And . . . you're such a good girl . . .'

She reached out and put a hand on his face. 'None of that matters now, Michael. The nightmare is over. And so you should put the nightmare of Derrynamuck behind you also. Your comrade would not have wanted you to spend your life weeping inside for him. He wanted you to live. And God in his mercy has spared you to live. And we have a new life to prepare for.'

He could only stare at her, at this lovely eighteen-year-old girl who was his wife.

She moved closer and her hands gently drew his head to her stomach, as if willing him to feel the triumph of life inside her. He brought his arms tightly around her and as the anguish spilled out of him he buried his face in the beloved body that held his unborn child.

When Cullen shambled into the cottage that afternoon, he took one look at the two of them in the rocking-chair and nodded his head. Oho, but I'll swear the cold weather is thawing at last, praise be to God!

Mary sprang up from Michael's lap and blushed crimson as she closed the book.

'No, go on, go on,' Cullen said. 'Don't mind me at all. Go on reading your book, treasure.'

'Michael was reading it to me,' Mary said. 'It's one of the ones we got in Dublin. I'll start the supper.'

'Arrah, but you're a great woman for the cooking, so you are.' Cullen took off his greatcoat and hung it up, then rubbing his hands together he moved to his seat by the right of the inglenook, withdrew his pipe and tobacco from his jacket pocket and filled the bowl. Lifting a taper from the fire, he lit the pipe, his blue eyes fixed merrily on Michael as he sucked noisily for some minutes and swiped the clouds of smoke away.

'She told you then?'

'Told me what?' Michael stretched his legs and crossed them at the ankles.

'Christmas turkeys, can't I see that she told you! So now . . .' the old man's cheeks hollowed and expanded as he sucked and blew at the pipe, 'if you're going to be a daddy, what am I going to be?'

Michael smiled as he thought about it. 'Some sort of very distant uncle, I think.'

'A godfather,' Mary said. 'You will be the child's godfather, John.'

'A godfather? Oh, well now . . .' the old man chuckled. 'I'll take him fishing as I did you, Michael.'

'It might be a girl,' Michael said.

'Aw! Deed it won't!' Cullen took the pipe out of his mouth and protested sourly. 'Faith, but what would I do with a girl? 'Tis boys that like the rambling and fishing and learning the Irish history. And we don't need another girl, do we? We have our darling Mary.'

'Did you go to Eadstown?' Michael asked.

'Aye. I got ye more clothes and the things you asked for. The bag is dropped there by the door. I went to Donard an' all.'

'Donard?'

'Aye, to the tavern. Had a jewel of a time with some of the boys. A travelling man was supping in there. It seems George Fenton is living in Wexford now. He daren't come back to Wicklow, of course. General Moore's Proc still stands.'

Mary hung the cooking pot on the crane. 'Who is George Fenton?' she asked.

'A militiaman, treasure, and a villain of the first order.' Cullen sucked at his pipe and began to chuckle. 'Oho! Wait'll I tell you, Michael. There's a song being sung in all the taverns of Wicklow about you.'

'A ballad about how I died a hero?' Michael said dryly.

'Oh, no! The yeomen in there were laughing as how you were dead, but the people won't have it at all. Dead? The darling Michael of Imaal dead? Not until we see his body with our own two looking eyes will we believe it, they sez. Oho!' The old man's eyes gleamed with the memory. 'The yeos were looking mighty uneasy at the end of it all. Specially when the blacksmith and the keeper started singing the ballad.'

Michael sat up with a frown and Cullen explained, ' 'Tis because of the rumour, do you see? Someone got hold of a rumour that after you were seen running across the snow, you were seen a week later in the County Clare with some of your boys. Wait now!'

The old man held up his hand and closed his eyes. 'I learned

the words so's I could sing them to you. It has a nice marching
air to it.

'He is gone, he is gone
To the county of Clare,
Fresh men for to muster
And arms to prepare.'

Michael threw back his head and laughed. Mary laughed
too. As long as they thought he was dead or in County Clare, he
would be left in peace with her.

That night as Mary prepared to undress, she blew out the
candle and peered at Michael in the firelight. He was lying in
the bed with his hands behind his head watching her. 'Close
your eyes,' she ordered.

Michael closed his eyes, knowing, if the last few weeks were
anything to judge by, she would only get undressed under the
covers if he didn't, and that often took an age of bouncing and
tutting. He listened to her movements and half-opened his eyes
as she reached to put on her nightgown. He saw the new lush-
ness to her body, how fuller she was at the breast already swelled
with the milk of pregnancy. He closed his eyes quickly as she
turned and climbed into bed.

They lay in each other's arms for a time just talking quietly
about their future. Two or three months, he reckoned, that he
would stay in hiding. Two or three months he would stay here
with her, day in and day out.

'It will take you at least that time to get fully fit again, maybe
even longer,' she whispered hopefully.

He smiled at her. 'Despite the ballads, the militia are convinced I'm dead, and Cullen is going to spread the word that, in
his opinion, I truly am dead. That should give us some time
together, some peace.'

There was a long pause, then she slid her arms around his
shoulders and stretched out and cleaved to him, but he was
hesitant, uncertain. 'Are you sure it's all right?' he whispered.

'Yes, except six weeks before and six weeks afterwards.'

'When is the baby due?'

'Not for months, a little under six months, the end of
August.'

He made love to her with an excess of tenderness: and from
that night he knew he would never walk away from her again,

knew he would kill anyone who ever tried to take her from him, or ever harmed her, or ever hurt her, with even a word.

There was little sleep that winter night, for it was the homecoming after the war. A time for giving and holding, reassuring and promising, and loving, in a peaceful kind of way. And when at last she fell asleep, there was a look of contentment on her face that he had not seen for a long time.

Dawn filtered in through the small lace-covered window. He watched the shaft of light grow brighter, then slipped out of bed and dressed quietly, moving through the old man's slumbering living-room to take a solitary walk on the nearby hills.

The land was desolate, his existence unrecognised by all but the sheep who rested under the mearing dykes. The birds of the season had not yet woken. The air was fresh, but there was no shivering wind. Beyond him the green and brown mountains lay fold on fold against the lightening sky. He gazed round at the austere beauty of the wilderness and breathed in the peaceful solitude of the hills.

The agony of Ireland would go on. And so would he. He would not die for his country. He would *live* for his country. A young man with a green cravat and over fifty bullet wounds in his body had willed that he should. A young girl with his unborn child in her body willed that he should, and all the new happiness in his heart willed that he should.

And he would! They would not beat him, not this year or next. They would never catch him, not in five years or twenty. And that would be his supreme revenge on his enemies, every man jack bastard one of them!

Smug they were now, smug as red-feathered roosters vainly strutting like lords of the roost. But Imaal was *his* barnyard, and one day the cock of the walk would be back, with a flash of game spurs that would send them arunning like puckered-skin chickens. Already his face smiled at the challenge of it, his teeth white and clenched with the pleasure of it.

But the smile passed. That was something for the future. He had promised the present to the girl back in the house. And God knows, he had little enough else to promise her, his own precious Mary.

Suddenly a bird chirped, and another, then he heard the querulous cry of a curlew from the direction of some riverstream on Lugnaquilla. He mused away an hour, before turning back towards the house, still limping a little, still slightly stiff in his limbs after his agony in the snow-drenched mountains.

A sudden triumphant smile broke on his face. But he was still free, free to live and love and, one day, spring back to the heights of his own green mountains again.

He came slowly to the small white thatched cottage surrounded by willow trees and wilderness. Through the window he saw the old man bent over the fire, pumping at the bellows, blowing the smoored turf into flames. The bedroom door was closed. She was still asleep in the warm bed where, in a few minutes, he would tiredly join her.

At the door he turned to look back at the mountains lying fold on fold against the skyline. The air was cold, but a warming winter sun was rising over the Glen of Imaal.

BOOK TWO

Part One

He planted flowers o'er her grave,
And there passed hours by.
'Twas a strange sight, that dark night,
To see the strong man cry.

'A Story of Imaal' (Ballad of Michael Dwyer)

Chapter Twenty-One

In the shadowy stillness of the small green wood, rich with the fragrance of pines, a young man stood as motionless as a hawk marking its prey. In his hands he held a gaming-gun in readiness, his face shadowed by the brim of a black hat pulled low on his brow.

Slowly he raised the gun almost level with his cheek, the barrel angled downwards, his eyes fixed unwavering on the tawny hare. He gently pulled back the flintlock mechanism, making only a slight click, and prepared to fire. Then – a chaos of noise erupted behind him. The hare dashed for cover. A black cloud of cawing rooks screamed into the air.

He turned abruptly towards the noise and ran swiftly to the edge of the wood, where he spied a small hunting party some way off. His eyes fell on the barking dog galloping wildly across the field, a red setter, half-mad with panic, pursued by a shouting man on horseback.

The setter frantically skidded right, then left, then plunged forward again.

'You unmanageable hound!' the horseman shouted, then spotting the young man by the trees, 'Catch him! Don't just stand there, man! Catch him!'

He hesitated, not used to taking orders, but he could see something had badly upset the dog. He stepped out a few paces, whistling in a long and low way. The setter's ears pricked uncertainly, he skidded to a trot, looked around and bounded over to him, eyes wide and tongue hanging.

'There's a good boy,' the young man said softly, rubbing the russet head. 'Calm down now, calm down. Nothing to be frightened of. Nothing at all.'

The setter shuddered and shook himself, his animal instinct telling him he would suffer no harm from this human. Panting with relief, he shook himself again and moved his head to lick the back of the hand gently stroking him – and it was then that the bloody wound on his flappy ear came to view.

The young man glanced up as the horseman drew rein. An elegantly dressed man only a few years older than himself. He recognised him instantly as William Hume, the son of the late Mr Hume of Humewood. He quickly turned his face back to the setter.

'Setters are an unpredictable breed,' Hume exclaimed angrily. 'This one keeps turning a bit mad. He's spoiled a good day's sporting for me.'

'He's been hit – either by a whip or the graze of a bullet – on the ear.'

'What?'

'Aye, just a small nick. But enough to make him think he was maybe for the kill and not the fox.'

'Damn the bloody blockhead who did that!' Hume cried, looking over his shoulder in the direction of the hunting party. 'Whoever it was should be horsewhipped. That setter is a very valuable dog – my late father's favourite.'

'Well, he seems calm enough now.'

'Yes, thanks to you.'

Hume's eyes raked over the young man kneeling and petting the dog, taking in every detail of him from head to foot. A tall fellow, strong-made but light-limbed. He wore shoes, black wool stockings and leather breeches. His upper body was clothed in a black knitted jersey of the type fishermen wore. But he was not a fisherman, for bathe as often as they may, fishermen always carried the smell of the fish with them.

There was something else about this fellow, something that made Hume uneasy as his eyes moved over the black hat to the black hair curling around his neck. Then Hume realised what it was that bothered him – the hat! The insolent fellow had not thought to remove it in the presence of a gentleman! Not even briefly to touch his forelock.

Oolaloo 'For'ard away!'

Hume jerked round in the saddle. 'Sounds as if they've spotted the varmint again,' he said, excitement in his voice. 'A big one he is too; an old dog fox with a greying brush, so he must have eluded many a hunt. But we'll catch the clever old thing this time.'

The young man glanced up at Hume's turned back, then in the direction the noise came from, the noise of the hunt in full cry, yelping hounds baying with blood-lust. 'Sounds as if they

336

are near the river,' he said. 'Horses and hounds are likely to get bogged down in the banks there, I reckon. And if the fox once slides into the water, as the clever old thing surely intends, then his scent will be lost.'

He again bent to smooth the dog, the smile on his face hidden under the low brim of his black hat.

Hume turned back. 'Yes, I fear you may be right there,' he said sourly. 'You are obviously experienced in hunting the fox?'

'Only if he has asked for it by attacking the fowl in the yard. I've never hunted him for pleasure. I prefer to hunt game that will provide a good breakfast or supper.'

Hume laughed. 'And old Reynard could never do that! You are a farmer?'

'A farmer's son, sir.'

Hume smiled, warmed by the fellow remembering his manners and rightly addressing him as 'sir'. And that black hat would soon be whipped off when he disclosed who he himself was.

'Well, I am William Hoare Hume of Humewood, the new Member of Parliament for Wicklow, and a captain of the Humewood Cavalry Corps.'

'An honour to meet you, sir,' the young man replied, his lips smiling as he touched a finger to the brim of his hat, but did not remove it.

'Your own name?' Hume demanded.

'Byrne, sir.'

Hume frowned. There were hundreds of Byrnes in Wicklow. He was about to ask which Byrne of which district, when the young man said quietly: 'I was very sorry to hear about your father, Mr Hume, about the way he was killed at the end of last year.'

Hume was taken aback at the sincerity in the voice, for he had not expected any tenant's son, undoubtedly a papist, to be sorry about the death of one of the Protestant landed gentry.

'Why are you sorry?' he demanded.

'Because Mr Hume senior was a fair man,' came the reply. 'And from what I have heard, it was a deliberate murder, provoked through a personal and bitter enmity between two men, and nothing to do with the cause of the rebellion.'

Mr Hume's young face clouded at the memory of his father. 'A terrible, terrible business,' he said sadly. 'Shot in cold blood while out sporting one morning. It was Michael Dwyer that did it.'

'Michael Dwyer?' The noise of the hunt filled the pause. 'Then why did they hang Moore of Killalish for the deed? And 'tis said Moore confessed at the gallows that he did it.'

'True, but the militia still insist it was Dwyer.'

The young man shrugged. 'The militia would blame the Crucifixion on Dwyer if they could. But I doubt if a condemned man would tell a lie on the threshold of eternity. If Moore said he killed your father, then I would imagine he did, and not Dwyer.'

'Maybe so, maybe so,' Hume said with a sigh. 'Moore of Killalish even confessed to me, at the end, that it was him who did it. But the militia still insist he was lying. Did you know Dwyer?'

'I never did come face to face with him myself,' the young man said. 'Did you ever see him, sir?'

'Once or twice, as a boy, but not since I left Wicklow for school in England. A very quiet lad as I remember. Turned into a wild and vicious character by all accounts.'

'So they say, sir.'

'Well, at least Wicklow is rid of him. They say he died in a cave somewhere up in the mountains near Corragh. The eagles and hawks will have done for him by now.'

'One would imagine so, sir.'

Impetuously, Hume decided he liked this young man, who had tamed his dead father's beloved mad setter into tranquil contentment, lying on its belly, front paws out.

'Look here, you must allow me to reward you for your trouble,' Hume said benevolently, 'for assisting me in catching the dog.' He withdrew some silver from his pocket.

'No, no, I want nothing!'

The smile disappeared from William Hume's face at the man's sharp tone. The god-like thrill of handing out money to the peasant classes turning to pique at this ungrateful rebuff of his generosity.

'But you did me a service! The dog had turned mad and would have disappeared for weeks, or even altogether, if you had not caught and calmed him.'

'Just being neighbourly,' the young man answered over his shoulder as he turned and strolled away. 'Good hunting to you, Mr Hume.'

The dog rose to his feet and slunk after him, as if hoping the man on horseback wouldn't notice, but after a pat on the head, he was ordered back to his master.

The dog did not obey, just stood there watching the young man until he had disappeared into the shadows of the wood from which he had first emerged.

Leaning on the window ledge of the tavern in Donard, the red-coated soldier stood watching the girl as she moved from stall to stall down the busy square. It was market-day, the square crowded with hawkers selling everything from dairy produce and small pigs to wool and sewing threads.

It was not the girl's beauty that drew the soldier's attention, made him pick her out from the crowd. It was the way the people responded to her, every single one of them, in a way bordering on absolute homage.

She seemed unaware of it, her manner modest and restrained, her expression preoccupied as she sorted through the various coloured cards of sewing threads while the old hag sitting behind the wooden box smiled up at her lovingly.

She was young, no more than nineteen or twenty. She wore a long blue cloak that hid her figure, but from the angles of her smooth face and delicate nose and chin, and the tall way she carried herself, he guessed that that body hidden beneath the cloak was slender. Her black hair hung long and straight in a simple style to her waist. And when she turned her head, and her eyes lingered for a thoughtful moment on the tavern, he saw they were large and dark.

He was fascinated by her, wondering who she was, and why the people treated her with such deference as if she were some Celtic queen who had graced their shabby square. She might be lovely, but she was still a peasant girl, probably the daughter of an Imaal farmer.

Still, he could not take his eyes off her. If she had betrayed some sign of being a doxie, given some hint in her manner, by look or laugh, that she was the type who would not mind enjoying a night or two of soldier's pay, he might have even considered approaching her, striking up an acquaintance.

But she was clearly no doxie. She had the look of a gentle madonna, with a touch of that dark Celtic pride that could be withering and hostile. He was the wrong man, in the wrong place, for a girl like her. Even without speaking to her, he instinctively knew there would be an infinite gulf between them.

And the realisation of that made him suddenly resent the girl.

There were two or three other redcoats in the tavern, a number of the hated militia too, but the eyes of the tavern keeper were fixed on Captain Woollard of the 38th Regiment, standing by the window. He watched carefully as the captain turned, and beckoned with an authoritative hand to a yeoman named Hawkins sitting near the fire.

Sergeant Hawkins was of the Humewood (Upper Talbotstown) Yeoman Cavalry. He had been born in the Glen of Imaal, the son of a farming family who rented a hundred and twenty acres of land from the Humes of Humewood, and he knew all the inhabitants of this part of County Wicklow. He joined Woollard at the window.

'Who is that girl?' Woollard asked.

Hawkins bent and peered. 'Mary Doyle,' he answered. 'The daughter of William Doyle of Knockandarragh.'

'A farmer?'

'Aye.'

'Does he hold a special position in the community?'

'Who, Doyle?' Sergeant Hawkins laughed. 'Only when he's had a good few drinks and starts his singing.' Hawkins laughed again. 'And can that man drink! I reckon he was weaned on the stuff.'

Captain Woollard looked perplexed. 'So why do the people treat her as they do, as if she were someone special.'

Sergeant Hawkins gave the question a little thought. He leaned an elbow on the ledge and stared at the girl.

'Ask any other yeoman that question,' he said, 'and they would not be able to tell you. But I think I can. She was the sweetheart of Michael Dwyer, before he was killed. And because the people adored him, they now adore her. She reminds them of him.'

'Michael Dwyer!' Woollard spat the name. So that was her claim to fame. He was disappointed, for he felt nothing but contempt for these people and their heroes. And Dwyer was a local hero that Woollard was sick to the bowels hearing about.

Most of the tales were embellished with hatred and vindictiveness, for Dwyer had always beaten the militia, who were poor soldiers, sloppy and cowardly in the extreme.

'He was a savage, and against the law,' Woollard said. 'He would have been caught and hanged eventually, if the Eighty-ninth had not shot him while running away.'

Sergeant Hawkins was not a fast-talking man. He was also extremely fair and honest. He said slowly: 'With all respect to you, sir, but Michael Dwyer was no savage. No man knew him as well as I did, for our families grew up alongside each other in Imaal, and I never knew him to do a mean or unmanly act. And even after the rebellion when he carried on his mountain warfare, I could not censure him for that. He was hunted and hounded mercilessly by certain factions of the militia, bent on murdering him. What else had he to do but fight back?'

'I was not aware you had sympathy for the rebel,' Woollard responded curtly.

'Is it Dwyer ye are talking about, Sergeant Hawkins? Oh, 'tis an ill wind that whispers his name!'

Captain Woollard spun round. He saw that the man addressing them was not tall, but thick-set and strong, getting on in years, leaning on a blackthorn stick. His hair, eyebrows and side-whiskers were white and bushy, his eyes a very clear shade of blue. He wore the breeches and gaiters of a mountain shepherd, a rug-cloak slung across his shoulders. Woollard wondered how long he had been standing behind them, listening. He was about to tell him to be off, when the man spoke again.

'A right bastard he was – Dwyer! And any yeoman who felt sympathy for him is a fool of the first order. Some ignorant folk round here may try and let on that he was fighting against injustice and in defence of the people against the brutality of the militia, but truth is – the bastard was nothing more than a disgrace to humanity. Aye, aye: I could tell you a tale or two about Michael Dwyer that would cure your sympathy in no time.'

Despite himself, Captain Woollard was interested. He knew the man was probably only looking for a free drink, but, he decided, why not? He called over to the surly tavern keeper for a bottle, and when he came with it, Woollard did not miss the look of hatred he fired at the white-haired old man.

'Oh yes, sir,' said the old man, sitting down on a stool near by and sipping his drink, 'I knew Dwyer well – before he died, that is. And let me tell ye, it was him, and him alone, that turned this here hair of mine white! Persecuted me he did, persecuted me something sinful, until one day I could take no more, and at Baltinglass Fair, I lifted this here stick and hit him such a cracking larrup on the head it nearly left him a corpse; troth, it did.' The old man sniffed proudly at the memory.

Woollard looked at Hawkins, who nodded. He had seen the old man do it. And the emnity between him and Dwyer had been legend ever since.

'Who is he?' Woollard asked when the white-haired old man had stepped unsteadily out of the tavern, after consuming a good portion of the bottle of whiskey. 'He never stopped talking long enough for me to ask his name.'

'John Cullen,' Hawkins replied. 'An old shepherd who lives way up in the wilderness of the sheep hills. He has only his dog and goat for company and very few mortals venture up there, so he has little else to think about while sitting by his hearth or tending his sheep on the hills, but his brooding hatred of Dwyer.'

A sudden commotion outside abruptly diverted both men's attention back to the window. The girl was now standing by the wooden box of a woman selling balls of wool. The white-haired old man was shouting at her, waving his stick in the air.

'Good Lord!' said Woollard. 'Looks like he might hit her!' He rushed out of the tavern followed by Sergeant Hawkins, who clutched his arm.

'Don't intervene,' Hawkins warned quietly, 'unless he strikes her. Otherwise the people will be glad to turn on you. The old man too, if you attempt to take her side.'

Both men paused a little way back from the group of people who had moved closer to the old man and the girl, listening with expressions of horrified fascination.

'You're a fool, a fool,' the old man shouted, 'to be wasting your youth mourning that bastard. And ye may as well know the truth of it – for I *knows* the truth of it, and truth is – Dwyer was making a fool of you, using you like a common doxie. The lass he really loved was the daughter of Reilly of Coolamaddra. Aye, and rumour has it that he would have married her if he hadn't been shot!'

The girl made no answer, but her pale cheeks had stained with a red flush, her dark eyes flickering.

'And serves you right!' the old man cried. 'You and Reilly's daughter along with you. Sluts, the both of you, *sluts!*'

Within seconds the old man was converged upon and seized by two young men who unceremoniously lifted him off his feet and carried him bodily away from the girl while the furious women jeered and booed him.

'Let me go, you gouts!' the old man screamed. 'Let me go!'

The girl had turned and stood looking after the two men who dumped the old man at the end of the square and ordered him to be off – or else! And when she turned back, Woollard saw her face contained no anger, but a strange look of disbelief.

He felt a pang of sympathy for her, but then his head overruled all his other instincts and he found himself agreeing with the old man. Serves her right, for getting mixed up with a rebel.

For a moment, by the way she clutched at her stomach and breathed deeply, he feared she was going to faint. But then she noticed him looking at her, and instantly she seemed to collect herself, her chin lifting slightly, before she turned to speak to the plump rosy-faced woman behind the box of wools.

'Do you have any other colours?' she said softly. 'Any *light* colours?'

'Ah, no,' the woman replied apologetically. 'Only the black and the brown. 'Tis the dye, d'ye see. The dyes for other colours is more costly than the black and the brown. But I may have them next time.'

'I bought too much black last time,' the girl said. 'Will you take back what I have not used?'

Woollard waited for the woman to scowl a refusal, for there were no people more shrewder than these market dealers. But the woman smiled rosily and cried, 'Sure I will, me lovey! As long as it's an unused ball.'

And when the girl took out three balls of black wool from the goatskin bag under her cloak, the woman happily counted the money into the girl's hand in refund.

'I'll likely have some blue next time,' the woman said brightly. 'Or maybe even white or yella.'

The girl nodded and walked on, and Captain Woollard watched the woman's eyes following her lovingly as she moved through the crowded square, the people parting and smiling at her, with the same attitude of absolute homage as before.

Whatever the vicious old shepherd had said about Dwyer being in love with the other girl, these people seemed to think different.

From the shadows of the trees the young man watched the hunting party that had failed to catch the clever old fox. He watched them as their horses formed a procession and made its way uphill before breaking into a free trot on the open meadows beyond.

He turned to go, moving out of the shadows, then mused away the time as he strolled along the wild and hilly paths that would lead him home. The game bag on his back contained two pheasants and a rabbit.

He smiled to himself, glad the old fox with the greying bush had escaped the hounds. Hume had been right. He must have escaped many a hunt in his long life, and deserved some credit for his skill.

He breathed deep into his lungs and gazed over the deserted hills. He had been out since the chilly dew of morning and now the afternoon was fresh and warm with the smell of May blossom in the air.

He sprang down from a ridge on to another path below, then stopped abruptly, his attention attracted by the distant screams of a female.

He moved in the direction of the screams, towards an old sand quarry which bordered the beaten pathway.

When he reached the edge he saw a young peasant girl struggling with two of the militia, the bodice of her dress torn in two. One laughed savagely, then bent his head as if biting her. Slight as she was, the girl struggled wildly until one of them began to punch her mercilessly in the stomach.

For a moment he stood stunned as he watched them fling her violently to the ground, one holding her down, kneeling at her head and clamping a hand over her screaming mouth while the other tugged at the belt around his waist and prepared to mount her.

As the leather tongue of the belt came free of its buckle, and the soldier yanked at the buttons on his breeches, a bullet hit him straight between the shoulder blades.

The second militiaman looked up, eyes flashing wide with shock. He reached for the pistol in the holster at his waist, hand flaying wide as he careened backwards from the bullet in his chest.

That was the last of his ammunition – two bullets – but it had been enough.

He jumped down into the quarry and ran to the girl, kicking the body of the militiaman aside and knelt down beside her. 'Are you badly hurt?' he asked.

At first she was speechless from terror, but as her panic died and her pain struck sharp, she rolled on to her side and clutched on her stomach, moaning.

It took some minutes for her to stop moaning, but when her gulping breathing eased, and thick fair lashes fluttered, she lifted her eyes to him, eyes as blue as the cornflower.

'What happened?' she whispered.

'They're both dead,' he whispered back.

She breathed out a long quivering sigh of relief, and, as if unaware of her torn bodice, lay back and closed her eyes. He found nothing provocative in the way she lay back. He could see she was in deep shock, and also startlingly pretty. She looked like a fair young angel, only fifteen or so, sweet and delicate and lily-pale.

He bit on his lip as he knelt on one knee looking down at her. He dared not touch her. His eyes moved over her torn bodice and bare young bosom, there were teeth marks and blood above her left breast. She put him in mind of a new spring flower, crushed and bruised by a careless boot.

He was glad he had killed them.

Being stopped in meadow or on hill by squires and landlords or landlords' sons was a commonplace suffering for peasant girls. If they refused to submit or screamed and ran away, the rent would be refused on next quarter day and the family evicted for non-payment. The landed class had it all sewn up and there was little anyone could do about it. But militiamen – so-called law officers – who thought they could beat and rape a young girl at their leisure!

Damnation or not – he was glad he had killed them.

But he could not delay here much longer.

'Do you think you can walk?' he asked softly.

'Yes,' she whispered, but did not move.

He laid down his gun and put his hands under her shoulders, lifting her to a sitting position, one hand on her back while the other reached for the shawl that lay in a heap a few feet away. He draped it around her and covered her nakedness, then said firmly: 'Come now. Stand up, and I'll take you home.'

She was so dazed it took him some time to discover where she lived. He practically had to carry her over the hills. She staggered and fell continually until he caught his arm around her waist, talking to her quietly about everyday things but getting no response. She felt very small and fragile against him, like a shaking young fawn.

345

They stopped at a stream and he made her drink a few handfuls of the cool water, and wash her face. She seemed to get better then.

'Can we rest here awhile?' she asked.

He was reluctant, but agreed. 'A short while,' he said.

He remained crouched by the stream while she sat a few feet away, her back against a tree. Silence fell, broken only by the sound of birdsong. From the branch above her head a wren sang loudly. He turned on his heel and listened, wondering as he always did, how such powerful notes could come from a bird as tiny as the wren.

'Why?' she said in a small voice. 'Why did they treat me like that? As if I was some filly in a field they could just beat and jump on.'

He didn't answer her at first, his interest seemingly caught by the antics of the wren above her head, but he could feel her eyes on him.

'Because they are animals themselves,' he said quietly. 'Bulls – dressed as men.' He lowered his eyes and looked at her. 'And because . . . you are very pretty.'

She looked away with a crimson flush, shrugged, and looked back at him. 'Would they have done it if I was ugly?'

He took off his hat and shook loose his black hair. 'How can I answer that? You are not the first, you know. The best thing you can do now is try and forget it. But never walk so far abroad alone.'

She sat staring at him with her pink mouth slightly open, her brow furrowed as if something about him puzzled her.

'What's the matter?' he asked warily.

She tilted her golden head to the side as she scrutinised him, then her entire face lightened as it came to her.

'I know you,' she said. 'You're Michael Dwyer.'

'Who me?' He laughed. 'Of course I'm not. Do I look like a ghost?'

'Not a bit, but you are him,' she insisted. 'I know it for sure. I used to see you when I was a little girl, a few years ago, when you used to play in the hurley matches with the other lads.'

'Ach, you're confusing me with some childhood memory.'

'And I saw you playing in the ball-kicking match against the Carlow boys. Do you remember that? Wicklow won handsomely.' Her smile was wide, her voice excited. 'You didn't die then? But what was the trail of blood you left in the snow?'

346

Now that she smiled he saw her dimples, and again thought how pretty she was, in a baby-faced way. But give her another year or so and she would be breathtaking. His eyes moved over the gloss of her sunny hair, long and pale as the primrose. She had that moon-like, quiet beauty of the blue-eyed and fair. Aye, another year or so and she would no doubt be running up these hills after sunset where some love-struck lad would be waiting for her.

Through the haze of his thoughts he had been looking at her, and she dimpled in a smile again. 'Is it right that Sam McAllister took the bullets to help you escape? Is it true your family removed his body from the hillside at Derrynamuck and buried him in a proper grave at Kilranelagh? Where have you been these last few months?'

'So many questions!' He returned the hat to his head. 'Come now, it's time we left.'

'Michael Dwyer, who would believe it?' she mused as they walked on. When he made no answer she looked at him thoughtfully. 'Would you like to know my name?' she asked.

'If you'd like to tell me.'

'It's Etty – Esther.'

'That's nice. I have a sister called Etty – Esther.'

'Will you be playing in any more of the hurley matches?'

'Oh, I doubt it.' He smiled sidelong at her. 'I'm supposed to be dead.'

'Is it true what they say – you got married?'

'Aye, I did.'

'Is *she* pretty?'

'She's beautiful. She's expecting a baby. Though you never would know it to look at her.'

He halted as four white cottages came into view. He looked down the hill. 'Is that it? Is that where you live?'

'Aye, the last house but one.'

'I'll leave you here so. Will you be able to make the rest of your way on your own?'

She nodded, then of a sudden she clutched at her stomach, her mouth twisting in pain.

'What's wrong?'

'They . . . they punched me. It's hurting.'

He closed his eyes briefly, reluctant to go any closer to the houses with her. But then he sighed, and took her arm in a resigned manner.

347

'I'll see you down to that tree by the first house,' he said.

He held her elbow as they moved downhill, listening silently as she told him bits and pieces about her family. As she spoke, he realised he knew her father and brothers well, but he had never met any of the females, woman or child.

At the tree he stopped and looked at her carefully. Her pain and shock were gone. She was breathing and speaking normally.

'You all right now?'

'Aye, just a bit sore where they punched me, but I'll be fine.' She held out a small hand to him and smiled into his face. 'Goodbye, Michael Dwyer, and thanks.'

'You're welcome,' he said lightly, turning to go.

'See you, Michael,' she called after him.

He looked over his shoulder and nodded.

'Aye, see you, Etty.'

His eyes scanned the surrounding land as he walked away. There was nothing left in his gaming-gun or pistol and he had no more ammunition on him. If any further trouble presented itself, he would have to rely on his wits to get him out of it.

He glanced over his shoulder and saw the girl still standing by the tree, her primrose hair shining in the sunlight. In that moment she looked to him as sweet and fair as an angel.

She lifted a hand and waved.

Smiling, he waved back, but as he moved on quickly he thought of the two militiamen and found himself hoping that his coming child would not be a girl. It had not really mattered to him before today, but now he realised what a terrible worry it would be if he had a daughter, and fervently hoped that Mary would birth a boy.

But if it was a girl, he decided, he would teach her to defend herself, right well!

Old man Cullen plodded up the path to his cottage. Inside, the house was neat and clean, with those certain touches that only a woman can bring to a house, a bowl of dried flowers here, a lace circle on the table there, a warm cosiness everywhere.

But it was empty.

He leaned his stick against the wall, threw off his rug-cloak and hung it on a hook in the corner, and sat down on his chair to the right of the inglenook. He lifted the poker and stirred the smoored turf into flames, then lit his long-pipe and sat gazing into the fire as he smoked, recalling every word of his

348

conversation with Hawkins and the officer, not to mention the fine whiskey he had drunk, before the lads had dumped him at the edge of the square with an abundance of furious threats and a few winks.

He hunched his shoulders and chuckled. Musha – it had been a great day!

He was still chuckling when Michael came in some minutes later and looked at him curiously. 'What has you so happy?'

'Ah, treasure, I've had a jewel of a time in Donard, telling the soldiers what a bastard you were. Troth, if you could have just heard me! Have you had a good day?'

'I've had better,' Michael said grimly.

'Then take off your bag and hat and come and sit down,' Cullen said gently. 'Will I put the kettle on to boil?'

Michael nodded, and Cullen smiled. And if Captain Woollard had seen the gentle face and heard the kindly tone of the white-haired old man at that moment, he would never have believed it was the same man who had drunk his whiskey that morning.

'Did you meet up with Mary?' Michael asked.

Cullen lost his smile, a worried frown moving on to his brow. 'I did, but I'm not sure if I didn't get a bit carried away with all the play-acting by the time I seen her. I'd had a few drinks, d'ye see. I hope I didn't upset her. She looked a bit shocked when I'd finished.'

Michael glanced round sharply as he pulled the game bag from his back. 'What did you say to her?'

'Well,' Cullen looked at him a bit sheepish. 'I told her that the lass you truly loved was the daughter of Reilly of Coolamaddra. And it was her you might have married if you hadn't been killed.'

Michael smiled. 'I shouldn't worry about that. Mary knows only too well where my heart lies.'

'But that's not all . . . I called her a slut.'

Michael frowned at him from under his lashes. 'Now that was going too far,' he said coldly.

'I know, treasure, I know.' Cullen rubbed a hand over his white hair and shook himself unhappily. 'But they were listening, d'ye see, the militia! And I wanted to make a good display of it – and I did too! 'Troth, no mortal in that square today would ever believe that Mary has been living here with me for the past few months. Ever since you were killed.'

'Will you stop saying that!' Michael could not help smiling at the way Cullen spoke with utter conviction. No wonder people really thought he was dead – those who were supposed to think it, anyway.

'I think I'll go down the hillside and watch for her,' he said suddenly. 'You can make yourself useful by taking the rabbit out of that bag and preparing it for cooking.'

'Did ne'er a nice pheasant stroll across your path today?' Cullen queried. 'I have a fancy for a bit of roasted pheasant. We had rabbit last night.'

'And grateful you should be that you did,' Michael said reprovingly. 'There's many a poor family in Wicklow that would be thankful for a taste of any kind of meat to go with their potatoes.'

Cullen knew he was right, but a person couldn't help having fancies, and his fancy tonight was not rabbit!

When Michael had gone out of the door, the old man shrugged his shoulders and sighed, then moved to his feet and sidled over to prepare the rabbit. Still, Mary would do wonders with it when it came to the cooking. She had a knack with the herbs that was magical. A twist of this herb, a shake of that, a handful of another, and by the time it was cooked, the smell alone would have his mouth watering.

And then he unstrapped the bag and saw the flash of blue feathers on the two pheasants. Oho! He chuckled in delight and rubbed his hands together. Boys-oh-boys, but it was true! Unlike many another poor family in Wicklow, he and Mary ate as richly as royalty with the food that Michael brought back to them.

Carefully scanning the surrounding land as he went, Michael had only gone a short distance from the house when he saw her, the dark girl in the blue cloak just a few feet away on the hilly path below. He stood for a moment watching her, and as he did, even the fair loveliness of young Esther paled into insignificance.

He gave the whistle of a song thrush, soft and melodious. She looked up, and they smiled together.

He jumped down, anxious to know if Cullen had really upset her, but when he reached her she dropped her bag and clung to him in a tight embrace and a flurry of kisses that left him laughing.

'What brought this on?' he murmured.

'Absence,' she answered. 'I feel as if I've been away from you for a lot longer than a day.'

He lifted her bag in one hand and took her hand in his other and led her on up the path.

'And was it a good day or a bad day?' he asked quietly.

'A good one. I still have some of the money you gave me in the purse left over, but ... I treated myself to some more lavender water.'

'Ach, Mary, the bedroom reeks of that stuff whenever you've had a bath in there. Why can't you use carbolic soap like everyone else?'

'Carbolic soap is not very romantic,' she said sullenly. 'And anyway,' she added with a smile, 'I also bought yourself and Cullen a twist of tobacco each.'

He looked at her. 'You're not angry with him then? He's worried you might be.'

'Nay! He played his part well. For a minute he even had me believing him. But 'tis how it should be, Michael, him convincing everyone that he would shoot you on sight if you ever came near him – if you were still alive.'

They both laughed at that; then a worried frown came on Mary's face. 'Did you meet anyone today? Anyone who might recognise you?'

'No,' he lied, deciding to make no mention of either the meeting with Hume or the incident with the girl. If Mary knew he had shot two men, even militiamen, she would be very upset for days. But perhaps if she had been there, and seen what he had seen, she might have understood. As it was, he decided to spare her and say nothing.

That night in their bedroom she teased him terribly about Reilly's daughter at Coolamaddra. But once the candles were snuffed and he had finally managed to silence her beneath the bedcovers, he gave her the love that was hers alone, in bed or out of it.

Three evenings later, Cullen came bursting into the cottage in a fury. He stared redly at Michael.

'You never told us what happened with you and young Esther Costello the other day!'

'Etty?'

'Aye, Etty Costello. As purty as a primrose.'

Michael threw a glance at Mary, who had paused in the act of

351

stirring the cooking-pot on the crane over the fire.

'Nothing happened!' Michael snapped at Cullen, turning his back on his wife and making eyes at the old man, attempting to warn him off mentioning any dead militiamen in front of Mary.

But Cullen was too upset and angry to notice. He blurted out the whole story, in every detail, as told by Etty to her father, who had now told Cullen.

'You did right to shoot them!' Cullen cried angrily. 'But 'tis a pity you didn't come along a few minutes earlier! The bla'guards roughed the poor child up something cruel, something cruel! Her daddy said her whole stomach was black from the punches they gave her.'

'Oh, the poor girl,' Mary cried in a distressed tone. 'The brutes! To treat a young girl like that.'

' 'Tis a pity you didn't come along a few minutes earlier,' Cullen cried again. 'Oh, sorra that you didn't. Sorra, sorra, sorra . . .'

'I went as soon as I heard her,' Michael said. 'I stopped them as quickly and in the only way I could.'

Cullen nodded his head up and down several times, then he looked cloudily at Michael.

'Aye, she said you treated her very kindly. She said it over and over to her mother and father, that you treated her very kindly. But prepare yourself for this, treasure. Young Etty had a haemorrhage in her stomach the same night and died from it. She was buried in her grave this afternoon.'

Chapter Twenty-Two

Mary had spent the afternoon collecting herbs; her basket was full of young sorrel leaves which grew profusely in Imaal. She walked easily up the hilly path towards Cullen's cottage without any sign of breathlessness, although she was almost six months with child.

She gazed about her in the vast silence of the wilderness, an immense green silence that stretched for miles around these hills, disturbed only by the warbling of birds and intermittent calls of animals. It was a solitude that reassured her, lulled her into a sense of peacefulness as her eyes scanned the undulating landscape dappled white with hawthorn blossom. Down below she could see fields of oats still as green as grass stalks. She put a hand to her breast and inhaled the sweet air, suddenly exalted at the joy of her life up here in the wilderness.

As she drew near to the top of the path and the house came into view, she saw Michael sitting on a stool outside it, reading a book in the sunshine, his back propped against the wall, his legs stretched and crossed at the ankles, his head bowed. She smiled as she looked at the key to her happiness. Up here she enjoyed peace, pleasure, and companionship. What more could she ask for?

A sparrowhawk rose up from a pine tree with a fierce shrilling cry and startled her, but worse was the stillness that followed the cry, as if all the world had paused in its breathing; and then she heard the rhythmic sounds, drawing closer and closer.

Her heart beat wildly and she looked at her beloved, his head bent over his book, calm and motionless, as the redcoated soldiers appeared on the ridge above him. Her blood raced around her brain, and she wondered if it was all a mirage of her imagination. They seemed afar off, outlined against the sky.

She watched the mirage of a detachment of soldiers moving in double column down towards the steep path that ran a few yards from the house. Amidst the feverishness of her brain she found herself thinking that they could not have come from the old mountain road above her head, but must have come across the mountains from the right.

Michael's dark head was still lowered over his book. At times she was sure he went deaf with the engrossment of his reading. She felt her legs weakening under her and reached for the support of a tree, hidden by the branches as she watched, her head and heart pounding as she saw Michael lift his head and glance at the soldiers marching only a few yards away from him, and calmly returned to his book. A number of the soldiers turned their heads towards the cottage and the man sitting outside it, but the column marched on along the path without hesitating, continuing down the far hillside in the direction of Leitrim, becoming smaller and smaller until they eventually drifted away. And then she knew it had all been a mirage of her imagination, and suddenly she did not feel so happy with her life up here anymore.

'Life in the lush stillness of the wilderness,' Cullen had once told her, 'can be as full of fanciful notions as life in a vast desert of sand, full of dream-like images and voices that exist only in the mind.'

Michael looked up again as she slowly approached him, concern tightening his face as he noted the paleness of hers. He sprang to his feet and in an instant was beside her.

'Are you all right, Mary?'

'The soldiers,' she managed. 'Did you see any soldiers, Michael?'

'Aye, I heard them before I spied them on the ridge. I knew from their perfectly ordered tramp they were an English regiment. And so they were.'

'What? Did you truly see them? Are you sure they were real?'

'Only a fool doubts what he sees with his own eyes,' he said.

'Then why,' she said weakly, 'why did they just pass on? Why did they not search the house?'

'Well,' he said, smiling, 'they most definitely would have searched the house if it had been deserted. But they obviously saw no reason to suspect a house where the occupant was not frightened or started away on their appearance.'

'Oh, is that why,' she whispered, then fainted.

Later that night, old man Cullen sat in his favourite chair to the right of the inglenook, smoking a long-pipe as he studied the fire. These past few months had been a time of great companionship for him; every morning setting off to his sheep at Leoh after breakfast, returning in the afternoons to a warm house and the smell of bacon or a roasting pheasant, or whatever game Michael had managed to shoot.

Aye, his little house had become a home. And he was beginning to wish that things would stay as they were for ever, and let reality and the rest of the world go to hell or high water.

He turned his eyes to the girl sitting opposite him at the fireside, her head bent industriously over the fine Irish linen she was carefully stitching.

She too, he thought, had been very contented these past few months, delighted at having Michael all to herself and secretly living with him up here instead of lodging in harbourers' houses. Bustling around the house as busy as a bee, keeping it as clean and nice as his darling mother had always done. And Michael had not been idle either. Troth, he hadn't!

He had rethatched the roof, strip by strip, ensuring the house would have no dampness in its walls when the baby came. He had even managed to plant the potato garden before St Patrick's Day. The seeds had to be down before the 17th if the potatoes were to have St Pat's blessing and flour in the taste. He had even managed to get over to Eadstown and help his father with the spring sowing. And how he had managed that still made the old man and many another laugh.

He had dirtied his face with earth and whitened his hair with flour, then covered it with a large scarecrow's hat, dressing himself in the tattered old cloak and clothes of a beggar, leaning on a stick and smoking a long-pipe as he took to the road; touching his hat with a wheezy 'Top of the mornin'' to the militia as they passed.

But the biggest laugh was when he had finished helping out at Eadstown. After a stay of two days his devilish humour had got the better of him and he could not resist plodding in his beggarly clothes into the tavern and sitting down amongst the militia – after placing handfuls of smelly old wet pig straw in his pockets.

'Ach, but it's a grand day!' he had wheezed at the soldiers from under his hat. 'Musha, but wouldn't the heavenly scent of thim spring flowers make ye think of what it's going to be like when we sit down with the angels come when.'

355

The militia had ignored and edged away from the dirty-faced, white-haired old man who was sniffing the air with delight while stenching the place out. 'More like sitting with Paddy's pigs!' one had muttered.

And according to the tavern keeper, he had wheezed and sniffed on with nerves of steel, sliding closer and muttering to the militia if there was 'Any chance of an oul wee drink?' before they lost their patience and turfed him over to the keeper, who was about to throw him out, telling him he *stank*, when he answered quietly in a young voice: 'Aye, just like a dead man.'

It had taken just one glimpse at the laughing eyes under the hat for the keeper to change his mind, after nearly having a heartstroke, urging the beggar over to the counter.

'Ach, sure maybe I will give the old devil a drink after all. But away from the people mind. 'Tis a clean house I run. And only one drink at that, and only because I'm a born Samaritan and pity unfortunates.'

' 'Tis a saint in the making ye are and no mistake!' wheezed the beggar gratefully. 'God bless ye and all yer descendants.'

And he had sat alone by the counter, in the isolation of his stench, drinking away contentedly, his head lowered as if studying the contents of his glass while the militia discussed and told tales about Michael Dwyer, their favourite topic. Many a hunt had been made for his body, but parts of the mountains were too treacherous to search. The tavern keeper and those local men who had been given the nod and wink, egged them on, enjoying every minute of it, asking which parts had been searched.

'What say you, old beggar?' provoked the keeper with a grin.

'I'm a County Kildare man myself,' came the wheezing reply. 'Never heard of the varmint.'

'What – never heard of the Rebel Captain of the Wicklow Mountains?'

'Naaaaaay,' he wheezed, rising to his feet with a shrug and a shake. 'But to the wind with him anyway. Myself also. For I'm a gintleman of the road and I'm heading up Ballintruer way and 'tis a long way and all.'

He then politely fingered the side of his hat as he passed the militiamen and wheezed out of the tavern. And the drinks and laughter had flowed and bubbled, long after the unsuspecting militia had also vacated the tavern.

Cullen puffed happily on his long-pipe, smiling to himself.

Derrynamuck had not damaged his nerves a bit, not a fray; they were as cool and steady as ever.

'Heck, sure I don't know,' Cullen muttered, as if in reply to a question.

'What don't you know?' said Mary in a low gentle voice, her head still bent over her stitching, embroidering a yellow butterfly on a small white petticoat.

'What? Oh, nothing, treasure,' Cullen murmured, as if waking from a dark study. He glanced at her, at her bent head with its smoothly combed length of black hair gleaming in the candlelight, then turned his eyes back to the fire, watching the flames and glowing embers.

He smiled subtly to himself. Sure wouldn't you think it was the Virgin herself sitting there sewing. Looking like butter wouldn't melt in her mouth. Huh! Women were such frauds! Over these past few months he had come to learn that Mary was not entirely the gentle creature of perfection he had first thought her. She could be a very frivolous person, adorning her hair in tortoise-shell combs, and at times laughing much too merrily for a girl in her condition.

He glanced at Mary with grave disapproval.

Mary's head came up from her sewing, but her eyes were turned towards Michael sitting at the table, frowning as he read a newspaper by the glow of a candle. She was very proud to have a husband who could read and write. Very few of the older men in Wicklow could. And only a small number of Michael's comrades had come from families comfortable enough to send them to the barn-school and later a scholastic priest. Neither John Mernagh nor Martin Burke could write their name, depending always on Hugh Vesty or Michael to read and explain things to them.

And Michael would read anything: books, pamphlets, anything which told him of the world outside the Wicklow Mountains. But his favourites were the newspapers which carried the latest about Napoleon and Nelson, and the unrest and talk of revolution amongst the workers in England who were presently incensed by the latest extravagance of the Prince of Wales.

Michael had explained it to herself and Cullen – England was almost bankrupt due to the cost of the war with France, but Parliament still had to find the money to meet the cost of the Prince's wine and clothes bills, which every year were enormous. Poverty was rife in the rural areas, and half of London was homeless. And now the dandy Prince had commissioned the building of an elaborate dome in a place called Brighton, to the cost of *seventy thousand pounds*. And for what? – to house his horses! The English people were very angry.

Mary's eyes were still on Michael, wondering why he was frowning so sharply, looking at the newspaper as if he could not quite believe what he had just read.

'Is it something else about the Prince of Wales?' she asked quietly.

Michael slowly looked up. 'They've agreed to sell us,' he said incredulously. 'The British Government has agreed to sell us off!'

'Eh?' Cullen removed the pipe from his mouth and turned round in his chair. 'What are you saying?'

So Michael explained it to them. The aftermath of the rebellion had left the Irish prisons overcrowded, despite the fact that great numbers had been dispatched to serve as seamen in the British fleet. But now the rumour was fact – Britain and her administrators in Ireland had made a deal with the King of Prussia – agreeing to the disposal of prisoners by sentencing them to serve in his army, and those males who were too old, or too young, or simply did not fit the cut of a soldier, were sold at so much per head to work in Prussia's mines.

'They have agreed to *sell* us!' Michael cried. 'The British Government, who complain loudly and pompously about Negro slaves in America, are *selling* the Irish to Prussia! And his Germanic Majesty – our fine and noble King George the Third – has agreed to sell off his Irish subjects like so many head of cattle to his German relatives!'

He threw the paper down and moved over to the fireplace, standing with feet apart and arms folded, eyes blazing with anger as he stared into space, looking tall and strong and every bit the rebel captain again.

Cullen stared at him in mute horror, but Mary dipped her head and silently resumed her stitching, tears of anguish moistening her eyes. First young Esther Costello, now this. What next? Things always happened in threes, and the third would be the one that did it, ended her peace and the wedded idyll she had enjoyed for little more than three months.

Cullen finally found his voice. 'Ach, pay no heed to what you read in the papers, 'tis all lies!' but Michael had moved across to the bedroom, kicking the door shut behind him.

*　　*　　*

Herr Schouler, the Prussian agent, had arrived in Dublin to make his selection of Irishmen, studying each prisoner as a farmer would a ram or a bullock.

Schouler was furious when he later saw the Secretary of State, Lord Castlereagh.

'Lord Castlereagh! Our agreement was that I could have my choice of the reb-ells! Now General Johnson tells me that *he* will pick out the prisoners, and it is all the rogues and thieves I must have. *Nein! Nein! Nein!*'

Castlereagh flicked an elegant hand. 'Herr Schouler, there must be some mistake. It is my most ardent wish that as many rebels as possible be removed from this island and dispatched to Prussia.'

'*Ya!* And we agreed a price for reb-ells! General Johnson does not choose the men for me, because he does not know the quality of men for which I have orders. If the young, well-looking, and tall men are picked out first for the English ships, the old and little men I can make no use of. And if all the rogues and thieves are to be chosen for me, I cannot agree to that.'

'But of course not, Herr Schouler,' Castlereagh concurred silkily.

'My earlier talks with you was of Irish reb-ells, not rogues and thieves! I should be highly punishable in the eyes of the King my master if I was to send him for the Prussian army picked rogues and thieves instead of reb-ells!'

'Please calm down, Herr Schouler, I am sure we can come to some agreement of mutual satisfaction.'

'I *must* have Irish reb-ells for the King my Master! I will not take old rogues and little thieves! *Nein! Nein! Nein!*'

'Herr Schouler!' Castlereagh exploded. 'Irish reb-ells you want! Irish reb-ells you shall have!'

Quickly drawing in a steadying breath, Castlereagh adjusted the silk bow of his neckcloth, and forced a smile. 'Now,' he said smoothly, 'how about a cup of English tea while we discuss the matter?'

Chapter Twenty-Three

At his Lodge in Phoenix Park, the Viceroy, Lord Cornwallis, was still suffering a hail of public abuse from the high-ranking gentry for being altogether too harsh on the militia. Cornwallis defended himself stoutly in a letter to London.

> 'On my arrival in this country I put a stop to the burning of houses and murder of the inhabitants by the yeomen, or any other person who delighted in the amusement. I also stopped flogging for the purpose of extorting confessions; and to the free quarters of soldiers which comprehended universal rape and robbery throughout the country. I stopped all this, and if this be a crime I freely acknowledge my guilt.'

Although he sincerely believed he had, the Viceroy had stopped nothing. In Wicklow the house-burning season started a few days later. The militia marched through the villages in search of rebels, setting fire to hillside dwellings and occasionally shooting any man who stood out against them.

Once again men were being forced back up the mountains in droves, only this time they had no captain to command them or organise their systems of defence. And as the days moved on, many became angry and confused.

'Where is Dwyer?' they demanded. ' 'Tis hard to know which tales to believe any more. Is he dead or alive or what?'

But neither Hugh Vesty nor any of Michael's principal men would give them the satisfaction of a straight answer.

'He must be dead!' some decided.

'He's alive!' others insisted. 'Wasn't it he who answered the cries of the girl and dealt with her persecutors?'

'Nay, the militia have it right, 'twere a couple of vagabones did that. Didn't the girl say so herself before she died, and didn't her daddy tell the militia so too?'

'Aye, but who was ever known to tell the militia the truth?'

And so it went on; while Hugh Vesty and the others maintained their silence, not sure if the captain would ever be willing to come down from the mountains again, leave his little paradise and enter the fight again, even if it was in defence of his own people, his own friends.

It was usual for many of the farmers to send their sheep up to the grazing lands of Wicklow under the care of shepherds. But now the militia had begun to kill sheep at whim again, deciding a good meal of lamb or mutton tasted better when it did not have to be paid for.

Two yeomen had just completed this venture and were on their way back down the hills when they came across a twelve-year-old boy with a haversack on his back.

One of the yeomen was Ned Valentine. 'What have you got in the bag?' he demanded.

'A loaf of bread,' said the boy, 'and a flask of buttermilk.'

'Where are you taking it?'

'To my daddy at Aughavannagh. Himself and some other men are cutting turf there.'

'Liar!' Valentine snapped. 'You're taking it to feed rebels. Come now, admit it!'

The boy stared at him in white horror. 'No!' he cried. ' 'Tis for my daddy cutting the turf.'

Valentine narrowed his eyes in sudden cunning as he looked at the boy. 'Tell me, is it true what some are whispering – that Dwyer is alive?'

'Ach no, sir! He's as dead as Moses.'

'How can you be so sure?'

The boy shrugged. 'Well I can't be truly sure, seeing as nobody's found his bones, but everyone I know says he is dead. Even my daddy. He says some are pretending the Reb-chief is alive just to worry the militia.'

Valentine's eyes were sparkling, his face bright. The boy was not ready for his instantaneous response, almost falling over as the bag was ripped from his back. 'We'll have to confiscate this,' Valentine said. 'It's evidence that you were endeavouring to supply rebels with food. You're under arrest.'

Two Protestant gentleman had come riding along the road; a Mr Henry Evebank and a Mr Goodwin. They muttered a few words between themselves, then challenged Valentine.

'What are you doing with that boy?' Mr Evebank demanded.

'What is it to do with you, sir?' Valentine snapped.

'He's but a child. What crime could he possibly have committed?'

'He's a damned rebel caught in the act of taking supplies to his friends still out under arms.'

'I wasn't! I was taking it to my daddy cutting turf at Aughavannagh.'

'Let the child go on his way,' Mr Goodwin ordered. 'You know very well who the boy's father is and where he lives.'

'And there is an easy way to find out if he is lying,' Mr Evebank suggested. 'Go along to the bog at Aughavannagh and see if his father is cutting turf there. If not, you can find the boy at his home later and call him to account.'

After a moment's hesitation, Valentine nodded. 'All right, we'll go to the bog – but we'll take him with us!'

'You will not harm him,' Mr Evebank said sternly.

'Why should we harm him if he's telling the truth? But if he's lying – he'll be on the next ship learning the ropes.'

The boy looked greatly relieved, knowing his daddy was cutting the turf. The two gentlemen rode on, their eyes occasionally straying to the yeomen; one dragging a dead sheep and the other pushing the young boy in front of him, in the direction of Aughavannagh.

The following morning his father and a group of searchers found the boy under a hawthorn bush, shot through the head. The bag of bread beside him.

Mary was not sure what had awakened her. For a brief moment, eyes blinking, she wondered if she had been dreaming. Then she heard the sound again.

The tap-tap-tap against the window glass.

The bedroom was in darkness, she was alone in the bed, but she could hear his movements as he quietly and swiftly dressed; the snap of his belt-buckle, the shrugging on of his jacket. It was only when he moved to the window that she saw him clearly, his face calm but unreadable as he looked out and examined the sky as if quickly noting the weather. Outside the night was bright and calm, but she could feel the storm of tension in the air.

The third thing had happened.

He paused for a moment to check the pistol in his belt. Then the latch on the bedroom door clicked; seconds later he had slipped out of the house like a lover slipping out to meet a maid.

The old man was still asleep in his settle-bed in the corner of the living-room when she entered and moved quickly to the front door, opened it and ran down to the low stone wall, quiet as a shadow.

The entire land was drenched in moonlight, but she could see no sign of him. She stood like a silent ghost in her nightgown, trembling. Then she saw him some distance down the hilly path below, Hugh Vesty Byrne beside him.

They were running.

She saw them again a short time later, as they crossed a moonlit meadow below.

They were running more swiftly now. In the direction of Aughavannagh.

She turned and walked back to the house. The old man was sitting up in his bed when she entered.

'Has Michael gone out?'

'Aye.'

'To his men?'

She nodded. 'Hugh Vesty came for him.'

The two were silent for a time, glooming in harmony. They had been a good threesome, like the eagle and the dove and the old happy thrush living together in peace. But now they knew the eagle of the mountains was about to leave the nest.

'Go back to sleep,' Mary whispered, bolting and chaining the door. 'He'll not be returning tonight.'

The dark fields around the house in Fearbreaga, some miles before Aughavannagh, was well manned with armed picquets. John Mernagh and Martin Burke jerked alert at the sound of footsteps, then rushed to give a hard grasp of the hand to their captain.

A large group of neighbours was gathered outside the house. They fell silent abruptly when the four men approached, all eyes on the captain who walked through them as if they were not there, and entered the house.

The kitchen was empty but for two people. By the fireside sat a youngish woman with a face as pale as a ghost, her hands in her lap, staring into the fire in a vacant tearless trance. According to Hugh Vesty, she had been like that since the hour they brought her dead boy home.

Behind her stood another woman, a generation older, quietly murmuring prayers as she sprinkled holy water over her daughter.

'Where is Dary?' Michael whispered.

The older woman glanced up. She was silent for some time before answering. 'My son-in-law is in the bedroom,' she finally whispered back. 'You'd better go on in yourself. He'll not believe me if I tell him it's you. He's not up to believing much any more.'

Hugh Vesty and the others remained near the front door while Michael retired to the bedroom. He was in there a long time. When he came out he looked at the older woman still murmuring her prayers, and his eyes moved to the white-faced woman sitting in the chair – she was stirring out of her vacant trance, a puzzled frown on her face as she began to look slowly around the room, as if searching for something she had lost.

Michael froze where he stood. For she brought back a memory to him. A memory he had not had in a long time. He had been sixteen, alone on the farm when the cow gave premature birth to her calf. His father was in yonder fields with his younger brothers, his mother at market with the girls.

Cumbersomely, still in pain from the birth, the cow had bent over her calf, smelling and licking it. Suddenly she had lowed and moved away to the corner of the field and stayed there. The calf was dead, still-born. Michael had stood looking sadly across at the cow, flicking her tail against her flanks wearily, still in pain, and thought the best thing he could do for her was bury the calf as quickly as possible.

When he returned from the nearby meadow the cow was lowing loudly, looking searchingly around the field. On the corner ground where she had moved to, was the afterbirth bag. And now it had been delivered, she was looking for her calf.

She began stumbling round the field, smelling the ground where her calf had lain, putting her head over the hedge here and there, lowing madly, searching and not finding until she became as wild as a bull. He offered her a drink of warm milk, but she ran away in fury, attempting to break through the hedge, sniffing in the direction of the meadow; she knew her calf was there.

In the end he took his spade and led her out through the gate and up to the meadow. And there he lifted the newly dug earth and let her see. The long lashes on her big old face moved up

364

and down, and then she jiggled with delight at the sight of her calf, straining down her neck to lick him lovingly.

After that she had looked so stupid, that great bulk of a lovely cow, just standing and staring at her calf for a long time, and then her dull old brain grasped why he had not responded to her love. Suddenly she fell down on her knees, her big body covering the hole containing her calf, and she had raised her head and cried and cried in such a terrible and mournful way it had echoed over the hills for hours, until she lost her voice from hoarseness.

And now this white-faced woman was also looking searchingly around the room for her offspring, lying dead in the bedroom.

'Let's go,' Michael whispered urgently to the others, and they all silently left the house. The door swung back on its hinges and stood open behind them, but none of the neighbours dared enter without permission.

A buzz of chattering rose up when they came out and pushed through the crowd of neighbours. They had reached the edge of the field when a group of men ran after them. One caught Michael's arm. He spoke breathlessly, urgently: 'None of us know where've you been. But we do know it won't be easy for you if you come out again. So it's been suggested that a subscription be levied amongst the people to help you buy ammunition, and any other rations of food and drink will be supplied to you and your men as before, as regular as the soldiers in the barracks.'

Before Michael could answer, another man grabbed roughly on his arm. 'Do you know what we're saying to you, Dwyer? Do you know?'

'I'm not a fool,' Michael answered, shrugging the man's hand away. Once again he was being asked to lead his small army of men and take up the role of defender of the local population against the militia and yeomanry forces.

The man grabbed his arm again. 'Can't you see? It's them or us! They've made that penny plain. Only this time they've started on the children. Two down already.'

'Look,' Michael said irritably, 'will you just leave me be and let me move on.'

'Listen, brother, you and Dary were good friends. And now his boy—'

'Get out of my way!' Michael snapped.

The man remained where he was, utterly perplexed, then turned on his heel and marched off. The huddle of neighbours stared after the four rebels in bewildered silence. They had only walked a few yards when a scream rose up from the house behind. A woman's scream.

'*Oh, mercy, Jesus!*'

'Keep walking,' Michael whispered urgently. 'She's reached the bedroom and come back to her senses and I don't want to be around for it.'

The armed picquets fell silently into pairs and followed at a distance in irregular intervals. It was not until the leading four reached the vicinity of the Lugnaquilla that anyone spoke.

'What did Dary say to you?' Hugh Vesty murmured.

'Very little,' Michael answered. 'He was too choked over the boy to say much. But the last thing he said to me was: ". . . as surely as God hears me, I'm asking you to come out, stay out, and make them pay." '

'Those were his very words?'

'Those were his very words.'

'And what did you say?'

Michael looked up at the sky for a moment. The stars had long grown dim, and now the dawn was spreading its light over the land. It was going to be a warm June day. He looked at his four companions and asked: 'Do you know what day this is?'

'Aye, Thursday.'

'Oh, it's more than just Thursday,' Michael said. 'It's the first day of summer horse-racing at Davidstown. And not only that. It's the day of the Blue Ribbon.'

'The Blue Ribbon?' Hugh Vesty scratched his head and smiled. 'Sure now, isn't it just typical of you to remember a thing like that.'

Daylight streaked into the bedroom, inching its way over to the bed. Mary threw back the covers and prepared her mind for the day. She could hear old man Cullen bustling about in the living-room.

'Is that you up, Mary?' he called.

'There's only me in here,' she reminded him.

'Do you want your bowl of warm water?'

'Aye.'

Five minutes later the door opened a few inches, and Cullen's hands placed a bowl of water on the floor before the door closed quickly again. Mary cleansed herself and dressed, then moved out to the kitchen where, to her surprise, Cullen had already prepared the breakfast.

'You were right then,' Cullen said as they sat down to bowls of hot milk and oatmeal. 'About him not coming back last night.'

'Aye, I may as well go over to Bushfield this very day,' she said tiredly.

'And what business have you over at Bushfield?'

'Business with the bootmaker. I slipped over there one day and ordered Michael a new pair of mountain boots to replace the pair he lost at Derrynamuck.'

Cullen was astonished. 'And have you the money to pay for the boots?'

'Aye, I saved it from the purse he gave me.'

'Musha, but you're a grand and thrifty woman altogether,' Cullen declared. 'And who did you say the boots were for?'

'My brother, who else?' She laid down her spoon and looked sad. 'It will be so hard to leave here,' she murmured, 'so hard to go back to the unsettled life of harbourers' houses.'

'Aye, lass, aye. But we chose our man and we chose our side and now we must face it and look bravely. And listen, won't you be able to come back here now and again for your little trysts, just like before?'

'Even when the baby arrives?'

'And why not? Isn't there plenty of room in here for three? Oh, hear me, Mary, when that little lad arrives, he'll always find a hundred thousand joyful welcomes waiting for him in *this* house.'

'And if the little lad turns out to be a little lass?' Mary queried.

'Ach, Mary, this is no time or place for a girl to be born. A lad has more chance, he can fight back.'

'But if it is a girl – what then?'

'Then, then, the same waits for her too. A hundred thousand joyful welcomes.'

Mary smiled. 'Do you mean that?'

'Oh I do, treasure, I surely do,' Cullen insisted, then sat scowling as if he had just eaten a bowl of last year's rhubarb.

The evening sun was far down in the west. The Blue Ribbon had been won by a gelding trained in Kildare and sired by the famous Green Dancer.

The races were over, most of the people gone, only a few

hucksters remained, packing up what was left of their wares and preparing to leave. One girl, a gypsy type selling little brass bells and charms, nodded and chatted as Michael questioned her. Soon the other remaining hucksters had formed a group beside her, grinning and slapping the latecomer on the back, then raising their arms to point north-west.

'Just as I predicted,' Michael said on returning to his principal men on the hillside. 'Some mules will always choose the same old watering-hole.'

From the open window of Plant's tavern at Castleruddery the uproarious laughter of the revellers inside could be heard.

Michael strolled up to the window, stood for a moment looking inside, then moved along and entered the tavern. Around the fireplace sat a group of locals drinking and talking. He strode quickly past them towards a table near the rear of the taproom and sat down on an empty stool amidst a group of yeomen playing cards.

'Any room for another player, avics? What is it? Fifteen or Twenty-five?'

The yeomen all looked up and stared at him.

'Hell's flames,' one said. 'Is it you, Dwyer?'

'Aye. Who were you expecting to join you – the Devil?'

'Ach, no,' said Hugh Vesty, sliding up behind him, ' 'tis not cards they use when they play games with the devil.'

The yeomen's stampede to the back door was sudden and noisy. Michael darted back to the front of the tavern-house where his men were waiting.

'Catch them at the rear,' he commanded.

House by house the inhabitants of Castleruddery and the surrounding neighbourhood rushed out to watch the sport as the yeomen ran over the fields like hares and the rebels chased like hounds.

Ned Valentine was running the fastest. He looked wildly over his shoulder and saw two rebels swiftly closing in on him.

'Hell's flames!' he cried again.

Angrily, Michael pushed Hugh Vesty out of his way. 'Go your own trail and find your own fox,' he cried. 'Valentine is mine.'

Chapter Twenty-Four

John Cullen was still up when Michael came in many hours later. Mary was in bed but not asleep. She could hear him talking urgently to Cullen in the living-room, and instantly knew that he had already gone back to that life on the mountains which he would not allow her to share.

Life on the run.

'If that's how it must be!' Cullen was saying fretfully. 'If that's how it must be! Musha, no place will be safe for you now awhile . . . Have you eaten at all? Mary left some food simmering here in the pot for you in case you came back. Shall I lift it up for you?'

'Yes, and quickly,' she heard him answer as he reached the bedroom door.

'Aye, and I'll have some more meself, there's plenty left. Arrah . . .' Cullen added gloomily, 'God knows when I'll eat such fine cooking again.'

She sat up as he entered the room, which was in darkness except for the light from the fire. 'Where have you been?' she demanded curtly.

'Mary, it's been a long night and a long day and 'tis a long story,' he said by way of explanation. 'Now you must get up and dress. I'm moving you out of here tonight.'

'Tonight?'

'I'm afraid so.'

'Why?'

'By dawn every redcoat and militiaman will be back on the hunt for me. I want you to stay at the old couple's house for a few days. Then I'll move you on.'

'Why can't I just go home to Mammy?'

He paused then sat down on the bed. 'Best not to. In case they have any suspicion of you being associated with me. Best to hide where they would not think of looking for you.'

'They wouldn't think of looking for me here. You neither.'

'No, but Cullen hating me as he does, they may come and ask him to give them the wink if he spies me.'

'My,' she snipped, 'but you think of everything, don't you?'

'Well I do try,' he answered, sensing the rising misery behind her sulky face and sharp tone. 'When did you say the baby was due?'

'End of August.'

'Then at the beginning of August I will take you home to your mammy. I promise I will. By then the heat may have cooled.'

She looked at him darkly. 'You might have given me a little warning that this was going to happen so sudden.'

'I didn't know it was.'

'Yes you did,' she whispered harshly, flaring into a passion and pushing her tears away. 'Last night you knew. But you just slipped out without even a nudge or a word.'

'Ah, Mary, all I knew last night was that—'

He could say no more, for she had pulled his face down to kiss his mouth fiercely.

Cullen sat at the table frowning as he stared at Michael's untouched plate. His own second helping had long been eaten. 'Quickly,' he muttered in a tone as sulky as Mary's had been. 'That's what he said when I asked if I should serve it up. Do it quickly.' And now it was cold.

Abruptly he stood up and walked boldly to the bedroom door. 'Will I put this food back in the pot for ye or what?' he shouted. ' 'Tis turned cold. Will I heat it up again or no? Answer me.'

But nobody did. So he grunted over to the table and put the food back in the pot, then sat crouched over the fire scowling, his humour as black as the soot in the chimney at the certain news that his birds were migrating.

All in all, he grumbled in thought, it had been a devil of a day and the two in there had treated him very badly. One threatening him with a girl and now the other ignoring him. And if himself had so much time to spend in delay he could have spent some of it talking with him awhile, not locked in there with her.

He pushed the poker into the red depths of the fire, then moved back to the table and poured himself a tankard of ale from the jug. Sitting down at the fire again he warmed the ale with the hot poker and sat sipping, with brooding eyes, for over an hour.

When the bedroom door finally opened it was Mary who

crept into the living-room. She had a shawl over her nightgown and her hair as wild as brambles.

'What ails you?' Cullen cried angrily. 'Keeping him in there all this time. He told me he had to be away within the hour.'

'Hush!' she whispered sternly. 'Michael is sleeping.'

Cullen gaped at her in astonishment. 'God forgive you, woman of no sense, but I'm beginning to think young Kearns was right about you. You'll get him killed yet. And why is he sleeping when he should be away?'

'He's only human, you know.' She took down a plate and moved over to ladle herself a plate of the reheated lamb and turnip stew. 'He's had no sleep since the night before last.'

'He's had no food either,' Cullen declared, 'and now you're sitting down to eat his supper!'

'He's too tired to eat it,' she explained. 'And I'm very hungry. I'm eating for two.'

'Well, could you not let him eat it himself?' Cullen pouted. 'You don't have to do everything for him. And that lad has suffered great deprivation and hunger in his time.'

'Has he?' Mary's spoon halted in mid-air over the plate of steaming food. She frowned at the old man. 'In what way?'

'Down in Wexford, during the rebellion; he told me he once went five days with nothing inside him but goat's milk. Small wonder they were defeated.'

'Five days? Why did he not shoot something?'

'With all that war and gunfire and marching going on? Don't be docile! Any game within miles would have long run for cover.'

Mary put down the spoon and gazed at Cullen with such a forlorn and guilty expression on her face that his anger towards her suddenly vanished. He looked back at her with pity and tenderness, then nodded towards the plate.

'Ach, eat it up, treasure,' he said gently, then added with unintended crudeness, 'you've obviously satisfied his hunger in other ways.'

Mary blinked, wondering if he was scolding her again, then saw he was not. She stood up and lifted the plate and spoon. 'You're right,' she said in a determined voice. 'I'll wake him and make him eat it.'

When they were both ready to leave a short time later, Mary put her arms around Cullen impulsively and kissed him on the cheek.

371

'Huh!' he said. 'None of your female games with me.' But his tone was soft.

Michael did not say goodbye, for he would be back off and on and would continue to keep an eye on the old man. 'I'll see you in a few days or so,' he said, lifting Mary's bag in one hand and leading her out with the other.

'God spare you,' Cullen said, and glumly watched them slip away into the darkness.

The white-haired old couple who lived deep in the fastness of the glen were delighted to have Mary back with them, but Michael was very stern with the old woman. She patted his arm and gushed apologies in a sing-song voice, and assured him that she knew right well who Mary was. No, she would not fall into the wishful haze of imagining she was her dead daughter.

' 'Tis the flickering of the fire-flames in the shadow of evening when sits she across from me sewing,' the old woman whispered. 'Then I like to pretend the three of us are together again as we used to be. But I won't do it again. Aye, I promise! I promise on the name of all the saints and martyrs that ever walked this land. For sure I do. Now off you go and let us settle in awhile longer.'

Then holding her skirt she dipped a creaky knee and bobbed her white head and sang, 'Top o' the morning to you.'

'And the rest of the day to you,' he answered in kind, although it was not yet morning. The stars still glittered in the distance of the sky.

She stood at the door and watched him with her rheumy blue eyes as he walked away. She would liked to have told him the truth of it, but God willing, he would one day learn it himself, when he too was left sitting in the corner, left sitting on the edge of life.

She would have liked to have told him that there was great loneliness among the old, great loneliness. The young and even the not so young could look to the future, but the old could only look back; and sometimes, sometimes the memories became confused.

She shook her head and looked up at the stars, shining like the wings of so many angels who stood in distant groups watching the earth. She sighed. Still, heaven was waiting; the Land of the Ever Young.

'Praise be to God!' she whispered, then turned and creaked

indoors, her arms opening wide to the dark silent girl who smiled nervously at her.

'Welcome, child,' she crooned. '*Ceád mile failte.* You will not be lonely here, for I will comfort you, and talk long with you. And maybe you will learn something that I would have liked to tell that young man of yours. Aye, and many another young person too.'

'What is that?' Mary asked.

The woman's old blue eyes smiled, her voice became as soft as candleglow. 'That there is truly great wisdom among the old,' she said.

He had walked only two miles but he felt very tired. Every few steps his eyelids drooped heavily. Less than an hour's sleep he had had, lying between clean warm sheets, before she had woken him with her usual lilting little phrases of love, and rammed a spoonful of food into his mouth.

He would miss those clean warm sheets. He would miss that solid old four-poster that even the movements of their love-making could not creak. He would miss his darling girl. He suddenly realised that he was no longer tired, he was exhausted. He wanted to lie down where he stood.

He looked about him and decided he would do just that. The men up on Lugnaquilla could wait. Another hour or two of sleep would have him fit again. He had never needed much sleep, but he did need more than one hour in two nights. Wearily, he bent his steps up towards a deep crevice on a stone crag, hidden by overhanging purple heather.

There was still a mattress of old straw on the floor, for he had once spent a long summer night up here with Sam McAllister, a night when the two of them had talked and laughed and hardly slept at all, so mighty and witty had their humour been.

Late last summer that was. Long enough for some creature of nature to have made a home in the straw. He struck his flint and peered around, then stamped with his feet all over the straw, but there was nothing to see and nothing to hear and nothing scampered away. It was as empty as purgatory.

He sank down on the straw, stretched his tired limbs and closed his eyes. Instantly he was asleep, for long ago he had taught himself how to sleep immediately. But as he slept, a vision came to him, a vision of a young man from Antrim, wearing a green cravat.

Sam McAllister was calling him, bending over him and calling him. 'Wake up, Michael, wake up.'

He opened his eyes and stared all around, but there was no one there. He gave a superstitious shudder and closed his eyes again. 'Ah, Sam,' he whispered, 'you've never haunted me yet. Don't start now.'

Within minutes he was asleep again, and Sam McAllister was still bending over him. 'Wake up, Michael, wake up.'

It was definitely McAllister, same face, fresh and young, but no bullet wounds. Same voice, crystal clear. He looked at McAllister's arm, the left arm that had been smashed; it was undamaged. And then he said something that only Sam McAllister could say.

'Michael, wake up! Don't die in your shoes like a trooper's horse.'

His eyes flashed open, then looked from left to right. The deep crevice was empty of all but himself, and it was light outside. He lay blinking a few seconds, his whole being on edge. It was just a dream, but he was a Celt, and Celts knew all things were possible.

In one swift movement he rolled forward on to his heels, his head bent low as he crept outside and peeped over the brow of the crag, and saw the redcoats.

They were moving upwards – only another ten minutes or so and they would have reached his bed. He moved on to his stomach and slithered noiselessly around to the side of the crag where he was hidden from view to anyone below. But he could not stay there, the risk was too great. Neither could he move upwards, the climb was steep and a man had to be standing to do it.

Looking down to the land, he saw a possible way out, and moved to his feet to take it. He bent slightly, every muscle in his body held tight as he jumped the twelve-foot drop to the land below, landing as lightly as a robin on a rosebush.

Moving flat on his stomach, he slithered like a silent snake through the long fern and furze until he reached the high cover of an old whitethorn bush, and there he crouched hidden as the soldiers moved up, passing only inches from him. So close they might have heard his breathing, if they had stopped muttering amongst themselves long enough to listen.

He watched them climb on to the crag, lifting the overhanging heather with their bayonets and peering inside. Shaking their heads, one called to his commanding officer: 'Empty, sir. And very small. Not big enough for more than one or two men. Could be just the rain shelter of a hill shepherd.'

'Has it been occupied of late?'

'I wouldn't say so, sir. No sign of the makings of a fire. Just a layer of old straw.'

'Move on then.'

And they moved on, towards that part of the mountains where he had no camps and none of his men lay, for his camps had been chosen carefully, were almost inaccessible to the stranger.

Fools, he thought idly. If they had just taken the trouble to bend down and feel the layer of straw, they would have found that the straw was warm to the touch, signifying that a body must have been lying on it only minutes before.

He waited until they were well out of sight, then rose to his feet and moved on, his mind returning to the dream, the *unbelievable* dream. Was it Sam McAllister who had warned him? Or was it simply his own instincts?

It was Sam.

He was certain of it. He had seen him as clearly as if he were alive. Heard him as clearly as if he were alive. '*Wake up, Michael, wake up. Don't die in your shoes like a trooper's horse.*'

It was Sam.

By the time he reached a small mountain stream he was in a daze. He bent to water his face, then gazed slowly around him. Nobody would *believe* him. Nobody! But he would tell them anyway. He would tell his men, tell Mary, tell his mother and father and sisters and brothers, he would tell anyone who would listen.

And later, if God spared him, he would tell his son. He would tell his son that it was possible – for he had known it and still cherished it: the bond of brotherly love and comradeship that could exist between a Protestant Irishman and a Catholic Irishman; and it was only the Devil that sewed evil and hatred between them. But himself and McAllister had never allowed old Lucifer such a victory.

By noon, the news that travelled like wildfire all over Wicklow was certain and without doubt. Michael Dwyer was alive and back, and every soldier in Wicklow searching for him. The militia realised they should have listened to the people. He had been in County Clare with some of his boys after all.

The hunt was furious. A week went by, then two and three, but the game could not be tracked.

Towards the end of July, Michael was making a pre-arranged call at Reilly's house in Coolamaddra to collect some provisions for his men. As he approached quietly along the trees he saw Reilly's younger daughter sitting on the wall outside the house. She was singing to herself, as sweetly as a blackbird; and, as arranged, she was combing her chestnut hair.

It was safe to approach.

He strolled towards the wall and smiled at her. She did not smile back, just frowned at him sullenly, then turned her face to the sky and continued singing in a low voice:

'If I was a herring, I would not wait to be turned . . .'

A herring to catch a trout – instantly his eyes flashed to the house. A second later he had vaulted over the wall down into the hollow and was running for the fields when the six yeomen waiting inside the house dashed out and fired a number of unsuccessful shots after him.

'Did you warn him?' they shouted at the girl.

'What! Warn that villain who ditched me for another maid!' She tossed her head angrily. 'I never even spoke to the scoundrel. And I never will again, not as long as I live.'

The yeos were eyeing her suspiciously, uncertain.

'Who was this other maid? Was it the daughter of Doyle at Knockandarragh?'

'Nay! He only dallied with her at the Baltinglass Fair and on an evening or two afterwards.' She curled her lip contemptuously. 'Doyle's daughter was not for him. He found her very quiet and dull in her ways when she wasn't swirling her skirts and brazenly showing her legs at the dancing. He ditched her too, quick enough, and came back to me.'

'Who was it then? The last girl Dwyer ditched you for?'

'A girl from County Clare,' she said sulkily. 'That's why he went there after the business at Derrynamuck. A right hussy she sounds and all. Some say she even came back with him – living with him in sin!'

'Do you know what this girl looks like?'

'No, I don't, but as for ye lot—' she suddenly stormed, jamming her fists against her hips and shaking herself. 'If ye had been quicker on your feet ye would have caught him – him who led me up the mountain path then ditched me!'

She strutted furiously into the house where she flung herself into the arms of her sister and clung quivering until, with great sighs of relief, they heard the yeos march off.

'Oh, that was a close one,' her sister breathed.

'Aye, but wasn't I a genius to come up with that melodic warning? I hope Michael tells the other lads about it and all – especially Andrew Thomas.'

'Andrew Thomas? Is it him who's taken your fancy now?'

'Well, we have talked a bit lately, and I have always liked Andrew.'

'I thought it was Michael you would love to your grave.'

'Well, there's no sense in that now, is there? Not now he's married to Mary Doyle. And anyway . . .' She withdrew her looking-glass from the pocket of her dress and held it up as she pushed at a few chestnut curls. ' . . . Michael always treated me no warmer than a friend, but Andrew Thomas looks at me something smoky.'

At that moment Andrew Thomas was standing alone amidst an avenue of trees that led up to the great house of Thomas Hugo in Drummin, near the village of Annamoe. It was late evening, and the boughs of the ancient evergreens sheltered him from view. He was waiting for someone, someone who obsessed his thoughts.

The evening slipped into darkness, the glow from the lamps in the long windows cast beams into the shadows over the dark neatly cut lawn in front of the house.

Andrew smiled. Ruggedy Jack was responsible for that – the neatly cut lawn. Ruggedy Jack was very proud of his lawn. It was the only thing Ruggedy Jack ever had to be proud of. And if someone were ever to steal his tools, Ruggedy Jack would cut that lawn with his teeth rather than let its appearance shame him.

Poor old Ruggedy Jack.

Another hour drifted by, but he continued to wait, calm and patient. He passed the time recalling the lines of Irish poems his mother had taught him as a boy, beautiful poems that stilled his mind. Then his thoughts wandered over old ballads that told of Ireland's history.

Funny how the Anglo gentry had never grasped the secret

behind the Irish ballad. Funny how their noses would twist and their lips curl to see the peasants gathered and hear them sing for hours into the night. Some ballads were happy, but most were sad, and all contained the core of truth.

But what the gentry had not yet understood, and probably never would, was that to an oppressed people long forbidden an official education by the word of books, ballads were their vocal literature. And through them they recorded the events of history as they happened, and passed them on, in song, from generation to generation, so their descendants would know how it was, and how it had been, for their forebears.

In the distance he heard the sound of horses, the rolling of wheels. He jerked alert and peered through the trees. The carriage had turned into the avenue. For a minute he thought of what he intended to do, the ultimate sin, and he would burn for it. But then he stifled his conscience and raised the gun he was holding.

His arm was outstretched, the muzzle was pointed straight in front of him, and when the carriage rolled by, and the man at the window was level with the muzzle, he pulled the trigger.

The startled horses took fright and reared. By the time they reached the great doors the driver had managed to calm them. The driver shouted wildly, ran and banged on the doors. Servants rushed out, gasped in horror and rushed to help out the man inside the carriage – Thomas Hugo of Drummin, their master. The bullet had missed him, passed an inch from his nose and straight through the other window.

Another bullet cracked and flew. It would have hit Thomas Hugo straight between the shoulder blades if Ruggedy Jack had not heard the crack and pulled his master forward, a second before the bullet chipped Hugo's arm, removing the cloth of his coat and lodging in the wall beside the great doors. Blood began to ooze down his sleeve.

'Your arm this time, Hugo,' a voice cried. 'I'll have the rest of you yet!'

The servants ushered their terrified master inside.

Thomas Hugo of Drummin was a thickly built member of the landed gentry who, every season, was Master of the Hunt. When his wound had been dressed, he entered the drawing-room to find his daughter standing by one of the long windows, staring into the night.

'Was it him?' she asked.

'Yes, it was him,' he answered, white as a sheet.

'You'll have to go very carefully, Papa. He truly does mean to kill you.'

'I'll see the bastard hang first.'

Mary Hugo, a pale-faced girl with loops of dark hair coiled around each ear, turned searching eyes back to the window. Was he still out there? Was Andrew Thomas still lurking somewhere behind those trees?

'He will never forgive you,' she murmured.

The brandy decanter clinked behind her. 'Let the bastard go to hell.'

She stood silent, thinking of the young man she had known since childhood. Her first memories of him were of a small, skinny lad with thick brown hair and cheeky brown eyes. Now he was twenty-two, straight and well-made, and the last time she had seen him, his eyes had been flaming with disbelief and anger.

He had lived here a servant below stairs, serving his master devotedly and in every way possible. His master had never thanked him, but Andrew had never seemed to notice that. She has been greatly drawn to the young servant lad, liked being in his quiet company, often sat in the stables talking to him for hours. And one day, when she had sneaked off after him and persuaded him to teach her how to tickle a trout, he had whispered something in her ear, something that had made her very happy and very unhappy all at the same time. She had been thirteen then, and he fifteen, and to this day she had never told another soul what Andrew Thomas had whispered to her.

Then, one evening last year, before the rebellion broke, her father had hosted a supper for some of the yeomanry officers of the neighbourhood. She had been present, and was quite pleased to hear one mention that he had seen young Andrew Thomas shoot a sparrowhawk that very day. He showed great skill with a gun.

His fellow yeomen were not pleased; talk of a rebellion was rife then, in the previous spring of 1798. And as the night moved on they mentioned Andrew again, saying it might not be wise to leave a young man so skilled with a gun at large, in the home of a gentleman of property. They suggested that Andrew be arrested that night and dispatched to the fleet. In Ireland a man only had to be *suspected* of being disaffected to be sent to the fleet. A trial was unnecessary.

She had waited with breath trapped to hear her father refuse, refuse angrily, for Andrew Thomas had been his faithful servant from the day he had learned to walk.

'Perhaps you are right,' her father had said. 'Yes, you may as well take young Thomas with you when you leave.'

She had been the only person to see the serving-maid slip swiftly out of the room. She excused herself and hastily followed, down to the kitchen, just in time to see the maid bend and whisper in Andrew's ear. He had left immediately, pausing to take his master's favourite gun with him. At the door he had turned and looked at his master's daughter. 'I will be back,' he had promised. 'And I will kill him.'

Mary Hugo emitted a trembling sigh as she stared into the night with tear-filled eyes. The land outside was black. And Andrew Thomas had returned to fulfil his promise.

When Michael Dwyer heard about the assassination attempt, he was furious. He called Andrew Thomas to account.

When Andrew gave his explanation, Michael told him it was unacceptable.

'Why?' Andrew cried, hardly able to believe his ears.

'It was a cold-blooded murder attempt, the same as that on William Hume senior,' Michael said. 'I will not accept such behaviour from one of my men.'

'You have killed enough men in your day, Captain!'

'Aye – on the battlefield, soldier to soldier. When they come towards me, or after me, wearing the accoutrements of battle and try for my life or the lives of my men, then I fight them. But I am no hidden sniper! And I will not allow any cowardly sniper to remain in my division.'

'Hugo backs the shooting-and-burning militia! What's the difference—'

'The difference is premeditated and cold-blooded murder of a civilian. And you swore the oath of the United Irishmen, Thomas, you swore that you would not shed innocent or civilian blood!'

Andrew Thomas sought to argue, but his captain would not be swayed.

'I'm sorry,' Michael said quietly, 'but if you again attempt the murder of Thomas Hugo, you will afterwards go your own road, for I will not allow you to stay in this company.'

Andrew Thomas looked around at the small army of silent

men. Their faces more than anything else told him that Dwyer meant it.

He shrugged angrily and walked away, walked for hours until it was dark, then returned to camp. Most of the men were deep inside the huge cavern, candles were burning brightly and a fire flaming, the glow from the cavern's entrance unseen from the land below, for across and beyond this side of the Lugnaquilla was nothing but miles and miles of wilderness.

Outside the cavern a group of men were playing cards around a fire. They were Dubliners, half Protestants and half Catholics. There had been a series of raids in the capital, searching for United Irishmen who had taken part in the rebellion, and these twenty had managed to flee Dublin to join Dwyer in the mountains. They were a merry bunch, always singing and joking.

'How goes it, Andrew?' one called cheerily.

Andrew nodded silently to them as he passed into the cavern. He looked around, and saw the captain sitting away from the main body of men. As usual he was in the midst of his three staunch companions, Hugh Vesty, John Mernagh, and Martin Burke; an unbreakable foursome; each would risk their lives for the others.

The captain looked up at him, smiled and beckoned him over as if their angry exchange earlier had never happened. Hesitantly, he sauntered across, and the unbreakable foursome broke apart to let him sit amongst them.

Later, when they had all lain down to sleep, Andrew Thomas lay awake, his choice stark and hard before him; the choice between killing Hugo and staying with the captain and his men. He didn't know which he wanted most. All he knew was that he wanted both.

Two weeks after the assassination attempt, Thomas Hugo's arm was almost healed. Then luck decided to strike him a nice turn. He was breathlessly informed, by a very reliable and well-paid source, that Michael Dwyer and only two of his men were near Stranahely, on a low hip-edge of Table Mountain.

So Thomas Hugo, Master of the Hunt, collected together a hunting party.

'Right, men!' Hugo cried. 'Let's bring that croppy to the whip!'

They rode from Annamoe up Glenmalure and over the Black

Banks where they rode quietly and in single file through a small forest, their horses' hoofs covered in leather to quieten their steps, making barely a sound on the thick ancient layer of leaves. Before they reached the edge of the clearing, they stopped in the density of the forest and sat in silence for some long minutes, waiting and smiling at each other.

Then Hugo gave the signal, and they came out at a gallop, and succeeded in forming a circle around the ledge. Even to Hugo, the rebels appeared to be taken by surprise. The three sprang to their feet and sent down a volley as they ran for cover.

The huntsmen plunged their horses into the dykes and took shelter along the ditches. Only Hugo's large brown hat could be seen above the high hedge.

'You may as well surrender, Dwyer!' Hugo shouted. 'Any way down and we have you.'

In the silence that fell, the huntsmen's horses could be heard snorting.

'Do you hear me, Dwyer? I give you my word that nothing ill short of the law will befall you, if you throw down your arms and come in peacefully.'

In the continuing silence, Hugo's hat bobbed above the hedge in his impatience. 'Are you there, Dwyer?'

'I am, Hugo.'

'Then you must see that we have you surrounded and there is no way down. Now, will you surrender peacefully, or do we have to come and get you? Give me your answer!'

'Here it is, avic.'

The bullet whistled into Hugo's hat and carried it flying across the air. Hugo was so startled he fell off his horse into the ditch with a splatter of curses.

The huntsmen began firing.

The exchange of volleys went on for some short minutes, with the rebels' fire becoming more and more intermittent, then ceasing completely. At first the huntsmen were jubilant, sure the rebels had used up their ammunition. But on dismounting from their horses and clambering up the slopes, it slowly dawned on them that Dwyer and his men had been quietly moving up and up, toward the shoulders of Table Mountain, and now were gone.

Hugo had to be helped back on to his horse, emitting a furious string of oaths at being foiled in his quest to bring in the rebel captain.

'Damn him for a dog fox!' he bawled. 'Not only has he lost me a bounty of five hundred guineas, he has lost me a hat that cost a small fortune in Sackville Street!'

The three rebels were far away, moving across the high grassy slopes of Table Mountain. Michael shook his head in bewilderment.

'What an eejit that man is,' he said. 'Sitting there talking through his hat.'

'He's got no hat now,' Hugh Vesty reminded him. 'I think it flew all the way to Arklow.'

'Good enough for him,' Michael muttered. 'He's lucky I didn't decide to shoot his block off. Without his hat his brain will get an airing now anyway. Did you hear the stupid tongue of him? "Any way down and we have you!" Sure now, any fool knows that what can't go down, must go up.'

He gave a bemused sigh. 'And they say we're the ignoramuses.'

This time it was Andrew Thomas's turn to be furious when he heard. He rushed across the camp and pulled roughly on Michael's arm.

'You let Hugo get away! He came after you, gun in hand, and you played with him instead of shooting him!'

'That's right.'

Andrew sucked in a breath and clenched his teeth. 'I played fair with you, Captain. You offered me a choice of killing Hugo or staying with you, and I elected to stay with you. Now you insult me by playing games with Hugo and allowing him to bob away on his merry way home.'

'It was nothing to do with you, Andrew. You never entered my thoughts at the time.'

'Why did you not kill him?' Andrew demanded. 'Mernagh tells me that you could have done it if you had wished.'

'There was no need to kill him. He was no real threat to us, just a nuisance.'

Andrew was trembling, his eyes glistening with tears of rage.

'Forget Hugo,' Michael commanded softly.

'No!'

'Then he'll kill you long before you kill him. He'll mangle you up into a sick knot of hate without lifting a finger. Don't give any man that power.'

Andrew sagged at the truth of it, but he managed to rasp an

383

angry parting shot at Michael for letting him down.

'I'm beginning to think that what James Horan often says about you is right, Captain.'

'And what does James Horan often say about me?' Michael asked softly.

'That you have a particular partiality for the Protestants,' Andrew snapped, then turned quickly and marched off.

Hugh Vesty moved to Michael's shoulder. 'That boy is in bad pain,' he said. 'There's something more in it than he says. I think you should go after him and find out what it is.'

Michael looked at his cousin. 'At this minute he hates me more than he hates Hugo.'

'Ach, he doesn't. Andrew is one of our best. He needs help to get that large weight off his shoulders. And it should be you who goes after him, being his captain and all – I'm only a mere second in command.'

Michael finally found his man half a mile away, leaning back against a boulder and staring into space. He stuffed his hands into his pockets and took up position beside Andrew Thomas.

'All right,' he said quietly. 'So you spent your life serving at the heels of your master and he never gave you the time of the day. Most masters are like that with their servants. Didn't you know that?'

'He agreed to my disposal' – Andrew snapped his fingers – 'like that! Without even a moment's hesitation, he agreed they could send me off into a life of hell below deck' – Andrew snapped his fingers again – 'like that.'

'Then he's not worth a thought. Do as I advise, Andrew, and forget Hugo.'

'I can't.'

'For God's sake, Andrew – why not?'

'Thomas Hugo is my father,' Andrew Thomas said. 'He took my mother when she was a young kitchenmaid. She still works in his kitchens. He refused to let me have his surname, so she gave me his first – Thomas.'

'Ah, man!' Michael didn't know what else to say, so he put an arm around the shoulders of the younger man and pulled him close.

A very long time later, when they finally arrived back together at the camp, Hugh Vesty and Mernagh and Burke were waiting. They took one look at the face of Andrew Thomas and smiled in relief. It was just like the business with young Kearns again. All's well that ends well.

'Here, Andrew, drink this, it will settle you down nicely.' Hugh Vesty held out a small wooden cup almost full with pure white poteen.

'Mountain dew, drink it down,' Hugh urged briskly as Andrew held the cup and stared at its contents. 'Although you may find it a bit smoky. Mernagh only got it yesterday.'

Andrew tasted the brew, then eyes wide, made a deep rasping sound in his throat as he blew out the invisible flames.

'And a drop for you, Captain,' Mernagh offered, holding up a cup. Michael shook his head. 'I have something to do first. I'll be back in a while.'

James Horan was a big lad, and very malicious and quarrelsome of late. He was having a heated conversation with a few of the Dublin lads. He turned as Michael approached.

'Ah, here's the man himself! He'll lay the bones of this argument once and for all because he was there. Listen, Captain, do you remember—'

'You're out of this company, Horan. You have two minutes to pick up your things and get out.'

Horan's face straightened muscle by muscle. 'Why?' he rasped.

'You're a pissed-up bloody troublemaker, that's why.' Michael motioned with his head. 'Look over there.'

Horan turned his head towards a group of men sitting away from the main body of small groups. They were Protestant deserters from the Antrim militia regiment once stationed in Arklow. Men from Sam McAllister's regiment. Men who found they could not fight their own countrymen during the rebellion and had deserted to the rebels.

'They used to sit amongst us before I took my leave,' Michael said. 'But when I came back I noticed how they sat apart. Now I know why. They're no longer comrades in arms, are they, Horan? Not on your tongue. They're just Protestants. Well let me tell you, boy, this camp is still United Irish, and those boys have risked their lives with us, just as Sam McAllister and the Little Dragoon and many others did before they died.'

'I don't want out,' Horan cried. 'It was just idle talk. I'll not bother with it again.'

'You're out whether you want it or not. This camp is no longer the place for you. You're turning bad inside and looking for a reason. Next you'll be looking for blood.'

James Horan looked at the ground for a few moments. When he looked up again the message had sunk in. His face was full of furious contempt.

'My, but you do love the Prods, don't you, Captain? First you start dreaming about one, then you let another ride off. Next I'll be hearing how proudly you wear your orange sash and sing the Lillibulero.'

Michael's face turned ashen. 'Run now and you'll be lucky to get out undamaged. Anyone else who feels the same and wants to go with him – move now!'

No one moved but Horan. He lifted his musket and hefted it on to his shoulder.

'And you know the rules, Horan,' Michael warned. 'A whisper about anything you know and every rebel in Wicklow and the surrounding counties will be looking for an informer. Remember what happened to Patrick Lynch after Derrynamuck. He's now in solitary confinement in Kilmainham – for his own protection from the people of Wicklow. He was lucky to make it to Dublin alive. Hear me, Horan, don't use your mouth to dig your grave.'

Horan shrugged and strolled off. He hadn't a clue where he would go, but he couldn't stay, not now he'd been given his marching orders. But he would go out defiant!

'Now why would I do that, Captain, when I can use my mouth to sing a true old song or two instead.'

Then, as he passed the group of Protestant deserters, he smiled maliciously and began to sing:

> 'Ara! what makes the noose creak and swing?
>   Lillibulero, bullen-a-la.
> Ho! by my soul 'tis a Protestant wind
>   Lillibulero, bullen-a-la.'

Every Protestant and Catholic stared in edgy silence. James Horan looked around the camp and grinned brazenly, then stumbled into a half-run before falling flat on his face from the force of the kick to his backside.

'Get up and get out!' Michael snapped.

Horan scrambled to his feet and turned around, humiliation and rage dripping from every pore. 'Oh, do me a favour, Captain Big Man. Go back to your bed and curl up with a dream of your darling Prod McAllister—'

'Don't you even mention his name,' Michael warned, eyes flaming. 'His name is too good for your filthy tongue! And as big as you are, Horan, you could never in a lifetime be the man that McAllister was.'

'Oh no? Well there's something you should know, Dwyer. What McAllister did at Derrynamuck was not for you. No, sir! The bastard knew he was finished and just wanted to go out in a blaze of glory.'

It was all over in two swift moves. The blow to Horan's stomach sent him gasping to his knees, but it was the force of the boot slamming up to his jaw that broke it and laid him back unconscious.

'He'll have to stay with us now,' Hugh Vesty said to Michael after Horan had been carried far into the cavern.

'But soon as he's fit again he goes.' Michael was still white-faced with anger.

'He might not be fit for months,' Hugh said, but Michael did not hear him, because, as he usually did when he was angry, he had wandered off alone.

'I shouldn't have said anything,' Andrew Thomas said quietly to Hugh Vesty. 'But I was that mad myself over the business with Hugo, and Horan got me all fired up about the captain, telling me how he made the men let Joseph Holt go just because he was a Protestant and even though he was a traitor.'

'Joseph Holt was a great United commander in his day,' Hugh Vesty said sternly. 'Never forget that, boy. And the business with Horan would have flared soon enough. I've had to speak to him myself about that tongue of his. Michael is right – Horan has turned bad inside. And it takes only one bad apple to rot an entire barrel. We have enough to do fighting the armies of the oppressor without faction-fighting amongst ourselves. We're supposed to have put all that behind us when we became United men.'

Hugh lifted his drink, then looked squarely at the man sitting beside him. 'So, what about Hugo?'

Andrew Thomas gave no answer for a long time. Then he shrugged. 'What's done is done,' he said. 'I reckon if I don't forget Hugo, I'll end up turning as bad inside as Horan. I've decided to let him go to Hades.'

Hugh Vesty grinned. 'Smart thinking. Save your passion for

Reilly's daughter at Coolamaddra, and leave the devil to deal with Hugo.'

Less than thirty-six hours later, Andrew Thomas was dead. In the company of only two others, for they never travelled in large groups for fear of drawing attention to themselves, he travelled over to the house of Edward Byrne on the northern slope of Derrybawn Mountain to collect provisions for the camp. The rain had been falling since morning, the ground heavy.

They headed on to Matthew McDaniel's house at Castle Kevin. McDaniel was one of those given the job of procuring ammunition for the rebels with the money supplied through levy by the people of County Wicklow. It was still raining and very dark when they had packed their sacks, so they decided to rest up at McDaniel's for the night.

The following morning, breakfast over, they lifted their sacks in readiness to leave, grinning and making faces at Matthew McDaniel, who appeared to be peering in through the living-room window at them, but was actually peering into a small looking-glass perched on the window while shaving his face by the full light outside.

Suddenly, Matt McDaniel gave a shout and disappeared. They came out of the door to see what he was up to, and saw him running for his life and a troop of the Rathdrum Cavalry spurring towards the house.

The three rebels dropped their sacks and scattered in different directions. Andrew took the left-hand, downward path, slipped as he crossed a stream. He scrambled to his feet and fired a shot at his pursuers; his gun did not go off. He fired again, a dull click and no more; the powder had got wet in the stream. For a second he just stared in disbelief at his master's favourite gun, the gun he himself had nicknamed 'Roaring Bess'.

'You never failed me before!' the approaching yeomen heard him cry, a moment before he disappeared like an experienced fox, hard pressed, through the trees; and eventually lost them.

He might have made it, had he not been seen by a yeoman named Lieutenant Weekes, an immensely lanky man whom the rebels had nicknamed 'Long Weekes', as he pushed through a sloe hedge on to rushy ground which led to a pond where Weekes was crouched duck-shooting.

388

Weekes turned, saw a young man with a gun, an obvious rebel, saw him about to make a run for it, and quickly brought him down with a shot in the thigh. The pursuers from the Rathdrum Cavalry came along a few minutes later. For a moment they looked down at Andrew Thomas, then lunged into kicking him unconscious, before emptying their firelocks into him.

'I say!' declared Long Weekes, the son of a Reverend. 'There was no need to finish the business with such barbarous brutality!'

Thomas King of Kingston, a magistrate who lived two miles from Rathdrum, spent most of his leisure hours busily writing reports to his friends at Dublin Castle. He employed a number of spies, paid them poorly, and occasionally they gave him as much information as he had paid for.

He rushed into his study and almost knocked over the ink-stand in his haste to report:

A rebel of note has been killed. Who he was, I have not yet been able to find out, but the rumour is that Dwyer's party are grieving much at his death and all the Females on the mountains who favour the rebels are wearing black ribbons by way of mourning.

Two days later, the magistrate held another report in his hand, although he could not truly believe its contents. He stood by the window gawping after the young woman who walked slowly down the lane, Mary Hugo.

His wife poked a sharply chiselled face round the door. 'What did she want with you, Mr King? She was very curt with me!'

The magistrate was still in shock. 'She has signed a sworn statement for the authorities at Dublin Castle. But I don't believe it. I *refuse* to believe it. Here, here, read it for yourself.'

His wife stepped in brusquely and did read it, but far too short-sightedly for the bursting magistrate to await her reaction.

'See,' he cried, his finger prodding the paper, 'she has sworn that the body now lying dead in the Flannel Hall at Rathdrum is the body of the late Andrew Thomas of Drummin and for the taking of whom a reward was offered by the government and says that he was born and reared in the same house as her and that, and that – she is his half-sister!'

'Well!' Mrs King curled back and stared at her husband. 'Oh, how wicked. How very, very wicked! What are you going to do with the statement?'

'I will have to send it to Dublin Castle! They rely on my reports and would not like it if I kept anything from them.'

'Then let this be a lesson to you, Mr King,' she said sternly, flouncing towards the door. 'And take heed when I speak to you in future. I *told* you I did not like that young woman, and now events have proved that I was right about her. She is a wicked, wicked person to dictate and sign a scurrilous statement like that.'

Chapter Twenty-Five

Mary's stay with the old couple was much happier the second time around. The white-haired woman was very kind to her; spending much time in teaching her the 'old' remedies and cures. She had even taken Mary to a secret holy well where she was urged to drink the water and make a wish for a safe birth for herself and the child.

And she had started to bloom; within days of going to the old couple, she suddenly bloomed and bloomed until she was as big as a late summer rose. She wondered if it was all the raspberry-leaf tea the old woman kept making her drink. She felt so relaxed in mind and body she often dozed off in the day, but hardly slept at night with the baby's movements.

At the beginning of August, as promised, Michael came just before dawn to take her home to Knockandarragh, and found the old couple in a frantic state and Mary in the pains of labour. She was standing in her nightgown by the table, bent almost double, one hand gripping the edge of the table and the other pressed into her back.

'But it's not due for weeks,' he said in confusion. 'Are you sure it's not just backache?'

'It's not any kind of ache,' Mary cried. 'It's pain!'

'She'll not be able to travel,' the old woman said to Michael. 'But she must keep on her feet a while longer. Now you go running for the doctoring woman quick as you can.'

Suddenly he was terrified to leave her. He put an arm round her. 'Will I, Mary?'

She looked at him and nodded urgently. 'It started before I went to bed last evening, but I thought it was just very bad backache, before the stabs of pain woke me.'

'I'll be back in no time,' he assured her, then shot out of the door and started to run, across the yard and through the small wood near by, speeding through the trees until he came to the edge of the clearing where he suddenly stopped dead – and stared at the unexpected figure of a woman stalking towards him; a great dark vulture of a woman, as strong as an ox and knocking on six foot two. For a moment he almost side-stepped behind a tree in fright, but she had seen him – Midge Mahoney!

'Oho!' she cried in glee. 'They say the early bird catches the worm – and now I have you!'

He wondered what she was doing so far from her own abode, then remembered she was a niece of sorts to the old couple.

She let out a teasing laugh and bellowed towards him. 'Ach, surely I don't frighten ye now – a big lad like you!'

'I've no time for wrestling with you, Mrs Mahoney,' he said plaintively. 'I have to get to the doctoring woman.'

'What for?' Then her face sharpened, she looked at him hawk-like. 'Has Mary started?'

'Aye, early. And she's in bad pain.'

'Oh, the poor lamb!' Suddenly her whole demeanour changed at the news that one of her sisters was suffering. As lusty and brutal as she could be with men, Midge was terribly tender-hearted towards her own sex.

'Then you don't need no doctoring woman – not when Midge Mahoney is at hand.' She shook herself like a fierce mother hen and began striding in the direction of the old couple's house.

'Well don't just stand there!' she cried over her shoulder. ' 'Tis you that put her in that condition, so you may come back and help me.'

She began to stride again. He caught up and looked at her warily. 'Do you know anything about birthing babies?'

'Nothing at all.' She fired a derisive glance at him. 'I only birthed four of my own. Four lads that are turning into great lovely brutes of men like their father.'

He thought of Midge's timid little husband only half her size and said nothing, recalling to mind Midge's four boys – all hawks in her own image.

When they returned to the house Mary was still on her feet, doubled up in pain and tears spilling down her cheeks.

'Ach, my lovely lamb!' Midge cried, gathering Mary inside her arms. 'Into the bedroom now and I'll have the sharp edge off your pain in no time.'

Midge turned and fired a command at Michael. 'You – make yourself useful! Go and collect some marigolds.'

He stared at her. 'Marigolds?'

'No other will do,' Midge said, leading Mary away. 'And when you have a handful collected, bring them back to me, then start hefting in the water.'

Michael looked in sceptical wonderment at the white-haired old woman, who nodded her head solemnly. 'Marigolds,' she confirmed. 'Midge has the ancient knowledge.'

Michael turned to the old man. 'Will you do something for me, Paudeen? Will you go to Eadstown and tell my mother to come here – as swiftly and as secretly as she can.' He looked at the bedroom door. 'I don't trust that witch with my wife.'

'She'll not fare better with anyone else,' the old man said. 'Midge can work wonders with her flowers and plants. She knows more than the doctoring woman – she has the gift.'

'Do as I ask!' Michael pleaded. 'Fetch my mother.'

The old man nodded genially and reached for his hat. 'I'll go on the donkey. He's a swift old thing.'

When Michael returned with the marigolds, Midge came out of the bedroom with an anxious expression on her face. 'It's not going to take as long as I thought,' she said to the old woman. Michael watched as Midge pulled the green leaves off the marigolds and deftly began to chop them in shreds.

The old woman creaked over to the table with three or four small glass jars of chopped-up plants, then an iron milk-pot, then a jug of steaming water. Midge lifted a spoonful from each bottle and dropped the contents into the pot, then sprinkled in a handful of the chopped marigold leaves.

'Now give it just a second or two of brewing on the fire,' Midge ordered the old woman. 'Then we'll temper it down with a little cold water.'

Mary groaned out in pain as another contraction knifed her body.

Midge looked at Michael and snapped a command. 'You! Go in and hold her hand till I'm ready.'

He winced as he stepped into the bedroom and saw her, her eyes glazed with pain. She gripped his hand so tightly, digging her nails into his palms, he winced again.

'Don't leave me,' she pleaded.

'Never,' he promised, and kissed her hand passionately.

'You – out!' Midge ordered, carrying in a cup of her brew. 'Now, my darling girl, drink this and the nightmare will vanish.'

The old woman creaked in behind her, and held Mary's head up while Midge held the cup to her lips and made her drink.

393

He hovered at the door watching. Within minutes the glazed look of pain disappeared from Mary's eyes and she relaxed down on the bed with a dreamy sigh of relief.

'There now,' Midge declared with satisfaction. 'I think we mixed the ingredients just right. Too much of one or the other can cause problems, you know.'

'Aye, to be sure.' The old woman nodded her head in solemn agreement.

Midge sat down on the edge of the bed and gently held Mary's slender hand inside her own large-knuckled two. Mary smiled dreamily at the big woman in drugged adoration.

Midge smiled back tenderly, then turned a wry face to her old aunt. 'Did you hear about that gentry woman who picked up a whisper of our knowledge of the marigolds? Aye – thought she was clever she did, knowing one of our secrets. And when she got badly sick, she ate a handful of marigold leaves and swelled up the size of a house. Aye – writhing in agony for days she was and the Quality doctor unable to do anything for her.'

Midge sniffed. 'I could have made up a mixture and relieved her in no time, but when I learned who she was, I remembered once hearing that particular madam declaring that us Irish-women were good for nothing but making babies. So I decided not to disappoint her by offering to make anything else.'

The morning was well on when Michael's mother appeared like a silent vision from nowhere. She spoke to him distantly as she threw off her cloak then turned and entered the bedroom leaving him in mid-sentence.

She stared down at Mary for a silent moment, then looked sternly at Midge.

'What have you given her?' she demanded.

Midge was reluctant to discuss the exact details of her potions. She was also instantly subdued by the presence of this cool, efficient-mannered woman, whom she had known for many a long year.

'Well?'

Midge shrugged. 'Sure it's her first and hardest and longest,' she said. 'A little easing of her pain for a while is no harm. Is it now?'

'The old and pagan practices are gone,' Mrs Dwyer said coldly.

'Well, begor, and who says so?' Midge cried indignantly, flaring into a pet passion. 'There's no virtue in pain. And if I can give a little help to one of my poor sisters suffering the punishment of Eve – then I will and bedamned!'

Across the bed the two women stared at each other in a dark look that held centuries of female anger and female sympathy in its depth. Then a ghost of a secret smile moved reluctantly on Mrs Dwyer's lips, and Midge smiled too.

Michael watched in puzzlement. He had seen that look pass between women before. A secret way of communicating that seemed to speak volumes without words.

'But not a drop more,' his mother said softly to Midge. 'She will need all her wits and strength to deliver the child. It will not be able to come without her help.'

Midge nodded in agreement, and turning her head and seeing him standing there, she perked up in female superiority. 'You – out! And make sure there is plenty of water hissing and steaming when we need it.'

Before he could reply she had marched over and slammed the door in his face.

Evening was falling. The old man, long returned, was now kneeling humbly beside his white-haired old wife on the hearthmat, quietly murmuring the rosary together for a safe and successful birth.

Michael stood by the closed bedroom door, silently watching them, inwardly distraught. The water was hissing and steaming. The awful screams from inside the bedroom made him want to cry. What had Midge called it – the punishment of Eve?

He looked at the old couple who never halted in their litany. No wonder they appealed for succour to a more influential woman.

'. . . Blessed art thou amongst women, and blessed is the fruit of thy womb, Jesus.'

'Holy Mary, Mother of God, pray for us sinners now and at the hour of our death . . .'

The screams became worse. He could stand no more. He wandered outside and stood against a tree not far from the house. The screams reached out to him. He bent and lifted a stone, then withdrew the knife sheathed inside the top of his boot and began to sharpen it, slowly and methodically. His frustration and impotence were boiling to danger point when the screams abruptly ceased.

He stood waiting, like a stone statue, terrified to go near the house which had fallen into sudden silence. He had known since his childhood that some women, and some babies, did not survive the pain and travail of birth.

He waited for what seemed like hours.

Then Midge Mahoney came out carrying a bowl of water which she threw violently towards the field, then turned back indoors.

She came out again carrying a bucket this time, and sent the water flying in the same violent motion towards the field.

The third time she came out she was carrying a kettle. She stalked towards the rain-barrel, then saw him standing there in the dusky shadows of evening.

'Lord save us!' she cried. 'In all the excitement we forgot about you!'

He had never hit a female in his life, but he wanted to hit her. Only hours before he had felt a new respect and liking for her. Now he glared at her in sheer hatred, but she didn't seem to notice.

'A girl child!' she crooned, smiling rapturously. 'And so beautiful after she was washed that your mother and me cried all over her.'

There was a great deal of bustle and smiles between the old couple when he entered, like two excited children who had suddenly experienced a great event in their humble and humdrum lives.

His mother came out of the bedroom and stood for a moment pinning her hair back into a neat knot. She looked as careless as he had never seen her. The sleeves of her dress were rolled up high, the buttons of her bodice thrown open at the neck.

'Mary?' he asked.

His mother turned and smiled at him. 'Go in and see for yourself.'

She had been washed and tidied up. She looked as fresh and peaceful as if her pain had never been. She lifted adoring eyes from the swaddled bundle in her arms, then seeing who it was, a nervous smile twitched on to her face.

'A girl,' she said.

'I'm glad,' he lied.

'A lovely girl,' she repeated.

A half-smile of pretended delight hovered about his mouth.

'Come and see.'

He moved over to the bed, then bent and gently pulled back

the swaddling and looked into the tiny face of the child.

And the world stood still.

Sheer wonder came into his eyes. Six months of knowing a child was expected, three months of hoping for a boy, had not been long enough to prepare him for this first sight of his daughter.

Her blue eyes stared back into his unseeing; blue eyes that would shortly turn to brown or hazel. Her skin was smooth and tawny pink, her hair soft and thick and silky black like Mary's; her little rosebud mouth shaped as if she was saying a silent ooo.

'Your mother and Midge say she's a full nine months,' Mary whispered. 'So the doctoring woman must have got it wrong. She must have been conceived not long after we were married.'

It was an effort to tear his eyes away, but he managed to look at Mary, smiling joyously and swallowing his breath. 'Isn't she tiny?' he quivered.

'She is, but then she's a colleen and not a buachaleen.' Mary sniffed her offspring with loving pride and covered the tiny face with gentle kisses.

'You can hold her if you like,' she said suddenly.

'Can I?'

'Aye.'

She placed the child in his arms. He held her nervously, unable to speak as he stared down at the little scrap of magic that he and Mary had concocted between them. The baby turned her face into his chest in blind curiosity, her little mouth working in a searching movement; then her lips began to quiver and her face screwed up and she let out a yell of disappointment.

'Maybe she's hungry,' Mary said anxiously. He quickly handed the bawling child back to her, then sat down on the edge of the bed and propped his head against the bedpost and watched as she uncovered and attempted to feed the child at her breast.

Strangely, there was no embarrassment between them, these two country people, for although unwedded men may blush at the glimpse of a bare leg or ankle, a husband watching his wife feeding her child was as natural as watching a ewe suckling her lamb.

But the sharing of it, the newness of it, filled them both with a silent awe as they looked at the child that belonged to them both. They looked at each other, and both knew what the other was thinking, and their new happiness was tinged with a sadness as they realised the struggle that lay ahead.

Then he realised the child was getting fretful, Mary too, moving about on the pillows and wincing as if in pain.

'What is it?'

'I don't know how to do it!' she cried, her face hot with shame at such an admission. 'And it hurts so.'

The baby yelled fretfully, and kept on yelling.

'I'll get my mother,' he said quickly, and fled out of the door. His mother came at once, told him to leave them alone for a while.

'Huerta, my lovely girl!' Mrs Dwyer murmured to the baby as she positioned her correctly against Mary's breast. 'You have to learn to do it right, otherwise your poor mammy will end up as sore as can be . . . there now!'

Soon both mother and child were feeding more easily, the rosebud mouth sucking contentedly, a tiny palm pressed into the soft milky flesh.

Mrs Dwyer smiled.

'I feel so foolish,' Mary whispered. 'Not knowing how.'

'And why should you know? The ways of motherhood don't always come so easily or naturally as men may think.'

Mary lifted sooty eyelashes and looked at her mother-in-law. She had always been slightly afraid of her, until this day. She could be so cold, so unemotional at times, you never knew how she was truly feeling. It was only during the birth, when they had struggled and suffered together, that she had discovered just how soothing and tender this woman could be.

Mrs Dwyer suddenly smiled again, a soft smile of amusement. 'I remember a young black cow we had once, lovely she was, and very young going through her first birth. And so natural, they tell us, is motherhood to animals, that when her new-born calf smelled the milk and tried to suckle her, she darted away in fright.'

Mary started to laugh, then laughed and laughed with such relief the baby whined indignantly.

'So it is with women,' Mrs Dwyer said gently. 'The ways of motherhood do not flow into us as naturally as the milk. We must learn from each other.'

The two women looked at each other and a flicker of a new intimacy showed in each face. They smiled in silent understanding. Then the older woman lifted the baby to the other side, and again nodded in satisfaction.

'Will you send Michael back in?' Mary whispered.

'I will, for I think he's had a hard day of it. Midge has treated him something contemptuous. She always hates men badly before a child is born, then loves them madly again as soon as the pain is over and the joy begins.'

'I do like her,' Mary said.

'So do I,' Mrs Dwyer agreed. 'But she's still a terrible woman!'

Midge was on her third glass of poteen. She herself had brought the bottle to the old couple last Christmas but they had never touched it, believing drink to be sinful. Midge was talking and laughing so heartily that, as always, every bulging proportion of her great body shook. The old couple paid no attention to her, just smiled foolishly at each other, for the glass of poteen she had forced them to drink had gone to their heads. The old man stood up and sat down again, then wondered why he had done so.

Midge turned her attention to Michael, sitting beside her on the settle. She ogled him silently for a minute then edged her massive body closer until he was jammed up against the high wooden arm.

'As I recall, Michael asthore, the rule of abstinence is six weeks before and six weeks after – three months. Isn't that a long old time for a lusty young stallion to go without his oats?' She fumbled slyly at his thigh and blinked her eyes wickedly. 'Doesn't it make you glad you're a rebel and not a priest?'

Michael scrambled to his feet and out of her clutches as his mother walked back into the room. She glared coldly at Midge, then motioned him with her head to go back inside.

'Now Mrs Mahoney . . .' He didn't wait to hear his mother's words, but as he closed the bedroom door behind him, Midge boomed out a laugh that made the rafters shake.

'A terrible woman,' he murmured as he moved back to the bed and sat down on the edge, then smiled as he again feasted his eyes on his daughter. She had collapsed in sleep, a bubble of milk still on her upper pink lip.

'I'll teach her all the good things,' he whispered passionately. 'I'll teach her how to tickle a fish and make a wish when she holds her first ladybird. I'll teach her to hear the heartbeat of the land and see the sun flaming through the wings of a butterfly . . .'

Mary whispered: 'I thought you would be disappointed with

a girl child, but I can see that if I'm not careful, she may end up weaning your affection away from me.'

Still smiling, he looked at her, and the smile wiped from his face as he saw she was not jesting in any way. Her eyes were dark and sullen, and for the first time he knew the frightening extent of what Sam McAllister had once called 'Mary's obsession'.

And it did frighten him. For the weight of responsibility it put on his shoulders was heavier than any five hundred guineas. Her emotional dependence on him was total. It had been so since the day they married, and seemingly not even the birth of the child had changed that.

'Don't be silly,' he said. 'Love of a daughter is different to love of a wife.'

The expression on her face changed, became odd and a little strained.

'I was only jesting . . .' She began to mumble in agonised shame, and suddenly the hardness of her unsettled life, hiding and running, always having to be one degree smarter than the soldiers, the constant terror of it all, and the exhaustion wreaked on her body by the birth crashed down on her.

'It's so unfair!' she cried. 'All you did was fight for the freedom of your country and the protection of your people. It's so unfair . . .'

Suddenly she glared at Michael like a wild woman. 'And I *know* what they did to Andrew Thomas! You lied to me, Michael, you *lied* to me. You are a *liar*. The old couple went over on the donkey to find out if it was really true what they did to Andrew Thomas, like many more did. When they came back I overheard them talking and praying about it. When Andrew's mother pleaded to have his body to bury, they gave it to her – after they had hacked off his head! And they'll not be satisfied until they do the same with you!'

The screaming voice and the wailing of the child brought Mrs Dwyer and Midge rushing into the room.

'Dear God,' Mrs Dwyer murmured, reaching to take the crying child. 'I was not expecting anything like this to happen for days. And then nothing like this!'

'Give me back my baby!' Mary screamed. 'They'll not stick her on top of a bayonet as they do other babies!' She pushed back the covers and rushed at Mrs Dwyer with such vicious strength that Michael had to grab her and propel her back on to the bed. He was trembling, every inch of him, with shock.

'I'll have to make a potion,' Midge said quietly, stone-cold sober.

'Yes,' Mrs Dwyer said.

'Take the child outside,' Michael shouted to his mother. 'Quickly!'

Michael managed to hold Mary down but she struggled so fiercely in shrieking hysteria he was forced to slap her hard across the face.

She stared up at him in a long blank silence, then rolled her head upon the pillow and emitted great grinding heaving sobs that echoed through every part of the house and the desolate field beyond.

The old couple hovered anxiously by the doorway, then moved away. Within minutes the litany of the rosary was heard again.

Midge rushed in carrying a cup of her brew. 'Come now, darling girl, drink this and life will look rosier and not so black.'

'Is it the stuff you gave her before?' Michael asked as Midge forced Mary to sit up and drink between sobs.

'No, that was for easing pain in the body, this is for easing the tension of her nerves.' When the drink was taken and Mary lay back, Midge said sadly: 'Any girl would crack at the edges after what she's had to put up with. You at Derrynamuck and all. She should never have been told about Andrew Thomas. Even I vomited when I heard of it – and I wasn't pregnant or had a husband on the run from the same butchers that caught young Andrew.'

She looked at him, then sighed, and said quietly. 'I've been over here a few times in the past weeks. I've talked long with this lass of yours, and her real trouble, her *real* sickness, is that she holds too high an opinion of you. No man is worth that anguish in my book. All bottled up inside her it was. Now it's all come out with the child.'

Mary was lying in heavy-lidded silence, but tears still streamed down her cheeks. Her hand reached for his, gripped it tight.

'Leave us alone,' he said to Midge, and Midge did.

Now her eyes were soft and misty, no anger, but no happiness either. And he was acutely aware that he was the cause of all her pain. If he had not joined the United Irishmen, if he had kept his nose deep in the mud and licked the horse-dung off their boots whenever they asked, he might now be living in peaceful humiliation with his wife and child on a few rented acres that could never be his, no matter how hard he worked.

> All men are born and continue free and equal in respect of their rights. The aim of all political associations is the preservation of the natural and imprescriptable rights of man. And these rights are liberty, equality, property, security, and the right to resist oppression.

That had been the dream. That had been the failure.

He slipped an arm under her shoulder. She turned her face into his chest and allowed him to rock her gently.

'A baby needs a father and a future,' she said drowsily.

'Yes.'

'I need you.'

'Yes.' Never had he understood her so well. She had given him everything, everything she had to give, and now she asked for just one small thing in return – his continued survival. She depended totally on it.

'It will be all right, Mary, I promise.'

She twisted in his arms, eyes closed. 'Do you, Michael? Do you promise?'

'I do.'

'You're not lying again?'

'No.'

Finally she drifted into sleep. He looked towards the window now black with night. Survival – such a hard thing to ask of a man to whom survival was a day-to-day business, and a night-to-night achievement.

Hugh Vesty, John Mernagh and Martin Burke came anxiously looking for him a short time later. He left with them, promising to return as soon as he could. Midge assured him she would come every day to keep an eye on Mary and help out.

When he reached the camp the men all congratulated him and started a celebration. Some were dismayed at his lack of enthusiasm and subdued manner, but then they whispered it must be because the child was not a son.

The moon glided slowly on its course through the night sky. In the rebel camp the music was merry, the jokes witty. But deep

402

in the wild fastness of the Glen of Imaal, the black-haired girl stood by her window, her sleeping baby in her arms, her dark eyes fixed in a melancholy stare on the dark outline of the hills, as if in a trance. Her body was rocking gently, her voice crooning softly.

> 'I know my love by his way of walking,
> I know my love by his way of talking,
> I know my love by his coat of blue;
> But if my love dies what shall I do?'

Chapter Twenty-Six

The ship creaked noisily. The wind wheeled down from the north, a bitter wind for late September. It breezed coldly over Wicklow and Wexford to the harbour of Passage in Waterford.

Groups of sombre and silent people watched from hilltop and harbour wall as the captain and crew of the ship busily shook out all their canvas to the wind, now favourable for sailing. There were three hundred men on board, tall and well-made young men from the counties of Wicklow, Wexford, Waterford, and Kildare. Country-bred boys with bodies lean and strong from swinging scythes in Irish grainfields, destined now to swing pickaxes in Prussia's mines.

Herr Schouler was very pleased with his latest selection. On the quayside he turned and said farewell most graciously to the government official sent down from Dublin Castle.

'You will speak, please, to Lord Castlereagh, and give to him my warmest thanks in the name of the King my master.'

'Of course, Herr Schouler.'

The two men smiled, inclined their heads in a bow of farewell.

The groups of sombre and silent people watched from hilltop and harbour wall until the ship sailed out of Passage, destined for Danzig, its hold packed with three hundred slaves, sold at so much a head by His Majesty's crown servants in Ireland.

'From now on,' Michael said softly, 'they will not speak in the language of the oppressor, for the Prussian slave-masters may understand. They will speak only in Gaelic. And those men who know only a few words of their native language because their masters at home forbade them to speak it will now spend every moment on every lapping wave learning, learning, learning.'

The men sitting around the table looked at him over the flickering flames of the candle.

'And how will that help them?' Hugh Vesty asked. 'Apart

from being able to console each other in Gaelic. Their hands and feet will still be chained.'

'It will give them, at least, freedom of speech, and within that freedom they may see and discuss opportunities that could effect their escape. And many will contrive their damnedest to escape. I am sure of that.'

Every man around the table wished them luck. There were six of them, staying at the house of a harbourer, John Martin of Kilranelagh, a land-steward of Mr Greene of Greenville House.

John Martin was at the table with them, playing cards and engrossed in the conversation of the rebels. He looked contented, for there was nothing he enjoyed more than sitting with men in a card game and listening to man-talk: politics, wars, cards, kings and jacks. He loved it.

Around the hearth his wife and three daughters sat gossiping as they sewed.

'Jacks are high,' Mernagh said, shuffling to deal again.

Hugh Vesty consulted a paper at his elbow, then looked at the proprietor of the house. 'And according to my notes, Martin old boy, that's three chickens and a hog that our Rory has won from you.'

'Three chickens and a hog? I'm down that much?' John Martin stared at Rory Derneen, whom he had always thought of as being something of a young gentleman – a rather pretty young gentleman – turned into a rebel. 'Where did you learn to play such sharp cards?' he demanded dourly.

Derneen smiled. 'In my cradle.'

Hugh Vesty grinned. 'That's right, Rory. I reckon you could win the crown off the King of England if he would just agree to a game.'

John Martin turned his gaze away from Derneen, and, for the umpteenth time that night, stared longingly at the bottle of red-sealed parliamentarian whiskey which he had been trying to win from the rebels for over an hour.

' 'Tis not a leprechaun's shilling,' he said to Derneen. 'It can be taken, even off a knave like you.' He rubbed his hands at the challenge. 'I'll win it if I have to stay up all night.'

'Good for you, if you can manage it,' Hugh Vesty said. 'We've had that bottle for months and not lost it yet.'

'Well tonight's the night,' Martin returned. 'I'll win it even if I have to lose my wife and daughters in the process.'

The men all glanced towards the four muslin-frilled females at the hearth.

'You may keep your wife,' Rory Derneen said. 'But if you lose your daughters, I put all three in my pocket and take them away with me. Is that agreed?'

John Martin nodded happily. 'Agreed!'

The three daughters, who had paused in their chatter to listen with heads bent, exchanged a silent and significant look with each other, then with their mother.

Mrs Martin snorted and called out brightly, 'Isn't that grand now? The head of our house thinks so highly of his womenfolk who wait on him hand and foot, that he's ready to lose them in a card game for a bottle of parliamentarian whiskey!'

'Oh, stop your yammering, woman,' her husband snarled irritably. ' 'Tis not a serious consideration or risk, for I intend to win. And as head of the house, let me remind ye that it is not your place to interrupt or comment on my conversation when I am in the company of men.' He glared at her coldly. 'Ye'll not do it again, woman. I forbid it!'

'Indeed now.' Mrs Martin laughed jocularly and looked at the younger men around the table. 'Boys-oh-boys, but that's a real man you have in your midst now,' she advised them. 'Listen well to him, and he will teach you how to give your women fair stimulation on ways to be loyal and loving to ye.'

Martin knew that she was taunting him, in front of the men too. In front of the *men* too! The shame of it almost choked him. He showed his teeth to her and was about to reply cuttingly, when a breathless youth hurried into the room from the hallway, and stood panting at the table beside Dwyer. Underneath his cloak the youth was dressed in the elegant livery of a footman.

'What is it?' Michael asked.

'Military operation in search of you, planned for tonight. The Thirty-eighth Regiment and a corps of yeos.'

'Are you sure?'

The youth nodded. 'I heard them talking to Mr Greenville.'

'What time do they plan to move?'

'Nine o'clock.'

Michael glanced at the clock on the dresser. 'It's that now.'

'I couldn't get away any earlier,' the youth explained. 'I had to pretend a gippy stomach and pretend I was about to get sick all over Mr Greenville's Indian hall carpet before I was ordered below stairs.'

'Did you hear their planned route of march?'

'No. But they feel sure you are hereabouts. You were spotted earlier by a yeo out riding.'

'Thanks, avic. We'll not forget this. Now high-tail it back before you are missed.'

The youth was gone in a flash of heels. Michael sat mentally working out all routes to the area.

'There is only one,' he said. 'One certain route whereby the enemy must come. But a few good men properly placed should cut the whole of them off.'

'And what shall I do?' John Martin asked.

'Get one of your daughters to tie you in a chair,' Michael replied. 'If things turn out badly, we forced ourselves on you against your will.'

Then the men stepped outside to the silence of the hills, a natural silence that had become their greatest ally, for it carried the sound of their whistling bird calls for miles. To the stranger the whistling would have genuinely sounded as those of birds, but to the rebels each wavering note carried a message.

Less than half an hour later, after a series of calls from restless nightingales and irritable owls, twenty more rebels had mustered to Michael's assistance in a field near Martin's house, where he instructed them in his plan, then divided them into four sections.

Three small parties hurried away, under the separate command of Hugh Vesty, John Mernagh, and Martin Burke.

Those men left behind followed Michael to an unfrequented avenue not far distant. Here he placed them in alternate positions behind the hedges, ensuring their cross-fire could not injure one another in the darkness which would soon fall.

He walked backwards up the avenue, his eyes roving the hedges to make sure all men were well enveloped in the cover of bushes and trees, stopping at the top of the avenue where Rory Derneen stood behind a hedge in the foremost sentry position.

Michael put a hand on his shoulder and moved him back a few paces. 'You stand well behind me,' he whispered. 'You are one man I don't want to lose.'

Surprise was evident on Derneen's face at this unexpected sentiment from the captain, who was now training his musket over the hedge and positioning himself for firing.

407

'And why would you not want to lose me in particular?' Derneen asked. 'As a matter of interest only.'

'Because if we lose you, avic, we lose a very good provider.' Michael smiled. 'Three chickens and a hog – and nearly three daughters!'

'Ach, I was only jesting about the daughters, I have my own darling to be true to,' Derneen said with a smile, then added seriously, 'but I'm surely going back to collect the chickens and the hog – fair play and fair game. They'll make us a nice supper one of these nights.' Then he also took up firing position and stood in readiness.

The night was cold, unseasonably cold, and darkness came. The two lines of men down the avenue waited in silence.

They had been waiting for over half an hour when Rory Derneen suddenly broke the silence.

'Isn't it a terrible thing they do to hogs, though?' he whispered. 'Gelding them and depriving them of a love life with some little piglet, and rearing them just for meat.'

Michael slowly turned his head and stared at Rory Derneen.

'Still,' Derneen sighed. 'I suppose that's how all animals finalise in the end. As meat. But the poor hog never gets a bit of happiness beforehand.'

'Shove the hog!' Michael rasped. 'Now whisht, and be ready as soon as you hear even the faintest footfall.'

Time passed slowly as they waited and, although it was extremely cold, not a whisper could be heard save the fluttering of the beech leaves along the hedgerows. They had taken their positions at half past nine – it was now one o'clock.

'Listen, Captain,' Derneen finally whispered. 'I don't think they're acoming. Not a hint of a footfall of any mortal, never mind the enemy.'

Michael made no answer just continued waiting for his enemy.

'Captain—'

'We wait!'

At two o'clock soft whistling was heard over the hills.

'Hear that?' Derneen whispered. 'Even Hugh Vesty thinks we should quit. And truth to tell, Captain, even if the enemy were to come along this freezing minute, my fingers are too cold to crook the freezing trigger. Same for all the other men, I expect.'

'Aye . . . perhaps you are right.'

408

Michael passed down the lines and across the fields and consulted with his principal men. When he returned, the men were all greatly relieved to hear the command to fall out being given. Shivering with cold from standing without motion for so long, they all headed for the fire at John Martin's house. Once inside, Michael withdrew from his haversack two bottles of poteen. A round of it quickly revived their flagged spirits and warmed their blood again, making them drowsy with tiredness.

John Martin was not a bit tired, he had fallen into a few hours' warm sleep while tied up in a comfortable chair near the fire. The females of the house were all tucked up in bed. Martin yawned, and smiled as he rubbed his arms and hands when Rory Derneen untied him.

'Shall we play the game now?' John Martin asked eagerly. 'For the bottle of parliamentarian?'

'Do I look fit and snappy for a card game?' Derneen cried irritably. 'Or do I look frozen stiff after standing like a stone statue in the cold night for over five hours?'

'You don't want to play cards then?' Martin queried.

'No!'

'Ah, come on, avico, just one game?'

'Go piss at a star!' Derneen yelled, then threw himself down on a fairly good chaise longue on the far side of the room. 'I'm jacked,' he moaned. 'I was up most of last night too. O God, I'm jacked.'

'Jacks were high, last we played,' Martin said dolefully, looking towards Michael and the others.

"Tis a big enough house you have,' Michael said. 'Can these men squeeze in here for tonight? They're tired and cold.'

'Sure they can, avic,' Martin replied. 'Let them spread themselves around any place they can find. Wait now, there's a few straw ticks in one of the bedrooms. I'll bring them out.'

The men fell down on the ticks and floor and were soon asleep. The candles were snuffed, the house fell into darkness and the four leaders sat tiredly around the glow of the fire, quietly discussing the false information.

'Not false,' Michael said. 'Not from him. He either got the night or the neighbourhood wrong.'

'Every minute out there was like an hour,' Hugh Vesty said. 'But my lads never made a word of complaint.'

The proprietor of the house stood looking at the four men talking quietly around the fire, and knew all chance of the card game was gone. 'Well now,' said John Martin, 'I think I'll just nip out and look at a star before I retire to bed. I'll be back in a—'

He was pushed back into the room by one of the two lads on outpost duty who rushed in from the hallway. 'They're coming, Captain, on yonder hills!'

The four leaders sprang to their feet, then had a little difficulty rousing some of the sleeping men who groaned at the thought of going out into the cold night again. Rory Derneen was sleeping so soundly, Michael had to shake him violently before getting a response.

'Ach, I'm near dead, Captain.'

'You will be if the yeos get you.'

Michael pushed John Martin back into his chair and swung the rope around him, tying him securely and yanking the knots tight. Then he went to the door and, standing by it, ordered every man out.

As the men quickly and quietly filed past him, Michael looked back into the room and saw Rory Derneen still sleeping soundly. He went over and jabbed him with the butt of his musket.

'Get up for your life, man.'

'Ah, Captain . . .' Derneen forced open a bleary blue eye. 'Leave me be. The sleep has such a lovely hold of me I can't seem to banish it.'

Michael pulled him to a sitting position and slapped him a stinging back-hander across the face. 'There now, has that banished it?'

'Oh it has, Captain, and my poor head along with it.' A few seconds later Derneen was running after the others, who only had time to take cover in the fields as a number of the yeomanry corps rode in their direction.

As soon as they were close enough, a rebel fired. A shout rose up from the yeos, and realising they had a welcoming committee, the whole party immediately turned and rode off at a gallop.

'Some military operation,' Rory Derneen yawned. 'One man was all it took to send them off. The rest of us could have stayed in slumber.'

'Back to your original defence positions!' Michael commanded.

Derneen moaned as the three other sections took off. 'Holy Saint Patrick,' he muttered, 'here we go again.'

410

'Derneen and I will try to skirmish,' Michael said to his men as they lined the avenue, 'but if they come agalloping, you know what to do.'

Michael turned to Derneen. 'Come along – I'm changing our position to a forward one.' He set off on a swift run beyond the avenue into a field where a very large rock stood perpendicular in the centre, between six and seven feet high, placed there for the cows to rub against. They took up positions either side of the rock and waited, raising their guns at the sound of a troop of horses, then took aim as the 38th came into view.

Derneen in his enthusiasm moved forward a few steps and slammed the trigger so the butt kicked against his shoulder.

'Rejoin,' Dwyer called to him, as superbly calm at the onset of battle as ever, even though the redcoats were now closing in, hammering forward in a gallop.

Michael let out a high vibrant whistling sound, and the three other sections under the command of Hugh Vesty, John Mernagh, and Martin Burke, appeared on different parts of the hills.

'Fire!' The four leaders yelled in unison. 'Fire, fire, fire, fire!'

Preconcerted, the rebels' fire came from four directions and the only line the military commander could form was a disorderly retreat, thinking they were completely surrounded by great numbers. 'There's hundreds of the bastards!' he roared, turning his horse around. 'Go! Go! Go!'

The drumming of hoofs died in the distance, complete silence fell over the land.

'Now run!' the leaders commanded. And the entire body of rebels took off in different directions, disappearing into the darkness of the night like fleeting ghosts.

Michael sprinted back towards John Martin's house with Rory Derneen ten paces behind. When they entered the house John Martin was still in his chair, tied up securely, his face questioning in the firelight.

Michael smiled, and flicked into his lap the bottle of sealed parliamentarian whiskey.

'For you, avic,' he said.

'Me?' Martin tried to struggle out of his binds. 'For me?'

'But mind,' Rory Derneen warned. 'I'll be back for the chickens and the hog. Fair play and fair game.'

And so they swiftly disappeared again, and when the military returned with reinforcements a short time later, all they found was a dark house surrounded by dark deserted fields and not a hint of a rebel in sight or earshot.

Captain Woollard crashed into the house, marched into the living-room and stood staring at the man tied in the chair, a bottle of whiskey in his lap.

'Was Dwyer here?'

'Rebels were here,' Martin confessed. 'Rebels for sure, but who they were I couldn't say, for isn't it just out of a coma I've come.' He nodded down to the bottle in his lap. 'They must have hit my head with that, knocked me clean out.'

He aimed an angry spit at the fire. 'Vicious bastards. They hate me just for being a loyal land-steward to Mr Greene of Greenville House.'

Woollard halted at that. He could not manhandle an employee of Mr Greene without possible consequences. And the dozy bloody clod truly looked as if he might have been clobbered.

'Would you be so kind as to untie me, sir?' John Martin asked politely.

'Go piss at the moon!' Captain Woollard shouted in furious frustration, and marched outside.

'I'd try for a star anyway,' Martin grumbled sulkily. 'If someone would just untie me.'

Minutes later his wife and three mobcapped daughters appeared in the doorway.

'Well don't just stand there like gawping hens,' Martin shouted. 'Cut my bonds and let me loose!'

'Of course we will, our manly hero!' Mrs Martin bustled gaily into the room. 'But not until we decide which one of us lowly females shall perform such a noble task.'

Martin pitched his brows in puzzlement as his daughters breezed in carrying a plate of scones, a jug of lemon water, and four glasses. 'What the blazes are you doing?' he cried.

The three daughters chuckled and sat around the table while Mrs Martin lit the candles, then sat herself and shuffled the cards.

'What are you doing?' Martin shouted again. 'Put down those cards and come and untie me.'

Mrs Martin ignored him and smiled at each of her daughters. 'Now then, darlings,' she said in a jocular tone, 'whoever has the highest score at breakfast time, wins the honour of deciding if and when we should untie him. Is that agreed?'

The daughters nodded happily. 'Agreed!'

'Good!' Mrs Martin levelled a long and wicked smile at her gaping husband as she dealt out the cards with an experienced hand.

'Queens are high,' she said.

Michael and Derneen were far away, running through the darkness together, then with a salute of farewell, split in opposite directions.

Michael headed towards the old couple's house where Mary was still living, quite content and blissfully drooling over Mary-Anne, who was now almost eight weeks old.

Mary's yearnings for him to spend more time with her and the child had conflicted with the need to keep his survival unendangered until a week ago, when he and Hugh Vesty had erected a false timber ceiling in the bedroom which would facilitate a quick hoist up to concealment in case of a random search.

The old couple made no objection, so pleased and rejuvenated were they by the girl and her child. They cared little about the risk and possible penalties of being discovered as harbourers. 'Sure we were as dull as dead anyway,' the old woman said calmly to Michael, 'before Mary came and brought new life into our existence.'

And so, when he tapped on the window, old Paudeen happily got out of his bed and let him in, then chained and rebarred the door and shuffled back to bed and sleep again.

The house was warm after the cold outside; the fires in living-room and bedroom were banked down for the night in a slow smoulder of little piles of glowing turf under a weight of smoored ashes.

In the bedroom the baby was sleeping soundly. Michael sat on the edge of the bed and began to undress. Mary stirred and stretched over to peer into the wooden cradle beside the bed, then moved back to make room for him.

'Have you met any trouble since I seen you last?' she whispered as always.

'Not a bit,' he said, and she questioned him no further. She had come to know that in his short times with her he sought only peace and a space of forgetfulness. She also knew that her gentleness and natural lack of aggression always lulled and restored him.

'Stay with me,' she whispered when they woke in the morning. 'Stay with me and Mary-Anne for a few unbroken days.'

She felt the sudden tension in his body, and sensing his refusal stopped his mouth with her own. As always, the efforts of his cold reason were washed away by the warm softness of her persuasion.

And he stayed, time and time again, as often as he could, for he truly adored her. He lied to her continuously, swearing he had glimpsed neither hilt nor hide of a redcoat in weeks, often only hours after escaping death by inches or minutes.

Although the daily round of her life was secret and hidden, Mary continued to be happy living with the old couple, and he was happy for her, agreeing she could stay for so long so no one suspected she was there. And in her new contentment, the nineteen-year-old mother bloomed with a new radiance. She was beautiful, he told her so every time he made love to her, which was often. So it was not too much of a surprise when shortly after Christmas, Mary discovered she was expecting another child.

Chapter Twenty-Seven

In the spring of the new century of 1800, Martin Burke married a Wicklow girl named Rachel, leaving John Mernagh as the only single man in the unbreakable foursome.

The militia and yeomanry forces still carried out occasional atrocities in Wicklow, and would have indulged in outright carnage had it not been for the fear of reprisals from Michael Dwyer and his small force. House burnings became less frequent, as did rape; for the militia knew that the reprisal for rape was certain death. Of all crimes, the one beyond all toleration to the rebels was the brutal violation of their girls and women.

And so life began to stabilise a little. Reports on Dwyer continued to flow into the secret service files at Dublin Castle. One report even admitted that he had put a halt to religious faction-fighting amongst the young men of the country, pointing out to those who indulged in it that, when real fighting was needed during the rebellion, they had been very noticeable by their absence.

The Castle officials carefully read every report on Dwyer, especially those sent in by Thomas King, the resident magistrate at Rathdrum, and the latest contained only bad news, as usual.

Be assured that from the day Dwyer appeared as a Rebel of note I have used every means I could devise to bring him in. But he is very cautious and 'tis almost impossible to get acquainted with his movements. Had I not a very particular Influence in another way over my spies (being a magistrate) I should often be inclined to think they were deceiving me, but as I have nothing definite to warrant that conclusion, I still have hopes.

While Dwyer remains in Imaal he thinks himself perfectly safe. The inhabitants make no secret of harbouring him – he walks about in open day, and every man watches for him by day as well as by night, and none would give the smallest information which could be used to any good effect. You know most of the men of the Rathdrum Troop – there is nothing they would not do or attempt, was there any prospect of getting Dwyer, but while the inhabitants of Imaal continue his Protection, nothing can be done there by any man from this side.

Captain Myers, the inspector of yeomanry, also sent a report on Dwyer to the Viceroy's military secretary, Colonel Little-hales, giving more or less the same information and concluding: '. . . the attachment and fidelity of the country people to him are without parallel.'

Michael and Hugh Vesty were strolling through the moonlight on the north side of the Keadeen Mountains. At length they stopped in the midst of the dark dense wilderness by a large rock next to an equally large bush of heath.

Michael turned his back to the rock, struck it with his heel, and called out a command. Less than a minute later, the bush of heath was lifted aside, quite detached from the surface, and a flickering gleam of a candle appeared.

The young man who held the candle let out a cry of greeting, then proceeded to light them through a passage leading into a large cavern inside the mountain which had its own natural airlets. The interior was afloat with candleglow and, as was usual in every cavern they used, the walls had been well lined with moss to protect them from loose clay and damp. There were twelve men inside and, as usual, their arms and accoutrements were hung up in military order.

Thomas Halpin was sitting near the rear of the cave playing cards with three men. He had stopped playing as soon as the command was heard and the lad had run to see who it was.

Now, as the two men walked into the interior, Halpin's eyes were riveted on the tall young man with black hair – the Reb Chief himself.

Halpin's heart began to thump wildly, a rush of perspiration came to his face. He had waited seven days for this meeting, seven long impatient days, and now the waiting was over. He took in every detail of Dwyer, his firm figure and manly appearance; and in that first instant, that brief instant when an image is flashed onto the mind in an indelible first impression, his description of Dwyer would have been: 'a military officer in civilian clothes'.

Then he noticed the Rebel Captain was viewing him with a curious eye and Halpin got to his feet, feeling slightly faint in case the decision would go against him.

James Doyle of Ballynecor, the man in command of this particular group, was talking to Dwyer and waving a hand towards Halpin as he explained who he was. Then Doyle beckoned Halpin over.

Halpin braced himself, walked across and stopped directly in front of Dwyer and Hugh Vesty.

'He wants to join us,' James Doyle said to Michael. 'He's been with us seven days now. I explained that the decision was yours. He has brought us two guns – a musket and a fowling piece – and a supply of powder.'

Halpin smiled, but Dwyer was still viewing him with a long, cool look. Michael saw before him a man of about thirty-eight years old and five foot six high, brown hair and blue eyes, long face, long sharp nose, round- and narrow-shouldered and weakly built.

'Why do you wish to join us?' he asked.

Halpin's lips had gone dry under the measuring gaze. James Doyle nudged him with an encouraging grin. 'He won't eat you or shoot you – just explain to him what you explained to us.'

Halpin nodded, then explained. He was a Munster man who had lived in Wicklow since 1798. He was first employed by Henry Allen of Greenan who owned a factory there which was burned by Joseph Holt because he suspected Allen was going to allow the military to use it as a barracks. After the rebellion Mr Allen had claimed over £5000 in compensation from the government for the loss of his factory, but Lord Cornwallis would not allow it after evidence was submitted by yeomen that Allen was himself a United Irishman. An awful unlucky man was Mr Allen – got done by both sides.

Halpin smiled, but when he saw Dwyer was still watching him coolly, he flushed and continued his explanation. When the rebellion had flared he had burned to join it, but not being a Wicklow man, and not being part of a 'young' set of lads, the opportunity never came to him; it was all the young men who were taking off in groups to join up.

He had then gone to work at the mansion of Mr Fawcett of Ballynockan near Rathdrum. Not long after going there he became friendly with the family of Brian Devlin of Croneybeag, them that are relations of the Dwyers of Eadstown, and the daughters had often discussed their first cousin Michael Dwyer, of whom they were very proud. Anne Devlin, in particular, spoke of him often.

Halpin paused, still no reaction from Dwyer, but Hugh Vesty Byrne asked indignantly, 'Did they not talk about me? I'm their first cousin too, you know.'

Halpin smiled, but before he could digress, Dwyer, in a neutral voice, told him to continue, and he quickly did.

He was employed as a gardener by Mr Fawcett, who was extensively engaged in planting his grounds with young trees and shrubs. He had liked working there, and did a fine job of it, but then Mr Fawcett discovered that he had allowed some rebels to shelter in the garden-house and he had almost lost his job. Only his promise never to do it again had saved him. But then . . . well, after that he had got into a bit of financial trouble, and ran up some debts in Mr Fawcett's name. When Mr Fawcett declared he knew nothing about the debts, investigations were made, and the bailiffs came to the garden-house to take him, but he fled. He didn't know where to go, what to do. Then a neighbour suggested: 'The best thing you can do is to go to the boys on the mountains.'

Halpin moved his hands in a pathetic gesture. 'And, well, I thought that would be great, because I always longed to be one of the boys. And, well, I hope now that you will decide to take me in . . . I'm prepared to fight if need be, do whatever task you may give me . . .' He flushed a deep embarrassed red. 'I know you may think I'm a bit old to be a rebel, but I hope that won't disqualify me.'

'Where did you get the guns and the powder?' Dwyer asked.

'I sneaked back during the night and stole them from Mr Fawcett,' Halpin said. 'I may as well be honest about it. But I felt I ought to bring something with me . . . as a contribution towards my food and that. I'm sure there are lots of ways I can help you, I can fix broken guns, I can cook, I can—'

Dwyer cut him short. 'I think we have your situation now.'

Halpin looked at him. 'You'll . . . take me in?'

'Well, I have little admiration for thieves and swindlers,' Dwyer said neutrally, 'but you did risk your employment by giving shelter to rebels. You may stay here with this group, for now.'

Thomas Halpin beamed, began to gush his thanks, but Dwyer was already walking away from him.

'Go back and play your hand,' James Doyle said, motioning his head towards the card-playing group Halpin had been sitting with. 'Looks like the men have held the game for you.'

Halpin flopped back down in delight amidst the three men, who slapped him on the back and told him they knew there would be no problem.

Thomas Halpin was so overjoyed with his luck that he won the next three games, but throughout his eyes kept straying to Dwyer, Byrne, and James Doyle of Ballynecor as they stood in a group quietly talking together. The three soon sat down on one of the straw beds and started up their own card game. Dwyer propped his back against the cavern wall, leaning languidly back from the hips as he surveyed his cards, eyes half closed as his lips moved in low conversation.

'Drink?'

A rebel had taken out a hip-flask and handed it to Halpin. 'Take a slug then pass it around, Tom,' he murmured.

Halpin looked at the flask, took a deep slug of the whiskey, passed it on. Then he laughed and said: 'Isn't it great all the same? Isn't it great!'

'The whiskey?'

'No – myself being one of the boys on the mountains.' He laughed again and thumped his knee. 'If my old father in Munster could only see me now – one of the rebel boys – he'd be right proud of me!'

The three rebels looked at him as if thinking his father must have very little to be proud of. ' 'Tis a hard life,' one murmured. 'You never know the day you might be killed. Are you playing your hand or what?'

'Eh? Oh, sure . . .' Halpin looked down to see he had three aces and two jacks. He smiled, and studying the face of each man surveying their cards, Halpin knew the game was his. Then he saw Dwyer and Byrne suddenly move to their feet and walk out of the cave with a salute of farewell to James Doyle of Ballynecor.

'Is the captain not lying with us here tonight?' Halpin asked curiously.

'Who knows?' a lad named Browne replied. 'He comes and goes and he doesn't trouble himself to confer with us. All we know is that he is the chief and he never lets us down and is never long acoming when we whistle a signal of trouble. Let's see you?'

Halpin laid down his cards and let him see – three aces and two jacks – a full house. 'Can you beat that?'

'Nah!'

Browne threw down his two pairs and Halpin collected the pennies. 'Well, I'm for a stretch,' he said. 'I'm done in. All that worry about whether the captain would take me in or not.'

He moved over to where the straw mats were laid out and threw himself down under a blanket. Shortly afterwards the entire group were lying down and most of the candles snuffed.

The lad on the straw mat next to Halpin was fussing with his blanket, the one named Browne who had given him the whiskey. 'When will the captain be back?' Halpin whispered.

'Who knows?' Browne shrugged. 'He usually lays at headquarters, or at some harbourer's house. But sometimes he does sleep here. He may be back in an hour, or not for a few days. Who knows? But if he needs us, he knows how to fetch us.'

'Listen, brother,' Halpin whispered. 'Have you e'er a drop of whiskey left in your flask?'

Browne fussed with his blanket again then handed over the flask. 'You may finish it,' he whispered.

'Thanks.' Halpin smiled, held up the flask. 'To the boys,' he whispered gleefully, then gulped and drained, wiped his mouth, and leaned closer to Browne. ''Tis from Wexford you said you come from, eh?'

'Aye, the rich corn country.'

'Have you been a rebel since the Ninety-eight?'

Browne chuckled. 'Man, I was born a rebel. I come from a long line of rebels. When my mother crooned me to sleep she always did so with a rebel song.'

'Why was that?'

'Curse you for an ignoramus.' Browne peered curiously at Halpin. 'Did you never learn your history down in Munster?'

'I never learned nothing much of anything,' Halpin confessed.

'Then I shall tell you my history for a start,' Browne whispered, rising on to his elbow and resting his head on his hand.

'Go ahead.' Halpin leaned closer until their heads were close together like whispering conspirators.

'From the days of Strongbow,' Browne said, 'my family lived at Rathronan Castle in Wexford. We were a grand family, a rich family. But when the Devil came to Ireland carrying a Bible in

420

his hand, we fought with the confederacy against Cromwell, and lost, and were dispossessed of our home, everything. In his victory Cromwell gave Rathronan Castle as a gift to one of his soldiers, a man called Ivory. And that man called Ivory very generously took the Brownes back on to the lands of Rathronan Castle – as labourers – as his tenants. *Le Brun* we were called then, until we were forced to anglicise to Browne.'

'That's a hell of a story,' Halpin whispered. 'But I've heard similar many times before, except few came from castles. But now, lookit here, old pal – I'll call you *Le Brun* if it'll make you feel any better.'

'Just call me in the morning,' Browne said, turning over and fussing with his blanket again. 'I'm a very heavy sleeper.'

Halpin lay back with one arm under his head and wondered where the captain and his second-in-command had gone so late. From the reaction of the other men, it appeared as if those two often drifted in and out of the various camps, although Halpin only knew about this particular camp. The main camp, the one they called 'headquarters' could not be told to him until he had been sworn in under oath – as one of the United boys.

One of the United boys! He smiled to himself and snuggled down to sleep.

The following day James Doyle kept Thomas Halpin busy cleaning guns while others went out shooting game in the high woods of the mountain.

In the early afternoon John Harman came in, and after being introduced to Thomas Halpin and shaking his hand, Harman said to Doyle: 'I've just received intelligence that some of the yeos were heard swearing this morning that as soon as the day is done, they will go tonight and shoot the parish priest of Imaal.'

'Bastards,' Doyle muttered. 'We'll have to send a detachment there so.'

A great idea suddenly came to Thomas Halpin. He jumped to his feet. 'I say, boys, why don't we go tonight and shoot their minister Weekes?'

John Harman swung round and glared dangerously at Halpin. 'I'll blow the head off any man that injures Reverend Weekes.'

'But . . .' Halpin looked stunned, 'but . . . wasn't it Reverend Weekes's son that brought down Andrew Thomas with a shot in the leg?'

'No mind about what his son does,' Harman snapped.

'Reverend Weekes is good and decent. So you better keep your stupid tongue in your stupid mouth, man!'

'Sorry, sorry, didn't mean it really,' Halpin muttered weakly, and slouched back to his guns and rags. He'd only been trying to talk and act like his idea of a rebel.

Halpin was relieved when John Harman eventually left, and delighted when Dwyer and Hugh Vesty came in close on evening time. Neither seemed to notice him sitting in the corner, so busy were they organising the men in low voices and giving them orders of some kind.

Then Dwyer strode over to him. 'Now you – Thomas Halpin.'

'Aye,' Halpin jumped to his feet, surprised that the captain had remembered his name.

'How well can you cook?' Dwyer asked.

'Quite well.'

'Good. Now here's what I want you to do. About two miles from here is a small crevice. I'll tell you in detail where to find it. Inside you will find, wrapped in a tablecloth, a large joint of beef and some other provisions. I'm told it is there now. Collect them, then come straight back and start cooking.'

'Aye.' Halpin nodded. 'But what about the lad who normally does the cooking?'

'No.' Dwyer shook his head. 'Every single one of these lads is needed somewhere else tonight with Hugh Vesty. And I need this cavern cleared. There will just be myself here all night.'

'Just you here all night?' Halpin could not believe it. 'Just you – alone? And me?'

'Just me and you,' Dwyer confirmed, then smiled. 'And two men coming down from Dublin to talk business. 'Tis them I want you to cook a palatable meal for. And while they are here, will you do guard duty outside? You can sleep when they've gone.'

'I'll do whatever you say, Captain,' Halpin snapped keenly. 'Now where do I find the beef and stuff?'

Dwyer grinned at his keenness and patted his shoulder. 'Not yet, wait till I see to these lads and then I'll come back and tell you where.'

Halpin waited around as each man collected his gun and took off with Hugh Vesty. Suddenly there was only himself and the captain left inside the cavern. 'Come on, avic,' Dwyer said urgently. 'The city boys will be here in a few hours and I want to have a sleep before they come, as I shall probably be up all night discussing business. And, man, I am already very tired.'

'Then you go ahead and have a sleep,' Halpin said kindly. 'But now listen . . . they've taken all the guns. I'll need a gun if I'm going abroad.'

'And maybe get stopped for being armed?' Dwyer laughed. 'Are you crazy? Even the yeos know that no one goes sporting at night. Now look, the reason I've picked you to go down there is because you're not known as a rebel, and therefore not likely to be followed back.'

'What about when I stand guard duty? I'll need a gun then, won't I?'

'I'll give you one of mine.'

'Oh, right, right.'

Halpin listened carefully and nodded several times as he was given instructions. Then Dwyer escorted him to the entrance of the cavern. 'It will be dark when you get back,' he said, 'and I'll be sleeping. But if you kick hard against the rock it will echo through and wake me, and I'll come to light you in with a candle. All right?'

'Don't you worry about a thing, Captain.' Halpin's thin lips snapped out every word like a command. 'You just rest and leave it to me. But listen . . . the boys said only a captain or higher could do it officially, so will you take the time to swear me in as a United man when I get back?'

Dwyer gave him a long measuring look. 'I'll think about it while you're gone. Now go.'

The bush of heath was placed firmly back in position and Halpin ran off like a bandy rabbit scurrying after a fieldmouse.

Darkness had well fallen when Halpin returned to the cavern, protesting frantically as he stepped into the interior lit by a single candle.

'I tell you he was here! I swear it! He was planning to settle down for a sleep!'

Captain Woollard peered around the cave which had been stripped bare – no straw mats, no moss on the walls, no remains of a fire, nothing to indicate it had ever been used by anybody as a shelter.

The cave was filled with redcoats. Halpin staggered amongst them with his hands to his dazed head. 'The fire was there . . . the straw mats were along here . . . that's where Dwyer sat playing cards . . . the moss, where in damnation is the moss?'

'And where's the bush of heath that was supposed to be at the entrance?' Woollard demanded. 'That's also gone – if it was ever there!'

'But why would I lie?' Halpin cried. 'It took me weeks to wangle my way through the people and get to this small group. Then seven days I lay here waiting for my prize. Seven days when I was kept a prisoner and not allowed outside again until Dwyer had given me the once over. The only times they let me out was to relieve myself, and even then I had a guard on me.'

'And after all that,' Woollard said sneeringly, 'Dwyer comes along, a man with five hundred jinglers on his head, and tells you that he's going to be all alone and sleeping, with no body-guards nearby – then sends you out with that valuable infor-mation. I knew you were lying!'

'But he was here, I swear it! They were all here – Hugh Vesty Byrne, John Harman, James Doyle, eleven other rebels.'

'No rebels were here,' Woollard snapped. 'You've just wasted our time to justify your pay.'

He turned to go, taking the candle with him, and in the swift beam Halpin's eyes noticed something on the floor in the far corner.

'Wait! Wait!' He darted over to the corner and felt blindly, then clutched. 'Wait! I've found something that'll prove they were here!'

Captain Woollard was standing at the entrance with the candle still in his hand when Thomas Halpin scrambled towards him and held out a book. Looking greatly surprised, Woollard passed the candle to Halpin, who held it up while the captain read the title, opened the front cover and jerked his head down to peer at a name written in ink on the flyleaf – *Hugh Vesty Byrne*.

'What's it say?' Halpin whispered, peering also, but totally illiterate.

Captain Woollard suddenly bashed Halpin's head with the book. 'You fool! The bastards were here right under your nose, but it was you they smelled!'

Halpin dropped the candle as the book whacked him left and right. He let out a cry and protected his head with his hands until Woollard began kicking him, then Halpin started to run.

When the redcoats had scrambled back down the craggy slopes and out of sight, the fourteen rebels standing motionless behind the trees and watching, stepped out and began their rugged journey through the darkness over to headquarters on Lugnaquilla.

'God, I'm sorry about the book,' Hugh Vesty said to Michael. 'I took it out last night to read before I slept – and forgot it when you suggested checking Halpin out. I picked it up again today, but left it down while I was stripping the moss.'

Michael shrugged. 'No matter. At least we found him out for sure. Pity about the cavern though. It was a good and comfortable hideout. We'll not be able to go anywhere near it again.'

'What made you suspect him?' Browne asked.

'His name, as soon as I heard it,' Michael answered. 'Yesterday the new list of "Rebels Still in Arms on the Wicklow Mountains" was published. Fifty-four names were on it. And the last name was Thomas Halpin.' He looked in astonishment at the group of men walking each side of him. 'Now isn't that a funny thing? The government knew Halpin had joined the rebels even before we did!'

'We reckon he must have expected to hang around for a while,' Hugh Vesty said. 'Sifting out whatever information he could – and being a listed rebel, harbourers and picquets would trust him. But when he got his chance at the captain so soon, he couldn't resist it.'

'The blatherumskite,' Browne said. 'Is that where you went last night? To check him out?'

'Aye,' Michael said. 'We went across Wicklow to my cousin Anne Devlin at Croneybeag, one mile from Rathdrum. She warned us off Halpin straight away. She's convinced he is a spy and informer, employed by Thomas King. Her younger brother, Little Arthur, has spotted Halpin slinking into the magistrate's house a number of times.'

'Two shillings a day, Mr Halpin!' Thomas King declared. 'That is the price we agreed. A very generous amount if I may say so. And that is the price Dublin Castle allows me for you.'

'Bedamned to the Castle then!' Halpin cried angrily. 'I'm now a marked man, a known informer. The risk I took is worth more than two shillings a day!'

'And that two shillings a day will continue to be paid only as long as you remain useful,' King informed him coldly. 'And how, I wonder, may you continue to be useful to me now? Now that you have become a known informer?'

The implication of the magistrate's words knocked Halpin's

aggression clean out of him. He fidgeted about and scowled, then looked at King sharply. 'What are you saying?'

'Simply that you will have to change your occupation. From a spy – to a prosecution witness.'

'Eh?' Halpin stared at him as if he was mad. 'A witness in open court!'

'It is your choice, Mr Halpin. You may remove to the barracks and live there as a protected witness on a very generous allowance of two shillings a day. Or you may go your own road and take your chances with a population that favours the rebels . . . a population that will shortly know how you tried for Dwyer's capture.'

There was a silence. Halpin slouched over to the window, gnawing his nails as he looked out.

'I can assure you, Mr Halpin,' said King in a gentle tone, 'that you will not be harmed while under my protection.'

Halpin slowly turned to him, all the blood seemed to have drained out of his face.

Thomas King threw a glance at the clock on the mantel. 'Come along,' he said brusquely, 'it's almost my breakfast time. If you are to serve as a prosecution witness we will need accused men in the dock.'

He adjusted his wig and sat down in the chair at his desk. 'Dwyer,' he snapped, lifting his quill. 'What did you manage to learn about him?'

'Nothing,' Halpin muttered, 'I could learn nothing about him at all.'

King looked up, disbelieving.

' 'Tis the truth!' Halpin insisted. 'Even his men seem to know only what they see of him, when they see him. Dwyer confides in nobody save a small group of his principal men.'

'Does he look like the two pictures drawn of him by the artists?'

'Well, neither picture looks anything like the other,' Halpin grunted, 'and neither picture looks anything like Dwyer. Not as I saw.'

Thomas King laid down his quill and folded his arms on the desk. 'You are beginning to spoil my appetite for breakfast, Mr Halpin. You really will have to do better than this if you wish to secure my protection.'

'I'm only telling you what I saw and heard,' Halpin said defensively.

'And so far you've heard nothing worth a spit!' King cried. 'And there's still the matter of the debts you ran up in Mr

Fawcett's name, don't forget those! Even the mildest court in England would give you the rope or life in Botany Bay for such a crime – but we in our benevolence are giving you two shillings a day!'

'Yes, sir,' Halpin stammered nervously, 'and very kind it is too, but—'

'It's Dwyer's woman that interests me now,' King snapped. 'I'm intrigued to know if you heard her name mentioned?'

'I did!' Halpin brightened. 'I heard her name was Mary.'

'Mary what?'

'Just Mary, I heard no other.'

'Good God, man!' King's fist banged down on the desk with impatience. 'Every second Catholic girl in Ireland is called Mary. What else did you hear about her?'

'Only that she's a sweet-looking wench and Dwyer would kill any man that looked crooked at her. So she's obviously more to him than just a whore to lay with. I did ask her surname but they freezed up as if they had said too much already.'

'They consider her a dangerous subject for idle discussion?'

'You've hit on it exactly!' Halpin nodded his head vigorously.

'Is she from County Clare, did they say?'

'They didn't say,' Halpin admitted lamely.

The magistrate pulled a cambric handkerchief from the pocket of his morning robe and dabbed at the exasperation on his forehead. 'Let us forget Dwyer's whore for now,' he said tiredly, 'and move on to any other snippet of information you might have overheard.'

'I did hear one interesting thing,' Halpin said suddenly. 'It seems a letter was sent down to Dwyer from Dublin, signed by many names and assuring him of continued support as long as he stays out and free. And with the letter was a sum of money.'

'You pox-faced wretch!' King cried angrily. 'Why did you not tell me this in the first place? Did you hear any of the names on the letter?'

'No particular name was mentioned as I heard. Only that the letter came from the Dublin Executive Committee of United Irishmen.'

'Good God!' King sat back and stared at the ceiling. 'Good God!' he said again, then lowered his eyes to Halpin. 'The twelve men in the cave? Do you know their names? Could you identify them if they were brought in?'

'I most surely could,' Halpin drawled, complacent now he

realised he had given some valuable information which would ensure his maintenance and protection. 'I could name and identify every one of the bastards.'

'Then, Mr Halpin, I think we should get you to a safe place of concealment until you are needed as a crown witness.' King moved to his feet and the window. Halpin watched him as he scanned the garden.

'Dublin, I think,' King said at last. 'As soon as we have breakfasted I will arrange a carriage and military escort to take you to Dublin Castle, where you will be placed under the protection of Major Sirr, the Chief of Police, until you are needed back in Wicklow.'

Some weeks later, Thomas King sat down in his study and wrote another report to Dublin Castle, full of his usual bad news.

Notwithstanding that His Majesty's troops are diligently in quest of him, Dwyer remains safe and his haunts are so very secret it is next to impossible to find him out. I am confidentially informed that every man watches danger for him, and all the people on that side of the mountains insist on saluting Dwyer as he walks about in broad daylight, continually side-stepping the militia.

All the men from the Rathdrum Yeomanry Troop are well known and should any of them venture over there in disguise – and in no other way could Dwyer ever be got, except by previous and certain information where he could be met on his own by a strong party – such disguised person would instantly be found out by Dwyer, as happened recently. Now a suspicious stranger only has to appear in the vicinity of Imaal and the whistling and bird calls echo over the hills and throughout the glen like a concerto.

Part Two

Twenty men from Dublin town,
   At night gathered round the fire
Brimming poteen we toss down
   To our Captain, Michael Dwyer.

Sláinte, Michael, brave and true,
   Then there rings a wild 'Hurrah!'
Also we drink, dear land, to you,
   Eire, sláinte geal go bráth.

'Twenty Men from Dublin Town', Arthur Griffith

Chapter Twenty-Eight

In the old couple's house, on a warm night in the month of July, the gentle white-haired old woman said her last rosary and drifted away in sleep to the Land of the Ever Young. Her husband, Paudeen, was heartbroken; as was Mary.

Midge Mahoney came and took her grieving old uncle back to her own house with her for a while, but all knew he would not last long without his soul-mate.

Michael took Mary home to Knockandarragh, and at the height of summer in late August, John Doyle breathlessly climbed the steep ravines and gave him the news that Mary had gone into labour.

Six men were collected to act as picquets outside the house at Knockandarragh. When Michael entered the house he found Mary's parents babbling and flapping excitedly and his mother the only sensible person present. She came towards him with a smile.

'You have a son,' she said.

Before Michael could reply, a strong hand thumped him hard on the back and almost sent him toppling off his feet. 'I have a grandson!' William Doyle roared. 'Are you not going to congratulate me?'

Michael shrugged his shoulders back into place and turned towards the man who was grinning at him like a horse yawning. 'Congratulations,' he said, then whisked over to the hallway which led to the bedrooms. At Mary's door he hesitated, then slowly creaked it open.

She was bright-eyed and flushed and he saw straight away that she was as giddy as a girl in her first romance. 'A boy!' she cried. 'A darling little boy. Come and see!'

Once again she held out the child to him and he took the small bundle in his hands. His eyes gloated over the sleeping face, the tiny clenched fists.

'I think he knows he is born in Ireland,' Michael finally

whispered. 'Look at his little hands, all clenched and set up for battle.'

'Isn't he bonnie though?' She couldn't resist whipping the baby back and tucking him into her once more. 'What would you like to name him?'

'John,' he said. 'After my own daddy.'

The door opened and William Doyle poked his head inside, searching out another look at his grandson and grinning stupidly. Someone yanked him away.

'John William,' Mary whispered. 'And say the two names or he'll be hurt.'

When darkness came the house in Knockandarragh was full with people. Michael's father was quietly delighted as he looked on his first grandson, but William Doyle was still loudly exclaiming his ecstasy to all who would listen.

The two grandmothers were busily handing round plates of food. Michael dispatched his brother-in-law to fetch John Cullen. When the old man arrived clutching his fiddle, and saw the child, he nodded his head up and down.

'A lad, as I prayed it would be. Amen, I say, for a prayer answered, Amen.' His eyes misted. 'John, is it? Troth, but I never dreamed youse would name him for me.' Neither Michael nor Mary had the heart to correct him.

In the living-room, Michael passed money to Mary's brother and sent him up to the tavern at Donard for some bottles of refreshment. When John Doyle returned, he was followed into the house only seconds later by Pat O'Riordan, who got very excited when he saw the whiskey.

'Is he still as mean as ever?' Michael whispered to William Doyle.

'Mean? That man wouldn't spend Christmas! But we must take our friends as we find them. And Pat is the best friend I ever had.'

'You could do worse than O'Riordan,' Michael supposed.

'Not much,' Doyle said gloomily. 'But still, no matter. My grandson is born and I want you all to celebrate with me!'

'O'Casey the blacksmith sends his felicitations,' John Doyle said, 'but he said he couldn't do the walk down here on account of the weakness in his legs.'

'I know that weakness,' William Doyle grunted. ' 'Tis called poteen.'

'He gave me a present for Mary.' John pulled out a twist of

paper from his pocket and laid it on the table. Mrs Doyle opened the paper and stared at the contents in puzzlement. 'What is it – tobacco?'

' 'Tis two ounces of leaves from China that make a drink called *chah*,' John told her. 'O'Casey got it from a smuggling man who said it makes a drink like the tea from India the gentry drink, but is not at all like our own and much better.'

'Oh, musha, I'll make some up for Mary so.'

'Huh!' William Doyle cried. 'I'd be whipped a cripple before I'd drink any *chah* from China.' He lifted a bottle of whiskey. 'Now then, who's for a drop of the right stuff?'

Hugh Vesty, Mernagh, and Burke, took it in turns with the three others to do outpost duty while the occupants of the house drank the health of the baby. Michael sat holding his one-year-old daughter, Mary-Anne, who was yawning tiredly after the excitement of cooing at all these strange people.

'Faith and troth,' Cullen declared, 'they say when a man and a maid get wed they become one, but from what I've observed they usually become three or four or more.' He stuck his fiddle under his chin and before long a party was in full swing.

Mary did not even hear the music, so enchanted was she with her son. She scarcely heard her mother enter the room. 'Drink this,' Mrs Doyle said. 'It's been sent to you from China all the way and is supposed to make you feel as fit as a young war horse.'

Mary almost choked on her first taste; became distressed almost to tears when her mother kept insisting she drink more. ' 'Twill poison me!' she cried.

'Hush now, pet,' her mother soothed. 'If you upset yourself you're liable to sour the sweet milk in your breasts. I'll bring you a nice cup of our own tae mór.'

Outside the door Mrs Doyle took a taste of the China *chah* and thought it tasted damned nice. She decided to make some more up for the neighbour-women who had come acalling, and bring Mary a cup of the usual herbal beverage made from the leaves of Ireland's own tae mór plant and chamomile.

When she returned to the living-room Mrs Doyle found her husband and Pat O'Riordan dancing together, clapping their hands and hopping and jigging, moving far apart then towards each other with heads down like two charging bulls. Mrs Doyle laughed at their antics, and sent up a 'Whoosh!' when it seemed the two might crash.

At the end of the dance William Doyle mopped his forehead and was moving towards the bottles when he noticed Michael's gun leaning against the wall. He frowned and turned to his son-in-law.

'You haven't been shooting any ducks with that, have you?'

'Ducks?'

'Aye, male ducks – drakes.'

'No, why?'

'Have you not heard about the curse?' Doyle shook his head gravely. 'Oh 'tis all around the country about some woman named Nell Flaherty who's put a terrible curse on whoever it was killed her pet drake. Wait now and Pat'll tell you. He knows it by heart.'

Doyle turned and put a hand over the glass journeying up to O'Riordan's mouth. 'Pat, the curse that woman Nell Flaherty made, how did it go?'

O'Riordan paled and shuddered. 'Oh, wisha, 'tis a terrible curse for any woman to send forth of a day. And God help the man it falls upon. The travelling man who brought it to us in the tavern, a man from Limerick way, said this woman Nell marched right into the centre of the village and stood for all to see and hear as she threw the curse to the wind.'

'Tell him how it goes, Pat.' Doyle was getting impatient, he reached for a drink. 'Tell this son-in-law of mine.'

O'Riordan, shivering nervously, cleared his throat and recited the woman's curse as she had shouted it and he had been told it.

'May his pigs never grunt! May his cat never hunt!
May a ghost ever haunt him at dead of night!
May his hens never lay! May his horse never neigh!
May his goat fly away like an old paper kite!
May he swell with the gout! May his teeth all fall out!
May he roar, yell and shout with the pain of headache.
May his hair stand like horns and his toes with many corns,
The monster that murdered Nell Flaherty's drake!'

'Listen to that now.' Doyle looked warningly at his son-in-law. 'See what could befall you if you don't mind whose duck you're shooting.'

'A terrible curse like Nell's could befall you,' O'Riordan whispered gravely.

'Sure now,' said Michael calmly, 'I always heard that a curse comes home to roost on the person that made it.'

Doyle and O'Riordan stared at him, then stared at each other with mouths open. As big as they were, they looked like two children who had just had their favourite party game spoiled.

Michael looked with innocent eyes from one to the other. 'Isn't that what they say? A curse always comes home to roost.'

'Well now . . .' said Doyle, then frowned at O'Riordan.

'Oh, well now . . .' said O'Riordan, then frowned at the floor.

Michael spied his mother coming into the room carrying a bundle of swaddling flannel. He moved away from the two confounded men and asked her: 'Is Mary left on her own?'

'Aye, but don't think of going in to her. The baby is changed and fed, Mary-Anne is asleep, and Mary also needs to sleep now. Leave them be.'

He did not argue with her, just nodded, but continued loitering by the door as she moved into the crowded living-room. He looked towards Doyle and O'Riordan, who were still frowning, as if trying to decide whether the curse would go where intended, or come home to roost. Then, panting with the effort of thought, both reached for a drink. They drank half a bottle between them in a few minutes.

Seeing his mother in deep conversation with Mrs Doyle, Michael moved to open the door and was about to slip out to the hallway leading to the bedrooms when O'Riordan suddenly cried: 'My soul from the devil! But I have it – I have the answer! Where are you, Dwyer?'

Michael turned and glared venomously at O'Riordan.

From his seat on the settle, O'Riordan smiled back at him triumphantly. ' 'Tis said that only the curse of the *innocent* brings no evil on those that utter it.'

William Doyle was astounded. He took O'Riordan by the hand and began to praise him. 'Oh, begor, you clever varmint, but aren't you right! And Nell Flaherty and her drake were innocent. So the curse stands.'

O'Riordan nodded. 'It does! Horns and corns and swelling with gout and teeth dropping out – the lot!'

Doyle looked over his shoulder and with a smirk of satisfaction regarded Michael. 'Well that settles it. There's no more to be said.'

'No more to be said,' O'Riordan repeated.

Then the two of them, almost in a state of delirium, laughed and knocked back their drinks.

'Now then, Michael . . .' Doyle cried, smirking smugly at his empty glass. 'You thought you were right but you were wrong and no hard feelings, boy. And to prove I hold nothing against you, one way or another, I'm inviting you to join me in a long and hearty drink, to celebrate the birth of my grandson.'

O'Riordan nudged Doyle, who looked around, and saw Michael was gone.

'Upon my soul!' Doyle cried. 'He was nippy enough with his mouth when trying to confuse me about the curse, but where is his mouth now that I want to drink with him?' He stared at O'Riordan. 'Isn't he the strangest son-in-law for a man to have, Pat?'

'He is,' O'Riordan agreed good-naturedly. 'He is indeed.'

A candle was flickering inside a table-lantern when Michael entered the silent bedroom. He saw that she was fast asleep, the baby in the rocker beside her. A drawer had been made into a bed for Mary-Anne, his best-beloved child.

He pulled the chair nearer to the bed and sat for a time watching the girl in the bed. The memory of her sudden brainstorm after the first birth was still clear in his mind.

The music and gaiety in the living-room went on. There was joy in the house, the joy that always comes with the birth of a child. Only this bedroom was dim and silent.

From the living-room he could hear William Doyle singing loudly and passionately. The words were blurred at the edges from drink, but he recognised the song as Doyle's favourite, 'My Love from Aughavannagh'. It had forty-two verses, even more when you counted the verses Doyle made up and added on. He loved the song and his singing of it so much that he couldn't bear it to end.

Michael sat back in the chair, deciding to remain where he was. The candle was guttering low. In a kind of languorous ecstasy he sat watching them sleep, his wife, his daughter and his son . . . his son.

He looked at the little chubby form of Mary-Anne in the bed-drawer beside the cradle. She was his first-born, his delight, his pride – but his son was his hope. Maybe by the time he had grown to a young man, things would have changed for the better in Ireland.

At the first threads of dawn, his son whimpered, then cried hungrily. Mary stirred and opened her eyes, and, seeing her husband sitting there, smiled knowingly and assured him, 'I feel fine.'

When Michael finally returned to the living-room it was still full with people. Cullen was slumped in sleep on a chair in the corner, his fiddle under his chin. Mrs Doyle was still surrounded by neighbour-women at the table, holding court around a pot of the China tea and all praising it to glory while bidding to best each other with horrific tales of their own childbearing days.

William Doyle had dissipated all his earlier horse-like energy. He sat scowling at his son-in-law like a peevish bulldog.

' 'Tis unmanly and unnatural and uncalled for,' he growled. ' 'Tis the most unmanly thing I ever knew of. 'Tis shame you have brought on the surname of my grandson!'

'What grieves you now?' Michael asked, moving over to the hearth where a neighbour-woman was lifting hot griddle breads off the gridiron. As he helped himself to one, William Doyle stretched his legs and folded his arms and enlarged upon his grievance against his son-in-law.

' 'Tis shame you have brought on me too. Shame that'll be known all over Wicklow by nightfall. These neighbours of mine will see to it. Troth, scandal travels faster than the horses on a mailcoach! And the scandal will be that Michael Dwyer, the sire of my grandson, chose to spend the entire night in a room with a woman and two bairns instead of acting like a man and staying with the men and celebrating with a toss of the right stuff.'

He bowed his head and gloomed. 'Faith, but I'll never live it down. A son-in-law as unsociable as an Englishman. And what have you been doing all this time, may I ask?'

'Sitting in the dark,' Michael answered truthfully.

Doyle winced at the shame of it. He sat looking at the ground for several moments, then shrugged and muttered dolefully, 'I used to know another man who preferred sitting in the dark instead of jollying with the men, but he was a lame monk.'

Pat O'Riordan tittered.

Doyle jerked round. 'Whát are you tittering about, you great spawn of a beggar-woman.'

O'Riordan tittered again, swayed backwards and forwards,

then rolled on to the floor and lay unconscious in a blissful drunken stupor.

'Now there's a man who knows how to celebrate!' Doyle cried admiringly. ' 'Tis him should have been my son-in-law!'

'Let's go,' Michael whispered to John Mernagh, 'while Doyle is searching for another drink. I think he intends to join O'Riordan and drink his grievance into a coma.'

As they slipped out, Mernagh looked back at O'Riordan's prostrate form. 'That man shouldn't drink,' he said. 'There's two essential rules to drinking and O'Riordan follows neither of them – pay your share for it and know how to carry it.'

Michael shrugged. 'God help him though, alone and lonely as he is. The drink is killing him but he'd be dead without it.'

Outside in the field he saw his mother perched on a stool milking a red cow. As he approached her, he got the scent of the pure sweet milk as it fell like a shooting waterfall into a whirlpool of white froth. The cow stood in docile contentment, almost asleep with the pleasure of being milked by a gentle-fingered, crooning woman.

'This poor girl was crying piteously to be milked,' his mother said, looking up. 'I've decided to make myself useful and stay around here for a day or two. That lot in there are too busy enjoying themselves to remember that work on a farm never stops. How is Mary now?'

'She says she feels fine.'

'Well, I reckon she'll need some help too. I'll go in to her shortly.'

He rubbed the cow's forehead. 'Has Daddy gone home?'

'Aye, he said he'll speak to you about the boy in his own time.'

Michael was disappointed. 'Has he been gone long?'

'Since the fifty-fourth verse of "My Love from Aughavannagh". He couldn't cope with another line of it. Doyle didn't even see him go, so tight were his eyes shut with the ecstasy of his own voice. I couldn't make out a word he was singing.'

They smiled together, then she bowed her head, crooning again, her fingers had never stopped working as she talked, the milk kept falling as sweetly as a lullaby.

'I'll be off so.' He patted the cow's side, then slyly brushed a tender finger against his mother's cheek before striding on towards the trees where his men stood silently waiting for him.

When they returned in a quiet fashion to the camp, the rest of the men were awake and waiting. Many came forward to greet him, but seeing his expressionless face, none dared to ask the result.

Michael gazed around at the men, then his face split into a wide smile and his fist shot victoriously into the air.

'*I have a son!*'

The men roared their cheers, and the real celebration began.

The afternoon came on mild and beautiful; but all decided it was time to send for the moonshine.

The detachment of men sent out for the purpose came back carrying two kegs and were accompanied by the man who had distilled it. He was a fine big tall man and strode along as if he was the king of his trade. Not only did he make the most exquisite brew ever tasted, he knew every historical detail about the making of it since way back when:

'Our Viking invaders who came around eight hundred and six and stayed awhile, they were the men who taught us the secret of brewing the magical nectar,' he told the men sitting around him and sipping.

'I know all about them,' Hugh Vesty the history expert said. 'It was them who named our own Wicklow for us – Wyking alo – which means Viking meadow. Though how you can call these uplands a meadow is beyond me!'

'And it was the Danes who taught us how to put the white froth on a drink,' the distiller-king said, returning to the subject of his own expertise. 'But there was one drink the Danes made, the secret ingredient of which no one could get out of them – a drink as pure and clear as a golden pond, with the pure white head on it – heather beer.'

The men all looked at each other; none had heard of it.

'And so the time came when there was only one Danish chieftain left on these shores,' the distiller-king continued, 'the others all having been routed by the Celts. And it was put to this last remaining chieftain, very nicely, that his life would be spared if he told the secret ingredient of the *beer* drink. But, begor, he died rather than tell it!'

He sat back and blithely regarded the mesmerised men. 'Indeed! Many suspected the secret ingredient was heather, so it was called heather beer, but none learned how to make it, not like the Danes, so the people decided, ah well, they may as well forget it and concentrate on malting the barley.'

The flute which had been crooning softly was now joined by a happy fiddle and the clinking of spoons; a bodhran began to thump, thump, thump and the music turned from easy to itchy.

The distiller-king didn't even hear the music, his mind intent on the perfection of his brew. 'Now then,' he said, finishing his drink and moving to open a second cask, 'I want you lads to taste and give your opinion on this particular keg. It has a quality and texture so fine and excellent, I am prepared to stake my reputation on it.'

Michael was smiling and looking across the camp. 'If it's all the same to you, avic, I think we'll get the Dublin boys' opinion on it first. As you can see from the way they're dressed, their velvet coats and breeches and all, many were fine bucks of the gentry before they joined us here.'

The Dublin men were clapping in time to the music; they stopped when Michael approached with a grin and the keg.

'Moonshine, boys. Its maker would be greatly obliged for your verdict on its quality.'

'Sure we'll give it a try anyway,' the Dubs agreed pleasantly.

When it was poured they sat studying the colour of it in their wooden cups. 'This moon looks mighty pale in the face to me,' one said. 'As pale and clear as a silver lake.'

'Well then,' said another. 'Are we all ready – down the hatch!'

Michael laughed at their wide-eyed reaction and gave them a toast as he joined them in another cup of the exquisite substance.

'Good health, boys, one and all, and may God keep up our luck.'

'*Sláinte!*' the Dublin men chorused merrily. 'Down the hatch!'

Another round was poured. Michael raised his cup and toasted again.

'And here's that we may never see hell or the hangman.'

'*Sláinte!*' the Dubs all sang. 'Down the hatch!'

'And here's to you all, as fine as you are.'

'*Sláinte* – down the hatch!'

'And here's to me, as bad as I am.'

'*Sláinte* – down the hatch!'

By the time Michael had proposed his umpteenth toast, the Dubs were all cock-eyed. Then one blinked his eyes, focused on the captain, and suddenly remembered with a yelp of delight just why they were celebrating. He stumbled to his feet and proposed another toast.

'Here's to the man that has a bonnie son.'

Another Dubliner scrambled to his feet and merrily held up his cup. 'And the blazes to any man that has a bonnie daughter – and won't give her to me!'

Chapter Twenty-Nine

A meeting of the most determined croppy hunters took place at a lodge in Rathdrum. Dwyer had to be caught! And so far only one band of men had proved equal to the task – the High-landers. The plan was agreed. Set a Celt to catch a Celt. Scottish soldiers or Irish rebels – they were all savages underneath.

Michael was shooting game on Knockamunnion with only five of his men when he heard the frantic bird calls and whistles of warning echoing over the mountains. He ran to a crag and, in the grey of the morning, saw a detachment of Highland infan-try only a few yards below, ascending at a furious pace. 'Too many to stand and fight,' he said as he ran back to the men. 'Separate and confuse!'

'Who are they?' asked Hugh Vesty. 'Yeos or English?'

'Neither,' Michael smiled. ' 'Tis the gallant Scotsmen!' Des-pite Derrynamuck, he still considered the Highlanders to be the best soldiers in Ireland. Moments later the Highlanders appeared on the ridge. Their colonel let out a shout, 'There's t'canny laddie!'

And the chase was on, fanning in six differing directions.

Each of the five other rebels soon confounded their followers as they disappeared, seemingly into thin air, down the ravines into the many secret caverns in these their own mountains, but the group of staunch Highland lads chasing Dwyer never let him out of their sight. They could run as fast, jump as far, and were every bit as expert and natural climbers as he was.

The chase continued through morning to afternoon, the whole day, across the mountains; in and out through wood and glen, over the Glenealo River and across to the lovely valley of Glendalough with its two small lakes lying in the hollow of its pine-covered hills.

Michael was running towards a stone tower that had been built almost a thousand years earlier as a fortress against the

Danes. The door was high, ten feet up in the wall, with a scaling rope still hanging from it, put there no doubt by the children who played in the tower. He glanced over his shoulder and frowned to see the Highlanders still close on his tail. No time to scale up and pull the rope inside with him without them seeing. No sense in being trapped.

He sprinted on through the trees, up towards the ruins of a monastery where Mass had been said by St Kevin's monks centuries before England had even heard of Christ. In and out through the ruins they chased him, and on and on until he reached the trees of the Upper Lake where he suddenly gave the Highlanders the slip.

They looked around them in bewilderment, then searched high and low, refusing to accept defeat after tracking their game so long and so far. Eventually they grounded their arms in fury and exhaustion.

'He's a Hieland born laddie, nae doot,' said one. 'Knew every larch and hole of the mountains back awa'.'

The seven men sat down for a breather, and held a council of war.

'Och!' exclaimed the youngest Highlander, a fair-haired lad named Sandy. 'I cannae help but think o' the days when my ain clansmen were chased o'er the Hielands by soldiers. We gi' yon tiger a good run o' it. Let's push awa' back to barracks.'

'Hold yer wheesht, mon. Five hundred English guineas. Think o' that!'

While they sat and thought of it, a strange noise reached them. A bump-bump-clop-clop sound which they could not discern.

' 'Tis over yonder!' cried one.

They jumped to their feet and held their weapons in readiness as the sound drew nearer, then stared in awe as a grotesque sight emerged from a young grove of larches. Sitting in a wooden box came a legless cripple pulling himself along at amazing speed with the aid of two hand-stools which he used to push the ground behind him.

'Aha, my gallant Sawnies!' the cripple cried as he bumped towards them. 'And is it a copper or a shilling ye have for a poor deformed one like meself?'

The Scotsmen stared at the miserable piece of humanity. Pity was their first emotion as they stared down at the two stumps of legs which had been snapped off at the thighs by the steel jaws of a poacher's mantrap when the cripple was eighteen years old.

Pity was their first emotion, but on closer inspection they saw the long bony face had a cruel look to it and the eyes held a malicious gleam.

The cripple dribbled a cackling laugh. 'No mind about coppers or shillings. Would ye be interested in guineas? Five hundred of the darlings. And me for a rightful share.'

'Five hundred guineas? D'ye ken where he be?'

The cripple nodded. 'Aye, but before I tell ye, do I have yer word on my share of the reward?'

'Wha' kind of mon are ye?' said the youngest Highlander tiredly. 'Selling oot yer ain clansman?'

'Hold yer wheesht, Sandy. Let the mon speak.'

'Dwyer's no clansman of mine!' the cripple shouted furiously. 'I hate the varmint! Detest and despise him something aggravating. Do I get me share of the money if I tell ye where he is?'

'Aye. One tenth part.'

'Tenth? But there be only seven of ye?'

'Aye, but wha' about our colonel and captain?'

The cripple set down his hand-stools and rubbed his long bony hands together as if wringing soapsuds from them, then said: 'He's up there, in St Kevin's Bed. I seed him go up there a few times before, when he was a youth, with some of his pals. I seed him go up there only a few months ago, with that other varmint, Hugh Vesty Byrne. But this time – I seed him go up alone.'

'Dwyer? Definitely Dwyer?'

'Aye, the Reb-Chief himself. I seed him get away from ye by slipping into the lake and swimming underwater like a mermaid. Then, while ye were sitting and gossiping, I seed him climb up to the Bed as swift as a cat.'

The Highlanders rushed down to the borders of the lake with the cripple bumping after them. They stared across the water to the historic hiding place – St Kevin's Bed – a cave high up the face of the cliff where the young monk had hidden in the sixth century, a perilous climb.

'Wha' can a mon do up there?' asked the youngest Highlander.

'He can sit and wonder how he's going to get back down again!' cackled the cripple.

'Have ye been up there?'

'Feck yer gab, ye Scotch beggar!' screamed the cripple, banging his hand-stools on the ground in fury. 'How in hell's flames could I get up there!'

'I'll gi' ye a blow in the weisin' if ye call me a Scotch beggar, ye Irish Iscariot. Why d'ye hate yer ain countrymon so anywa'?'

'I don't hate all of him!' the cripple cried peevishly. 'Leastaways, not the top half of him.' He began to grumble angrily. 'I used to seed them at the hurley matches and ball-kicking games. All them young men running over the green grass on their long strong legs. Dwyer's legs annoyed me something vexatious. I used to see him like I seed him this evening, running like the wind through the trees, swinging the hurley bat and laughing his head off when they won the contest. I knowed he was laughing at me. I knowed it as sure as my name is Danny of the Lake.'

He wrung and pulled at his hands as if he was strangling some invisible person. 'But after Dwyer's, the legs I hate the most are on Hugh Vesty Byrne. I seed him once pole-vault over a wall six feet high with no problem. Then I seed him and Dwyer trying to ride the horses standing up – not sitting like gentlemen, but feet balanced on the horses' haunches and arms spread as the horses cantered along. And they was laughing, even when they fell off they was laughing. Curse them!' he screamed in sudden savagery. 'Curse them to hell and beyond! And ye Jocks can give me a shilling now on account of my imparting the intelligence to ye! Youse shameless hoors – going around in yer skirts!'

The Highlanders quickly gathered a shilling together and threw it into the box. Anything to get rid of the horrible deformed man who screamed like a woman.

'The mon's demented,' said one, when the box had bumped away into the shadows. Darkness was falling and they realised no more time could be wasted if they were to bring Dwyer in.

They looked again up towards the high cave inside a projecting rock that hung over the water.

'We cannae even be sure he's up there. Mebbe the cripp' just said tha' on account of our kilts?'

'Och, nae. He hates the rebel's knee-breeches mair. He be looking a' 'em longer.'

They quickly formed their plan. Although it was a hazardous

and dangerous climb, they were all cragsmen and thought they could do it if Dwyer had, although not if they carried their muskets – the powder would get wet in the water.

They stripped off their coats, then, armed with only bayonets, they left their guns behind and slipped into the still waters of the lake and swam across to the crag's foot at the opposite side. There they separated into two groups, three started the climb to the right of the Bed, four to the left; their plan being to converge on Dwyer from each side of the ledge.

From where he stood just inside the cave, Michael could not see the Highlanders moving upwards, but he knew they were coming, having watched them swim across the lake.

He smiled to himself. It took a Celt to understand a Celt, and the Jocks could be every bit as superstitious as the Irish. Such a pity he had lost his sea-whistle at Derrynamuck.

He glanced up at the darkening sky; a purple hue hung over the land like a lamenting shadow; the moon was rising slowly from behind a few wisps of cloud, like a ghost rising out of smoke.

He waited a few long minutes, then cupping his hands around his mouth he sent out a high shrill scream like the cry of a soul burning in hell. The noise echoed and reverberated across the dark waters of the lake.

'Hoot!' cried one of the Highlanders almost losing his balance. 'Wha' was tha'?'

Again the high-pitched quivering wail echoed over the dark lake, freezing six of the seven Scotsmen to the face of the cliff in numbed terror.

'Isnae a mon made a sound like tha',' one cried. 'Isnae a mortal!'

'Och, ye bluidy bairns,' snapped the seventh. ' 'Tis Dwyer actin' the fool an' hopin' t'frighten us wi' the shreikin' cry o' ghostly bogles. Stave on!'

Only duty to the regiment, and nothing short of duty, forced the other six to continue upwards. They had almost reached the ledge of the saint's bed when Dwyer suddenly appeared on the ledge and stood calmly smiling down at them for a moment – then disappeared, came back to the ledge with a run, and jumped past them down into the water.

Over their shoulders they gaped down at him as he swam across to the opposite shore. 'Bluidy hellfire!'

Too late the Highlanders realised their mistake. They had left their guns behind and no guard!

446

'Och, nae, Dwyer!' one shouted as Michael lifted the stacked muskets and moved to throw them into the dark waters. 'Dinnae droon our weapons, mon! Just b'thankful ye got awa' an' free!'

'Aye!' Michael shouted cheerily, 'Scot-free!'

'Nae need t'make it personal, mon.'

'Did the Glengarrys tell you about Derrynamuck?' Michael shouted.

'Aye.'

'Then you'll understand why I can't oblige you, avics.' Michael consigned the muskets to the depths of the lake, then, turning away, almost stumbled over the legless man in the box.

'Hello there, Michael me hearty,' the cripple cooed in a whisper. 'I was just coming to see if it was ye or yourself the Jocks were seeking. I was just on me way to warn ye anyhow.'

Michael moved into the trees and retrieved the gun he had hidden there before going underwater along the edge of the lake. He came out again into the early moonlight and examined the gun with an experienced eye, while Danny looked on, beads of sweat beginning to form on his frightened face.

'You saw me, didn't you, Danny. You saw me take to the lake. You saw me go up to Kevin's Bed. You told the kilties where I could be found.'

'No, no!'

'Lucky for me you didn't see where I hid the gun.'

He looked at Danny, his eyes as cold as ice. He placed the muzzle of the gun against Danny's heart, 'Cripple or no, you're an informer, Danny, and you know the fate of informers.'

'No! No!' Danny screamed. 'In the name of Saint Kevin I'd never inform on one of me own race. What? Inform on the Reb-Chief of Wicklow? On the Glen-King of Imaal? Nay, never! And not to those shameless hoors in skirts! Did ye see them climbing up to the Bed and showing off their big wet legs?'

Inwardly Michael recoiled at Danny's sickness. He glanced over his shoulder at the sound of the Highlanders splashing back into the water, then looked again at the man in the box, at the long bony face that could have been sixty but was only thirty-five. He drew away the gun.

'I reckon I'd be doing you a kindness to kill you, Danny, but I wouldn't have you on my conscience. Go to the devil your own way.'

Danny stabbed him an evil glance between the eyes, but said nothing.

'At least I know where we stand now, Danny, you and me.'

'Stand?' As abruptly as Danny's fear had vanished, his anger came back. '*Stand? Stand?*' He screamed like a fox and grabbed at one of the legs standing before him. Michael tried to jump back but gasped in shock as Danny's teeth bit savagely into his knee. He raised his hand and whapped the cripple hard across the neck which brought a howl and instant release.

Michael shuddered, and moved away from the man who screamed as if insane. He turned and ran on; had only gone a short distance when he heard Danny's voice ringing out in renewed rage, and knew the Highlanders had reached the banks.

'Ye hoors! Ye let him get away! Ye shameless Scotch hoors in yer stupid skirts! Give me the boys in red coats any day to ye lot – at least they managed to run down their game at Castle Kevin when I gave them the word. Only one they bagged, Andrew Thomas, but at least they didn't lose their guns like ye shites! Scotchmen me eye! Botchmen!'

'Oh, mon, ye've asked fer it!' young Sandy hissed in rage. He lifted his foot to boot the cripple in the face but Danny was quicker. He whipped up the club he always carried in his box and swung it, sending the Highlander sprawling.

'Kill me, would ye?' Danny screamed at the others, holding the club up threateningly. 'Six more of ye against a poor cripple! Even Dwyer, bad as he is, couldn't hurt a poor legless cripple. But then Dywer is a man – not like ye hoors in skirts!'

Still waving the club, Danny let out an angry peel of laughter. 'Hoors! Hoors! Hoors!'

'God almighty!' a Highlander whispered, backing away from the grotesque man in the box. 'I'm no' even dead, but already I know what the Devil looks like. In God's name, come awa' lads. The mon's a demon from hell.'

Danny watched them narrowly as they helped Sandy to his feet and dragged him away. He listened to their movements and voices and knew they were heading in the direction of Lugduff Mountain.

The darkness was now like a blanket over the mountains of Glendalough. The moon sent silver beams over the dark waters of the upper lake around St Kevin's Bed.

Danny grinned and turned his box down towards the water, then cackled to himself as he wondered what the Highland hoors would do if, on their journey back, they happened to hear the haunting tune of bagpipes and meet the gliding ghost of Lugduff?

He lifted a bottle out of his box, threw back his head and took a long gulping slug, then recorked it and wiped his mouth and chin. He put the bottle away and sat motionless, staring with evil eyes at the dark rippling waters of the lake. He often sat at night staring at the lake, for deep in its depths lay the bones of the gamekeeper who had set the man-trap that had taken his legs.

He heard a quiet movement in the dense undergrowth beside him and shifted his narrow eyes sideways in fear . . . it was a badger, nosing its way along the ground. Suddenly there was no fear in Danny's eyes, they became bright and glowing with yearning.

He sat motionless, quietly smiling as the badger nosed closer, and when it was near enough, Danny swung up his arms and brought the club down, blow after savage blow, until the badger lay battered and bloody and dead.

He sat again, his anger spent, looking over the lake surrounded by pine trees and wilderness. He stared at the rippling water as if hypnotised. There was no other motion, no other sound.

Then he heard the footsteps coming through the trees, strong footsteps that did not try to disguise themselves. He quickly pushed his box around and raised his club, grinning slyly when the tall young man strode into the moonlight.

'Ho, ye rascal! Ye gave the botchmen the slip, did ye? Well, fair play to ye, Michael me hearty!'

Michael stood a few paces off, staring down at him with eyes that seemed aflame.

'So it was you that sent them to get Andrew Thomas. You traitorous bag of scum! I'd take my chances with you any day, Danny, but Andrew Thomas, I'll not forgive you for him.'

'What are you talking about?' Danny cried in amazement. 'I know no Andrew Thomas.'

'But you knew Matt McDaniel's house at Castle Kevin. And you knew three rebels were lying there. And it was you who told the boys in red coats where to find them. And you knew it was Andrew Thomas they caught.'

'Me?'

'I heard you with my own ears, Danny. I heard you boasting it to the kilties.'

'Did I?' Danny shrugged indifferently. 'I have a poor memory these days.' He unplugged the bottle in his box and held it to lips. 'So, ye've come back to kill me, eh? Come back to kill an informer. Then get on with it!'

He took a deep draught, then looked at Michael through almost-closed eyes savagely. 'Well, what ails ye? What are you waiting for?'

Danny was not a clever man, but he possessed that genius of cunning quite common in those bordering on madness. He knew Dwyer was capable of killing an informer but not a cripple.

And when Michael suddenly let out an angry breath then walked a few paces down to the lake's edge, Danny knew he was right in his deduction. If Dwyer was ever going to kill him as an informer, he would have done it earlier, when it was himself who had been betrayed.

Michael studied the waters of the lake and spoke quietly without turning round. 'I reckon I'd be doing you a kindness if I killed you, Danny,' he said again.

Danny shrugged. 'I reckon you would. But go ahead, kill half a man and feel proud of it.'

Michael moved to one of the stone boulders along the edge of the lake and sat down, a few feet away and facing Danny, looking at him with a mixture of revulsion and pity. But all Danny saw was the long gun Dwyer held in both hands, the muzzle pointing at the ground and out of harm's way.

'You've turned bad inside, Danny, real bad. And if there's one thing I hate to see, it's a man turned rotten.'

'Then look in your mirror, boy. From what I hears you're as bad as they come.'

Michael glanced at the waters of the lake then brought his gaze slowly back to the cripple.

'There's bad and bad, Danny. You should know that, all the time you spend sitting in that box looking at the ways of nature. Even the birds of the air defend their territory and fight to protect their own. But real badness, in man or beast, is nothing to do with situation and everything to do with heart . . . And when the rot starts the signs are clear, same as they are in nature; the bird that fouls its own nest, then wrecks it. The sheepdog that begins nipping his sheep, then ends up tearing their throats out. The man who clasps hands with his comrades, then steps out and sells them like Judas.'

450

'Well I couldn't do that, could I?' Danny said plaintively. 'Step out.'

'You still grinding that old bone? Man, you haven't heard or heeded a word I've been saying. Sure you've got no legs, but worse, you've got no heart, it's all withered up and rotten inside you. As dead as that poor badger you just beat to death.'

'Never liked badgers,' Danny said, taking another drink. 'And any heart I once had went with my legs.'

He held up the bottle as if measuring its contents against the light of the moon. 'But seeing as ye know so much about the ways of nature and the ways of badness, then ye should also know that only a wicked rooster will sneak into another cock's barnyard and lie with one of his hen-wives.'

Michael frowned in puzzlement. 'What the hell are you talking about?'

'Pat O'Riordan of your own Imaal,' Danny said. 'Only the other day I heard he got wed and brought a mate home to his nest. A lovely black-feathered hen that already had a chicken. And now she's clucked another one. But only this afternoon, I learned that ye were the rooster on that roost, not O'Riordan.'

Michael looked at the cripple with eyes half closed. Danny laughed contemptuously. 'And ye talk to me about badness. That's boiling!'

'Who told you such nonsense?' Michael said softly.

'What's that?' Danny snapped angrily, as if he resented the question. Then he shrugged. 'Nobody told me.'

'So where did you get the notion that the children are mine?'

'Oh, no notion in it! 'Tis the truth and no mistake.'

Danny paused with the bottle to his lips and bared his teeth in a savage grin. The conversation had lulled him into a calmness and he was enjoying it, sharpening his wits against the bright young spark who thought he was so clever.

'This afternoon it was I learned it. Only a few hours before ye and the kilties showed. I was behind those trees, keeping my eye on the lake as is my fashion, and watching two men fishing. They were talking together about the christening that O'Riordan is having for the second child this Sunday, at the chapel at Rathdangan. According to O'Riordan, everyone will be there. Then one man laughed and said, "But will the *father* of the child be there?" And as they talked on, I realised they were talking about the Reb-Chief himself.'

Michael looked calmly at the cripple, his eyes now as remote and cool as the lake.

'Way I see it,' Danny drained the bottle in a gulp, 'you and her must have been mating long before she went to the priest with O'Riordan. Although I reckon now that she never went anywhere with O'Riordan. I reckon you've had her tucked away in some little nest somewhere, and this business on Sunday is just a trick to take the militia off her scent.'

Danny cackled. 'But I'm smart, boy, smarter than most of the militia who're as stupid as flies in a whiskey bottle. A lot of them do reckon the children might be a gentleman's by-blows, and O'Riordan is happy enough to make a respectable woman of her, as long as he gets the next shot.' Danny shrugged. 'Sure half the bloody population of Ireland are gentry sired.'

Michael suddenly shivered. A chill wind blew over the lake and his clothes were still wet from his swim.

'Finished,' Danny said, throwing the bottle into the undergrowth. Then he chuckled and rolled his tongue in his cheek, all the fine cunning of his mind mulled by the warming whiskey in his belly.

'Come now, Michael me hearty, admit I have the cat by the tail. I'll not tell a soul. Admit those two shots came from no gentry gun but your own.'

Michael looked at him, a small enigmatic twist to his lips, and Danny smiled in the certainty that he was right, a slow delighted smile. But he had to be sure.

' 'Tis right then, the child to be christened on Sunday is yours, eh?'

'Yes, the child is mine.'

'And the woman? Is she yours too?'

'The woman too,' Michael confirmed, then slowly raised up the muzzle of the gun and shot the informer in the place where his heart had once been.

Chapter Thirty

At the little village chapel of Rathdangan, at a place where four roads meet, the christening Mass went off without a hitch, except no christening took place, only the Mass. The seven-week-old son of Michael and Mary Dwyer had been baptised secretly a week after his birth, in the presence of both parents, in the parlour of the priest's house at Green's River.

The military waiting on their mounts outside the little chapel didn't know that. And when the people began to come out, Captain Woollard's eyes sought keenly for a woman holding a newborn.

He recognised her at once, the girl in the square at Donard. She wore a large tortoiseshell comb in her dark hair, gypsy fashion, and, despite having a child, she was as slim as an unbroached filly. He sat more erect on his horse as he stared at her. Primitive in mind and race she might be, but she was outstanding amongst the sombre huddle of people around her. He looked amongst them for the one who might be the father, but there were no young men present, only middle-aged and old men.

He kneed his horse forward and within seconds the military had formed a cordon around the entrance to the church. Everyone fell silent and looked at the soldiers, their faces cold and sullen, like a people under siege.

Woollard surveyed them, his expression pure arrogance. A number of the women moved to form a silent second inner cordon around the girl holding the child, and Captain Woollard knew at once that he and his soldiers would likely be torn to pieces by these females if they as much as touched her.

'Is the child illegitimate,' he said down to the girl, 'or are you married?'

'No grandson of mine is ill-anything!' William Doyle cried, pushing forward. 'And is it insulting a virtuous woman ye'd be on a Holy Sunday?'

Woollard coolly regarded the sturdily built man who had a strong face, great rakish dark eyes, and a voice like a foghorn.

'Where is the husband then?'

'God save your honour, but isn't he looking at you.' William Doyle nudged O'Riordan forward and spoke through the corner of his mouth. 'Act like a half-wit,' he whispered unnecessarily.

O'Riordan stumbled forward in genuine terror, twisted the hat in his hand a few times, then offered a red twitching smile to the officer.

'Are you this woman's husband?'

'I am, sir.' O'Riordan tugged his forelock with a trembling hand.

Captain Woollard could not believe it. His eyes moved to the tall beautiful girl, then back to the ungainly heap of an ignorant-looking man beside her; at least twice her age.

'Pat here,' cried William Doyle, putting an arm fondly around O'Riordan, 'is the son-in-law I've always wanted. And no finer husband could my daughter or indeed any woman wish to have. Always up at the crack of dawn and out on his farm working like the land-slave he is. As fine as any man ever bred in Imaal.'

Woollard was staring scornfully at O'Riordan, whose head was now bowed in embarrassment at such praise.

'As fine as any man ever pulled on breeches!' Doyle clasped O'Riordan tighter. 'No matter about the colour of his face. I wish I could grow apples the red of Pat's face. And so what if his hair stands up here and there like horns – 'twas not him that shot the woman's pet duck! I'd swear that before a judge and jury and even—'

'Michael Dwyer?' interrupted Woollard. 'Your daughter knew him, I'm told.'

'Knew him?' Doyle squared his shoulders and glared at the redcoat with a colossal air of offence. 'What do you mean she *knew* him?'

'What I say. She knew him well enough to dance with him and be considered his companion at one time.'

'Oh, is that what you mean?' Doyle's wrath instantly fell with his shoulders. 'Sure stone the crows,' he said in a bewildered tone, ' 'tis hard to be knowing the true meaning of words these days. His Reverence in there was just telling us about a place called Genesis where Adam knew Eve and she conceived

. . . But my saintly daughter never knew Michael Dwyer that well, not before she was married – to Pat here.'

Woollard sniffed at the big nonsensical man – a typical specimen proving the English notion that all Irishmen were ignorant thick-headed peasants was in fact based on truth and not prejudice.

He decided to speak directly to the girl. 'Just how well did you know Michael Dwyer?'

'Knew him only long enough to find out what a rascal he is!' William Doyle answered, then regarded the officer with a look of sneering disdain. 'Dwyer? Tch! A womanish sort of fellow in my opinion – likes sitting with women and bairns. What sort of man is that? And no respect for the traditions of our county either. In the old days a Wicklow boy always courted a Wicklow girl, but not the rebel Dwyer! No, that gypsy had to wander as far as County Clare to find a girl good or bad enough for him. Isn't that right, people?'

The people all nodded in murmured agreement.

'Do you know any of his hideouts?'

'Faith, I don't!' Doyle declared. 'And don't want to neither. Why should a sensible man like myself be foolish enough to seek out trouble. But I'll tell you this, my good man, if that—'

But Woollard had heard enough. 'Thank you and good day!' he snapped.

'And the same to ye!' Doyle replied, then turned brightly to the crowd. 'Isn't he a very civil young man all the same? Wishing us a good day. Well, anyone who wants to may come along with meself and Pat now. There's going to be some acelebrating at my abode!'

Captain Woollard motioned with his head to his men and they side-stepped their mounts away from the huddled crowd, then sat on their horses along the edge of the fields where the corn was all reaped and stood in stooks, watching the people as they drifted towards their homes. The people from north Imaal piled into two hay wagons which trundled down the country road.

'What do you think?' Woollard asked the young lieutenant sitting alongside him. 'Do you think she is married to that stupid-looking man?'

'I think she is, sir, if the father says so.'

'He could have been lying.'

'He could have been, but matches like that are not unusual

among these natives, especially the agricultural tribes. So many of their young men die in their continual war against us that many fathers prefer to settle a land-match for the girl and ignore her plea for a love-match. But once the marriage tie is made, it is accepted by both as forever binding.'

Captain Woollard looked at him in surprise. 'You sound like an expert on the subject.'

The soldier shrugged. 'I should be, sir. I spent over six months up in Connaught after the French landed.'

'And became acquainted with the natives?'

'Just one, sir.'

When the soldier said no more, only sat with a blank face watching the last few stragglers standing in chatting groups, Woollard said impatiently: 'Well?'

'A girl, sir. She was lovely looking, and very dainty, except for the fact that she wore a broken old pair of men's boots under her skirts. She had no real shoes, you see. The Connaught people are poor almost to starving, have been since Cromwell shunted them to the barren patches where nothing grows. I was even thinking of marrying her, and buying her a pair of shoes, but her father quickly agreed a match with a man from miles away. Neither she nor I saw him until he came over the hill for the wedding. He was that old, sir, older than her father, and very bent from working the land.'

'Awful,' Woollard muttered, then looked curiously at his lieutenant. 'Were you really that willing to surrender to the foe?'

'I was hoping she would surrender to me, sir.'

'Then why didn't you just whip her back to barracks and swiftly break her in before her father could do anything about it?'

'She wouldn't have come, sir. She was a good girl, not a doxie.'

'Too many good girls in this rotten place,' Woollard muttered glumly. 'All Mary Virgins and very few Magdalenes. Black-haired, was she?'

'No, sir, golden.'

'Ah, a Viking throwback. Good God, I saw one the other day that looked like a chieftain herself. A magnificent fair trollop with yards of yellow hair and a skirt so thin you could see she had thighs as strong as any Viking or Highlander. But when I spoke to her she ran away like a frightened kitten, God damn

456

her! God damn them all! Did your Connaught girl have thighs like a Viking?'

'I doubt it, sir, she was petite as a faery.'

Woollard glanced at the handsome young face still staring blankly at the deserted chapel. A face as blank as the voice.

'Oh come now, lieutenent,' he said in a teasing tone, 'don't tell me she turned her back on a fine young soldier like you, and went with the bent old codger?'

'She had no choice, sir. Her family lived solely from the profits of a potato garden the size of a handkerchief, but the man she was matched with had fertile land, four whole fields of it, if only rented. Besides, her father would have killed her for even associating with an English soldier. The only time he ever saw me, he stared at me as if I was the ghost of Cromwell himself. Accused me of stealing his land. Accused me of shunting his people to starve in the barren hell of Connaught. Then he ordered the girl inside and slammed the door in my face. Yes, sir, he would have killed her first.'

'Awful moody people these Irish. Won't accept that bygones should be bygones.'

'Last I saw of her, she was walking back over the hill with the bent old man, as his wife, still wearing her broken old boots.'

'Well,' Woollard said in a cheering tone, 'now you will think twice before getting involved with any other native girl while you're here.'

'I'll not even think about it once, sir.'

'Jolly good!' Woollard turned his horse around. 'But don't sound so forlorn, boy. Think of England! And besides, where could your little romance have led? She would never have fitted into English society, not even in shoes. She would have been despised. Remember that.'

'Yes, sir.'

Woollard raised his hand and signalled the column to move.

'I'll remember it every time I see a fine lady wearing fine shoes and hear her complaining about having to make another tedious journey with her husband to his Irish estates on the rich fertile lands of Longford or Drogheda . . . sir.'

Woollard responded with a tolerant sneer. 'Wonderful victory Cromwell had at Drogheda.' Then he breathed deep in his lungs and fixed his eyes on the mountains as they rode in slow double file past the reaped cornfields. 'Well, there are still

457

plenty of young men left in Wicklow,' he said. 'Athletic-looking bastards every one of them, and most are up those mountains with Dwyer – a ruddy hard bugger to catch.'

'Yes, sir.'

'Damn it all!' Woollard cried irritably. 'At times I think I'd give my commission just to get a glimpse of the insurgent chief.'

When the military party had ridden well out of sight, the detachment of armed men concealed amongst the corn stooks, who had observed the whole proceedings with guns primed and aimed, broke cover and shook themselves down.

'Did you hear that now?' Hugh Vesty said to Michael. 'That there redcoat would give his commission just to see you.'

'And who the blazes would want his commission?' Michael asked.

Hugh Vesty thought about it, then smiled. 'You're right, who the blazes would? Now, come on – let's go and see our wives and children.' He strode off eagerly and Michael could not help smiling as he followed. Hugh Vesty's wife Sarah had now also given birth to a boy, and Hugh was delighted as could be, and already planning his history lessons.

The Mass-attenders had long gone. The rebels broke away in pairs and disappeared into the hills towards Lugnaquilla. At Camara, Michael and Hugh Vesty, with Mernagh and Burke following close behind, turned off towards the isolated land of Knockandarragh where, all going well, their wives had arranged to meet them.

The house at Knockandarragh was once again filled with people. In the centre of the room the table was furnished with numerous uncut loaves and plates of butter, cheese, ham, and cold pork, and tumblers for cold ale or seasonal blackcurrant juice, the cost of which Michael's father had agreed to pay half, even though he did not attend, seeing as it was all a charade – and just another excuse for Doyle to revel.

William Doyle was standing in a pool of importance by the fireplace, master of all the news, which he imparted with great aplomb to those neighbours who had come just to hear the gossip.

'The husband?' Doyle cried. ' "God save your honour," says I, "but isn't he looking at you" – and me knowing himself was beyond in the cornfields doing just that.'

The laughter was lively when the four rebels walked in. Michael smiled warmly at O'Riordan and patted his shoulder. 'You did a grand job, Pat.'

'And what about me?' Doyle demanded. 'In all modesty but truth you have to admit that it was me carried the whole thing off.' He smiled rakishly at all the neighbour-women.

Michael looked at the laden table and ale casks. 'What are you celebrating?' he said curiously to Doyle.

'What do you think – a christening.'

'A christening?' Michael looked perplexed. 'And who was christened?'

'Nobody.' Doyle was all puzzlement. 'You know that right well.'

Michael looked at Hugh Vesty with a sly gleam in his eye. 'It seems foolish, doesn't it, to celebrate a christening without someone getting watered.'

Doyle let out a roar when he was suddenly scooped off his feet as lightly as if he was a sack of oats, then carried struggling and shouting through the room of gaping neighbours.

'Put me down! Ah here! Fair play now!' But Michael and Hugh Vesty continued out to the yard and across to the long cattle-trough where Doyle was dumped in the water without ceremony.

'God Almighty!' Doyle roared, trying to get up, then slipping back again until his head and every screed of his clothing was soaked. 'God Almighty!'

The sight of him was so ludicrous that the neighbours were all carried away into an ecstasy of hilarious laughter. Even Mrs Doyle, holding her grandson, was laughing; but the one laughing the most was Mary. Her laughter floated merrily over the rooftop, while her father struggled and slipped and spluttered.

'*God Almighty!*' Doyle roared up at Michael. 'Why the blazes did you do that?'

'You only got what you asked for,' Michael told him. 'Slandering the father of your grandchildren – a womanish sort of fellow indeed!'

'Devil roast you, I was only playing the game!' Doyle cried as Mernagh, Burke and O'Riordan helped him out. 'Oh would ye look at me clothes!' Doyle stood staring down in horror at his soaked Sunday best, while Michael and Hugh Vesty doubled up in laughter.

'He wanted a christening and he got it!' Hugh Vesty cried, thumping Michael in the chest.

Still laughing, Michael turned towards the house, and saw Mary looking at him with approval. Her cheeks were flushed from her merriment. He approached her slowly and smiling, the sly gleam back in his eye.

'No, no,' she said with laughing lips, backing away. 'No, don't . . .'

'To the devil with this for a story,' William Doyle muttered. 'I'll not live this down in a hurry.'

'William, oh, William,' O'Riordan said plaintively. 'Don't get upset now. He's just in good humour because the whole thing went off as planned.'

'Holy Moses,' said Doyle, slumping wearily down on the edge of the trough and wiping the water from his face. 'Holy Moses, if he does things like this in a good humour, what would he do in a bad mood?'

They heard a scream of excited laughter and looked round to see Michael chasing Mary through the field. A loud cheer rose up from the neighbours when he caught her and kissed her passionately in full view of them.

'Look at him,' Doyle grunted. 'As playful as a buck hare with a doe rabbit, and not an ounce of remorse in him. He's turned my fine celebration into a rowdy debauch.'

Still dripping from head to foot, he turned and stared dolefully at O'Riordan, his hair a matted mass about his face. 'Isn't he the *wurrst* son-in-law a man could have, Pat?'

'He is,' O'Riordan agreed pliantly. 'He is, by jiminy. He is indeed.'

The priest from Green's River was at the Dwyers' house at Eadstown that night when Michael slipped in. No one noticed him, all their backs to the door as they gathered round the priest seated on the settle reading a newspaper that Michael's father had pushed into his hands.

'Tell me, is it true, Father?' John Dwyer said anxiously. 'Tell me it is *not* true. There are many words there that I don't understand.'

Father Richard's eyes, deep and far-seeing, opened slightly as he looked up. 'Ah, here is your wayward son,' he said, handing the paper back to John Dwyer. 'I would like to hear him tell you what it means – him that had the benefit of an elementary education from a barn-master, but more from a scholastic priest.'

'Michael . . .' John Dwyer held out the paper to his son.

Michael took it, read it, then contemptuously flicked the paper on to the flames of the fire.

'What difference will it make to us?' he said to the priest coldly. 'On a practical level it will make no difference at all. We will still be denied every right of the citizen, no right to own land, no right to vote, no right to public assembly, no right to any of the natural and unalienable rights of man!'

'The natural and unalienable rights of man . . .' The priest recognised the words and sighed sadly. 'So, you have found a new doctrine?'

The family looked at each other in blank bewilderment. The priest turned to the fire and held his hands out to the blaze. 'So tell us, Michael, in the true parrot-fashion of the inflamed disciple, the philosophy of Thomas Paine that led thousands of young Irishmen to their futile deaths in 1798.'

'It also inspired America to freedom and France to overthrow the tyrants.'

'Good God!' the priest cried. 'The man is not only an Englishman, he is an atheist! If you begin by believing part of what he says, you will end up believing *all* of what he says!'

'I believe,' Michael said steadily, 'that men are born free and equal in respect of their rights. And those rights are liberty, property, safety, and the right to resist oppression.'

'Very good,' the priest commended in a sarcastic tone.

'Don't you sneer down your nose at me,' Michael said irreverently. 'I have been fighting for those rights since the spring of ninety-eight! Now you sin in your heart and lie with your tongue and tell me that you do not agree with those words also!'

'I do,' the priest admitted, 'but it does not have to be achieved with the gun and the sword. There is another way, and it is coming. You say it will make no difference, but it will. To us as people, it will. If not as patriots.'

'Father, please . . .' John Dwyer was losing his patience. 'What it says in the newspaper, explain it in its truth not its words.'

'The Irish Parliament is to be dissolved, and we are to join with England in an Act of Union that will elevate us from slaves to citizens.'

'But . . . but it says . . .' John Dwyer had read it differently,

'it says Ireland will now be ruled solely by English politicians –
direct from the Parliament at Westminster.'

'English Crown servants still ruling us from Dublin Castle,'
Michael said. 'What difference will it make? We will still be the
most cruelly oppressed nation in the world.'

'Wrong,' the priest corrected. 'It is all going to change. You
see, the Bishops of the Catholic Church in Ireland have agreed
to the Act of Union . . . in exchange for Catholic emancipation.'

The priest looked around at the family, smiling joyously.
'Yes, yes . . . in exchange for the emancipation of our people.'
He looked at Michael. 'What say you now, revolutionary? Is
this not a better way to achieve the natural and unalienable
rights of man?'

Michael met the eyes of the priest, look for look; then turned
and strolled through the kitchen towards the scullery at the
back, loudly whistling a tune the United Irishmen had whistled
many times while marching to battle in 1798, the tune of the
French Revolution, 'The Marseillaise'.

'He may whistle "The Marseillaise" now,' the priest said,
unperturbed, 'but come the Union . . .' He smiled.

'Is it true, Father?' Mrs Dwyer asked incredulously.
'Emancipation is truly coming for the Catholics at last?'

The priest stood up and laughed. 'It is true! Not our liberty
as patriots, but the liberty of being treated as citizens in our
own land.'

'Oh my,' said Mrs Dwyer in the daze of a miracle. 'Oh my,
my, my!'

The vote was passed through both Houses of Parliament, and
on 1st January 1801, the Act of Union between Ireland and
England was established.

The three hundred members of the dissolved Irish Home
Parliament were now reduced to a small delegation at
Westminster, and amongst the great numbers of that political
House, they were hard to find in the crowd.

Catholic emancipation did not follow. William Pitt had
genuinely tried to bring it about, some believed, but King
George would not even consider Pitt's Irish relief measures,
flaring into a bout of insanity whenever they were mentioned.
The King's refusal to consider emancipation of the Irish
Catholics was given colossal approval by the ruling Tory Party
of the British Parliament, and Pitt resigned as Prime Minister.

462

Lord Cornwallis was heartbroken. He had convinced both sides of the divide that they would benefit from the Union. Under Pitt's instructions, he had wheeled and dealed, promising peerages and government pensions to the land barons who insisted on recompense for abandoning their political privileges. He had secured government posts for defunct members of the Irish Parliament, secured bishoprics for others, and bargained huge financial bribes to secure the vote. He had grumbled privately about 'trafficking with the most *corrupt* people on earth', blind to his own part in the corruption. But he had also truly believed that the Union was the answer to the Irish problem. 'What we have now,' he said, 'is not a Union with Ireland, but a union with the Protestant party of Ireland.'

To the seven-eighths majority in Ireland, the only difference the Union brought was a new Viceroy and a new administration at Dublin Castle – and a new flag! The English cross of St George and the Scottish cross of St Andrew, were now joined by the Irish cross of St Patrick – in a single flag known as the Union Jack.

'Jacks are high,' said Hugh Vesty Byrne.

'Not me,' said John Mernagh, viewing the cards in his hand.

'Nor me,' said Martin Burke.

'What about you, Michael?' Hugh Vesty asked. 'Can you open with a pair of jacks or higher?'

Michael looked up vaguely. 'I'm thinking about the priest,' he said. 'He truly believed them. He truly believed they were going to grant us emancipation and treat us as citizens. He was not expecting King George to piss in his eye.'

He looked at the men anxiously. 'I'm worried about him. I think I'll go over there and see if he's all right. He's done me many favours, even though we disagree on many things.'

The priest was stumbling unsteadily along the banks of Green's River. His eyes bloodshot from lack of sleep, his grey hair straggling down his back. His bones hurt violently. He was stiff from walking – walking here and there and everywhere – seeking respite from his rage and finding none.

'Oh, what fools we were,' he muttered to the ground. 'They spit on their own people, so why should they not spit on us whom they despise.'

He raised his eyes from the ground and let out an ironic

laugh. 'By God, you are right, Mr Paine! They govern not in service of the people, but in *contempt* of the people.'

He stumbled on. 'And yes, Mr Paine, after all, what is this thing called a crown? And if the crown makes a king, what does that make the goldsmith who made the crown? And when they, the politicians and placemen and pension-men and lords of the chamber bow down and worship that crown, why do they not see the daily labour of the people who pay for it in taxes. Why do they spit on them?'

He let out another small laugh. 'You see, my young revolutionary, I too have read Thomas Paine, and see him for the dangerous man that he is.'

And as he walked, looking around at the wild hills, he saw the haze of people marching to the mountain top. As they always did in his dream. But now they were no longer singing joyous hymns, they were singing a war cry. He stared at them and trembled to his bones. Then he sprang to life and rushed to join them, stumbling in his movements. A young man came out of the crowd, walking towards him, a dark-haired young man holding a long gun at his side.

'Yes!' the priest cried, reaching to take the gun. 'It is the only way now. They have sown the wind so must reap the whirlwind!'

'What ails you?' the young man said. 'Are you sick in your head or what? Stumbling and raving like a madman.'

Then the haze cleared, the face came into focus, and his sleep-starved mind stabled on a shaky balance. 'So it is you,' he whispered. 'You have come to taunt me with "The Marseillaise". You have come to gloat over my stupidity and shame.'

'Ach, stop talking like a fool and come along now. Your house is just beyond.' Michael took his arm. 'We should get you to bed, I'm thinking.'

The priest awoke three days later, with no memory for what had passed. He opened his eyes and looked up at the dark girl bending over him. She smiled, then with a litany of gentle phrases, forced him to sit up and spoon-fed him a bowl of broth.

'It tastes good,' he said. 'Was I sick, Mary?'

'Just bone-tired and mind-weary, Father,' Mary said softly.

Then it all came back to him. The betrayal. The lies he had believed, and encouraged so many others to believe. He wondered if he had said anything in the turmoil of his dreams.

'Did I . . . say anything . . . in my sleep?'

Mary threw a glance at Michael standing over by the wall.

464

'No, nothing at all, Father,' she replied quickly. 'You slept like a corpse.'

'And now, it seems, I am restored to life again.'

He looked bleakly at the young couple who had helped him, and whose future was as dangerously uncertain as his own. How could he, as their pastor, help them in return? And then he realised there was only one way.

'Listen to me now,' he said softly, 'listen while I tell you what our beloved Redeemer said in the Gospel of Saint Matthew . . . Love your enemies, bless them that curse you, do good to them that hate you, and pray for them that use you and persecute you.'

Both stared at him silently.

Then the sorrow of it all rose in him, and his eyes misted.

'Oh, Father,' Mary whispered, 'why are you crying?'

'Not for myself, child, not for myself.' He looked up and smiled. 'There, you see, a tear and a smile. One usually follows the other in the up and down of life. Is that not so?'

'That is so,' Mary agreed.

The priest was silent for a long moment, then he sighed deeply and pulled the bed covers high up over his misery. He lay back and closed his eyes.

'Thank you both,' he said. 'But now you may leave me. I will be fine. I will rise soon and pay a visit to some of the hearty men of the parish who enjoy arguing with me. Just like himself there.'

Mary reached out and touched his hand. 'Father . . .'

'God bless the two of you,' he whispered. 'May you live to see your children's children.'

Michael motioned with his head to Mary.

Outside the house he looked into her anxious face. 'Nay,' he said dismissively. 'It was just a brainstorm, but it's cleared now. The stubborn old martyr has a good few sermons left in him yet.'

In the bright winter sunlight, they walked back along the riverbank, hand in hand, with the three companions who followed their captain with avid loyalty close behind.

At the hedge of a field, the five of them paused to watch a lone young bull having a fierce fight with his shadow, running in circles and charging and snorting in fury.

'Which one do you think will win?' Hugh Vesty murmured.

The five laughed, and walked on.

Chapter Thirty-One

To the fury of the ruling class, the new Viceroy of Ireland, Lord Hardwicke, soon made it very clear that, in the same way Lord Cornwallis had refused to be dictated to by generals of the army or officers of the militia, he in turn would not be dictated to by the land barons. He was an Englishman, and intended to rule as an Englishman, and as an Englishman he would not bow to the whims and wishes of the Irish gentry.

With all the hullabaloo of the Union, and the recall of many English regiments, Michael Dwyer began to entertain a small hope that maybe the Castle authorities would forget all about him.

They did not forget him, but they were no longer very troubled about him. The rebellion was long over and all radical movements crushed. So as long as Dwyer continued to confine his military strategy to one of defence and not attack, and as long as he continued to confine himself to his own mountains of Wicklow, he posed no real threat to country or government.

Nevertheless, the militia and yeomanry forces were kept on full pay and incentive to capture Michael Dwyer and bring him in. But the English regiments had been taken off the offensive and were now mainly employed in policing the country.

But as the summer of 1801 wore on, Michael Dwyer's popularity with the people of Wicklow began to wane into confusion. He had started behaving strangely, acting completely out of character. They had known him since his boyhood and, although now a rebel captain, he had never been unnecessarily quarrelsome or suffered from blood-lust; and neither had he ever taken a penny or a potato that was not his own, or that was not given freely to him.

But now – and they could scarcely believe it – Michael Dwyer was sending out raiding parties at night to steal from the people – his *own* people.

Oh sure, the newspapers constantly referred to him as a

466

bandit and a thief and every other degrading name imaginable, but the people knew they were just the usual lies of government-paid editors.

But who could say they were lies now? Now that Dwyer was truly sending out raiding parties who stole from anyone, enemy or ally, and used brute force if resistance was made.

Then, out of the blue, an anonymous tip-off was sent to Colonel Antrobus of the Somerset Fencible Regiment, believed to be from a rebel closely connected with Dwyer, informing him that the house of a man named Keogh in Glenmalure was going to be robbed by Dwyer that very night.

And that very night, a party of soldiers was concealed around Keogh's house, with more waiting in the darkness of the tensely silent living-room. The family were huddled in a bewildered frightened group in the bedroom.

When the masked party finally came along and entered the house, a soldier instantly rose and shot the leader while the others were surrounded.

'Well damn my eyes!' cried the soldier when the candles had been lit and he was able to stare at the dead man. 'This ain't Dwyer – this is Henry Moody, a yeoman from Hacketstown!'

The entire robbing party consisted of yeomen from Hacketstown and Rathdrum. The newspapers had given Dwyer the name of being a plunderer, and so the yeomen had used his name to cover their misdeeds.

The people rejoiced, many cried openly and apologised profusely to the Dwyer family at Eadstown and the Doyles at Knockandarragh for their lack of faith. The Doyles accepted the apologies with forgiving good humour, but the Dwyers neither accepted or rejected them, just carried on about their business, coldly aloof.

Colonel Antrobus announced that the yeomen would be charged and brought to trial for robbery. Thomas King, the resident magistrate at Rathdrum, was furious at such an outrage. He remonstrated with Colonel Antrobus about charging formerly loyal yeomen, but Antrobus would not be swayed. The robbing party were tried by court martial, convicted, and sentenced to a period of imprisonment.

And that was that.

But still the robberies continued, by Michael Dwyer, and brute force was still being used against any who put up resistance.

The people didn't know what to think. If it was Dwyer, and all the victims said it was, then why was he doing it? They, the people of his own Wicklow, had always kept him and his men as well supplied with rations and levies as the soldiers in the barracks!

Some finally plucked up the courage to voice the worst of their suspicions: three years of life as a rebel on the run had finally taken its toll; Michael Dwyer had turned bad.

Down the winding path at the side of John Cullen's house, Michael sat on the grass bank with his arms on his knees staring into the bubbling water of the Lech River. Mary sat beside him. Neither had spoken for some time. Occasionally she stole glances at his face, and her heart ached for him. Nothing had ever caused him so much annoyance and upset as this gang of unprincipled ruffians which was going about Wicklow robbing under his name.

He thought he had tracked them down. And when he discovered they were yeomen, he had sent a tip-off to the barracks. The military, he had explained to her, would never have believed it was the yeos doing the robberies, and not him, unless they had seen it for themselves.

But now it seemed that more than one gang was conveniently using his name. He didn't care what the papers said, or what the soldiery thought, but he cared deeply what his own people thought. And he knew they didn't know what to think any more.

Mary stroked Michael's arm. 'Will you stay for supper?' she asked.

He turned and looked vaguely into her brown eyes, shook his head. 'No, I have to go. I told Hugh Vesty I would only stay one night and I've been here two already. If I don't show soon, himself and the lads will be out looking for me.'

The evening summer sun was still high in the west. He stood up and walked away, pulling Mary behind him, for as always she hated the moment of parting and dragged it out as long as she could.

Even when he had disappeared from her sight she remained looking at the hills, unaware that time was passing and Cullen was calling to her, her mind travelling with him through the stony places that led to the hidden valleys and his men.

* * *

The rebel camp was currently on Knockamunnion, a green shoulder of Table Mountain, dense with pine trees and rippling streams. Michael walked along the hilly paths in slow melancholy. Near Stranahely he passed the isolated house of a small farm worked by a middle-aged man named Malone. Malone was in his front yard as he approached, but at Michael's salute, the man only nodded curtly, then turned to go back inside.

'Malone!' Michael snapped.

The farmer turned and stood in dour silence as Michael walked up to him.

'What is wrong with you, Malone? Why do you greet me so sourly?'

When Malone gave no answer, Michael gritted his teeth angrily and said with feeling. 'Surely you know that I would never foul my own nest and turn on my own people!'

Malone looked at him. 'You have never sent out, or been part of, a night raid of robbery?'

'Sure I have,' Michael admitted. 'After the battle of Hacketstown when we were so in need of arms, I raided a number of yeomen's houses and relieved them of their weapons. The yeomanry muskets were paid for by the people's taxes and were employed in murdering those same people who paid for them. We believed we had a right to take them, for our own and the people's protection. We could not be expected to face the enemy unarmed.'

'And you have never raided the people for private gain?'

'Never. Not me nor any of my trusted companions. Anything we ever wanted that could not be given freely was always paid for. If we could not pay, and the people could not give, we did without.'

Malone looked shrewdly into his face, then nodded. 'I believe you.'

'I'm obliged that you do,' Michael said coldly, then moved to walk on. Malone caught his arm. 'We're just about to have supper, will you join us?'

'If you'll not be offended, I won't.'

'Please?' Malone said. 'I feel bad for believing the worries about you. But if you sit and share my table, I'll know we're friends again as always.'

Michael shrugged. 'A glass of ale then, but nothing more. I'm behind time and my comrades will be wondering about me.'

When he entered the neatly kept and well-furnished house, Mrs Malone smiled at him without a trace of rancour or suspicion. 'Ah! Musha! Is it ye, Michael? Come in and feel welcome.'

She was a nice-faced woman of about thirty-six with a smile as warm as the fire she stood by, stirring the contents of a large copper cauldron. In her youth Mrs Malone had been a natural beauty of the dark kind and was still a very handsome woman. Also in the room were her two daughters aged eleven and twelve, and her thirteen-year-old son.

Michael knew them all, but he had never met the strange young maiden who was sitting by the fire.

Mrs Malone began to talk to him animatedly, but Michael's eyes were riveted on the young woman with a head of chestnut ringlets under a cute straw bonnet and dressed in a frock of blue and white striped muslin. She was tall too, judging the distance from the muslin crease at her hip-line to the toe of her shoe . . . a long-legged person.

She bowed her head shyly under his gaze and Malone finally interrupted his wife and introduced the young woman.

'Oh, dear me, yes!' Mrs Malone cried. 'Wasn't I forgetting my manners.'

Malone was astute enough to give Michael a false surname in the introduction, but the young woman was a stranger. She had been employed as companion to an old lady in Dublin, but now that the lady had died, leaving her homeless and destitute, she was travelling to seek lodgings with a relative in Talbotstown, some many miles away, and had got lost. She was very tired from her travelling and feared being abroad after dusk, so had stopped and asked if she could lodge with the family overnight. They had naturally made her welcome.

As he drank his ale and talked with Malone, Michael could not keep his eyes off the girl, pausing to listen intently when she spoke to Mrs Malone in her husky voice, asking how on earth did a doctor ever get up to these wild hills by carriage or horse?

'Dear me, darling!' Mrs Malone laughed. 'I've never seen a real doctor round these parts. We women rely on each other. Mind you, there are doctors in the towns, I'm told, but they don't trouble themselves with us natives. But still, God is good in showing us nature's way of healing. Will you stay for supper, Michael?'

Michael hesitated, his eyes still on the girl.

'We have a nice piece of brawn, and there's a blackberry pie, and the potatoes are cooked now.'

Michael smiled. 'Aye, I think I will stay. Thank you kindly.'

Mrs Malone provided a nice table, and throughout the meal as her husband talked and laughed, she couldn't help noticing the way the rebel kept staring at the girl who studiously avoided his eyes.

All the nice warmth left Mrs Malone's face, her lips pressed together tightly. She had never believed that Michael Dwyer had turned bad or turned on his own people, but this was a different kind of badness, a badness she hated to see in any man with a wife and children, and he was not even trying to hide it. His eyes kept straying to the girl as if she were a magnet, and whenever she spoke, which was not often, he listened to every word she said as if her voice fascinated him.

And yet, in comparison to Mary Doyle she was like a painted doll next to a fresh summer flower. But then, many a man had been led astray by the lure of new pastures and forbidden fruit . . . Oh, look at that – now his eyes were on her breasts, like firm peaches under the tightly buttoned bodice. Mrs Malone took a gulp of blackcurrant juice and almost spat it across the table at him.

After supper they adjourned back around the fire and, although it was now dark, the rebel made no move to leave. As much as Mrs Malone would have liked to, it would be the lowest of manners to hint that he should be making tracks. Her husband hadn't seemed to notice a thing, just kept laughing and talking to the cool-eyed philanderer as if he were his best-loved friend.

Mrs Malone sat in her chair knitting, head bent as she listened to the rebel politely ask the girl questions about herself. Her accent was not wholly Dublin, he said. No, she replied huskily, she had been born in France of a French father and Irish mother . . . Her father had been killed during the Terror, and her mother had fled with her to Ireland, but had died of fever shortly after arriving in Dublin. The girl had then been fortunate enough to have been taken in by a lady of quality who brought her up as a companion, on the proviso that she never again spoke French. The old lady hated the French.

'Is that right?' Michael said softly, smiling. 'And now you're heading for Talbotstown? Whereabouts in Talbotstown?'

Mrs Malone put the end of a knitting needle against her teeth

471

and sat that way for some time, gazing into the fire with brooding eyes that had a deep sadness in them. Only this afternoon she had ventured down to the village well to draw water, for although there was plenty of streams about, the water-well was a meeting-place for the mountain women who longed to have a chat with other females, but felt they needed an excuse to sit and idle an hour. And only this afternoon herself and two others had idled the time sitting on the stone wall of the well, chatting about the love story of Michael Dwyer and Mary Doyle.

In this land and time of arranged marriages, they had talked softly and wistfully about the way Mary had defiantly run away that October night and secretly married him, pledging to link her destiny with his, to share his dangerous and uncertain life in hill and valley and harbourer's house, and all for love.

The women had shuddered at the romance of it, and spoke of his great love for her too, and they had all nodded and agreed that their 'Mary of the Mountains' was worthy of such love, for with her long raven hair, tall proud body, and dark gentle eyes, she was truly a daughter of their race. And the women beside Mrs Malone had swung their feet against the wall and sighed with a gentle sadness for their own great love story that had never happened, and now never would.

And then they had all sat for a time singing songs and watching the day go by, all thinking of the love story of Michael Dwyer and Mary Doyle, for Mary's defiance gave them hope for their daughters, who might one day know the ecstasy of love, even if their mothers never had.

Mrs Malone clicked the needle against her teeth and started knitting again, her brow furrowed. But what would she tell her friends now? How could she break their simple-natured hearts and tell them that the rebel captain – whom Mary Doyle had faithfully married and faithfully stuck by through all the perils of his life – was now showing a very keen interest in a paint-and-powdered floozy with a hint of a foreign accent!

She looked up again when her son brought out his flute and began to play an old romantic song. Then her husband took down his fiddle and her two daughters treated their female guest to a display of dancing.

The rebel smiled and clapped them, and said he liked to dance himself. He suddenly leaned towards the young woman and said: 'Will you dance with me?'

She seemed startled, then smiled and coyly shook her head in refusal.

'Why not? Just a step or two anyhow?'

The girl coyly refused again, and again he smiled strangely and asked, 'Why not?'

She tilted her chin and cleared her throat. 'I really don't think I should.'

'Of course you should,' he said, catching her hand and forcing her up, then pulling her to the centre of the floor, he smiled provocatively, 'Ach, don't be shy now.'

The rigidity left the girl's body and her face took on an expression that might have been a smile.

Michael turned to Malone and asked him to strike up a fast beat. The boy came in with a few sweet blasts on his flute and the girls laughed merrily as he whirled and twirled the young woman almost off her feet.

Mrs Malone sat fuming as she watched the rebel frolicking with the girl. It was as if some shameless mania had taken hold of him. And the way he was whirling and twirling the girl so fast it looked like he was trying to make her fall. Dear me, God preserve us, it did and all. Into his arms of course! And his poor wife nursing his baby son at some harbourer's house. Mrs Malone's palms itched to leap up and whap him, the girl too, for now the hussy was laughing and enjoying it.

And then, as the girl twirled and almost stumbled, the rebel reached out and caught her under the arms to steady her, and it was then, that Mrs Malone's sharp eyes saw his hand slyly touch one of her breasts.

She would not have it! She jumped up and reached for a copper pot hanging over the fireplace to wallop him with it. Her friends would expect it. Every married female in Wicklow would applaud her! She turned with pot raised like an avenging angel – just in time to see the rebel slip out his foot and trip the girl into a tumble on to the floor.

Well, as God's alive, if Mrs Malone could have helped the girl she would have done, but as if in a dream she stood rooted to the spot in horrified disbelief.

The music ceased abruptly, Malone jumped to the assistance of his female guest, but Dwyer shouted him back, bending over the girl sprawled between his feet and shrieking as if her back might be broke.

A second later the rebel had seized the girl's dress and ripped the bodice apart, shoving his hand inside and angrily bouncing one hard orange on the floor, then another, yanking loose the wide tape of flannel covering, and laying bare the smooth flat chest of a young man.

'Stop screaming like a woman and get to your feet!' Michael rasped. He yanked the youth to his feet and slammed him against the far wall. 'I knew you were not a female as soon as I saw you. I couldn't believe it, but I knew it. Now what's your game and why have you come here?'

The youth became terrified, began protesting a whole string of reasons for his predicament, then Michael lost his patience.

'Outside!' he commanded, then dragged the youth out to the back yard where he was again slammed hard against a wall.

'Feet apart!'

The youth's knees instinctively jammed together, his eyes as wide as a terrified horse.

'*Feet apart!*' Michael hissed.

He put his hands on the youth's shoulders and rammed his knee between the youth's knees. 'Now, I can smell dirty business here. One false answer to my questions and this knee of mine goes up hard and without mercy. You understand me?'

Five minutes later the youth was dragged back inside and the family stood gaping in silent astonishment as Michael pushed him into the bedroom, whipped up a sheet and began tying him to the bedpost. Never had they seen Dwyer in such a rage.

'What's going on?' Malone asked as Dwyer tightly knotted the sheet around the youth's wrists, then gagged his mouth. 'Why is she – he here?'

'To set you up, avic. You're going to be robbed, this very night, by Michael Dwyer and his banditti. His job was to slip out of bed after you had all retired, unchain the door so they could just walk in, then act all innocent and go on her – his merry way tomorrow to meet up with them again for the next job.'

'Oh!' Mrs Malone stared with eyes as wide as saucers at the girlish-looking young man, his chestnut wig and cute bonnet askew, his face painted and powdered perfectly.

'He's a play-actor from Dublin,' Michael said. 'Got kicked out for being light-fingered and fell in with a gang of real robbers.'

'Oh, Michael darling,' Mrs Malone cried. 'Will you ever forgive me for lifting the pot and almost smashing—'

'No time for prattle,' Michael rasped. 'They may be here shortly. Now here's what you do. Put all the children into this bed, and you stay in here with them, Mrs Malone.'

'I'll not leave my children in here with him,' she cried. 'What if he breaks free?'

'Not from those knots. Those knots have held strong men scaling up and down mountain ridges.'

Minutes later the children were in bed, the candles snuffed, and the house in darkness. Michael stood like a shadow by the living-room window.

'Do you know who they are?' Malone whispered.

'Yes.'

'Do you want a drop of whiskey to steady your nerves?' Malone queried.

'No.'

'Do you mind if I have some?'

'Go ahead. But only enough to steady you.'

They waited all through the night. Mrs Malone crept anxiously out a number of times, returning swiftly to her children, then the sound of her light snoring betrayed she had fallen asleep.

In the last flush of darkness, Michael stepped back from the window and whispered: 'Here they come.'

The latch on the unbarred door quietly lifted only minutes later. A man crept in, then another, and another, five in all, through the open door.

Malone was snoring loudly in the settle-bed by the far wall. The leader of the gang, whose face was blackened and wore a large winter scarf around his neck, bent down to light a candle from the fire. As it flamed, Michael saw the youth had not been lying about the identity of his fellow criminals.

'Get up, ye bastard!' the leader hissed at Malone, who woke as if stupid, and stared in pretended surprise at the five men with blackened faces.

'Where do you keep your money?'

'Money?' Malone slunk down the bed. 'I have no money.'

'Sure you do. We've checked you out. Now save us time and trouble and tell us where you keep your box.'

'What'll you do if I don't?'

An amused laugh. 'Well you know the saying, avic. Your money or your life. And believe me, we're not jesting.'

'Who are you?'

'Captain Dwyer at your service, my good man. And these here are my faithful comrades, Hugh Vesty Byrne, John Mernagh, Martin Burke, and—'

'And Farrell Reily,' Michael finished, slamming the door with his foot.

The five men jolted round and stared at the brace of pistols pointing at them. 'Make a move and I take at least two of you,' Michael said. 'Now, you know the saying, avic? Hands up!'

Five pairs of hands shot up at the sound of both pistols being cocked.

'Relieve them of their weapons,' Michael said to Malone. 'But take them from behind.'

'You proddy-loving pig!' James Horan hissed. 'I should have knifed you in your sleep when I had the chance.'

Michael was looking at the blackened face of Farrell Reily, the one-time close companion of Michael Kearns who had left the rebel camp shortly after Horan.

'Oh, Reily,' Michael said sadly. 'It grieves me to see you like this.'

When Reily made no answer, Michael addressed Malone. 'Wake your boy and bring him in here dressed and ready for a run.'

When the boy came out, he made to sling an angry jab at Horan's belly, but his father held him back.

'Now here's what you do, son. Go to the house of William Jackson at Brusselstown.'

'You want me to go to Billy the Rock?' the boy cried nervously.

Malone looked at Michael, then nodded at his son. 'Yes, Billy the Rock. Tell him that the robbing party using the name of Dwyer are here, disarmed. But he's to bring no other yeomen except his son John Jackson, Sergeant Hawkins, and . . .' He looked questioningly at Dwyer.

'Thomas Morris,' Michael said. 'Repeat the names.'

When the boy did so efficiently, James Horan let out a roar of rage. 'So that's what you're going to do, Dwyer? Hand us over to Protestant yeomen?'

'I can think of no worse fate for you,' Michael replied coldly. 'In your night raids you killed two harmless Protestant civilians who didn't even put up a resistance to your robbery.'

'The bastards have been killing us long enough,' Horan raged. 'Living off our backs, supporting the English butchers.

Oh yes, Captain Big Man, I had it right about you, you'll be singing the Lillibulero yet! You pig!'

The boy rushed back in. 'Shall I take the pony, Da? I could make swifter speed on the pony and I can ride him bareback.'

'Look, will you just go!' Michael urged the boy, but the split-second diversion was enough for the five men who sprang for their lives and suddenly fell on Dwyer in one brutal swoop and almost broke his wrists in their frenzy to bash the guns from his hands. Both pistols went off, both bullets penetrating the wooden floor. Malone stood floundering.

'Take Dwyer outside and put him up against the wall,' James Horan roared. 'Boys-o-boys, my day has come! This is going to be my dream come true!'

The four dragged Dwyer out through the door and now it was his turn to be slammed up against the wall. Dawn was breaking and the sky a dull grey. Michael maintained his composure and looked at Horan as if he was slime.

Horan laughed viciously. 'Would you just look at the cocky bastard, boys? And you know what – I've just had an idea! Why don't we do to this pig what he was going to do to us – hand him over to the militia in Rathdrum or Baltinglass. Those bastards hate him so much they'd hang him up, cut him to pieces, then kneel down and drink his blood as it dripped.'

Three of the men holding his arms laughed; the fourth, Farrell Reily only smiled weakly.

'But let's not give the bastards all the fun,' Horan laughed. 'Let's break a few bones and spill a bit of blood ourselves beforehand.'

Horan bent his body almost double and clenched his fists in readiness to blast straight up to the chin. 'Here we go,' he grunted.

Swift as a knife-flick Michael swung up his boot in such a savage kick to Horan's face it sent him flying and broke his jaw again.

'You always did talk too much, Horan.'

For a moment the four men stared at Horan sprawled in agony, blood spilling out of his mouth, then fists began to pound into Dwyer's body, two throwing left and rights, while the other two held him hard against the wall. Boom, boom, boom, into the stomach, the chest, the solar plexus. Boom, boom, boom!

'Now it's my turn!'

477

One of the gang holding Dwyer eagerly swopped places with his exhilarated companion and stood setting his fists for a big one to the stomach. And then it thudded home – vooooooom!

'Now it's my turn!'

Heaving and doubled up in pain, Dwyer raised dazed eyes to the youth with the painted face. His chestnut wig and bonnet were neatly back in place.

Mrs Malone appeared at the door and wailed: 'He threatened to shoot me afterwards if I didn't cut him free! He threatened to knife my children!'

'And you did right to heed him,' one of the gang assured her. 'You see, missis, our Louis here may be pretty as a picture, but underneath that dress, he's a natural-born killer.'

The youth stood before Dwyer, smiling viciously, his eyes flashing venom. 'Hold him firm against the wall,' he ordered in a strong manly voice. 'Dancing boy and me have a score to settle.'

'Now, Louis,' Farrell Reily protested in a weak voice. 'None of your funny business.'

'Shut your mouth, crab-face!' Louis snapped, then smiled leeringly at Dwyer. 'Feet apart!' he commanded.

Dwyer drew on his heaving breath and spat in his face.

'Kick his feet apart!' Louis yelled. And the men instantly obeyed, as if more terrified of this painted youth than James Horan. 'Now you, Hughes,' Louis commanded, 'grab his hair and hold his head up.'

Then Louis stepped up close and clamped his hands each side of Michael's face with a seductive smile. '*Cherie!*' he hissed.

Whatever funny business Louis had in mind was thwarted by a bullet which smashed through the wall above their heads, sending limestone fragments showering down on them.

Louis swung round and the four jerked their heads in the direction of the gunshot. Hugh Vesty Byrne stood on the high bank reloading. Mernagh and Burke stood a few feet apart with guns aimed.

'Let him down to the ground nice and easy,' Hugh Vesty shouted, pulling back his flint. 'The next is for you, lover-boy, if you make one false move.'

'Who me?' Louis said in his most girlish voice, hands coyly clutching his torn bodice.

The three were in the yard in seconds, and, seeing reinforcements had arrived, Malone came out. He felt ashamed for not going to Dwyer's assistance but he wasn't sure what to do. He was useless with guns and not good enough with his fists to take on five bruisers. And he did, after all, have a family to protect first and foremost.

'Rope!' Hugh commanded, and when Malone ran to the barn and returned with a coil of hemp, 'Tie their hands behind their backs, good and tight.'

Then Hugh Vesty stood to peer into the blackened face of Farrell Reily. 'Oh, Reily!' he said in a disappointed tone. 'Now what do you think a good lad like Kearns would say if he saw you like this, and knew how you've been acting, eh? He rated you, Reily. Considered you a good friend. But if he were to come along here this minute, man, he would spit in your eye.'

'I never touched Dwyer,' Reily cried. 'I held him, but I couldn't hit him. I swear it.'

'Are you the gang of robbers using Michael's name?' Hugh asked. 'Is this what it's all about?'

Farrell Reily nodded sheepishly. 'But on the Book, Hugh Vesty, I wish I'd never got into it. I wish I'd never listened to Horan. And I wish to God I'd never met that crazy half-Frenchman. I wish I'd never left our camp.'

'I do understand your remorse,' Hugh said softly, then slung a powerful blow into Reily's stomach, making him bellow like a bull and double over. 'But I understand the hurt inflicted on my poor cousin over there even better,' Hugh snapped. 'I may even kill you for this, Reily, before the day is dark. Michael saved your life three times in battle that I know of, you ungrateful bandy-arsed punkawn!'

Michael was on one knee, drawing in deep breaths, his face very white. Mernagh and Burke were bent over him, each with a hand on his shoulder. The gang of four were all tied up, as was the one in the dress and bonnet. James Horan was still sprawled and moaning in agony.

Hugh Vesty squatted down before his cousin and looked into his face. 'Good job we came out looking for you, avic.'

Michael managed a weak smile, 'I always was a lucky fella,' then winced as he tried to rise, sank back to his knee, head down.

An uncertain quietness had fallen over the yard as the two cousins spoke low together. Hugh Vesty helped Michael to his feet and called to Malone to bring out his cart. 'We'll take this lot across to Billy the Rock,' he said.

'He's likely on his way,' Malone said. 'My boy went

arunning as soon as the fists started flying.'

When Michael entered the living-room, Mrs Malone was already pouring a kettle of hot water into a bowl. 'Sit down now and let's see if any bones are broken,' she said.

His entire stomach and midriff area had been punched purple, but only one rib seemed to be possibly cracked. She tutted and murmured as she rubbed witchhazel and lily of the valley oil into his flesh, then cut strips of linen, dipped them in the hot water and wrapped them tightly around his lower ribs.

'You have a hard body,' she commented. 'Lucky for you.'

'Aye, I'm dowsed in luck,' he answered wryly. 'Ever since the day as a childybawn when I was captured near a faery rath by them that's in it.'

'On with you!' she laughed, then burst into tears. 'Would they have killed my man, do you think?'

'Who knows?' he shrugged, then stiffly pulled on his shirt. 'Best thing to do now is forget it. They'll not be troubling anyone again. Not in Wicklow anyhow.'

Outside in the yard the gang were being loaded on to the cart. James Horan lay stretched and moaning, trying to speak. Farrell Reily sat on the hay-strewn cart staring in silent pleading at Hugh Vesty, who ignored him and motioned with his gun to the others to climb aboard.

Malone was forced to drive his cart slowly down the rugged hill-path. The armed rebels walked alongside in escort, occasionally pulling on the wheels to stop it rolling too fast.

Mrs Malone watched them go, Wicklow boys all four of them, and her heart beat proud. She was sure if they had not come along, she would be a widow this livelong day.

'Now here's what we do,' she said to her two young daughters. 'We'll milk the cow, feed the hens, have some breakfast ourselves, then set off to tell the people what happened this long night and clear up the confusion about the robberies.' Then she laughed merrily and ushered her girls indoors.

'And to think,' she suddenly cried, smiling joyously at her daughters, 'that he had no notion of being unfaithful to his Mary after all!'

The two girls began to titter and rub shoulders as their mother flung an arm around each and embraced them passionately to her breast. 'Oh musha, my darlings – but 'tis still a love story we have going on there if I'm not mistook! A real love

480

story and, God help us, there's few enough of them around.'

She shuddered in ecstasy at the thought of it, then swept the girls aside and busied herself with breakfast. And as she did so, she praised God aloud for not allowing the Devil to steal in and lay out dead her own man. For although he was not the great love of her life and dreams, over the years she had become damned fond of him.

William Jackson had been given the nickname of 'Billy the Rock' simply because of a conspicuously large rock that stood in the field across from his house.

The cart had travelled some two miles when Billy came riding along, accompanied by three more mounted yeomen, his son John Jackson, Thomas Morris, and Sergeant Hawkins.

Michael was looking at the two younger men, John Jackson and Thomas Morris. Both were the same age as himself, and the three had grown up as neighbours and friends since childhood. All had been of a sporting turn and had spent much time in shooting and coursing over the mountains together. Such a strong attachment had sprung up between the three that the houses of Morris and Jackson, although Protestant, had been as open to Michael as his own home. Then the rebellion broke, sides had been chosen, and Morris and Jackson took the king's shilling in exchange for a red coat.

As they drew closer Michael then looked at John Jackson's father, Billy the Rock.

Billy the Rock – his great shouting voice that could rattle the glass of any window whether in anger or laughter, came back to Michael. Billy the Rock – who had made him drink his first cup of whiskey, then roared with laughter to see the eyes rolling in his eleven-year-old head. But that was long past and best forgotten. Billy the Rock was now also a yeoman in a red coat.

Billy was a thick-set man, heavy in his saddle, with a face that could be coarse or genial, depending on his mood. His face was wary as he approached.

The cart stopped, the rebels waited calmly, though prudently cocked their guns.

Billy the Rock's face suddenly cleared as he rode close and saw the bound men in the cart.

'The boy was telling the truth then,' he said to Dwyer. 'On the way we wondered if we might be riding into a trap.'

'Escort them off,' Michael said tonelessly.

481

'Will you testify against them?' Sergeant Hawkins asked Malone.

Malone nodded. 'I surely will.'

'We'll leave you to it so,' Dwyer said as he and the rebels began to move away, walking backwards. Michael knew he was safe, but a man with five hundred guineas on his head couldn't entirely trust anyone.

Billy the Rock and Sergeant Hawkins saluted in silent farewell and turned their horses round. Thomas Morris and John Jackson stayed as they were, both looking embarrassed.

Thomas Morris was a sturdy young man with a face that usually wore a cheerful grin, but now was straight and moody. He urged his horse forward.

'Michael . . .'

'Aye.'

With every step Michael took back, Morris's horse moved forward. 'Our houses, Jackson's and mine, are still open to you . . . secretly of course.'

'I'll remember that,' Michael kept moving backwards, 'in an emergency.'

'And if we ever meet on a battlefield—'

'Oh sure!' Michael agreed with immense weariness. 'We'll aim at each other but make sure to shoot high – same as we did at Hacketstown and Humewood.'

Morris grinned.

Jackson smiled.

Dwyer turned away and walked off with his comrades without looking back.

The cartload of men were driven to the English barracks at Hacketstown. Captain Woollard rode into the yard a moment later and sat watching the bound gang as they were ordered to climb down.

Sergeant Hawkins explained the situation to him, even admitting that it was Dwyer who had handed them over.

'What's that wench doing with them?' Woollard asked, looking with keen interest at the rather gorgeous Louis. 'Is she a whore?'

'She's a man in female attire, sir,' Hawkins replied.

'O my sainted arse!' Woollard exclaimed wearily. 'The wenching situation in this country gets worse by the day. Still, every man to his own amusement.'

'This one here needs attention.' Billy the Rock leaned over the side of the cart and looked down at James Horan, who was still moaning. 'Jaw's broke by the looks of it.'

'And who did that?'

'No idea, sir.'

Woollard rode up to Malone sitting on the bench. 'Do you know who broke the jaw of the man in the cart?'

'Couldn't say, sir.' Malone answered blankly. 'All I know is that the gang entered my house for the purpose of robbing me. Same gang who were robbing alongside that party of yeomen.'

'Not alongside,' Billy the Rock said musingly. 'It's my feeling they got the idea from the yeomen and took it up after they had left off. Using Dwyer's name again, of course.'

'Well, whoever did what,' Woollard said scornfully, 'in my opinion, the whole bloody boiling of them are cruel savages devoid of any feelings of basic humanity.'

'What shall we do with this one?' Billy the Rock pointed to James Horan. 'He's in pain and clearly in need of attention.'

Captain Woollard back-stepped his horse and sat peering down at the moaning man. 'Good Lord, yes, he does need taking care of. The poor man must be relieved of his misery as soon as possible.'

Then Captain Woollard withdrew his pistol and shot Horan point blank through the heart.

'This doesn't let Dwyer off,' he said to Hawkins and Jackson. 'As soon as we have breakfasted, we'll scout the area where you last saw him.'

Hawkins and Jackson jerked out of their shock, and pretended compliance.

'Yes, sir. Of course.'

'Jolly good!' Captain Woollard smiled with a sudden upwelling of good humour. 'And if we find him, we'll shake his hand in gratitude then fire a nice British cartridge up his arse.'

He looked towards the mess hut with a curious sniff. 'I say, is that gammon and eggs I smell? Or is it the usual slop our king provides for his glory boys?'

Chapter Thirty-Two

For almost nine months Michael Dwyer's name had not appeared in a newspaper. Then the *Hibernian* brought him to public notice again in an article that endeavoured to be informative and impartial, yet trembled with exasperation:

> At the breaking out of the late Rebellion, Michael Dwyer, being about six or seven and twenty years of age, ranged himself under the banners of insurrection; and though always foremost in danger, had the good fortune to retire unhurt through all the battles of that deplorable contest. When the rebellion was put down, Dwyer withdrew, accompanied by a chosen band, into the fastnesses of his native mountains, where he has since kept his ground, bidding defiance to all the parties sent out from time to time against him.
>
> It must be a matter of astonishment that an active, powerful and vigilant Government could never succeed in exterminating this banditti from the mountains, however difficult, and inaccessible they may at first appear. The rebel, who is intimately acquainted with the topography of the place, has his regular videts and scouts in all the most advantageous points, who, on the appearance of alarm, or the approach of strangers, blow their whistles, which resound through the innumerable caverns, and are the signal for a muster. They are generally superintended by the chief himself, or his cousin of the name of Byrne, a determined fellow in whom alone he places confidence. Both are adepts at disguising their faces and persons and are thought to pay frequent visits to the metropolis – Dwyer is an active and vigorous fellow, and said to be wonderfully patient of fatigue, and fearless of every kind of danger.

By the time 1801 had passed into 1802, the Protestants of Wicklow were as unhappy about the Union as the Catholics. Unlike the previous Irish Parliament, England forbade them any say in government except the vote of their representative, who was invariably ignored at Westminster.

By the early spring of 1802, the Protestant and Catholic farmers of Wicklow were as good friends again as ever. They discussed their differences and the space of their hostile separation since the rebellion . . . In 1798 the Catholics were told that the Protestants intended to murder them, and they would not take that lying down . . . In 1798 the Protestants were told the Catholics intended to murder them, so what could they do but join the yeomanry forces and assist the English troops?

No one could quite remember who had told who, but when a rumour is whispered on the wind, it breezes into every household. Then all concluded that the English Executive at Dublin Castle was to blame – using the old system of divide and conquer to secure its imperial rule.

And so life stabilised as all abandoned their past prejudices and prepared excitedly for the spring planting, during which long idle discussions were held on the prospect of the autumn harvests.

In that same spring of 1802, the war between England and France ended with a peace treaty signed at Amiens. The Protestant and Catholic farmers greeted this news with an indifferent shrug and returned to talk of husbandry of the land, their eyes fixed keenly on the fertility of the soil as summer progressed. But even as the men reaped the harvest of barley and corn in the fields, and their women and children helped to collect the cut stalks of the grain which would be used as dry straw for fresh bedding, roof thatching, and animal fodder, the search for Michael Dwyer continued.

He had just stepped into the house of Laurence Mangan at Talbotstown when Mangan's daughter, Grania, cried a warning that an English regiment was riding down the road.

Mangan and Michael looked at each other; there was no way out, the house backed into the high ground of the hill-face and there was nothing but solid rock beyond the fireplace. If he attempted to run he would be seen the length of the road.

Grania rushed over to Michael and clutched on his arm. There were only the three of them in the house. Minutes later a hammering came on the door. Mangan opened it.

'Routine search,' Captain Woollard said with a bored air.

Mangan opened the door wider. 'This house belongs to Mr Hume of Humewood,' he said, thereby warning the officer that it could not be burned down at whim. 'My tenancy is with Mr Hume.'

Captain Woollard ignored him as a number of redcoats moved through the house, opening the settle-bed, moving the pine table and black-oak furniture, searching in and under the beds in the rooms off the kitchen.

Throughout, Captain Woollard stood officiously beside the silent Mangan whose very countenance fumed at such indignity. His daughter, on the other hand, was looking at the military officer with mild curiosity. She was a handsome girl with golden hair. Her eyes were blue, her lips naturally red, and her figure well shaped, as clearly emphasised by the tight black bodice laced under the white cotton cups of her breasts.

Involuntarily, Woollard smiled at her, and she smiled back. He looked down the room at the searching soldiers and wondered about her. Most of these females were rebel-lovers; but there were those few who – when confronted with a handsome officer in his scarlet uniform – instantly contracted a dose of scarlet fever.

Woollard stood taller in his uniform and found himself sympathising with such females: how could a rebel dressed in the country style, ever compare with the splendid scarlet gallants of His Majesty's army?

He looked at her and smiled again. She turned her eyes to the fire but a flush stained her oval cheeks, Woollard noticed, a *scarlet* flush!

His posture relaxed into one of arrogant charm. He moved a step or two towards the hearth and addressed a question to her: 'What is your name, miss?'

'Her name is Grania,' Mangan snapped.

'Gran – ya.' Woollard repeated the name as if it belonged to an angel, but before he unleashed all the seductive power of his charm, he decided to clarify one point: 'Are you one of those females afflicted with a favouring disposition towards the rebels?'

Her eyes widened a fraction and sought those of her father.

'Well, are you?' Woollard murmured softly, placing his scarlet-coated body in front of her father and shielding her face from his view.

'*Tá a lá go dona. An bhfuil tú fuar?*' she answered, her voice a soft, musical soprano.

Woollard stared at her in enchanted puzzlement.

'She doesn't speak English,' Mangan said. 'The wife was ill when she was born so I sent her down to be reared by my sister in Cork. She came back only a year or so ago speaking only the Gaelic. Not as much as ten words of English can she speak.'

'What did she say to me in Gaelic?' Woollard queried.

'She says it's a very bad day. Are you cold?'

'A bad day? Am I cold?' Woollard looked out at the sultry late September day, then stared curiously at the girl who smiled sweetly at him.

'She's also simple-minded,' Mangan said in slow sadness. 'Spends most of her time talking in Gaelic to the hens and pigs.'

The girl looked from the officer to her father with the awkwardness of one in the presence of those whose language they cannot understand.

Mangan rapidly translated in Irish what they had said. She placed her chin on her shoulder and blushed scarlet again, then uttered a silly giggle like a child of five.

Captain Woollard fell instantly out of love with her. He realised his men were all staring at him, waiting for his command. The place had been searched without success.

'Search the outhouses and surrounding land!' Woollard snapped at them, then glared scornfully at Mangan and the girl before marching out also.

'A right piss-off this is,' Captain Woollard muttered in disgust to his lieutenant as he relieved himself against a hedge adjoining the property. 'How can an officer ever hope to rise to glory in this bogland – searching houses and chasing bloody rebels and no other action?'

'And the rebels always seem to have the advantage in a chase, sir, knowing every inch of the land as they do – especially Dwyer.'

'I'll have that clever bastard on a triangle one of these days,' Woollard said, buttoning his breeches. 'I'll flog him myself until there's not an inch of skin left on his spine. Bloodybacks they call us – well I'll make his back so bloody he'll be screaming for me to kill him. Then I'll hand him over to the Rathdrum Militia and let them stick him like a pig and slice him up between them.'

'If we ever catch him, sir.'

487

Woollard turned and stared at his aide. 'I do believe, lieutenant, that you take great joy in irritating me. Of course we'll catch the bastard eventually. How many times have I told you that in any game of war, when it comes to deciding a victory, God always wears a red coat.'

'He didn't in America, sir.'

Woollard looked pained. 'I despair of you, lieutenant, I really do! Why – in the name of England – did you ever join the army?'

'My father bought me a commission, sir. It was either the army or lose my inheritance.'

'Then you must be daft in the loft if you think a wise old father like that would ever have accepted an Irish trollop in a pair of old broken boots!'

The other soldiers returned. 'No rebels around here, sir.'

'Then let's go!' Woollard snapped, then as he mounted his charger, 'And I warn you, lieutenant, if you persist in irritating me I'll have you cashiered for cowardice.'

'Yes, sir. Very good, sir,' the soldier answered drolly.

'Oy there!' Woollard checked his mount as Mrs Mangan turned in from the road and began to walk across the yard towards the house.

'You, woman – halt!'

'Me, sir?' she asked, turning to face him.

'Do you have knowledge of Dwyer's whereabouts?' Woollard demanded without preamble. 'Answer me truthfully now, and don't even think of antagonising me,' he warned, 'or I'll shoot you.'

'Shoot me, sir? Oh, God save us – what was the question again?'

'Do you have you any knowledge of Dwyer's whereabouts?'

'I do,' she replied with a nod. 'I was told only ten minutes ago.'

'Well?'

'Well, sir, 'tis said that Moiley the Bogeyman ate him a few days ago.' She regarded Woollard with a woebegone look that said, 'Wasn't that a terrible way to go?'

'*For'ard!*' Woollard screamed at his troop, then rode off at a gallop as if fearing the very real possibility of shooting her.

Grania stood by the window watching them with wide blue eyes until they had disappeared from view, then she turned and looked up towards the roof-tree and wide oak ceiling beams where Michael had been lying flat on his back directly over their heads, squeezed under the roof.

'All clear,' she said, and he swung down to the ground with a jump and smiled a smile of gratitude especially for her.

He was dressed in country style of brown whipcord breeches into which a black linen shirt was tucked and fastened with a wide leather belt accoutred /with military pouches and cartridge-box. On his shoulders he wore a cross-belt that held a brace of pistols each side of his chest which were hidden by a brown jacket.

The girl laughed again, for she had guessed Woollard's thoughts when he had preened to a taller and firmer stance in his scarlet regimentals.

'God help any maid that's foolish enough to fall into bed with him,' she said, 'for the poor lass is likely to end up kneeling at his feet in praise and ordered to tell him *exactly* just how wonderful he was, and just how very grateful she is for the honour.'

Michael looked at Grania in mild surprise, for she was an unmarried maid and not supposed to know about such things, but then he remembered she was on the verge of marriage with one of his comrades; a good-looking lad who had lately returned to camp looking unusually tousled, and followed orders as if in a dream.

Mrs Mangan came in carrying a red hen which she had picked up in the yard. 'Oh, is it ye, Michael,' she said indifferently, her near-miss with a bullet completely forgotten as she held up the ruffled red hen who was trembling violently and appeared to have had some of her feathers torn out.

'Would ye look at the poor darling,' Mrs Mangan cried. 'A beautiful hen she was when I bought her last week, and the rooster fell head-over-heels in love with her, but his other wives are mad with jealousy and keep pecking and clawing at her something vicious. Will you have a glass of buttermilk or ale, Michael?'

'If you'll not be offended, I won't,' he said, then quickly thanked her husband, who assured him that every villager in Wicklow was behind him, and he could trust his life with every single one of them.

'And as for me,' Mangan added, 'I have to be saying that I'm fiercely proud to have had you under my roof.'

They both laughed at that, and Michael moved to the door

where Grania stood guard by the gate to make sure all was clear. She gave him the nod, and he went out to her. He thanked her again by hugging her tightly and lifting her off her feet.

'On with you!' Grania laughed in flushed embarrassment. 'I'm already spoken for – and you're a married man that has two children.'

'Nay, that's not true.' He shook his head and smiled. 'I have three children.'

'Three? Since when?'

'Since a week ago.'

'My!' she said in a teasing tone, 'but you do keep that girl busy! What is it now—'

'Three children in four years,' he said softly. 'Our first two were born quite close together, but there was a gap of two years before our second son Peter was born a week ago.'

She smiled and suddenly gripped his hands tightly in both of hers. 'Congratulations, Michael, congratulations, asthore.'

' 'Tis Mary who deserves any congratulating,' he murmured.

'Yes,' she breathed, looking into his eyes, for in that moment she saw the depth of his feelings for his wife. 'You're a happy man,' she whispered. 'You're still in love with her.'

He shrugged. 'She's everything a man could want in a wife: courageous and loyal, beautiful, good-tempered, and very loving.'

She sighed. 'I hope my man can say the same when we've been married four years. Will you give him my love?'

He released his hands and backed away with a grin. 'I'll leave you to do that.'

Mr William Hume of Humewood sent for his tenant, Sergeant Hawkins of the Upper Talbotstown Yeomanry Corps. When Hawkins arrived, Mr Hume received him in his study.

'A friend from London is over on a visit,' Hume said. 'He wishes to have a crack at the excellent game we have here. You are cognisant of the best shooting ground, Hawkins, are you not?'

'Indeed I am, sir.'

'Excellent! Just as I thought. Now report here before first light in the morning to accompany us.'

Hawkins looked pleased, he loved a good sport; then an idea came to him. 'May I bring the young son of Ned Byrne of Fearbreaga, sir? He can hear and smell the game a mile off.'

Hume hesitated. 'Is he trustworthy?'

'He was too young to be an insurgent in 1798, if that is what you mean.'

'Is he a supporter of Dwyer?'

Hawkins shrugged. 'They all are, sir, but it doesn't mean he bodes any ill against you. Young Byrne is a very decent and likeable young lad.'

'You trust him?'

'I do.'

William Hume sighed. 'Well, if a yeoman trusts him, then I suppose I can. But he must not be allowed to carry a gun. Now, Hawkins, be here dark and early. I want my English friend to have an excellent time while he is in Ireland, an excellent time. Three days shall we allow? Three days sporting?'

'Three days should bring in a nice bag,' Hawkins agreed. 'Although we will have to make some recompense to Ned Byrne for losing his son's labour on the farm for three days.'

'Naturally, naturally,' Hume replied brightly.

The following morning was fine and frosty, perfect for a shoot. Ned Byrne's fifteen-year-old son, aware of Hume's rewarding nature, was happy enough to go along, and the party of four set off sharp and early and were on the shooting-ground at Aughavannagh not long after the darkness had lifted.

The Englishman was a fine young fellow, full of good humour and eager for the sport. They had been on the ground only a few minutes when, turning a hill, they saw six other sporting men in the distance, carrying guns.

'It seems we are not the only hunters out this early,' Hume remarked, then, as his red setter bounded away to leap madly at the tall young man leading the hunting party, he stared – and recognition dawned.

'I say, that's the fellow who calmed my poor injured setter for me. What did he tell me his name was now . . . Do you know him, Hawkins?'

'Yes, sir.' Hawkins pulled Hume aside and whispered in his ear. 'It's Michael Dwyer, sir.'

'Dwyer—' Hume went rigid with fright, his face blanched into a sickly paleness and his breathing quickened. It was on a morning such as this, in 1798, that his father had been killed while out sporting.

'Calm yourself, Mr Hume,' Hawkins said quietly. 'We are in no danger.'

Hawkins motioned with his head to young Byrne of Fear-breaga, who ran up to the party of men who had turned to look into the far undergrowth, a shot rang out, and a rebel sprang into a race with Hume's setter to collect the dead game while young Byrne spoke to Dwyer.

'Well?' Hawkins asked when he came back.

'Yes, w-well?' Hume stammered, ushering the lad aside so the Englishman could not hear.

'He says to crack away, sir. They apprehend no fear of us and we should apprehend no fear of them; he says we should crack away while the game is wild and running.'

Another shot rang out. Hume trembled to his boots. The Englishman looked totally bewildered, not having been told there were Irish rebels in these parts.

A few moments later Dwyer himself strolled casually down to them, leading back the setter and leaving his party behind. This time he removed his hat.

'Good morning, Mr Hume.'

'Oh, eh, yes indeed.' Hume pretended no recognition or knowledge of the man's identity.

The Englishman looked him over, from the gaming-gun in his hand down to the buckskin breeches and boots and assumed he was some sort of land-steward. 'Is it pheasant they are shooting up there?' he asked.

'Well it's surely not butterflies,' Dwyer answered in an amused drawl. 'You are an Englishman?'

'I have that honour,' came the bright reply. 'Here on a short holiday.'

'May I ask what you think of our country?'

Hume was astounded at the impertinence of the rebel, but the Englishman seemed quite unperturbed. 'A beautiful country! Quite beautiful. Yes, I must confess I am enjoying my stay here very well so far. The air and relaxation have been a damned tonic after the hubbub of old London.'

He smiled fondly at Hume and slapped him on the back. 'No offence, Willie, old chap, but Sutton and Thetford still insist you are pigging it here in some wilderness. I'll soon put them to rights!'

Hume flushed. 'Thank you, Kit, but I think that would be pointless,' he said in a resentful quiet tone.

'Devil take all those beggars in Dublin, though! Quite gave me the wrong impression when I landed. Reminded me of the

London wit who said he never knew what the English beggars did with their old discarded rags, until he came to Ireland.'

'Oh, we heard that jest,' Dwyer said brightly. 'But did you ever hear the response of one our Dublin wits on the matter?'

'No . . .' The young Englishman smiled, eager for the souvenir of gossip. 'Do tell.'

'Ireland may have beggars in rags – but England has a king insane.'

'Oh, I say, that's a bit below the belt.' The Englishman smiled in a very superior manner, then suddenly relented. 'Of course the man *is* completely batty – and worse – he's becoming less like a king and more like a national debt!' He turned to Hume. 'Did you know, Willie, that he's presently allowed to take one million pounds a year out of the seventeen million Parliament collect in taxes? *One million!* Now, as a liberal-minded man and a devout Whig—'

'Yes, eh, well,' the Member of Parliament for Wicklow looked whitely apprehensive as he looked at the rebel.

But Dwyer seemed to be enjoying the young Englishman. For strangely enough, although he hated redcoats, and hated the British Parliament, he was totally uncontaminated by any fanatical feelings of hatred towards ordinary Englishmen, rich or poor. And this detached sentiment was also felt by most of his comrades.

But William Hoare Hume didn't know that. He was sure he and his English friend were about to be dispatched at some unsuspecting moment by this rebel who only had to give the signal to his party of sharp-shooters.

'Have you done much sporting?' Michael asked the genial young Englishman.

'Did a bit of grouse-shooting up in Scotland. Lovely country, except for the people, of course. Very dour and grim in the best of their humours. The Scotsman who took us out as a guide had the set face of a Puritan elder and never uttered one word for the entire two days he was with us. Quite took the enjoyment out of it all.'

'Ach, you were just unlucky,' Michael told him. 'Some are as bright and merry as Christmas.'

'Yes, eh, well,' Hume said nervously. 'Shall we seek out the pheasant?'

'A nice stag's head is what I'm after,' the Englishman exclaimed. 'A red one, to stuff and put on my wall back in

England – will always remind me of you, Hume!'

'Ha ha ha ha!' Hume laughed miserably, knowing his friend had made an unfortunate gaffe.

'The red deer are never killed in this land,' Michael said quietly, 'except by ignorant foreign visitors and plundering invaders.'

'What? Not kill the deer, not even one?' The Englishman made an exaggerated face of gross disbelief.

'It is an unwritten law of old,' Sergeant Hawkins explained quietly. 'Ordered by Finn.'

'And who is he – some upstart of a country bumpkin magistrate?'

'We are allowed to course the red deer in a chase,' young Byrne piped up solemnly, 'but it must reach no *kill* while poetry is our heritage and Ireland our land.'

'Take my advice,' Michael said to the Englishman, 'and content yourself with the pheasant.'

'Oh, well!' the Englishman declared good-naturedly. 'A pheasant or a peasant, I'll have to shoot and stuff something in Ireland to bring back and show what a fine shot I am.'

Hume burst into a peal of tense laughter, bordering on hysteria. A country silence filled the pause, the lads on the hill now stood waiting to know if they should advance or retreat away from the gaming grounds.

Michael nodded at Hawkins, tousled young Byrne's hair, then saluted Hume and his friend in farewell with a touch of his hat.

'Good sporting to you, gentlemen.'

'Oh, maybe so, maybe so now,' Hume replied with a huge smile of relief as the rebel strolled away.

'A pleasant enough fellow,' declared the Englishman, still in the bliss of his ignorance. 'But a little strange, perhaps?'

Hume stiffened. 'Strange?'

'Rather lofty in his manner, I thought. Telling us not to shoot the deer then striding off as if he was some lord of the acres.'

'Oh, they're all like that in these hill parts,' Hume assured him quickly. 'All think they are descendants of Irish kings or Gaelic lords. One has to humour them, you know, for the sake of peaceful relations.'

'Whisht, sir!' young Byrne whispered, holding up his hand. He stalked forward a few paces into the trees, then beckoned the others to follow him. 'Stand well covered and ready,' he hissed.

The three men quietly prepared their guns, excitement boiling in their blood, then Hawkins stood well back, firmly holding the setter as all waited for what seemed a very long time while young Byrne stood with head cocked and eyes half closed. Suddenly he made a sound with his mouth like that of a pheasant cock yearning amorously for a mate.

Nothing happened, but he smiled and made the sound again, clucking loudly and seductively . . .

. . . and out he came, along the beaten path, a great big pheasant-cock making angry noises and strutting like a furious army general ready to savage the rival making wooing calls to his wives.

Suddenly he stopped strutting and looked about him, his head stretching high out of his neck, jerking from left to right. He made an irritable noise in his throat and shook his feathers; then clucking angrily he scraped the ground furiously with one leg, preparing for battle.

From where he was concealed, young Byrne raised his catapult and let fly with an iron pellet at the same time as the Englishman fired.

'I say!' Hume cried. 'Good shot, Kit, old chap, good shot!'

The Englishman scrambled forward and picked up the prize pheasant by the neck. 'Oh, look at the size of him,' he cried, 'and the plumage!' His face was beaming with radiant astonishment. 'Wait till they hear it was my very first shot of the trip, what? And he'll make a wonderful stuff!'

Hawkins and young Byrne peered at the pheasant, then looked slyly at each other. Hawkins shook his head, the lad nodded agreeably. It would be very unsporting to point out that the pheasant-cock bore no bullet wound, just a small black bruise in the centre of its forehead where he had received his death blow.

'Good work, boy,' William Hume exclaimed in delight. 'Where did you learn to make a sound like that?'

' 'Tis an old trick,' the lad said, then smiled mischievously. 'The dames will be out soon, sir, if I woo them a bit more. They'll be out looking for their lord or his rival. They'll not care which, as long as he's amorous.'

'A pair!' the Englishman cried excitedly. 'Perhaps I could stuff a pair – a lord and his dame – put them in matching glass cases in the dining-room.'

'Good God, man, is it really necessary to be in such disgusting good humour all the livelong day!' Hume's patience had suddenly deserted him without warning.

The Englishman stared at him, then smiled slowly in understanding. 'Willie, you old devil, don't tell me that you're jealous because I got the first kill?'

'I'm delighted you got the first kill,' Hume cried, taking out a handkerchief and mopping his brow. 'But devil take it, Kit, here in Ireland any game we kill is usually sent straight to the kitchen, not the taxidermist!'

The Englishman looked totally taken aback. 'No need to get so temperamental, dear chap.' He looked about him, crestfallen. 'Oh, damn it,' he said quietly, 'I do hate arguing and you Irish are so good at it. I know, let's split the difference, stuff only one, and shake hands and be friends again, what?'

Hume nodded and smiled a shade guiltily as his hand was warmly grasped. 'Good old Kit, so patient.' Hume grasped the hand tighter. 'I am glad you came.'

Kit smiled self-consciously. 'I cannot endure ill-feelings between old school chums, or indeed anyone. I hope I have not offended.'

'Not intentionally, Kit, never intentionally.'

'So now back to the game, eh?' Kit turned and flung an imperious finger towards young Byrne. 'You, boy! Do that seductive noise again and make those feathered whores come strutting. Then tonight, Willie, old chum, you and I should get gloriously drunk and find ourselves a couple of damsels who might oblige us with the pleasure of a jolly good rogering!'

Hawkins, who had just taken a gulp of whiskey from his hip-flask, choked and sprayed the contents of his mouth all over William Hume.

But William Hume didn't seem even to notice. He collapsed back against a tree and began to laugh until tears ran from his eyes.

As soon as his friend had returned to England, William Hume, Member of Parliament for Wicklow and Captain of the Humewood Cavalry, informed all his associates that he was planning a campaign to bring in Michael Dwyer. He made a number of half-hearted midnight raids on houses but all to no avail. Hume wrote to the Castle explaining the result.

In one house, he explained, while searching the room off the kitchen he found the bed still warm, and the family could not account satisfactorily for the person or persons who had been sleeping in it. He was convinced it was Dwyer; but now the country was no longer under martial law, and without definite evidence, he could do nothing to the family on mere suspicion.

He also had to live in Wicklow, Hume explained, depending on the peaceful goodwill and labour of his many tenants. He was fully persuaded that as the entire population was determined to protect Dwyer, it was impossible to arrest him.

Inside Dublin Castle, the new Under-Secretary of State, Alexander Marsden, found he had inherited a wide range of spies and informers from the former administration.

Thomas King, the resident magistrate at Rathdrum, continued to send in his indignant reports:

> If gentlemen like Mr Hume, our Knight of the Shire, will temporise with rebels, what can be expected but they live publicly in that country without fear of apprehension. Dwyer walks about in open day, but seldom comes on this side of the great body of mountains.
>
> Above all the cause of Loyalty was much injured by granting a pardon to John Jackson, a Yeoman who was clearly convicted of harbouring Dwyer, the consequence has been that Dwyer is as free in every Yeoman's house there (if I am rightly informed) as he can wish – his greatest place of resort is with one Morris who lives at Boleycarrigeen, and frequently lies in the same bed. He is often at Wilson's at Knockanarigan, Jackson's, and William Murray not far from Ballinaclay, all Yeomen – I find these names upon report so often repeated that I have no doubt on the subject.

Alexander Marsden threw down the report. He was now convinced more than ever that Michael Dwyer posed no threat to the safety of the country or government. He was simply an embarrassment. His defiance and evasion of capture had caused many red faces in military circles.

Marsden swept the reports on the Wicklow rebels aside. He was far more interested in the other reports sent to him from his network of spies on the Continent, who kept him well informed of the Irish *emigré* 1798 leaders now living in Napoleon's

France. These were the truly dangerous men that Marsden feared – Irish Protestants of the class – politically inflamed intellectuals bent on achieving an Irish Republic modelled on the French and American system.

These were the men Marsden hated beyond measure. Their betrayal of their own superior class alone suffused him with an anger he could barely control. Their nonsensical theory that Irishmen of every religious persuasion could stand shoulder to shoulder as equals and united was more than ludicrous, it was insulting – insulting to every respectable member of the class.

Rebels of the peasant farming class, like Dwyer, did have a few understandable grievances to justify their rebellious nature, but rebels of the superior class born with a silver spoon to feed their mouths had no justification for their views at all – and if any of these United *emigré* leaders dared to return to Ireland, Marsden intended to see every one of them hanged for treason.

A fine lesson that would be. A perfect discouragement to any other members of the class who might have similar notions about an American-styled democracy where Johnny was considered to be as good as his master.

Johnny as good as his master?

Never.

Chapter Thirty-Three

The pretty Sarah, wife of Hugh Vesty Byrne, had grown up some fifteen miles away from Imaal in the vicinity of Rathdrum. The first time she had ever set eyes on Mary Doyle was on the night of her wedding to Michael Dwyer. The two girls had spoken very little to each other that night, for Mary had no eyes or words for anyone but her husband.

Sarah had not particularly liked the new bride that night. Sarah had looked at Mary with her shy smile and soft brown eyes and thought Michael had made the biggest mistake of his life. In truth, Mary Doyle was the loveliest girl Sarah had ever seen, but she looked timid and doltishly dependent – qualities that filled Sarah with contempt, for although she herself was a frailly built girl, she had been as ready as any man to risk her life for liberty in 1798.

In view of all that had happened since then, Sarah smiled now at her thoughts that night in October 1798. Mary lived a harder life than any other female in Wicklow, and over the years had proved herself in all ways admirable, bearing all her difficulties and discomforts without complaint. And she was now Sarah's dearest friend.

'Thank God, they're all asleep now,' Mary murmured tiredly. 'Are you coming to bed soon, Sarah?'

From where she was sitting on an old settle, Sarah looked up from her contemplation of the fire and silently nodded at the girl sitting on the edge of the bed in the dark shadows of the room, pulling a comb through the tangle of dark hair around her shoulders. Her dress was folded neatly on the back of a chair, her arms and shoulders were bare; she sat in a white petticoat which revealed the swell of full milky breasts that had recently given sleepy comfort to a suckling infant.

They were in a harbourer's house deep in Glenmalure, at a relative of Hugh Vesty's. The largest of two bedrooms had been given over to the two young women and their children, while the parents of the family willingly insisted on sleeping on a straw pallet in the small open loft above the living-room.

Sarah and Mary shared the bed, while their children slept on a straw tick on the floor, and the two babies snuggled side by side under warm blankets in a big wicker laundry basket beside the bed. Like Mary, Sarah had also borne three children: Philip, Michael, and baby Rose. And like Mary, Sarah adored her husband.

Sometimes Sarah raged at Hugh Vesty against the hardness of their lives, the long separations, the pregnancies that resulted from a few nights of love that were the more ecstatic because they were brief and stolen. And he would apologise sadly, and she would be filled with guilt at her outburst, for the women at least had the joy of the children, but all the time the hunt for the men went on, English regiments, militia regiments, Rathdrum and Baltinglass yeomanry; and occasionally, rebels were killed.

And therein lay the anger and the heartache. To the world at large they had only the name of rebels, but to Hugh Vesty and Michael and the people of Wicklow, they were friends with individual names, friends with mothers and fathers and sisters and brothers, some with baby children, friends shot down like vermin – and some, like Andrew Thomas, brutally mutilated.

'Sarah,' Mary whispered, suddenly, 'what is wrong, darling?'

Mary moved from the bed to sit on the settle and put an arm around her friend. It was not the first time they had comforted each other. Over the years the similarity of their situations had drawn them towards each other. More and more they sought out each other's company, for both knew the loneliness and desperation of being wife to a hunted rebel. Both knew the feeling of being cut off from everything that was normal and secure in the general run of life. And when one or the other allowed their fears to overwhelm them, they would put their arms around each other in the way of all women seeking and giving comfort, and whatever the problem the other would whisper: 'I know, I know, I have felt the same also.'

Sarah pushed back her tears and clutched Mary's warm dry hand. They were so different in many ways. Mary would never rage at Michael about the hardness of her life. His love was all she considered, his love fulfilled her, the memory of their last time together sustained her until the next, and knowing his pride and delight in his children, she would go on bearing them happily and placidly, and in return he worshipped her like a queen.

But it seemed to Sarah that, as different as she and Mary were, only with each other could they honestly speak their minds and share the burden of the struggle, say the things that a woman says only to another woman. Their friendship had grown slowly but surely, a friendship almost as deep and as solid as that shared by their two husbands; and now, beneath that friendship, both knew there was love.

'It's all a dream . . .' Sarah whispered. 'A dream that one day it will be all right . . . that the redcoats will go from our country, that the fanatical militia will leave us alone, that we can return with our men and babies to our farms and live in peace . . . but it's all a dream isn't it?'

'I don't know,' Mary whispered. 'I used to dream, of a house and hearth of my own, but now I just live from day to day.'

She shrugged, then moved off the settle and knelt down to rake the ashes over the red embers of the fire. In the firelight her beauty had a wild quality, but when she turned and looked at Sarah, Sarah noticed the dark shadows of fatigue under her eyes.

'You look tired,' Sarah murmured.

Mary nodded, and gazed back at the fire. She was tired, so very tired of her nomadic life. Sometimes she wondered just how long she could carry on. She was no great heroine full of bravery and courage, she was just an ordinary girl with ordinary needs and three small children to rear.

She had relinquished all her dreams in the days after Derrynamuck, especially her great dream of escaping with him to America. She knew he would never go, never leave Wicklow, and after Derrynamuck she had vowed that she would never again ask him to. He had his own dream which he carried before him like some eternal flame, and everything else had to be sacrificed to it. And the tragedy of it, she knew, was that his dream would never come true, no matter how many men tried to make it so. Thousands of young men had the same dream in 1798, thousands of young men who had not lived to see the closing days of that summer of rebellion, all in vain, all in vain . . .

So how would it all end? She dared not think about it. She could only live from day to day, always wondering if this would be the day they brought her the news of his death, always wondering if she would ever see him alive again, and every day that she did not see him she counted as lost. He lived a constant battle, his days ending in neither victory nor defeat, and often happily with her. She no longer minded those times when he gave most of his attention to the children, for she loved the children almost as much as she loved him, and they were three more strong links in the emotional chain that bound him to her.

She shrugged, as she often did of late, an unconscious gesture of the acceptance of her life. This was it, this was how it would go on, and this was how she had chosen it . . . and there was a sense of victory in that. Other women were bargained off in an arranged match and lived secure lives of loveless misery, but she had made her own choice, and despite everything, she had no regrets.

Mary turned her head; her voice soft and puzzled. 'Isn't it a funny thing, Sarah, how the yeomanry in Imaal and the surrounding neighbourhoods have become more friendly towards Michael? Almost every man jack of them seems to be on his side now. Do you know why?'

Sarah made a vague gesture. She was at a loss to understand it herself. Mary was right, though. Of late the Imaal yeomanry seemed as determined that Michael should remain free and uncaptured as the people were.

The relaxed attitude of the Imaal yeomanry was indeed a strange thing, an unexpected development, and in the early spring of that year of 1803, Michael asked Billy the Rock the reason why.

Billy the Rock threw back his head and laughed heartily. There were three other men in his farmhouse parlour besides Dwyer: his son John Jackson, Thomas Morris, and Sergeant Hawkins of the Upper Talbotstown Corps. And the fact that Dwyer was here alone amongst them proved his faith and trust in them.

'Sure we're friends and neighbours,' Billy the Rock said. 'Have been since you three lads were weans. Is that a good enough reason?'

Not for the realistic Michael Dwyer. 'No, sir, it is not. I smell a conspiracy of some kind.' He sat back and stretched his legs then looked at Morris and Jackson, who were also sitting round the table drinking.

John Jackson and Thomas Morris had harboured Michael

many times in the past eighteen months, and had been found out by spies of Thomas King. Both had been charged under court martial with harbouring Michael Dwyer in their homes. Thomas King sat as magistrate, and evidence was produced maintaining that Thomas Morris had not only harboured Dwyer and entertained him handsomely, but had actually shared the same bed with him.

Jackson and Morris were found guilty and sentenced to five hundred lashes each, to be inflicted in stages of one hundred. Before the first hundred could be thrashed, Reverend Ryan of Donoughmore intervened. He petitioned the Castle on behalf of his two parishioners, insisting in all sincere belief that it was a trumped-up charge – as loyal yeomen who had fought at Hacketstown lived in daily fear of the rebel chief, so it was ridiculous to believe they would harbour him, let alone settle down to sleep in the same bed as him!

The sentence was overruled and both were pardoned. And rumour had it that for weeks afterwards, Thomas King stumped around in purple fury muttering all kinds of abuse against the interfering ecclesiastic divine from Donoughmore.

'I can accept old friendship as a reason for you two,' Michael said to John Jackson and Thomas Morris, 'and even you, Billy, and even you, Sergeant Hawkins, but not the whole damned Imaal Yeomanry Corps!' He shook his head and smiled cannily. 'Yes, sir, I smell a conspiracy.'

Morris and Jackson grinned. Sergeant Hawkins smiled subtly as he pared his fingernails on a seat by the window. Billy the Rock stared at Michael with a blank poker face.

'Conspiracy? You're talking crazy, boy. Every yeoman outside this house would shoot you down if they saw you.'

'Is that right?' Michael said. 'Then how come two yeos from the Upper Talbotstown walked right past myself and Hugh Vesty this morning? Two of them came along the road towards the two of us, and as we closed they carried on past us with their eyes to the sky and without speaking.'

'Those men,' Billy the Rock, explained in a fatherly tone, 'are like us. Before the rebellion they were what you might call – neutral Protestants.'

'They're still bloody yeomen,' Michael declared. 'But all seem more intent on farming their land than finding rebels lately.'

Thomas Morris, reaching for the bottle on the table, said:

'Tell him the truth, Billy. He'll work it out for himself soon enough, seeing as he smells something already.'

Michael looked at Billy the Rock, who sat back and folded his arms. There was silence for several seconds, then Billy explained.

'You've become the prize goose that lays the golden eggs for the yeos, boy. Attempting to capture you is a lucrative business. Very few now believe that you can be taken. But if by some miracle you were to be captured, the present standard of living for most yeomen would suddenly drop, and a good source of income would come to an end. Every yeoman would be put back on occasional small expenses – but while you remain out and free, they remain on full incentive and full pay.'

Michael stared at each man in the room with grudging admiration. 'Good God,' he said slowly. 'You are entirely disreputable.'

'So are you,' Billy reminded him gently. 'You're the most disreputable man in Wicklow.'

'Listen here,' Michael said, 'I was born disreputable. But you lot were born part of the privileged class – and now are officers of the bloody law!'

'We tell you why most of the heat is off you, boy,' Billy said. 'And is it complaining you are?'

Michael grinned. 'Not a bit.' He sat back in his chair. 'But it's a little hard to take – after years of defeating the yeos, I now find that I'm helping to make them rich.'

'A fact of life they've come to realise,' Billy said logically. 'If they can't make money out of Dwyer with a share of the reward for his capture, then make it another way by helping him to stay free.'

'It's disgusting!' Michael said indignantly.

Billy the Rock threw back his head and laughed. 'But now, in all fairness, it's not only the money. Many fear reprisals if they did manage to capture you; and apart from that, since the Union most feel little allegiance to this new government.'

'And you will still have to be extremely careful,' Morris said in sudden seriousness. 'The fanatical Rathdrum and Baltinglass Corps are still pledged to your murder. Their minds are so poisoned with sectarian hatred, they would hunt you on no pay at all. And the English regiments and Scottish Highlanders are duty bound to take you if they find you, and kill you if they have to.'

Michael gave a smile of wry amusement. 'I have heard that before.'

'Then there's the bounty-hunters,' John Jackson said. 'And there's never been a shortage of avaricious fiends who are

504

happy to take bribes from the secret service funds and become spies on their own people and co-religionists – remember Thomas Halpin?'

'Halpin!' Sergeant Hawkins snorted contemptuously and came over from the window to refill his glass. 'Halpin testified against a man he claimed to have seen standing sentry for rebels and handing a gun to them. And the man was convicted and sent to New Geneva, even though the magistrate, Thomas King, had it on record that at the time Halpin was supposed to have seen the accused doing all this, the accused had been physically locked up in prison, and was only just released.'

'Thomas Halpin . . .' Michael's eyes had turned dark. 'He's the proof that Saint Patrick never did drive all the snakes out of Ireland. But if that reptile ever slithers across my vision, I'll give him more than a trip to New Geneva.'

'One other thing,' Morris said. 'It's now common knowledge, even amongst the English regiments, that Mary Doyle's children are your children.'

'Mary Dwyer,' Michael corrected softly. 'Her name is Mary Dwyer. And has been since 1798.'

A week later intelligence was sent to Michael informing him that Thomas Halpin had returned to Wicklow and had spent the past five nights at the barracks, during which time he had identified three young men as being three of those rebels he had seen in the cave on the Keadeen Mountains.

Michael arranged for several people to watch the barracks and let him know as soon as the informer came out. He then learned from a friendly yeoman that Halpin had also returned for the purpose of setting Dwyer for a capture, and had spent the past four nights, accompanied by two of the militia in disguise and disguised himself as a wigged and bonneted woman, going around the taverns with a good deal of money in his pocket with which to pay the people for information about '. . . my long-lost cousin, Michael Dwyer'.

'Did the people take the money?' Michael asked.

'Sure they did, and they gave Halpin plenty of information, about everything and everyone, except Michael Dwyer.'

Then, on the sixth morning of Halpin's visit to Wicklow, a youth ran breathlessly up to Michael with information that had passed along the road from farmer to farmer, and over the hills from shepherd to shepherd: Halpin, back in his own clothes, had been escorted from the barracks as far as the road leading up to Dublin, and was now continuing his journey alone.

Michael set off at a sprint, running like the wind and jumping over ditches and skidding down hills until he came to the Dublin road, and eventually got a view of the informer – swinging along for all the world as if he had never perjured any young men to the hell-hole of New Geneva and slavery in a Prussian mining camp; and now had tried again to set up Dwyer for a capture.

When Halpin was only fifty perches ahead, he turned and spied his pursuer. Letting out a yelp he jumped into a run and a vigorous chase commenced, until Dwyer was easily running down his game. Halpin withdrew a pistol, turned and fired wildly over his shoulder, then dropped the gun as he scurried on as swiftly as a rabbit.

When Halpin was well within range, Michael stopped, raised the gun, aimed at Halpin's leg, and pulled the trigger – and the world blew up before his eyes in a thundering burst of red-hot pain. He reeled over to a tree in blind agony. Through the haze of his pain, he saw Halpin coming slowly back to him.

'You're dead,' Halpin cried in astonishment, looking at the blood spreading over Dwyer's shirt. 'Holy Jakers, but you're dead this time, Dwyer! And listen, won't it be me that collects the reward!'

Halpin was almost jigging with joy. Michael turned away from him, his brow pressed against the tree, taking deep breaths as if summoning the strength for one last attack. With one hand he fumbled at the pistol in his belt, remembered it was unloaded, opened it, then plucked a bullet from the cartridge-pouch in his belt.

Peering closer, Halpin suddenly saw that it was only Dwyer's left hand, pressed against his chest, that was injured, and his right was fingering a pistol. Then he saw him spit the bullet into the barrel and almost jumped out of his shoes.

Halpin had run so fast he was well out of pistol-range when Michael eventually moved away from the tree and aimed, then slowly lowered the gun and watched with half-closed eyes as the reptile disappeared from view, towards Dublin.

He turned and looked at the ground and the fallen musket which had blown up in his hand; the barrel had burst at the moment of firing. He shoved the pistol back in his belt and turned back towards Imaal, taking deep breaths and walking slowly until he had mastered his pain and his demeanour again became normal.

He walked for some time over the lonely hills and at length saw Lawler the tailor coming towards him. Lawler instantly jumped to a salute, then stared at the blood on the captain's shirt.

'Do you have your tailor's kit with you?' Michael asked.

'Never without it,' Lawler answered in puzzlement, holding up his bag.

'Scissors?'

'Aye.'

Michael held up his blood-soaked left hand, the thumb had been shattered and was joined to the hand only by a thread of skin.

'Then would you mind cutting this away,' Michael said, 'for it can be no further use to me.'

Lawler inspected the hand which was bloody and slightly burned but generally undamaged except for the thumb which was beyond repair; he took out his scissors and removed it.

The pain was almost unbearable. Michael took deep breaths and closed his eyes as Lawler lifted spare strips of linen from his bag and began to carefully dress the hand in a neat bandage.

'God sakes,' Lawler tutted, 'but you must be in agony. And what about that blood on your shirt?'

'Just blood from the hand,' Michael assured him, then in response to Lawler's questions told him about Halpin and the bursting gun.

When Thomas Halpin reached Dublin he rushed straight to the Castle and into Major Sirr's office in the lower courtyard. He explained everything that had happened to Dublin's Chief of Police, who had sent him down to Wicklow on such a hazardous mission.

'I went in search of the rebel, as agreed, and after five nights without success I spied him this morning, sitting alone and dreaming in the sun, and I closed in; but as I cocked my pistol, Dwyer took to his heels without even knowing who was near him.'

'A cautious man!' Major Sirr sat curling one of his moustaches around his finger. 'Took to his heels without even knowing who was near him?'

'But I pursued him, Major Sirr, I did that! I fired several shots and chased him across two rivers and countless hills, then

I lost him. I would have carried on the pursuit but for the fatigue of the long hunt and the fact that Dwyer can run all day without missing a breath.'

Major Sirr sat thoughtful, he uncurled his moustache, then curled it again.

'I did my best, sir,' Halpin said plaintively. 'I did as much as any human could. But it wouldn't be safe for me to return to Wicklow ever again, not even as a witness in a trial.'

Major Sirr was deeply disappointed at the failure of the mission, but Halpin had done his best, and a man could do no more than that. A sudden idea occurred to him. A broad smile came on his face as he voiced it.

'You did your best, Halpin. And for that you deserve a reward.'

'I do?' Halpin was all eyes in surprise.

'Indeed you do. I have a sudden notion to take you on to my staff.'

'But I am on your staff, Major Sirr,' Halpin said in a puzzled tone. 'I have been for a long time now, as a spy on the Dublin sedition-mongers in the taverns.'

'And so I am offering you promotion.' Major Sirr enjoyed being benevolent to his minions. He sat laughing soundlessly like a panting bull dog. 'How would you like to wear a red coat and white breeches and have all Dublin cowering at your feet?'

Halpin was astonished into speechlessness, then finally he managed to stammer a response.

'A militiaman?'

Major Sirr nodded.

Halpin seemed overcome. He staggered to a chair and sat down, overwhelmed by his amazing good fortune. Then on an impulse of wild joy he fell to his knees and shuffled across the floor until he was kneeling before the major and kissing his hand.

'I'll not let you down, Major Sirr, sir! I'll be the best militia-man that ever marched the streets of Dublin, so I will! The first blatherumskite I hear singing a seditious song I'll lock in mana-cles and throw in the grid without mercy!'

The major looked at the man grovelling at his feet and resisted a sudden urge to kick him. Then he remembered all his good work at the Wicklow trials and his efforts in pursuing the notorious Dwyer, and gently patted him on the head instead.

'Very good. Very good. Lock them in manacles and throw

them in the grid without mercy. That's what I like to hear from my men. That's the kind of enthusiasm that gets results. But now, before you rise off your knees, my good man, whip off your neckcloth and give my boots a spit and rub, will you?'

Halpin looked down at the major's dull boots, then up at his face.

'It would be an honour, Major Sirr, sir!' he said with an emotional quiver in his voice. He whipped off his neckcloth and within seconds he was spitting and polishing away.

Chapter Thirty-Four

For two weeks Michael went around with his arm in a sling, during which time Mary tended and changed the dressings on the wound every night. By the end of the third week he had discarded the sling, and at a month's end he had taught himself to handle his musket as if the left thumb had never been lost. But still, the loss annoyed him.

'The Ninety-eight Rebellion and almost five years on the run and I never suffered an injury until now. And I did it myself! That's what annoys me so.'

'It was not your fault,' Mary said defensively, 'it was the fault of the gun.'

'The gun was mine so the fault is mine,' he told her. 'But do you know the worst thing about it? Halpin saw my injured hand. Halpin saw the thumb hanging off beyond repair.'

'So?'

'It makes me more easy to identify, even in disguise. Because now the soldiery will be keeping their eyes open for a man who is without a thumb on his left hand.'

Mary made no answer and showed no sign of anxiety. Almost every yeoman on this side of the mountains seemed now to be on Michael's side, and she was nursing a secret hope that before long they would be able to start living a normal life again, in the peace of their own Imaal. She was also beginning to think that Michael, like her, was tired of the struggle. He had the heart of a lion and didn't know the meaning of fear, but more and more he seemed to want to be with his children, and more and more he had started longing for the land . . . the eternal land that grips a man's soul with a passion that never cools.

This past spring she had noticed the change in him, noticed how keenly his eye had been watching, not for the militia, but the weather: sun, wind, and rain, and how it affected the growth of the crops, the behaviour of the animals, and she knew memories of his youth were arousing in him, memories of the days when the land was his mistress and his whole being moved in tune with the seasons of nature; and it was as if a new hope was growing in him too . . . How would it all end? she wondered.

The following morning Michael was dallying with his second favourite girl on the grass outside Cullen's house. She ran towards him on her little four-year-old legs, carefully cupping the ladybird in her dimpled hands. He bent down, his eyes opening wide with awe as she let him peek at the red and black beetle sitting motionlessly on her palm.

'Make a wish, Mary-Anne,' he whispered.

'I wish . . . I wish . . .' she let out a ripple of excited laughter that mingled with the sun on the grass. 'What will I wish?'

'Wish that one day you will own acres and acres of land.'

She looked at him with dark disappointed eyes which were almost hidden by the mop of black curls falling around her face. 'Don't want that wish,' she said sulkily.

'Then wish for whatever you want.'

She peeped in at the ladybird in her cupped hands before throwing back her head and singing in a high childish voice. 'I wish I was a *blue* bud that flies over the twees!'

Mary was standing at the door watching them. She saw him laughing, then waited for his answer when their daughter asked solemnly, 'When will my wish come twoo, Dada, when?'

Mary saw him look up at the sky for his answer – then suddenly rise to his feet and stand to stare at the ridge where Hugh Vesty, John Mernagh, and Martin Burke had appeared, all moving to jump down on to the path below.

She saw him reach down and swing up the child and carry her towards the three men whose voices reached Mary, though not all their words.

'. . . Robert Emmet is back from France . . . A number of the United Irish leaders are back with him . . . another attempt for liberty is going to be made . . . Miles Byrne has joined Emmet, and now Emmet wants to meet you . . . He sent Arthur Devlin and James Hope, they're waiting in the care of others to talk with you . . . three miles back a way . . .'

Mary turned back into the house, clutching her arms around her waist as if the warmth of the sun had suddenly gone behind the clouds and left her feeling chilly. Her eyes were dark and moody and there was despair in them. How would it all end? It would never end!

She asked him no questions, not even when he returned from his meeting with the two visitors and told her that he was going to Dublin, nor when he returned from Dublin, for she knew that he would not tell her anything worth knowing anyway. He didn't even know that she had overheard his conversation with the men when they had brought him Emmet's summons.

All through that month of May and the following month of June she sought no explanation nor made any complaint when he spent less time than usual with her. There seemed to be a great deal more activity amongst the young men of Imaal, but it could just have been the onset of summer. Young men always gathered to parley and frisk and jest on the hills in summertime. Even the older men sat on the walls and talked until after the midnight hour; the women too, young and old. The whole world came out of doors when summer's heat was in the air.

And her brain became hot and weary as she shut her mind to the hurricane that was slowly unfurling its cyclone in preparation to blast her life into chaos again. She knew it was coming, just as surely as the shepherd knows a storm is moving closer in the distance, even though the thunder is still too far away for him to hear, yet in his bones he knows it is acoming.

Her sleep became troubled. She had terrifying dreams that woke her in the night. But in daylight she shut her mind and sought refuge within the shelter of her outer placidity, refusing to allow words of discussion to give substance to her fears. Only when a dream is manifest in words does it take on the possibility of reality. She pretended not to hear him when he told her he was going to Dublin again, and would not be back in Wicklow for a number of days. She pretended greater absorption in the corduroy breeches she was making for him from the roll of cloth her father had acquired in Wicklow Town for her. She made all her family's clothes, as well as any dressmaker or tailor in Dublin . . . She lifted her head after he had gone and thought about Dublin, and her thoughts rarely strayed from Dublin for the next three days.

It was not to Dublin that Michael went, but a lonely country house on the outskirts, on Butterfield Lane in Rathfarnham. There were ten men sitting around the table in the dining-room, a number of maps and papers on the table, but only one of the men was speaking, pausing when a young woman entered the room carrying a candelabra and set it on the table.

The light flared up, making Michael realise the evening had grown dark without him noticing it. In the golden glow of the candles he looked up at the face of the girl, Anne Devlin, his cousin, whose family had moved from Wicklow to County Dublin. He watched her as she moved the candelabra nearer to the papers on the table, then sat down again in the vacant chair beside the black-haired, brown-eyed young man who was her new master. She settled herself beside Robert Emmet as if she were his second in command and not his servant.

Robert Emmet was a Protestant of the ruling class, and the youngest revolutionary officer to sit on the secret Executive Council in 1798. His brother Thomas Emmet had been one of the founders of the United Irish movement with Wolfe Tone and Thomas Russell. He was twenty-five years old, had an extremely intelligent face, yet his face wore none of the arrogance so characteristic of many revolutionaries.

Michael saw Emmet glance at Anne only briefly before returning his eyes to the paper on the table, covered in his own handwriting, and continued to read the words aloud in his soft, cultured voice:

> 'People of Ireland, you are now called upon to show the world that you are competent to take your place among nations; that you have a right to claim the world's recognizance of you as an independent country, by the only satisfactory proof you can furnish of your capability of gaining your independence – by your wresting it from England with your own hands. We war not against property, we war against no religious sect, we war not against past opinions or prejudices, we war against English dominion.'

The men around the table murmured their comments, but Michael kept his eyes fixed on the young general of the secret army who had calmly read the proclamation of revolution as if it were a solemn prayer.

Then Emmet's dark eyes, with their serious intellectual expression, were looking straight at Michael.

'You appear very thoughtful, Captain. Is there anything in the draft proclamation which you do not agree with?'

'I agree with everything in the proclamation,' Michael

replied quietly. 'But . . . I would like to hear the last few lines again.'

Emmet looked down, then repeated: 'We war not against property, we war against no religious sect, we war not against past opinions or prejudices, we war against English dominion.'

'So, this time,' Michael said, 'they will not be able to say our fight is a religious one.'

'Oh, but our fight is a religious one,' Emmet said firmly. 'If we succeed, we intend to remove all the penalties from which the people now suffer because of their religious beliefs. In short, Captain, we fight that all of us may have our own country; and that done, each of us shall have our own religion.'

'A new Jerusalem,' Michael said wryly.

'A new Ireland,' Emmet said with a smile.

By the middle of July, Mary's nerves were ready to snap. She was sitting alone by the fire when Michael entered. The children were asleep in the bedroom; Cullen had not returned from his eight-mile round trip to the tavern.

'I want you to tell me,' she snapped, quivering with tension.

'Then you should have asked me to tell you,' he said gently.

'Why didn't you tell me anyway?'

'I thought you preferred not to know. That is the impression you have given.'

'I know about Emmet. Have you agreed to join him in his rebellion?'

'A mutual reliance has been agreed between us,' he admitted.

'You will go to Dublin for it?'

'No, we are not to stir until Dublin has made its move.'

She stood up and stoked the fire, then remained staring at it. 'It is true, then?' she whispered. 'We are on the eve of another break-out?'

'No, it is not planned for some months yet; not until the autumn, sometime in November.'

The silence lasted for at least a minute, then he moved and put his hands on her shoulders. With a sigh she turned and moved inside his arms. They leaned one against the other in silence, a calm moment of love without passion, and she relaxed in the solidity of their love and forgot the uncertain future ahead . . . summer had not yet reached its zenith, and autumn was a long way off.

A weeks later, on the evening of Sunday, 24th July, a number of breathless young men running at speed arrived in the vicinity of Imaal. One was John O'Neill, who had moved to open his own dairy business in Dublin after marrying Michael's sister Cathy. Dark night had fallen when they were brought to a harbourer's house at Rostyduff, and gave Dwyer the news.

'Emmet was betrayed! All our plans are broken! The whole business erupted months before time and Dublin was in chaos last night. But 'tis clear Emmet had traitors in his camp. Now it's all over bar the shouting and the manhunts.'

'Where is Emmet now, do you know?'

'Aye, he's where the most of us are now – on the run.'

The next few days found Michael constantly out on the hills with his principal men, keeping a sharp look-out for the arrival of news from Dublin, and news of Emmet, who was still in the country.

In the long silences on the sun-shadowed hills, Michael found himself thinking a great deal about Emmet, a young aristo, polite and trusting, who believed fervently in the words that his fellow Protestant, Theobald Wolfe Tone, had spoken only five years earlier at his trial; that the aims of the United Irishmen were: 'To assert the independence of our country, to unite the whole people of Ireland, to abolish the memory of past dissensions and to substitute the common name of Irishman in place of the denominations of Protestant and Catholic.'

Emmet had passionately believed that was possible. And Michael too had dreamed of being part of it when it came to pass. Dreams of young men, dreams on wings, chasing the mythical phoenix of victory, the phoenix rising in glory from the embers of defeat, the symbol of the United Irishmen.

Now, Emmet too was just another bird in flight, fleeing from the clutches of the hawks, and Michael was hoping that he would fly to the hills of Imaal, and to the protection of himself and his men.

But Emmet never came; and events took a turn that had Michael Dwyer looking out for no one but himself and his Wicklow comrades; and Mary knew that all her worst fears were about to be realised.

The alarm created in Dublin Castle by Emmet's exposed

conspiracy was great, especially when it was revealed that seventeen counties had been prepared to join him in rebellion. The powers of government went into action immediately. Martial law was proclaimed; the act of Habeas Corpus was suspended and hundreds indiscriminately arrested and imprisoned without charge.

Then the Castle turned its attention from Dublin to Wicklow. They knew that by some accident or default Michael Dwyer had been in his mountains and taken no part in the trouble in Dublin, but they also knew that he must have been privy to Emmet's conspiracy and encouraged him. Their biggest fear now was an invasion by the French who had promised to support Emmet, and if a French force were to land, and Michael Dwyer was still at liberty, they decided he could constitute a threat to the whole country. They became more convinced of this when an officer of the 38th Regiment wrote to Under-Secretary Marsden.

Wicklow is quiet for the present, although it is well known to the best informed that Dwyer could, at half an hour's warning, draw to his standard nineteen out of every twenty of the inhabitants.

The Chief Secretary William Wickham also read the letter, then placed it before the Viceroy Lord Hardwicke.

'The capture of Michael Dwyer alone would make the difference of an army to us,' Wickham said.

Lord Hardwicke agreed. 'If this man were to remain in the fastness of Wicklow at the time of a French landing, there is no doubt that a formidable insurrection requiring a powerful force to put it down will instantly break out there. I am still very uneasy about Cork, Limerick, and Kerry, but Dwyer is my nightmare. From the information we have received, there is no doubt that if things had gone to plan, he would have raised his musket to assist Emmet.'

Three days later, Lord Hardwicke issued a government proclamation which stated: 'Michael Dwyer stands charged with repeated acts of High Treason and with furthering the Rebellion that lately broke out in Ireland.'

Five hundred pounds was offered for his apprehension and a further five hundred for information leading thereto. One hundred pounds was offered for information in respect of those aiding, abetting, harbouring or concealing the said Michael Dwyer, and all were warned of the dire results that would follow any attempts to aid or conceal him.

A general order was sent out to all officers commanding the military forces in Wicklow to 'punish according to martial law not only Dwyer himself but anyone assisting or sheltering him'.

Lord Hardwicke then sent a copy of the proclamation to the Home Secretary in London.

> I beg leave to send you enclosed the copy of the Proclamation issued on Tuesday offering large rewards for apprehending Michael Dwyer the noted rebel, who still maintains himself in the fastness of the County of Wicklow, and has acquired an extraordinary ascendancy over the inhabitants of those parts.
>
> I am in great hopes that if neither the rewards offered in the Proclamation, nor the threats by which they are accompanied, should be attended with success, then some more active measures which I have concerted with the Commander of His Majesty's Forces will tend ultimately to secure this man and enable me to bring him to punishment.

When, after a month, the proclamation brought no results or information, a military offensive against Dwyer was put into action. Large detachments of soldiers and spies were sent to the mountains to try to trap him. Soldiers in twos and threes were free-quartered all over Wicklow in the houses of suspected harbourers, and every member of the house subjected to close scrutiny. They could not take out a vessel for water, nor go any distance from the house without being watched.

When this offensive also brought no results, the Castle put their final plan into action.

Michael's mother was feeding hens in the yard when the hammering of hoofs made her turn and look towards the bohereen that led to the home fields.

'God in Heaven . . .' she whispered.

Within minutes the farmhouse at Eadstown was surrounded by soldiers on horse and foot and every member of the family arrested, including Michael's mother. She was sent, accompanied by Maíre and Etty, under military escort to Dublin and all three were confined in the women's section of Kilmainham Gaol. Michael's three brothers, James, Peter and John, were sent to the hold of a prison tender lying in Dublin Bay. His father was sent to the prison at New Geneva, near Passage, in Waterford.

At the same time as the house in Eadstown was being surrounded, so was the Doyles' house at Knockandarragh. By that evening every relative of Michael Dwyer, and several of his neighbours, had been arrested and sent to prison. But the one person who eluded the search – the one person they had hoped to arrest and use as their main hostage and weapon against Dwyer – was his wife.

From dawn to dawn the soldiers searched every habitation, no matter how isolated, even John Cullen's house at Knockgorragh, but Mary Dwyer could not be found. In the days that followed, the military officers had no option but to report to the Castle that she was proving as elusive as Dwyer himself. Wherever he had her concealed, it was beyond their reach.

The Castle was disappointed, but not without hope. They waited eagerly for Dwyer's response to the arrest of his family and relatives. But the only response they received was from his twenty-five-year-old brother James, imprisoned in a little sloop of war in Dublin Bay, who sent a communication to the government, challenging them to bring his mother to trial for the heinous crime for which she had been arrested and imprisoned – that of being the mother of a son who would not surrender or allow himself to be arrested.

The challenge went unheeded.

Chapter Thirty-Five

Winter came early to Wicklow. By the end of November the country lay under deep snow, making travel for the military parties almost impossible. The soldiers remained free-quartered in the houses, wrapped up against the cold as they doggedly followed the inhabitants in and out; but a halt had been forced on the searches through the valleys and mountains bound by snow.

Lord Hardwicke was getting desperate. On 22nd November the House of Commons had debated the recent trouble in Ireland, and the opposition party did not hesitate to point out scathingly the logic of a government that dismissed Emmet's rebellion as nothing more than a contemptible riot, yet needed the powers of martial law to keep the country under control.

In France, Napoleon made no secret of his sympathy for the Irish, declaring that his heart was deeply grieved by the stories that were reaching him from Ireland. Persecution was wide-spread, but the spirit of the people was unyielding. He announced in Paris that he would never make peace with England until the independence of Ireland was recognised.

The French journalists took up the theme, and made great satire of a British government that had shouted their horror at the executions on the guillotine during the French Revolution, yet considered the recent public executions of young Irishmen in Dublin's Thomas Street to be quite civilised and found no horror in the fact that the city's dogs had been seen lapping up the blood.

The words of the radical Englishman Thomas Paine were repeated for the benefit of all.

The heads stuck upon spikes, which remained for years upon Temple Bar in London, differed nothing in horror to the scene from those carried about on pikes in Paris: yet this was done by the English government. Lay then the axe to the root – and first teach *governments* humanity!

The cobblestones of Thomas Street in Dublin truly had been soaked in blood. Lord Hardwicke's *conciliatory* administration in Ireland had lost all credibility; he realised his administration needed a propaganda victory to restore it. To this political end, he looked again towards Wicklow and the intractable rebel who would not allow himself to be arrested.

A relative of Dwyer's, an aunt, was released from Kilmainham and given a letter for Michael Dwyer bearing His Excellency's seal. The letter urged him to throw himself upon the *mercy* of the government, and surrender. The terms of surrender offered were a safe retreat out of Ireland with his immediate family.

Lord Hardwicke waited as the letter was no doubt passed from hand to hand along the mysterious trail that led to Dwyer. He was willing to rid Ireland of Michael Dwyer at any price. He wrote to the Home Secretary in London, explaining the reasons for his offer of surrender terms.

I offered him a retreat from the Kingdom with his family, a measure which I thought right to take, on account of the little hope I have been advised to entertain of apprehending him by any ordinary means. And the fact of him having taken an active part in the late Insurrection seemed to present a fair pretext for removing from the country a very dangerous rebel, by an act of leniency, which the loyal party of the country could not possibly disapprove. He thought proper, however, to reject my offer, trusting, as I have reason to believe, to his being able to make a new effort on the landing of the French, an event which he is taught to consider as very near, and represents to his associates as certainly to take place before the close of winter.

The falling snow was Michael's greatest ally. While it continued to fall he was able to move swiftly across the mountains. When it lay on the ground smooth and ordered he was forced to take the precaution of defacing his footsteps as he went.

He had spent a long time turning over in his mind Hardwicke's terms of surrender. For Mary's sake he felt he should have considered it even longer, but he knew that he could never accept the offer, for it made no provision for his principal men. How could he make terms for himself alone, and desert the men who had stood by him faithfully throughout? Men like Hugh Vesty, John Mernagh, and Martin Burke.

The imprisonment of his family and relatives had shaken him badly. For a time he had descended into utter despair at the thought of his mother in prison. Then his sister Cathy, who now lived in Dublin and had not been arrested, sent a message to say his mother did not want him to play the Castle's game on her account. Maíre and Etty had given Cathy the same message.

He was torn by his responsibility to them as well as his men, and although he showed no outward sign of it, the whole situation left him depressed and confused, torn in all directions between emotional ties to his family and his friends. The only thing he was certain of was that no redcoat would ever lay hands on his wife and children, and no redcoat would take him.

His friends in the villages knew how difficult his situation had become, but to his surprise it was his Protestant acquaintances who offered to do anything they could to help him, risking imprisonment as they did so. He had accepted Billy the Rock's offer to harbour Mary and the children, for no soldier would ever think of looking for her in the house of a staunch Protestant yeoman like William Jackson. She had stayed with Billy throughout the weeks the military had searched for her, and Billy had shielded her well, but now that the search was off, she was back in the wilderness with John Cullen at Knockgorragh.

Michael himself withdrew to the most inaccessible parts of the mountains with his friends, determined to avoid capture at all costs by refusing to sleep in any house, even Cullen's. The weather was severe and the snow deep; but the cold, he told himself, would do no more than harden his determination to beat his enemy, every man jack of them.

As always in winter, the rebels had separated to make the best they could for themselves, but ten men remained in hiding with Michael in a cave near Oakwood. Eight of them lay deep in the heart of the cave, quite warm as they slept around the heat of a brazier, while Michael and Hugh Vesty were out in the cold dawn fishing for breakfast.

There had been a snowstorm in the night, piling the snow in great heaps on the banks. They crouched at the edge of a small lake which was frozen over but for the large hole they broke in it with the butts of their muskets.

'It's a good thing fish are notoriously deaf,' Michael remarked, and Hugh Vesty laughed; once the activity under the water had settled down again, both set to the task, and after an hour five fish lay on the ice.

'That'll do,' Hugh said, shivering. 'They're big enough to give a decent-sized half apiece to every man.'

Late in the afternoon Michael set off to see Mary and his children. Hugh Vesty advised against it, but he was shrugged aside.

'Sure, look at him!' Laurence O'Keefe shook his head as Michael trudged away through the snow. 'The man is crazy. Why does he have to keep checking on them all the time?'

'It's easy for you to talk,' Hugh Vesty snapped. 'You have neither chick nor child to worry about. You have only yourself.'

'Well you have three children too, Hugh Vesty,' argued O'Keefe, 'but I don't see you venturing across the mountains at all times of the day and night to check on them like he does.'

'Because, you bloody fool, I'm not the man the military are bent on catching. My wife and children are safe enough, but Michael's mother and father and brothers and sisters are all now in prison. Mary's family too. All hostages. But the Castle knows – and Michael knows – that if they were to get his wife or even one of his children, then they have him!'

Wrapped up well against the cold, Michael trudged through the white wilderness and green pine forests in the direction of Knockgorragh. His black greatcoat, woollen scarf around his face, and hat pulled low over his brow, all helped to keep the bitter cold from cutting into him, as well as obscuring his identity; although there was not another soul to be seen across the panorama of white mountains. As he slid down the slopes he glanced up at the fleecy sky, darkening in the east, and knew it would be snowing again before nightfall.

He travelled south-west past the Three Lakes, round Table Mountain and into the Glen of Imaal.

At the ridge above Cullen's house he paused, and stared in surprise at a hunched figure shuffling away from the house, muffled against the cold. He stood in silence, and was even more surprised to see the figure making tracks not down to the lowlands and habitations, but up towards the uninhabited mountains.

'Father . . .'

The parish priest of Imaal glanced up, and sang out his usual greeting. 'Musha, Michael, are you alive yet?'

'I am, Father,' Michael responded in kind. 'Are you?'

'More or less,' the priest replied. 'More than tomorrow and less than yesterday.'

'What are you doing here?'

'Come down and I will tell you,' the priest called.

Michael made the jump down on the soft snow, glancing over the priest's shoulder towards the house. 'Is all well inside?'

The priest nodded. 'As well as can be expected.' Clouds of breath issued from his mouth in the chill air. 'But now, it's glad I am that Providence sent you down here, for I was on my way up to find you.'

Michael pulled down the wool of his scarf. 'Up the mountains?' His voice was incredulous.

'Up the mountains,' the priest confirmed. 'And no doubt climbing on my knees before I found you.'

'You would never have found me,' Michael informed him. 'But why did you want to?'

The priest glanced back at the house and saw old man Cullen peering through the window. 'Come over to the barn,' he said urgently. 'What I have to say is for your ears alone.'

Michael blinked, half nodded, and found himself following the old priest over to the barn. As he neared the house he looked at Cullen by the window and shrugged his bafflement. Cullen shrugged back, then quickly made the sign of the cross over himself with one hand by way of warning, and Michael instantly knew that despite his warm greeting, the priest was on the warpath.

Inside the barn the priest sat down on a bale of straw and Michael stood watching him as he loosened his muffler.

'So,' Michael said warily, 'why were you prepared to tramp through all the snow and miles to find me?'

'To persuade you to surrender.'

Again Michael looked at him incredulously. 'You must be having another brainstorm, I'm thinking.'

'Surrender, Michael,' the priest urged. 'It is the best thing now.'

'You must be crazy! Do you think I've spent over five years holding out against the army and the yeomanry just to surrender

523

because you think I should? Go home, Father, before you catch your death of cold.'

The priest looked with tired eyes at his angry face, then clasped his hands on his lap and spoke slowly and deliberately.

'I did not come to argue with you, Michael, I came to reason with you. It was last week that John Cullen told me about Lord Hardwicke's offer, and I thanked God for it. No man could be as lucky as you, I thought to myself. Whether you make your own luck, or you are charmed as the people say, I do not know. All I know is that at the close of summer the government were obliged to enter into a system of example by the brutal execution of young Robert Emmet in order to convince the world the Irish could be controlled under their imperial hand. But now that the blood of the sacrificial lamb has been spilled, they need another example, this time of their *mercy*. And so they have chosen you as their scapegoat.'

The priest nodded. 'Yes, yes, the sacrificial lamb and the scapegoat, both have their uses. The scapegoat, in case you didn't know, was named after the goat which, in ancient Jewish religious custom, was allowed to escape into the wilderness after the high priest had symbolically lain all the sins of the people upon it.'

'But I'm no goat, scape or otherwise,' Michael said coldly. 'I'm a man, and as a man I shall continue to do what I think is right. And neither you nor the Castle will persuade me different.'

'But a man must always be ready to consider the necessity of change if he wishes to survive,' the priest continued reasonably. 'And you are a survivor. You have proved that time and time again. The Castle know you are a survivor, and so for their own purposes they offer you certain survival.'

'I've survived well enough with their hindrance,' Michael said dismissively. 'I'll continue to survive without their help.'

The priest continued reasonably. 'It would be wrong for me or anyone to ascribe your attitude to the mere wantonness of youth or the intoxication of vanity. In the first instant, you are no longer a youth, you are twenty-nine years old, almost thirty, a father of three children. In the latter instant, you have been known to be intoxicated by the beauty of a woman and the imbibing of spirits during a celebratory frolic, but never by your own esteem. So, deprived of the wantonness of youth or the intoxication of vanity, the only reason left for your refusal to surrender is downright bloody-mindedness!'

'Wait a minute,' Michael said. 'I don't believe this. When atrocities were committed on the people of Wicklow during the rebellion and the years following it, who did they look to for protection? When the militia sallied out to give you one more flogging for the hell of it, who stopped them? *We did!* Who gave the people a small sense of self-respect because some of their own were still holding out a resistance against all the odds? *We did!*'

'Yes, Michael, you have served your cause well. You fought gallantly in the rebellion of 1798, and throughout the aftermath you and your comrades were the only safeguard the local people had in the face of such terrible acts of savagery – and now you are regarded as a hero. Your exploits are already part of local legend. You have become a heroic symbol of bravery and defiance – but the time has come to stop being a hero, and be the *man* that you say you are.'

Michael studied the pale and aged face of the priest. 'I'd not be much of a man if I let them beat me now, and humbly surrendered.'

'For God's sake, what can you possibly hope to achieve by staying out?'

'Freedom.'

'Indeed. Your own freedom? Or your country's freedom?'

'I have the first, the second will come.'

'The devil it will – not in my lifetime and not in yours. The men in ninety-eight tried it, Emmet tried it, but generation after generation of men will keep trying and dying before the bell of freedom ever rings in Ireland.'

'Defeat is not always wrong!' Michael cried. 'Even by trying we achieve a measure of victory. All I have ever fought for is the natural and basic rights of man. The right to own our own farms. The right to live in peace and be able to provide a decent living for our families, not hand the greatest measure of our crops over to an English landlord who will then invest that money in England and leave Ireland impoverished. The right to consume our own beef and corn – not stand by meekly and see it shipped to England while the Irish live on potatoes. The right to make the English people see that they are *not* the chosen people. And it is *not* the fair hand of God that allows an Irish child to die of famine at the same moment an English child sits at a full table and consumes Irish beef! It is *not* the fair hand of God that wills that – it is the thieving hand of the British Government!'

Michael stared at the priest a bit wild-eyed. He was rising into a fury and he did not want that. He wanted to see his wife and children. He turned to walk out of the barn.

'Wait!' the priest called. 'Wait!' He jumped up and snatched Michael's arm. 'Look at me, man! Look at me and tell me how long you think you can live like this. How long you think you can you keep up a resistance with only a small army of men against an Empire. How long? How long?'

'How long?' Michael snapped angrily. 'I'll tell you how long I can hold out. One day the future children of Wicklow will see a very old man wandering over those mountains with a gaming-gun in his hand – and it will most likely be me!'

'All right.' The priest nodded and passed a hand tiredly across his eyes. 'I have tried reason, now I must resort to rage.'

Michael looked at him, wryly; but the priest's voice thundered through the barn in genuine black anger.

'There is more in life to consider than the rights of man! The *rights* of man, indeed! What about the *duties* of man? No rights were ever given to man that were not accompanied by duty. A man who adheres to his duties is far more honourable, far more admirable than the man who insists on his rights! You are an Irish Catholic, boy, and you have no rights, not in Ireland. But you do have duties.'

He waved a hand towards the land beyond the open barn door. 'Forget the great dream of reform in Ireland and look to your own locality of Wicklow. Look at the poor people now placed under an intolerable burden supporting so much sol-diery. No recompense do they get from the government for feeding the soldiers free-quartered in their houses and who must be fed before even their own children. And without com-plaint they are suffering this – because of you!'

Michael took the verbal blow with no words and no reaction.

'But if you care not about your duty to them, think of your duty to your parents, to your brothers and sisters, all confined in prison – because of you! Think of your relatives, removed from their farms and families and confined in the wet and stinking hold of prison ships – because of you!'

Michael was unable to cover his reaction this time. 'By God,' he said harshly, 'it is not only the Castle that wants to turn me into the scapegoat and heap the suffering of Wicklow on my back – so do you.'

'I am reminding you of your duty to these people because, as your pastor, it is *my* duty to do so. I am a priest, I too have taken an oath. And my duty is to the care and situation of my whole flock, not just one. If you must know, Michael, there have been many times when I have heard of your escapes and clapped my hands in glee. The rebel in me cheered you all the way. But I can no longer cheer you, not any more. My respect and admiration for you ended the moment I heard that you had turned down Lord Hardwicke's very generous offer.'

Michael's dark stare went right through the priest. 'To hell with your respect, to hell with your admiration. I have never asked nor looked for either, but I once gave you both – as a priest and as a man. Now I would not give you the touch of my hat. I've listened to you long enough, but I'll never listen to you again. From this day you are no longer a priest to me – you are a traitor!'

He turned to go, then flashed back in anger. 'Every bit as much a traitor as the Catholic Archbishop of Dublin who purchased his own secure position by selling us out for the Union, and now preaches English supremacy and decrees it as the will of God – let him shake hands with Cromwell in hell!'

'I am not a traitor,' the priest whispered whitely, 'and neither is Bishop Troy.'

'No? Then explain why Troy sent out a letter to be read in all Catholic chapels reminding the Irish Catholics of their *religious* obligation of loyalty to the King, and their *religious* obligation to give respect and obedience to all those constituted by Divine Providence to govern us? Religious obligation, indeed. Divine Providence, indeed. I say he is a big fat traitor! And as you read out his sickening letter, you too are a traitor.'

'I did not read out the letter, I could not.' The priest sagged down on to the bale of straw, too old and too cold and too tired to take much more. A verbal whipping could rip sharper than any cat o' nine tails. 'Bishop Troy knew nothing of Emmet's conspiracy,' he said, 'but the oligarchy at the Castle are now saying that the Catholic bishops not only backed it, but organised it.'

'So the letter was to save his own skin?'

'In part, but not entirely. You cannot judge a man or a nation without knowing their history. Troy and myself were both

527

priests during the Penal Days. To have lived through them is to have lived through a nightmare more horrific than Dante's visions of Hell. But like a man who is given a morsel of food after a long famine, some of our priests think we now enjoy a feast of British blessings. They see our present condition as a great sign of British benevolence and government conciliation, because, although we are not one dead body nearer to emancipation, it is no longer a crime of death to practise our faith.'

'The priest at Rathdangan read out the letter. As did all the other priests in Wicklow.'

'Well I did not and could not. How could I tell my people that it was their *religious* obligation to give respect to an oppressive regime that rules them?'

'So by not reading out the letter, you have disobeyed your archbishop?'

'Yes.'

'He will threaten you with eternal damnation,' Michael warned. 'He may even defrock you.'

The priest shrugged. 'Then I will borrow a pair of your breeches that Mary makes and sews so well and carry on as before. Once a priest, always a priest. But at the end of the day, I am subject to a higher power than the archbishop.'

The priest smiled wearily, and Michael felt a flash of shame. 'I apologise,' he murmured. 'I shouldn't have called you a traitor.'

'I have been called worse.'

Michael looked narrowly at the priest. 'Why did you really come here?'

'To ask you to surrender.'

'Then I'll give it to you straight,' Michael said impatiently, 'one last and final time – I will never surrender.'

'What about your wife?'

Michael was halfway out of the barn. He turned and stared at the priest. 'What about my wife?'

The priest stood up and walked towards him, drawing in his breath as if preparing for one last attack with the weapon of reason.

'Your wife brings me back to the original point of my reasoning with you, before you confused me with other argumentative issues. You have obviously abandoned your duty to your parents and relatives, but are you also going to abandon your duty to Mary? Is your love of your lofty ideal so much greater than your love for her? I think it must be. Is your affection and duty to your comrades so much more important than your duty to her? I think it must be. And in that case, you should never have married her and vowed to forsake all others for her. In truth, Michael, you have forsaken nothing or no one for her. The vows you made at your wedding have turned out to be lies.'

'That's unfair,' Michael burst out. 'I have always put my wife's welfare and protection before my own. I love my wife . . . in a way that you couldn't possibly understand.'

'A strange love it is, then. A selfish love it is, then. That girl has given you as much as any woman could ever give, and what have you given her in return? Nights of pleasure from time to time obviously, but no days of happiness, no days of contentment free of worry. In the past five years she has borne you three children and lived every day the life of a fugitive.'

'You make it sound wretched,' Michael said quietly. 'It was never like that. We have known much happiness, despite the hardship. We have known great happiness, in each other, and in our children.'

The priest snorted. 'I'll wager the happiness was all on your side, the hardship on hers. So well for you to live amongst the companionship of your men while she is left alone with your babies in the back room of some harbourer's house. And however kind and friendly the harbourers may be, a woman with children needs the stability of a permanent place to live. A permanent nest to settle her young at night. A permanent place to hang her pots and pans. Good God, even the travelling gypsy women who settle nowhere still have their own little permanent wagons to live in by day and by night.'

Michael opened his mouth to speak, but no words came, for suddenly he understood. Suddenly it all became clear to him why the priest had been ready to search the mountains to find him. And having found him so close to the house, had embarked on his long rigmarole about rights and duty without coming straight to the truth of it.

'Mary asked you,' he said at last. 'It was Mary who asked you to ask me to surrender, wasn't it?'

The priest sighed, as if a great weight had been lifted from his shoulders. 'Yes, it was Mary. She could not ask you herself. It seems she made a vow to you in the days after Derrynamuck and she has never broken it.'

Michael could only stare at the priest, trying to remember

what the vow had been . . . and then it came back to him. She had vowed never to ask for more than he could possibly give her, and now she was asking him to give up the very principles of his existence, and surrender to the Castle.

'You must know how grieved she is to ask this of you,' the priest said, 'for she has always take great pride in your defiance and bravery. She too defied her father when she ran away and married you, and she has never regretted her choice. Her love for you then was like a rushing river that has now swelled into an ocean. She has tried very hard to be a fit mate for you, but she has three small children and she is tired of her nomadic life. And now that the Viceroy is being so magnanimous by offering you a safe retreat from the kingdom with your immediate family to a country of your choice, she sees a chance of her dream coming true – a life of peace and freedom waiting for you all in the friendly land of America. And she cannot understand why you won't take it.'

His lack of response, the paleness of his face, gave the priest hope. He put a gentle hand on his shoulder and spoke softly.

'For over five years she has been true to you. Now it is your turn to be true to her. You have told me how much you love her, and she has told me how much you love your children, and now is your chance to prove it. Now is your chance to prove which means most to you – being a hero of the people, being a faithful comrade, or being a husband and father.'

The priest moved to leave, pulling his muffler around him. 'Now I must go. I have done what I see as my duty, done what I promised faithfully to Mary that I would do. Cullen knows nothing of this, by the way. Mary and I spoke in private in the bedroom. I will leave you to your decision. But whatever you decide, I would remind you of the words of Saint Paul to the Corinthians: Take heed, lest this liberty of yours becomes a stumbling-block to them that are weaker than you.'

Michael still made no response, and the priest moved out of the barn. He had only been gone a few seconds when he reappeared in the doorway, pulling down his muffler.

'There is something else you should know,' he said, his voice flat. 'Because you love your wife . . . in a way that you say I could not possibly understand . . . she is expecting another child.'

It was maybe half an hour later when Mary walked into the

barn without the cover of even a shawl over her dress. She had made a guess at his response when he had stayed in the barn. He was always reluctant to face her when he was angry. He was standing where the priest had left him, leaning against the wall. She stared at him, white-faced and shivering. He looked back at her in silence.

Silence, that dark silence that Mary had come to know so well. No words were needed, for suddenly she knew it was the end, the final and bitter end. The life had gone out of his face and she could see his soul dying in his eyes.

A pang of pain and a sense of her own betrayal assailed her. A maelstrom of memory flashed back of their life gone by, a memory of that golden summer years ago, the summer of 1798, when he had regularly travelled over nine miles of difficult and deserted mountains from the rebel camp in Glenmalure just to see her, a sash of green around his waist denoting his rank as a field officer, smiling defiance in his eyes and careless of the dangers that surrounded him.

A memory of that same year when she had first lain with him as his bride in a candlelit bedroom and his rapturous eyes had moved over her with delight, and how he had looked at his baby daughter with such transparent love on his face, such smiling pride as he watched his first-born son grow from a baby into a boy, then another son, chubby and contented, the drowser of the family.

Days, months, years of running together, living together in the spaces between that hunted life up in the distance of the mountains where men primed their muskets and refused to face defeat. Days, months, years, all leading up to this awful moment.

She wound her arms around his neck and kissed his face sadly. He pulled her shivering body into the shelter of his own and returned her embrace, in silence.

They eventually spoke to each other, briefly and quietly. He spent only a few minutes in the house, just long enough to take his children in his arms and grip them tight to his body. First Mary-Anne, who at sight of him had jumped up excitedly and run to cling to his legs. He reached down and lifted her up, tousled her mop of black curls and smiled into her liquid black eyes. She laughed her excited laugh and he saw love in her eyes, love for him, simply because he was her daddy. She was too young to understand that he was a hero.

Three-year-old John was the next to be hauled up until he stood with a child on each arm and looked at the wooden object John proudly held up.

'Dada, look . . . Uncle Cullen whittled me a whistle,' the small boy cried, pushing the wooden whistle between his father's lips. Michael blew it and Mary-Anne screamed when the sound blasted into her face. John thought her discomfort hilarious and let out a gleeful laugh until the room was filled with their noise.

Then Michael felt a tugging at his legs and looked down to see fourteen-month-old Peter balancing and swaying on his chubby legs like a drunken little man, gurgling and clawing for some of the attention.

He set the other two down and swung Peter high in the air above his head, and he chuckled down at him. He brought the boy down and laid him across his shoulder, then slowly he turned and looked across the room at Mary.

'What did the priest say?' Cullen asked, puzzled at the silent stare that was passing between husband and wife. 'What's going on, Michael?'

Michael did not answer Cullen, he couldn't. He was unable even to look at his old friend. When Cullen spoke to him again he barely heard the words. He hastily restored Peter to his mother then turned and quickly left the house without a word of farewell to anyone.

Mary rushed to the door and watched him go. He went quickly, running and skidding over the snow as if fearing he might change his mind if he allowed himself to think about it a second longer.

It was the end, and now it had come she felt only a terrible sorrow for him, for he would never believe that it was hopeless, had always been hopeless. The fight for this heartbreaking, tragic country had been fought and lost and would never be won. But he would never believe that, not to his dying day, not even if God himself decreed it.

She stood at the door crying uncontrollably, her bewildered children looking at her in frightened silence, but Cullen was at the end of his patience.

'What ails you,' Cullen demanded, 'crying like that? And where's himself gone in such a hurry – slipping and sliding over the snow without even a glance or a word to myself?'

'He's gone to see Billy Jackson,' Mary murmured. 'To tell him that he's prepared to surrender.'

When she finally glanced round, Cullen's face was as white as his hair.

'It is the best thing now,' she whispered.

'But . . . but,' the old man seemed short of breath, then disbelieving, 'but he's always said that he would not desert his comrades. I've heard him saying that so often, heard him with my own two hearing ears.'

'And he'll not desert his comrades,' she assured him. 'He'll agree to a peaceable surrender on the terms the Viceroy has offered, but on the condition that Hugh Vesty, John Mernagh, Martin Burke, and their wives and children are also included in the terms.'

Cullen was all of a fluster. His hands moved over his face. He stepped outside and looked all around him, his eyes bewildered as he tried to imagine the Wicklow Mountains without Michael Dwyer. Since boyhood he had hunted and wandered up there, and for five and a half years the silent hills had seemed alive with his presence, aflame with his defiance. Even without seeing him, Cullen always knew he was up there, somewhere.

Of a sudden, in the imagery of Cullen's mind, the mountains were no longer white and cold, but green and lush with spring, covered in yellow gorse and purple heather. Lambs bleated lazily, herons cried over the lakes, and larks and thrushes disturbed the peaceful solitude with their melodious chatter. Everything was wild and tangled and familiar, and Cullen remembered how Michael had always loved this green and tangled land, loved it with the passion that never cools.

Michael had always believed he would live here and die here; he had never yearned to make his home and fortune some place else. He had never truly been anywhere outside Wicklow, except once to Wexford and thrice to Dublin. He had never even seen County Clare. How would he ever survive out in the alien world? A world where the Irish luck given to him long ago by the faeries would lose its magic.

Cullen turned back to Mary, his eyes and voice brooding. 'And if the Viceroy agrees about the other lads, treasure, where will youse all be going to?'

'There is only one place an Irish person will choose to go outside Ireland,' Mary answered softly, 'and don't you know that well, old man. If the Viceroy agrees, we shall go to the United States of North America.'

Chapter Thirty-Six

No one answered him, for no one could quite take in what he had just told them. The men in the cave all looked at each other, then back at him. He sat staring in front of him, eyes stilled on the flames of the fire.

'What about us?' Laurence O'Keefe asked. 'What are we to do?'

'You must do the best you can for yourselves,' Michael replied quietly. 'I have to consider my father, my mother, my brothers and sisters, my relatives and in-laws, my wife and children, and my comrades who have been with me since the beginning. But I cannot be every man's friend and keeper.'

O'Keefe and the others looked from Dwyer to Hugh Vesty, John Mernagh, and Martin Burke – the unbreakable foursome. All at some time or another had risked their lives for each other, and even now, at the end, were not to part.

'If it's any consolation,' Michael said, 'Billy the Rock assures me that the present military operations will be suspended once the four of us surrender. The heat will be drawn off Wicklow. He is convinced that many of you will be able to slip back to your homes and carry on with life without any Imaal yeoman bothering you. Most will choose to forget that you were ever rebels. Very few of the Wicklow yeomanry feel any allegiance to this government, except the old rancorous true blues at Rathdrum, Baltinglass, and Hacketstown, of course. You will have to take your chances with them, but so you would if you were not rebels. Some things never change.'

The rest of men drew away from the foursome into their own group and held a council on the subject of what they should do. In the end all agreed they could not blame the captain, who had other responsibilities beyond them. Most decided to stay where they were until after the proposed surrender had actually taken place, for few truly believed that Dwyer would be able to do it at the last. But if he did, they would wait until the military activities in Wicklow had ceased, then head back to their homes and take their chances.

Only one man decided to leave the camp there and then, and to everyone's surprise it was one of the unbreakable foursome – John Mernagh. He had not uttered one word since Dwyer's return, and now he looked at him as if waking up out of a trance, his eyes dull with contempt.

'You make whatever arrangements for surrender you want, Captain, but leave me out of it. You forget that I have no wife or child, and need not surrender to emotional involvement, or the damned and bloody Castle. If I have to, I'll keep up the fight on my own. In other words, Captain, you can take my name off your surrender terms, *and go to hell!*'

The whole cave fell into a silence that centred on the captain, who breathed softly to himself then closed his eyes for a moment.

'You must do what you think fit,' he said tonelessly.

'Too right I will!' yelled Mernagh, and grabbing up his things, turned and flung himself out of the cave.

'Maybe I should go with him,' O'Keefe said somewhat sadly. 'It wouldn't be right to let the poor bastard fight the whole British Empire on his own.'

'What about you two?' Michael murmured to Hugh Vesty and Martin Burke when O'Keefe had run after Mernagh. 'I made provision for you because I felt I could not secure terms only for myself and desert you. But you are men with minds of your own, and can go your own roads if you wish.'

'And let you have all the fun in America?' Hugh Vesty shrugged. 'Don't be crazy, boy.'

Martin Burke smiled quietly, 'Don't fret, Michael. Mernagh will be back at your side soon enough. How many dark nights in the past has he upped and left us to go and form his own army, but he was always back for breakfast.'

'It only happened once,' Hugh Vesty said in all fairness, 'and then only because John got furiously drunk. But once common sense returned, he returned.' He grinned. 'Aye, Martin, you have the right of it. Mernagh will be back, I'm thinking.'

Michael hoped they were right. He cared deeply for John Mernagh and would have liked to have gone after him and talk it over. In the past five and half years they had been good comrades and Mernagh had proved himself as loyal as Hugh Vesty. But everything had changed now, and in the last extremity every man had the right to choose his own way.

Billy the Rock was already at William Hume's house at
Humewood. Billy was still in shock at Dwyer's sudden and
dramatic capitulation, but he managed to hold up the paper and
read out the terms proposed.

'In response to Lord Hardwicke's offer that he will be given a
safe passage out of the kingdom in return for his peaceable
surrender,' Billy said, 'he agrees to such surrender on the condition that his parents, brothers and sisters, and all those presently confined in prison for no other reason than being related
to him, are released. Also, that Hugh Vesty Byrne and Martin
Burke, together with their wives and children, as well as John
Mernagh and his cousin Arthur Devlin, are included in the
terms of his surrender. And the country of their exile to be the
United States of North America.'

William Hume was very excited; the fact that Dwyer had
chosen to surrender only to him would elevate his standing
with the peasants and farmers and people of his own Wicklow.
It was a declaration of trust, for, according to the practice of the
time, whoever accepted a man in surrender was then responsible for his fate until the agreed terms of surrender were
carried out. By this act, Hume knew that Michael Dwyer was
entrusting his life to him, and Hume was determined that such
faith would not be in vain.

'There is one other condition,' Billy said. 'From the moment
of his surrender he asks that his wife and children be allowed to
lodge with him and on no account are they to be separated.'

'A strange request,' Hume said.

Billy shrugged. 'I suspect it was made by her. I doubt she
would allow him to go as far as Dublin without some guarantee
that she will be allowed to join him soon after.'

'Well,' Hume said thoughtfully, 'if the Castle agree to the
rest of the terms, I can't see why they would not agree to that
also. Some of the United leaders in 1798 had their wives with
them while awaiting deportation.'

Within the hour Hume had set off in his carriage for Dublin
Castle where he discussed the matter with Lord Hardwicke,
and two days later he hastened to Brusselstown to give Billy the
Rock the news that Lord Hardwicke had agreed the terms. By
the mercy of government, Michael Dwyer and his four named
associates would be allowed a safe retreat from the kingdom

with wives and children on condition of their peaceable surrender to William Hoare Hume, Member of Parliament for Wicklow.

So, on the black and cold night of 16th December, at a place called the Three Bridges, Michael Dwyer met William Hume alone and in secret, handed over his gun in surrender, and the two walked back together to the estate at Humewood, where hot food and warm red wine were waiting to be served to both of them.

Neither of them slept. They spent the long night in reflective conversation, and by grey dawnlight the two, if not friends, had developed a certain respect for each other.

By mid-morning a cavalcade of mounted yeomen was ready to escort him on the forty-mile journey to Dublin Castle, and Michael was amused to see that nearly all were yeomen who, at one time or another, had been accused, not unjustly, of befriending him. William Hume was obviously determined that he should reach his Dublin destination safely.

William Hume remained behind at Humewood to await the surrender of the others. He assured Michael that as soon as his own surrender at the Castle was completed, he would personally arrange for Mary and the children to join him in Dublin. Then Hume gave him one of his very best horses, and surrounded by his servants, stood by the high iron gates of Humewood and watched the rebel captain and his escort ride off.

Michael's face was calm and without expression as they rode through the snow towards Donard. It was his last journey through his own Imaal; and, like his life, the mountains of his beloved Wicklow were shrouded in dark mist.

The news of his surrender had spread like wildfire. Every mile along the route people came out and stared up at him as he rode by. To them it was the end of an era. But it was not the end they had expected. Surrender was not a fitting end for a hero. And to them, he was the greatest hero that had ever lived in Wicklow since the great chieftain lord, Feagh McHugh O'Byrne.

For over five years Michael Dwyer had been what every Wicklow youth dreamed of being – a man who owned no master, a man who refused to bend the servile knee. And they had thought he would die as undaunted as he had lived. Nay, surrender was not the end they had expected, nor the end that great stories and great ballads were made of.

Riding by, he looked in silence at the faces of all the people he knew, and he knew every one, every face a part of his life that was now over. They shouted up to him, words of gratitude, words of encouragement, words of farewell, words that trailed off like the last few notes of a sad song . . .

At Blessington he yearned to look back, turn and take one last look at the wild mountains that had been his playground, his battleground, and had sheltered him so well. But he kept his eyes fixed on the road ahead. There was no point in looking back at the man he had once been.

Part Three

She took and kissed the first flower once,
And sweetly said to me:
'This flower comes from the Wicklow Hills,
Dew, wet and pure,' said she,
'Its name is Michael Dwyer—
The strongest flower of all;
But I'll keep it fresh beside my breast
Though all the world shall fall.'

'The Three Flowers', Norman G. Reddin

Chapter Thirty-Seven

Shortly after his arrival at Dublin Castle he was given a brief interview before members of the Privy Council, then Under-Secretary Marsden informed him that he was to be transferred to Kilmainham Gaol – on a charge of high treason.

Michael stared at Marsden in disbelief, and his eyes turned as cold as ice. 'You forget one thing, Mr Marsden – all Wicklow knows about my surrender terms. All Wicklow knows that Lord Hardwicke made the offer and I accepted and submitted in good faith. If you persist in this treachery, you will be responsible for bringing danger and disgrace to the name of William Hume.'

'The terms of your surrender as agreed with William Hume will be honoured,' Marsden said, as if faintly shocked at the accusation of a double-cross. 'The official charge of high treason is simply for public reassurance that even rebels like you can eventually see the futile error of your ways. Wicklow may know you entered into secret terms with the government, but the world does not. And when we talk about the world, we mean, of course, England.'

'Give me back six minutes,' Michael said, 'and all the soldiers in the Empire will not take me in six years.'

'We will give you a clean and well-furnished cell in Kilmainham Gaol,' Marsden said in bland tones, 'where you will be given the status and privileges of a first-class State prisoner. You will also be allowed to enjoy the company of your wife and children there, until a ship is available to take you out of the kingdom.'

'And my relatives?'

'Will be liberated within a very short time,' Marsden said dismissively. 'We have no further need of them.'

Michael breathed softly to himself. He was still angry, very angry that the Castle were going to use him in their usual propaganda to show the world how decent they were in their handling of the Irish savages. But he was also very relieved that his surrender terms would be met and his family liberated. The fact that scores of men and women had been arrested and thrown into prison merely for being *relatives* of a rebel would not be told to the world, for then the world might think the Irish had a true grievance against those who governed them after all, instead of being a barbaric and troublesome race incapable of gratitude to those who endeavoured to teach them civilised behaviour. So it had always been in the war between the two islands; while the government silenced free speech and controlled the newspapers and thereby the ears of the world, the British story suffered no contradiction and would always be believed.

'How long can I expect to be confined in Kilmainham Gaol?' he asked.

'Not too long, hopefully, for we are very anxious to get you out of Ireland.' Marsden's grey eyes glazed over until their expression was hard to read. 'But however long you remain in Kilmainham, I think you will find that we shall treat you well.'

And they did. Within days of being transferred to Kilmainham, Mary and the children joined him in his large and well-furnished cell and for the first time in six years they spent the entire festival of Christmas together, albeit behind bars. But both had the satisfaction of knowing that all their Wicklow relatives had been set free and were now back in the comfort of their homes, including Michael's father, who had been released from New Geneva in Waterford.

On New Year's Day, 1804, Mary began to wonder about the life that awaited them in America.

'Did Mr Hume say to which part of America we would be sent?' she asked. 'Did he say New York?'

Michael shook his head vaguely as he placed more logs on the fire in the corner of the cell. 'I think he mentioned a place called Baltimore, wherever that may be.'

'Baltimore,' Mary repeated, then her face broke into a sunburst of a smile. 'It sounds Irish, doesn't it? Baltimore.'

'Aye,' he smiled back at her. 'I suppose it does. There's a Baltimore in Cork.'

It was still dark, not yet dawn, the room lit only by the flames of the fire that had to be kept alive in defence of the winter chill permanently in the air.

Mary sat on the side of bed, relieved and happy in herself as she looked over at the small curly heads of her three children asleep in a bed along the opposite wall. This was how they would live from now on, all together, day in and day out. And when they reached the land of the free she would have him all to herself, just him and the children all to herself in some little thatched cottage in Baltimore in America. No harbourers in the next room, no soldiers on the hills, no comrades looking for their leader.

She bit her lip thoughtfully. Were the houses in America thatched, she suddenly wondered, or were they mansions with long windows that required a great deal of lace for curtaining? Ach, no matter, she would settle for either. By all accounts it didn't take long for a hard-working man to get rich in America.

Her eyes rested on the dark hair and sleeping innocent face of Mary-Anne, Michael's favourite child, and Mary wondered if maybe their daughter would end up a very rich and grand lady by marrying one of the Boston Irish? A gentleman prisoner on the floor above, a wealthy young lawyer named St John Mason, had told her that the Boston Irish were some of the richest people in the world.

'Is Boston anywhere near Baltimore, do you know?' she asked Michael.

Michael didn't know the answer to her question, and didn't query the point of it either. He sat down on the bed beside her, his eyes looking up to the barred window of their cell at the sky beyond.

After a life so long and free on the mountains he found the stone walls of the prison crushing. But the unease that had followed his interview at the Castle was dropping away, the unease of not knowing whether they were planning a double-cross or not. So far, Marsden had not been lying – they had treated him well, providing him with the company of his family, adequate fuel for the fire, sufficient food and drink, and no reason for complaint.

Except that he was not allowed access to the joint cell of Hugh Vesty and Martin Burke, who had not been quite so well treated, given the status of 'second-class' political prisoners and placed in a narrow cell with sparse comfort and sparse diet. His only consolation on their behalf was that things would improve for them once they were all out of this prison.

'What are you thinking?' Mary asked.

543

'How long it will take for our ship to come in,' he murmured.

Time passed – weeks, months. He became very uneasy at their long detention and demanded to know why the conditions of his surrender had not yet been fulfilled. His inquiries were set aside with one plausible explanation after another.

Summer came, warm and humid; and with it the birth of Mary's child, a delicate little girl born in the infirmary of Kilmainham. They named her Esther.

Again Michael demanded to know why the terms of his surrender had not yet been fulfilled. The response as always was negative, but he attacked and pressed for an answer on all occasions. He requested an explanation from Dr Trevor, the superintendent of the gaol.

'I know nothing about it,' Dr Trevor snapped, 'other than that the Castle are trying to engage a ship.'

'Ships are going to America all the time.'

'Trading ships that have room for three or four passengers and no more. Very few have enough space to accommodate five men, three women, and seven children. The Castle are trying very hard to engage the right ship, I can assure you of that.'

Dr Trevor hurried away, and avoided him henceforth.

Harvest time came, cool and dry; and Dr Trevor spent part of each day watching Michael Dwyer from behind the thick drapes of his office window, watching and waiting for some little sign that the man's patience was ready to break. He watched every day without fail, for every day Dwyer and his companions took a good deal of exercise at ball playing and the like in the yard below.

The governor of Kilmainham Gaol was John Dunne, but Dr Trevor was the inquisitor-general and the Castle's chief spy. Trevor had given good service to the government over the years, and in return had received not only large sums from the secret service funds, but a variety of well-paid offices.

He was superintendent of Kilmainham Gaol; physician of Kilmainham Gaol; a justice of the peace; agent of transport ships; recruiting agent for army and navy, and in this latter office he regularly toured the prisons persuading prisoners that a life on the high seas or marching across the world carrying a musket in His Majesty's service would be far more enjoyable than a high hanging.

And a high hanging was what Dr Trevor dreamed of whenever he looked down at Michael Dwyer. He hated the rebel
with undiluted venom. Since Dwyer's arrival at Kilmainham
he had disrupted the very life of the prison. For years Dr Trevor
had maintained the natural order of prison life – misery,
degradation, dull eyes in dull faces, men brought so low that
complaint and lament was their natural conversation – but
Dwyer had changed all that, for despite the frustration of his
long wait, the rapscallion still enjoyed a sense of humour and a
bit of fun.

Dr Trevor watched Dwyer in the yard below who was grinning broadly as he gave orders to a gentleman prisoner named
John Patten, then ran down the other end of the yard to confer
with John Mernagh, another Wicklow rebel who had speedily
joined his leader in Kilmainham after Christmas.

Dr Trevor jerked round as the governor, John Dunne, entered
the room. 'Is it our rebel chief you are watching again?' the
governor asked wryly.

'Look at him!' Trevor cried. 'He's at it again – these games
of his cannot be allowed to continue! This is the seventh or
eighth match at ball he has organised amongst the men in the
past month. His effect on the second-class prisoners is deplorable.'

'In what way?'

'In what way, sir? In the most unsatisfactory way. According
to the turnkeys, these men at night are as tired as ploughboys at
harvest time, falling down on their mats in sleep before the
doors are even locked.'

The governor, a Lancashire man, looked down to the recreation ground at Dwyer and his companions, all active fellows,
playing a match with sixteen others while the rest of the yard
looked on with great interest and pleasure.

Such enjoyment, the governor knew, was anathema to a man
like Dr Trevor, who had been described by one suffering prisoner as 'a monster in human shape'. Another had stated that
Trevor had treated him 'with such cold-blooded cruelty it
nearly brought my life to its termination'.

And John Dunne, as governor, knew both had been speaking
the truth, indeed Dr Trevor had become known as the 'Tyrant
of Kilmainham'. He too despised Dr Trevor, but he was power-
less to act against him, for Trevor was answerable only to the
Castle, who continually ignored the complaints sent to them

about his brutality, especially against the women prisoners.

And now it seemed that the superintendent's venom was to be sprayed in full force at Michael Dwyer. And John Dunne knew why. It was not only Dwyer's ball games that infuriated Dr Trevor, it was his wit against the turnkeys that he used in such a manner that no one ever knew if he was serious or not.

Then there was also the business of Trevor's ring of informers that Dwyer had effectively broken – men sent out to the recreation ground under guise of being political prisoners, but in truth planted there for the purpose of picking other prisoners' brains in the hope of discovering the names of rebels still at liberty.

These informers – Trevor's men – were suspected by the real prisoners and all had been pointed out to Dwyer. And according to gossip, when the informers went out and mixed with the men watching the ball game, cheering with them, Dwyer had seemingly selected one at a time for friendly attention at the end of each match, sidling up to him and asking in pretended earnest, 'Do you know any of the informers, avic? I'm told there are some of the reptiles skulking amongst us. If you know who they are, will you point them out to me?'

And so terrific was the reputation of Michael Dwyer that now not one of Trevor's men would set foot on the recreation ground while he and his friends were on it, and the rest of the prisoners had enjoyed seeing the rebel chief sending the informers sneaking away in a hurry.

'He's a tyrant!' Trevor snapped. 'A damned tyrant and no less!'

The governor turned his eyes from the men in the yard and stared at Dr Trevor. 'Oh come, Dr Trevor,' he said coldly, 'I cannot support your charge. Apart from Dwyer's enthusiasm for the ball games, I find him, on the whole, a rather quiet and peaceable man.'

'Do you indeed? I find his manner rather pert! And why should he not be quiet and peaceable when he has his woman and brats to keep him company in his cell? Is it not a pretty thing that this rebel received the privileges usually only accorded to *gentlemen* prisoners?'

'He is not technically a prisoner,' the governor said by way of reminder. 'The government made surrender terms with him and he remains here while awaiting deportation.'

'I know nothing of his surrender,' Trevor snapped, 'except

that he made it when he could hold out no longer.'

Trevor moved away from the window then, but he was back standing by it the following day, his eyes piercing and dangerous as they watched Dwyer playing with a five-year-old female brat in the yard.

'One false move from you, my boyo,' Trevor whispered, 'just one false move, one act of insubordination is all I need, then I will have you.'

A few days later, during their recreation period in the yard, a gentleman from the first class spoke quietly to Michael, and showed him a written memorial complaining about the system of cruelty and abuse that was being carried on inside Kilmainham Gaol by Dr Trevor, and the deplorable conditions.

Michael looked at the names at the bottom of the paper, many were gentlemen of first-class status: St John Mason, a lawyer and cousin of Robert Emmet, John Patten, brother-in-law of Robert Emmet, Philip Long, banker to Robert Emmet – fourteen from the first class in all, and forty-one from the second class – all from the wing that housed the political prisoners, otherwise known as *State* prisoners.

The memorial stated that 'a system of avaricious and malignant severity is practised in this prison which calls aloud for, and might be sufficiently demonstrated, by a fair and impartial investigation'.

'St John Mason,' said the prisoner to Michael, 'is going to try and get one of his barrister friends to slip it to a judge on the bench. And once the barrister gets it into the judge's hand, the judge is obliged by law to do something about it.'

'So what do you want me to do about it?' Michael whispered.

'Sign it.'

'I can't do that.'

'Why not? Can't you write?'

'I can write well enough, but that's not the problem. Each man on that list is complaining about his treatment here in Kilmainham, but as far as it is possible inside a prison, I have been treated well.'

'And how long do you think that will last?'

'Until I board my ship.'

'You must be stupid or crazy, man, to trust the Castle. There won't be any ship. Can't you see – you were a big fish they finally baited in their net, and they'll make you pay, Dwyer.

Somehow and someway, they will have their revenge on you.'

Michael looked around the men in the yard, then at the guards, then up to the windows while he spoke. 'I have William Hume's oath of honour that my surrender terms will not be violated,' he said firmly. 'But my surrender is not the issue here. I have been treated well so far, and therefore I cannot sign that paper.'

'Look at the three names at the end.'

Michael glanced down at the three names: Hugh Vesty Byrne, John Mernagh, and Martin Burke.

'While you have been enjoying first-class privileges, they have been living in deplorable conditions.'

'They tell me so,' Michael answered softly, 'and they are the reason I cannot add my name to the list.'

'I don't understand you.'

'Then I'll explain it to you, avic. If that memorial is to have any effect with men of influence on the outside, it has to be seen as a genuine and truthful account of life in here. But if my name is on it, enjoying the privileges that I do, wife and children allowed to lodge with me and so on, then it will be disbelieved and seen as nothing more than a list of complaints from a bunch of ungrateful malcontents. It will not receive the attention it deserves.'

'Ah . . . now I understand you.'

'I'm glad that you do,' Michael said, and strolled away.

The yard was empty, being so early in the morning, but Michael Dwyer was already out in the air as usual, as if the confines of his cell was something he could not bear in daytime.

And Dr Trevor was watching as usual. He had no knowledge of the prisoners' memorial that contained not only complaints about the severity of the prison but a personal indictment against him. A memorial that Michael Dwyer had declined to sign.

Dr Trevor watched him playing with his female brat again, saw him chase her down the yard, heard her excited screams.

As his eyes followed them, Trevor saw something else which made his blood boil – down the far end of the yard a small boy with black curly hair was feeding bits of bread to a cluster of tame pigeons. Now wasn't that a pretty thing – government bread being wasted by one of Dwyer's brats!

Then he saw the boy running towards Dwyer on his four-year-old legs, saw Dwyer swinging him up on to his shoulders, saw the two of them smiling, the girl also, as the three stood watching the birds happily eating away.

Trevor sent for a turnkey who came at the double. Trevor beckoned him over to the window.

'Do you see those pigeons down there?'

'Oh yes, sir,' replied the turnkey. 'They belong to a prisoner who's been training them for months.'

'Kill them,' Trevor said.

'Beg pardon, sir?'

'You heard me!' Trevor fiercely retorted. 'Collect four guards with four guns and tell them to go out to that yard and shoot those birds immediately.'

Trevor watched as the guards entered the yard, aimed their guns and killed the tame pigeons while Dwyer's brats stood bawling their eyes out.

Trevor nodded to himself, smiling as he watched Dwyer stare in disgust at the guards, utter a few words to them, then take his wailing children back inside.

The turnkey returned, and spoke to Dr Trevor's back.

'The guards want to know what they should do with the pigeons, sir. Should they take them to the kitchen?'

'No. Tell the guards to leave the dead birds where they lie. They must not be removed from the yard, not under any circumstances. Understand?'

'No, sir . . . I mean, yes, sir.'

'What did Dwyer say to the guards? Was it a complaint?'

'It was, sir. He said if they were forced to kill the birds, they might at least have given him time to remove the children before they did it.'

'Remove the children indeed! From my prison they should be removed.' Dr Trevor frowned. 'But I'll need a better complaint from Dwyer than that.' He looked at the turnkey. 'What other weaknesses has he? Apart from his children?'

'He's developing a bad need for liquor, sir. And not ale. He's beginning to need spirits.'

'And are we supplying his need?'

'Oh yes, sir. Just like you ordered. He can't seem to sleep at night without a noggin of whiskey to help him.'

'And when he wakes up? Does he need whiskey then?'

'Not yet, sir. But if word of his ship doesn't come soon, then I reckon it won't be long before he'll need it to face another day within these walls.'

'How long before he is totally dependent on it?'

'Hard to say, sir. He's a quiet enough fellow, for all his wild reputation, but I reckon it's his wife who's keeping him calm, her and the liquor.'

'Her and the liquor? And if we denied him both at a stroke—' Trevor turned to face the turnkey and smiled cunningly. 'What have you learned about the wife?' he asked.

'She's queer in the head, sir. A tasty wench, but not quite the full shilling. She thinks this place is one of Dublin's luxury hotels.'

'Does she indeed?' Dr Trevor's wide eyes invited the turnkey to elaborate on his opinion, and the turnkey obliged with a shrug.

'I knew she was a bit loony after her first day in here. For a start, she brought her own soap but requested a bowl. When I brought it, she asks if we could supply her with a full bucket of water every morning to warm up for washing. Then after breakfast she asked for more water to wash up the plates, and when I told her to use the water they'd washed themselves in, she refused and asked for fresh. So I asked her if she thought this was a luxury hotel and I was a bleeding chambermaid, but she turned to himself, and he said nothing, but the look he gave went right through me. And ever since she's had water for washing and fresh water for washing the plates. The governor said she could.'

'The governor—'

'Allowed her more soap when her own ran out, and now she gets a regular supply as well as being provided with a broom to sweep out her cell. All the turnkeys laugh at her, not when himself's around, of course, but I reckon she's more to be pitied than laughed at. Mind, she aggravated me something sorely last week when she took her broom and viciously pushed out a turnkey who did me a favour by carrying in her bucket of water – she said he had lice crawling on his hair and she didn't want him near her children or baby. Then I asks her if it was maybe a nursemaid in white starches she would prefer as a turnkey, but she starts sobbing and wailing and says all she wants is to go to Baltimore or back to the mountains of Wicklow.'

Dr Trevor was smiling, the turnkey had given him an idea.

'It's not decent, sir, having women in a male prison, women that can't be treated as prisoners, if you understand.'

'I understand perfectly,' Trevor murmured.

'I mean . . .' the turnkey scratched his head, 'if she were a real bona fide woman prisoner, I could just give her a punch or a kick and life would be easy. But I can't very well do that with him around. He can see no fault in her queer and fancy ways, but then he gets the pleasure of her in his bed at night while all I get is tears and complaints and requests for more bleeding water.'

'How much daily food rations is Dwyer allowed?' Trevor asked, his mind working furiously.

'Same rations as all the other first-class prisoners,' the turnkey shrugged, 'except Dwyer has to share his with his family. Every day I give his wife one pound of bread, half an ounce of tea, three ounces of sugar, half pint of milk, and one pound of beef or pork.'

Divided between two adults and three children and a baby, it provided no more than a cup of tea and a meat sandwich daily, but Trevor considered it far too generous, especially when the brats could save enough of the bread to feed to birds. He hmmned to himself. The total cost of such an allowance was three shillings a day, three shillings a day that could go into his own pocket, if his idea went as planned.

'Has Mrs Dwyer had her rations today?'

'Yes, sir, first thing this morning. Just after I humped in her bleeding bucket of water. A nice thing it is that rebel prisoners can wash and shave before I get a chance to even scratch meself after my breakfast.'

Trevor scowled. Lord Hardwicke might insist that Dwyer's conditions should not be interfered with while awaiting his ship, but Mr Marsden was not such a lily as His Excellency. Mr Marsden was still a formidable power at the Castle. He knew the amount of every bribe that had been paid to government officials to secure the Union, for he had been the Castle's pay-clerk. He knew every trick, every secret of everyone, and apart from His Excellency, very few would dare to stand or speak against the Under-Secretary. Very few could manage to even look him in the eye, and as long as they kept their eyes averted, Marsden remained the real power at Dublin Castle. And Marsden was Trevor's employer.

'Take the water in as usual tomorrow,' Trevor told the turnkey, 'but leave the business of the food rations to me.'

* * *

The following morning a new attendant carried the Dwyers' food rations in to their cell; a convicted prisoner from the felons' side. He was no more than a filthy bundle of rags with lice crawling all over him.

With horrified eyes Mary stared at the crust of grime on his hands and face as he set down the tray of rations, but before she could utter a word, he suddenly grabbed the portion of cooked meat in his filthy hands, tore off a piece, shoved it hungrily into his mouth, and scurried out.

His foul smell lingered, but as Michael stared at the meat he had left, he saw it was putrid. The smell of it almost made him sick as he carried it to the door and called for the turnkey.

The turnkey rushed to report the matter to the Tyrant of Kilmainham.

'Dwyer has made an official complaint, sir.'

'A complaint? An *official* complaint?' Dr Trevor looked shocked. 'And what could he have to complain about, may I ask?'

'About the food, sir. He says it was served in an offensive manner as well as being rotten and foul-smelling.'

'Served in an *offensive* manner? Oh, you are right, my good man, these savages think this is a ruddy hotel. I run the best prison in the Western world and my meat is as fine as that served in the Castle. Did he eat the meat?'

'No sir. He just handed it back to me.'

'Was he abusive?'

'No, sir. Just asked for it to be removed. He suggested it might be given to the rats, as a way of killing a few of them off.'

Dr Trevor almost collapsed with frustration and fury. 'That is not good enough! I need a better complaint than that!'

'Why not just invent one, sir?'

'Invent one? With that turnip of a governor on my back! John Dunne is just waiting for an opportunity to expose me to Lord Hardwicke. The man is overburdened with notions of morality and humanity. He should not be in the prison service. He should have stayed in Lancashire and tended docile sheep instead of hardened men. No . . . when Dwyer finally loses his temper and breaks the rules, I want the governor either to see it, or hear of it from men he trusts, men he relies on to tell him the truth.'

'What about Dwyer, sir?'

'Oh, get out!' Trevor fiercely retorted. 'I'll think about Dwyer tonight. In the meantime, tell him he must do without meat today, but he should find everything satisfactory tomorrow.'

When the turnkey had gone, Dr Trevor mustered his humour and marched down the corridors. There were more prisoners than Dwyer who needed his attention.

His face was soft and gentle when he entered the solitary cell of a fifty-year-old man with long black hair rapidly turning grey all over. The man sat on the stone ledge under the high barred window, as still and silent as if he were in a trance.

'And how are we today, Mr Devlin?' Trevor said kindly.

Brian Devlin made no answer.

'I have some news for you,' Trevor said kindly. 'I performed an autopsy on your son's head at the time of his death, to discover the cause, but it is only now that the Castle have given me permission to tell you the result.'

Brian Devlin moved his head and looked at Dr Trevor with staring eyes of hatred.

'You killed my nine-year-old boy!' he rasped. 'You made him walk and walk in the pouring rain even though you knew he was half-blind and suffering with gaol fever. To call yourself a doctor is an obscene joke – and now you tell me that you did an autopsy on my son's head!'

Devlin sprang at Dr Trevor, but was brought down to his knees by the pull of the chains and irons around his ankles.

'I did an autopsy,' Trevor confirmed, his voice still kindly. 'And the verdict has been accepted officially as "Death by Visitation from God" – in lay terms, natural causes.'

After a very long time, Brian Devlin crawled off his knees and resumed his seat on the stone ledge.

'Oh, Devlin,' Trevor exclaimed, 'this hostility is getting us nowhere. It upsets you and it hurts me, for I was deeply grieved at the death of your boy. But I would like to make it up to you. I would like to become a friend to you and the rest of your family. I would like to help you all. What say you – shall we bury the hatchet and let bygones be bygones?'

When Devlin made no answer, Dr Trevor took a wad of money out of his pocket and held it before the prisoner.

'You are an uncle to Michael Dwyer. Tell us everything you know about him and agree to testify against him in court. You needn't tell everything. All you need describe are details of all the innocent people you saw him kill in cold blood and before your very eyes. In return we shall give you freedom and protection and make you rich. A wise man would know what to do. Only a fool would refuse it.

Brian Devlin met Trevor's eyes. 'A pox on you and your

money. I would rather die than lie under oath.'

Dr Trevor's face split into a wide grin. 'Then, you case-hardened old villain, you shall be hanged!'

He strutted out of the cell and down the corridor, unaware of the figure of John Dunne standing in the shadows.

The governor motioned to the turnkey, who relocked the cell, then turned and nodded.

'You heard every word that Trevor said?' the governor whispered.

'I did, sir. And a nice state of affairs it is when a prison doctor spends his days going round the cells telling prisoners they're going to be hanged.'

'None of these men have yet been charged with any crime,' John Dunne said, 'and if they are charged and brought to trial, it will be a judge and jury and the rule of law that decides if they will be hanged, not Dr Trevor.'

'Trouble is, sir, while they're in here, Dr Trevor is the rule and law.'

The governor nodded; that was true. But somehow the man had to be stopped. Not only was he starving prisoners and pocketing the money allowed for their food, he solicited, threatened, starved, and bribed uncharged prisoners to become soldiers and enlist in the army. But it was his treatment of some of the prisoners on the women's side that was totally inhuman. To allow Trevor to attend them as a doctor was an obscenity. And the Under-Secretary of State allowed it.

St John Mason, barrister-at-law and cousin of Robert Emmet, wrote to Richard Brinsley Sheridan in London, in the hope of publishing an indictment against Dr Trevor's personal conduct and administration of Kilmainham Gaol, which he hoped would be brought up in the Parliament at Westminster. Mason described Trevor very charitably as 'one whose sleepless hours are consumed in plotting against human happiness and human life'.

And in Kilmainham, Dr Trevor lay awake; plotting against the human happiness of Michael and Mary Dwyer. By dawn he had come up with another idea to spoil their tempers and appetites.

After the turnkey had brought in the water, another new attendant brought in their food rations. This time he was fairly clean, and the meat was fresh, a succulent joint of roasted beef from which their portion had not yet been sliced off.

Michael was sitting on the bed endeavouring to get Peter's chubby two-year-old legs into a pair of breeches. Mary sat at the table holding baby Esther. Mary-Anne and John sat each side of her, their eyes wide with awe as they stared at the giant who had brought in their food.

'I'll slice a nice big piece for you, shall I, ma'am?' the attendant said pleasantly to Mary, taking up a huge, very long-bladed knife.

This time it was Michael who froze and paled as he stared at the massive man, a man who had been pointed out to him on the first occasion he had seen him walking with Dr Trevor along the corridors of Kilmainham Gaol. He was Tom Galvin, the public executioner and hangman.

'Hello, me young hearties,' Galvin said brightly to Mary-Anne and John. 'Yez are a bit young to be in prison, ain't yez? You ain't rebels I hope?'

Both stared back at him, too young to have learned what rebels were.

Galvin smiled at John and held up the huge knife. 'Do you like my knife, boy? Ain't it a beauty?'

John nodded nervously at the giant. ' 'Tis a big one.'

'Aye, and a famous one. This is the knife that hacked off a rebel's head on Thomas Street.'

Peter yelled in fright when he was suddenly flung down on the bed and Michael sprang at the hangman.

Seconds later the guards rushed in on cue, and all the children were screaming as the guards pounced and seemed to need all their strength to pinion Dwyer to the wall.

Dr Trevor entered the cell and pretended to look shocked and appalled. 'This is not the kind of behaviour we expect from first-class prisoners, Dwyer. Good gracious, no! If you wish to create ructions then I am afraid you will have to be removed from the first-class to more appropriate accommodation elsewhere.'

'I demand the fulfilment of my terms!' Michael screamed in rage. 'I did not surrender to William Hume for the privilege of spending my life caged in a prison! I demand that the government either fulfil my terms or admit it was all a double-cross.'

'Terms?' Dr Trevor looked at each of the guards with a disbelieving smirk; then scornfully at Dwyer. 'The government made terms – with you? I know nothing about your terms.'

'You damn well do know about my terms!'

'*Your terms! Your terms!*' Trevor screamed back, his eyes popping out of his head. 'I know what your terms are better than you do yourself – you have no terms at all! There is no robber or highwayman could make better possible terms than saving his life, and the capital offence is where a rebel like you should be!'

'And a devil like you should be back with your horn-headed father in hell!'

'Remove him to the felons' side and have him double-bolted,' Trevor ordered.

'No! No!' Mary screamed, throwing herself at the guards, who coldly pulled back the fingers gripping her husband's arm and pushed her aside. Her screams and those of the children brought Michael back to his senses.

'I'll go quietly,' he said in a low voice to Trevor. 'Tell them to unhand me and I'll go quietly.'

Trevor was startled by his sudden change of demeanour. 'Why should I allow you to go quietly?'

'Because my children are watching,' Michael hissed.

After a moment's consideration, the sides of his mouth turned down, Trevor nodded to the guards. 'Let him come quietly.'

The guards were grinning at their victory over the noted rebel.

'I will be back soon,' Michael said brightly to the children, flashing a message with his eyes to Mary, asking her to play the game. 'We are all friends again, see?' He looked at the grinning guards. 'And I will be back soon.'

Mary-Anne and John clung sobbing to his legs, but he restored them to their mother and firmly told them there was nothing to cry about, nothing at all.

Then he moved out of the cell and walked quietly down the corridor with guards before and behind and each side of him, and Dr Trevor strutting like the ex-army man that he was, five paces behind.

'Dr Trevor, sir!'

The superintendent spun round to face Tom Galvin, who was still very sour at being attacked by Dwyer and not getting the opportunity of using his knife before the guards came. But then, on reflection, Galvin was glad the guards had come in on signal, for he was not really a fighter, he was only used to dealing with men whose hands were chained.

'What shall I do with this now?' the hangman asked, holding up the tray of beef.

'What you have been paid to do with it, Mr Galvin,' Trevor retorted. 'Serve it to the rest of the first-class prisoners.'

'Yes, sirrah!'

Galvin threw back his head and roared with laughter as he visualised the stunned faces of the prisoners when the public hangman walked into their cells. He laughed all the way down the corridor, for the whole situation delighted his gallows-style sense of humour.

When Dr Trevor returned to the corridor an hour later, little Mary-Anne was still standing by the cell door, staring down the dark passage where her daddy had gone, hiccupping sobs to herself as she waited vigilantly for his return.

Trevor paused, stood for a moment looking down at the child, who stared back at him from under her mop of curls in terror, then he passed on and looked calmly at Mary as he entered the cell.

When she looked up, he bowed. 'Madam,' he said reverently.

'Yes?' Mary whispered.

'I would be deeply grateful,' he said in a languid voice, 'if you would kindly do me the pleasure of removing yourself and your brats from this prison within the hour.'

For a few seconds Mary said nothing then, her voice very quiet, 'I'll not go anywhere without my husband. It was agreed that I could stay with him.' Her gaze was bitter. 'Where I belong.'

Trevor's smile was mocking, almost pitying. 'No, madam, you belong back in Wicklow, but he belongs on the scaffold.'

'He'll die of suffocation anyway,' Mary cried savagely, 'if he's kept caged in this prison much longer!'

'Then you must pray for him,' Trevor said with gentle scorn.

By that evening, Mary had been turned out of the prison with her children, Michael was securely bolted on the felons' side, and Dr Trevor ended the day in blissful contentment as he smoked his long-pipe and pondered on the day's work.

It had taken longer than expected to get Dwyer where he wanted him, and where he should have been from the day he entered Kilmainham eleven months ago; on the felons' side, in the company of murderers, highwaymen, and pimps.

And Dwyer's health would suffer in a very bad way for a time – deprived of the liquor he had come to need so badly to help him sleep. Just the thought of Dwyer shaking with his craving made Trevor almost swoon with pleasure.

The pity was that he would not be able to keep him there for long, not for more than a few weeks. The bastard had the status of a political prisoner and would eventually have to be sent back to the rebel wing – but not to the first class. His status would be reduced to second class, and although deprived of the liquor and the company of his beloved wife, he would be consoled by the company of his dear comrades, Byrne, Burke and Mernagh, all back together with their leader in one cell. And then the next stage of the plan could be put into operation . . . *Ley fuga*.

Dr Trevor smiled. In stalemate situations of this kind, *ley fuga* was the best solution – prisoner shot in the act of escape. It had worked many times before, and it was the easiest way to get rid of the four rebels in one swift move – plan their escape for them, and shoot them as they attempted it.

But every coin had two sides, and within minutes Trevor was frowning. Of course, Lord Hardwicke had every intention of putting Dwyer on a ship, as soon as he could procure one.

Trevor sat back and took a long reflective chew on his pipe, then he inhaled deeply and blew out the smoke with a slow smile.

Still, Lord Hardwicke would be spared the trouble and have no further need to procure a ship . . . if his plan of *ley fuga* succeeded.

Chapter Thirty-Eight

Since the day of Michael Dwyer's imprisonment fifteen months previously, Lord Hardwicke had been pressing the Home Office in London for a ship. And now, at last, in the spring of 1805, he had received word from Lord Hawkesbury that a ship had been engaged and would leave England within two months.

Everyone in the Castle breathed a huge sigh of relief; and Alexander Marsden sent for Dr Trevor.

'Inform the prisoner,' Marsden said, smiling, 'that a ship has been engaged and will soon be on its way.'

Trevor looked crestfallen. 'How soon?'

'The ship is called the *Tellicherry*,' Marsden said. 'It will hold one hundred and eighty passengers, including Dwyer and his associates. We have hopes of it docking at Cork sometime at the beginning of June. So, with any luck, we should be rid of the rebel captain by the end of summer.'

Dr Trevor had the sly look of a cunning old fox when he stepped into Michael Dwyer's cell, a cell he shared with Hugh Vesty. It was a hell-hole containing nothing but a pile of straw for sleeping; the window was unglazed, making the night temperature sub-zero in winter, and the door was always locked.

A hell-hole the other prisoners had complained about in a signed memorial of protest, which had not included the name of Michael Dwyer. He had signed the second memorial to be sneaked out, but the complaints were largely ignored as a list of 'gross exaggerations'. And so the prisoners were served continually with food that was uneatable: the meat putrid and vegetables rotten; and the plates often washed in the turnkey's emptied privet bucket.

A hell-hole in which Michael's treatment at the hands of Dr Trevor had become worse and worse as the days passed, until it developed into a mental battle of wills between the two of them.

The inquisitor-general had even concocted a plan to provide an excuse to have him and his three comrades shot while attempting to escape.

As soon as the escape plan had been whispered to him, Michael had jumped at the chance, and had even succeeded, with Hugh Vesty and the others, in getting as far as the governor's empty office. About to escape down the coal-hole beneath, the simple easiness of it all suddenly made him suspicious. He scrambled up to the window and saw a large guard of soldiers with fixed bayonets outside the prison wall; some were simply waiting, others were priming and loading . . . *ley fuga*.

It was an old prison trick, and in their desperation they had almost fallen for it; and for weeks afterwards Dr Trevor had stalked Kilmainham in a black rage of frustration.

He was a lot calmer now as he looked down at the two rebels sitting on their straw and playing cards.

'Well, Dwyer,' Trevor said brightly, 'it seems your ship is about to come in.'

Michael did not lift up his head but turned a wry face to Hugh Vesty. 'What do you say, avic? Should we believe him?'

Hugh Vesty shook his head. 'No, sir, we should not. The man is incapable of telling the truth. You only have to look at his eyes to see they've gone crooked with his roguery.'

'Very funny, very funny,' Trevor declared, quite used to their sarcasm. 'You boys will never lose your dry tongues and humour, will you? But maybe a long dose of the salty sea air will dry them up completely.'

Trevor held up the sheet of paper bearing the government seal. 'This is the official notice which orders me to inform one Michael Dwyer, Hugh Vesty Byrne, John Mernagh, Martin Burke, and Arthur Devlin, to prepare themselves to sail out of the kingdom – in accordance with the surrender terms agreed by the aforementioned Michael Dwyer.'

Trevor hefted a defeated sigh. 'As you know, Dwyer, I have always been of the opinion that the whole lot of you should be hanged, but what can I do now but accept the situation and pray the ship will sink? The same ship that has been arranged by Lord Hardwicke himself. A ship called . . .' Trevor looked down at the paper ' . . . the *Tellicherry*.'

Michael leaned forward and peered at the paper which was undoubtedly genuine. He could hardly believe it. 'America . . .' He looked at Hugh Vesty, his voice full of wonder. 'Do you hear that, avic? As long as it has taken, our ship is truly coming in at last, to take us to America.'

'America?' Dr Trevor could no longer contain his laughter at the joke. 'You will never be seen in America, Dwyer. Do you think the government are such damned fools as to send you to the rebel states of America from which you might come back when you please to rise another rebellion?'

Michael looked at Trevor stunned. 'But William Hume—'

'William Hume took too much upon himself when he promised you America,' Trevor said contemptuously. 'He overestimated his influence with the Castle. Lord Hardwicke did agree to spare your life and give you a passage out of the kingdom in return for your peaceable surrender, but the day after you obliged, His Excellency wrote to London requesting a convict ship for Botany Bay – and that is where you are going – to the penal colony of Botany Bay. You and your comrades and one hundred and seventy-five more along with you. And seeing as the ship will be overcrowded, your wives and children, of course, will not be going with you.'

Trevor laughed again at the disbelief on their faces.

It was Hugh Vesty who finally spoke. 'If what you say be the true intention of your government, then they are what we always took them to be, a corrupt and perfidious set, and they have a ready and willing tool in you!'

'All Ireland knows the terms agreed on my surrender,' Michael said, coming out of his shock, 'and the blatant violation of those terms by the government will be published to the world. Have no doubt on that.'

'The government,' Trevor said, 'has asked me to present you with an ultimatum, Dwyer. Either publicly declare your willingness to go to New South Wales, or stand trial for high treason.'

'I'll stand my trial,' Michael snapped. 'And as every rebel trial is rigged – I'll have my speech in the dock and publicly tell the bastards what I think of them.'

'Oh, they've had enough of that kind of speech,' Trevor said blithely. 'You'd be gagged and dragged away after your first sentence. What you should concentrate on now, my boyo, is the event that usually takes place after a trial – the high hanging.'

Michael managed a contemptuous smile. 'If you are trying to terrorise me with visions of the noose, Dr Trevor, then you haven't yet learned just how callous I am.'

'Callous enough to allow your precious wife and children to stand and watch you swing in the wind?' Dr Trevor looked deeply shocked. 'Oh yes, they would be brought to watch. And every yeoman in Rathdrum and Baltinglass would be cheering as they wept. And as a physician I feel I should tell you that many a young wife has had to be committed to the insane asylum after witnessing such a scene. Now . . . how do you think your poor devoted wife would cope?'

As soon as Dwyer sprang to his feet, the waiting guards rushed in. Dr Trevor escaped the rough and tumble and rushed back to the Castle to report the result to Alexander Marsden.

'He'll never agree to go willingly in public,' Trevor opined.

'Then you must persuade him!' the Under-Secretary snapped. 'That is what the secret service funds pay you for!'

'Why not just bring him to trial and execution?' Trevor demanded. 'It's no more than he deserves. I have threatened him with no less.'

Marsden flopped down in his chair and looked at Dr Trevor with cool grey eyes.

'We cannot bring him to trial and execution without exposing a flagrant breach of his surrender terms. And those terms were his life and a passage out of the country. But never once, in any newspaper article, was it mentioned that the passage was to America. So if we can send him off to Botany Bay with as little trouble as possible, and with his agreement, the whole sorry business and Michael Dwyer himself will be quickly forgotten.'

'Then I have no choice but to continue my efforts to persuade him.'

'Do!' Marsden said. 'And remind him that any decision he makes affects not only himself, but the friends he sought fit to include in his surrender terms. Remind him that if he is brought to trial, they will be too. If he is hanged, they will be too. But if he agrees to go to the sunny climate of Botany Bay, they will too.'

'That's a fair enough argument,' Trevor agreed. 'I'll go back now and use my powers of persuasion.'

In Kilmainham, Dr Trevor used all his powers of persuasion on Michael Dwyer. He was removed to the worst cell in the dungeons, double-bolted to the wall, and loaded down with four stone of irons. The only window in the cell opened on to the corridor and was kept closed. He was taken off the food allowance and allowed only bread and water and one pint of milk a week. And all to persuade him to agree to be transported to Botany Bay.

After two months, Dr Trevor reported to Marsden that the rebel was still holding out as strong as ever.

'I thought his cell in the dungeons would do the trick,' Trevor said despondently. 'There is little air in there as the window is on the corridor wall and is kept locked. For a man who was reared on the fresh air of the mountains it must be sheer torture, but the bastard is every bit as callous as he said he was.'

Marsden looked worried.

'And that's not the worst of it,' Trevor informed him. 'Hugh Vesty Byrne, John Mernagh, Martin Burke, and Arthur Devlin have all been double-bolted on the felons' side, but they too are holding out – none will agree to show the public that they are willing to forgo the promise of America and go to Botany Bay as a more just and appropriate penance for their crimes.'

'They'll agree to go if their leader does,' Marsden said, 'and we need him to agree soon. The *Tellicherry* is already at anchor in the cove of Cork.'

'You'll just have to transport him by force then,' Trevor said. 'What else can you do?'

'I'd better bring in the newspapers to help us,' Marsden said. 'They can start a campaign against the rebel captain which should bring public opinion to our view. In situations of this kind, the newspapers have never failed us yet.'

'I should think not!' Trevor exclaimed. 'Considering the vasts amount of money you pay them. I'm told Cody of the *Post* is receiving a salary of four hundred pounds from the secret service funds – more than myself!'

'And he is worth every penny,' Marsden snapped, and could not help thinking just how essential to any good government was the system of having the newspaper editors in their pay. The editor of the *Dublin Post* in particular rarely ever published a word without submitting it first to the Under-Secretary of State. And so the next edition carried the following:

> The offender who has been so long in Kilmainham
> Gaol called Captain Dwyer of the Mountains has
> refused to go to Botany Bay. He requests to be sent to

America, he and three of his myrmidons with their families and the expense of such a voyage to be defrayed for them, an audacious request with which the Government will naturally not comply.

William Hoare Hume had been away in London attending Parliament. On his return he went immediately to Dublin Castle and furiously demanded to see Lord Hardwicke.

'This places me in a very unpleasant and potentially dangerous position in County Wicklow,' Hume explained, 'if the terms I promised Michael Dwyer to induce his surrender are not kept. All the newspapers have done is make public that the promises I gave have been broken. Do you not understand that I stand in very great danger of being assassinated!'

It was a problem, Lord Hardwicke agreed, but he was determined that Michael Dwyer and his men sail out of Ireland on the *Tellicherry*.

'And what about Dwyer's wife?' Hume demanded. 'He would never have surrendered only I agreed, as you did, that his wife and children would be allowed to go along with him. And I assure you that it will provide no service to the country to leave her in Wicklow after he is gone. She has me tormented over him already. I put it to you plainly, my lord, if Mary Dwyer is left in Wicklow, there will be no shortage of those anxious to carry out her revenge on the man and men she believes have betrayed her husband.'

William Hume's face was the colour of beet, the sweat beginning to glisten on his brow.

'And if I may say so, my lord, it is a betrayal. The only reason you offered him surrender terms in the first place is because you were informed by the military commanders that he would never be taken by other means.'

A compromise was eventually agreed, a compromise that Dwyer might find acceptable, and which would demonstrate to the whole country the *mercy* of its government.

Michael was brought into Dr Trevor's parlour to see William Hume. He had lost stones in weight and his hair was an untidy mass of black curls around his shoulders.

'Well, damn my eyes,' Michael rasped with a crack of a smile. 'Is it Judas or Mr Hume himself?'

'I have not betrayed you, Dwyer,' Hume said with feeling. 'I believed you were to be sent to America, but now I am told that I misunderstood, that I made assumptions I had no right to make. It is my belief that we have both been . . . misled.'

'I sent you three letters which you chose to ignore,' Michael said. 'Three letters written to you in the most respectful terms, asking you to honour the pledges you made to me.'

'And I forwarded those letters directly to the Castle with a note of my own, asking for you to be sent out as soon as possible.'

'And now they intend to send me out, and not to America, but to Botany Bay, and the sacred honour of William Hume is set at nought.'

'Not quite at nought,' Hume said quietly. 'I have been to see Lord Hardwicke on your behalf and he has now agreed to a compromise . . . You and your comrades will go to New South Wales, not as convicts, but as free men. On arrival in Sydney you will each be given a land grant of a hundred acres. Think of it, man! – a new life for you all, with land of your own, land that will belong to no man but you – one hundred acres of it.'

Dr Trevor, standing quietly in the corner, almost fainted, and had to slump down in a chair when William Hume continued.

'And in view of your long detention in prison, which is another breach of the surrender terms, the government has agreed that we should compensate you with the sum of two hundred pounds to help you purchase the farming implements you will need to begin your life in New South Wales. Your comrades will each receive one hundred pounds for the same breach, and for the same purpose. I think it is a very fair compromise, and a wonderful opportunity for you.'

'One hundred acres of my own land is indeed like a dream come true,' Michael admitted, 'but the wonder fades when I remember that land would be in a British colony, ruled by the British Parliament and its administrators, and ruled by redcoats. How can I be sure that as soon as I land there, I will not be double-crossed again and immediately linked to a chain gang?'

'Here are the papers,' William Hume showed them to him. 'All are signed and sealed by His Excellency and show that the five of you are to be admitted into the colony as free men. New South Wales has plenty of convicts – it is free men willing to work hard for their fortune and turn the settlement into a country that New South Wales needs.'

'And our wives can come with us?'

'Certainly.'

Michael looked long at William Hume. 'They will never agree to let us go to the free states of America, will they?'

'No,' Hume said emphatically. 'But you have to admit, this is a very good second-best.'

Michael shrugged realistically. 'I reckon it's the best I can hope for.'

After a silence, he said tiredly to Hume: 'Will you advise Mary of this so-called compromise, and ask her to prepare herself and the children for our departure.'

William Hume paled. 'My dear fellow . . . I don't think you understand . . . although you will be transported as free men, the *Tellicherry* is a *convict* ship. It is overcrowded already. Your wife may go with you . . . but not your children.'

Michael blinked a number of times, as if he couldn't quite take the last in. 'We'll not go without them,' he said incredulously. 'Are you crazy? How could Mary and I have any kind of new life without the four new lives we have created?'

'You must understand,' Hume said in flustered tones, 'it would not be safe for them to go on a convict ship that might break out in fever. Convict ships usually do break out in the most terrible fevers, and children catch it the first. They could very well die before they even reached New South Wales. At least here, in the care of your family, they would be safe. When they have grown into young adults they could join you out there. You will have made your fortune by then and be able to send them their passage money.'

'No.' Michael shook his head emphatically. 'I'd rather let my children see me hanged than let them think I willingly deserted them. And my father has enough to house and feed without my four as well.'

Dr Trevor sat back and listened, his humour brighter as Hume reasoned, then argued, then almost lost his temper as the battle of words became more angry and more heated.

'No!' Michael cried. 'I can forfeit my country but never my children!'

'Perhaps I had better speak to your wife,' Hume said wearily.

'Well, if I won't agree, she is even less likely to agree.'

William Hume flopped his arms in defeat. 'I have done everything I can. I can do no more. I will convey the Castle's offer to your wife and the wives of Hugh Vesty Byrne and Martin Burke. After that, the people of Wicklow will know I have achieved the best I could for you; a passage out of the country as a free man.'

As soon as William Hume had left the room, Dr Trevor summoned the waiting guards and the prisoner was returned to the cell in the dungeon where he was double-bolted again, loaded down with irons and continued on his starvation diet.

A week later Dr Trevor visited him again. 'Hugh Vesty Byrne has agreed to go to New South Wales under the government's new terms,' he informed him. 'So have Burke, Mernagh and your cousin Arthur Devlin.'

'Good luck to them so,' Michael answered.

'Don't be a fool, Dwyer! They can agree to nothing without you. If the government is forced to send you out as a convict they will be sent as convicts also. The only reason they have not been brought to trial is because they were included in your surrender terms. It is up to you, Dwyer. Are you going to deny your faithful comrades a chance of a new life as free men?'

'I'll not agree to go without my children,' Michael said, stubbornly. 'So bugger off!'

Dr Trevor had no alternative but to report his intractable attitude to Alexander Marsden.

'Tell him he can take his blasted children then!' Marsden snapped. 'The other prisoners are already being loaded on to the *Tellicherry* at Cork and yet Dwyer and his men remain in Kilmainham. We are running out of time, Dr Trevor, and we do not wish Dwyer to force our hand. This administration is in enough trouble as it is.'

'What?' Trevor stared at Marsden open-mouthed. 'Dwyer can take his children?'

'He can take his children,' Marsden repeated. 'I no longer care who he takes as long as he goes and is seen to go willingly.' He looked coldly at Trevor. 'And you can take that look off your face – Dwyer is the least of your problems now. While you have been concentrating on the Wicklow rebels, St John Mason, the cousin of Robert Emmet, has been gathering evidence which he hopes to get published, exposing the suffering of political prisoners in Kilmainham Gaol.'

'Huh!' Trevor was not in the least alarmed. 'Mason may have been a talented young barrister-at-law before he became a rebel, but he holds no clout in this city any more. In response to his last signed memorial, Judge Day examined the prison and found it very satisfactory.'

'Only because you were given a week's warning and had time with your underlings to put on a show and send out for the best food the city could provide – a fact that is now known in all the wrong quarters.'

Marsden's grey eyes were glittering. 'Mason is relentless in his determination to bring you down. With his lawyer's hand he has written down every abuse, every act of violence, every act of obscenity. And he has finally succeeded in getting his message to men of influence on the outside. Now one of the noisiest lawyers in Ireland, Mr Daniel O'Connell, has threatened to lay the conditions of the State prisoners in Kilmainham before people in authority and have the matter brought up in Parliament. A baseless threat, you may say, but now there is also a rumour that over in England, Richard Brinsley Sheridan, a most respected member of the Westminster Parliament, is seeking to raise the subject of prison abuses in Ireland before the Commons – in particular, Kilmainham Gaol.'

Dr Trevor was struck speechless, and remained so when Marsden gave him the worst news of all.

'Also, an allegation has been made that both you and I own the bakery that supplies food to Kilmainham Gaol. Do you see the headlines that could make: the Under-Secretary of State and the prison superintendent own the bakery that receives large amounts of government money for supplying food to the starving prisoners in Kilmainham Gaol! They will say we are worse criminals than the inmates!' Marsden looked as if he was going to be sick, his face as pale as a sheet. 'The allegation shall be denied as a slanderous lie, of course.'

'But . . . surely you can deal with them, Marsden? You have great power here in Ireland.'

'But not in England. Not since the Emmet affair. Why else, despite my years as Under-Secretary, was I not promoted to Chief Secretary when Wickham resigned with all that nonsense of not wishing to dip his hands in any more Irish blood. I should have been given the post as Chief Secretary, I *earned* the post as Chief Secretary – but they sent Evan Nepean over instead. No, Dr Trevor, I cannot, as you say, deal with them. Not very easily, anyway.'

And in that moment Dr Trevor knew that Alexander Marsden would not hesitate to send the superintendent of Kilmainham to the wall, if the situation and his own reputation required it.

When Mary arrived at Kilmainham, Dr Trevor greeted her in a very subdued and contrite manner.

568

'Mrs Dwyer,' he said respectfully, 'I have done wrong to you in the past, and now feel compelled to ask your pardon and forgiveness.'

Mary spoke softly. 'I don't think I could ever forgive you.'

'I understand,' Trevor replied wearily. 'Yes, I do. But could you, perhaps, find it in your heart to at least try?'

'Why should I?'

Trevor shrugged. 'Because I once thought you and your husband and your kind were despicable. Now I realise it is the men in high places who are truly the despicable ones. They use men like me to do their dirty work, then throw us to the wall when we are of no further use. Now it is them I despise. Now it is you I would like to help, by making amends, and doing something decent for a change.'

Mary's confusion showed on her face. 'How can you help me now?'

'In a very practical way.'

Dr Trevor was at his most gentle when he personally came to bring Michael Dwyer up to his parlour and give him the wonderful news that he could take his children with him to New South Wales.

Michael was so relieved he smiled in genuine gratitude at the infamous tyrant, and even accepted the glass of whiskey Trevor shoved in his hand.

A different Michael, full of strength, might have taken the opportunity to throw the whiskey in Trevor's face, but weakened and wearied by his starvation diet and long confinement, he no longer cared enough. All he wanted to get out into the fresh air with his wife and children and start a new life.

'Drink up,' Trevor urged gently. 'I know how you must need it; but believe me, it was the Castle who ordered me to double-bolt you and load you with irons. Yes, yes, they are a savage set and I'm suddenly sick to the heart of doing their dirty work.'

Michael looked at Trevor first in shock, then suspiciously. He took a drink of the whiskey which burned down to his empty stomach, and went dizzily to his head.

'I remonstrated very hotly with the Castle on your behalf,' Trevor explained, topping up the glass. 'I told them that any man – any man – who had seen you with your children – as I did here in Kilmainham, could not possibly expect you to leave without them.'

569

Michael narrowed his eyes. 'What little game are you playing this time?'

'No game, no game,' Trevor said quietly and tiredly. 'It happens to men, you know, to the most unlikely of men too. One morning they wake up and take a good look at their life, at themselves, and they don't like what they see . . . And I suddenly don't like the man that Dublin Castle and Kilmainham Gaol have made me.'

'An overnight conversion, eh? An old devil like you?' Michael chuckled, then laughed outright.

Dr Trevor accepted the insult meekly. 'It has happened to better and worse men than me. It happened to Saint Paul on the road to Damascus. Yet before that day he was violent in the extreme against the Christians. Was it not he who ordered the stoning of Stephen, the first Christian martyr? And yet, after Damascus, when he saw the badness of his ways, he became a Christian martyr himself.'

Michael stared at him, listening to the bizarre words and unable to believe or make sense of them. Trevor talked on in a low contrite voice, but Michael had stopped listening. He looked around the room which appeared very cluttered and colourful after his bare cell, then he turned his eyes to the window and sat staring, his mind going blank.

He was only vaguely aware of Trevor moving to his feet and going to the door. Then a hand touched his face and he heard her voice.

He came back to life at once, turned, and slowly stood up and stared at her; still the loveliest thing he ever saw. And then she was in his arms, kissing him in full view of Dr Trevor, and he didn't care.

Dr Trevor found the loving reunion quite unbearable. 'I think, my dear girl,' he said finally, 'that we should give the poor man time to breathe and recollect his strength. We are very short of time, and we have to discuss the subject of your children.'

He carried over a chair and placed it beside Mary. The two sat down again, but Mary would not let go of Michael's hand. She was suddenly nervous, and very unsure of herself.

'I have brought you a new set of clothes,' she told him. 'I made them myself.'

'You have heard that we can all go together?' Michael said to her. 'As they originally agreed.'

'Aye. Dr Trevor told me yesterday.'

'Yesterday.' Michael looked from one to the other. 'So why was I not told until today?'

'Because I have been seeking a way to help you both,' Trevor said gently, then looked at Mary. 'Perhaps you will explain.'

It was only then he noticed how thin she had become, how black her eyes looked against her pale skin, and there was a continual trembling about her mouth as she spoke.

Mr Hume, she explained, had told her about the government's compromise that did not include the children. At first she had been in an agony of confusion, for she would not let him go without her, but neither could she leave her children. But then, the more she thought about the danger of the convict ship, the fever and contagion that killed many adults on board those ships, she knew she could never agree to let her babies travel on such a vessel whether the government agreed or not. What was she to do? She thought she might die with the suffering of her mind. She could see no answer to it, until she came to the prison yesterday after receiving word from Dr Trevor, and he now had come up with a solution.

Michael turned his eyes to the reformed tyrant, who suddenly looked very tired and old.

'It is the only solution to your wife's dilemma,' Trevor said softly. 'As you know, I am the agent of transport in Ireland. There is another vessel leaving for New South Wales three months after the *Tellicherry*. A trading ship containing cargo and supplies needed in the colony. Passengers such as military men and their families will be travelling on it. I can arrange for your children to be sent out after you on board that ship, accompanied by one of your relatives as chaperon.'

Mary turned huge black eyes to Michael. 'It's a wonderful solution,' she said breathlessly. 'The only acceptable solution. Don't you see, Michael, I *cannot* allow the children to travel on a convict ship full of prostitutes and men and women riddled with all kind of diseases. But a trading ship with officers and their families would be free of all sickness.'

Michael looked at her as if she had been uttering the same sort of bizarre words as Trevor had done earlier. 'Then . . . why could you not wait and travel with the children later in the trading vessel?'

'I can't,' she said, tears in her voice and eyes. 'The Castle insist I must go with you. Mr Hume insists I must go with you. And Michael . . . I *want* to go with you!'

He wanted her to go with him too. But he was so confused, so bewildered, it was all too much to take in his weary and weakened state. He was unable to cope with the confusion of it all. After holding out in his irons long enough for the Castle to agree about the children, now Mary was asking him to go without them. He turned his eyes to the window, not knowing what to do.

'I'll not risk my children dying,' she said vehemently. 'And Dr Trevor has given his solemn word that he will make sure the children travel on the trading vessel. He has given his oath on the Bible.'

Again Michael looked at Trevor suspiciously. 'Why are you doing this? You have done your best to abuse and torture and starve me, even hoped to have me shot dead in the act of escape. Why should you now want to help me or mine?'

'I understand your lack of faith,' Trevor replied softly. 'I can hardly blame you for it. But you are right, nothing is given in this life without something in exchange. Everything has a price. And in return for sending your children after you on the trading vessel, I expect a favour from you in return.'

'What favour?'

'Not a very big favour. Just a simple letter acknowledging my efforts to help you. We can discuss the details later. But now you must make your decision. It is something only the two of you can worry over and decide. I shall not try to influence you in any way. And now I will leave you alone for a short while.'

He stood up, nodded his head at Mary. 'The cutter engaged to take the five men to Cork is leaving Dublin Bay tomorrow. If you want to make any last final arrangements about your children, you will have to leave here fairly soon, and make your own way to Cork. The *Tellicherry* will soon be leaving Ireland, and the government are determined that your husband will be on it.'

'When?' she asked. 'When will the ship be leaving?'

'In a matter of days.'

When the door had closed, both looked at each other in helpless anguish and impotence as they considered the decision before them. Their children ranged from ten months to six years. How could they leave them? But could they expose them to the dangers of a long voyage on a convict ship? Could they take even the smallest risk on their children's lives when Dr

Trevor had promised to send them on only a few months later in the care of one of their relatives?

And Dr Trevor had promised it, if Michael repaid him with only one small favour.

Some short minutes after his departure, Dr Trevor returned. 'Well?' he asked, looking at them both. 'Have you decided?'

Michael had enough sense to remain silent. He knew that if he was forced to say the words he would weep. Mary answered for him, then sat looking around her in tear-drenched puzzlement, every part of her shaking, as if suddenly wondering why the bottom had fallen from her world.

What had happened? It had all seemed so simple when she had asked him to surrender. Why had it all gone so terribly wrong?

Her mind was still in a turmoil when she finally left the prison to make her arrangements and say a last tearful farewell to her parents and her children. She knew she would never see her parents again; and yet, as painful as that was, it was nowhere near the pain she felt when she thought of the eleven months that she would be parted from her babies, eight months on the sea and three months following. Eleven long months and twelve thousand miles between them.

Her father and mother travelled with her to the farmhouse at Eadstown where she handed her children into the care of Michael's mother. Everyone tried to be cheerful and said encouraging words to Mary as she whispered lilting little phrases of love to one child and another, then stood crushing her handkerchief between her palms as she stared at her baby daughter sleeping in her own mother's arms.

Michael's mother dealt with the situation as she always did, employing herself busily and efficiently with the numerous things that had to be done in a house where four little ones had come to stay. But when she finally paused to take a sip of the tea she had poured out for everyone, she suddenly made a choking sound in her throat and the cup crashed down on to the table. For a moment tears glistened in her eyes, but before anyone could notice them, she moved hastily over to the sink and began pummelling away at the washing, her brows contracted, as if nothing on earth was more important than the job she had in hand.

The rest of the family stood around the kitchen but no one spoke. Even William Doyle was lost for a sentence as he sat in moping silence, dressed in his finest coat and holding a new hat. He would not allow anyone else to take his daughter all the way to Cork harbour, and he intended that when she took her last look on him as she sailed into exile, she would remember him at his best.

'Where is himself?' he said suddenly, looking around for Michael's father, whom he had only just noticed was not present.

'He's gone to Dublin,' Mrs Dwyer murmured, without turning round. 'Gone with a hope and a prayer of being allowed to say a last goodbye to our son.'

His prayer was answered. John Dwyer stood in a corner of the empty yard of Kilmainham Gaol, a helpless look on his face as he watched his son's face turn a sickly pale. A second later Michael turned away, put his hands against the wall and vomited.

John Dwyer could not blame him. He too would have vomited after writing such a letter, the price Dr Trevor had exacted in return for sending Michael's children after him in the safety of a trading vessel.

He took out a linen square and handed it to his son, then said quietly: 'He obviously intends to use the letter in some way.'

'Oh, he does,' Michael whispered. 'He intends to show it to the world.'

'Then take heart from that, for if he shows it to the world, then the world will know of his promise to you. He will not be able to go back on it.'

Michael closed his eyes for a brief moment, self-disgust overwhelming him. His head ached and the yard still tilted at a sickening angle.

'I know one day I will look back and say it was worth it,' he said shakily. 'The day my children join me in Botany Bay. But truth to tell, Daddy, at this minute I feel a high hanging would have been easier and less shameful.'

John Dwyer stared at his first and favourite son, saw the tears of shame in his eyes, and the pain in his own heart swelled so much he had to turn away.

'Aye,' he said bitterly. 'It is not always those who die on the battlefield or on the gallows that suffer the most. But who would ever believe that?'

A guard stepped into the yard and called out. It was time to go, to the cutter waiting in Dublin Bay.

Both men ignored him.

John Dwyer looked up at the August sun. It was promising to

be a very warm day and he was already hot in his Sunday suit. The misery in his heart, the ache of parting was no less than a bereavement, for he knew he would never see Michael again after this day. He looked at the sky again, hugging his sorrow tightly, frightened it would escape him. He dared not weaken; the first thing Michael had asked of him when he arrived, was that he should not weaken and make it harder for both of them.

'I have no money left and nothing to give you,' he said finally, 'except these . . .' He took from his pocket a small piece of whitewashed stone from the wall of the house in Eadstown, and a small lump of turf from the fields around it. 'Two small pieces of home to take with you,' he whispered.

Michael nodded and took the mementoes of Imaal. He was silent for a moment, then said in a soft voice. 'I was thinking last night of the time on the high meadows when we hunted the dog fox together. Do you remember that, Daddy, the night we finally caught that vicious old chicken-killer?'

'The fox that ran across the moon?' John Dwyer smiled. 'You were my hero that night, boy.'

They stood in silence, miserably conscious that their life together was almost finished for ever.

Michael started as another memory struck him. 'I nearly forgot . . . I have something for you.' He reached into his pocket and withdrew a fold of money and pressed it into his father's hand.

John Dwyer was struck speechless as he stared at the money.

'One hundred pounds,' Michael said, 'to help with the expense of the care of my children until they can join us.'

'Where . . . where did you get this money?'

'William Hume and the government decided to compensate me for my two years' imprisonment and the breach of my surrender terms with two hundred pounds. It seems I will need to purchase farming implements and other goods for my new life in New South Wales.'

His father shook his head. 'Take it back so. I don't want any money for the care of my own grandchildren.'

'I want you to have it,' Michael insisted, turning away as the guard called again, less politely this time. His father had no choice but to follow him across the yard.

The guard held the door open for them and again spoke urgently about the carriages that were waiting to convey him and his comrades to the docks. John Dwyer muttered an apologetic response, but Michael did not condescend to exchange a word with any of his guardians who attempted to speak to him as he re-entered the dark interior of Kilmainham Gaol.

They came out into the bright sunlight again a short time later, but this time Michael was in the company of his three comrades and the waiting crowd outside the gates roared their cheers. A few seconds later Arthur Devlin was brought out to join them, and the five walked towards the waiting carriages which had armed guards front and back and either side of them.

Again Michael tried not to look back as he moved to climb inside the carriage, but the yearning was just too great. He turned and looked back, his eyes searching over the heads of the blur of people until his eyes rested on the lonely figure of his father standing by the inner gate of Kilmainham Gaol.

His father nodded, his mouth doing its best to smile.

Michael grinned bravely, then waved as the carriage pulled away. And that was the last memory of him that his father cherished through every day and month and year of his life that followed.

'Written by Michael Dwyer's own hand,' Dr Trevor said, placing a sheet of paper before Alexander Marsden.

Marsden looked at the paper, then cocked an eyebrow. 'Are you sure it was written by him?'

'Positive.' Dr Trevor smiled. 'I stood beside him as he wrote it.'

Alexander Marsden studied the handwriting; he had read other letters written by Michael Dwyer, letters Dwyer had managed to send out from Kilmainham to William Hume, and which Hume had forwarded to the Castle. Those letters had been written in a firm hand, but the hand that had written this letter addressed to Dr Trevor was very shaky indeed.

Most Respected Sir,
    With a heartfelt gratitude and fully sensible of how far I am from deserving any kindness from you, I make bold to return my sincere thanks for your kindness to me, and the consolation you gave me by promising to send my children after me to Botany Bay. Your own humane mind will tell you that there is nothing so distressing to parents as parting from their children, especially me who had the misfortune to forfeit them and their country.

I declare to you that I never was sorry until now for offending the Government, until I see their kindness in forgiving the injuries done to them by those guilty of such offences. Now I am sorry to the bottom of my heart for having offended so good a Government, this I declare to be my real sentiments at this moment and will be till the hour of my death, for I never saw my error until now, but I sincerely lament it and still hope for your humanity that I may expect my children in Botany Bay and shall find myself happy in earning their bread, and they and I shall be forever bound to pray for your welfare.

I remain your most humble
and much obliged servant
Michael Dwyer.

'Does that not testify to my kindness?' Trevor exclaimed. 'Let Daniel O'Connell and Richard Brinsley Sheridan stuff that in their pipes and smoke it!'

Marsden was not impressed. 'Your rejoicing, Trevor, is as nauseating as the humble pie you have obviously forced this man to eat and choke on,' he said scornfully. 'Not even Richard Brinsley Sheridan would believe these to be the true sentiments of Dwyer, but the blackmail in them is evident. The man is clearly prepared to go to any lengths to secure a reunion with his children.'

Dr Trevor stared at Marsden with eyes popping. The Under-Secretary had to be the most complex and unpredictable man he had ever known.

'And what reason would Sheridan have for doubting the sincerity of the letter?' Trevor demanded. 'He has never met Dwyer. All he knows of him is the impression created in the press which, as you of all people should know, is hardly favourable.'

'You have made a grave mistake,' Marsden informed him coldly. 'When Richard Brinsley Sheridan stands up in the House of Commons and petitions the members to agree to an investigation into the treatment of Irish State prisoners in Kilmainham Gaol, another Member of Parliament intends to stand up and support him. A man who knows Dwyer well, and will never believe that he underwent such a dramatic change of sentiment in the short time between the writing of *this* letter, and the letters Dwyer wrote to him only months ago complaining of his treatment in Kilmainham Gaol. Any fool can see your hand in this, Dr Trevor.'

'Who the devil are you talking about? Which Member of Parliament?'

'The Member for Wicklow!' Marsden cried. 'William Hoare Hume.' He threw the letter across the desk with a glare of contempt. 'If I honestly thought you were abusing your position in Kilmainham Gaol, Dr Trevor, it would be my duty to have you removed within the hour.'

Trevor's first instinct was to laugh in Marsden's face, then a wiser notion occurred to him. Marsden was frightened, and needed to be calmed in his fears. And not only was Marsden frightened, he was utterly ruthless and utterly treacherous.

Trevor smiled slyly. 'Dear Mr Marsden, upright and honest Mr Marsden, would I ever abuse my position or your very great trust in my talents by allowing some bogman-lawyer or melodramatic playwright-politician to cast aspersions on your honour or mine? Good gracious, no! And to assure you of such, I have here a letter from another prisoner, testifying to my kindness.'

Dr Trevor withdrew the letter from his medical bag and handed it to Marsden, who stared in disbelief at the name on the letter – Brian Devlin, the fifty-year-old prisoner who had vociferously and continuously attributed the death of his nine-year-old boy to the inhumane conduct of Dr Trevor.

'The handwriting and spelling are poor,' Dr Trevor said, 'but a comparison before witnesses would prove it was written by Devlin's own hand.'

Marsden could only stare at the letter from Brian Devlin, which thanked Dr Trevor in the most humblest terms for his kindness and humane attention! He slowly laid down the letter and stared for some time at his desk-top, then said in a low voice: 'You have Devlin's young daughter confined in a solitary cell.'

Trevor smiled sadly at the truth of it. 'I do, Mr Marsden, but it was you that put her there, was it not? Poor Devlin is quite at his wits' end about her, but I have assured him that she will come to no harm under *my* protection.'

Marsden shrugged in a noncommittal way. 'What do you hope to achieve by these letters?'

'Vindication of any slanderous lies that may be made against me in any Parliamentary investigation.'

Marsden smiled, but the smile was simply a movement of his lips. 'And the governor, John Dunne, has he also written a letter testifying to your humanity towards the prisoners?'

'The governor?' Dr Trevor looked at Marsden in sudden horror. 'Oh, dear me, with all the business of the letters I clean forgot the dreadful business which brought me here. Our wonderful governor from the grime of Lancashire was very ill last night, so ill that I was deeply concerned for him. The terrible pains in his stomach caused him to struggle violently on his bed, so violently in fact, that I was forced to call two of my attendants to hold him down while I administered a very effective medicine which I hoped would alleviate his pain and encourage a rapid recovery. But alas, the poor man died a few hours later.'

A silence hung in the room.

'How sad, how very sad,' Marsden whispered, then turned away to stare at the light of a summer morning shining through the window. 'Please convey my deepest regrets to his wife.'

'Certainly. Now if you will excuse me, I must return to my poor prisoners. Good day, Mr Marsden.'

Dr Trevor had reached the door when Marsden suddenly spoke again. 'One last question before you leave, Dr Trevor . . . I am curious about your promise to the rebel captain . . . do you truly intend to send his children after him?'

Again Dr Trevor smiled sadly. 'It would be a terrible cruelty not to do so, considering his very real love for them.'

The answer was so ambiguous, Marsden was left none the wiser when Dr Trevor swung himself and his medical bag through the door.

Chapter Thirty-Nine

In Cork harbour, the *Tellicherry* was almost ready to set sail.

A number of communications were sent to the Castle informing Mr Marsden that 166 convicts were securely on board; 130 men and 36 women. The convict list should have been more, but as the fever which was reigning in the *Renown* lying alongside had now crept into the *Tellicherry* it was decided to put no more on, especially as enough space had to be allocated to Michael Dwyer and his associates, a space which would keep them separate from the convicts and still in security.

Among the communications was a report from Dr Harding, who had inspected the *Tellicherry* and found the men's prison not sufficiently ventilated. He also found the women's prison very small, but decided that

> . . . as most generally sleep in other parts of the ship, it is of no consequence, but for the danger of spreading the fever. On the *Tellicherry* I saw a soldier (who informed me he was ill for two days) lying in the berths with the other soldiers and women. If they are not more circumspect and cautious about contagion the consequences must be very bad.

Then Marsden received a communication which made him smile with satisfaction and relief. Michael Dwyer and his associates had been received on board. So far they had behaved very well, except with the barber who had been denied his earnings of sixpence a head; Dwyer had slapped the barber's face when he attempted to touch his hair, saying the government had agreed that they would not be shaved or put with the convicts or put in irons or treated in any way as convicts.

For their accommodation they had been given one of the hospitals on the *Tellicherry*, a space big enough to accommodate them adequately, which they acknowledged.

Marsden's face showed no expression when he read the last few lines:

I shall request Captain Cuzens not to put them in irons at present, when he is at sea he will of course do what he considers most proper.

The *Tellicherry* lay far out in the waters of Cork harbour. Up and down its decks the crew were preparing to weigh anchor and set sail.

Mary stood in a nightmare of anxiety beside Michael on the deck, both staring silently towards the distant shore, both thinking the same thought, both wondering if Dr Trevor would truly keep his promise. Neither was yet capable of speaking calmly or intelligently about their children to the other.

Consumed as she was by her own worries, Mary cast pitiful eyes at the dejected faces of Hugh Vesty and Martin Burke standing each side of them; neither of their wives had come to Cork to sail into exile with them.

Mary was not too surprised that Rachel Burke had not come, for she had seemingly lost interest in Martin after his first few months in prison. But Sarah Byrne . . . Mary could not believe that Sarah, her dear friend Sarah, who had shared and cared with her in the days gone by, had now turned her back on Hugh Vesty. She had always believed that Sarah was as faithful and devoted to her man as she was.

Hugh Vesty had always believed that too. He stared towards the harbour in the far distance like a man in a trance. Michael put a hand on his shoulder, with the intention of giving comfort, but suddenly his hand gripped Hugh Vesty's shoulder hard as his keen eyesight detected a small boat rowing towards the *Tellicherry* with a female in it. The boat was almost half a mile away, but he could clearly see the bonnet of a female.

'Hugh . . .' he whispered, pointing to the boat.

Hugh jerked alert and stared and stared, then in a fever of excitement shouted up to the captain on the bridge. 'It's my wife! You can't sail yet! She has government permission to sail with us!'

Captain Cuzens was well aware of that, and being a conscientious and good-natured man, agreed to let the *Tellicherry* lie while waiting for its final passenger.

Mary was delighted, not only for Hugh Vesty, but herself.

Now she would have her dear friend for female company and solace when they reached the alien new land on the other side of the world. She stood with hands pressed to each side of her smiling face, but as the boat drew near, and the quarter-master ordered the chair to be lowered over the side, the smile slowly faded from Mary's face, her eyes widening; then a sound like a choking cry escaped her lips.

Michael also stared at the occupants of the boat, just managing to catch Mary, who suddenly slumped against him as Sarah stepped on board with her children.

'I couldn't leave them!' Sarah cried, seeing their reaction. 'I couldn't leave my children, not for the eight months of the voyage nor the three months in following. I couldn't leave them for that long – not for eleven hours, never mind eleven months!' She turned to her husband with a look of desperation. 'I had to do it, Hugh, risk the fever and the dangers. I couldn't leave them behind.'

Hugh Vesty could only smile at her with love and relief. But the sight of the children had reduced Mary to an agony of breathing. She looked wildly at them with dilated nostrils, her bosom heaving. How could she endure the length of the voyage with these children to remind her of the four she had left behind?

As the slow swelling pain became unbearable she broke down completely, emitting great grinding heaving sobs that echoed over the ship, evoking deep pity in everyone who heard her.

Grief and frustration struggling violently within him, Michael looked up at the captain, although he knew it was futile even to think it, let alone ask. The journey to Wicklow and back would take almost a week.

The small-boat was rowing away. Captain Cuzens gave signal to the ships of the East India fleet waiting to escort the *Tellicherry* as far as Madeira.

The convict ship sailed out of Cork on the evening tide. And it was then that Sarah moved with the others to the ship's rail and reached to take Mary's hand in her own. Mary gripped it tightly, her other hand clasped in Michael's as the Wicklow group stood in sombre silence and stared at the land shrinking away. They were sailing southward, at six knots an hour; out of sight of land after the ship had cleared the headlands of the bay.

Ireland of the Sorrows was no more. They were no longer

citizens of their homeland, but then they never had been. Each in their own silent way said farewell to the land all had loved and most had fought for. Each in their own silent way said goodbye to Ireland.

Mary was not even aware that Sarah's hand had slipped away as one by one the others left the breezy deck and the Dwyers alone. They stood together, watching the rise and fall of the sea, but thinking of the land, the solid dry land of the Glen of Imaal.

In Imaal the sun would be setting behind the hills. In the farmhouse at Eadstown four little children would be feeling sleepy now, maybe still wondering where their mammy had gone. Gone with their daddy.

And as the wind sung around the rigging of the three-masted ship and the sky darkened over the sea, Mary-Anne's familiar little questioning voice floated over the waves to Mary . . . asking the same questions she had asked night after night in the months after they had been forced out of Kilmainham Gaol and back to Wicklow . . . *'And where has Daddy gone? Is it far, far away? Is it somewhere down the dark passage in Kilmainham Gaol in Dublin town?'*

And Michael's mother would no doubt hush and pet and give the answer always given to Irish children who asked where their daddies had gone. 'He's gone to find the crock of gold at the end of the rainbow. And when he finds it, darling, he will send for you.'

And the answer would satisfy, as it always did at sleepy evening-time when the hills were draped in blue shadows and the stars began to twinkle in the sky. But in the harsh light of morning the questions would be asked again.

Where had their daddy gone? Was it far, far away? Was it somewhere down the dark passage in Kilmainham Gaol in Dublin town?

From the bridge, the captain of the ship watched the couple standing alone on the deck, wrapped into each other, like one person and not two. It was clear they were fond of each other, very fond indeed.

Good luck to them, Captain Cuzens thought, unaware that he was the most humane captain ever to master a convict ship. Good luck to them, they would need it where they were going.

But he puzzled over the rebel's frantic assurances to his sobbing wife earlier – that their children would be following in three months on a trading vessel. Three months? Trading vessel? No trading vessels ever left Ireland for New South Wales. Any goods the colony needed were shipped direct from England. And from what he had been told, there would be no more convict ships leaving Ireland for at least five years, maybe even longer. It had taken over two years to engage the *Tellicherry*. Most of Britain's ships were needed in the war with France.

The woman began to cry again, her head falling on the rebel's shoulder. His hand moved over her dark hair as he spoke, soothing her with words that could not be heard against the swish of the sea. Unlike her he had masterly control over his emotions and would not readily break down. Perhaps he would though, Captain Cuzens thought, if he knew the truth of it. Someone in that Dublin Castle had played a very cruel joke on him.

He obviously loved the woman, his wife, and it was well that he did, for it would be up to him to supply the strength they would both need in the time ahead. That's if the two of them even made it to New South Wales. No convict ship ever made it to the antipodes with a full cargo. There was always a number of deaths on the way, no matter how well run the ship.

As the ship rolled on its course towards the other side of the world, with nothing for the eye to see but waves cutting their crests and the fine spray of foam, Captain Cuzens saw the couple often, standing together on deck and gazing beyond the ocean. There had been no need to put any of the rebels in irons or restrict them to their quarters, so good was their behaviour so far.

The Wicklow group spent hours all together on deck during the day, the men often improvising a hurling game with old pieces of wood and a ball made of knotted hemp; a number of times they had cheekily fired the ball towards the captain, but it was always a crew member who raised a deck-scrub or a brush had sprang to send it rebounding back to a tumultuous cheer of approval. The crew, who had viewed the rebels suspiciously at first, were now quite civil and pleasant to them.

The two women were not so active, the captain observed. Hugh Byrne's wife looked quite ill at times, often lying under the awning while Dwyer's wife sat near by and cared for the children. And so determined was Captain Cuzens that his ship would have the lowest mortality rate of any convict ship, he occasionally sent the sickly woman nutritious food from his own table.

But it was the couple, the rebel chief and his wife, who interested him the most. Especially at night, for at night they always came up on deck alone. Sometimes they would stand together in their usual position, but mostly they would sit closely on one of the rope coils, their eyes on the sky, as if carefully watching the stars.

They were watching the North Star. Night after night they watched it sinking lower and lower until the night finally came when it was gone, never to be seen again. After that they looked to the sky no more. Soon there would be new stars in the heavens, the stars of the Southern Cross. But however beautiful the stars of the Southern Cross, they were not the same stars that twinkled and gleamed and could be seen by four little children in the Glen of Imaal in Wicklow.

BOOK THREE

Part One

I wish you slept where your kin are sleeping—
   The green green valley is sweet;
And the holy mountains their strange watch keeping
   Would love you lying still at their feet,
The soft grass for your winding sheet.

You would sleep sweet with your lips smiling,
   Dreaming, and hearing still
The bonny blackbird with songs beguiling,
   The rain's light feet on the hill,
The children's laughter merry and shrill.

    'Ballad for Michael Dwyer', by Katherine Tynan

Chapter Forty

Twenty years later, in 1825, two dark-haired young Irishmen stood on the deck of the *Marquis of Huntly* and cheered with the rest of the passengers when a sliver of land was seen on the horizon. After almost seven months at sea, even the smallest glimpse of land was a truly beautiful sight to land lovers.

The land swelled into high dark cliffs as they skimmed through the Bass Straits. John and Peter Dwyer were becoming restless with excitement at the prospect of seeing their father again. Neither could even remember what he looked like, but they had grown up in Wicklow listening to his legend. The Insurgent Captain of the Wicklow Mountains. Even if he had not been their own daddy, the tales and ballads would have still made their blood race, their hearts thump with pride as they listened to the accounts of his bravery remembered in song.

More cliffs appeared in the distance; someone announced that they were the headlands of Botany Bay. All morning they coasted along the cliffs which suddenly terminated in a precipice, called the South Head, on which stood the lighthouse and signal station. The North Head in the distance was a similar cliff, and between the two the ship entered the deep blue waters of Port Jackson, one of the most beautiful harbours in the world.

As they passed the North Head, one of the crew pointed out the Quarantine Ground where a fever ship was moored. John and Peter Dwyer stared at it full of pity for the passengers who had finally reached their destination after such a long voyage, only to be imprisoned indefinitely in the hold of the fever ship. Above the Quarantine Ground they saw a hill of tombstones marking the burial places of those who had come this far, but had been destined never to set foot alive on land again.

But excitement came back on their faces as they looked again towards the harbour of Sydney, their eyes roving the many bays and inlets of the estuary and the pure white sand which formed the beach, looking almost silver against the deep blue of the water. It was nothing like they had imagined, it was far more pleasing to the eye than they had ever hoped, this foreign country in which their parents had lived for over twenty years, and which now was to be their home too.

Their excitement turned to impatience when the *Marquis of Huntly* dropped anchor and lay for a time within sight of the quays but too far away to disembark. A small group of people was gathered on the quayside waiting, but as the lads no longer knew what their parents looked liked, it was impossible to pick out any familiar figure. Presently the harbour master came on board to examine their papers, followed by a doctor who examined their bodies. Then, at last, passed as fit and healthy, and being fare-paying passengers, they were part of the first few to climb into the boat that took them ashore.

It was the woman on the quayside that John Dwyer saw first. Instantly he knew she was his mother. A tall and dark-haired, still-beautiful woman who stared at him as if he was a ghost come to haunt her. Suddenly her eyes lit up with a strange wild gleam and a delighted cry escaped her lips as she moved towards him.

'Michael,' she said breathlessly. 'Oh, Michael . . .'

John turned to Peter, and saw the same stunned look on his brother's face that stiffened his own. They knew of their mother's obsession for their father, and had often been told of John's physical resemblance to him, and now she had confused the two, both knew at once that their father must be dead.

'Mary . . .' A man came forward and caught her arm. A tall man with fair hair. A priest. He spoke to her gently.

'Your sons are here at last,' he said. 'Your sons, John and Peter.'

She came back to herself and stared at them, an apologetic smile moving her lips. Like a woman in a dream she put a hand to each of their faces, then stared again at the young man with black hair who looked just as her husband had looked on the day she had married him all those years ago.

'Welcome to Sydney,' the priest said brightly, taking control of the situation. 'I am Father Therry, a friend of your parents. But come, come, meet your brother and sisters. They have been wild with impatience for days waiting here in Sydney for your ship to come in.'

John and Peter turned towards the three young people

standing a few feet away. All smiled uneasily as they looked at the brothers and sisters they had never met. Father Therry introduced the Australians: eighteen-year-old James, seventeen-year-old Bridget, and thirteen-year-old Eliza.

Of all the three, James seemed over the moon at finally meeting his two Irish brothers, but Bridget and Eliza shrieked with joy at the news that their Irish sisters Mary-Anne and Esther were following, would already have set sail, and should arrive in New South Wales in about six months.

Mary-Anne – the thought of his sister made John's face stiffen again. Mary-Anne had spent her life dreaming of the day she would go to New South Wales. But John knew she was not interested in sisters or brothers or even her mother. Mary-Anne was coming here in search of the man she had always loved above all others.

'Daddy?' John finally said to his mother. 'Why is Daddy not here?'

His mother lost her smile as she looked at him. Never had he seen eyes that looked so sad; huge brown eyes that misted over like the Wicklow Mountains at dusk.

'I thought he would live for ever,' she whispered. 'He was that strong, stronger in heart and mind and body than all his comrades. But his comrades are alive and well, and he is dead.' She nodded her head and looked around her with a vacant air as if she still could not believe it. 'Yes, yes. My Michael is dead.'

'When?' Peter cried, the realisation that their journey had been in vain suddenly rendering him heartbroken. 'When did he die?'

Mary couldn't remember. To her it seemed an eternity ago. James, Bridget and Eliza moved around her like a comforting blanket while Father Therry answered for her, his voice subdued.

'Your daddy never forgot his children in Ireland. His greatest sorrow was the mistake of leaving you behind, and his greatest dream was to see you all again, bring you here to live with him. He would have done it from the first day he landed if he could. But it was not to be. This is not the time or place to tell you of his fortunes here in New South Wales. But at least I can tell you that he died a natural death in his home, just a few months ago.'

Just a few months ago. John and Peter were close to tears. After all these years, they had come just a few months too late.

'A natural death? A natural death!' Mary glared at the priest, her voice harsh. 'You never saw the weals of the lash on every inch of his back. You were not even in the colony then! And as long as I live, Father Therry, and as much as you preach to me about forgiveness, I will never forgive William Bligh, that bully of the *Bounty* who persecuted not only Fletcher Christian but also my husband!'

Six months later it was two dark-haired young women who stood in excited anticipation on the deck and stared around the beautiful harbour as their ship entered Port Jackson. They were bonneted and gloved and had changed into their finest dresses. Mary-Anne wore green plaid which suited her attractive dark looks. Esther wore blue and looked a timid young thing next to her imposing and volatile sister.

Mary-Anne peered towards the quays and, for a moment, thought she saw her long-lost and long-loved Daddy. But she soon realised the man standing alone could not be him; he was too young. And then she let out her usual excited laugh and waved a hand as the small-boat drew nearer to the shore and she recognised the familiar features of her brother John.

It was a happy and noisy reunion. Other people on the quayside turned to look at the two young women laughing and jumping up and down and knew at once who they were.

Irish!

Only the Irish could laugh and joke and jump up and down after one of the most hazardous and lengthy sea journeys in the world. The English, at least, had the decency and good manners to land in respectable and sallow exhaustion.

In answer to his sisters' babble of questions, John told them that the family were all anxiously waiting for them at the house at Cabramatta. It was impossible for them all to come, never knowing for certain the actual day or week that an expected ship would come in.

'Yes, yes, we know!' Mary-Anne laughed. 'It's all in the wind, all in the wind. If I had a shilling for the number of times we were told that on our journey I'd be rich now.'

The three walked along the quays. 'Everything is different here,' John said. 'There are English and Irish and Scots, and the place is mainly Protestant. But it's not like back home . . . here there is no national or religious hatred. It's a new country in a new world, and although the inhabitants will never forget their original homelands, most are now beginning to think of themselves as a new race. As Australians.'

Mary-Anne looked sharply at her brother, and saw he had already fallen in love with New South Wales. 'So it is not the hell-hole they say it is?' she said.

'Only if you are a convict.'

Esther finally managed to get a word in as John led them up to a waiting horse and trap. 'What are the brother and two sisters like?' she asked curiously.

John smiled. 'Oh they're grand, just grand. James is a very fine young man, and clever too. You will like them, Essie, especially the girls.'

Mary-Anne's face turned dark with resentment as she thought of the two daughters who had grown up with her daddy when she had been left behind with relatives. All she had known of him in that time was the number of letters he had written to her over the years, and they had been few and far between, since it could take three or four years for a letter to reach Ireland from New South Wales and vice versa. Even so . . . whenever a ship did come, there was always a letter on it, a letter full of love and promises, but no money for a sailing ticket.

Reading her expression, and guessing her thoughts, and not wanting to be the one to tell her, John hastily bustled her up to the bench of the trap, and spent the journey informing his sisters of some of the things he had learned about New South Wales.

'Everything is topsy-turvy here,' he told them with a smile. 'Instead of the falling of the leaves in autumn, here we have the stripping of the bark which peels off the gum trees in long ribbons at certain seasons.'

'Is it always this hot?' Mary-Anne tugged at the bodice of her thick plaid dress.

'This is quite cool,' John replied. 'When we arrived it was summer and hot beyond endurance. Peter and I spent the first few weeks flopped in continual exhaustion. And the rains are not the soft mists of Ireland, but great battering rains that drench you to the skin in seconds.'

Mary-Anne looked around her curiously as they drove along and saw a few one-storey houses dotted here and there. It was twenty miles from Sydney to the family home near the banks of George's Creek at Cabramatta. Deprived of the sea breeze, the road inland to Cabramatta was several degrees warmer than Sydney. John pointed out a number of orange groves and vineyards as they rode along. Peaches were very cheap and almost abundant, he told them, as were all kinds of melons, but apples were very expensive as they mostly had to be imported from Van Diemen's Land.

The noise which had been in the air from shortly after they started their journey began to grate on Mary-Anne's nerves.

'What is that noise?' she demanded.

'Grasshoppers,' John said, now quite used to the chirruping, creaking, and whirring of the varmints. 'Millions of them, and all invisible. Their sound used to drive me crazy but in all my searches I've never managed to see one of them. I'm told they are more like dust-hoppers and live beneath the dust on the road. Now I no longer notice their noise.'

'Look!' Esther smiled with delight as they turned a bend and caught a glimpse of the Blue Mountains in the distance. Mary-Anne also smiled at the nicest view she had seen so far . . . mountains covered from base to peak in forests of tall trees.

In reply to their questions, John told them that no one had yet managed to discover what was on the other side of the mountain range, so dense was the bush, but many believed it was China. John then told a famous tale which made the two girls roar with laughter; and as she listened and laughed, Mary-Anne wondered if it was one of her daddy's humorous tales.

'There was a convict,' John said, 'an Irish convict, who managed to escape into the bush. Someone had told him that if he made his way over the Blue Mountains it was only then a fair walk to China. So off he set, deciding he could fare no worse in China where he would be free at last of redcoats. He had been assured that there were definitely, most definitely, no redcoats in China.

'He walked for days, cutting his way through the bush; until, at last, in the vast tangled wilderness, he descended down a hill into a clearing and saw a number of strange-looking habitations and knew he had reached China. He approached the first building cheerily, and got the shock of his life when out stepped an officer from the New South Wales Corps from Sydney. The convict greeted him without fear, for he was free now. "A long life to you, Colonel," he said curiously, "but what brought your honour to China?" '

John smiled. 'The poor devil ended up back as a convict-servant in the barracks, insisting he'd been short off his mark; just another day of walking would have taken him to China all the way.'

Esther twisted sideways to see completely into his face. She loved her eldest brother John very much and was pleased to see how much he liked this new land.

'Not being a convict yourself,' she said, 'is there anything about New South Wales that you *don't* like?'

'There is, Essie, there is. I hate the dust, the flies, the ants, and the intense heat of summer. And then there are the locusts – in summer they cling in swarms to the bark of trees, and the noise they make . . . rattle, rattle, rattle, is terrible. But even that you get used to after a while.'

'What about the people?'

'The people are like most people, good and bad, and bad and good. The people on the whole are friendly enough, but the entire country seems to be permanently drunk.' He looked at Esther gravely and nodded. 'Ireland is temperance in comparison. And the women have bigger thirsts than the men!'

'The women?' Mary-Anne laughed in disbelief but John told another story to prove his point.

'Our brother James was born a year after Mammy and Daddy arrived in the colony. Mammy was weak and not in good spirits after the birth, so to help her, Daddy got a female convict assigned to them as a nursemaid, and also bought Mammy a bottle of her favourite lavender water to cheer her, even though it cost more than a gallon of rum would have cost. The following morning Mammy looked for her lavender water and found the convict-maid gulping it. Aye, they'd drink anything that looks like liquor, and if it's not liquor, they drink it anyway. Daddy thought it amusing, but Mammy dismissed her there and then, so grieved was she at losing her precious luxury of lavender water.'

Mary-Anne could well believe it. If there was one thing she had never forgotten about her mother, it was her smell of lavender water.

They had driven for miles along a country road with nothing to see each side but the monotonous scenery of rows and rows of gum trees. Awful they were, for they had very little foliage, and even that was a dull and sapless-looking green.

At last, they reached Cabramatta. The girls jerked

alert when in the distance they saw a house.

'This is it,' John said as they approached a long, low, white-painted building of ten windows with a spacious veranda in front of it and a small neat garden at each side. The door and all the window shutters were painted green, as were the wooden railings each side of the drive leading up to the house.

Mary-Anne had intended to be suitably superior when she met her younger Australian sisters. After all, she was the eldest, was twenty-six years old, had been married, and was now a widow, a *young* widow. Oh yes, twenty-six was old for a maiden but young for a widow. And now she had come to claim the only man in her life, to live out her days making up for lost time with him, and if her Australian sisters thought to prevent her from taking first place in his paternal affections – then they had another think coming! By the hand of St Patrick they did!

But when Bridget and Eliza came running out of the house, Mary-Anne sat looking coolly at them only for a second, then leaped from the trap and was squealing and jumping up and down with excitement and laughter every bit as much as Esther, Bridget and Eliza.

Two parrots sitting on the branch of a nearby tree fluttered their splendid colours and squawked in unison with the girls.

Then Mary-Anne saw her mother standing silently by the door.

'*Mammy!*'

The parrots squawked again and began to move in an excited side-step along the branch of the tree, pausing to look at the emotional scene below, inspecting the newcomers first with one eye, then with the other.

'Why, Mammy, you have hardly changed at all!' Mary-Anne said through her tears when the hugging had eased. 'Hardly at all!'

'Such flattery is irresistible,' her mother said with a laugh, tears spilling down her face when Mary-Anne insisted it was true.

'This is a great day for me, Mary-Anne,' she said softly, 'having all my children with me again . . . all my children . . .'

'And Daddy?' Mary-Anne cried in cheerful indignation, looking beyond her mother to the large comfortably furnished but empty living-room behind her. 'Where is he now that he's not here to greet his first and favourite daughter?'

Mary didn't answer, just stood staring at her daughter, the

598

colour fading from her face. Slowly she turned agonised dark eyes to her son John, who had promised to relieve her of this.

John stood with head bowed, fingers twisting the brim of the felt hat in his hands and looking as if he would like to shrink inside his clothes. He had broken his promise to his mother, had been unable to prepare the way and lighten the burden for her. But then – his mother didn't know Mary-Anne as well as he did. His mother didn't know anything of the years of childhood and youth that Mary-Anne had spent sitting on hills, under sun and under stars, talking of the past and dreaming of the future, of the sea, and of a land far, far away. His mother didn't know that Mary-Anne had come twelve thousand miles to see her daddy, and nobody else.

In the thick silence Mary-Anne also looked at her brother John, then at the faces of her other brothers and sisters, new and old; only Esther looked as perplexed as she herself felt.

Suddenly, Mary-Anne knew – knew the first dull ache of failed ambition, then the splintering pain of shattered dreams.

She stood staring at her mother with eyes gleaming. Her bosom and breath heaved as if someone was choking her. A slow whining sound moved from the pit of her stomach and crawled up to her heaving throat, and erupted in a high-pitched sound that sent the parrots fluttering and flying under and over the branch of the tree, chattering and screaming as Mary-Anne lunged screaming at her mother, the mother who had left her four children behind when she sailed into exile with their father, the mother whom Mary-Anne had always blamed for the desertion, and no one else.

'You *bitch*!' she screamed. 'You let me cross three oceans and twelve thousand miles to come here knowing there was nothing and no one to come for!'

Her mother staggered back and muttered something incoherent. Then she gasped with pain. James moved sharply and caught her about the body, shoving Mary-Anne roughly aside as he did so, for their mother had fainted.

Holding her slumped body securely in his arms, James turned his head over his shoulder and glared with angry hazel eyes at Mary-Anne.

'If you ever dare speak to my mother like that again,' he warned in a cold voice, 'I will kill you stone dead.'

Mary-Anne's throat contorted violently, but she was speechless. She stared at the eighteen-year-old young man they had said was named James, a stranger she had met only minutes before, a stranger who had referred to her mother as *his* mother.

And then a great wave of despair engulfed her as she realised that it was she who was the stranger. A stranger who had once been a child sobbing by a cell door and watching her daddy walking down a long dark passage in Kilmainham Gaol in Dublin Town, and she had waited and waited, all through that day and all through the years, to see him smiling at her again as he came back to her out of the long darkness. But he never did. And now he never would.

'John!' she gasped, needing the comfort and protection of someone she knew well, the comfort of family against the sudden loneliness of this strange place and these strangers.

'John!' she gasped again; and John was at her side immediately, as were Peter and Esther, until the four Irish children who had been left behind, stood in a small group and watched Bridget and Eliza follow their brother James as he carried their mother into the house, the house in Cabramatta which the three had grown up in, with their parents, Michael and Mary Dwyer.

The four were still standing in a group outside on the veranda when the three came out of the house again.

Mary-Anne stood within John's arms, her head against his shoulder. For a minute or so the two sides stood looking at each other silently, then James shrugged, still angry.

'This was not how Daddy would have wished it,' he said quietly. 'This would have grieved him sorely.'

'You don't understand,' Mary-Anne cried harshly. 'You don't understand because you don't know about Ireland. We were their children in Ireland. We lived on the run with them, in harbourers' houses all over the Wicklow hills. We lived in Kilmainham Gaol with them. Esther was born in Kilmainham Gaol. Anything we didn't know about our parents, things that happened when we were too young, or before we were born, was told to us later, by those who were there . . . Michael Kearns of Baltinglass, who made it to Dublin but not America; John Cullen before he died; Thomas Morris and John Jackson; Billy the Rock; scores of others; all had their own tales to tell us about our parents – Michael and Mary Dwyer – who said they would send for us a few months later, but nearly twenty years passed before they did.'

As Mary-Anne spoke, the expression on the three Australians' faces slowly changed from anger to sadness. James looked steadily at his sister.

'And for that, you blamed Mother?'

'Not only for that,' she said with quiet honesty. 'The thing I blamed her for most of all was the surrender. Only for that we would have all stayed together in Wicklow. They would never have caught him. And you three—'

'Would still have been born,' James told her. 'If not here then there. You may look at us like some distantly related strangers, Mary-Anne, or possibly even half-brother and half-sisters. But we are not, we have the same mother and father, and they would have been our parents too, regardless of where we had been born.'

'You three were the lucky ones,' Mary-Anne said bitterly.

'And you four were the beloved ones,' James said. 'The ones they always pined for. We had our moments, too, of feeling second-best.'

'Mary-Anne . . . Etty . . .'

All turned to look at their mother standing in the doorway, her face pale and pinched – and smiling.

'Mary-Anne . . . Etty, this is a great day for me, having all my children with me again . . . all our seven children together . . . it was what we often talked of, and always dreamed of, and now here you all are.'

Still smiling, as if all memory of Mary-Anne's attack had been lost in her faint, she opened her arms to her two daughters from Ireland, and it was Mary-Anne who reached them first.

'Oh, Mammy,' she wept. 'I blamed you. Every day I blamed you.'

'So did I,' her mother said, rocking her weeping daughter's head on her shoulder. 'So did I, Mary-Anne.'

Mary released a hand and held it out in welcome to Esther, who was standing in timid silence, 'And I was never able to forget any of you, and God knows, sometimes for the sake of my sanity, I did try.'

It took weeks for Mary-Anne to find out the full story of her parents' early life in New South Wales. And not from their mother, who seemed reluctant to talk about her husband at all, and on the rare occasions that she did, always seemed to lapse into a world of her own private visions, until the length of her silences became unendurable.

'Hugh Vesty is the man,' James said one evening to Mary-Anne. 'Himself and Sarah will tell you anything you want to know. Just as they always told us anything we wanted to know about Ireland.'

Mary-Anne looked at him in surprise. 'What did they tell you about Ireland?'

James smiled. 'Everything.'

Hugh Vesty Byrne's farm was a wide and rambling building surrounded by outhouses and cattle-pens and acres and acres of land – land that belonged to Hugh Vesty.

'We have to keep the calves locked securely in the byre at night,' Hugh Vesty said, 'because of the danger of the dingos.'

Mary-Anne shuddered as they walked back towards the house. Dingos were the native dogs and very numerous in number. She had soon learned that dingos didn't bark but howled, and at night the sound of their howling from the neighbouring forests had a most eerie tone.

'I used to hate foxes,' Hugh Vesty said, 'but now I often long for a glimpse of one. There are no foxes here. You know that of course. No cunning red foxes to pit your wits against, just wiry old sandy-coloured dingos. Old Reynard is a gentleman in comparison to those savages.'

He paused and stared over the land into the distance, a trace of a distant smile on his face, as if seeing again the red brush of a fox lolloping through the luxuriant green grass of the Wicklow hills on a cold and frosty morning.

Mary-Anne's gaze wandered over Hugh Vesty's face. A lean-faced man, fair hair turned grey at the sides. A man who had loved history. A man who had been a part of Ireland's history.

'Tell me, Hugh . . . Tell me . . .'

His mind preoccupied, Hugh misunderstood, for those were the words young James Dwyer always used when he wanted to know about the past. 'Tell me, Hugh, tell me . . .'

'About Ireland?' Hugh Vesty shrugged. 'That was all in the long-ago. All part of another time and another world. A world that ended for me on the day our ship sailed away from the Cove of Cork . . .'

Mary-Anne hesitated as Hugh Vesty paused to stroke a bay colt standing by the paddock fence, but then she asked: 'Were you on Spike Island, Hugh? In the prison on Spike Island in the bay of Cork?'

Hugh Vesty furrowed his brow. 'The prison on Spike Island in the bay of Cork? Nay . . . but I was in the prison on Norfolk Island in the Pacific Ocean, about a thousand miles away from here. Myself and Michael were there for six months, before they sent us to Van Diemen's Land.'

'Michael . . . ?' Mary-Anne prompted, for Hugh Vesty was proving as reluctant to speak about the early days in New South Wales as was her mother.

'Michael was my cousin, do you know.' Hugh absently stroked the colt's neck in a slow motion, his mind already back in the long-ago. 'My cousin and my comrade. It was on Norfolk Island that he showed them what kind of a man he was. A man who would never bend the knee. The monsters in charge of us were man-killers, and they only liked creatures that grovelled at their feet for easy kicking. Many did in the end, of course. But not myself . . . and not my cousin . . .

'One day they had him, my cousin Michael, tied to the flogging frame, and all of us made to watch. Two of the man-killers stood at a distance with whips ready, one on each side of him, so they could thrash from right to left.

'Then with a shout they went to work, thrashing his naked back with their flails, first one then the other, as hard and as regular as any two farmers threshing in the fields at harvest time. The count got to thirty and blood and flesh were flying off the steel ends of their cats into our faces. Some of the lads were moaning as if they themselves were being whipped, others were shouting with rage and abuse, for Michael was a popular kind of fellow with them all. But Michael himself never made a sound, never uttered a moan, although we could see him flinching from the blows.

'The man-killers set to work again on the twenty still to go, and you could see the beasts they were by the enjoyment on their faces, for only the cruellest animals enjoy torturing their prey. On they thrashed with their whips until his shoulders were ripped to shreds, and no doctor present, for a doctor only had to be present when the count was over fifty.

'At fifty he had still not uttered a sound, not even a whimper, so the bastards broke the rules and flayed on, seething with evil frustration, for as much as they enjoy the flogging, their true moment of ecstasy is when they hear the screams. At sixty they paused for a breather, and it was then Michael turned his head and looked at

603

them with a look as cool and defiant as ever I saw on him in Wicklow.

' "Thrash away until Doomsday, avics," he told them, "but you will never make me sing." '

Hugh Vesty paused in his stroking of the colt's neck. He looked vacantly around him at his acres of land. 'There was another time,' he said, then broke off, and tears formed.

A bright log fire was crackling and blazing merrily on the white painted hearth. A leg of ham was smoking over the fire, for ham and eggs seemed to be the continual diet in New South Wales. On a hot plate to the side of the hearth was an iron dish filled to overflowing with hot mealy potatoes peeping through their cracked and peeling skins.

'He gets carried away and forgets who he is talking to,' Sarah Byrne said apologetically to Mary-Anne. 'Hugh's mind has always dwelt in the past. Truth be known, he probably thought he was back on the Wicklow hills talking to his comrades. I ask your pardon for him, Mary-Anne, for I am sure Hugh forgot that he was telling that horrible tale to Michael's daughter.'

Mary-Anne nodded, convinced that Hugh Vesty had not even been aware of her hasty departure. 'I'm fine now, Sarah. Truly I am.'

When Hugh Vesty wandered in some minutes later, Sarah rushed to greet him and Mary-Anne could hear her admonishing him in hushed tones.

'Crying and shaking she was, mortally upset at what you told her. 'Tis one thing telling the lads those kind of things, Hugh, but not womenfolk. Do as her own family do and speak no more of it.'

'Oh no,' Mary-Anne cried. 'I want you to speak of it, Hugh. I want you to tell me . . . tell me everything . . .'

But Sarah would not allow any more conversation about the early days until after supper was eaten. She moved to the back door and rang a large brass bell which clanged over the fields and brought her tribe of children in to the house. Mary-Anne counted eight from Catherine, who was about eighteen, down to three-year-old Sylvester. But two of the older children who had been born in Ireland, Michael and Rose, were missing. 'Helping out over at John Mernagh's place,' Hugh said.

Later, much later, when all had gone to bed, Mary-Anne was disappointed when Hugh Vesty said goodnight also and retired. He had to be up at dawn and the land was a hard task-master.

Mary-Anne looked in appeal at Sarah, who had settled herself near the lamp on the table, her knitting in her hand. 'I always sit up by myself for an hour or so at night,' Sarah said softly. 'Helps me to wind down before sleep.'

Mary-Anne realised that Sarah must have ordered Hugh Vesty off to bed and allow any further reminiscences to be a gentle matter between women.

'What happened on the ship?' Mary-Anne asked. 'Word came back to Ireland that Michael Dwyer had staged a mutiny on the *Tellicherry* at San Salvador and the captain and all the crew were killed. It was brought back by an Irish seaman and for a time no one could be sure if the rumour was true or not.'

'A mutiny? On the *Tellicherry*?' Sarah looked amazed. 'Oh my, but that Irish seaman must have been dishing out truth from a bowl of wishful thinking.' She shook her head. 'Nay, there was no trouble whatsoever on the *Tellicherry*, not from Cork to Sydney, and not from any of us. We had the best captain ever sailed the seven seas, Captain Cuzens. He treated us fair and well, and we did not repay him with anything other than respect.

'We were not classed as convicts,' Sarah went on, 'but free-settlers destined for Botany Bay, and so we were housed in clean comfort, away from the convicts, in the ship's hospital quarters. It was a well-run ship and we lost only six convicts from fever, five men and one woman, and that was the lowest loss any ship ever had on reaching Sydney. Captain Cuzens was very pleased, of course, but the smooth passage only served to sadden your mammy and daddy even more, added to their regrets, for they knew then that ye four would have suffered no ill effects if you had sailed with us. Oh, how they regretted leaving you behind . . . Only for that they would have been happy on reaching Sydney and facing the prospect of starting a new life, for we were treated well on our arrival.'

'You were?' Mary-Anne said, surprised.

'Oh yes, we were,' Sarah said, and as she sat back and gazed into the past, Mary-Anne let her talk on and on without interruption.

'At the time we arrived in Sydney in 1806, Philip Gidley King was the Governor of New South Wales. He ordered the five United Irishmen to go and see him at Government House

at Paramatta, and there gave them a long lecture on his knowledge of the capricious disposition and turbulent nature of the
Irish, followed by his encouragement that they would settle
down and work hard as free-settlers in New South Wales and
become worthy British subjects. He gave each of them a government land grant of a hundred uncultivated acres at Cabramatta;
and each grant of land was situated next door to the other,
which pleased the men greatly.

'You see, we didn't know it then, although we know it now,
that Britain wanted the settlement to grow into a self-sufficient
country, and for that to happen, New South Wales needed
married men with children and the prospect of more children.
In hindsight, I am sure that is why the Castle reneged on the
surrender terms first offered to Michael and sent us all here
instead of America, so bad was the need in Australia and few
would come voluntarily . . .

'The convicts sent out were all single and mostly male, and
they provided the free labour needed to build roads and buildings and so on. But married men who arrived with their wives
were the ones who would have the children and be more likely
to work hard on the land in order to provide a decent standard
of living for their families – families that would, as I say, help
the settlement to grow into a country.

'Well now, they were not disappointed in us, for no people
worked harder in that first year than we did. Although we
arrived in the month of February, it was summertime here. We
lived in tents for a few months while the men built the houses
on each grant of land, all helping each other. Each house was
made entirely of timber, the boards cut evenly and lapped one
over the other and nailed to upright posts which came from the
bole of gum trees which, as you know, are available in plenty.
Often we sighed for the pine trees of Wicklow but, however,
the houses were finished and lathed and plastered within, then
whitewashed inside all over.

'With some of the money the Castle had paid us for their
breach of faith and with which to buy farm implements to work
the new land, Mary had bought some lovely coloured material
when we moored at San Salvador – one of the crew got it for
her – and she made curtains for each house. With a bright fire
crackling in the white hearth, begor, at night you could pretend
you were back in Wicklow.

'We were proud of our little houses then, but even more so

later on when we took the time to travel beyond our own land and see the land of others. Begor, but the industry was poor and lazy, especially those owned by single men who had come out as convicts and earned their ticket of leave. Wretched huts or hovels built of heaps of turf, or slats of wood nailed haphazardly together and plastered with mud to keep them weatherproof, and the window no more than a gaping hole. Oh aye, whoever said it did say it right – a man with children will work hard to make the world a better place, but a man without children sees only his own future, and many, God help us, are very short-sighted.'

Mary-Anne shifted restlessly. It was all very interesting, but not what she wanted to hear.

'I want to know what happened to my daddy,' she said softly.

Sarah gave a half smile. 'Sure I know that you do, darling. Shall we have some tea?'

Mary-Anne nodded in a resigned sort of way, for she had soon discovered that tea at every opportunity was the colonial custom amongst the women of New South Wales.

The tea made and poured, Sarah placed her elbows on the table, and over the rim of her cup, stared into the glow of the lamp and continued.

'Hard as we tried, not one of us could fault the British system in New South Wales in so far as their treatment of settlers went. Because as settlers, we were entitled to draw free provisions from the Government storehouse for the first eighteen months in order to help us get established. That was very fair we thought. And despite Governor King's long lecture about knowing all about the Wicklow men and their rebel activities in the past, the fact that he did not separate them to different parts of the colony, but allotted them land grants next to each other, showed that he had faith in them and no real misgivings. Nay, for all his talk about the capricious Irish, Gidley King knew that when it came to crop growing and horse rearing we were the best in the world.'

Sarah chewed her lip. 'Although he was not too pleased when he learned that Michael had quickly discovered a way of turning peaches into cider and cider into brandy. But he let him off with a warning. Peaches are so abundant here, we discovered that if a peach stone is thrown into the ground, a large quantity of fruit may be gathered from the tree that shortly shoots up without any subsequent culture. Michael still made the cider, but he never again broke the rules and made the brandy – not that I know of anyway. In truth, I am sure he did not, for his intentions were truly to become a peaceable and prosperous citizen of the land he had been banished to, for the term of his natural life.

'However, it was Michael who was the one who went into Sydney on any business that needed doing, for he never lost his love of rambling for miles as was his habit in Wicklow. Even at the end, when something was on his mind, he would ramble almost as far as the Hawkesbury. But in the early days into Sydney he would go, and bedad, he became good friends with a number of the English soldiers in the New South Wales Corps. But then, in Ireland he had many a friend in the English and Scottish camps too. He was that kind of man. And it is still hard to figure it all out, for no one really knew, except him, who his friends were.

'I remember Hugh Vesty once telling me about the time in Wicklow that himself and Michael were down near the Three Bridges when around the bend came four Highlanders from the Duke of York Regiment. Hugh nearly had heart failure at the sight of them so close, but they passed by without recognising who the two were – or so Hugh thought – until one of them turned his head and called back, "Make sure that you are nowhere near Glenmalure tonight or the next few days, Dwyer, for we shall be going there in search of you." And Michael calls back, "I wasn't planning to go anywhere near Glenmalure, Cameron, but thanks for warning me anyway." '

Sarah smiled. 'Oh, the tales I could tell about the happenings in Wicklow . . . Another unlikely friend of his turned out to be a captain in the Somerset Fencibles—'

'The New South Wales Corps . . .' Mary-Anne said, turning the conversation back to the land they were in. 'What about them?'

'Good men some of them. And I'll tell you for why. At the end of the first year Michael had managed to clear forty acres of his uncultivated land, so determined was he to succeed and make his land profitable, for only then would he be able to send for his children in Ireland. It was a dream that spurred him to work from dawn to dusk, for Captain Cuzens had told him during the voyage that Dr Trevor had tricked him, and not to live in hopes of seeing another ship from Ireland for at least three to five years.

'Months later Michael and Hugh had a fair number of acres planted with maize and wheat and the early crops were looking good. Michael drove us all mad doing his arithmetic, but no matter which way he did his sums, he reckoned it would take him at least five years of hard work before he would have enough money to send for his children. But each day was a day less, and on he worked, as they all worked. But then a terrible thing happened in New South Wales. Governor King announced that his term in the colony was over, and a new Governor was already on the seas. And when he arrived, the new Governor of New South Wales turned out to be none other than William Bligh, the former captain of the *Bounty*.

'Bligh was not long in the colony when he showed signs of unbalanced hatred for two groups of people – the soldiers of the New South Wales Corps, and the five Wicklowmen that lived at Cabramatta. You see, in 1800, Bligh had been sent to Dublin by the British Admiralty for the purpose of making surveys of Dun Laoghaire harbour and the surrounding coasts – he was a great man for drawing maps apparently. But while in Dublin he saw the proclamation and knew all the gossip about the Insurgent Captain of the Wicklow Mountains.

'Next thing we knew, Michael, Hugh Vesty, Mernagh, Burke, Arthur Devlin, and two English convicts were arrested and charged with planning to raise a rebellion in New South Wales as a reprisal for the defeat on Vinegar Hill.'

Sarah looked into the astonished eyes of Mary-Anne and nodded. 'Aye, it would have been laughable but for the ugly fact that the men faced death if found guilty.'

'But . . . the English convicts,' Mary-Anne said. 'How could they have been accused of planning a rebellion in return for Vinegar Hill?'

'They were accused because Bligh wanted them accused. You see, the *Bounty* was not the only mutiny that Bligh had suffered. Some years later there was a second mutiny at the Nore. The crew were caught and tried, some hanged, some transported to Botany Bay, and these two English convicts were mutineers from the Nore. Captain William Bligh was obviously a man who could never write "paid" against a crime or a grudge.'

The silence that followed was so long, the faraway look in Sarah's eyes so dark, that Mary-Anne got to her feet and made more tea. When she placed the steaming cup in front of Sarah, Sarah did not seem to notice.

'Whenever I think back to that time,' she said quietly, 'the time of that trial in May 1807, I think not of our men, but of myself and Mary. She had not long given birth to James then, her first child born in the new land. The arrests of our men was a savage blow to us, made worse because we could not even begin to understand the why of it.

'However, in Sydney the evidence against them was being gathered, and two convicted murderers who were serving their time as *lifers* were brought forward by Bligh as the two main prosecution witnesses, and he later gave them both a free pardon for their testimony at the trial. It was held in the Criminal Court before Judge Atkins and six military officers.

'Well, first the charge was read out: *Instigating many people to revolt from their allegiance and to rise in open rebellion.*'

Sarah sighed and eyed her tea-cup morosely. 'Cons and ex-cons by the score were marched in to give their evidence. All claimed they had heard the Wicklowmen rousing other Irish in the taverns to make ready for a rising and steal the guns of their masters. The two convicted lifers admitted they were turning king's evidence and had planned to take part in the rebellion, stimulated as they had been by the persuasive powers of Michael Dwyer, whose plan, they said, was to seize the barracks, kill all the leading gentry and start a general massacre.

'There was a terrible commotion when that was said. By that evening members of the leading gentry had arrived in Sydney and all were clamouring for the immediate hangings of the Wicklow men.'

Sarah shuddered at the memory. 'Then, it came, the time for the defence. Michael represented himself. But Mary and myself had not been lazy, indeed not! No two women were as relentless as us, and poor Mary carrying little James everywhere with her. I also found it hard because I was fair advanced in pregnancy myself. But Mary and I lost no time in going to see all our land-holding neighbours who had known us since our arrival, not the hovel dwellers, but the decent ones. And strange as it may seem to some, it was our English neighbours who travelled into Sydney and the court and gave firm evidence in the Wicklowmen's defence.

'One by one the Englishmen stepped forward and testified to the peaceable nature and hard work of the Wicklowmen. Then Michael, who acted in his own defence, as did the others, recalled a number of the prosecution witnesses and questioned them carefully on their testimony. Hugh questioned a number of them too, only he asked the questions in a different way, and that's when the cracks in their testimonies began to show. All the witnesses, including the Englishmen, were questioned by the officers on the bench. Then they retired from Friday to Monday to consider their verdict.

'Five days the trial lasted, but that break from Friday to Monday was the longest time I ever knew, and Mary was almost unbalanced in her terror. I had more trouble calming her down than could be imagined. She was shaking like a leaf on a tree in autumn when the court resumed and the officers and Judge Atkins gave the verdict.

' "Michael Dwyer – not guilty.

' "Hugh Byrne – not guilty.

' "Martin Burke – not guilty.

' "John Mernagh – not guilty."

'I stopped listening after that, so gushing with floods of tears were myself and Mary, and never did I like six military officers so much as those sitting in judgement at that trial. Fair men, good men, Englishmen, who had the courage to be just and lawful. Which goes to prove that men should be judged solely on their characters and not their nationality.'

Mary-Anne was all of a fluster. It was not the verdict that she had expected. 'But the flogging on Norfolk Island! Van Diemen's Land! When did that happen?'

Sarah looked at her coldly. 'Didn't I tell you that William Bligh could never write "paid" against a grudge! As soon as the men stepped out of the court he had them re-arrested and refused to set them free. He refused to accept the verdict of the court. He accused Judge Atkins of being drunk throughout the trial of the Irish State prisoners. He accused the six military officers of the New South Wales Corps of being drunk! Well, by God, there was a terrible commotion. Michael told Bligh that he was not an Irish State prisoner, that he had come to the colony without conviction, that he still had not been convicted of any crime, and therefore was still a free settler and a free man under the law!'

' "The law!" Bligh shouted. "Damn the law! My will is the only law in New South Wales!"

'The next day they were taken before a bench of civic magistrates and tried again on the same charge. We knew what the verdict would be even before it came, because according to

Mr Blaxland, a very decent and fair English gentleman, Bligh selected only those magistrates who did his will; and so the Wicklowmen were found guilty, along with the two English convicts who had been charged with them.

'It was Lieutenant Minchin, one of the officers who sat in judgement at the first trial, who came and sadly gave us the news – hard labour in a penal prison for as long as Governor Bligh decreed. Two were to be transported to Norfolk Island, two to the Derwent, and the others to Port Dalrymple. Michael was also sentenced to receive a thousand lashes, to be inflicted in stages, as was Thomas McCann, one of the Nore mutineers.'

Sarah put a hand to her brow and smoothed it wearily, as if the memories were tiring her badly.

'I could not take it in. I lay in a trance for days, and indeed, only a week later I gave premature birth to Catherine. But Mary . . . poor Mary . . . she never strayed from her position down at the harbour where they had Michael imprisoned on Bligh's own ship, the *Porpoise*, begging and crying to see him, but she was denied any sympathy or consideration.

'We later learned through Mr Blackland, who travelled to and from England, that Alexander Marsden's brother, William Marsden, who had lived for some time in Wicklow but was at that time Secretary to the Admiralty in London, had said – even to Mrs Bligh in England – that although others had been appalled and outraged at the news of a projected massacre by the Wicklowmen, he considered it nonsense and that the informers were the people he distrusted most. Hugh Vesty Byrne he said he would believe nothing against.'

Sarah sighed. 'A fairer man than his brother it would seem. But transported in chains our husbands were . . . And how Mary and I managed after that was something like a nightmare, our families broken up, our cultivated land left to smother under weeds. We would not have managed at all only for the kindness of our English neighbours. But no one in the whole wide world could console Mary . . . poor Mary . . . her devotion to Michael had always been a matter for comment . . .

'But then, after about nine months, when she heard that he had been moved from Norfolk Island to Van Diemen's Land what did she do? She did what no other woman in her right mind would do. She took up her little son James and somehow managed to get herself on a trading vessel destined for Hobart and followed Michael all the way to Van Diemen's Land.'

Chapter Forty-One

They talked until almost dawn. At least, Sarah Byrne did.

Mary-Anne listened without interruption, staring wide-eyed at the yellow bowl of the lamp on the table, a bowl of bitter visions. She could imagine it all vividly, but not objectively, for the people suffering in this piece of human history were not characters in a story or a song, but her parents, Michael and Mary Dwyer.

'Went to find her husband in Van Diemen's Land,' Sarah said. 'And for a time I never knew what had happened to her. Did she ever make it there? Did she ever find him? Did tragedy befall the ship she was on? All I could do was pray. The last was my biggest fear, for ships were always going down in the waters to Van Diemen's Land. Some due to pirates, some due to a host of other reasons.

'But here in New South Wales things were getting worse and worse under Governor Bligh. Some would say they got better. It depended on who you were and where you were. He was a demon to the convicts and the small land-holders, but he was adored by the gentry and leading land-owners on the Hawkesbury, which was the very best area in the colony. Bligh was a man who favoured only one side of a community, a divisive man, a man who had a temper and a tongue on him that would raise a blister on a brick.

'In the end it was the soldiers and officers of the New South Wales Corps that he raised – to mutiny. Led by their officers they marched to Government House, and there Major Johnstone – one of the officers who sat on the bench at our husbands' first trial – read out a document informing Governor Bligh that he had been judged unfit to rule the colony, and that the military were assuming command until a new governor could be sent out from England. Bligh was put under house arrest and the whole of Sydney seemed to be cheering; but the Hawkesbury, of course, was glumly silent.

'When the news finally sank in, I went to Major Johnstone, who had assumed the role of Acting-Governor, and requested that the convictions of Bligh's kangaroo court on our husbands be quashed. He agreed, and Colonel Patterson who was then embarking for Van Diemen's Land was ordered to inform the Wicklowmen that they could return. You see, although they were originally separated and sent to Norfolk Island, the Derwent, and the coal mines, after six months or so they all ended up together in Van Diemen's Land.

'Well, they came back. First my Hugh Vesty, who saw, for the first time, our daughter Catherine, born some eighteen months previously. Then back came John Mernagh and Martin Burke, then Arthur Devlin; but not Michael, and not Mary, who had reached there safely and found who she went looking for.'

'Why did they not come back?'

'Why? Because Mary was so terrified of Governor Bligh she would not allow Michael to return to New South Wales until Bligh had left not only Government House, but the colony itself. And so they stayed in Hobart, where Colonel Patterson, who was the commanding officer there, gave Mary new accommodation and Michael government work. And it was while they were in Hobart that Mary gave birth to Bridget.

'Bridget was born in Van Diemen's Land?'

'Aye, Mary went off with one little child in her arms and fourteen months later came back with two.' Sarah sniffed. 'But then, you being a widow and all, Mary-Anne, you'll not blush when I say that Michael and Mary were always that way inclined with each other.'

Mary-Anne blushed, but Sarah did not notice. 'And knowing Mary as I do, I can imagine how she must have near smothered him with her embraces the first opportunity she got him alone, and well, as you know, being inclined as they were, need I say more . . .'

Sarah sniffed again, and Mary-Anne could not help thinking that as inclined as her daddy and mammy had been, they had not produced as many children as Hugh Vesty and Sarah – eight she had counted, and two were away, and Sarah was pregnant at this minute!

'So then,' Sarah said, a new light beginning to shine in her eyes, 'in that year of 1810, the great man himself came to New South Wales as Bligh's replacement. Oh, Mary-Anne, it would take me a another night and a day to extol the virtues of Lachlan Macquarie! An army officer he was, in his late forties, and 'tis said that his family once owned a castle in Scotland before their fortunes changed and he was reared on an impoverished farm in the Hebrides. He brought with him his lady wife, and his own Seventy-third Regiment who had fought with him in India, and some of them, would you believe, were Irish.

'So Bligh was sent home to England, and poor Major Johnstone was also sent home for court martial for leading the mutiny – although he got off lightly and was soon back in the colony with his friends again.

'But it was in that year of 1810 that the reign of Governor Lachlan Macquarie began. A man who was everything that Bligh was not. A man with a great deal of common sense and humanity. A *gentleman*. But with none of the pompous pretensions of the gentry who liked to think of themselves as the "elite" and thought all convicts should remain convicts for life.

'But Lachlan Macquarie was not of their ilk. He believed in giving a man a fair chance. And that included the convicts. When he announced his new policy to the colony, he said that in his view, good conduct had to be recognised and rewarded. For if good conduct produced no benefit to a man and did not lead him back to his place in society, then why should he ever abandon bad conduct?'

Sarah sat back, eyes glowing with admiration. 'Oh, aye, Lachlan Macquarie was not only a man fit to rule a colony, he was a man fit to rule a nation.'

'Is that when my parents came back to New South Wales?'

Sarah nodded. 'Governor Macquarie sent for them. And when they returned he summoned the five Wicklowmen to Government House at Parammata, and after a long discussion, gave them all confirmation of their pardons, as well as the official papers for their land grant at Cabramatta, and even assigned them two convicts each to help them restore their land.

'And so for a few months life was good again for your daddy, who was back hoeing and sowing his land and doing his arithmetic. But then Michael got a summons to go to Government House and Mary was sure that ill-fortune was about to descend upon them again. She could never forget the night when the summons had come from Governor Bligh and Michael had

615

ended up in chains. So you can imagine her shock when Michael returned and told her that he had been asked to become one of Macquarie's newly reorganised police force.'

Sarah smiled. 'Well, I tell you, Michael was near sick at the thought of being a policeman. To him it was like becoming a militiaman. Especially as he would have to wear the dark blue uniform when on duty. He had been given time to think about it, and he declared to us all that he would never do it. If he had not worn the green uniform that Emmet sent down to him in Wicklow, he would not wear Macquarie's blue uniform in New South Wales.

'We all disagreed with him, especially Hugh Vesty, who pointed out that we need never fear the law kicking in our doors again, not if the local lawman was our own cousin and comrade. Mary, too, encouraged him to accept the offer, if only to remove her constant fear of his sudden arrest. She was also very proud, because one of the reasons put forward in the offer was Michael's ability to read and write, which a great number in the colony still cannot do, myself included.

'And so it was that Michael became a policeman. I think he always knew that he would have to, if only to prove to Macquarie that his rebel days were truly over. And he did the job well, treating the Irish convicts with great humanity and kindness, as you can imagine. And only a year later Macquarie made Michael the Chief of Police of the George's River and Liverpool District.

'John Mernagh, his side-kick from Wicklow, also became a policeman, so did Martin Burke. And Lachlan Macquarie never had a day's trouble with the Irish in this area during his whole eleven years in New South Wales, not when the men in charge of policing the district were ex-rebels who had been part of the sharp-shooting force on Vinegar Hill.'

Sarah smiled at Mary-Anne. 'A clever man, that Lachlan Macquarie, wouldn't you say?'

'From an outlaw to a policeman,' Mary-Anne could not help smiling at the irony of her daddy's life. 'But to me,' she said, 'growing up as I did with only his legend, he will always be the rebel on the Wicklow Mountains.'

'Because he had no other choice on the Wicklow Mountains,' Sarah said. 'But Governor Macquarie wanted to shape this colony and make it a good place for people to live and build their futures.' Her eyes were glowing again, as they always did whenever she thought or spoke of Lachlan Macquarie.

'In that first year after Michael became part of his police force,' she said, 'Governor Macquarie himself twice dropped into the Dwyer homestead at Cabramatta for refreshment. On the first occasion he explained that himself and his guide had been out inspecting the farms around George's River and Harris Creek and had got lost in the forest for three hours before riding on to Dwyer's land.

'On the second occasion, he said that he had been inspecting the outlying area of George's River with the intention of creating a town. That second time he was accompanied by Mrs Macquarie and Captain Antill.

'Elizabeth Macquarie was a lovely lady. Although in her first year here she shocked the mock gentry greatly, by giving a party on Saint Patrick's Day for all the Irish convicts in her husband's service. A lovely lady, as I say, and she seemed quite relaxed in Mary's home at Cabramatta. Mary in turn lost some of her nervousness and spoke to Governor Macquarie about a matter that had been troubling her. You see, whatever happened to Mary during her time in Van Diemen's Land, when she returned she had become very religious. And so, as Governor Macquarie was at his most convivial and charming, she mentioned to him that there was a large number of Catholics in New South Wales, and not one Catholic church or priest to serve them.

'Lachlan Macquarie very gently assured her that she need not worry about the large number of Catholics in New South Wales, because it was his intention that by the time he had finished his term as Governor, he would have turned them all into Protestants.'

Sarah chuckled. 'And Mary believed him! Not knowing that the reason Lachlan Macquarie was in the area that afternoon was because himself and Captain Antill had been marking out a square for the Catholic Church he intended to build in his newly created town of Liverpool.'

'He sounds indeed like a good man,' Mary-Anne said.

'Aye, a man like General John Moore. Two of a kind. Both soldiers and both great men. Although in the end it was in Sydney that the first Catholic Church was built.'

'And my parents were happy from then on?'

'With each other they were always happy,' Sarah said quietly, a sad expression on her face. 'As you know, or must have been told, it was a love story with them two from start to finish, from the first day they met in Wicklow until they parted at your daddy's grave in Sydney. Have you been there yet?'

'Not yet,' Mary-Anne said. 'I want to know about his life first, before I go and face his death.'

'Well yes, as you ask, they were happy enough in those years after coming back from Van Diemen's Land. But they still had their problems, financial problems, like every other farmer in New South Wales. Despite being a policeman Michael still depended on the land as his main source of income, but the soil was not good fertile soil and repeated cropping only seemed to tire it and not rejuvenate it. Then in 1813 there was a terrible drought which parched and killed the land, as well as killing thousands of sheep and cattle. Water! Blessed water! Not man nor animal nor land can survive without it.

'Well, the drought lasted for almost three years, and when the rains finally came in 1815 it was glorious! Everyone was running and dancing and laughing in the rain until they were soaked to the skin. But then the laughing stopped, because the rain didn't stop, and the floods from the Blue Mountains destroyed all the new crops and stock and drowned a number of the settlers . . . Such hard days for the people of New South Wales, lean and hard days . . . Your daddy was despairing of ever saving enough money to send for you four . . . But all we could do was face it like Christians and start again when the weather stabilised, which it did in 1818.

'But then came that terrible business with Arthur Devlin . . . that nearly killed Michael so it did . . . that was when his past caught up with him.'

'What business was that?' Mary-Anne sat alert.

Sarah paused, and rubbed her hands over her eyes. When she drew them away, she said tiredly: 'It was after Lachlan Macquarie had left New South Wales. And it was the test the entire Irish population in the colony had been waiting for, the test the gentry had been waiting for, and the test that Michael must surely have known would come one day.

'The court of magistrates issued an order for the arrest of Arthur Devlin on charges of treason-felony, and anyone found harbouring Arthur Devlin would suffer the utmost rigour of the law. And Michael being the Chief, it was his responsibility to secure Arthur Devlin's arrest.

'Well now, as you know, Arthur Devlin was one of the

Devlins of Wicklow and a cousin to Michael. Arthur Devlin had been with him on Vinegar Hill and many another battle of the Irish Rebellion of 1798. In 1803 Arthur Devlin had fought with Robert Emmet against the powers of Dublin Castle. Arthur Devlin had been included in the surrender terms Michael had given to William Hume of Humewood, and had been with Michael in Kilmainham Gaol before sailing out with him on the *Tellicherry*. And Arthur Devlin had been in prison with him in Van Diemen's Land . . . For Michael to arrest Arthur Devlin on a charge that would undoubtedly lead to him being hanged . . .'

Sarah nodded her head slowly up and down. 'Aye, Mary-Anne, the expression in your eyes tells me that you have guessed rightly what happened. Michael couldn't do it. He had the chance of arresting Arthur Devlin, but he just couldn't do it. Arthur Devlin went into hiding, and was proclaimed as a missing and wanted person.

'It was the test, and Michael had failed it, and so for him there was a reckoning. Some of the leading land-holders got ugly, saying there was Irish politics in it. He had failed in his duty as a policeman, and he was asked to hand in his policeman's coat, after eleven years of being the Chief of Police of the George's River and Liverpool District.

'Michael obliged, and truth to tell, he was relieved, for he had never felt completely comfortable in the blue coat, not from the first day he donned it. Oh look—' Sarah nodded towards the windows, 'dawn is coming! Shall we have another cup of tea, Mary-Anne, before snatching a few hours' shut-eye?'

Mary-Anne lifted her dark eyes from the lamp on the table and looked at Sarah directly.

'What made my daddy die?' she said.

'He just got sick, Mary-Anne. After being out in the bush a few days he got sick, and was sick for a week or so, and then he died. Mary won't have it that it was as simple as that. She still claims that it was his years in the prisons in the Pacific Ocean that put him in an early grave. But nothing she says will ever bring him back to her, and that is her continual heartbreak. For although she is now forty-five years old, in her heart she is still the same girl who ran away from home that October night in 1798 to marry him, the same girl who followed him all the way to Van Diemen's Land.'

Sarah reached out across the table and lifted Mary-Anne's hand in both of hers and clasped it tight. 'Understand this, daughter of Mary Dwyer. Whatever you may learn about your daddy, good or bad, bad or good, and however you may think you loved him, the one who truly loved him was his wife Mary. And always at the back of her mind was the fear that he would die, and she would be left in the world without him. And now that has come to pass. So I am asking you, Mary-Anne, daughter of Michael Dwyer, to be gentle with your mother, be good to her, be kind to her, because . . . because I don't think Mary will live for very much longer.'

Chapter Forty-Two

Mary lived to see her children's children. She lived for thirty more years. She lived to see her daughter Mary-Anne married in New South Wales to a Wicklow man named Patrick Grace and give birth to four children. She lived to see John and Peter married before they both moved to Bungendore and settled down on their own land with their families. She saw Bridget married to a bank manager named John O'Sullivan. Esther married another Wicklow man named Owen Byrne, and both set up their own business, the Lake George Hotel, and were now prosperous members of the New South Wales community. James married a girl called Jane and moved to the district of Lachlan. The youngest, Eliza, ran away from home at fifteen in a fit of romance and she too was now married and a mother.

Her family scattered all over New South Wales, Mary was left alone in the house her husband had built at Cabramatta, which he had extended over the years to twelve rooms. A lonely empty house surrounded by forests where the dingos howled at night, and memories of another time and another place came to life again in the flames of a crackling fire.

Each of her children wanted her to go and live with them; the choice was hard, but in the end she chose to go and live in Goulborn with her third daughter, Bridget, the daughter she had conceived and given birth to in Van Diemen's Land.

The O'Sullivans' house in Goulborn was spacious and comfortably furnished, as would be fitting for a banker. The lace curtains on the open long windows hung limply in the heat of summer, the air outside full of the noise of bees, and exquisitely coloured butterflies flitting everywhere.

Mary sat by the open window staring wide-eyed over her life. She knew the end was near, and was glad of it. Looking back, she had not done very much of note in her allotted time, except leave her beloved Ireland, and give seven children to Australia.

And they in turn were giving more children to Australia, young men and women who were helping to shape a colony into a country. Yes, it would be to these early settlers that Australia would one day look back, as a piece of history, and wonder how it had been.

They would look back and try to imagine themselves into a world of convicts, and think how terrible those early days in Australia were; yet the convicts in Australia always had more hope than the oppressed people of Ireland, because the convicts always knew there would be an end to their bondage, seven years, fourteen years, even the lifers could earn their ticket of leave with good conduct; but for the people of Ireland there seemed no end to their agony.

There had been a terrible famine there ten years before, in 1846, a famine in which over one million Irish had died; corpses on the roadsides, dead children with green lips from eating grass; mass famine graves.

And yet – in that year of the potato failure and terrible famine, enough corn and beef to feed the whole of Ireland three times over, had been exported as usual to England; while emigrant ships left Ireland weekly, packed with over two million skeletal hopefuls on their way to food in America.

'*They are going, going, going,*' the London Post had written cheerfully, '*and very soon the Irish will be as scarce on the banks of the Shannon as the American Indians on the banks of the Potomac.*'

And Jesus said – *Love thy neighbour!* Her eyes moved down to the missal on her lap. She still could not read more than a word here and there, although she pretended to Michael that she could read now, and he was very pleased with her progress, not knowing that she was learning the pages of her missal by memorising his words and not by reading them.

In the distance she heard the sound of a horse's hoofs hammering away and she looked up, a sunburst of a smile breaking on her face as she saw the distant and dark figure of a young man riding towards the house. He was still quite far off, but she knew it was him. She grabbed up her stick and moved out to meet him, not shuffling or hobbling, but slowly and sedately; she didn't truly need the brass-topped stick, but it had been given to her a year before by Bridget, and she felt obliged to use it, and now was fond of its company.

She stepped out to the veranda and watched him for a

moment. No hat on his head as usual, black curls flying in the breeze of his horse's speed.

'Michael!' she cried joyously, waving her stick like an Irish child with a hawthorn branch.

He slowed to a canter as he approached, then drew rein and grinned down at her, before leaping from his saddle and tying the horse to the veranda rail.

'Michael,' she said, 'have you have come to escort me to Mass?'

'I have indeed,' he said, smiling. He bent and kissed her cheek, and she looked up at him adoringly.

'Michael,' she said, 'why is it that you always make me feel young again?'

'My natural charm,' he said seductively.

She frowned at that, but then she smiled again, for she knew it was a manner he used only with her, and no other female. From as far back as she could remember he had always had a special kind of love for her. And oh, how she had loved him! Of all the children of her children, this one had always been her favourite grand-child – Michael, now twenty-five years old, son of her own son John, and the first young man to be ordained a priest into the new Benedictine order in Australia.

He paused, and looked up at the sky for a moment, as she saw that his face was very tanned. But then it would be, for he spent most of his time riding all over New South Wales to tend the scattered population of Catholics who lived too far away to attend church for their marriages, baptisms, and requiems.

'I see you are ready and waiting,' he said, glancing from her bonnet and shawl to the missal clutched in her hand. 'Did Bridget leave the trap?'

'No,' Mary answered. 'She took the trap and left the chaise.'

John and Bridget O'Sullivan were away from home with their children, visiting James in Lachlan, and were expected back late that night. But two kind and faithful servants were in residence in the house to see to all Mary's needs. One of them, Teresa, now came out on to the veranda and greeted Michael with a delighted smile.

'Good morning, Father, is it to Mass you'll be taking your grandmother now?'

'And not only my grandmother, Teresa, but yourself and Molly as well.'

'Good gracious, Father, but ye'll be turning us all into saints yet!'

And with that Teresa skipped away and returned in less than a minute with Molly, both of them bonneted and wreathed in smiles, for they took great pride in being the only two Catholic servant girls who were regularly escorted to Mass by the priest himself. And himself a fine young specimen of a priest at that!

'I'll return to share breakfast with you,' he told Mary as he helped her into the chaise, 'but after that I must leave. I have to ride over to Bungendore this afternoon.'

Mary nodded, for he spent his life riding here and there from dawn to dusk and never showed any sign of fatigue whatever. 'And what hymn have you planned for me today, Michael,' she asked, never managing to call her grandson 'Father'.

'A special hymn, Grandmother,' he said with a smile. 'One that will please you greatly.

'The twenty-third psalm?'

'No.'

' "O Glorious Redeemer"?'

'No.'

' "Hail Queen of Heaven"?'

'No.'

'Oh, Michael!' she said indignantly, banging her stick on the floor of the chaise. 'Stop teasing me now!'

He threw back his head and laughed. 'Wait and see,' he said, climbing up to bench and lifting the reins. 'Wait and see.'

Mary sat in the front row of St Mary's Church, Teresa and Molly each side of her, all eyes on young Father Dwyer as he said Mass; and it was a very different young man who stood before the altar to the one who had ridden up to the house like a wild and carefree horseman earlier that morning. He looked slowly and reverently around at his congregation then stood with arms open, palms forward, in a gesture of welcome.

'*Dominus vobiscum*,' he said. 'The Lord be with you.'

'*Et cum spiritu tuo*,' the people answered. 'And with you.'

'*Sursum corda*,' the priest smiled. 'Lift up your hearts!'

Memories, memories. Mary's mind drifted back to another time and another place, and a young French priest in a secret penal chapel on the Quays of Dublin. Memories, memories, ghosts that had haunted her for thirty years moved through the mist before her eyes as in the background she could dimly hear voices saying the Pater Noster and the Credo. Then she heard music, beautiful music that touched her very soul and quickened her breathing.

'The hymn, ma'am.' Teresa nudged, knowing how much Mrs Dwyer loved her hymns and always joined in the singing of them, however quietly.

Mary turned her eyes towards the choir, but they sat silently as a young boy of about ten years old rose to his feet at the pulsing sound of the organ. She knew him to be the son of a convict-servant from Wexford, the son of a man who had died in Ireland's famine and whose mother, ten years ago, had been transported, although pregnant, for stealing corn. A ten-year-old boy whom her grandson had taken under his wing, as if he were his own son, the only kind of adoptive son a priest could have. The boy now stood alone and sang with a voice so full of beautiful and innocent purity that Mary closed her eyes and felt her heart race with the mixed emotions of agony and ecstasy.

> 'Hail, glorious Saint Patrick,
> Dear saint of our isle,
> On us thy poor children
> Bestow a sweet smile;
> And now thou art high
> In the mansions above,
> On Erin's green valleys
> Look down in thy love.'

The choir rose for the chorus:

> *On Erin's green valleys,*
> *On Erin's green valleys,*
> *On Erin's green valleys*
> *Look down in thy love.*

As the organ played and the boy prepared to sing again, Mary looked towards the young priest at the altar, and saw her grandson smiling at her, a smile that took her right back to the Glen of Imaal in Wicklow, her eyes misty with mourning for the hills and vales that she would never see again.

> 'Thy people, now exiles
> On many a shore,
> Shall love and revere thee
> Till time be no more;
> And the fire thou hast kindled

Shall ever burn bright.
Its warmth undiminished,
Undying its light.'

Mary leaned on her stick and tried to stand as the choir and
the entire congregation rose to its feet and joined in the chorus
that rose up to the dim arches and wooden rafters of the church.

On Erin's green valleys,
On Erin's green valleys,
On Erin's green valleys
Look down in thy love.

'Well, Grandmother,' the young priest said with a smile as
he came out of the vestry and walked towards the front row of
chairs when the Mass was over. 'Did you approve of the hymn
today?'

Mary had not managed to rise to her feet to join in the
chorus. Teresa and Molly were standing in front of her.

'Oh, Father . . .' Teresa turned a tear-stained face to Father
Dwyer, then herself and Molly moved aside from the woman
who sat as if she was sleeping, but as her grandson stared at her,
he knew that Mary Doyle Dwyer had heard her last hymn.

Three days later Father Dwyer officiated at his grandmother's
Requiem Mass; then at the funeral which was led by the Bishop
of Sydney's carriage and attended by large numbers who followed the cortege into Devonshire Street Cemetery where
Mary Dwyer was finally laid to rest in the same grave as her
husband.

The people stood in a large silent crowd and watched as one
by one the children and grandchildren of Michael and Mary
Dwyer stepped forward and sprinkled holy water into the
grave. They were all there, those who should and could have
been there – all the old and elderly friends who had come to
this land from Wicklow under the surrender terms offered to
their captain.

And perhaps it was for them that the priest ended the burial
service with the hymn that Michael Dwyer, in his last dying
moments in the house at Cabramatta, had requested be sung at
his own burial, but which was not, because no one in the colony
had known the words.

But the young Benedictine priest had learned them long ago. And so, with a quiet but resonant voice, Michael's grandson stood by the grave in Devonshire Street Cemetery, and sang the Corpus Christi.

> 'Come then, good Shepherd, bread divine,
> Still show to us thy mercy sign;
> Oh, feed us still, keep us thine;
> So we may see thy glories shine
> In the fields of immortality . . .'

After a silence, the priest then held up his hand over the mutual grave of his Wicklow-born grandparents, and said the farewell.

'The body lies in the dust of the earth, but the spirit is free again. May God, who has called you, bid you welcome, into that place where Lazarus is poor no longer. May his angels greet you, and lead you home to Paradise, and establish you in that bliss which knows no ending.'

EPILOGUE

Some thirty years later again, when he was no longer the youngest, but the most famous Benedictine priest in New South Wales, Father Dwyer, who had become Dean Dwyer, attended a celebration in Sydney held in honour of his grandfather. The events were reported in the Sydney *Freeman's Journal*, copies of which were sent back to the people of Ireland, and many a flush of pride mantled a Wicklowman's brow as he read the words from Australia.

> Sixty years ago there passed away in our city one who, in his own sphere, had led a life as adventurous, heroic, and full of romance as any recorded in the history of struggling nationalities. Michael Dwyer, the insurgent chief of the Wicklow mountains, was exiled to this colony in 1805, and now sleeps his last long sleep in Devonshire Street Cemetery – far from the hills of his own Imaal. But still the patriot chieftain cannot be said to occupy a grave in the land of the stranger. His descendants are still amongst us, and by them, as well as his countrymen, the memory of the dead patriot is kept green and fresh as in his own shamrock land; and many years will pass away ere this gallant Kosciuszko of Irish history is forgotten.

In Ireland a number of monuments were erected to Michael Dwyer in the county of Wicklow, but in Australia, in 1898, on the centenery of the 1798 Rebellion, a procession was attended by over 100,000 Irish who travelled from all over Australasia. The procession started at Devonshire Street Cemetery where the coffins of Michael and Mary Dwyer were removed into a hearse and taken to Waverley Cemetery where they were reburied beneath a beautiful white marble and bronze monument topped by a Celtic cross, draped with the green flag of Ireland and the blue and white flag of Australia.

At the graveside stood the grandchildren, great-grand-children, and great-great-grandchildren of Michael and Mary Dwyer. The monument was not only a tribute to Michael and Mary Dwyer, and all those others who had been transported after the 1798 Rebellion, it was a tribute to all the young Irish men and women who had left their own oppressed country, and helped to build a nation, in return for the chance they had been given, and the freedom they had found, in the new land of Australia.

*Tadeusz Kosciuszko – Leader of rebellion for the freedom of Poland in 1794.

SHORT BIBLIOGRAPHY

Diary of Sir John Moore, edited by Major-General Sir J.F. Maurice, 1904

Charles Cornwallis, Memoirs and Correspondence

The Viceroy's Postbag: Whitehall Papers and Correspondence of the Earl of Hardwicke, Michael MacDonagh, 1904

Luke Cullen Papers and Manuscript, National Library of Ireland

Memoirs of Miles Byrne, edited by his widow. Paris, 1863

Memoirs of Joseph Holt, edited by T. Crofton Croker, 1838

Michael Dwyer, by Charles Dickson

Life of Robert Emmet, by R.R. Madden, 1856

Vice-Admiral William Bligh, by George Mackaness, 1931

Irish in Australia, by James Hogan, 1887

Lachlan Macquarie, by M.H. Ellis

Historical Records of Australia

Newspapers:

Saunders Newsletter – 15th August 1798

Freeman's Journal – 30th June 1798

Wicklow People – various dates, 1938

Sydney Gazette – various dates, 1807 and 1810

The Honey Plain

Elizabeth Wassell

'If you behave like a bastard,
you turn women into bitches!'

Dermot O'Duffy has a reputation as a philanderer. His marriage to the beautiful flame-haired Fiona has long since grown cold and bitter.

Then along comes Grania — a young painter who challenges his antics — and together they embark on a mad-cap affair around Ireland, just ahead of a posse including the jilted Fiona, her angry father, and an oily popinjay called Doyle.

Fast-paced, funny and vivid, Elizabeth Wassell's first novel is a memorable quest for love in our cynical times.

'In *The Honey Plain* Elizabeth Wassell has written a realistic novel with a mythological presence; a satiric-comic novel with a serious feel; and a rattling good yarn bristling with ideas. Essentially, though, *The Honey Plain* is a touching love story, well wrought and well told.'

Brendan Kennelly

ISBN 0 86327 595 8

Available from:
Wolfhound Press
68 Mountjoy Square
Dublin 1

Tread Softly on my Dreams

Gretta Curran Browne

'An epic novel.'
IT Magazine

Set against the background of a country in turmoil,
Tread Softly on my Dreams is the passionate and
powerful story of one of Ireland's most famous rebels
— Robert Emmet.

Intrigue, deceit, idealism and patriotism pave the
route to the 1803 Revolution.

Robert's devotion to his dream will change the lives
of all those who love him. Sacrifice and tragedy await
the courageous Anne Devlin, while romance blossoms
between Robert and the fragile Sarah Curran.
But can love survive amid the turbulent
fight for freedom?

ISBN 0 86327 648 2

Available from:
Wolfhound Press
68 Mountjoy Square
Dublin 1

The Hungry Earth
Seán Kenny

'Turlough's journey of self-discovery in both the past
and present is a strikingly original one, at once
haunting and enlightening.'

Irish Echo, US

In this stunning first novel, Seán Kenny fruitfully
combines realism, history, and time-slip sequences
with the shocking flavours of a psycho-thriller.
Macabre humour leavens the spiritual bankruptcy and
quest of a very contemporary character, whose routine
work, social life, and extra-marital affairs with young
women are about to turn round forever.

ISBN 0 86327 479 X

Celtic Fury
Seán Kenny

The author of *The Hungry Earth* once again blends
supernatural occurrences and sexual intrigue in a story
that searches out the heart of the Irish condition — a tale
that will linger in your mind long after the last line. . . .

ISBN 0 86327 607 5

Available from:
Wolfhound Press
68 Mountjoy Square
Dublin 1